M. R. James' Dark Choices Volume 2

M. R. James' Dark Choices Volume 2

A Selection of Fine Tales of the Strange and Supernatural Endorsed by the Master of the Genre

Including Three Novellas 'A Beleaguered City,' The Turn of the Screw,' and 'The Man-Wolf,' Two Novelettes 'Mr. Justice Harbottle' and 'Squire Toby's Will,' Six Short Stories, and One Ballad

M. R. James'
Dark Choices
Volume 2
A Selection of Fine Tales of the Strange and Supernatural
Endorsed by the Master of the Genre

Including Three Novellas 'A Beleaguered City,' 'The Turn of the Screw,' and 'The Man-Wolf,' Two Novelettes 'Mr. Justice Harbottle' and 'Squire Toby's Will,' Six Short Stories, and One Ballad

FIRST EDITION

Leonaur is an imprint
of Oakpast Ltd

ISBN: 978-0-85706-447-9 (hardcover)
ISBN: 978-0-85706-448-6 (softcover)

http://www.leonaur.com

Publisher's Notes

The opinions of the authors represent a view of events in which he was a participant related from his own perspective, as such the text is relevant as an historical document.

The views expressed in this book are not necessarily those of the publisher.

Contents

Introduction

An introduction in a Leonaur book is so rare as to be noteworthy. The Leonaur Editors believe that the text—and the reputation of most authors—is usually enough to alert the non-academic reader as to the value of the contents of the book about to be read. Not all our readers agree (and we have the correspondence to prove this), but our view remains that if the promise of a dessert with a cherry topping was never made then no one has justification for bridling at the absence of the cherry—the same principle obviously applies to our books and introductions. So having clearly established our deep conviction in this broad principle—conceived after hours of serious and sometimes fraught consideration—what follows is an *introduction*, the proverbial exception to the rule.

The presence of an introduction here is, however, a matter of necessity rather than a general change of policy on our part. The book you are now holding is part of a five volume anthology, a collection of tales by a diverse collection of authors. Anthologies must have a *raison d'être* and it is incumbent on us, as the editors, to explain what that is—so much is only fair. The idea for this anthology occurred to one of the Leonaur editors as he was working on the recently published Leonaur edition of *The Collected Supernatural and Weird Fiction of M. R. James*. For the sake of brevity your editors will assume that any reader who is about to embark upon reading this anthology, having presumably been drawn to it by its title, will not need to have anything about the biography and works of M. R. James recounted to them. For those yet 'in the dark,' if the pun is excused, it is enough to point out that in the echelons of authors of supernatural fiction James' name is at the forefront. His work is timeless, unmistakable, of the highest literary order, emulates none but is sufficiently well regarded by his peers among other fine writers of the genre to be stylistically adopted for their own excursions into the story-telling of the other worldly. As a consequence this style became known as 'Jamesian' which as far as we know is not a distinction accorded to any other author of chilling tales.

What struck the Leonaur editor working on the James collection was that M. R. James not only wrote supernatural fiction but that he also wrote about it quite extensively. Unsurprisingly, given his academic status, it was also a subject about which he knew a great deal and given his own abilities it seems reasonable to expect that his opinions and verdicts carry an indisputable weight of authority—despite the implied subjectivity of critical examination and assessment.

In letters, articles and introductions M. R. James gave his views as to which authors and which stories he regarded most highly. Irrespective of the medium we are fortunate that his opinions remained consistent. The Leonaur editors have principally drawn upon James' article 'Some Remarks on Ghost Stories,' written by him for the December 1929 issue of *The Bookman*, as their inspiration for bringing together this *M. R. James' Dark Choices* anthology series. This article references many writers and their works—approvingly and otherwise—and encapsulates James' assessment of the genre; other of James' non-fiction on the subject of supernatural fiction has been occasionally referenced by us to illuminate the opinions and preferences established in this principal article.

In the main, James dealt with the stories he discussed in 'Some Remarks on Ghost Stories' chronologically by date of publication. We have not followed his example in arranging the tales in our anthology series. In order to create volumes of similar length some consideration had to be given to the extent of each of the pieces, which range from novels to novellas to short stories and it was equally necessary to give some regard to the balance of each book. Where James extolled the merits of several works by the same author these have been distributed throughout the five volumes—as far as possible—to avoid over-emphasis on a single author in any one volume and for the sake of variety of style and ultimately for the enhancement of reader enjoyment. We have given very careful attention to James' words in 'Some Remarks on Ghost Stories,' because the citing of an author or tale is not necessarily an accolade—and on at least one occasion James' praise is decidedly faint.

Simply put the Leonaur editor thought that if one was in search of a good ghost story, it was not possible to go far wrong with the spirit hand of M. R. James as a guide. The word 'spirit' is, of course, applied advisably because the five volumes of this anthology were *not* actually compiled by James whilst he was on this side of the veil and the Leonaur editors are claiming no special powers with which they might elicit information and help from him from beyond the misty curtain. In short this anthology series is a 'bit of fun,' and such a motivation seems entirely appropriate to us because, at most levels, the writing and reading of spooky stories—with a few notable exceptions is also about the fun and frisson of a good scare—followed by a broad smile.

Readers may be reassured that M. R. James really did make written reference to the authors and stories that comprise *M. R. James' Dark Choices.* There is no author or story within the pages of these anthologies that M. R. James did not endorse to one degree or another; so is M. R. James the editor of this anthology? 'No' is the short answer, the Leonaur editors have compiled these anthologies. James simply approved of the stories included and left us his views on them in his own writings on supernatural fiction.

It is our belief that as many anthologies are edited by those who owe their renown to being nothing more than the editors of anthologies this one has much to recommended it; it is different because these are the 'dark choices' of someone who was himself a *master* of the genre. We hope you will agree and enjoy every spine chilling tale.

About This Book

The first piece in this second volume is 'A Beleaguered City' by Mrs. Oliphant. James selected two Mrs Oliphant stories as worthy of special praise particularly as outstanding examples of 'the religious ghost story.' The other is 'The Open Door' which appears in volume three of this anthology series. James considered Mrs Oliphant—together with two of her female peers—to have 'some sufficiently absorbing stories to their credit.' If this remark does not in isolation seem especially effusive in its praise it may be worth pointing out that James' opinions tended to be sober even at the height of his enthusiasms and these remarks are nevertheless decidedly warmer than the cool criticisms of those works and writers for whom he had little regard—irrespective of commercial success or the accolades bestowed upon them by others. James appears, with some justification to be fair, to have been sufficiently sure of his ground and subject as to be able to pronounce his verdicts without 'fear or favour.'

Margaret Oliphant (1828-1897) was a prolific Scottish author who wrote fiction and non-fiction. Among her many works are novels, novellas, short stories, biographies, travel books, histories and literary criticisms. The novella featured in this volume is an intriguing take on the spooky story. Within 'The Beleaguered City' the dead are making themselves felt everywhere as their unseen influence and presence increasingly pervades the everyday lives of the citizens.

Henry James' (1843-1916) famous 'The Turn of the Screw,' the second story in this volume, needs scant introduction by us. M. R, James' reaction to the tale is open to some interpretation because it is one of the last references he makes in his article. James acknowledged that his approach to his subject was 'a series of rather disjointed reflections' and he concludes—presumably since he had not made reference to it previously in its proper place—by asking his readers to believe that he 'has read, 'The

Turn of the Screw'.' We are inclined to think that James felt he could not leave such a highly regarded work out of his appraisal and that he, in common with virtually everybody else, knew it for the masterpiece it is. For this reason Henry James' tale of the creeping corruption of innocence, the absence of which among great supernatural fiction would otherwise be a conspicuous omission, is included here. It could be that M. R. James' acknowledgement is nothing more than a bald statement of fact, but in context that seems unlikely and we have judged that the remark is simply another example of James' taciturn style.

'The Man-Wolf' is another story from the writing partnership of Erckmann-Chatrian. As noted in the first volume of this series, James, who believed that the best writing in the supernatural fiction genre came from the British Isles—although he qualifies his opinion by suggesting that may be because of his lack of knowledge of foreign authors, felt Erckmann-Chatrian to be especially noteworthy among non-English supernatural fiction writers. He tells us 'I should feel myself ungrateful if I did not pay tribute to the supernatural tales of Erckmann-Chatrian.' James cites no fewer than five Erckmann-Chatrian tales including this welcome excursion into to the full-moon world of werewolves. Apart from supernatural and horror stories Erckmann-Chatrian wrote much historical fiction with military themes. Their novels and stories set in the age of Napoleon and the Franco-Prussian War are particularly highly regarded. James said of their stories: 'it is high time that they were made more accessible than they are.' Fortunately for us these wonderful stories have been available in English for some time and are admired by the wider audience that James had hoped for.

There are three stories in this volume from the pen of the grandfather of the ghost story, J. Sheridan Le Fanu (1814-1873). Le Fanu was prolific and virtually his entire literary output was devoted to ghostly and gothic tales. Not only was he the first author to concentrate on the genre, with works published in the first half of the nineteenth century, he was also, according to James, the undisputed master of it. James was, in fact, so impressed by Le Fanu's work that he wrote an introduction for a collection of his tales. Some readers may find the mid-Victorian wordiness of Le Fanu's prose unpalatable and 'heavy going;' James assertion that Le Fanu was 'an artist in words' indicates he would disagree with that perspective, after all both he and Le Fanu were products of the same Victorian world. Without doubt, J. Sheridan Le Fanu wrote enough supernatural fiction to understand how to give his readers a real fright—on cue—even today. So James awarded the *palm d'or* to Le Fanu as the finest supernatural writer of his day and further asserted that three of his stories, including 'Mr. Justice Harbottle' in this volume, are 'unsurpassed.' Also here are 'Squire Toby's Will' and the atmospheric Dutch horror that is 'Schalken the Painter,' both of which James considers close to Le Fanu's best. James wrote: 'I do not think that there are any better ghost stories anywhere than the best of Le Fanu'—leaving the reader in doubt about the magnitude of his regard for Le Fanu's efforts.

E. F. Benson's (1867-1940) contribution to this volume is the curiously titled short story, 'Spinach.'

It is inevitable that no collection of classic ghost stories can be complete without a contribution by Charles Dickens (1812-1870). Of course, it should be remembered that these selections are made by M. R. James and his sometimes idiosyncratic and highly singular verdicts owe fealty to no one's opinion but his own. It may be that that as a result of its continual exposure and the fact that the name of its principal character, 'Scrooge' has all but become a by-word for anyone mean and miserly, that 'A Christmas Carol' would be considered by many as the archetypal ghost story and so James' first choice. Readers might therefore be surprised to learn that James takes the view: 'I do not call 'A Christmas Carol' a ghost story proper.' Instead he cites among a few others the highly atmospheric tale of inexorable approaching doom that is, 'The Signal Man' from, *Mugby Junction*. This is, ultimately, a selection that few would take issue with because it is a fine example of the art of the short story irrespective of genre.

James recommended two stories by American F. Marion Crawford (1854-1909) in his article and *M. R. James' Dark Choices* includes both of them. The first, 'The Upper Berth' appears in volume one of this anthology series and James considered it to be Crawford's finest work. Second place though, 'some distance behind' according to James was accorded to the story in this volume, 'The Screaming Skull.'

Irish writer, Mrs Riddell makes her second appearance in this anthology series, with, 'Hertford O'Donnell's Warning,' as does another Victorian female writer of ghostly fiction from volume one, Rhoda Broughton, with her short story, 'Behold, it was a Dream.' These are both our selections based on James' declared esteem for the stories of these two ladies without giving specific titles.

This volume concludes with another example of a creepy tale within verse, 'Young Benjie' by Andrew Lang.

The Leonaur Editors

A Beleaguered City

By Mrs. Oliphant

Chapter 1

The Narrative of M. Le Maire: The Condition of the City.

I, Martin Dupin (*de la Clairière*), had the honour of holding the office of *Maire* in the town of Semur, in the Haute Bourgogne, at the time when the following events occurred. It will be perceived, therefore, that no one could have more complete knowledge of the facts—at once from my official position, and from the place of eminence in the affairs of the district generally which my family has held for many generations—by what citizen-like virtues and unblemished integrity I will not be vain enough to specify. Nor is it necessary; for no one who knows Semur can be ignorant of the position held by the Dupins, from father to son. The estate La Clairière has been so long in the family that we might very well, were we disposed, add its name to our own, as so many families in France do; and, indeed, I do not prevent my wife (whose prejudices I respect) from making this use of it upon her cards.

But, for myself, *bourgeois* I was born and *bourgeois* I mean to die. My residence, like that of my father and grandfather, is at No. 29 in the Grande Rue, opposite the Cathedral, and not far from the Hospital of St. Jean. We inhabit the first floor, along with the *rez-de-chaussée*, which has been turned into domestic offices suitable for the needs of the family. My mother, holding a respected place in my household, lives with us in the most perfect family union. My wife (*née* de Champfleurie) is everything that is calculated to render a household happy; but, alas! one only of our two children survives to bless us. I have thought these details of my private circumstances necessary, to explain the following narrative; to which I will also add, by way of introduction, a simple sketch of the town itself and its general conditions before these remarkable events occurred.

It was on a summer evening about sunset, the middle of the month of June, that my attention was attracted by an incident of no importance which occurred in the street, when I was making my way home, after an inspection of the young vines in my new vineyard to the left of La Clairière. All were in perfectly good condition, and none of the many signs which point to the arrival of the insect were apparent. I had come back in good spirits, thinking of the prosperity which I was happy to believe I had merited by a conscientious performance of all my duties. I had little with which to blame myself: not only my wife and relations, but my dependants and neighbours, approved my conduct as a man; and even my fellow-citizens, exacting as they are, had confirmed in my favour the good opinion which my family had been fortunate enough to secure from father to son.

These thoughts were in my mind as I turned the corner of the Grande Rue and approached my own house. At this moment the tinkle of a little bell warned all the bystanders of the procession which was about to pass, carrying the rites of the Church to some dying person. Some of the women, always devout, fell on their knees. I did not go so far as this, for I do not pretend, in these days of progress, to have retained the same attitude of mind as that which it is no doubt becoming to behold in the more devout sex; but I stood respectfully out of the way, and took off my hat, as good breeding alone, if nothing else, demanded of me. Just in front of me, however, was Jacques Richard, always a troublesome individual, standing doggedly, with his hat upon his head and his hands in his pockets, straight in the path of *M. le Curé*.

There is not in all France a more obstinate fellow. He stood there, notwithstanding the efforts of a good woman to draw him away, and though I myself called to him. *M. le Curé* is not the man to flinch; and as he passed, walking as usual very quickly and straight, his *soutane* brushed against the blouse of Jacques. He gave one quick glance from beneath his eyebrows at the profane interruption, but he would not distract himself from his sacred errand at such a moment. It is a sacred errand when any one, be he priest or layman, carries the best he can give to the bedside of the dying. I said this to Jacques when *M. le Curé* had passed and the bell went tinkling on along the street. 'Jacques,' said I, 'I do not call it impious, like this good woman, but I call it inhuman. What! a man goes to carry help to the dying, and you show him no respect!'

This brought the colour to his face; and I think, perhaps, that he might have become ashamed of the part he had played; but the women pushed in again, as they are so fond of doing. 'Oh, *M. le Maire*, he does not deserve that you should lose your words upon him!' they cried; 'and, besides, is it likely he will pay any attention to you when he tries to stop even the *bon Dieu?*'

'The *bon Dieu!*' cried Jacques. 'Why doesn't He clear the way for himself? Look here. I do not care one farthing for your *bon Dieu*. Here is mine; I carry him about with me.' And he took a piece of a hundred *sous* out of his pocket (how had it got there?) '*Vive l'argent!*' he said. 'You know it yourself, though you will not say so. There is no *bon Dieu* but money. With money you can do anything. *L'argent c'est le bon Dieu!*'

'Be silent,' I cried, 'thou profane one!' And the women were still more indignant than I. 'We shall see, we shall see; when he is ill and would give his soul for something to wet his lips, his *bon Dieu* will not do much for him,' cried one; and another said, clasping her hands with a shrill cry, 'It is enough to make the dead rise out of their graves!'

'The dead rise out of their graves!' These words, though one has heard them before, took possession of my imagination. I saw the rude fellow go along the street as I went on, tossing the coin in his hand. Once time It fell to the ground and rang upon the pavement, and he laughed more loudly as he picked it up.

He was walking towards the sunset, and I too, at a distance after. The sky was full of rose- tinted clouds floating across the blue, floating high over the grey pinnacles of the Cathedral, and filling the long open line of the Rue St. Etienne down which he was going. As I crossed to my own house I caught him full against the light, in his blue blouse, tossing the big silver piece in the air, and heard him laugh and shout '*Vive l'argent!* This is the only *bon Dieu*.' Though there are many people who live as if this were their sentiment, there are few who give it such brutal expression; but some of the people at the corner of the street laughed too. '*Bravo, Jacques!*' they cried; and one said, You are right, *mon ami*, the only god to trust in nowadays.'

'It is a short *credo*, *M. le Maire*,' said another, who caught my eye. He saw I was displeased, this one, and his countenance changed at once.

'Yes, Jean Pierre,' I said, 'it is worse than short—it is brutal. I hope no man who respects himself will ever countenance it. It is against the dignity of human nature, if nothing more.'

'Ah, *M. le Maire!*' cried a poor woman, one of the good ladies of the market, with entrenchments of baskets all round her, who had been walking my way; 'ah, *M. le Maire!* did not I say true? it is enough to bring the dead out of their graves.'

'That would be something to see,' said Jean Pierre, with a laugh; 'and I hope, *ma bonne femme*, that if you have any interest with them, you will entreat these gentlemen to appear before I go away.'

'I do not like such jesting,' said I. 'The dead are very dead and will not disturb anybody, but even the prejudices of respectable persons ought to be respected. A ribald like Jacques counts for nothing, but I did not expect this from you.'

'What would you, *M. le Maire?*' he said, with a shrug of his shoulders. 'We are made like that. I respect prejudices as you say. My wife is a good woman, she prays for two—but me! How can I tell that Jacques is not right after all? A *grosse pièce* of a hundred *sous*, one sees that, one knows what it can do—but for the other!' He thrust up one shoulder to his ear, and turned up the palms of his hands.

'It is our duty at all times to respect the convictions of others,' I said, severely; and passed on to my own house, having no desire to encourage discussions at the street corner. A man in my position is obliged to be always mindful of the example he ought to set. But I had not yet done with this phrase, which had, as I have said, caught my ear and my imagination. My mother was in the great *salle* of the *rez-de-chausée*, as I passed, in altercation with a peasant who had just brought us in some loads of wood. There is often, it seems to me, a sort of *refrain* in conversation, which one catches everywhere as one comes and goes. Figure my astonishment when I heard from the lips of my good mother the same words with which that good-for-nothing Jacques Richard had made the profession of his brutal faith. 'Go!' she cried, in anger; 'you are all the same. Money is your god, *De grosses pièces*, that is all you think of in these days.'

'*Eh, bien, madame*,' said the peasant; 'and if so, what then? Don't you others, gentlemen and ladies, do just the same? What is there in the world but money to think of? If it is a question of marriage, you demand what is the *dot*; if it is a question of office, you ask. Monsieur Untel, is he rich? And it is perfectly just. We know what money can do; but as for *le bon Dieu*, whom our grandmothers used to talk about—'

And lo! our *gros paysan* made exactly the same gesture as Jean Pierre. He put up his shoulders to his ears, and spread out the palms of his hands, as who should say, There is nothing further to be said.

Then there occurred a still more remarkable repetition. My mother, as may be supposed, being a very respectable person, and more or less *dévote*, grew red with indignation and horror.

'Oh, these poor grandmothers!' she cried; 'God give them rest! It is enough to make the dead rise out of their graves.'

'Oh, I will answer for *les morts!* they will give nobody any trouble,' he said with a laugh. I went in and reproved the man severely, finding that, as I supposed, he had attempted to cheat my good mother in the price of the wood. Fortunately she had been quite as clever as he was. She went upstairs shaking her head, while I gave the man to understand that no one should speak to her but with the profoundest respect in my house. 'She has her opinions, like all respectable ladies,' I said, 'but under this roof these opinions shall always be sacred.' And, to do him justice, I will add that when it was put to him in this way Gros-Jean was ashamed of himself.

When I talked over these incidents with my wife, as we gave each other the narrative of our day's experiences, she was greatly distressed, as may be supposed. 'I try to hope they are not so bad as *Bonne Maman* thinks. But oh, *mon ami!*' she said, 'what will the world come to if this is what they really believe?'

'Take courage,' I said; 'the world will never come to anything much different from what it is. So long as there are *des anges* like thee to pray for us, the scale will not go down to the wrong side.'

I said this, of course, to please my Agnès, who is the best of wives; but on thinking it over after, I could not but be struck with the extreme justice (not to speak of the beauty of the sentiment) of this thought. The *bon Dieu*—if, indeed, that great Being is as represented to us by the Church—must naturally care as much for one-half of His creatures as for the other, though they have not the same weight in the world; and consequently the faith of the women must hold the balance straight, especially if, as is said, they exceed us in point of numbers. This leaves a little margin for those of them who profess the same freedom of thought as is generally accorded to men—a class, I must add, which I abominate from the bottom of my heart.

I need not dwell upon other little scenes which impressed the same idea still more upon my mind. Semur, I need not say, is not the centre of the world, and might, therefore, be supposed likely to escape the full current of worldliness. We amuse ourselves little, and we have not any opportunity of rising to the heights of ambition; for our town is not even the *chef-lieu* of the department,—though this is a subject upon which I cannot trust myself to speak. Figure to yourself that La Rochette—a place of yesterday, without either the beauty or the antiquity of Semur—has been chosen as the centre of affairs, the residence of *M. le Préfet!* But I will not enter upon this question. What I was saying was, that, notwithstanding the fact that we amuse ourselves but little, that there is no theatre to speak of, little society, few distractions, and none of those inducements to strive for gain and to indulge the senses, which exist, for instance, in Paris—that capital of the world—yet, nevertheless, the thirst for money and for pleasure has increased among us to an extent which I cannot but consider alarming.

Gros-Jean, our peasant, toils for money, and hoards; Jacques, who is a cooper and maker of wine casks, gains and drinks; Jean Pierre snatches at every *sous* that comes in his way, and spends it in yet worse dissipations. He is one who quails when he meets my eye; he sins *en cachette*; but Jacques is bold, and defies opinion; and Gros-Jean is firm in the belief that to hoard money is the highest of mortal occupations. These three are types of what the population is at Semur. The men would all sell their souls for a *grosse pièce* of fifty *sous*—indeed, they would laugh, and express their delight that any one should believe them to have souls, if they could but have a chance of selling them; and the devil, who was once supposed to deal in that commodity, would be very welcome among us. And as for the *bon Dieu—pouff!* that was an affair of the grandmothers—*le bon Dieu c'est l'argent.* This is their creed.

I was very near the beginning of my official year as *Maire* when my attention was called to these matters as I have described above. A man may go on for years keeping quiet himself—keeping out of tumult, religious or political—and make no discovery of the general current of feeling; but when you are forced to serve your country in any official capacity, and when your eyes are opened to the state of affairs around you, then I allow that an inexperienced observer might well cry out, as my wife did, 'What will become of the world?' I am not prejudiced myself—unnecessary to say that the foolish scruples of the women do not move me. But the devotion of the community at large to this pursuit of gain—money without any grandeur, and pleasure without any refinement—that is a thing which cannot fail to wound all who believe in human nature.

To be a millionaire—that, I grant, would be pleasant. A man as rich as Monte Christo, able to do whatever he would, with the equipage of an English duke, the palace of an Italian prince, the retinue of a Russian noble—he, indeed, might be excused if his money seemed to him a kind of god. But Gros-Jean, who lays up two *sous* at a time, and lives on black bread and an onion; and Jacques, whose *grosse pièce* but secures him the headache of a drunkard next morning—what to them could be this miserable deity? As for myself, however, it was my business, as *Maire* of the commune, to take as little notice as possible of the follies these people might say, and to hold the middle course between the prejudices of the respectable and the levities of the foolish. With this, without more, to think of, I had enough to keep all my faculties employed.

Chapter 2

The Narrative of M. le Maire Continued: Beginning of the Late Remarkable Events.

I do not attempt to make out any distinct connection between the simple incidents above recorded, and the extraordinary events that followed. I have related them as they happened; chiefly by way of showing the state of feeling in the city, and the sentiment which pervaded the community—a sentiment, I fear, too common in my country. I need not say that to encourage superstition is far from my wish. I am a man of my century, and proud of being so; very little disposed to yield to the domination of the clerical party, though desirous of showing all just tolerance for conscientious faith, and every respect for the prejudices of the ladies of my family. I am, moreover, all the more inclined to be careful of giving in my adhesion to any prodigy, in consequence of a consciousness that the faculty of imagination has always been one of my characteristics. It usually is so, I am aware, in superior minds, and it has procured me many pleasures unknown to the common herd.

Had it been possible for me to believe that I had been misled by this faculty, I should have carefully refrained from putting upon record any account of my individual impressions; but my attitude here is not that of a man recording his personal experiences only, but of one who is the official mouthpiece and representative of the commune, and whose duty it is to render to government and to the human race a true narrative of the very wonderful facts to which every citizen of Semur can bear witness. In this capacity it has become my duty so to arrange and edit the different accounts of the mystery, as to present one coherent and trustworthy chronicle to the world.

To proceed, however, with my narrative. It is not necessary for me to describe what summer is in the Haute Bourgogne. Our generous wines, our glorious fruits, are sufficient proof, without any assertion on my part. The summer with us is as a perpetual *fête*—at least, before the insect appeared it was so, though now anxiety about the condition of our vines may cloud our enjoyment of the glorious sunshine which ripens them hourly before our eyes. Judge, then, of the astonishment of the world when there suddenly came upon us a darkness as in the depth of winter, falling, without warning, into the midst of the brilliant weather to which we are accustomed, and which had never failed us before in the memory of man! It was the month of July, when, in ordinary seasons, a cloud is so rare that it is a joy to see one, merely as a variety upon the brightness.

Suddenly, in the midst of our summer delights, this darkness came. Its first appearance took us so entirely by surprise that life seemed to stop short, and the business of the whole town was delayed by an hour or two; nobody being able to believe that at six o'clock in the morning the sun had not risen. I do not assert that the sun did not rise; all I mean to say is that at Semur it was still dark, as in a morning of winter, and when it gradually and slowly became day many hours of the morning were already spent. And never shall I forget the aspect of day when it came. It was like a ghost or pale shadow of the glorious days of July with which we are usually blessed. The barometer did not go down, nor was there any rain, but an unusual greyness wrapped earth and sky. I heard people say in the streets, and I am aware that the same words came to my own lips: 'If it were not full summer, I should say it was going to snow.' We have much snow in the Haute Bourgogne, and we are well acquainted with this aspect of the skies.

Of the depressing effect which this greyness exercised upon myself personally, I will not speak. I have always been noted as a man of fine perceptions, and I was aware instinctively that such a state of the atmosphere must mean something more than was apparent on the surface. But, as the danger was of an entirely unprecedented character, it is not to be wondered at that I should be completely at a loss to divine what its meaning was. It was a blight some people said; and many were of opinion that it was caused by clouds of *animalculae* coming, as is described in ancient writings, to destroy the crops, and even to affect the health of the population. The doctors scoffed at this; but they talked about malaria, which, as far as I could understand, was likely to produce exactly the same effect. The night closed in early as the day had dawned late; the lamps were lighted before six o'clock, and daylight had only begun about ten! Figure to yourself, a July day!

There ought to have been a moon almost at the full; but no moon was visible, no stars—nothing but a grey veil of clouds, growing darker and darker as the moments went on; such I have heard are the days and the nights in England, where the sea-fogs so often blot out the sky. But we are unacquainted with anything of the kind in our *plaisant pays de France*. There was nothing else talked of in Semur all that night, as may well be imagined. My own mind was extremely uneasy. Do what I would, I could not deliver myself from a sense of something dreadful in the air which was neither malaria nor *animalculae*. I took a promenade through the streets that evening, accompanied by M. Barbou, my *adjoint*, to make sure that all was safe; and the darkness was such that we almost lost our way, though we were both born in the town and had known every turning from our boyhood. It cannot be denied that Semur is very badly lighted.

We retain still the lanterns slung by cords across the streets which once were general in France, but which, in most places, have been superseded by the modern institution of gas. Gladly would I have distinguished my term of office by bringing gas to Semur. But the expense would have been great, and there were a hundred objections. In summer generally, the lanterns were of little consequence because of the brightness of the sky; but to see them now, twinkling dimly here and there, making us conscious how dark it was, was strange indeed. It was in the interests of order that we took our round, with a fear, in my mind at least, of I knew not what. *M. l'Adjoint* said nothing, but no doubt he thought as I did.

While we were thus patrolling the city with a special eye to the prevention of all seditious assemblages, such as are too apt to take advantage of any circumstances that may disturb the ordinary life of a city, or throw discredit on its magistrates, we were accosted by Paul Lecamus, a man whom I have always considered as something of a visionary, though his conduct is irreproachable, and his life honourable and industrious. He entertains religious convictions of a curious kind; but, as the man is quite free from revolutionary sentiments, I have never considered it to be my duty to interfere with him, or to investigate his creed. Indeed, he has been treated generally in Semur as a dreamer of dreams—one who holds a great many impracticable and foolish opinions—though the respect which I always exact for those whose lives are respectable and worthy has been a protection to him. He was, I think, aware that he owed something to my good offices, and it was to me accordingly that he addressed himself.

'Good evening, *M. le Maire*,' he said; 'you are groping about, like myself, in this strange night.'

'Good evening M. Paul,' I replied. 'It is, indeed, a strange night. It indicates, I fear, that a storm is coming.'

M. Paul shook his head. There is a solemnity about even his

ordinary appearance. He has a long face, pale, and adorned with a heavy, drooping moustache, which adds much to the solemn impression made by his countenance. He looked at me with great gravity as he stood in the shadow of the lamp, and slowly shook his head.

'You do not agree with me? Well! the opinion of a man like M. Paul Lecamus is always worthy to be heard.'

'Oh!' he said, 'I am called visionary. I am not supposed to be a trustworthy witness. Nevertheless, if *M. Le Maire* will come with me, I will show him something that is very strange—something that is almost more wonderful than the darkness—more strange,' he went on with great earnestness, 'than any storm that ever ravaged Burgundy.'

'That is much to say. A tempest now when the vines are in full bearing—'

'Would be nothing, nothing to what I can show you. Only come with me to the Porte St. Lambert.'

'If *M. le Maire* will excuse me,' said M. Barbou, 'I think I will go home. It is a little cold, and you are aware that I am always afraid of the damp.' In fact, our coats were beaded with a cold dew as in November, and I could not but acknowledge that my respectable colleague had reason. Besides, we were close to his house, and he had, no doubt, the sustaining consciousness of having done everything that was really incumbent upon him.

'Our ways lie together as far as my house,' he said, with a slight chattering of his teeth. No doubt it was the cold. After we had walked with him to his door, we proceeded to the Porte St. Lambert. By this time almost everybody had re-entered their houses. The streets were very dark, and they were also very still. When we reached the gates, at that hour of the night, we found them shut as a matter of course. The officers of the *octroi* were standing close together at the door of their office, in which the lamp was burning. The very lamp seemed oppressed by the heavy air; It burnt dully, surrounded with a yellow haze. The men had the appearance of suffering greatly from cold. They received me with a satisfaction which was very gratifying to me. 'At length here is *M. le Maire* himself, they said.

'My good friends,' said I, 'you have a cold post tonight. The weather has changed in the most extraordinary way. I have no doubt the scientific gentlemen at the *Musée* will be able to tell us all about it—M. de Clairon—'

'Not to interrupt *M. le Maire*,' said Riou, of the *octroi*, 'I think there is more in it than any scientific gentleman can explain.'

'Ah! You think so. But they explain everything,' I said, with a smile. 'They tell us how the wind is going to blow.'

As I said this, there seemed to pass us, from the direction of the closed gates, a breath of air so cold that I could not restrain a shiver. They looked at each other. It was not a smile that passed between them—they were too pale, too cold, to smile: but a look of intelligence. '*M. le Maire*,' said one of them, 'perceives it too;' but they did not shiver as I did. They were like men turned into ice who could feel no more.

'It is, without doubt, the most extraordinary weather,' I said. My teeth chattered like Barbou's. It was all I could do to keep myself steady. No one made any reply; but Lecamus said, 'Have the goodness to open the little postern for foot-passengers: *M. le Maire* wishes to make an inspection outside.'

Upon these words, Riou, who knew me well, caught me by the arm. 'A thousand pardons,' he said, '*M. le Maire*; but I entreat you, do not go. Who can tell what is outside? Since this morning there is something very strange on the other side of the gates. If *M. le Maire* would listen to me, he would keep them shut night and day till that is gone, he would not go out into the midst of it. *Mon Dieu!* a man may be brave. I know the courage of *M. le Maire*; but to march without necessity Into the jaws of hell: *mon Dieu,*' cried the poor man again. He crossed himself, and none of us smiled. Now a man may sign himself at the church door—one does so out of respect; but to use that ceremony for one's own advantage, before other men, Is rare—except In the case of members of a very decided party. Riou was not one of these. He signed himself In sight of us all, and not one of us smiled.

The other was less familiar—he knew me only in my public

capacity—he was one Gallais of the Quartier St. Médon. He said, taking off his hat: 'If I were *M. le Maire*, saving your respect, I would not go out Into an unknown danger with this man here, a man who is known as a *pietist*, as a clerical, as one who sees visions—'

'He is not a clerical, he is a good citizen,' I said; 'come, lend us your lantern. Shall I shrink from my duty wherever it leads me? Nay, my good friends, the *Maire* of a French commune fears neither man nor devil in the exercise of his duty. M. Paul, lead on.' When I said the word 'devil' a spasm of alarm passed over Riou's face. He crossed himself again. This time I could not but smile. 'My little Riou,' I said, 'do you know that you are a little imbecile with your piety? There is a time for everything.'

'Except religion, *M. le Maire*; that is never out of place,' said Gallais.

I could not believe my senses. 'Is it a conversion?' I said. 'Some of our Carmes *déchaussés* must have passed this way.'

'*M. le Maire* will soon see other teachers more wonderful than the Carmes *déchaussés*,' said Lecamus. He went and took down the lantern from its nail, and opened the little door. When it opened, I was once more penetrated by the same icy breath; once, twice, thrice, I cannot tell how many times this crossed me, as if someone passed. I looked round upon the others—I gave way a step. I could not help it. In spite of me, the hair seemed to rise erect on my head. The two officers stood close together, and Riou, collecting his courage, made an attempt to laugh. '*M. le Maire* perceives,' he said, his lips trembling almost too much to form the words, 'that the winds are walking about.' 'Hush, for God's sake!' said the other, grasping him by the arm.

This recalled me to myself; and I followed Lecamus, who stood waiting for me holding the door a little ajar. He went on strangely, like—I can use no other words to express it—a man making his way in the face of a crowd, a thing very surprising to me. I followed him close; but the moment I emerged from the doorway something caught my breath. The same feeling seized me also. I gasped; a sense of suffocation came upon me; I put out my hand to lay hold upon my guide. The solid grasp I got of his arm reassured me a little, and he did not hesitate, but pushed his way on. We got out clear of the gate and the shadow of the wall, keeping close to the little watch-tower on the west side. Then he made a pause, and so did I. We stood against the tower and looked out before us. There was nothing there. The darkness was great, yet through the gloom of the night I could see the division of the road from the broken ground on either side; there was nothing there.

I gasped, and drew myself up close against the wall, as Lecamus had also done. There was in the air, in the night, a sensation the most strange I have ever experienced. I have felt the same thing indeed at other times, in face of a great crowd, when thousands of people were moving, rustling, struggling, breathing around me, thronging all the vacant space, filling up every spot. This was the sensation that overwhelmed me here—a crowd: yet nothing to be seen but the darkness, the indistinct line of the road. We could not move for them, so close were they round us. What do I say? There was nobody—nothing—not a form to be seen, not a face but his and mine. I am obliged to confess that the moment was to me an awful moment. I could not speak. My heart beat wildly as if trying to escape from my breast—every breath I drew was with an effort. I clung to Lecamus with deadly and helpless terror, and forced myself back upon the wall, crouching against it; I did not turn and fly, as would have been natural. What say I? *did* not! I *could* not! they pressed round us so. Ah! you would think I must be mad to use such words, for there was nobody near me—not a shadow even upon the road.

Lecamus would have gone farther on; he would have pressed his way boldly into the midst; but my courage was not equal to this. I clutched and clung to him, dragging myself along against the wall, my whole mind intent upon getting back. I was stronger than he, and he had no power to resist me. I turned back, stumbling blindly, keeping my face to that crowd (there was no one), but struggling back again, tearing the skin off my hands as I groped my way along the wall. Oh, the agony of seeing the door closed! I have buffeted my way through a crowd before now, but I may say that I never before knew what terror was. When I fell upon the door, dragging Lecamus with me, it opened, thank God! I stumbled in, clutching at Riou with my disengaged hand, and fell upon the floor of the *octroi*, where they thought I had fainted. But this was not the case. A man of resolution may give way to the overpowering sensations of the moment. His bodily faculties may fail him; but his mind will not fail. As in every really superior intelligence, my forces collected for the emergency.

While the officers ran to bring me water, to search for the *eau-de vie* which they had in a cupboard, I astonished them all by rising up, pale, but with full command of myself. 'It is enough,' I said, raising my hand. 'I thank you, *Messieurs*, but nothing more is necessary;' and I would not take any of their restoratives. They were impressed, as was only natural, by the sight of my perfect self-possession: it helped them to acquire for themselves a demeanour befitting the occasion; and I felt, though still in great physical weakness and agitation, the consoling consciousness of having fulfilled my functions as head of the community.

'*M. le Maire* has seen a what there is outside?' Riou cried, stammering in his excitement; and the other fixed upon me eyes which were hungering with eagerness—if, indeed, it is permitted to use such words.

'I have seen—nothing, Riou,' I said. They looked at me with the utmost wonder. '*M. le Maire* has seen—nothing?' said Riou. 'Ah, I see! you say so to spare us. We have proved ourselves cowards; but if you will pardon me, *M. le Maire*, you, too, re-entered precipitately—you too! There are facts which may appal the bravest—but I implore you to tell us what you have seen.'

'I have seen nothing,' I said. As I spoke, my natural calm composure returned, my heart resumed its usual tranquil beating. 'There is nothing to be seen—it is dark, and one can perceive the line of the road for but a little way—that is all. There is nothing to be seen—'

They looked at me, startled and incredulous. They did not

know what to think. How could they refuse to believe me, sitting there calmly raising my eyes to them, making my statement with what they felt to be an air of perfect truth? But, then, how account for the precipitate return which they had already noted, the supposed faint, the pallor of my looks? They did not know what to think.

And here, let me remark, as in my conduct throughout these remarkable events, may be seen the benefit, the high advantage, of truth. Had not this been the truth, I could not have borne the searching of their looks. But it was true. There was nothing—nothing to be seen; in one sense, this was the thing of all others which overwhelmed my mind. But why insist upon these matters of detail to unenlightened men? There was nothing, and I had seen nothing. What I said was the truth.

All this time Lecamus had said nothing. As I raised myself from the ground, I had vaguely perceived him hanging up the lantern where It had been before; now he became distinct to me as I recovered the full possession of my faculties. He had seated himself upon a bench by the wall. There was no agitation about him; no sign of the thrill of departing excitement, which I felt going through my veins as through the strings of a harp. He was sitting against the wall, with his head drooping, his eyes cast down, an air of disappointment and despondency about him—nothing more. I got up as soon as I felt that I could go away with perfect propriety; but, before I left the place, called him. He got up when he heard his name, but he did it with reluctance. He came with me because I asked him to do so, not from any wish of his own.

Very different were the feelings of Riou and Gallais. They did their utmost to engage me in conversation, to consult me about a hundred trifles, to ask me with the greatest deference what they ought to do in such and such cases, pressing close to me, trying every expedient to delay my departure. When we went away they stood at the door of their little office close together, looking after us with looks which I found it difficult to forget; they would not abandon their post; but their faces were pale and contracted, their eyes wild with anxiety and distress.

It was only as I walked away, hearing my own steps and those of Lecamus ringing upon the pavement, that I began to realise what had happened. The effort of recovering my composure, the relief from the extreme excitement of terror (which, dreadful as the idea is, I am obliged to confess I had actually felt), the sudden influx of life and strength to my brain, had pushed away for the moment the recollection of what lay outside. When I thought of it again, the blood began once more to course in my veins. Lecamus went on by my side with his head down, the eyelids drooping over his eyes, not saying a word.

He followed me when I called him: but cast a regretful look at the postern by which we had gone out, through which I had dragged him back in a panic (I confess it) unworthy of me. Only when we had left at some distance behind us that door into the unseen, did my senses come fully back to me, and I ventured to ask myself what it meant. 'Lecamus,' I said—I could scarcely put my question into words—'what do you think? what is your idea?—how do you explain—' Even then I am glad to think I had sufficient power of control not to betray all that I felt.

'One does not try to explain,' he said slowly; 'one longs to know—that is all. If *M. le Maire* had not been—in such haste—had he been willing to go farther—to investigate—'

'God forbid!' I said; and the impulse to quicken my steps, to get home and put myself in safety, was almost more than I could restrain. But I forced myself to go quietly, to measure my steps by his, which were slow and reluctant, as if he dragged himself away with difficulty from that which was behind.

What was it? 'Do not ask, do not ask!' Nature seemed to say in my heart. Thoughts came into my mind in such a dizzy crowd, that the multitude of them seemed to take away my senses. I put up my hands to my ears, in which they seemed to be buzzing and rustling like bees, to stop the sound. When I did so, Lecamus turned and looked at me—grave and wondering. This recalled me to a sense of my weakness. But how I got home I can scarcely say. My mother and wife met me with anxiety. They were greatly disturbed about the Hospital of St. Jean, in respect to which it had been recently decided that certain changes should be made. The great ward of the hospital, which was the chief establishment for the sick in the town, had hitherto been so placed in communication with the chapel that mass was heard daily by all the patients—a thing which some had complained of as an annoyance disturbing their rest. So many, indeed, had been the complaints received, that we had come to the conclusion either that the opening should be built up, or the office suspended.

Against this decision, it is needless to say, the Sisters of St. Jean were moving heaven and earth. Equally unnecessary for me to add, that having so decided in my public capacity, as at once the representative of popular opinion and its guide, the covert reproaches which were breathed in my presence, and even the personal appeals made to me, had failed of any result. I respect the Sisters of St. Jean. They are good women and excellent nurses, and the commune owes them much. Still, justice must be impartial; and so long as I retain my position at the head of the community, it is my duty to see that all have their due. My opinions as a private individual, were I allowed to return to that humble position, are entirely a different matter; but this is a thing which ladies, however excellent, are slow to allow or to understand.

I will not pretend that this was to me a night of rest. In the darkness, when all is still, any anxiety which may afflict the soul is apt to gain complete possession and mastery, as all who have had true experience of life will understand. The night was very dark and very still, the clocks striking out the hours which went so slowly, and not another sound audible. The streets of Semur are always quiet, but they were more still than usual that night. Now and then, in a pause of my thoughts, I could hear the soft breathing of my Agnès in the adjoining room, which gave me a little comfort. But this was only by intervals, when I was able to escape from the grasp of the recollections that held me fast.

Again I seemed to see under my closed eyelids the faint line of the high road which led from the Porte St. Lambert, the broken ground with its ragged bushes on either side, and no one—no one there—not a soul, not a shadow: yet a multitude! When I allowed myself to think of this, my heart leaped into my throat again, my blood ran in my veins like a river in flood. I need not say that I resisted this transport of the nerves with all my might. As the night grew slowly into morning my power of resistance increased; I turned my back, so to speak, upon my recollections, and said to myself, with growing firmness, that all sensations of the body must have their origin in the body. Some derangement of the system—easily explainable, no doubt, if one but held the clue—must have produced the impression which otherwise it would be impossible to explain. As I turned this over and over in my mind, carefully avoiding all temptations to excitement—which is the only wise course in the case of a strong impression on the nerves—I gradually became able to believe that this was the cause. It is one of the penalties, I said to myself, which one has to pay for an organisation more finely tempered than that of the crowd.

This long struggle with myself made the night less tedious, though, perhaps, more terrible; and when at length I was overpowered by sleep, the short interval of unconsciousness restored me like a cordial. I woke in the early morning, feeling almost able to smile at the terrors of the night. When one can assure oneself that the day has really begun, even while it is yet dark, there is a change of sensation, an increase of strength and courage. One by one the dark hours went on. I heard them pealing from the Cathedral clock—four, five, six, seven—all dark, dark. I had got up and dressed before the last, but found no one else awake when I went out—no one stirring in the house,—no one moving in the street. The Cathedral doors were shut fast, a thing I have never seen before since I remember. Get up early who will, Père Laserques the sacristan is always up still earlier. He is a good old man, and I have often heard him say God's house should be open first of all houses, in case there might be any miserable ones about who had found no shelter in the dwellings of men.

But the darkness had cheated even Père Laserques. To see those great doors closed which stood always open gave me a shiver, I cannot well tell why. Had they been open, there was an inclination in my mind to have gone in, though I cannot tell why; for I am not in the habit of attending mass, save on Sunday to set an example. There were no shops open, not a sound about. I went out upon the ramparts to the Mont St. Lambert, where the band plays on Sundays. In all the trees there was not so much as the twitter of a bird. I could hear the river flowing swiftly below the wall, but I could not see it, except as something dark, a ravine of gloom below, and beyond the walls I did not venture to look. Why should I look? There was nothing, nothing, as I knew.

But fancy is so uncontrollable, and one's nerves so little to be trusted, that it was a wise precaution to refrain. The gloom itself was oppressive enough; the air seemed to creep with apprehensions, and from time to time my heart fluttered with a sick movement, as if it would escape from my control. But everything was still, still as the dead who had been so often in recent days called out of their graves by one or another. 'Enough to bring the dead out of their graves.' What strange words to make use of! It was rather now as if the world had become a grave in which we, though living, were held fast.

Soon after this the dark world began to lighten faintly, and with the rising of a little white mist, like a veil rolling upwards, I at last saw the river and the fields beyond.

To see anything at all lightened my heart a little, and I turned homeward when this faint daylight appeared. When I got back into the street, I found that the people at last were stirring. They had all a look of half panic, half shame upon their faces. Many were yawning and stretching themselves. 'Good morning, *M. le Maire*,' said one and another; 'you are early astir.'

'Not so early either,' I said; and then they added, almost every individual, with a look of shame, 'We were so late this morning; we overslept ourselves—like yesterday. The weather is extraordinary.' This was repeated to me by all kinds of people. They were half frightened, and they were ashamed. Père Laserques was sitting moaning on the Cathedral steps. Such a thing had never happened before. He had not rung the bell for early mass; he had not opened the Cathedral; he had not called *M. le Curé*.

'I think I must be going out of my senses,' he said; 'but then, *M. le Maire*, the weather! Did anyone ever see such weather? I think there must be some evil brewing. It is not for nothing that the seasons change—that winter comes in the midst of summer.'

After this I went home. My mother came running to one door when I entered, and my wife to another. '*O mon fils!*' and '*O mon ami!*' they said, rushing upon me. They wept, these dear women. I could not at first prevail upon them to tell me what was the matter. At last they confessed that they believed something to have happened to me, in punishment for the wrong done to the Sisters at the hospital. 'Make haste, my son, to amend this error,' my mother cried, 'lest a worse thing befall us!'

And then I discovered that among the women, and among many of the poor people, it had come to be believed that the darkness was a curse upon us for what we had done in respect to the hospital. This roused me to indignation. 'If they think I am to be driven from my duty by their magic,' I cried; 'It is no better than witchcraft!' not that I believed for a moment that it was they who had done it. My wife wept, and my mother became angry with me; but when a thing is duty, it is neither wife nor mother who will move me out of my way.

It was a miserable day. There was not light enough to see anything—scarcely to see each other's faces; and to add to our alarm, some travellers arriving by the diligence (we are still three leagues from a railway, while that miserable little place, La Rochette, being the *chef-lieu*, has a terminus) informed me that the darkness only existed in Semur and the neighbourhood, and that within a distance of three miles the sun was shining. The sun was shining! was it possible? it seemed so long since we had seen the sunshine; but this made our calamity more mysterious and more terrible. The people began to gather into little knots in the streets to talk of the strange thing that was happening. In the course of the day M. Barbou came to ask whether I did not think it would be well to appease the popular feeling by conceding what they wished to the Sisters of the hospital. I would not hear of it. 'Shall we own that we are in the wrong? I do not think we are in the wrong,' I said, and I would not yield. 'Do you think the good Sisters have it in their power to darken the sky with their incantations?'

M. l'Adjoint shook his head. He went away with a troubled countenance; but then he was not like myself, a man of natural firmness. All the efforts that were employed to influence him were also employed with me; but to yield to the women was not in my thoughts. We are now approaching, however, the first important incident in this narrative. The darkness increased as the afternoon came on; and it became a kind of thick twilight, no lighter than many a night. It was between five and six o'clock, just the time when our streets are the most crowded, when, sitting at my window, from which I kept a watch upon the Grande Rue, not knowing what might happen—I saw that some fresh incident had taken place. Very dimly through the darkness I perceived a crowd, which increased every moment, in front of the Cathedral. After watching it for a few minutes, I got my hat and went out. The people whom I saw—so many that they covered the whole middle of the *Place*, reaching almost to the pavement on the other side—had their heads all turned towards the Cathedral. 'What are you gazing at, my friend?' I said to one by whom I stood.

He looked up at me with a face which looked ghastly in the gloom. 'Look, *M. le Maire!*' he said; 'cannot you see it on the great door?'

'I see nothing,' said I; but as I uttered these words I did indeed see something which was very startling. Looking towards the great door of the Cathedral, as they all were doing, it suddenly seemed to me that I saw an illuminated placard attached to it, headed with the word '*Sommation*' in gigantic letters. '*Tiens!*' I cried; but when I looked again there was nothing. 'What is this?

it is some witchcraft!' I said, in spite of myself 'Do you see anything, Jean Pierre?'

'*M. le Maire*,' he said, 'one moment one sees something—the next, one sees nothing. Look! it comes again.' I have always considered myself a man of courage, but when I saw this extraordinary appearance the panic which had seized upon me the former night returned, though in another form. Fly I could not, but I will not deny that my knees smote together. I stood for some minutes without being able to articulate a word—which, indeed, seemed the case with most of those before me. Never have I seen a more quiet crowd. They were all gazing, as if it was life or death that was set before them—while I, too, gazed with a shiver going over me. It was as I have seen an illumination of lamps in a stormy night; one moment the whole seems black as the wind sweeps over it, the next it springs into life again; and thus you go on, by turns losing and discovering the device formed by the lights.

Thus from moment to moment there appeared before us, in letters that seemed to blaze and flicker, something that looked like a great official placard. '*Sommation!*'—this was how it was headed. I read a few words at a time, as it came and went; and who can describe the chill that ran through my veins as I made it out? It was a summons to the people of Semur by name—myself at the head as *Maire* (and I heard afterwards that every man who saw it saw his own name, though the whole *façade* of the Cathedral would not have held a full list of all the people of Semur)—to yield their places, which they had not filled aright, to those who knew the meaning of life, being dead. *Nous autres Morts*—these were the words which blazed out oftenest of all, so that everyone saw them.

And 'Go!' this terrible placard said—'Go! leave this place to us who know the true signification of life.' These words I remember, but not the rest; and even at this moment It struck me that there was no explanation, nothing but this *vraie signification de la vie*, I felt like one In a dream: the light coming and going before me; one word, then another, appearing—sometimes a phrase like that I have quoted, blazing out, then dropping Into darkness. For the moment I was struck dumb; but then It came back to my mind that I had an example to give, and that for me, eminently a man of my century, to yield credence to a miracle was something not to be thought of. Also I knew the necessity of doing something to break the impression of awe and terror on the mind of the people. 'This is a trick,' I cried loudly, that all might hear. 'Let someone go and fetch M. de Clairon from the *Musée*. He will tell us how it has been done.'

This, boldly uttered, broke the spell. A number of pale faces gathered round me. 'Here is *M. le Maire*—he will clear it up,' they cried, making room for me that I might approach nearer. '*M. le Maire* is a man of courage—he has judgment. Listen to *M. le Maire*.' It was a relief to everybody that I had spoken. And soon I found myself by the side of *M. le Curé,* who was standing among the rest, saying nothing, and with the air of one as much bewildered as any of us. He gave me one quick look from under his eyebrows to see who it was that approached him, as was his way, and made room for me, but said nothing.

I was in too much emotion myself to keep silence—indeed, I was in that condition of wonder, alarm, and nervous excitement, that I had to speak or die; and there seemed an escape from something too terrible for flesh and blood to contemplate in the idea that there was trickery here. '*M. le Curé*,' I said, 'this is a strange ornament that you have placed on the front of your church. You are standing here to enjoy the effect. Now that you have seen how successful it has been, will not you tell me in confidence how it is done?'

I am conscious that there was a sneer in my voice, but I was too much excited to think of politeness. He gave me another of his rapid, keen looks.

'*M. le Maire*,' he said, 'you are injurious to a man who is as little fond of tricks as yourself.'

His tone, his glance, gave me a certain sense of shame, but I could not stop myself. 'One knows,' I said, 'that there are many things which an ecclesiastic may do without harm, which are not permitted to an ordinary layman—one who is an honest man, and no more.'

M. le Curé made no reply. He gave me another of his quick glances, with an impatient turn of his head. Why should I have suspected him? for no harm was known of him. He was the *Curé*, that was all; and perhaps we men of the world have our prejudices too. Afterwards, however, as we waited for *M. de Clairon*—for the crisis was too exciting for personal resentment—*M. le Curé* himself let drop something which made it apparent that it was the ladies of the hospital upon whom his suspicions fell. 'It is never well to offend women, *M. le Maire*,' he said. 'Women do not discriminate the lawful from the unlawful: so long as they produce an effect, it does not matter to them.' This gave me a strange impression, for it seemed to me that *M. le Curé* was abandoning his own side.

However, all other sentiments were, as may be imagined, but as shadows compared with the overwhelming power that held all our eyes and our thoughts to the wonder before us. Every moment seemed an hour till M. de Clairon appeared. He was pushed forward through the crowd as by magic, all making room for him; and many of us thought that when science thus came forward capable of finding out everything, the miracle would disappear. But instead of this it seemed to glow brighter than ever. That great word '*Sommation*' blazed out, so that we saw his figure waver against the light as if giving way before the flames that scorched him. He was so near that his outline was marked out dark against the glare they gave. It was as though his close approach rekindled every light. Then, with a flicker and trembling, word by word and letter by letter went slowly out before our eyes.

M. de Clairon came down very pale, but with a sort of smile on his face. 'No, *M. le Maire,*' he said, 'I cannot see how it is done. It is clever. I will examine the door further, and try the panels. Yes, I have left someone to watch that nothing is touched in the meantime, with the permission of *M. le Curé*—'

'You have my full permission,' *M. le Curé* said; and M. de Clairon laughed, though he was still very pale. 'You saw my name there,' he said. 'I am amused—I who am not one of your worthy citizens, *M. le Maire*. What can *Messieurs les Morts* of Semur want with a poor man of science like me? But you shall have my report before the evening is out.'

With this I had to be content. The darkness which succeeded to that strange light seemed more terrible than ever. We all stumbled as we turned to go away, dazzled by it, and stricken dumb, though some kept saying that it was a trick, and some murmured exclamations with voices full of terror. The sound of the crowd breaking up was like a regiment marching—all the world had been there. I was thankful, however, that neither my mother nor. my wife had seen anything; and though they were anxious to know why I was so serious, I succeeded fortunately in keeping the secret from them.

M. de Clairon did not appear till late, and then he confessed to me he could make nothing of it. 'If it is a trick (as of course it must be), it has been most cleverly done,' he said; and admitted that he was baffled altogether. For my part, I was not surprised. Had it been the Sisters of the hospital, as *M. le Curé* thought, would they have let the opportunity pass of preaching a sermon to us, and recommending their doctrines? Not so; here there were no doctrines, nothing but that pregnant phrase, *la vraie signification de la vie.* This made a more deep impression upon me than anything else. The Holy Mother herself (whom I wish to speak of with profound respect), and the saints, and the forgiveness of sins, would have all been there had it been the Sisters, or even *M. le Curé*. This, though I had myself suggested an imposture, made it very unlikely to my quiet thoughts. But if not an imposture, what could it be supposed to be?

Chapter 3

Expulsion of the Inhabitants

I will not attempt to give any detailed account of the state of the town during this evening. For myself I was utterly worn out, and went to rest as soon as M. de Clairon left me, having satisfied, as well as I could, the questions of the women. Even in the intensest excitement weary nature will claim her dues. I slept. I can even remember the grateful sense of being able to put all anxieties and perplexities aside for the moment, as I went to sleep. I felt the drowsiness gain upon me, and I was glad. To forget was of itself a happiness. I woke up, however, intensely awake, and in perfect possession of all my faculties, while it was yet dark; and at once got up and began to dress.

The moment of hesitation which generally follows waking—the little interval of thought in which one turns over perhaps that which is past, perhaps that which is to come—found no place within me. I got up without a moment's pause, like one who has been called to go on a journey; nor did it surprise me at all to see my wife moving about, taking a cloak from her wardrobe, and putting up linen in a bag. She was already fully dressed; but she asked no questions of me any more than I did of her. We were in haste, though we said nothing. When I had dressed, I looked round me to see if I had forgotten anything, as one does when one leaves a place. I saw my watch suspended to its usual hook, and my pocket-book, which I had taken from my pocket on the previous night. I took up also the light overcoat which I had worn when I made my rounds through the city on the first night of the darkness.

'Now,' I said, 'Agnès, I am ready.' I did not speak to her of where we were going, nor she to me. Little Jean and my mother met us at the door. Nor did *she* say anything, contrary to her custom; and the child was quite quiet. We went downstairs together without saying a word. The servants, who were all astir, followed us. I cannot give any description of the feelings that were in my mind. I had not any feelings. I was only hurried out, hastened by something which I could not define—a sense that I must go; and perhaps I was too much astonished to do anything but yield. It seemed, however, to be no force or fear that was moving me, but a desire of my own; though I could not tell how it was, or why I should be so anxious to get away.

All the servants, trooping after me, had the same look in their faces; they were anxious to be gone—it seemed their business to go—there was no question, no consultation. And when we came out into the street, we encountered a stream of processions similar to our own. The children went quite steadily by the side of their parents. Little Jean, for example, on an ordinary occasion would have broken away—would have run to his comrades of the Bois-Sombre family, and they to him. But no; the little ones, like ourselves, walked along quite gravely. They asked no questions, neither did we ask any questions of each other, as, 'Where are you going?' or, 'What is the meaning of a so early promenade?' Nothing of the kind: my mother took my arm, and my wife, leading little Jean by the hand, came to the other side. The servants followed.

The street was quite full of people; but there was no noise except the sound of their footsteps. All of us turned the same way—turned towards the gates—and though I was not conscious of any feeling except the wish to go on, there were one or two things which took a place in my memory. The first was, that my wife suddenly turned round as we were coming out of the *porte-cochère*, her face lighting up. I need not say to anyone who knows Madame Dupin de la Clairière, that she is a beautiful woman. Without any partiality on my part, it would be impossible for me to ignore this fact: for it is perfectly well known and acknowledged by all. She was pale this morning—a little paler than usual; and her blue eyes enlarged, with a serious look, which they always retain more or less. But suddenly, as we went out of the door, her face lighted up, her eyes were suffused with tears—with light—how can I tell what it was?—they became like the eyes of angels. A little cry came from her parted lips—she lingered a moment, stooping down as if talking to someone less tall than herself, then came after us, with that light still in her face.

At the moment I was too much occupied to enquire what it was; but I noted it, even in the gravity of the occasion. The next thing I observed was *M. le Curé*, who, as I have already indicated, is a man of great composure of manner and presence of mind, coming out of the door of the Presbytery. There was a strange look on his face of astonishment and reluctance. He walked very slowly, not as we did, but with a visible desire to turn back, folding his arms across his breast, and holding himself as if against the wind, resisting some gale which blew behind him, and forced him on. We felt no gale; but there seemed to be a strange wind blowing along the side of the street on which *M. le Curé* was. And there was an air of concealed surprise in his face—great astonishment, but a determination not to let anyone see that he was astonished, or that the situation was strange to him. And I cannot tell how it was, but I, too, though preoccupied, was surprised to perceive that *M. le Curé* was going with the rest of us, though I could not have told why.

Behind *M. le Curé* there was another whom I remarked. This was Jacques Richard, he of whom I have already spoken. He was like a figure I have seen somewhere in sculpture. No one was near him, nobody touching him, and yet it was only necessary to look at the man to perceive that he was being forced along against his will. Every limb was in resistance; his feet were planted widely yet firmly upon the pavement; one of his arms was stretched out as if to lay hold on anything that should come within reach. *M. le Curé* resisted passively; but Jacques resisted with passion, laying his back to the wind, and struggling not to be carried away.

Notwithstanding his resistance, however, this rough figure was driven along slowly, struggling at every step. He did not make one movement that was not against his will, but still he was driven on. On our side of the street all went, like ourselves, calmly. My mother uttered now and then a low moan, but said nothing. She clung to my arm, and walked on, hurrying a little, sometimes going quicker than I intended to go. As for my wife, she accompanied us with her light step, which scarcely seemed to touch the ground, little Jean pattering by her side. Our neighbours were all round us.

We streamed down, as in a long procession, to the Porte St. Lambert. It was only when we got there that the strange character of the step we were all taking suddenly occurred to me. It was still a kind of grey twilight, not yet day. The bells of the Cathedral had begun to toll, which was very startling—not ringing in their cheerful way, but tolling as if for a funeral; and no other sound was audible but the noise of footsteps, like an army making a silent march into an enemy's country. We had reached the gate when a sudden wondering came over me. Why were we all going out of our houses in the wintry dusk to which our July days had turned?

I stopped, and turning round, was about to say something to the others, when I became suddenly aware that here I was not my own master. My tongue clave to the roof of my mouth; I could not say a word. Then I myself was turned round, and softly, firmly, irresistibly pushed out of the gate. My mother, who clung to me, added a little, no doubt, to the force against me, whatever it was, for she was frightened, and opposed herself to any endeavour on my part to regain freedom of movement; but all that her feeble force could do against mine must have been little. Several other men around me seemed to be moved as I was.

M. Barbou, for one, made a still more decided effort to turn back, for, being a bachelor, he had no one to restrain him. Him I saw turned round as you would turn a *roulette*. He was thrown against my wife in his tempestuous course, and but that she was so light and elastic in her tread, gliding out straight and softly like one of the saints, I think he must have thrown her down. And at that moment, silent as we all were, his '*Pardon, Madame, mille pardons, Madame,*' and his tone of horror at his own indiscretion, seemed to come to me like a voice out of another life. Partially roused before by the sudden impulse of resistance I have described, I was yet more roused now. I turned round, disengaging myself from my mother.

'Where are we going? why are we thus cast forth? My friends, help!' I cried. I looked round upon the others, who, as I have said, had also awakened to a possibility of resistance. M. de Bois-Sombre, without a word, came and placed himself by my side; others started from the crowd. We turned to resist this mysterious impulse which had sent us forth. The crowd surged round us in the uncertain light.

Just then there was a dull soft sound, once, twice, thrice repeated. We rushed forward, but too late. The gates were closed upon us. The two folds of the great Porte St. Lambert, and the little postern for foot-passengers, all at once, not hurriedly, as from any fear of us, but slowly, softly, rolled on their hinges and shut—in our faces. I rushed forward with all my force and flung myself upon the gate. To what use? it was so closed as no mortal could open it. They told me after, for I was not aware at the moment, that I burst forth with cries and exclamations, bidding them 'Open, open in the name of God!' I was not aware of what I said, but it seemed to me that I heard a voice of which nobody said anything to me, so that it would seem to have been unheard by the others, saying with a faint sound as of a trumpet, 'Closed—in the name of God.' It might be only an echo, faintly brought back to me, of the words I had myself said.

There was another change, however, of which no one could have any doubt. When I turned round from these closed doors, though the moment before the darkness was such that we could not see the gates closing, I found the sun shining gloriously round us, and all my fellow-citizens turning with one impulse, with a sudden cry of joy, to hail the full day.

Le grand jour! Never in my life did I feel the full happiness of it, the full sense of the words before. The sun burst out into shining, the birds into singing. The sky stretched over us—deep and unfathomable and blue,—the grass grew under our feet, a soft air of morning blew upon us, waving the curls of the children, the veils of the women, whose faces were lit up by the beautiful day. After three days of darkness what a resurrection! It seemed to make up to us for the misery of being thus expelled from our homes. It was early, and all the freshness of the morning was upon the road and the fields, where the sun had just dried the dew. The river ran softly, reflecting the blue sky. How black it had been, deep and dark as a stream of ink, when I had looked down upon it from the Mont St. Lambert! and now it ran as clear and free as the voice of a little child.

We all shared this moment of joy—for to us of the South the sunshine is as the breath of life, and to be deprived of it had been terrible. But when that first pleasure was over, the evidence of our strange position forced itself upon us with overpowering reality and force, made stronger by the very light. In the dimness it had not seemed so certain; now, gazing at each other in the clear light of the natural morning, we saw what had happened to us. No more delusion was possible. We could not flatter ourselves now that it was a trick or a deception. M. de Clairon stood there like the rest of us, staring at the closed gates which science could not open. And there stood *M. le Curé*, which was more remarkable still. The Church herself had not been able to do anything. We stood, a crowd of houseless exiles, looking at each other, our children clinging to us, our hearts failing us, expelled from our homes.

As we looked in each other's faces we saw our own trouble. Many of the women sat down and wept; some upon the stones in the road, some on the grass. The children took fright from them, and began to cry too. What was to become of us? I looked round upon this crowed with despair in my heart. It was I to whom everyone would look—for lodging, for direction—everything that human creatures want. It was my business to forget myself, though I also had been driven from my home and my city. Happily there was one thing I had left. In the pocket of my overcoat was my scarf of office. I stepped aside behind a tree, and took it out, and tied it upon me. That was something. There was thus a representative of order and law in the midst of the exiles, whatever might happen.

This action, which a great number of the crowd saw, restored confidence. Many of the poor people gathered round me, and placed themselves near me, especially those women who had no natural support. When *M. le Curé* saw this, it seemed to make a great impression upon him. He changed colour, he who was usually so calm. Hitherto he had appeared bewildered, amazed to find himself as others. This, I must add, though you may perhaps think it superstitious, surprised me very much too. But now he regained his self-possession. He stepped upon a piece of wood that lay in front of the gate. 'My children'—he said. But just then the Cathedral bells, which had gone on tolling, suddenly burst into a wild peal. I do not know what it sounded like. It was a clamour of notes all run together, tone upon tone, without time or measure, as though a multitude had seized upon the bells and pulled all the ropes at once. If it was joy, what strange and terrible joy! It froze the very blood in our veins. *M. le Curé* became quite pale. He stepped down hurriedly from the piece of wood. We all made a hurried movement farther off from the gate.

It was now that I perceived the necessity of doing something, of getting this crowd disposed of, especially the women and the children. I am not ashamed to own that I trembled like the others; and nothing less than the consciousness that all eyes were upon me, and that my scarf of office marked me out among all who stood around, could have kept me from moving with precipitation as they did. I was enabled, however, to retire at a deliberate pace, and being thus slightly detached from the crowd, I took advantage of the opportunity to address them. Above all things, it was my duty to prevent a tumult in these unprecedented circumstances.

'My friends,' I said, 'the event which has occurred is beyond explanation for the moment. The very nature of it is mysterious; the circumstances are such as require the closest investigation. But take courage. I pledge myself not to leave this place till the gates are open, and you can return to your homes; in the meantime, however, the women and the children cannot remain here. Let those who have friends in the villages near, go and ask for shelter; and let all who will, go to my house of La Clairière. My mother, my wife! recall to yourselves the position you occupy, and show an example. Lead our neighbours, I entreat you, to La Clairière.'

My mother is advanced in years and no longer strong, but she has a great heart. 'I will go,' she said. 'God bless thee, my son! There will no harm happen; for if this be true which we are told, thy father is in Semur.'

There then occurred one of those incidents for which calculation never will prepare us. My mother's words seemed, as it were to open the flood-gates; my wife came up to me with the light in her face which I had seen when we left our own door. 'It was our little Marie—our angel,' she said. And then there arose a great cry and clamour of others, both men and women pressing round. 'I saw my mother,' said one, 'who is dead twenty years come the St. Jean.' 'And I my little René,' said another. 'And I my Camille, who was killed in Africa.' And lo, what did they do, but rush towards the gate in a crowd—that gate from which they had but this moment fled in terror—beating upon it, and crying out, 'Open to us, open to us, our most dear! Do you think we have forgotten you? We have never forgotten you!'

What could we do with them, weeping thus, smiling, holding out their arms to—we knew not what? Even my Agnès was beyond my reach. Marie was our little girl who was dead. Those who were thus transported by a knowledge beyond ours were the weakest among us; most of them were women, the men old or feeble, and some children. I can recollect that I looked for Paul Lecamus among them, with wonder not to see him there. But though they were weak, they were beyond our strength to guide. What could we do with them? How could we force them away while they held to the fancy that those they loved were there? As it happens in times of emotion, it was those who were most impassioned who took the first place. We were at our wits' end.

But while we stood waiting, not knowing what to do, another sound suddenly came from the walls, which made them all silent in a moment. The most of us ran to this point and that (some taking flight altogether; but with the greater part anxious curiosity and anxiety had for the moment extinguished fear), in a wild eagerness to see who or what it was. But there was nothing to be seen, though the sound came from the wall close to the Mont St. Lambert, which I have already described. It was to me like the sound of a trumpet, and so I heard others say; and along with the trumpet were sounds as of words, though I could not make them out. But those others seemed to understand—they grew calmer—they ceased to weep. They raised their faces, all with that light upon them—that light I had seen in my Agnès. Some of them fell upon their knees. Imagine to yourself what a sight it was, all of us standing round, pale, stupefied, without a word to say!

Then the women suddenly burst forth into replies—'*Oui, ma chérie! Oui, mon ange!*' they cried. And while we looked they rose up; they came back, calling the children around them. My Agnès took that place which I had bidden her take. She had not hearkened to me, to leave me—but she hearkened now; and though I had bidden her to do this, yet to see her do it bewildered me, made my heart stand still. '*Mon ami*,' she said, 'I must leave thee; it is commanded: they will not have the children suffer.' What could we do? We stood pale and looked on, while all the little ones, all the feeble, were gathered in a little army. My mother stood like me—to her nothing had been revealed. She was very pale, and there was a quiver of pain in her lips. She was the one who had been ready to do my bidding: but there was a rebellion in her heart now.

When the procession was formed (for it was my care to see that everything was done in order), she followed, but among the last. Thus they went away, many of them weeping, looking back, waving their hands to us. My Agnès covered her face, she could not look at me; but she obeyed. They went some to this side, some to that, leaving us gazing. For a long time we did nothing but watch them, going along the roads. What had their angels said to them? Nay, but God knows. I heard the sound; it was like the sound of the silver trumpets that travellers talk of; it was like music from heaven. I turned to *M. le Curé*, who was standing by.

'What is it?' I cried, 'you are their director—you are an ecclesiastic—you know what belongs to the unseen. What is this that has been said to them?' I have always thought well of *M. le Curé*. There were tears running down his cheeks.

'I know not,' he said. 'I am a miserable like the rest. What they know is between God and them. Me! I have been of the world, like the rest.'

This is how we were left alone—the men of the city—to take what means were best to get back to our homes. There were several left among us who had shared the enlightenment of the women, but these were not persons of importance who could put themselves at the head of affairs. And there were women who remained with us, but these not of the best. To see our wives go was very strange to us; it was the thing we wished most to see, the women and children in safety; yet it was a strange sensation to see them go. For me, who had the charge of all on my hands, the relief was beyond description—yet was it strange; I cannot describe it. Then I called upon M. Barbou, who was trembling like a leaf, and gathered the chief of the citizens about me, including *M. le Curé*, that we should consult together what we should do.

I know no words that can describe our state in the strange circumstances we were now placed in. The women and the children were safe: that was much. But we—we were like an army suddenly formed, but without arms, without any knowledge of how to fight, without being able to see our enemy. We Frenchmen have not been without knowledge of such perils. We have seen the invader enter our doors: we have been obliged to spread our table for him, and give him of our best. But to be put forth by forces no man could resist—to be left outside, with the doors of our own houses closed upon us—to be confronted by nothing—by a mist, a silence, a darkness,—this was enough to paralyse the heart of any man.

And it did so, more or less, according to the nature of those who were exposed to the trial. Some altogether failed us, and fled, carrying the news into the country, where most people laughed at them, as we understood afterwards. Some could do nothing but sit and gaze, huddled together in crowds, at the cloud over Semur, from which they expected to see fire burst and consume the city altogether. And a few, I grieve to say, took possession of the little *cabaret*, which stands at about half a kilometre from the St. Lambert gate, and established themselves there, in hideous riot, which was the worst thing of all for serious men to behold. Those upon whom I could rely I formed into patrols to go round the city, that no opening of a gate, or movement of those who were within, should take place without our knowledge.

Such an emergency shows what men are. M. Barbou, though in ordinary times he discharges his duties as *adjoint* satisfactorily enough (though, it need not be added, a good *Maire* who is acquainted with his duties, makes the office of *adjoint* of but little importance), was now found entirely useless. He could not forget how he had been spun round and tossed forth from the city gates. When I proposed to put him at the head of a patrol, he had an attack of the nerves. Before nightfall he deserted me altogether, going off to his country-house, and taking a number of his neighbours with him.

'How can we tell when we may be permitted to return to the town?' he said, with his teeth chattering. '*M. le Maire*, I adjure you to put yourself in a place of safety.'

'Sir,' I said to him, sternly, 'for one who deserts his post there is no place of safety.'

But I do not think he was capable of understanding me. Fortunately, I found in *M. le Curé* a much more trustworthy coadjutor. He was indefatigable; he had the habit of sitting up to all hours, of being called at all hours, in which our *bourgeoisie*, I cannot but acknowledge, is wanting. The expression I have before described of astonishment—but of astonishment which he wished to conceal—never left his face. He did not understand how such a thing could have been permitted to happen while he had no share in it; and, indeed, I will not deny that this was a matter of great wonder to myself too.

The arrangements I have described gave us occupation; and this had a happy effect upon us in distracting our minds from what had happened; for I think that if we had sat still and gazed at the dark city we should soon have gone mad, as some did.

In our ceaseless patrols and attempts to find a way of entrance, we distracted ourselves from the enquiry. Who would dare to go in if the entrance were found? In the meantime not a gate was opened, not a figure was visible. We saw nothing, no more than if Semur had been a picture painted upon a canvas. Strange sights Indeed met our eyes—sights which made even the bravest quail. The strangest of them was the boats that would go down and up the river, shooting forth from under the fortified bridge, which Is one of the chief features of our town, sometimes with sails perfectly well managed, sometimes impelled by oars, but with no one visible in them—no one conducting them.

To see one of these boats impelled up the stream, with no rower visible, was a wonderful sight. M. de Clairon, who was by my side, murmured something about a magnetic current; but when I asked him sternly by what set in motion, his voice died away In his moustache. *M. le Curé* said very little: one saw his lips move as he watched with us the passage of those boats. He smiled when it was proposed by someone to fire upon them.

He read his Hours as he went round at the head of his patrol. My fellow townsmen and I conceived a great respect for him; and he inspired pity in me also. He had been the teacher of the Unseen among us, till the moment when the Unseen was thus, as it were, brought within our reach; but with the revelation he had nothing to do; and it filled him with pain and wonder. It made him silent; he said little about his religion, but signed himself, and his lips moved. He thought (I imagine) that he had displeased Those who are over all.

When night came the bravest of us were afraid. I speak for myself. It was bright moonlight where we were, and Semur lay like a blot between the earth and the sky, all dark: even the Cathedral towers were lost in it; nothing visible but the line of the ramparts, whitened outside by the moon. One knows what black and strange shadows are cast by the moonlight; and it seemed to all of us that we did not know what might be lurking behind every tree. The shadows of the branches looked like terrible faces. I sent all my people out on the patrols, though they were dropping with fatigue. Rather that than to be mad with terror. For myself, I took up my post as near the bank of the river as we could approach; for there was a limit beyond which we might not pass. I made the experiment often; and It seemed to me, and to all that attempted it, that we did reach the very edge of the stream; but the next moment perceived that we were at a certain distance, say twenty metres or thereabout.

I placed myself there very often, wrapping a cloak about me to preserve me from the dew. (I may say that food had been sent us, and wine from La Clairière and many other houses in the neighbourhood, where the women had gone for this among other reasons, that we might be nourished by them.) And I must here relate a personal incident, though I have endeavoured not to be egotistical. While I sat watching, I distinctly saw a boat, a boat which belonged to myself, lying on the very edge of the shadow. The prow, indeed, touched the moonlight where it was cut clean across by the darkness; and this was how I discovered that it was the *Marie*, a pretty pleasure-boat which had been made for my wife. The sight of it made my heart beat; for what could it mean but that someone who was dear to me, someone in whom I took an interest, was there?

I sprang up from where I sat to make another effort to get nearer; but my feet were as lead, and would not move; and there came a singing in my ears, and my blood coursed through my veins as in a fever. Ah! was it possible? I, who am a man, who have resolution, who have courage, who can lead the people, *I was afraid!* I sat down again and wept like a child. Perhaps it was my little Marie that was in the boat. God, He knows if I loved thee, my little angel! but I was afraid. O how mean is man! though we are so proud. They came near to me who were my own, and it was borne in upon my spirit that my good father was with the child; but because they had died I was afraid. I covered my face with my hands. Then it seemed to me that I heard a long quiver of a sigh; a long, long breath, such as sometimes relieves a sorrow that is beyond words. Trembling, I uncovered my eyes. There was nothing on the edge of the moonlight; all was dark, and all was still, the white radiance making a clear line across the river, but nothing more.

If my Agnès had been with me she would have seen our child, she would have heard that voice! The great cold drops of moisture were on my forehead. My limbs trembled, my heart fluttered in my bosom. I could neither listen nor yet speak. And those who would have spoken to me, those who loved me, sighing, went away. It is not possible that such wretchedness should be credible to noble minds; and if it had not been for pride and for shame, I should have fled away straight to La Clairière, to put myself under shelter, to have someone near me who was less a coward than I. I, upon whom all the others relied, the *Maire* of the Commune! I make my confession. I was of no more force than this.

A voice behind me made me spring to my feet—the leap of a mouse would have driven me wild. I was altogether demoralised. '*Monsieur le Maire*, it is but I,' said someone quite humble and frightened. '*Tiens!*—It is thou, Jacques!' I said. I could have embraced him, though it is well known how little I approve of him. But he was living, he was a man like myself. I put out my hand, and felt him warm and breathing, and I shall never forget the ease that came to my heart. Its beating calmed. I was restored to myself.

'*M. le Maire*,' he said, 'I wish to ask you something. Is it true all that is said about these people, I would say, these *Messieurs?* I do not wish to speak with disrespect, *M. le Maire.*'

'What is it, Jacques, that is said?' I had called him 'thou' not out of contempt, but because, for the moment, he seemed to me as a brother, as one of my friends.

'*M. le Maire*, is it indeed *les morts* that are in Semur?'

He trembled, and so did I. 'Jacques,' I said, 'you know all that I know.'

'Yes, *M. le Maire*, it is so, sure enough. I do not doubt it. If it were the Prussians, a man could fight. But *ces Messieurs là!* What I want to know is: is it because of what you did to those little Sisters, those good little ladies of St. Jean?'

'What I did? You were yourself one of the complainants. You were of those who said, when a man is ill, when he is suffering, they torment him with their mass; it is quiet he wants, not their mass. These were thy words, *vaurien*. And now you say it was I!'

'True, *M. le Maire,*' said Jacques; 'but look you, when a man is better, when he has just got well, when he feels he is safe, then you should not take what he says for gospel. It would be strange if one had a new illness just when one is getting well of the old; and one feels now is the time to enjoy one's self, to kick up one's heels a little, while at least there is not likely to be much of a watch kept *up there*—the saints forgive me,' cried Jacques, trembling and crossing himself, 'if I speak with levity at such a moment! And the little ladies were very kind. It was wrong to close their chapel, *M. le Maire*. From that comes all our trouble.'

'You good-for-nothing!' I cried, 'it is you and such as you that are the beginning of our trouble. You thought there was no watch kept *up there*; you thought God would not take the trouble to punish you; you went about the streets of Semur tossing a *grosse pièce* of a hundred *sous*, and calling out, "There is no God—this is my god; *l'argent, c'est le bon Dieu!*"'

'*M. le Maire, M. le Maire,* be silent, I implore you! It is enough to bring down a judgement upon us.'

'It has brought down a judgement upon us. Go thou and try what thy *grosse pièce* will do for thee now—worship thy god. Go, I tell you, and get help from your money.'

'I have no money, *M. le Maire*, and what could money do here? We would do much better to promise a large candle for the next festival, and that the ladies of St. Jean—'

'Get away with thee to the end of the world, thou and thy ladies of St. Jean!' I cried; which was wrong, I do not deny it, for they are good women, not like this good-for-nothing fellow. And to think that this man, whom I despise, was more pleasant to me than the dear souls who loved me! Shame came upon me at the thought. I too, then, was like the others, fearing the Unseen—capable of understanding only that which was palpable. When Jacques slunk away, which he did for a few steps, not losing sight of me, I turned my face towards the river and the town. The moonlight fell upon the water, white as silver where that line of darkness lay, shining, as if it tried, and tried in vain, to penetrate Semur; and between that and the blue sky overhead lay the city out of which we had been driven forth—the city of the dead. 'O God,' I cried, 'whom I know not, am not I to Thee as my little Jean is to me, a child and less than a child? Do not abandon me in this darkness. Would I abandon him were he ever so disobedient? And God, if thou art God, Thou art a better father than I.'

When I had said this, my heart was a little relieved. It seemed to me that I had spoken to someone who knew all of us, whether we were dead or whether we were living. That is a wonderful thing to think of, when it appears to one not as a thing to believe, but as something that is real. It gave me courage. I got up and went to meet the patrol which was coming in, and found that great good-for-nothing Jacques running close after me, holding my cloak.

'Do not send me away, *M. le Maire*,' he said, 'I dare not stay by myself with *them* so near.' Instead of his money, in which he had trusted, it was I who had become his god now.

Chapter 4

Outside the Walls.

There are few who have not heard something of the sufferings of a siege. Whether within or without, it is the most terrible of all the experiences of war. I am old enough to recollect the trenches before Sebastopol, and all that my countrymen and the English endured there. Sometimes I endeavoured to think of this to distract me from what we ourselves endured. But how different was it! We had neither shelter nor support. We had no weapons, nor any against whom to wield them. We were cast out of our homes in the midst of our lives, in the midst of our occupations, and left there helpless, to gaze at each other, to blind our eyes trying to penetrate the darkness before us. Could we have done anything, the oppression might have been less terrible—but what was there that we could do?

Fortunately (though I do not deny that I felt each desertion) our band grew less and less every day. Hour by hour someone stole away—first one, then another, dispersing themselves among the villages near, in which many had friends. The accounts which these men gave were, I afterwards learnt, of the most vague description. Some talked of wonders they had seen, and were laughed at—and some spread reports of internal division among us. Not till long after did I know all the reports that went abroad. It was said that there had been fighting in Semur, and that we were divided into two factions, one of which had gained the mastery, and driven the other out.

This was the story current in La Rochette, where they are always glad to hear anything to the discredit of the people of Semur; but no credence could have been given to it by those in authority, otherwise *M. le Préfet*, however indifferent to our interests, must necessarily have taken some steps for our relief. Our entire separation from the world was indeed one of the strangest details of this terrible period. Generally the diligence, though conveying on the whole few passengers, returned with two or three, at least, visitors or commercial persons, daily—and the latter class frequently arrived in carriages of their own; but during this period no stranger came to see our miserable plight.

We made shelter for ourselves under the branches of the few trees that grew in the uncultivated ground on either side of the road—and a hasty erection, half tent half shed, was put up for a place to assemble in, or for those who were unable to bear the heat of the day or the occasional chills of the night. But the most of us were too restless to seek repose, and could not bear to be out of sight of the city. At any moment It seemed to us the gates might open, or some loophole be visible by which we might throw ourselves upon the darkness and vanquish it. This was what we said to ourselves, forgetting how we shook and trembled whenever any contact had been possible with those who were within.

But one thing was certain, that though we feared, we could

not turn our eyes from the place. We slept leaning against a tree, or with our heads on our hands, and our faces toward Semur. We took no count of day or night, but ate the morsel the women brought to us, and slept thus, not sleeping, when want or weariness overwhelmed us. There was scarcely an hour in the day that some of the women did not come to ask what news. They crept along the roads in twos and threes, and lingered for hours sitting by the way weeping, starting at every breath of wind.

Meanwhile all was not silent within Semur. The Cathedral bells rang often, at first filling us with hope, for how familiar was that sound! The first time, we all gathered together and listened, and many wept. It was as if we heard our mother's voice. M. de Bols-Sombre burst into tears. I have never seen him within the doors of the Cathedral since his marriage; but he burst into tears. '*Mon Dieu!* If I were but there!' he said. We stood and listened, our hearts melting, some falling on their knees. *M. le Curé* stood up in the midst of us and began to intone the psalm: [He has a beautiful voice. It is sympathetic. It goes to the heart.] 'I was glad when they said to me, let us go up—' And though there were few of us who could have supposed themselves capable of listening to that sentiment a little while before with any sympathy, yet a vague hope rose up within us while we heard him, while we listened to the bells.

What man is there to whom the bells of his village, the *carillon* of his city, is not most dear? It rings for him through all his life; It Is the first sound of home in the distance when he comes back—the last that follows him like a long farewell when he goes away. While we listened, we forgot our fears. They were as we were, they were also our brethren, who rang those bells. We seemed to see them trooping into our beautiful Cathedral. Ah! only to see it again, to be within its shelter, cool and calm as in our mother's arms! It seemed to us that we should wish for nothing more.

When the sound ceased we looked into each other's faces, and each man saw that his neighbour was pale. Hope died in us when the sound died away, vibrating sadly through the air. Some men threw themselves on the ground in their despair.

And from this time forward many voices were heard, calls and shouts within the walls, and sometimes a sound like a trumpet, and other instruments of music. We thought, indeed, that noises as of bands patrolling along the ramparts were audible as our patrols worked their way round and round. This was a duty which I never allowed to be neglected, not because I put very much faith in it, but because it gave us a sort of employment. There is a story somewhere which I recollect dimly of an ancient city which its assailants did not touch, but only marched round and round till the walls fell, and they could enter. Whether this was a story of classic times or out of our own remote history, I could not recollect. But I thought of it many times while we made our way like a procession of ghosts, round and round, straining our ears to hear what those voices were which sounded above us, in tones that were familiar, yet so strange.

This story got so much into my head (and after a time all our heads seemed to get confused and full of wild and bewildering expedients) that I found myself suggesting—I, a man known for sense and reason—that we should blow trumpets at some time to be fixed, which was a thing the ancients had done in the strange tale which had taken possession of me. *M. le Curé* looked at me with disapproval. He said, 'I did not expect from *M. le Maire* anything that was disrespectful to religion.' Heaven forbid that I should be disrespectful to religion at anytime of life, but then it was impossible to me. I remembered after that the tale of which I speak, which had so seized upon me, was in the sacred writings; but those who know me will understand that no sneer at these writings or intention of wounding the feelings of *M. le Curé* was in my mind.

I was seated one day upon a little inequality of the ground, leaning my back against a half-withered hawthorn, and dozing with my head in my hands, when a soothing, which always diffuses itself from her presence, shed itself over me, and opening my eyes, I saw my Agnès sitting by me. She had come with some food and a little linen, fresh and soft like her own touch. My wife was not gaunt and worn like me, but she was pale and as thin as a shadow. I woke with a start, and seeing her there, there suddenly came a dread over me that she would pass away before my eyes, and go over to Those who were within Semur. I cried '*Non, mon Agnès; non, mon Agnès*: before you ask, No!' seizing her and holding her fast in this dream, which was not altogether a dream. She looked at me with a smile, that smile that has always been to me as the rising of the sun over the earth.

'*Mon ami*' she said surprised, 'I ask nothing, except that you should take a little rest and spare thyself.' Then she added, with haste, what I knew she would say, 'Unless it were this, *mon ami*. If I were permitted, I would go into the city—I would ask those who are there what is their meaning: and if no way can be found—no act of penitence.—Oh! do not answer in haste! I have no fear; and it would be to save thee.'

A strong throb of anger came into my throat. Figure to yourself that I looked at my wife with anger, with the same feeling which had moved me when the deserters left us; but far more hot and sharp. I seized her soft hands and crushed them in mine. 'You would leave me!' I said. 'You would desert your husband. You would go over to our enemies!'

'O Martin, say not so,' she cried, with tears. 'Not enemies. There is our little Marie, and my mother, who died when I was born.'

'You love these dead tyrants. Yes,' I said, 'you love them best. You will go to—the majority, to the strongest. Do not speak to me! Because your God is on their side, you will forsake us too.'

Then she threw herself upon me and encircled me with her arms. The touch of them stilled my passion; but yet I held her, clutching her gown, so terrible a fear came over me that she would go and come back no more.

'Forsake thee!' she breathed out over me with a moan. Then, putting her cool cheek to mine, which burned, 'But I would die for thee, Martin.'

'Silence, my wife: that is what you shall not do,' I cried, beside myself. I rose up; I put her away from me. That is, I know it, what has been done. Their God does this, they do not hesitate to say—takes from you what you love best, to make you better—*you!* and they ask you to love Him when He has thus despoiled you! 'Go home, Agnès,' I said, hoarse with terror. 'Let us face them as we may; you shall not go among them, or put thyself in peril. Die for me! *Mon Dieu!* and what then, what should I do then? Turn your face from them; turn from them; go! go! and let me not see thee here again.'

My wife did not understand the terror that seized me. She obeyed me, as she always does, but, with the tears falling from her white cheeks, fixed upon me the most piteous look. '*Mon ami,*' she said, 'you are disturbed, you are not in possession of yourself; this cannot be what you mean.'

'Let me not see thee here again!' I cried. 'Would you make me mad in the midst of my trouble? No! I will not have you look that way. Go home! go home!' Then I took her into my arms and wept, though I am not a man given to tears. 'Oh! my Agnès,' I said, 'give me thy counsel. What you tell me I will do; but rather than risk thee, I would live thus forever, and defy them.'

She put her hand upon my lips. 'I will not ask this again,' she said, bowing her head; 'but defy them—why should you defy them? Have they come for nothing? Was Semur a city of the saints? They have come to convert our people, Martin—thee too, and the rest. If you will submit your hearts, they will open the gates, they will go back to their sacred homes: and we to ours. This has been borne in upon me sleeping and waking; and it seemed to me that if I could but go, and say, "Oh! my fathers, oh! my brothers, they submit," all would be well. For I do not fear them, Martin. Would they harm me that love us? I would but give our Marie one kiss—'

'You are a traitor!' I said. 'You would steal yourself from me, and do me the worst wrong of all—'

But I recovered my calm. What she said reached my understanding at last. 'Submit !' I said, 'but to what? To come and turn us from our homes, to wrap our town in darkness, to banish our wives and our children, to leave us here to be scorched by the sun and drenched by the rain,—this is not to convince us, my Agnès. And to what then do you bid us submit ?'

'It is to convince you, *mon ami*, of the love of God, who has permitted this great tribulation to be, that we might be saved,' said Agnès. Her face was sublime with faith. It Is possible to these dear women; but for me the words she spoke were but words without meaning. I shook my head. Now that my horror and alarm were passed, I could well remember often to have heard words like these before.

'My angel!' I said, 'all this I admire, I adore in thee; but how is it the love of God?—and how shall we be saved by it? Submit! I will do anything that is reasonable; but of what truth have we here the proof?'

Someone had come up behind as we were talking. When I heard his voice I smiled, notwithstanding my despair. It was natural that the Church should come to the woman's aid. But I would not refuse to give ear to *M. le Curé*, who had proved himself a man, had he been ten times a priest.

'I have not heard what *Madame* has been saying, *M. le Maire*, neither would I interpose but for your question. You ask of what truth have we the proof here? It is the Unseen that has revealed itself. Do we see anything, you and I? Nothing, nothing, but a cloud. But that which we cannot see, that which we know not, that which we dread—look! it is there.'

I turned unconsciously as he pointed with his hand. Oh, heaven, what did I see! Above the cloud that wrapped Semur there was a separation, a rent in the darkness, and in mid heaven the Cathedral towers, pointing to the sky. I paid no more attention to *M. le Curé*. I sent forth a shout that roused all, even the weary line of the patrol that was marching slowly with bowed heads round the walls; and there went up such a cry of joy as shook the earth. 'The towers, the towers!' I cried. These were the towers that could be seen leagues off, the first sign of Semur; our towers, which we had been born to love like our father's name. I have had joys In my life, deep and great. I have loved, I have won honours, I have conquered difficulty; but never had I felt as now. It was as if one had been born again.

When we had gazed upon them, blessing them and thanking God, I gave orders that all our company should be called to the tent, that we might consider whether any new step could now be taken: Agnès with the other women sitting apart on one side and waiting. I recognised even in the excitement of such a time that theirs was no easy part. To sit there silent, to wait till we had spoken, to be bound by what we decided, and to have no voice—yes, that was hard. They thought they knew better than we did: but they were silent, devouring us with their eager eyes. I love one woman more than all the world; I count her the best thing that God has made; yet would I not be as Agnès for all that life could give me. It was her part to be silent, and she was so, like the angel she is, while even Jacques Richard had the right to speak. *Mon Dieu!* but it is hard, I allow it; they have need to be angels. This thought passed through my mind even at the crisis which had now arrived.

For at such moments one sees everything, one thinks of everything, though it is only after that one remembers what one has seen and thought. When my fellow-citizens gathered together (we were now less than a hundred in number, so many had gone from us), I took it upon myself to speak. We were a haggard, worn-eyed company, having had neither shelter nor sleep nor even food, save in hasty snatches. I stood at the door of the tent and they below, for the ground sloped a little. Beside me were *M. le Curé*, M. de Bois-Sombre, and one or two others of the chief citizens. 'My friends,' I said, 'you have seen that a new circumstance has occurred. It is not within our power to tell what its meaning is, yet it must be a symptom of good. For my own part, to see these towers makes the air lighter. Let us think of the Church as we may, no one can deny that the towers of Semur are dear to our hearts.'

'*M. le Maire*,' said M. de Bois-Sombre, interrupting, 'I speak I am sure the sentiments of my fellow-citizens when I say that there is no longer any question among us concerning the

Church; it is an admirable institution, a universal advantage—'

'Yes, yes,' said the crowd, 'yes, certainly! and some added, 'It is the only safeguard, it is our protection,' and some signed themselves. In the crowd I saw Riou, who had done this at the *octroi*. But the sign did not surprise me now.

M. le Curé stood by my side, but he did not smile. His countenance was dark, almost angry. He stood quite silent, with his eyes on the ground. It gave him no pleasure, this profession of faith.

'It is well, my friends,' said I, 'we are all in accord; and the good God has permitted us again to see these towers. I have called you together to collect your ideas. This change must have a meaning. It has been suggested to me that we might send an ambassador—a messenger, if that is possible, into the city—'

Here I stopped short; and a shiver ran through me—a shiver which went over the whole company. We were all pale as we looked in each other's faces; and for a moment no one ventured to speak. After this pause it was perhaps natural that he who first found his voice should be the last who had any right to give an opinion. Who should it be but Jacques Richard? '*M. le Maire,*' cried the fellow, 'speaks at his ease—but who will thus risk himself?' Probably he did not mean that his grumbling should be heard, but in the silence every sound was audible; there was a gasp, a catching of the breath, and all turned their eyes again upon me.

I did not pause to think what answer I should give. 'I!' I cried. 'Here stands one who will risk himself, who will perish if need be—'

Something stirred behind me. It was Agnès who had risen to her feet, who stood with her lips parted and quivering, with her hands clasped, as if about to speak. But she did not speak. Well! she had proposed to do it. Then why not I?

'Let me make the observation,' said another of our fellow-citizens. Bordereau the banker, 'that this would not be just. Without *M. le Maire* we should be a mob without a head. If a messenger is to be sent, let it be someone not so indispensable—'

'Why send a messenger?' said another, Philip Leclerc. 'Do we know that these *Messieurs* will admit anyone? and how can you speak, how can you parley with those—' and he too, was seized with a shiver—'whom you cannot see?'

Then there came another voice out of the crowd. It was one who would not show himself, who was conscious of the mockery in his tone. 'If there is anyone sent, let it be *M. le Curé*,' it said.

M. le Curé stepped forward. His pale countenance flushed red. 'Here am I,' he said, 'I am ready; but he who spoke speaks to mock me. Is it befitting in this presence?'

There was a struggle among the men. Whoever it was who had spoken (I did not wish to know), I had no need to condemn the mocker; they themselves silenced him; then Jacques Richard (still less worthy of credit) cried out again with a voice that was husky. What are men made of? Notwithstanding everything, it was from the *cabaret*, from the wine-shop, that he had come. He said, 'Though *M. le Maire* will not take my opinion, yet it is this. Let them reopen the chapel in the hospital. The ladies of St. Jean—'

'Hold thy peace,' I said, 'miserable!'

But a murmur rose. 'Though it is not his part to speak, I agree,' said one. 'And I.' 'And I.' There was well-nigh a tumult of consent; and this made me angry. Words were on my lips which it might have been foolish to utter, when M. de Bois-Sombre, who is a man of judgement, interfered.

'*M. le Maire,*' he said, 'as there are none of us here who would show disrespect to the Church and holy things—that is understood—it is not necessary to enter into details. Every restriction that would wound the most susceptible is withdrawn; not one more than another, but all. We have been indifferent in the past, but for the future you will agree with me that everything shall be changed. The ambassador—whoever he may be—' he added with a catching of his breath, 'must be empowered to promise—everything—submission to all that may be required.'

Here the women could not restrain themselves; they all rose up with a cry, and many of them began to weep. 'Ah!' said one with a hysterical sound of laughter in her tears. '*Sainte Mère!* it will be heaven upon earth.'

M. le Curé said nothing; a keen glance of wonder, yet of subdued triumph, shot from under his eyelids. As for me, I wrung my hands: 'What you say will be superstition; it will be hypocrisy,' I cried.

But at that moment a further incident occurred. Suddenly, while we deliberated, a long loud peal of a trumpet sounded into the air. I have already said that many sounds had been heard before; but this was different; there was not one of us that did not feel that this was addressed to himself. The agitation was extreme; it was a summons, the beginning of some distinct communication. The crowd scattered; but for myself, after a momentary struggle, I went forward resolutely. I did not even look back at my wife. I was no longer Martin Dupin, but the *Maire* of Semur, the saviour of the community. Even Bois-Sombre quailed: but I felt that it was in me to hold head against death itself; and before I had gone two steps I felt rather than saw that *M. le Curé* had come to my side. We went on without a word; gradually the others collected behind us, following yet straggling here and there upon the inequalities of the ground.

Before us lay the cloud that was Semur, a darkness defined by the shining of the summer day around, the river escaping from that gloom as from a cavern, the towers piercing through, but the sunshine thrown back on every side from that darkness. I have spoken of the walls as if we saw them, but there were no walls visible, nor any gate, though we all turned like blind men to where the Porte St. Lambert was. There was the broad vacant road leading up to it, leading into the gloom. We stood there at a little distance. Whether it was human weakness or an invisible barrier, how can I tell? We stood thus immovable, with the trumpet pealing out over us, out of the cloud. It summoned every man as by his name. To me it was not wonderful that this impression should come, but afterwards it was elicited from all that this was the feeling of each. Though no words were said, it was as the calling of our names. We all waited in such a supreme agitation as I cannot describe for some communication that was to come.

When suddenly, in a moment, the trumpet ceased; there was an interval of dead and terrible silence; then, each with a leap of his heart as if it would burst from his bosom, we saw a single figure slowly detach itself out of the gloom. 'My God!' I cried. My senses went from me; I felt my head go round like a straw tossed on the winds.

To know them so near, those mysterious visitors—to feel them, to hear them, was not that enough? But, to see! who could bear it? Our voices rang like broken chords, like a tearing and rending of sound. Some covered their faces with their hands; for our very eyes seemed to be drawn out of their sockets, fluttering like things with a separate life.

Then there fell upon us a strange and wonderful calm. The figure advanced slowly; there was weakness in it. The step, though solemn, was feeble; and if you can figure to yourself our consternation, the pause, the cry—our hearts dropping back as it might be into their places—the sudden stop of the wild panting in our breasts: when there became visible to us a human face well known, a man as we were. 'Lecamus!' I cried; and all the men round took it up, crowding nearer, trembling yet delivered from their terror; some even laughed in the relief. There was but one who had an air of discontent, and that was *M. le Curé*. As he said 'Lecamus!' like the rest, there was impatience, disappointment, anger in his tone.

And I, who had wondered where Lecamus had gone; thinking sometimes that he was one of the deserters who had left us! But when he came nearer his face was as the face of a dead man, and a cold chill came over us. His eyes, which were cast down, flickered under the thin eyelids in which all the veins were visible. His face was gray like that of the dying. 'Is he dead?' I said. But, except *M. le Curé*, no one knew that I spoke.

'Not even so,' said *M. le Curé*, with a mortification in his voice, which I have never forgotten. 'Not even so. That might be something. They teach us not by angels—by the fools and offscourings of the earth.'

And he would have turned away. It was a humiliation. Was not he the representative of the Unseen, the vicegerent, with power over heaven and hell? but something was here more strong than he. He stood by my side in spite of himself to listen to the ambassador. I will not deny that such a choice was strange, strange beyond measure, to me also.

'Lecamus,' I said, my voice trembling in my throat, 'have you been among the dead, and do you live?'

'I live,' he said; then looked around with tears upon the crowd. 'Good neighbours, good friends,' he said, and put out his hand and touched them; he was as much agitated as they.

'M. Lecamus,' said I, 'we are here in very strange circumstances, as you know; do not trifle with us. If you have indeed been with those who have taken the control of our city, do not keep us in suspense. You will see by the emblems of my office that it is to me you must address yourself; if you have a mission, speak.'

'It is just,' he said, 'it is just—but bear with me one moment. It is good to behold those who draw breath; if I have not loved you enough, my good neighbours, forgive me now!'

'Rouse yourself, Lecamus,' said I with some anxiety. 'Three days we have been suffering here; we are distracted with the suspense. Tell us your message—if you have anything to tell.'

'Three days!' he said, wondering; 'I should have said years. Time is long when there is neither night nor day.' Then, uncovering himself, he turned towards the city. 'They who have sent me would have you know that they come, not in anger but in friendship: for the love they bear you, and because it has been permitted—'

As he spoke his feebleness disappeared. He held his head high; and we clustered closer and closer round him, not losing a half word, not a tone, not a breath.

'They are not the dead. They are the immortal. They are those who dwell—elsewhere. They have other work, which has been interrupted because of this trial. They ask, "Do you know now—do you know now?" this is what I am bidden to say.'

'What'—I said (I tried to say it, but my lips were dry), 'What would they have us to know?'

But a clamour interrupted me. 'Ah! yes, yes, yes!' the people cried, men and women; some wept aloud, some signed themselves, some held up their hands to the skies. 'Never more will we deny religion,' they cried, 'never more fail in our duties. They shall see how we will follow every office, how the churches shall be full, how we will observe the feasts and the days of the saints! M. Lecamus,' cried two or three together; 'go, tell these *Messieurs* that we will have masses said for them, that we will obey in everything. We have seen what comes of it when a city is without piety. Never more will we neglect the holy functions; we will vow ourselves to the holy Mother and the saints—'

'And if those ladies wish it,' cried Jacques Richard, 'there shall be as many masses as there are priests to say them in the Hospital of St. Jean.'

'Silence, fellow!' I cried; 'is it for you to promise in the name of the Commune?' I was almost beside myself. 'M. Lecamus is it for this that they have come?'

His head had begun to droop again, and a dimness came over his face. 'Do I know?' he said. 'It was them I longed for, not to know their errand; but I have not yet said all. You are to send two—two whom you esteem the highest—to speak with them face to face.'

Then at once there rose a tumult among the people—an eagerness which nothing could subdue. There was a cry that the ambassadors were already elected, and we were pushed forward, *M. le Curé* and myself, towards the gate. They would not hear us speak. 'We promise,' they cried, 'we promise everything; let us but get back.' Had it been to sacrifice us they would have done the same; they would have killed us in their passion, in order to return to their city—and afterwards mourned us and honoured us as martyrs. But for the moment they had neither ruth nor fear. Had it been they who were going to reason not with flesh and blood, it would have been different; but it was we, not they; and they hurried us on as not willing that a moment should be lost. I had to struggle, almost to fight, in order to provide them with a leader, which was indispensable, before I myself went away. For who could tell if we should ever come back? For a moment I hesitated, thinking that it might be well to invest M. de Bois-Sombre as my deputy with my scarf of office; but then I reflected that when a man goes to battle, when he goes to risk his life, perhaps to lose it, for his people, it is his right to bear those signs which distinguish him from common men, which show in what office, for what cause, he is ready to die.

Accordingly I paused, struggling against the pressure of the people, and said in a loud voice, 'In the absence of M. Barbou, who has forsaken us, I constitute the excellent M. Felix de Bois-Sombre my representative. In my absence my fellow-citizens will respect and obey him as myself.' There was a cry of assent. They would have given their assent to anything that we might but go on. What was it to them? They took no thought of the heaving of my bosom, the beating of my heart. They left us on the edge of the darkness with our faces towards the gate. There we stood one breathless moment. Then the little postern slowly opened before us, and once more we stood within Semur.

Chapter 5

The Narrative of Paul Lecamus

M. le Maire having requested me, on his entrance into Semur, to lose no time in drawing up an account of my residence in the town, to be placed with his own narrative, I have promised to do so to the best of my ability, feeling that my condition is a very precarious one, and my time for explanation may be short. Many things, needless to enumerate, press this upon my mind. It was a pleasure to me to see my neighbours when I first came out of the city; but their voices, their touch, their vehemence and eagerness wear me out. From my childhood up I have shrunk from close contact with my fellowmen. My mind has been busy with other thoughts; I have desired to investigate the mysterious and unseen. When I have walked abroad I have heard whispers In the air; I have felt the movement of wings, the gliding of unseen feet.

To my comrades these have been a source of alarm and disquiet, but not to me; is not God in the unseen with all His angels? and not only so, but the best and wisest of men. There was a time indeed, when life acquired for me a charm. There was a smile which filled me with blessedness, and made the sunshine more sweet. But when she died my earthly joys died with her. Since then I have thought of little but the depths profound, into which she has disappeared like the rest.

I was in the garden of my house on that night when all the others left Semur, I was restless, my mind was disturbed. It seemed to me that I approached the crisis of my life. Since the time when I led *M. le Maire* beyond the walls, and we felt both of us the rush and pressure of that crowd, a feeling of expectation had been in my mind. I knew not what I looked for—but something I looked for that should change the world. The '*Sommation*' on the Cathedral doors did not surprise me. Why should it be a matter of wonder that the dead should come back? the wonder is that they do not. Ah! that is the wonder. How one can go away who loves you, and never return, nor speak, nor send any message—that is the miracle: not that the heavens should bend down and the gates of Paradise roll back, and those who have left us return. All my life it has been a marvel to me how they could be kept away. I could not stay indoors on this strange night. My mind was full of agitation. I came out into the garden though it was dark. I sat down upon the bench under the trellis—she loved it. Often had I spent half the night there thinking of her.

It was very dark that night: the sky all veiled, no light anywhere—a night like November. One would have said there was snow in the air. I think I must have slept toward morning (I have observed throughout that the preliminaries of these occurrences have always been veiled in sleep), and when I woke suddenly it was to find myself, if I may so speak, the subject of a struggle. The struggle was within me, yet it was not I. In my mind there was a desire to rise from where I sat and go away, I could not tell where or why; but something in me said stay, and my limbs were as heavy as lead. I could not move; I sat still against my will; against one part of my will—but the other was obstinate and would not let me go. Thus a combat took place within me of which I knew not the meaning. While it went on I began to hear the sound of many feet, the opening of doors, the people pouring out into the streets. This gave me no surprise; it seemed to me that I understood why it was; only in my own case, I knew nothing.

I listened to the steps pouring past, going on and on, faintly dying away in the distance, and there was a great stillness. I then became convinced, though I cannot tell how, that I was the only living man left in Semur; but neither did this trouble me. The struggle within me came to an end, and I experienced a great calm. I cannot tell how long It was till I perceived a change In the air, In the darkness round me. It was like the movement of someone unseen. I have felt such a sensation In the night, when all was still, before now. I saw nothing. I heard nothing. Yet I was aware, I cannot tell how, that there was a great coming and going, and the sensation as of a multitude in the air. I then rose and went into my house, where Leocadie, my old housekeeper, had shut all the doors so carefully when she went to bed. They were now all open, even the door of my wife's room of which I kept always the key, and where no one entered but myself; the windows also were open.

I looked out upon the Grande Rue, and all the other houses were like mine. Everything was open, doors and windows, and the streets were full. There was in them a flow and movement of the unseen, without a sound, sensible only to the soul. I cannot describe it, for I neither heard nor saw, but felt. I have often been in crowds; I have lived in Paris, and once passed into England, and walked about the London streets. But never, it seemed to me, never was I aware of so many, of so great a multitude. I stood at my open window, and watched as in a dream. *M. le Maire* is aware that his house is visible from mine. Towards that a stream seemed to be always going, and at the windows and in the doorways was a sensation of multitudes like that which I have already described.

Gazing out thus upon the revolution which was happening before my eyes, I did not think of my own house or what was passing there, till suddenly, in a moment, I was aware that someone had come in to me. Not a crowd as elsewhere; one. My heart leaped up like a bird let loose; it grew faint within me with joy and fear. I was giddy so that I could not stand. I called out her name, but low, for I was too happy, I had no voice. Besides was it needed, when heart already spoke to heart?

I had no answer, but I needed none. I laid myself down on the floor where her feet would be. Her presence wrapped me round and round. It was beyond speech. Neither did I need to see her face, nor to touch her hand. She was more near to me, more near, than when I held her in my arms. How long it was so, I cannot tell; it was long as love, yet short as the drawing of a breath. I knew nothing, felt nothing but Her, alone; all my wonder and desire to know departed from me. We said to each other everything without words—heart overflowing into heart. It was beyond knowledge or speech.

But this is not of public signification that I should occupy with it the time of *M. le Maire*.

After a while my happiness came to an end. I can no more tell how, than I can tell how it came. One moment, I was warm in her presence; the next, I was alone. I rose up staggering with blindness and woe—could it be that already, already it was over? I went out blindly following after her. My God, I shall follow, I shall follow, till life is over. She loved me; but she was gone.

Thus, despair came to me at the very moment when the longing of my soul was satisfied and I found myself among the unseen; but I cared for knowledge no longer, I sought only her. I lost a portion of my time so. I regret to have to confess it to *M. le Maire*. Much that I might have learned will thus remain lost to my fellow-citizens and the world. We are made so. What we desire eludes us at the moment of grasping it—or those affections which are the foundation of our lives preoccupy us, and blind the soul. Instead of endeavouring to establish my faith and enlighten my judgement as to those mysteries which have been my life-long study, all higher purpose departed from me; and I did nothing but rush through the city, groping among those crowds, seeing nothing, thinking of nothing—save of One.

From this also I awakened as out of a dream. What roused me was the pealing of the Cathedral bells. I was made to pause and standstill, and return to myself. Then I perceived, but dimly, that the thing which had happened to me was that which I had desired all my life. I leave this explanation of my failure[1] in public duty to the charity of *M. le Maire.*

The bells of the Cathedral brought me back to myself—to that which we call reality in our language; but of all that was around me when I regained consciousness, it now appeared to me that I only was a dream. I was in the midst of a world where all was in movement. What the current was which flowed around me I know not; if it was thought which becomes sensible among spirits, if it was action, I cannot tell. But the energy, the force, the living that was in them, that could no one misunderstand. I stood in the streets, lagging and feeble, scarcely able to wish, much less to think. They pushed against me, put me aside, took no note of me. In the unseen world described by a poet whom *M. le Maire* has probably heard of, the man who traverses Purgatory (to speak of no other place) is seen by all, and is a wonder to all he meets—his shadow, his breath separate him from those around him.

But whether the unseen life has changed, or if it is I who am not worthy their attention, this I know that I stood in our city like a ghost, and no one took any heed of me. When there came back upon me slowly my old desire to inquire, to understand, I was met with this difficulty at the first—that no one heeded me. I went through and through the streets, sometimes I paused to look round, to implore that which swept by me to make itself

1. The reader will remember that the ringing of the Cathedral bells happened in fact very soon after the exodus of the citizens; so that the self-reproaches of M. Lecamus had less foundation than he thought.

known. But the stream went along like soft air, like the flowing of a river, setting me aside from time to time, as the air will displace a straw, or the water a stone, but no more. There was neither languor nor lingering. I was the only passive thing, the being without occupation. Would you have paused in your labours to tell an idle traveller the meaning of our lives, before the day when you left Semur? Nor would they: I was driven hither and thither by the current of that life, but no one stepped forth out of the unseen to hear my questions or to answer me how this might be.

You have been made to believe that all was darkness in Semur. *M. le Maire*, it was not so. The darkness wrapped the walls as in a winding sheet; but within, soon after you were gone, there arose a sweet and wonderful light—a light that was neither of the sun nor of the moon; and presently, after the ringing of the bells, the silence departed as the darkness had departed. I began to hear, first a murmur, then the sound of the going which I had felt without hearing it—then a faint tinkle of voices—and at the last, as my mind grew attuned to these wonders, the very words they said. If they spoke in our language or in another, I cannot tell; but I understood. How long it was before the sensation of their presence was aided by the happiness of hearing I know not, nor do I know how the time has passed, or how long it is, whether years or days, that I have been in Semur with those who are now there; for the light did not vary—there was no night or day.

All I know is that suddenly, on awakening from a sleep (for the wonder was that I could sleep, sometimes sitting on the Cathedral steps, sometimes in my own house; where sometimes also I lingered and searched about for the crusts that Leocadie had left), I found the whole world full of sound. They sang going in bands about the streets; they talked to each other as they went along every way. From the houses, all open, where everyone could go who would, there came the soft chiming of those voices. And at first every sound was full of gladness and hope. The song they sang first was like this:

Send us, send us to our father's house.
Many are our brethren, many and dear.
They have forgotten, forgotten, forgotten!
But when we speak, then will they hear.

And the others answered:

We have come, we have come to the house of our fathers.
Sweet are the homes, the homes we were born in.
As we remember, so will they remember.
When we speak, when we speak, they will hear.

Do not think that these were the words they sang; but it was like this. And as they sang there was joy and expectation everywhere. It was more beautiful than any of our music, for it was full of desire and longing, yet hope and gladness; whereas among us, where there is longing, it is always sad. Later a great singer, I know not who he was, one going past as on a majestic soft wind, sang another song, of which I shall tell you by and by. I do not think he was one of them. They came out to the windows, to the doors, into all the streets and byways to hear him as he went past.

M. le Maire will, however, be good enough to remark that I did not understand all that I heard. In the middle of a phrase, in a word half breathed, a sudden barrier would rise. For a time I laboured after their meaning, trying hard and vainly to understand; but afterwards I perceived that only when they spoke of Semur, of you who were gone forth, and of what was being done, could I make it out. At first this made me only more eager to hear; but when thought came, then I perceived that of all my longing nothing was satisfied. Though I was alone with the unseen, I comprehended it not; only when it touched upon w hat I knew, then I understood.

At first all went well. Those who were in the streets, and at the doors and windows of the houses, and on the Cathedral steps, where they seemed to throng, listening to the sounding of the bells, spoke only of this that they had come to do. Of you and you only I heard. They said to each other, with great joy, that the women had been instructed, that they had listened, and were safe. There was pleasure in all the city. The singers were called forth, those who were best instructed (so I judged from what I heard), to take the place of the warders on the walls; and all, as they went along, sang that song: '*Our brothers have forgotten; but when we speak, they will hear.*'

How was it, how was it that you did not hear? One time I was by the river *porte* in a boat; and this song came to me from the walls as sweet as Heaven. Never have I heard such a song. The music was beseeching, it moved the very heart. '*We have come out of the unseen,*' they sang; '*for love of you; believe us, believe us! Love brings us back to earth; believe us, believe us!*'

How was it that you did not hear? When I heard those singers sing, I wept; they beguiled the heart out of my bosom. They sang, they shouted, the music swept about all the walls: 'Love brings us back to earth, believe us!' *M. le Maire*, I saw you from the river gate; there was a look of perplexity upon your face; and one put his curved hand to his ear as if to listen to some thin far-off sound, when it was like a storm, like a tempest of music! After that there was a great change in the city. The choirs came back from the walls marching more slowly, and with a sighing through all the air. A sigh, nay, something like a sob breathed through the streets. 'They cannot hear us, or they will not hear us.' Wherever I turned, this was what I heard: 'They cannot hear us.'

The whole town, and all the houses that were teeming with souls, and all the street, where so many were coming and going, was full of wonder and dismay. (If you will take my opinion, they know pain as well as joy, *M. le Maire*, Those who are in Semur. They are not as gods, perfect and sufficing to themselves, nor are they all-knowing and all-wise, like the good God. They hope like us, and desire, and are mistaken; but do no wrong. This is my opinion. I am no more than other men, that you should accept it without support; but I have lived among them, and this is what I think.) They were taken by surprise; they did not understand it any more than we understand when we have put forth all our strength and fail. They were confounded, if I could judge rightly. Then there arose cries from one to another: 'Do you forget what was said to us?' and, 'We were warned, we were warned.' There went a sighing over all the city: 'They cannot hear us, our voices are not as their voices; they cannot see us. We have taken their homes from them, and they know not the reason.'

My heart was wrung for their disappointment. I longed to tell them that neither had I heard at once; but it was only after a time that I ventured upon this. And whether I spoke, and was heard; or if it was read in my heart, I cannot tell. There was a pause made round me as if of wondering and listening, and then, in a moment, in the twinkling of an eye, a face suddenly turned and looked into my face.

M. le Maire, it was the face of your father, Martin Dupin, whom I remember as well as I remember my own father. He was the best man I ever knew. It appeared to me for a moment, that face alone, looking at me with questioning eyes.

There seemed to be agitation and doubt for a time after this; some went out (so I understood) on embassies among you, but could get no hearing; some through the gates, some by the river. And the bells were rung that you might hear and know; but neither could you understand the bells. I wandered from one place to another, listening and watching—till the unseen became to me as the seen, and I thought of the wonder no more. Sometimes there came to me vaguely a desire to question them, to ask whence they came and what was the secret of their living, and why they were here? But if I had asked who would have heard me? and desire had grown faint in my heart; all I wished for was that you should hear, that you should understand; with this wish Semur was full.

They thought but of this. They went to the walls in bands, each in their order, and as they came all the others rushed to meet them, to ask, 'What news?' I following, now with one, now with another, breathless and footsore as they glided along. It is terrible when flesh and blood live with those who are spirits. I toiled after them. I sat on the Cathedral steps, and slept and waked, and heard the voices still in my dream. I prayed, but it was hard to pray. Once following a crowd I entered your house, *M. le Maire*, and went up, though I scarcely could drag myself along. There many were assembled as in council. Your father was at the head of all. He was the one, he only, who knew me. Again he looked at me and I saw him, and in the light of his face an assembly such as I have seen in pictures.

One moment it glimmered before me and then it was gone. There were the captains of all the bands waiting to speak, men and women. I heard them repeating from one to another the same tale. One voice was small and soft like a child's; it spoke of you. 'We went to him,' it said; and your father, *M. le Maire*, he too joined in, and said: 'We went to him—but he could not hear us.' And some said it was enough—that they had no commission from on high, that they were but permitted—that it was their own will to do it—and that the time had come to forbear.

Now, while I listened, my heart was grieved that they should fail. This gave me a wound for myself who had trusted in them, and also for them. But I, who am I, a poor man without credit among my neighbours, a dreamer, one whom many despise, that I should come to their aid? Yet I could not listen and take no part. I cried out: 'Send me. I will tell them in words they understand.' The sound of my voice was like a roar in that atmosphere. It sent a tremble into the air. It seemed to rend me as it came forth from me, and made me giddy, so that I would have fallen had not there been a support afforded me.

As the light was going out of my eyes I saw again the faces looking at each other, questioning, benign, beautiful heads one over another, eyes that were clear as the heavens, but sad. I trembled while I gazed: there was the bliss of heaven in their faces, yet they were sad. Then everything faded. I was led away, I know not how, and brought to the door and put forth. I was not worthy to see the blessed grieve. That is a sight upon which the angels look with awe, and which brings those tears which are salvation into the eyes of God. I went back to my house, weary yet calm.

There were many in my house; but because my heart was full

of one who was not there, I knew not those who were there. I sat me down where she had been. I was weary, more weary than ever before, but calm. Then I bethought me that I knew no more than at the first, that I had lived among the unseen as if they were my neighbours, neither fearing them, nor hearing those wonders which they have to tell. As I sat with my head in my hands, two talked to each other close by: 'Is it true that we have failed?' said one; and the other answered, 'Must not all fail that is not sent of the Father?' I was silent; but I knew them, they were the voices of my father and my mother. I listened as out of a faint, in a dream.

While I sat thus, with these voices in my ears, which a little while before would have seemed to me more worthy of note than anything on earth, but which now lulled me and comforted me, as a child is comforted by the voices of its guardians in the night, there occurred a new thing in the city like nothing I had heard before. It roused me notwithstanding my exhaustion and stupor. It was the sound as of someone passing through the city suddenly and swiftly, whether in some wonderful chariot, whether on some sweeping mighty wind, I cannot tell. The voices stopped that were conversing beside me, and I stood up, and with an impulse I could not resist went out, as if a king were passing that way.

Straight, without turning to the right or left, through the city, from one gate to another, this passenger seemed going; and as he went there was the sound as of a proclamation, as if it were a herald denouncing war or ratifying peace. Whosoever he was, the sweep of his going moved my hair like a wind. At first the proclamation was but as a great shout, and I could not understand it; but as he came nearer the words became distinct. 'Neither will they believe—though one rose from the dead.' As it passed a murmur went up from the city, like the voice of a great multitude. Then there came sudden silence.

At this moment, for a time—*M. le Maire* will take my statement for what it is worth—I became unconscious of what passed further. Whether weariness overpowered me and I slept, as at the most terrible moment nature will demand to do, or if I fainted I cannot tell; but for a time I knew no more. When I came to myself, I was seated on the Cathedral steps with everything silent around me. From thence I rose up, moved by a will which was not mine, and was led softly across the Grande Rue, through the great square, with my face towards the Porte St. Lambert. I went steadily on without hesitation, never doubting that the gates would open to me, doubting nothing, though I had never attempted to withdraw from the city before. When I came to the gate I said not a word, nor anyone to me; but the door rolled slowly open before me, and I was put forth into the morning light, into the shining of the sun. I have now said everything I had to say. The message I delivered was said through me; I can tell no more. Let me rest a little; figure to yourselves, I have known no night of rest, nor eaten a morsel of bread for—did you say it was but three days?

Chapter 6

M. Le Maire Resumes His Narrative.

We re-entered by the door for foot-passengers which is by the side of the great Porte St. Lambert.

I will not deny that my heart was, as one may say, in my throat. A man does what is his duty, what his fellow-citizens expect of him; but that is not to say that he renders himself callous to natural emotion. My veins were swollen, the blood coursing through them like a high-flowing river; my tongue was parched and dry. I am not ashamed to admit that from head to foot my body quivered and trembled. I was afraid—but I went forward; no man can do more. As for *M. le Curé* he said not a word. If he had any fears he concealed them as I did. But his occupation is with the ghostly and spiritual. To see men die, to accompany them to the verge of the grave, to create for them during the time of their suffering after death (if it is true that they suffer), an interest in heaven, this his profession must necessarily give him courage.

My position is very different. I have not made up my mind

upon these subjects. When one can believe frankly in all the Church says, many things become simple, which otherwise cause great difficulty in the mind. The mysterious and wonderful then find their natural place in the course of affairs; but when a man thinks for himself, and has to take everything on his own responsibility, and make all the necessary explanations, there is often great difficulty. So many things will not fit into their places, they straggle like weary men on a march. One cannot put them together, or satisfy one's self.

The sun was shining outside the walls when we re-entered Semur; but the first step we took was into a gloom as black as night, which did not re-assure us, it is unnecessary to say. A chill was in the air, of night and mist. We shivered, not with the nerves only but with the cold. And as all was dark, so all was still. I had expected to feel the presence of those who were there, as I had felt the crowd of the invisible before they entered the city. But the air was vacant, there was nothing but darkness and cold. We went on for a little way with a strange fervour of expectation. At each moment, at each step, it seemed to me that some great call must be made upon my self-possession and courage, some event happen; but there was nothing.

All was calm, the houses on either side of the way were open, all but the office of the *octroi* which was black as night with its closed door. *M. le Curé* has told me since that he believed Them to be there, though unseen. This idea, however, was not in my mind. I had felt the unseen multitude; but here the air was free, there was no one interposing between us, who breathed as men, and the walls that surrounded us. Just within the gate a lamp was burning, hanging to its rope over our heads; and the lights were in the houses as if someone had left them there; they threw a strange glimmer into the darkness, flickering in the wind. By and by as we went on the gloom lessened, and by the time we had reached the Grande Rue, there was a clear steady pale twilight by which we saw everything, as by the light of day.

We stood at the corner of the square and looked round. Although still I heard the beating of my own pulses loudly working in my ears, yet it was less terrible than at first. A city when asleep is wonderful to look on, but in all the closed doors and windows one feels the safety and repose sheltered there which no man can disturb; and the air has in it a sense of life, subdued, yet warm. But here all was open, and all deserted. The house of the miser Grosgain was exposed from the highest to the lowest, but nobody was there to search for what was hidden. The hotel de Bois-Sombre, with its great *porte-cochère*, always so jealously closed; and my own house, which my mother and wife have always guarded so carefully, that no damp nor breath of night might enter, had every door and window wide open.

Desolation seemed seated in all these empty places. I feared to go into my own dwelling. It seemed to me as if the dead must be lying within. *Bon Dieu!* Not a soul, not a shadow; all vacant in this soft twilight; nothing moving, nothing visible. The great doors of the Cathedral were wide open, and every little entry. How spacious the city looked, how silent, how wonderful! There was room for a squadron to wheel in the great square, but not so much as a bird, not a dog; all pale and empty. We stood for a long time (or it seemed a long time) at the corner, looking right and left. We were afraid to make a step farther. We knew not what to do. Nor could I speak; there was much I wished to say, but something stopped my voice.

At last *M. le Curé* found utterance. His voice so moved the silence, that at first my heart was faint with fear; it was hoarse, and the sound rolled round the great square like muffled thunder. One did not seem to know what strange faces might rise at the open windows, what terrors might appear. But all he said was, 'We are ambassadors in vain.'

What was it that followed? My teeth chattered. I could not hear. It was as if 'in vain!' 'in vain!' came back in echoes, more and more distant from every opening. They breathed all around us, then were still, then returned louder from beyond the river. *M. le Curé*, though he is a spiritual person, was no more courageous than I. With one impulse, we put out our hands and grasped each other. We retreated back to back, like men hemmed in by foes, and I felt his heart beating wildly, and he mine. Then silence, silence settled all around.

It was now my turn to speak. I would not be behind, come what might, though my lips were parched with mental trouble.

I said, 'Are we indeed too late? Lecamus must have deceived himself.'

To this there came no echo and no reply, which would be a relief, you may suppose; but it was not so. It was well-nigh more appalling, more terrible than the sound; for though we spoke thus, we did not believe the place was empty. Those whom we approached seemed to be wrapping themselves in silence, invisible, waiting to speak with some awful purpose when their time came.

There we stood for some minutes, like two children, holding each other s hands, leaning against each other at the corner of the square—as helpless as children, waiting for what should come next. I say it frankly, my brain and my heart were one throb. They plunged and beat so wildly that I could scarcely have heard any other sound. In this respect I think he was more calm. There was on his face that look of intense listening which strains the very soul. But neither he nor I heard anything, not so much as a whisper. At last, 'Let us go on,' I said. We stumbled as we went, with agitation and fear. We were afraid to turn our backs to those empty houses, which seemed to gaze at us with all their empty windows pale and glaring. Mechanically, scarce knowing what I was doing, I made towards my own house.

There was no one there. The rooms were all open and empty. I went from one to another, with a sense of expectation which made my heart faint; but no one was there, nor anything changed. Yet I do wrong to say that nothing was changed. In my library, where I keep my books, where my father and grandfather conducted their affairs, like me, one little difference struck me suddenly, as if someone had dealt me a blow.

The old bureau which my grandfather had used, at which I remember standing by his knee, had been drawn from the corner where I had placed it out of the way (to make room for the furniture I preferred), and replaced, as in old times, in the middle of the room. It was nothing; yet how much was in this! though only myself could have perceived it. Some of the old drawers were open, full of old papers. I glanced over them in my agitation, to see if there might be any writing, any message addressed to me; but there was nothing, nothing but this silent sign of those who had been here. Naturally *M. le Curé,* who kept watch at the door, was unacquainted with the cause of my emotion.

The last room I entered was my wife's. Her veil was lying on the white bed, as if she had gone out that moment, and some of her ornaments were on the table. It seemed to me that the atmosphere of mystery which filled the rest of the house was not here. A ribbon, a little ring, what nothings are these? Yet they make even emptiness sweet. In my Agnès's room there is a little shrine, more sacred to us than any altar. There is the picture of our little Marie. It is covered with a veil, embroidered with needlework which it is a wonder to see. Not always can even Agnès bear to look upon the face of this angel, whom God has taken from her. She has worked the little curtain with lilies, with white and virginal flowers; and no hand, not even mine, ever draws it aside.

What did I see? The veil was boldly folded away; the face of the child looked at me across her mother's bed, and upon the frame of the picture was laid a branch of olive, with silvery leaves. I know no more but that I uttered a great cry, and flung myself upon my knees before this angel-gift. What stranger could know what was in my heart? *M. le Curé*, my friend, my brother, came hastily to me, with a pale countenance; but when he looked at me, he drew back and turned away his face, and a sob came from his breast. Never child had called him father, were it in heaven, were it on earth. Well I knew whose tender fingers had placed the branch of olive there.

I went out of the room and locked the door. It was just that my wife should find it where it had been laid.

I put my arm into his as we went out once more into the street. That moment had made us brother and brother. And this union made us more strong. Besides, the silence and the emptiness began to grow less terrible to us. We spoke in our natural voices as we came out, scarcely knowing how great was the difference between them and the whispers which had been all we dared at first to employ. Yet the sound of these louder tones scared us when we heard them, for we were still trembling, not assured of deliverance. It was he who showed himself a man, not I; for my heart was overwhelmed, the tears stood in my eyes, I had no strength to resist my impressions.

'Martin Dupin,' he said suddenly, 'it is enough. We are frightening ourselves with shadows. We are afraid even of our own voices. This must not be. Enough! Whosoever they were who have been in Semur, their visitation is over, and they are gone.'

'I think so,' I said faintly; 'but God knows.' Just then something passed me as sure as ever man passed me. I started back out of the way and dropped my friend's arm, and covered my eyes with my hands. It was nothing that could be seen; it was an air, a breath. *M. le Curé* looked at me wildly; he was as a man beside himself. He struck his foot upon the pavement and gave a loud and bitter cry.

'Is it delusion?' he said, 'O my God! or shall not even this, not even so much as this be revealed to me?'

To see a man who had so ruled himself, who had resisted every disturbance and stood fast when all gave way, moved thus at the very last to cry out with passion against that which had been denied to him, brought me back to myself. How often had I read it in his eyes before! He—the priest—the servant of the unseen—yet to all of us lay persons had that been revealed which was hid from him. A great pity was within me, and gave me strength. 'Brother,' I said, 'we are weak. If we saw heaven opened, could we trust to our vision now? Our imaginations are masters of us. So far as mortal eye can see, we are alone in Semur. Have you forgotten your psalm, and how you sustained us at the first? And now, your Cathedral is open to you, my brother. *Laetatus sum*,' I said.

It was an inspiration from above, and no thought of mine; for it is well known, that though deeply respectful, I have never professed religion. With one impulse we turned, we went together, as in a procession, across the silent place, and up the great steps. We said not a word to each other of what we meant to do. All was fair and silent in the holy place; a breath of incense still in the air; a murmur of psalms (as one could imagine) far up in the high roof. There I served, while he said his mass. It was for my friend that this impulse came to my mind; but I was rewarded. The days of my childhood seemed to come back to me. All trouble, and care, and mystery, and pain, seemed left behind.

All I could see was the glimmer on the altar of the great candlesticks, the sacred *pyx* in its shrine, the chalice, and the book. I was again an *enfant de choeur* robed in white, like the angels, no doubt, no disquiet in my soul—and my father kneeling behind among the faithful, bowing his head, with a sweetness which I too knew, being a father, because it was his child that tinkled the bell and swung the censer. Never since those days have I served the mass. My heart grew soft within me as the heart of a little child. The voice of *M. le Curé* was full of tears—it swelled out into the air and filled the vacant place. I knelt behind him on the steps of the altar and wept.

Then there came a sound that made our hearts leap in our bosoms. His voice wavered as if it had been struck by a strong wind; but he was a brave man, and he went on. It was the bells of the Cathedral that pealed out over our heads. In the midst of the office, while we knelt all alone, they began to ring as at Easter or some great festival. At first softly, almost sadly, like choirs of distant singers, that died away and were echoed and died again; then taking up another strain, they rang out into the sky with hurrying notes and clang of joy. The effect upon myself was wonderful. I no longer felt any fear. The illusion was complete. I was a child again, serving the mass in my little surplice—aware that all who loved me were kneeling behind, that the good God was smiling, and the Cathedral bells ringing out their majestic Amen.

M. le Curé came down the altar steps when his mass was

ended. Together we put away the vestments and the holy vessels. Our hearts were soft; the weight was taken from them. As we came out the bells were dying away in long and low echoes, now faint, now louder, like mingled voices of gladness and regret. And whereas It had been a pale twilight when we entered, the clearness of the day had rolled sweetly In, and now It was fair morning in all the streets. We did not say a word to each other, but arm and arm took our way to the gates, to open to our neighbours, to call all our fellow-citizens back to Semur.

If I record here an incident of another kind. It is because of the sequel that followed. As we passed by the hospital of St. Jean, we heard distinctly, coming from within, the accents of a feeble yet impatient voice. The sound revived for a moment the troubles that were stilled within us—but only for a moment. This was no visionary voice. It brought a smile to the grave face of *M. le Curé* and tempted me well nigh to laughter, so strangely did this sensation of the actual, break and disperse the visionary atmosphere.

We went in without any timidity, with a conscious relaxation of the great strain upon us. In a little nook, curtained off from the great ward, lay a sick man upon his bed. 'Is it *M. le Maire?*' he said; '*à la bonne heure!* I have a complaint to make of the nurses for the night. They have gone out to amuse themselves; they take no notice of poor sick people. They have known for a week that I could not sleep; but neither have they given me a sleeping draught, nor endeavoured to distract me with cheerful conversation. And today, look you, *M. le Maire*, not one of the sisters has come near me!'

'Have you suffered, my poor fellow?' I said; but he would not go so far as this.

'I don't want to make complaints, *M. le Maire*; but the sisters do not come themselves as they used to do. One does not care to have a strange nurse, when one knows that if the sisters did their duty But if it does not occur any more I do not wish it to be thought that I am the one to complain.'

'Do not fear, *mon ami,*' I said. 'I will say to the Reverend

Mother that you have been left too long alone.'

'And listen, *M. le Maire*,' cried the man; 'those bells, will they never be done? My head aches with the din they make. How can one go to sleep with all that riot in one's ears?'

We looked at each other, we could not but smile. So that which is joy and deliverance to one is vexation to another. As we went out again into the street the lingering music of the bells died out, and (for the first time for all these terrible days and nights) the great clock struck the hour. And as the clock struck, the last cloud rose like a mist and disappeared in flying vapours, and the full sunshine of noon burst on Semur.

Chapter 7

Supplement by M. de Bois-Sombre

When *M. le Maire* disappeared within the mist, we all remained behind with troubled hearts. For my own part I was alarmed for my friend. M. Martin Dupin is not noble. He belongs, indeed, to the *haute bourgeoisie*, and all his antecedents are most respectable; but it is his personal character and admirable qualities which justify me in calling him my friend. The manner in which he has performed his duties to his fellow-citizens during this time of distress has been sublime. It is not my habit to take any share in public life; the unhappy circumstances of France have made this impossible for years. Nevertheless, I put aside my scruples when It became necessary, to leave him free for his mission. I gave no opinion upon that mission itself, or how far he was right in obeying the advice of a hare-brained enthusiast like Lecamus.

Nevertheless the moment had come at which our banishment had become intolerable. Another day, and I should have proposed an assault upon the place. Our dead forefathers, though I would speak of them with every respect, should not presume upon their privilege. I do not pretend to be braver than other men, nor have I shown myself more equal than others to cope with the present emergency. But I have the impatience of my countrymen, and rather than rot here outside the gates, parted from Madame de Bois-Sombre and my children, who, I am happy to state, are in safety at the country house of the brave Dupin, I should have dared any hazard. This being the case, a new step of any kind called for my approbation, and I could not refuse under the circumstances—-especially as no ceremony of installation was required or profession of loyalty to one government or another—to take upon me the office of coadjutor and act as deputy for my friend Martin outside the walls of Semur.

The moment at which I assumed the authority was one of great discouragement and depression. The men were tired to death. Their minds were worn out as well as their bodies. The excitement and fatigue had been more than they could bear. Some were for giving up the contest and seeking new homes for themselves. These were they, I need not remark, who had but little to lose; some seemed to care for nothing but to lie down and rest. Though it produced a great movement among us when Lecamus suddenly appeared coming out of the city; and the undertaking of Dupin and the excellent *Curè* was viewed with great interest, yet there could not but be signs apparent that the situation had lasted too long. It was *tendu* in the strongest degree, and when that is the case a reaction must come.

It is impossible to say, for one thing, how great was our personal discomfort. We were as soldiers campaigning without a commissariat, or any precautions taken for our welfare; no food save what was sent to us from La Clairière and other places; no means of caring for our personal appearance, in which lies so much of the materials of self-respect. I say nothing of the chief features of all—the occupation of our homes by others—the forcible expulsion of which we had been the objects. No one could have been more deeply impressed than myself at the moment of these extraordinary proceedings; but we cannot go on with one monotonous impression, however serious, we other Frenchmen.

Three days is a very long time to dwell in one thought; I myself had become impatient, I do not deny. To go away, which would have been very natural, and which Agathe proposed, was contrary to my instincts and interests both. I trust I can obey the logic of circumstances as well as another; but to yield is not easy, and to leave my hotel at Semur—now the chief residence, alas! of the Bois-Sombres—probably to the licence of a mob—for one can never tell at what moment Republican institutions may break down and sink back into the chaos from which they arose—was impossible. Nor would I forsake the brave Dupin without the strongest motive; but that the situation was extremely *tendu*, and a reaction close at hand, was beyond dispute.

I resisted the movement which my excellent friend made to take off and transfer to me his scarf of office. These things are much thought of among the *bourgeoisie*. '*Mon ami*,' I said, 'you cannot tell what use you may have for it; whereas our townsmen know me, and that I am not one to take up an unwarrantable position.' We then accompanied him to the neighbourhood of the Porte St. Lambert. It was at that time invisible; we could but judge approximately. My men were unwilling to approach too near, neither did I myself think it necessary. We parted, after giving the two envoys an honourable escort, leaving a clear space between us and the darkness. To see them disappear gave us all a startling sensation.

Up to the last moment I had doubted whether they would obtain admittance. When they disappeared from our eyes, there came upon all of us an impulse of alarm. I myself was so far moved by it, that I called out after them in a sudden panic. For if any catastrophe had happened, how could I ever have forgiven myself, especially as Madame Dupin de la Clairière, a person entirely *comme il faut*, and of the most distinguished character, went after her husband, with a touching devotion, following him to the very edge of the darkness? I do not think, so deeply possessed was he by his mission, that he saw her. Dupin is very determined in his way; but he is imaginative and thoughtful, and it is very possible that, as he required all his powers to brace him for this enterprise, he made it a principle neither to look to the right hand nor the left.

When we paused, and following after our two representatives, Madame Dupin stepped forth, a thrill ran through us all. Some would have called to her, for I heard many broken exclamations; but most of us were too much startled to speak. We thought nothing less than that she was about to risk herself by going after them into the city. If that was her intention—and nothing is more probable; for women are very daring, though they are timid—she was stopped, it is most likely, by that curious inability to move a step farther which we have all experienced. We saw her pause, clasp her hands in despair (or it might be in token of farewell to her husband), then, instead of returning, seat herself on the road on the edge of the darkness. It was a relief to all who were looking on to see her there.

In the reaction after that excitement I found myself in face of a great difficulty—what to do with my men, to keep them from demoralisation. They were greatly excited; and yet there was nothing to be done for them, for myself, for any of us, but to wait. To organise the patrol again, under the circumstances, would have been impossible. Dupin, perhaps, might have tried it with that *bourgeois* determination which so often carries its point in spite of all higher intelligence; but to me, who have not this commonplace way of looking at things, It was impossible. The worthy soul did not think in what a difficulty he left us. That intolerable, good-for-nothing Jacques Richard (whom Dupin protects unwisely, I cannot tell why), and who was already half-seas-over, had drawn several of his comrades with him towards the *cabaret*, which was always a danger to us. We will drink success to *M. le Maire*,' he said, '*mes bons amis!* That can do no one any harm; and as we have spoken up, as we have empowered him to offer handsome terms to *Messieurs les Morts*—'

It was intolerable. Precisely at the moment when our fortune hung in the balance, and when, perhaps, an indiscreet word 'Arrest that fellow,' I said. 'Riou, you are an official; you understand your duty. Arrest him on the spot, and confine him in the tent out of the way of mischief. Two of you mount guard over him. And let a party be told off, of which you will take the command, Louis Bertin, to go at once to La Clairière and beg the Reverend Mothers of the hospital to favour us with their presence. It will be well to have those excellent ladies in our front whatever happens; and you may communicate to them the unanimous decision about their chapel. You, Robert Lemaire, with an escort, will proceed to the *campagne* of M. Barbou, and put him in possession of the circumstances. Those of you who have a natural wish to seek a little repose will consider yourselves as discharged from duty and permitted to do so. Your *Maire* having confided to me his authority—not without your consent—(this I avow I added with some difficulty, for who cared for their assent? but a Republican Government offers a premium to every insincerity), I wait with confidence to see these dispositions carried out.'

This, I am happy to say, produced the best effect. They obeyed me without hesitation; and, fortunately for me, slumber seized upon the majority. Had it not been for this, I can scarcely tell how I should have got out of it. I felt drowsy myself, having been with the patrol the greater part of the night; but to yield to such weakness was, in my position, of course impossible.

This, then, was our attitude during the last hours of suspense, which were perhaps the most trying of all. In the distance might be seen the little bands marching towards La Clairière, on one side, and M. Barbou's country-house (*La Corbeille des Raisins*) on the other. It goes without saying that I did not want M. Barbou, but it was the first errand I could think of. Towards the city, just where the darkness began that enveloped it, sat Madame Dupln. That *sainte-femme* was praying for her husband, who could doubt?

And under the trees, wherever they could find a favourable spot, my men lay down on the grass, and most of them fell asleep. My eyes were heavy enough, but responsibility drives away rest. I had but one nap of five minutes' duration, leaning against a tree, when it occurred to me that Jacques Richard, whom I sent under escort half-drunk to the tent, was not the most admirable companion for that poor visionary Lecamus, who had been accommodated there. I roused myself, therefore, though unwillingly, to see whether these two, so discordant, could agree.

I met Lecamus at the tent-door. He was coming out, very feeble and tottering, with that dazed look which (according to me) has always been characteristic of him. He had a bundle of papers in his hand. He had been setting in order his report of what had happened to him, to be submitted to the *Maire*. '*Monsieur*,' he said, with some irritation (which I forgave him), 'you have always been unfavourable to me. I owe it to you that this unhappy drunkard has been sent to disturb me in my feebleness and the discharge of a public duty.'

'My good Monsieur Lecamus,' said I, 'you do my recollection too much honour. The fact is, I had forgotten all about you and your public duty. Accept my excuses. Though indeed your supposition that I should have taken the trouble to annoy you, and your description of that good-for-nothing as an unhappy drunkard, are signs of intolerance which I should not have expected in a man so favoured.'

This speech, though too long, pleased me, for a man of this species, a revolutionary (are not all visionaries revolutionaries?) is always, when occasion offers, to be put down. He disarmed me, however, by his humility. He gave a look round. 'Where can I go? 'he said, and there was *pathos* in his voice. At length he perceived Madame Dupin sitting almost motionless on the road. 'Ah!' he said, 'there is my place.' The man, I could not but perceive, was very weak. His eyes were twice their natural size, his face was the colour of ashes; through his whole frame there was a trembling; the papers shook in his hand.

A compunction seized my mind: I regretted to have sent that piece of noise and folly to disturb a poor man so suffering and weak. 'Monsieur Lecamus,' I said, 'forgive me. I acknowledge that it was inconsiderate. Remain here in comfort, and I will find for this unruly fellow another place of confinement.'

'Nay,' he said, 'there is my place,' pointing to where Madame Dupin sat. I felt disposed for a moment to indulge in a pleasantry, to say that I approved his taste; but on second thoughts I forebore. He went tottering slowly across the broken ground, hardly able to drag himself along.

'Has he had any refreshment?' I asked of one of the women who were about. They told me yes, and this restored my composure; for after all I had not meant to annoy him, I had forgotten he was there—a trivial fault in circumstances so exciting. I was more easy in my mind, however, I confess it, when I saw that he had reached his chosen position safely. The man looked so weak. It seemed to me that he might have died on the road.

I thought I could almost perceive the gate, with Madame Dupin seated under the battlements, her charming figure relieved against the gloom, and that poor Lecamus lying, with his papers fluttering at her feet. This was the last thing I was conscious of.

Chapter 8

Extract From the Narrative of Madame Dupin de La Clairière (née de Champfleurie).

I went with my husband to the city gate.

I did not wish to distract his mind from what he had undertaken, therefore I took care he should not see me; but to follow close, giving the sympathy of your whole heart, must not that be a support? If I am asked whether I was content to let him go, I cannot answer yes; but had another than Martin been chosen, I could not have borne it. What I desired, was to go myself. I was not afraid: and if it had proved dangerous, if I had been broken and crushed to pieces between the seen and the unseen, one could not have had a more beautiful fate. It would have made me happy to go. But perhaps it was better that the messenger should not be a woman; they might have said it was delusion, an attack of the nerves. We are not trusted in these respects, though I find it hard to tell why.

But I went with Martin to the gate. To go as far as was possible, to be as near as possible, that was something. If there had been room for me to pass, I should have gone, and with such gladness! for God He knows that to help to thrust my husband into danger, and not to share it, was terrible to me. But no; the invisible line was still drawn, beyond which I could not stir. The door opened before him, and closed upon me. But though to see him disappear into the gloom was anguish, yet to know that he was the man by whom the city should be saved was sweet. I sat down on the spot where my steps were stayed. It was close to the wall, where there is a ledge of stonework round the basement of the tower. There I sat down to wait till he should come again.

If anyone thinks, however, that we, who were under the shelter of the roof of La Clairière were less tried than our husbands, it is a mistake; our chief grief was that we were parted from them, not knowing what suffering, what exposure they might have to bear, and knowing that they would not accept, as most of us were willing to accept, the interpretation of the mystery; but there was a certain comfort in the fact that we had to be very busy, preparing a little food to take to them, and feeding the others. La Clairière is a little country house, not a great *château*, and it was taxed to the utmost to afford some covert to the people. The children were all sheltered and cared for; but as for the rest of us we did as we could. And how gay they were, all the little ones! What was it to them all that had happened? It was a *fête* for them to be in the country, to be so many together, to run in the fields and the gardens.

Sometimes their laughter and their happiness were more than we could bear. Agathe de Bois-Sombre, who takes life hardly, who is more easily deranged than I, was one who was much disturbed by this. But was it not to preserve the children that we were commanded to go to La Clairière? Some of the women also were not easy to bear with. When they were put into our rooms they too found it a fete, and sat down among the children, and ate and drank, and forgot what it was; what awful reason had driven us out of our homes. These were not, oh let no one think so! the majority; but there were some, it cannot be denied; and it was difficult for me to calm down *Bonne Maman*, and keep her from sending them away with their babes.

'But they are *misérables*,' she said. 'If they were to wander and be lost, if they were to suffer as thou sayest, where would be the harm? I have no patience with the idle, with those who impose upon thee.' It is possible that *Bonne Maman* was right—but what then? 'Preserve the children and the sick,' was the mission that had been given to me. My own room was made the hospital. Nor did this please *Bonne Maman*. She bid me if I did not stay in it myself to give it to the Bois-Sombres, to some who deserved it. But is it not they who need most who deserve most? *Bonne Maman* cannot bear that the poor and wretched should live in her Martin's chamber. He is my Martin no less. But to give it up to our Lord is not that to sanctify it? There are who have put Him into their own bed when they imagined they were but sheltering a sick beggar there; that He should have the best was sweet to me: and could not I pray all the better that our Martin should be enlightened, should come to the true sanctuary? When I said this *Bonne Maman* wept. It was the grief of her heart that Martin thought otherwise than as we do. Nevertheless she said, 'He is so good; the *bon Dieu* knows how good he is;' as if even his mother could know that so well as I!

But with the women and the children crowding everywhere, the sick in my chamber, the helpless in every corner, it will be seen that we, too, had much to do. And our hearts were elsewhere, with those who were watching the city, who were face to face with those in whom they had not believed. We were going and coming all day long with food for them, and there never was a time of the night or day that there were not many of us watching on the brow of the hill to see if any change came in Semur. Agathe and I, and our children, were all together in one little room. She believed in God, but it was not any comfort to her; sometimes she would weep and pray all day long; sometimes entreat her husband to abandon the city, to go elsewhere and live, and fly from this strange fate. She is one who cannot endure to be unhappy—not to have what she wishes.

As for me, I was brought up in poverty, and it is no wonder if I can more easily submit. She was not willing that I should come this morning to Semur. In the night the Mere Julie had roused us, saying she had seen a procession of angels coming to restore us to the city. Ah! to those who have no knowledge it is easy to speak of processions of angels. But to those who have seen what an angel is—how they flock upon us unawares in the darkness, so that one is confused, and scarce can tell if it is reality or a dream; to those who have heard a little voice soft as the dew coming out of heaven! I said to them—for all were in a great tumult—that the angels do not come in processions, they steal upon us unaware, they reveal themselves in the soul. But they did not listen to me; even Agathe took pleasure in hearing of the revelation. As for me, I had denied myself, I had not seen Martin for a night and a day. I took one of the great baskets, and I went with the women who were the messengers for the day. A purpose formed itself in my heart, it was to make my way into the city, I know not how, and implore them to have pity upon us before the people were distraught.

Perhaps, had I been able to refrain from speaking to Martin, I might have found the occasion I wished; but how could I conceal my desire from my husband? And now all is changed, I am rejected and he is gone. He was more worthy. *Bonne Maman* is right. Our good God, who is our father, does He require that one should make profession of faith, that all should be alike? He sees the heart; and to choose my Martin, does not that prove that He loves best that which is best, not I, or a priest, or one who makes professions? Thus, I sat down at the gate with a great confidence, though also a trembling in my heart. He who had known how to choose him among all the others, would not He guard him? It was a proof to me once again that heaven is true, that the good God loves and comprehends us all, to see how His wisdom, which is unerring, had chosen the best man in Semur.

And *M. le Curé*, that goes without saying, he is a priest of priests, a true servant of God.

I saw my husband go: perhaps, God knows, into danger, perhaps to some encounter such as might fill the world with awe—to meet those who read the thought in your mind before it comes to your lips. Well! there is no thought in Martin that is not noble and true. Me, I have follies in my heart, every kind of folly; but he!—the tears came in a flood to my eyes, but I would not shed them, as if I were weeping for fear and sorrow—no—but for happiness to know that falsehood was not in him. My little Marie, a holy virgin, may look into her father's heart—I do not fear the test.

The sun came warm to my feet as I sat on the foundation of our city, but the projection of the tower gave me a little shade. All about was a great peace. I thought of the psalm which says, 'He will give it to His beloved sleeping'—that is true; but always there are some who are used as instruments, who are not permitted to sleep. The sounds that came from the people gradually ceased; they were all very quiet. M. de Bois-Sombre I saw at a distance making his dispositions. Then M. Paul Lecamus, whom I had long known, came up across the field, and seated himself close to me upon the road. I have always had a great sympathy with him since the death of his wife; ever since there has been an abstraction in his eyes, a look of desolation. He has no children or anyone to bring him back to life. Now, it seemed to me that he had the air of a man who was dying. He had been in the city while all of us had been outside.

'Monsieur Lecamus,' I said, 'you look very ill, and this is not a place for you. Could not I take you somewhere, where you might be more at your ease?'

'It is true, *Madame*,' he said, 'the road is hard, but the sunshine is sweet; and when I have finished what I am writing for *M. le Maire*, it will be over. There will be no more need—'

I did not understand what he meant. I asked him to let me help him, but he shook his head. His eyes were very hollow, in great caves, and his face was the colour of ashes. Still he smiled. 'I thank you, *Madame*,' he said, 'infinitely; everyone knows that Madame Dupin is kind; but when it is done, I shall be free.'

'I am sure, M. Lecamus, that my husband—that *M. le Maire*—would not wish you to trouble yourself, to be hurried—'

'No,' he said, 'not he, but I. Who else could write what I have to write? It must be done while it is day.'

'Then there is plenty of time, M. Lecamus. All the best of the day is yet to come; it is still morning. If you could but get as far as La Clairière. There we would nurse you—restore you.'

He shook his head. 'You have enough on your hands at La Clairière,' he said; and then, leaning upon the stones, he began to write again with his pencil. After a time, when he stopped, I ventured to ask—'Monsieur Lecamus, is it, indeed, those——whom we have known, who are in Semur?'

He turned his dim eyes upon me. 'Does Madame Dupin,' he said, 'require to ask?'

'No, no. It is true. I have seen and heard. But yet, when a little time passes, you know? one wonders; one asks one's self, was it a dream?'

'That is what I fear,' he said. 'I, too, if life went on, might ask, notwithstanding all that has occurred to me, Was it a dream?'

'M. Lecamus, you will forgive me if I hurt you. You saw—*her?*'

'No. Seeing—what is seeing? It is but a vulgar sense, it is not all; but I sat at her feet. She was with me. We were one, as of old—.' A gleam of strange light came into his dim eyes. 'Seeing is not everything, *Madame*.'

'No, M. Lecamus. I heard the dear voice of my little Marie.'

'Nor is hearing everything,' he said hastily. 'Neither did she speak; but she was there. We were one; we had no need to speak. What is speaking or hearing when heart wells into heart? For a very little moment, only for a moment, Madame Dupin.'

I put out my hand to him; I could not say a word. How was it possible that she could go away again, and leave him so feeble, so worn, alone?

'Only a very little moment,' he said, slowly. 'There were other voices—but not hers. I think I am glad it was in the spirit we met, she and I—I prefer not to see her till—after—'

'Oh, M. Lecamus, I am too much of the world! To see them, to hear them—it is for this I long.'

'No, dear *Madame*. I would not have it till—after . But I must make haste, I must write, I hear the hum approaching—'

I could not tell what he meant; but I asked no more. How

still everything was! The people lay asleep on the grass, and I, too, was overwhelmed by the great quiet. I do not know if I slept, but I dreamed. I saw a child very fair and tall always near me, but hiding her face. It appeared to me in my dream that all I wished for was to see this hidden countenance, to know her name; and that I followed and watched her, but for a long time in vain.

All at once she turned full upon me, held out her arms to me. Do I need to say who it was? I cried out in my dream to the good God, that He had done well to take her from me—that this was worth it all. Was it a dream? I would not give that dream for years of waking life. Then I started and came back, in a moment, to the still morning sunshine, the sight of the men asleep, the roughness of the wall against which I leant. Someone laid a hand on mine. I opened my eyes, not knowing what it was—if it might be my husband coming back, or her whom I had seen in my dream. It was M. Lecamus. He had risen up upon his knees—his papers were all laid aside. His eyes in those hollow caves were opened wide, and quivering with a strange light. He had caught my wrist with his worn hand. 'Listen!' he said; his voice fell to a whisper; a light broke over his face. 'Listen!' he cried; 'they are coming.'

While he thus grasped my wrist, holding up his weak and wavering body in that strained attitude, the moments passed very slowly. I was afraid of him, of his worn face and thin hands, and the wild eagerness about him. I am ashamed to say it, but so it was. And for this reason it seemed long to me, though I think not more than a minute, till suddenly the bells rang out, sweet and glad as they ring at Easter for the resurrection. There had been ringing of bells before, but not like this. With a start and universal movement the sleeping men got up from where they lay—not one but everyone, coming out of the little hollows and from under the trees as if from graves. They all sprang up to listen, with one impulse; and as for me, knowing that Martin was in the city, can it be wondered at if my heart beat so loud that I was incapable of thought of others!

What brought me to myself was the strange weight of M. Lecamus on my arm. He put his other hand upon me, all cold in the brightness, all trembling. He raised himself thus slowly to his feet. When I looked at him I shrieked aloud. I forgot all else. His face was transformed—a smile came upon it that was ineffable—the light blazed up, and then quivered and flickered In his eyes like a dying flame. All this time he was leaning his weight upon my arm. Then suddenly he loosed his hold of me, stretched out his hands, stood up, and—died. My God! shall I ever forget him as he stood—his head raised, his hands held out, his lips moving, the eyelids opened wide with a quiver, the light flickering and dying!

He died first, standing up, saying something with his pale lips—then fell. And it seemed to me all at once, and for a moment, that I heard a sound of many people marching past, the murmur and hum of a great multitude; and softly, softly I was put out of the way, and a voice said, '*Adieu, ma soeur.*' '*Ma soeur!*' who called me '*Ma soeur*'? I have no sister. I cried out, saying I know not what. They told me after that I wept and wrung my hands, and said, 'Not thee, not thee, Marie!' But after that I knew no more.

Chapter 9

The Narrative of Madame Veuve Dupin (née Lepelletier)

To complete the *procés verbal*, my son wishes me to give my account of the things which happened out of Semur during its miraculous occupation, as it is his desire, in the interests of truth, that nothing should be left out. In this I find a great difficulty for many reasons; in the first place, because I have not the aptitude of expressing myself in writing, and it may well be that the phrases I employ may fail in the correctness which good French requires; and again, because it is my misfortune not to agree in all points with my Martin, though I am proud to think that he is, in every relation of life, so good a man, that the women of his family need not hesitate to follow his advice—but necessarily there are some points which one reserves; and I cannot but feel the closeness of the connection between the late remarkable exhibition of the power of Heaven and the outrage done upon the good Sisters of St. Jean by the administration, of which unfortunately my son is at the head.

I say unfortunately, since it is the spirit of independence and pride in him which has resisted all the warnings offered by Divine Providence, and which refuses even now to right the wrongs of the Sisters of St. Jean; though, if it may be permitted to me to say it, as his mother, it was very fortunate in the late troubles that Martin Dupin found himself at the head of the Commune of Semur—since who else could have kept his self-control as he did?—caring for all things and forgetting nothing; who else would, with so much courage, have entered the city? and what other man, being a person of the world and secular in all his thoughts, as, alas! it is so common for men to be, would have so nobly acknowledged his obligations to the good God when our misfortunes were over? My constant prayers for his conversion do not make me incapable of perceiving the nobility of his conduct. When the evidence has been incontestible he has not hesitated to make a public profession of his gratitude, which all will acknowledge to be the sign of a truly noble mind and a heart of gold.

I have long felt that the times were ripe for some exhibition of the power of God. Things have been going very badly among us. Not only have the powers of darkness triumphed over our holy church, in a manner ever to be wept and mourned by all the faithful, and which might have been expected to bring down fire from Heaven upon our heads, but the corruption of popular manners (as might also have been expected) has been daily arising to a pitch unprecedented. The *fêtes* may indeed be said to be observed, but in what manner? In the *cabarets* rather than in the churches; and as for the fasts and vigils, who thinks of them? who attends to those sacred moments of penitence? Scarcely even a few ladies are found to do so, instead of the whole population, as in duty bound. I have even seen it happen that my daughter-in-law and myself, and her friend Madame de

Bois-Sombre, and old Mère Julie from the market, have formed the whole congregation.

Figure to yourself the *bon Dieu* and all the blessed saints looking down from heaven to hear—four persons only in our great Cathedral! I trust that I know that the good God does not despise even two or three; but if anyone will think of it—the great bells rung, and the candles lighted, and the *curé* in his beautiful robes, and all the companies of heaven looking on—and only us four! This shows the neglect of all sacred ordinances that was in Semur. While, on the other hand, what grasping there was for money; what fraud and deceit; what foolishness and dissipation! Even the Mère Julie herself, though a devout person, the pears she sold to us on the last market day before these events, were far, very far, as she must have known, from being satisfactory.

In the same way Gros-Jean, though a peasant from our own village near La Clairière, and a man for whom we have often done little services, attempted to impose upon me about the wood for the winter's use, the very night before these occurrences. 'It is enough,' I cried out, 'to bring the dead out of their graves.' I did not know—the holy saints forgive me!—how near it was to the moment when this should come true.

And perhaps it is well that I should admit without concealment that I am not one of the women to whom it has been given to see those who came back. There are moments when I will not deny I have asked myself why those others should have been so privileged and never I. Not even in a dream do I see those whom I have lost; yet I think that I too have loved them as well as any have been loved. I have stood by their beds to the last; I have closed their beloved eyes. *Mon Dieu! mon Dieu* I have not I drunk of that cup to the dregs? But never to me, never to me, has it been permitted either to see or to hear. *Bien!* it has been so ordered.

Agnès, my daughter-in-law, is a good woman. I have not a word to say against her; and if there are moments when my heart rebels, when I ask myself why she should have her eyes opened and not I, the good God knows that I do not complain against

His will—it is in His hand to do as He pleases. And if I receive no privileges, yet have I the privilege which is best, which is, as *M. le Curé* justly observes, the highest of all—that of doing my duty. In this I thank the good Lord our *Seigneur* that my Martin has never needed to be ashamed of his mother.

I will also admit that when it was first made apparent to me—not by the sounds of voices which the others heard, but by the use of my reason which I humbly believe is also a gift of God—that the way in which I could best serve both those of the city and my son Martin, who is over them, was to lead the way with the children and all the helpless to La Clairière, thus relieving the watchers, there was for a time a great struggle in my bosom. What were they all to me, that I should desert my Martin, my only son, the child of my old age; he who is as his father, as dear, and yet more dear, because he is his father s son?

'What! (I said in my heart) abandon thee, my child? nay, rather abandon life and every consolation; for what is life to me but thee?' But while my heart swelled with this cry, suddenly it became apparent to me how many there were holding up their hands helplessly to him, clinging to him so that he could not move. To whom else could they turn? He was the one among all who preserved his courage, who neither feared nor failed. When those voices rang out from the walls—which some understood, but which I did not understand, and many more with me—though my heart was wrung with straining my ears to listen if there was not a voice for me too, yet at the same time this thought was working in my heart.

There was a poor woman close to me with little children clinging to her; neither did she know what those voices said. Her eyes turned from Semur, all lost in the darkness, to the sky above us and to me beside her, all confused and bewildered; and the children clung to her, all in tears, crying with that wall which is endless—the trouble of childhood which does not know why it is troubled. '*Maman! Maman!*' they cried, 'let us go home.'

'Oh! be silent, my little ones,' said the poor woman; 'be silent; we will go to *M. le Maire*—he will not leave us without a friend.' It was then that I saw what my duty was. But it was with a pang—*bon Dieu!*—when I turned my back upon my Martin, when I went away to shelter, to peace, leaving my son thus in face of an offended Heaven and all the invisible powers, do you suppose it was a whole heart I carried in my breast? But no! it was nothing save a great ache—a struggle as of death. But what of that? I had my duty to do, as he had—and as he did not flinch, so did not I; otherwise he would have been ashamed of his mother—and I? I should have felt that the blood was not mine which ran in his veins.

No one can tell what it was, that march to La Clairière. Agnès at first was like an angel. I hope I always do Madame Martin justice. She is a saint. She is good to the bottom of her heart. Nevertheless, with those natures which are enthusiast—which are upborne by excitement—there is also a weakness. Though she was brave as the Holy *Pucelle* when we set out, after a while she flagged like another. The colour went out of her face, and though she smiled still, yet the tears came to her eyes, and she would have wept with the other women, and with the wail of the weary children, and all the agitation, and the weariness, and the length of the way, had not I recalled her to herself. 'Courage!' I said to her. 'Courage, *ma fille!* We will throw open all the chambers. I will give up even that one in which my Martin Dupin, the father of thy husband, died.'

'*Ma mère*', she said, holding my hand to her bosom, 'he is not dead—he is in Semur.' Forgive me, dear Lord! It gave me a pang that she could see him and not I.

'For me,' I cried, 'it is enough to know that my good man is in heaven: his room, which I have kept sacred, shall be given up to the poor.' But oh! the confusion of the stumbling, weary feet; the little children that dropped by the way, and caught at our skirts, and wailed and sobbed; the poor mothers with babes upon each arm, with sick hearts and failing limbs. One cry seemed to rise round us as we went, each infant moving the others to sympathy, till it rose like one breath, a wail of '*Maman! Maman!*' a cry that had no meaning, through having so much meaning. It was difficult not to cry out too in the excitement, in the labouring of the long, long, confused, and tedious way. '*Maman! Maman!*' The Holy Mother could not but hear it. It is not possible but that she must have looked out upon us, and heard us, so helpless as we were, where she sits in heaven.

When we got to La Clairière we were ready to sink down with fatigue like all the rest—nay, even more than the rest, for we were not used to it, and for my part I had altogether lost the habitude of long walks. But then you could see what Madame Martin was. She is slight and fragile and pale, not strong, as anyone can perceive; but she rose above the needs of the body. She was the one among us who rested not. We threw open all the rooms, and the poor people thronged in. Old Léontine, who is the *garde* of the house, gazed upon us and the crowd whom we brought with us with great eyes full of fear and trouble.

'But, *Madame*,' she cried, '*Madame!*' following me as I went above to the better rooms. She pulled me by my robe. She pushed the poor women with their children away. '*Allez donc, allez!*—rest outside till these ladies have time to speak to you,' she said; and pulled me by my sleeve. Then 'Madame Martin is putting all this *canaille* into our very chambers,' she cried. She had always distrusted Madame Martin, who was taken by the peasants for a clerical and a devote, because she was noble.

'The *bon Dieu* be praised that *Madame* also is here, who has sense and will regulate everything.'

'These are no *canaille*' I said: 'be silent, *ma bonne* Léontine, here is something which you cannot understand. This is Semur which has come out to us for lodging.' She let the keys drop out of her hands. It was not wonderful if she was amazed. All day long she followed me about, her very mouth open with wonder. 'Madame Martin, that understands itself,' she would say. 'She is *romanesque*—she has imagination—but *Madame*, *Madame* has *bon sens*—who would have believed it of *Madame*?' Léontine had been my *femme de ménage* long before there was a Madame Martin, when my son was young; and naturally it was of me she still thought. But I cannot put down all the trouble we had ere we found shelter for everyone. We filled the stables and the great barn, and all the cottages near; and to get them food, and to have something provided for those who were watching before the city, and who had no one but us to think of them, was a task which was almost beyond our powers.

Truly it was beyond our powers—but the Holy Mother of heaven and the good angels helped us. I cannot tell to anyone how it was accomplished, yet it was accomplished. The wail of the little ones ceased. They slept that first night as if they had been in heaven. As for us, when the night came, and the dews and the darkness, it seemed to us as if we were out of our bodies, so weary were we, so weary that we could not rest. From La Clairière on ordinary occasions it is a beautiful sight to see the lights of Semur shining in all the high windows, and the streets throwing up a faint whiteness upon the sky; but how strange it was now to look down and see nothing but a darkness—a cloud, which was the city!

The lights of the watchers in their camp were invisible to us,—they were so small and low upon the broken ground that we could not see them. Our Agnès crept close to me; we went with one accord to the seat before the door. We did not say 'I will go,' but went by one impulse, for our hearts were there; and we were glad to taste the freshness of the night and be silent after all our labours. We leant upon each other in our weariness. '*Ma mère,*' she said, 'where is he now, our Martin?' and wept.

'He is where there is the most to do, be thou sure of that,' I cried, but wept not. For what did I bring him into the world but for this end?

Were I to go day by day and hour by hour over that time of trouble, the story would not please any one. Many were brave and forgot their own sorrows to occupy themselves with those of others, but many also were not brave. There were those among us who murmured and complained. Some would contend with us to let them go and call their husbands, and leave the miserable country where such things could happen. Some would rave against the priests and the government, and some against those who neglected and offended the Holy Church. Among them there were those who did not hesitate to say it was our fault, though how we were answerable they could not tell. We were never at any time of the day or night without a sound of someone weeping or bewailing herself, as if she were the only sufferer, or crying out against those who had brought her here, far from all her friends. By times it seemed to me that I could bear it no longer, that it was but justice to turn those murmurers (*pleureuses*) away, and let them try what better they could do for themselves.

But in this point Madame Martin surpassed me. I do not grudge to say it. She was better than I was, for she was more patient. She wept with the weeping women, then dried her eyes and smiled upon them without a thought of anger—whereas I could have turned them to the door. One thing, however, which I could not away with, was that Agnès filled her own chamber with the poorest of the poor. 'How,' I cried, 'thyself and thy friend Madame de Bois-Sombre, were you not enough to fill it, that you should throw open that chamber to good-for-nothings, to *va-nu-pieds,* to the very rabble?'

'*Ma mère,*' said Madame Martin, 'our good Lord died for them.'

'And surely for thee too, thou *saint-imbécile!*' I cried out in my indignation. What, my Martin's chamber which he had adorned for his bride! I was beside myself. And they have an obstinacy these enthusiasts! But for that matter her friend Madame de Bois-Sombre thought the same. She would have been one of the *pleureuses* herself had it not been for shame.

'Agnès wishes to aid the *bon Dieu, Madame,*' she said, 'to make us suffer still a little more.' The tone in which she spoke, and the contraction in her forehead, as if our hospitality was not enough for her, turned my heart again to my daughter-in-law.

'You have reason, *Madame,*' I cried; 'there are indeed many ways in which Agnès does the work of the good God.' The Bois-Sombres are poor, they have not a roof to shelter them save that of the old hotel in Semur, from whence they were sent forth like the rest of us. And she and her children owed all to Agnès. Figure to yourself then my resentment when this lady directed her scorn at my daughter-in-law. I am not myself noble, though of the *haute bourgeoisie*, which some people think a purer race.

Long and terrible were the days we spent in this suspense. For ourselves it was well that there was so much to do—the food to provide for all this multitude, the little children to care for, and to prepare the provisions for our men who were before Semur. I was in the Ardennes during the war, and I saw some of its perils—but these were nothing to what we encountered now. It is true that my son Martin was not in the war, which made it very different to me; but here the dangers were such as we could not understand, and they weighed upon our spirits. The seat at the door, and that point where the road turned, where there was always so beautiful a view of the valley and of the town of Semur—were constantly occupied by groups of poor people gazing at the darkness in which their homes lay.

It was strange to see them, some kneeling and praying with moving lips; some taking but one look, not able to endure the sight. I was of these last. From time to time, whenever I had a moment, I came out, I know not why, to see if there was any change. But to gaze upon that altered prospect for hours, as some did, would have been intolerable to me. I could not linger nor try to imagine what might be passing there, either among those who were within (as was believed), or those who were without the walls. Neither could I pray as many did. My devotions of every day I will never, I trust, forsake or forget, and that my Martin was always in my mind is it needful to say? But to go over and over all the vague fears that were in me, and all those thoughts which would have broken my heart had they been put into words, I could not do this even to the good Lord Himself.

When I suffered myself to think, my heart grew sick, my head swam round, the light went from my eyes. They are happy who can do so, who can take the *bon Dieu* into their confidence, and say all to Him; but me, I could not do it. I could not dwell upon that which was so terrible, upon my home abandoned, my son—Ah! now that it is past, it is still terrible to think of. And then it was all I was capable of, to trust my God and do what was set before me. God, He knows what it is we can do and what we cannot. I could not tell even to Him all the terror and the misery and the darkness there was in me; but I put my faith in Him. It was all of which I was capable. We are not made alike, neither in the body nor in the soul.

And there were many women like me at La Clairière. When we had done each piece of work we would look out with a kind of hope, then go back to find something else to do—not looking at each other, not saying a word. Happily there was a great deal to do. And to see how some of the women, and those the most anxious, would work, never resting, going on from one thing to another, as if they were hungry for more and more! Some did it with their mouths shut close, with their countenances fixed, not daring to pause or meet another's eyes; but some, who were more patient, worked with a soft word, and sometimes a smile, and sometimes a tear; but ever working on. Some of them were an example to us all.

In the morning, when we got up, some from beds, some from the floor,—I insisted that all should lie down, by turns at least, for we could not make room for everyone at the same hours,—the very first thought of all was to hasten to the window, or, better, to the door. Who could tell what might have happened while we slept? For the first moment no one would speak,—it was the moment of hope—and then there would be a cry, a clasping of the hands, which told—what we all knew. The one of the women who touched my heart most was the wife of Riou of the *octroi*. She had been almost rich for her condition in life, with a good house and a little servant whom she trained admirably, as I have had occasion to know. Her husband and her son were both among those whom we had left under the walls of Semur; but she had three children with her at La Clairière.

Madame Riou slept lightly, and so did I. Sometimes I heard her stir in the middle of the night, though so softly that no one woke. We were in the same room, for it may be supposed that to keep a room to one's self was not possible. I did not stir, but lay and watched her as she went to the window, her figure visible against the pale dawning of the light, with an eager quick movement as of expectation—then turning back with slower step and a sigh. She was always full of hope. As the days went on, there came to be a kind of communication between us. We understood each other. When one was occupied and the other free, that one of us who went out to the door to look across the valley where Semur was would look at the other as if to say, 'I go.' When it was Madame Riou who did this, I shook my head, and she gave me a smile which awoke at every repetition (though I knew it was vain) a faint expectation, a little hope. When she came back, it was she who would shake her head, with her eyes full of tears. 'Did I not tell thee?' I said, speaking to her as if she were my daughter.

'It will be for next time, *Madame*,' she would say, and smile, yet put her apron to her eyes. There were many who were like her, and there were those of whom I have spoken who were *pleureuses*, never hoping anything, doing little, bewailing themselves and their hard fate. Some of them we employed to carry the provisions to Semur, and this amused them, though the heaviness of the baskets made again a complaint.

As for the children, thank God! they were not disturbed as we were—to them it was a beautiful holiday—it was like Heaven. There is no place on earth that I love like Semur, yet it is true that the streets are narrow, and there is not much room for the children. Here they were happy as the day; they strayed over all our gardens and the meadows, which were full of flowers; they sat in companies upon the green grass, as thick as the daisies themselves, which they loved. Old Sister Mariette, who is called Marie de la Consolation, sat out in the meadow under an acacia-tree and watched over them. She was the one among us who was happy. She had no son, no husband, among the watchers, and though, no doubt, she loved her convent and her hospital, yet she sat all day long in the shade and in the full air, and smiled, and never looked towards Semur.

'The good Lord will do as He wills,' she said, 'and that will be well.' It was true—we all knew it was true; but it might be—who could tell?—that it was His will to destroy our town, and take away our bread, and perhaps the lives of those who were dear to us; and something came in our throats which prevented a reply. '*Ma soeur*' I said, 'we are of the world, we tremble for those we love; we are not as you are.'

Sister Mariette did nothing but smile upon us. 'I have known my Lord these sixty years,' she said, 'and He has taken everything from me.' To see her smile as she said this was more than I could bear. From me He had taken something, but not all. Must we be prepared to give up all if we would be perfected? There were many of the others also who trembled at these words.

'And now He gives me my consolation,' she said, and called the little ones round her, and told them a tale of the Good Shepherd, which is out of the holy Gospel. To see all the little ones round her knees in a crowd, and the peaceful face with which she smiled upon them, and the meadows all full of flowers, and the sunshine coming and going through the branches: and to hear that tale of Him who went forth to seek the lamb that was lost, was like a tale out of a holy book, where all was peace and goodness and joy. But on the other side, not twenty steps off, was the house full of those who wept, and at all the doors and windows anxious faces gazing down upon that cloud in the valley where Semur was. A procession of our women was coming back, many with lingering steps, carrying the baskets which were empty. 'Is there any news?' we asked, reading their faces before they could answer. And some shook their heads, and some wept. There was no other reply.

On the last night before our deliverance, suddenly, in the middle of the night, there was a great commotion in the house. We all rose out of our beds at the sound of the cry, almost believing that someone at the window had seen the lifting of the cloud, and rushed together, frightened, yet all in an eager expectation to hear what it was. It was in the room where the old Mère Julie slept that the disturbance was. Mère Julie was one of the market-women of Semur, the one I have mentioned who was devout, who never missed the *Salut* in the afternoon, besides all masses which are obligatory. But there were other matters in which she had not satisfied my mind, as I have before said. She was the mother of Jacques Richard, who was a good-for-nothing, as is well known. At La Clairière Mere Julie had enacted a strange part. She had taken no part in anything that was done, but had established herself in the chamber allotted to her, and taken the best bed in it, where she kept her place night and day, making the others wait upon her.

She had always expressed a great devotion for St. Jean; and the Sisters of the Hospital had been very kind to her, and also to her *vaurien* of a son, who was indeed, in some manner, the occasion of all our troubles—being the first who complained of the opening of the chapel into the chief ward, which was closed up by the administration, and thus became, as I and many others think, the cause of all the calamities that have come upon us. It was her bed that was the centre of the great commotion we had heard, and a dozen voices immediately began to explain to us as we entered. 'Mère Julie has had a dream. She has seen a vision,' they said. It was a vision of angels in the most beautiful robes, all shining with gold and whiteness.

'The dress of the Holy Mother which she wears on the great *fêtes* was nothing to them,' Mère Julie told us, when she had composed herself. For all had run here and there at her first cry, and procured for her a *tisane*, and a cup of *bouillon*, and all that was good for an attack of the nerves, which was what it was at first supposed to be. 'Their wings were like the wings of the great peacock on the terrace, but also like those of eagles. And each one had a collar of beautiful jewels about his neck, and robes whiter than those of any bride.' This was the description she gave: and to see the women how they listened, head above head, a cloud of eager faces, all full of awe and attention!

The angels had promised her that they would come again, when we had bound ourselves to observe all the functions of the Church, and when all these *Messieurs* had been converted, and made their submission—to lead us back gloriously to Semur. There was a great tumult In the chamber, and all cried out that they were convinced, that they were ready to promise. All except Madame Martin, who stood and looked at them with a look which surprised me, which was of pity rather than sympathy. As there was no one else to speak, I took the word, being the mother of the present *Maire*, and wife of the last, and in part mistress of the house. Had Agnès spoken I would have yielded to her, but as she was silent I took my right.

'Mère Julie,' I said, 'and *mes bonnes femmes,* my friends, know you that it Is the middle of the night, the hour at which we must rest if we are to be able to do the work that is needful, which the *bon Dieu* has laid upon us? It is not from us—my daughter and myself—who, It is well known, have followed all the functions of the Church, that you will meet with an opposition to your promise. But what I desire is that you should calm yourselves, that you should retire and rest till the time of work, husbanding your strength, since we know not what claim may be made upon it. The holy angels,' I said, 'will comprehend, or if not they, then the *bon Dieu*, who understands everything.'

But it was with difficulty that I could induce them to listen to me, to do that which was reasonable. When, however, we had quieted the agitation, and persuaded the good women to repose themselves, it was no longer possible for me to rest. I promised to myself a little moment of quiet, for my heart longed to be alone. I stole out as quietly as I might, not to disturb any one, and sat down upon the bench outside the door. It was still a kind of half-dark, nothing visible, so that if anyone should gaze and gaze down the valley, it was not possible to see what was there: and I was glad that it was not possible, for my very soul was tired. I sat down and leant my back upon the wall of our house, and opened my lips to draw in the air of the morning.

How still it was! the very birds not yet begun to rustle and stir in the bushes; the night air hushed, and scarcely the first faint tint of blue beginning to steal into the darkness. When I had sat there a little, closing my eyes, lo, tears began to steal into them like rain when there has been a fever of heat. I have wept in my time many tears, but the time of weeping is over with me, and through all these miseries I had shed none. Now they came without asking, like a benediction refreshing my eyes. Just then I felt a soft pressure upon my shoulder, and there was Agnès coming close, putting her shoulder to mine, as was her way, that we might support each other.

'You weep, *ma mère*,' she said.

'I think it is one of the angels Mère Julie has seen,' said I. 'It is a refreshment—a blessing; my eyes were dry with weariness.'

'Mother,' said Madame Martin, 'do you think it is angels with wings like peacocks and jewelled collars that our Father sends to us? Ah, not so—one of those whom we love has touched your dear eyes,' and with that she kissed me upon my eyes, taking me in her arms. My heart is sometimes hard to my son s wife, but not always—not with my will, God knows! Her kiss was soft as the touch of any angel could be.

'God bless thee, my child,' I said.

'Thanks, thanks, *ma mère!*' she cried. 'Now I am resolved; now will I go and speak to Martin—of something in my heart.'

'What will you do, my child?' I said, for as the light increased I could see the meaning in her face, and that it was wrought up for some great thing. 'Beware, Agnès; risk not my son's happiness by risking thyself; thou art more to Martin than all the world beside.'

'He loves thee dearly, mother,' she said. My heart was comforted. I was able to remember that I too had had my day. 'He loves his mother, thank God, but not as he loves thee. Beware, *ma fille*. If you risk my son's happiness, neither will I forgive you.' She smiled upon me, and kissed my hands.

'I will go and take him his food and some linen, and carry him your love and mine.'

'You will go, and carry one of those heavy baskets with the others!'

'Mother,' cried Agnès, 'now you shame me that I have never done it before.'

What could I say? Those whose turn it was were preparing their burdens to set out. She had her little packet made up, besides, of our cool white linen, which I knew would be so grateful to my son. I went with her to the turn of the road, helping her with her basket; but my limbs trembled, what with the long continuance of the trial, what with the agitation of the night. It was but just daylight when they went away, disappearing down the long slope of the road that led to Semur. I went back to the bench at the door, and there I sat down and thought. Assuredly it was wrong to close up the chapel, to deprive the sick of the benefit of the holy-mass.

But yet I could not but reflect that the *bon Dieu* had suffered still more great scandals to take place without such a punishment. When, however, I reflected on all that has been done by those who have no cares of this world as we have, but are brides of Christ, and upon all they resign by their dedication, and the claim they have to be furthered, not hindered, in their holy work: and when I bethought myself how many and great are the powers of evil, and that, save in us poor women who can do so little, the Church has few friends: then it came back to me how heinous was the offence that had been committed, and that it might well be that the saints out of heaven should return to earth to take the part and avenge the cause of the weak.

My husband would have been the first to do it, had he seen with my eyes; but though in the flesh he did not do so, is it to be doubted that in heaven their eyes are enlightened—those who have been subjected to the cleansing fires and have ascended into final bliss? This all became clear to me as I sat and pondered, while the morning light grew around me, and the sun rose and shed his first rays, which are as precious gold, on the summits of the mountains—for at La Clairière we are nearer the mountains than at Semur.

The house was more still than usual, and all slept to a later hour because of the agitation of the past night. I had been seated, like old sister Mariette, with my eyes turned rather towards the hills than to the valley, being so deep in my thoughts that I did not look, as it was our constant wont to look, if any change had happened over Semur. Thus blessings come unawares when we are not looking for them. Suddenly I lifted my eyes—but not with expectation—languidly, as one looks without thought. Then it was that I gave that great cry which brought all crowding to the windows, to the gardens, to every spot from whence that blessed sight was visible; for there before us, piercing through the clouds, were the beautiful towers of Semur, the Cathedral with all its pinnacles, that are as if they were carved out of foam, and the solid tower of St. Lambert, and the others, every one. They told me after that I flew, though I am past running, to the farmyard to call all the labourers and servants of the farm, bidding them prepare every carriage and waggon, and even the *charrettes*, to carry back the children, and those who could not walk to the city.

'The men will be wild with privation and trouble,' I said to myself; 'they will want the sight of their little children, the comfort of their wives.'

I did not wait to reason nor to ask myself if I did well; and my son has told me since that he scarcely was more thankful for our great deliverance than, just when the crowd of gaunt and weary men returned into Semur, and there was a moment when excitement and joy were at their highest, and danger possible, to hear the roll of the heavy farm waggons, and to see me arrive, with all the little ones and their mothers, like a new army, to take possession of their homes once more.

Chapter 10

M. le Maire Concludes His Record.

The narratives which I have collected from the different eye-witnesses during the time of my own absence, will show how everything passed while I, with *M. le Curé*, was recovering possession of our city. Many have reported to me verbally the occurrences of the last half-hour before my return; and in their accounts there are naturally discrepancies, owing to their different points of view and different ways of regarding the subject. But all are agreed that a strange and universal slumber had seized upon all. M. de Bois-Sombre even admits that he, too, was overcome by this influence. They slept while we were performing our dangerous and solemn duty in Semur. But when the Cathedral bells began to ring, with one impulse all awoke, and starting from the places where they lay, from the shade of the trees and bushes and sheltering hollows, saw the cloud and the mist and the darkness which had enveloped Semur suddenly rise from the walls.

It floated up into the higher air before their eyes, then was caught and carried away, and flung about into shreds upon the sky by a strong wind, of which down below no influence was felt. They all gazed, not able to get their breath, speechless, beside themselves with joy, and saw the walls reappear, and the roofs of the houses, and our glorious Cathedral against the blue sky. They stood for a moment spellbound. M. de Bois-Sombre informs me that he was afraid of a wild rush into the city, and himself hastened to the front to lead and restrain it; when suddenly a great cry rang through the air, and someone was seen to fall across the high road, straight in front of the Porte St. Lambert. M. de Bois-Sombre was at once aware who it was, for he himself had watched Lecamus taking his place at the feet of my wife, who awaited my return there.

This checked the people in their first rush towards their homes; and when it was seen that Madame Dupin had also sunk down fainting on the ground after her more than human exertions for the comfort of all, there was but one impulse of tenderness and pity. When I reached the gate on my return, I found my wife lying there in all the pallor of death, and for a moment my heart stood still with sudden terror. What mattered Semur to me, if it had cost me my Agnès? or how could I think of Lecamus or any other, while she lay between life and death? I had her carried back to our own house. She was the first to re-enter Semur; and after a time, thanks be to God, she came back to herself.

But Paul Lecamus was a dead man. No need to carry him in, to attempt unavailing cares. 'He has gone, that one; he has marched with the others,' said the old doctor, who had served in his day, and sometimes would use the language of the camp. He cast but one glance at him, and laid his hand upon his heart in passing. 'Cover his face,' was all he said. It is possible that this check was good for the restraint of the crowd. It moderated the rush with which they returned to their homes. The sight of the motionless figures stretched out by the side of the way overawed them. Perhaps it may seem strange, to anyone who has known what had occurred, that the state of the city should have given me great anxiety the first night of our return.

The withdrawal of the oppression and awe which had been on the men, the return of everything to its natural state, the sight of their houses unchanged, so that the brain turned round of these common people, who seldom reflect upon anything, and they already began to ask themselves was it all a delusion—added to the exhaustion of their physical condition, and the natural desire for ease and pleasure after the long strain upon all their faculties—produced an excitement which might have led to very disastrous consequences. Fortunately I had foreseen this. I have always been considered to possess great knowledge of human nature, and this has been matured by recent events. I sent off messengers instantly to bring home the women and children, and called around me the men in whom I could most trust. Though I need not say that the excitement and suffering of the past three days had told not less upon myself than upon others, I abandoned all idea of rest.

The first thing that I did, aided by my respectable fellow-townsmen, was to take possession of all *cabarets* and wine-shops, allowing indeed the proprietors to return, but preventing all assemblages within them. We then established a patrol of respectable citizens throughout the city, to preserve the public peace. I calculated, with great anxiety, how many hours it would be before my messengers could reach La Clairière, to bring back the women—for in such a case the wives are the best guardians, and can exercise an influence more general and less suspected than that of the magistrates; but this was not to be hoped for for three or four hours at least. Judge, then, what was my joy and satisfaction when the sound of wheels (in itself a pleasant sound, for no wheels had been audible on the high-road since these events began) came briskly to us from the distance; and looking out from the watch-tower over the Porte St. Lambert, I saw the strangest procession. The wine-carts and all the farm vehicles of La Clairière, and every kind of country waggon, were jolting along the road, all in a tumult and babble of delicious voices; and from under the rude canopies and awnings and roofs of vine branches, made up to shield them from the sun, lo! there were the children like birds in a nest, one little head peeping over the other.

And the cries and songs, the laughter, and the shoutings! As they came along the air grew sweet, the world was made new. Many of us, who had borne all the terrors and sufferings of the past without fainting, now felt their strength fail them. Some broke out into tears, interrupted with laughter. Some called out aloud the names of their little ones. We went out to meet them, every man there present, myself at the head. And I will not deny that a sensation of pride came over me when I saw my mother stand up in the first waggon, with all those happy ones fluttering around her. 'My son,' she said, 'I have discharged the trust that was given me. I bring thee back the blessing of God.'

'And God bless thee, my mother!' I cried. The other men, who were fathers, like me, came round me, crowding to kiss her hand. It is not among the women of my family that you will find those who abandon their duties.

And then to lift them down in armfuls, those flowers of paradise, all fresh with the air of the fields, all joyous like the birds! We put them down by twos and threes, some of us sobbing with joy. And to see them dispersing hand in hand, running here and there, each to its home, carrying peace, and love, and gladness, through the streets—that was enough to make the most serious smile. No fear was in them, or care. Every haggard man they met—some of them feverish, restless, beginning to think of riot and pleasure after forced abstinence—there was a new shout, a rush of little feet, a shower of soft kisses. The women were following after, some packed into the carts and waggons, pale and worn, yet happy; some walking behind in groups; the more strong, or the more eager, in advance, and a long line of stragglers behind.

There was anxiety in their faces, mingled with their joy. How did they know what they might find in the houses from which they had been shut out? And many felt, like me, that In the very return, In the relief, there was danger. But the children feared nothing; they filled the streets with their dear voices, and happiness came back with them. When I felt my little Jean's cheek against mine, then for the first time did I know how much anguish I had suffered—how terrible was parting, and how sweet was life. But strength and prudence melt away when one indulges one's self, even in one's dearest affections. I had to call my guardians together, to put mastery upon myself, that a just vigilance might not be relaxed. M. de Bois-Sombre, though less anxious than myself, and disposed to believe (being a soldier) that a little license would do no harm, yet stood by me; and, thanks to our precautions, all went well.

Before night three parts of the population had returned to Semur, and the houses were all lighted up as for a great festival. The Cathedral stood open—even the great west doors, which are only opened on great occasions—with a glow of tapers gleaming out on every side. As I stood in the twilight watching, and glad at heart to think that all was going well, my mother and my wife—still pale, but now recovered from her fainting and weakness—came out into the great square, leading my little Jean. They were on their way to the Cathedral, to thank God for their return. They looked at me, but did not ask me to go with them, those dear women; they respected my opinions, as I had always respected theirs. But this silence moved me more than words; there came into my heart a sudden inspiration.

I was still in my scarf of office, which had been, I say it without vanity, the standard of authority and protection during all our trouble; and thus marked out as representative of all, I uncovered myself, after the ladies of my family had passed, and, without joining them, silently followed with a slow and solemn step. A suggestion, a look, is enough for my countrymen; those who were in the Place with me perceived in a moment what I meant. One by one they uncovered, they put themselves behind me. Thus we made such a procession as had never been seen in Semur. We were gaunt and worn with watching and anxiety, which only added to the solemn effect. Those who were already in the Cathedral, and especially *M. le Curé*, informed me afterwards that the tramp of our male feet as we came up the great steps gave to all a thrill of expectation and awe.

It was at the moment of the exposition of the Sacrament that we entered. Instinctively, in a moment, all understood—a thing which could happen nowhere but in France, where intelligence is swift as the breath on our lips. Those who were already there yielded their places to us, most of the women rising up, making as it were a ring round us, the tears running down their faces. When the Sacrament was replaced upon the altar, *M. le Curé,* perceiving our meaning, began at once in his noble voice to intone the *Te Deum.* Rejecting all other music, he adopted the plain song in which all could join, and with one voice, every man in unison with his brother, we sang with him. The great Cathedral walls seemed to throb with the sound that rolled upward, *mâle* and deep, as no song has ever risen from Semur in the memory of man. The women stood up around us, and wept and sobbed with pride and joy.

When this wonderful moment was over, and all the people poured forth out of the Cathedral walls into the soft evening, with stars shining above, and all the friendly lights below, there was such a tumult of emotion and gladness as I have never seen before. Many of the poor women surrounded me, kissed my hand notwithstanding my resistance, and called upon God to bless me; while some of the older persons made remarks full of justice and feeling.

'The *bon Dieu* is not used to such singing,' one of them cried, her old eyes streaming with tears. 'It must have surprised the saints up in heaven!'

'It will bring a blessing,' cried another. 'It is not like our little voices, that perhaps only reach half-way.'

This was figurative language, yet it was impossible to doubt there was much truth in it. Such a submission of our Intellects, as I felt in determining to make it, must have been pleasing to heaven. The women, they are always praying; but when we thus presented ourselves to give thanks, it meant something, a real homage; and with a feeling of solemnity we separated, aware that we had contented both earth and heaven.

Next morning there was a great function in the Cathedral, at which the whole city assisted. Those who could not get admittance crowded upon the steps, and knelt half-way across the Place. It was an occasion long remembered in Semur, though I have heard many say not in itself so impressive as the *Te Deum* on the evening of our return. After this we returned to our occupations, and life was resumed under its former conditions in our city.

It might be supposed, however, that the place in which events so extraordinary had happened would never again be as It was before. Had I not been myself so closely involved, It would have appeared to me certain, that the streets, trod once by such inhabitants as those who for three nights and days abode within Semur, would have always retained some trace of their presence; that life there would have been more solemn than in other places; and that those families for whose advantage the dead had risen out of their graves, would have henceforward carried about with them some sign of that Interposition. It will seem almost incredible when I now add that nothing of this kind has happened at Semur. The wonderful manifestation which interrupted our existence has passed absolutely as if it had never been.

We had not been twelve hours in our houses ere we had forgotten, or practically forgotten, our expulsion from them. Even myself, to whom everything was so vividly brought home, I have to enter my wife's room, to put aside the curtain from little Marie's picture, and to see and touch the olive branch which is there, before I can recall to myself anything that resembles the feeling with which I re-entered that sanctuary. My grandfather's bureau still stands in the middle of my library, where I found it on my return; but I have got used to it, and it no longer affects me. Everything is as it was; and I cannot persuade myself that, for a time, I and mine were shut out, and our places taken by those who neither eat nor drink, and whose life is invisible to our eyes.

Everything, I say, is as it was—everything goes on as if it would endure forever. We know this cannot be, yet it does not move us. Why, then, should the other move us? A little time, we are aware, and we, too, shall be as they are—as shadows, and unseen. But neither has the one changed us, and neither does the other. There was, for some time, a greater respect shown to religion in Semur, and a more devout attendance at the sacred functions; but I regret to say this did not continue. Even in my own case—I say it with sorrow—it did not continue. *M. le Curé* is an admirable person. I know no more excellent ecclesiastic. He is indefatigable in the performance of his spiritual duties; and he has, besides, a noble and upright soul. Since the days when we suffered and laboured together, he has been to me as a brother.

Still, it is undeniable that he makes calls upon our credulity, which a man obeys with reluctance. There are ways of surmounting this; as I see in Agnès for one, and in M. de Bois-Sombre for another. My wife does not question, she believes much; and in respect to that which she cannot acquiesce in, she is silent. 'There are many things I hear you talk of, Martin, which are strange to me,' she says; 'of myself I cannot believe in them; but I do not oppose, since it is possible you may have reason to know better than I; and so with some things that we hear from *M. le Curé*.' This is how she explains herself—but she is a woman. It Is a matter of grace to yield to our better judgement.

M. de Bois-Sombre has another way. '*Ma foi*,' he says, 'I have not the time for all your delicacies, my good people; I have come to see that these things are for the advantage of the world, and It is not my business to explain them. If *M. le Curé* attempted to criticise me in military matters, or thee, my excellent Martin, in affairs of business, or In the culture of your vines, I should think him not a wise man; and In like manner, faith and religion, these are his concern.' Félix de Bois Sombre is an excellent fellow; but he smells a little of the *mousquetaire*. I, who am neither a soldier nor a woman, I have hesitations. Nevertheless, so long as I am *Maire* of Semur, nothing less than the most absolute respect shall ever be shown to all truly religious persons, with whom it is my earnest desire to remain In sympathy and fraternity, so far as that may be.

It seemed, however, a little while ago as if my tenure of this office would not be long, notwithstanding the services which I am acknowledged, on every hand, to have done to my fellow-townsmen. It will be remembered that when *M. le Curé* and myself found Semur empty, we heard a voice of complaining from the hospital of St. Jean, and found a sick man who had been left there, and who grumbled against the Sisters, and accused them of neglecting him, but remained altogether unaware, in the meantime, of what had happened in the city. Will it be believed that after a time this fellow was put faith in as a seer, who had heard and beheld many things of which we were all ignorant? It must be said that, in the meantime, there had been a little excitement in the town on the subject of the chapel in the hospital, to which repeated reference has already been made.

It was insisted on behalf of these ladies that a promise had been given, taking, indeed, the form of a vow, that, as soon as we were again in possession of Semur, their full privileges should be restored to them. Their advocates even went so far as to send to me a deputation of those who had been nursed in the hospital, the leader of which was Jacques Richard, who since he has been, as he says, 'converted,' thrusts himself to the front of every movement.

'Permit me to speak, *M. le Maire*,' he said; 'me, who was one of those so misguided as to complain, before the great lesson we have all received. The mass did not disturb any sick person who was of right dispositions. I was then a very bad subject, indeed—

as, alas! *M. le Maire* too well knows. It annoyed me only as all pious observances annoyed me. I am now, thank heaven, of a very different way of thinking—'

But I would not listen to the fellow. When he was a *mauvais sujet* he was less abhorrent to me than now.

The men were aware that when I pronounced myself so distinctly on any subject, there was nothing more to be said, for, though gentle as a lamb and open to all reasonable arguments, I am capable of making the most obstinate stand for principle; and to yield to popular superstition, is that worthy of a man who has been instructed? At the same time it raised a great anger In my mind that all that should be thought of was a thing so trivial. That they should have given themselves, soul and body, for a little money; that they should have scoffed at all that was noble and generous, both in religion and in earthly things; all that was nothing to them. And now they would insult the great God Himself by believing that all He cared for was a little mass in a convent chapel. What desecration! What debasement! When I went to *M. le Curé* he smiled at my vehemence. There was pain in his smile, and it might be indignation; but he was not furious like me.

'They will conquer you, my friend,' he said.

'Never,' I cried. 'Before I might have yielded. But to tell me the gates of death have been rolled back, and Heaven revealed, and the great God stooped down from Heaven, in order that mass should be said according to the wishes of the community in the midst of the sick wards! They will never make me believe this, if I were to die for it.'

'Nevertheless, they will conquer,' *M. le Curé* said.

It angered me that he should say so. My heart was sore as if my friend had forsaken me. And then it was that the worst step was taken in this crusade of false religion. It was from my mother that I heard of it first. One day she came home in great excitement, saying that now indeed a real light was to be shed upon all that had happened to us.

'It appears,' she said, 'that Pierre Plastron was In the hospital all the time, and heard and saw many wonderful things. Sister Genevieve has just told me. It is wonderful beyond anything you could believe. He has spoken with our holy patron himself, St. Lambert, and has received instructions for a pilgrimage —'

'Pierre Plastron!' I cried; 'Pierre Plastron saw nothing, *ma mère*. He was not even aware that anything remarkable had occurred. He complained to us of the Sisters that they neglected him; he knew nothing more.'

'My son,' she said, looking upon me with reproving eyes, 'what have the good Sisters done to thee? Why is it that you look so unfavourably upon everything that comes from the community of St. Jean?'

'What have I to do with the community?' I cried—'when I tell thee, *Maman*, that this Pierre Plastron knows nothing! I heard it from the fellow's own lips, and *M. le Curé* was present and heard him too. He had seen nothing, he knew nothing. Inquire of *M. le Curé*, if you have doubts of me.'

'I do not doubt you, Martin,' said my mother, with severity, 'when you are not biased by prejudice. And, as for *M. le Curé* it is well known that the clergy are often jealous of the good Sisters, when they are not under their own control.'

Such was the injustice with which we were treated. And next day nothing was talked of but the revelation of Pierre Plastron. What he had seen and what he had heard was wonderful. All the saints had come and talked with him, and told him what he was to say to his townsmen. They told him exactly how everything had happened: how St. Jean himself had interfered on behalf of the Sisters, and how, if we were not more attentive to the duties of religion, certain among us would be bound hand and foot and cast into the jaws of hell. That I was one, nay the chief, of these denounced persons, no one could have any doubt. This exasperated me; and as soon as I knew that this folly had been printed and was in every house, I hastened to *M. le Curé*, and entreated him in his next Sunday's sermon to tell the true story of Pierre Plastron, and reveal the imposture. But *M. le Curé* shook his head. 'It will do no good,' he said.

'But how no good?' said I. 'What good are we looking for? These are lies, nothing but lies. Either he has deceived the poor ladies basely, or they themselves—but this is what I cannot believe.'

'Dear friend,' he said, 'compose thyself. Have you never discovered yet how strong is self-delusion? There will be no lying of which they are aware. Figure to yourself what a stimulus to the imagination to know that he was here, actually here. Even I—it suggests a hundred things to me. The Sisters will have said to him (meaning no evil, nay meaning the edification of the people), "But, Pierre, reflect! You must have seen this and that. Recall thy recollections a little." And by degrees Pierre will have found out that he remembered—more than could have been hoped.'

'Mon Dieu!' I cried, out of patience, 'and you know all this, yet you will not tell them the truth—the very truth.'

'To what good?' he said. Perhaps *M. le Curé* was right: but, for my part, had I stood up in that pulpit, I should have contradicted their lies and given no quarter. This, indeed, was what I did both in my private and public capacity; but the people, though they loved me, did not believe me. They said, 'The best men have their prejudices. *M. le Maire* is an excellent man; but what will you? He is but human after all.'

M. le Curé and I said no more to each other on this subject. He was a brave man, yet here perhaps he was not quite brave. And the effect of Pierre Plastron s revelations in other quarters was to turn the awe that had been in many minds into mockery and laughter. '*Ma foi*,' said Felix de Bois-Sombre, 'Monseigneur St. Lambert has bad taste, *mon ami* Martin, to choose Pierre Plastron for his confidant when he might have had thee.'

'M. de Bois-Sombre does ill to laugh,' said my mother (even my mother! she was not on my side), 'when it is known that the foolish are often chosen to confound the wise.' But Agnès, my wife, it was she who gave me the best consolation. She turned to me with the tears in her beautiful eyes.

'*Mon ami*,' she said, 'let Monseigneur St. Lambert say what he will. He is not God that we should put him above all. There were other saints with other thoughts that came for thee and for me!'

All this contradiction was over when Agnès and I together took our flowers on the *jour des morts* to the graves we love. Glimmering among the rest was a new cross which I had not seen before. This was the inscription upon it:—

À PAUL LECAMUS
PARTI
LE 20 JUILLET, 1875
AVEC LES BIEN-AIMÉS

On it was wrought in the marble a little branch of olive. I turned to look at my wife as she laid underneath this cross a handful of violets. She gave me her hand still fragrant with the flowers. There was none of his family left to put up for him any token of human remembrance. Who but she should have done it, who had helped him to join that company and army of the beloved? 'This was our brother,' she said; 'he will tell my Marie what use I made of her olive leaves.'

The Turn of the Screw

by Henry James

The story had held us, round the fire, sufficiently breathless, but except the obvious remark that it was gruesome, as, on Christmas Eve in an old house, a strange tale should essentially be, I remember no comment uttered till somebody happened to say that it was the only case he had met in which such a visitation had fallen on a child. The case, I may mention, was that of an apparition in just such an old house as had gathered us for the occasion—an appearance, of a dreadful kind, to a little boy sleeping in the room with his mother and waking her up in the terror of it; waking her not to dissipate his dread and soothe him to sleep again, but to encounter also, herself, before she had succeeded in doing so, the same sight that had shaken him.

It was this observation that drew from Douglas—not immediately, but later in the evening—a reply that had the interesting consequence to which I call attention. Someone else told a story not particularly effective, which I saw he was not following. This I took for a sign that he had himself something to produce and that we should only have to wait. We waited in fact till two nights later; but that same evening, before we scattered, he brought out what was in his mind.

"I quite agree—in regard to Griffin's ghost, or whatever it was—that its appearing first to the little boy, at so tender an age, adds a particular touch. But it's not the first occurrence of its charming kind that I know to have involved a child. If the child gives the effect another turn of the screw, what do you say to

TWO children—?"

"We say, of course," somebody exclaimed, "that they give two turns! Also that we want to hear about them."

I can see Douglas there before the fire, to which he had got up to present his back, looking down at his interlocutor with his hands in his pockets. "Nobody but me, till now, has ever heard. It's quite too horrible." This, naturally, was declared by several voices to give the thing the utmost price, and our friend, with quiet art, prepared his triumph by turning his eyes over the rest of us and going on: "It's beyond everything. Nothing at all that I know touches it."

"For sheer terror?" I remember asking.

He seemed to say it was not so simple as that; to be really at a loss how to qualify it. He passed his hand over his eyes, made a little wincing grimace. "For dreadful—dreadfulness!"

"Oh, how delicious!" cried one of the women.

He took no notice of her; he looked at me, but as if, instead of me, he saw what he spoke of. "For general uncanny ugliness and horror and pain."

"Well then," I said, "just sit right down and begin."

He turned round to the fire, gave a kick to a log, watched it an instant. Then as he faced us again: "I can't begin. I shall have to send to town." There was a unanimous groan at this, and much reproach; after which, in his preoccupied way, he explained. "The story's written. It's in a locked drawer—it has not been out for years. I could write to my man and enclose the key; he could send down the packet as he finds it." It was to me in particular that he appeared to propound this—appeared almost to appeal for aid not to hesitate. He had broken a thickness of ice, the formation of many a winter; had had his reasons for a long silence. The others resented postponement, but it was just his scruples that charmed me. I adjured him to write by the first post and to agree with us for an early hearing; then I asked him if the experience in question had been his own. To this his answer was prompt. "Oh, thank God, no!"

"And is the record yours? You took the thing down?"

"Nothing but the impression. I took that HERE"—he tapped his heart. "I've never lost it."

"Then your manuscript—?"

"Is in old, faded ink, and in the most beautiful hand." He hung fire again. "A woman's. She has been dead these twenty years. She sent me the pages in question before she died." They were all listening now, and of course there was somebody to be arch, or at any rate to draw the inference. But if he put the inference by without a smile it was also without irritation.

"She was a most charming person, but she was ten years older than I. She was my sister's governess," he quietly said. "She was the most agreeable woman I've ever known in her position; she would have been worthy of any whatever. It was long ago, and this episode was long before. I was at Trinity, and I found her at home on my coming down the second summer. I was much there that year—it was a beautiful one; and we had, in her off-hours, some strolls and talks in the garden—talks in which she struck me as awfully clever and nice. Oh yes; don't grin: I liked her extremely and am glad to this day to think she liked me, too. If she hadn't she wouldn't have told me. She had never told anyone. It wasn't simply that she said so, but that I knew she hadn't. I was sure; I could see. You'll easily judge why when you hear."

"Because the thing had been such a scare?"

He continued to fix me. "You'll easily judge," he repeated: "YOU will."

I fixed him, too. "I see. She was in love."

He laughed for the first time. "You ARE acute. Yes, she was in love. That is, she had been. That came out—she couldn't tell her story without its coming out. I saw it, and she saw I saw it; but neither of us spoke of it. I remember the time and the place-the corner of the lawn, the shade of the great beeches and the long, hot summer afternoon. It wasn't a scene for a shudder; but oh—!" He quitted the fire and dropped back into his chair.

"You'll receive the packet Thursday morning?" I inquired.

"Probably not till the second post."

"Well then; after dinner—"

"You'll all meet me here?" He looked us round again. "Isn't anybody going?" It was almost the tone of hope.

"Everybody will stay!"

"*I* will"—and "*I* will!" cried the ladies whose departure had been fixed. Mrs. Griffin, however, expressed the need for a little more light. "Who was it she was in love with?"

"The story will tell," I took upon myself to reply.

"Oh, I can't wait for the story!"

"The story WON'T tell," said Douglas; "not in any literal, vulgar way."

"More's the pity, then. That's the only way I ever understand."

"Won't YOU tell, Douglas?" somebody else inquired.

He sprang to his feet again. "Yes—tomorrow. Now I must go to bed. Goodnight." And quickly catching up a candlestick, he left us slightly bewildered. From our end of the great brown hall we heard his step on the stair; whereupon Mrs. Griffin spoke. "Well, if I don't know who she was in love with, I know who HE was."

"She was ten years older," said her husband.

"*Raison de plus*—at that age! But it's rather nice, his long reticence."

"Forty years!" Griffin put in.

"With this outbreak at last."

"The outbreak," I returned, "will make a tremendous occasion of Thursday night;" and everyone so agreed with me that, in the light of it, we lost all attention for everything else. The last story, however incomplete and like the mere opening of a serial, had been told; we handshook and "candlestuck," as somebody said, and went to bed.

I knew the next day that a letter containing the key had, by the first post, gone off to his London apartments; but in spite of—or perhaps just on account of—the eventual diffusion of this knowledge we quite let him alone till after dinner, till such an hour of the evening, in fact, as might best accord with the kind of emotion on which our hopes were fixed. Then he became as communicative as we could desire and indeed gave us his best reason for being so. We had it from him again before the fire in the hall, as we had had our mild wonders of the previous night. It appeared that the narrative he had promised to read us really required for a proper intelligence a few words of prologue.

Let me say here distinctly, to have done with it, that this narrative, from an exact transcript of my own made much later, is what I shall presently give. Poor Douglas, before his death—when it was in sight—committed to me the manuscript that reached him on the third of these days and that, on the same spot, with immense effect, he began to read to our hushed little circle on the night of the fourth. The departing ladies who had said they would stay didn't, of course, thank heaven, stay: they departed, in consequence of arrangements made, in a rage of curiosity, as they professed, produced by the touches with which he had already worked us up. But that only made his little final auditory more compact and select, kept it, round the hearth, subject to a common thrill.

The first of these touches conveyed that the written statement took up the tale at a point after it had, in a manner, begun. The fact to be in possession of was therefore that his old friend, the youngest of several daughters of a poor country parson, had, at the age of twenty, on taking service for the first time in the schoolroom, come up to London, in trepidation, to answer in person an advertisement that had already placed her in brief correspondence with the advertiser. This person proved, on her presenting herself, for judgment, at a house in Harley Street, that impressed her as vast and imposing—this prospective patron proved a gentleman, a bachelor in the prime of life, such a figure as had never risen, save in a dream or an old novel, before a fluttered, anxious girl out of a Hampshire vicarage.

One could easily fix his type; it never, happily, dies out. He was handsome and bold and pleasant, offhand and gay and kind. He struck her, inevitably, as gallant and splendid, but what took her most of all and gave her the courage she afterward showed was that he put the whole thing to her as a kind of favour, an obligation he should gratefully incur. She conceived him as rich, but as fearfully extravagant—saw him all in a glow of high fashion, of good looks, of expensive habits, of charming ways with women. He had for his own town residence a big house filled with the spoils of travel and the trophies of the chase; but it was to his country home, an old family place in Essex, that he wished her immediately to proceed.

He had been left, by the death of their parents in India, guardian to a small nephew and a small niece, children of a younger, a military brother, whom he had lost two years before. These children were, by the strangest of chances for a man in his position—a lone man without the right sort of experience or a grain of patience—very heavily on his hands. It had all been a great worry and, on his own part doubtless, a series of blunders, but he immensely pitied the poor chicks and had done all he could; had in particular sent them down to his other house, the proper place for them being of course the country, and kept them there, from the first, with the best people he could find to look after them, parting even with his own servants to wait on them and going down himself, whenever he might, to see how they were doing.

The awkward thing was that they had practically no other relations and that his own affairs took up all his time. He had put them in possession of Bly, which was healthy and secure, and had placed at the head of their little establishment—but below stairs only—an excellent woman, Mrs. Grose, whom he was sure his visitor would like and who had formerly been maid to his mother. She was now housekeeper and was also acting for the time as superintendent to the little girl, of whom, without children of her own, she was, by good luck, extremely fond. There were plenty of people to help, but of course the young lady who should go down as governess would be in supreme authority. She would also have, in holidays, to look after the small boy, who had been for a term at school—young as he was to be sent, but what else could be done?—and who, as the holidays were about to begin, would be back from one day to the other.

There had been for the two children at first a young lady whom they had had the misfortune to lose. She had done for them quite beautifully—she was a most respectable person—till her death, the great awkwardness of which had, precisely, left no alternative but the school for little Miles. Mrs. Grose, since then, in the way of manners and things, had done as she could for Flora; and there were, further, a cook, a housemaid, a dairy-woman, an old pony, an old groom, and an old gardener, all likewise thoroughly respectable.

So far had Douglas presented his picture when someone put a question. "And what did the former governess die of?—of so much respectability?"

Our friend's answer was prompt. "That will come out. I don't anticipate."

"Excuse me—I thought that was just what you ARE doing."

"In her successor's place," I suggested, "I should have wished to learn if the office brought with it—"

"Necessary danger to life?" Douglas completed my thought. "She did wish to learn, and she did learn. You shall hear tomorrow what she learned. Meanwhile, of course, the prospect struck her as slightly grim. She was young, untried, nervous: it was a vision of serious duties and little company, of really great loneliness. She hesitated—took a couple of days to consult and consider. But the salary offered much exceeded her modest measure, and on a second interview she faced the music, she engaged." And Douglas, with this, made a pause that, for the benefit of the company, moved me to throw in—

"The moral of which was of course the seduction exercised by the splendid young man. She succumbed to it."

He got up and, as he had done the night before, went to the fire, gave a stir to a log with his foot, then stood a moment with his back to us. "She saw him only twice."

"Yes, but that's just the beauty of her passion."

A little to my surprise, on this, Douglas turned round to me. "It WAS the beauty of it. There were others," he went on, "who hadn't succumbed. He told her frankly all his difficulty-that for several applicants the conditions had been prohibitive. They were, somehow, simply afraid. It sounded dull—it sounded strange; and all the more so because of his main condition."

"Which was—?"

"That she should never trouble him—but never, never: neither appeal nor complain nor write about anything; only meet all questions herself, receive all moneys from his solicitor, take the whole thing over and let him alone. She promised to do this, and she mentioned to me that when, for a moment, disburdened, delighted, he held her hand, thanking her for the sacrifice, she already felt rewarded."

"But was that all her reward?" one of the ladies asked.

"She never saw him again."

"Oh!" said the lady; which, as our friend immediately left us again, was the only other word of importance contributed to the subject till, the next night, by the corner of the hearth, in the best chair, he opened the faded red cover of a thin old-fashioned gilt-edged album. The whole thing took indeed more nights than one, but on the first occasion the same lady put another question. "What is your title?"

"I haven't one."

"Oh, *I* have!" I said. But Douglas, without heeding me, had begun to read with a fine clearness that was like a rendering to the ear of the beauty of his author's hand.

1

I remember the whole beginning as a succession of flights and drops, a little seesaw of the right throbs and the wrong. After rising, in town, to meet his appeal, I had at all events a couple of very bad days—found myself doubtful again, felt indeed sure I had made a mistake. In this state of mind I spent the long hours of bumping, swinging coach that carried me to the stopping place at which I was to be met by a vehicle from the house. This convenience, I was told, had been ordered, and I found, toward the close of the June afternoon, a commodious fly in waiting for me. Driving at that hour, on a lovely day, through a country to which the summer sweetness seemed to offer me a friendly welcome, my fortitude mounted afresh and, as we turned into the avenue, encountered a reprieve that was probably but a proof of the point to which it had sunk.

I suppose I had expected, or had dreaded, something so melancholy that what greeted me was a good surprise. I remember as a most pleasant impression the broad, clear front, its open windows and fresh curtains and the pair of maids looking out; I remember the lawn and the bright flowers and the crunch of my wheels on the gravel and the clustered treetops over which the rooks circled and cawed in the golden sky. The scene had a greatness that made it a different affair from my own scant home, and there immediately appeared at the door, with a little girl in her hand, a civil person who dropped me as decent a curtsy as if I had been the mistress or a distinguished visitor. I had received in Harley Street a narrower notion of the place, and that, as I recalled it, made me think the proprietor still more of a gentleman, suggested that what I was to enjoy might be something beyond his promise.

I had no drop again till the next day, for I was carried triumphantly through the following hours by my introduction to the younger of my pupils. The little girl who accompanied Mrs. Grose appeared to me on the spot a creature so charming as to make it a great fortune to have to do with her. She was the most beautiful child I had ever seen, and I afterward wondered that my employer had not told me more of her. I slept little that night—I was too much excited; and this astonished me, too, I recollect, remained with me, adding to my sense of the liberality with which I was treated.

The large, impressive room, one of the best in the house, the great state bed, as I almost felt it, the full, figured draperies, the long glasses in which, for the first time, I could see myself from head to foot, all struck me—like the extraordinary charm of my small charge—as so many things thrown in. It was thrown in as well, from the first moment, that I should get on with Mrs.

Grose in a relation over which, on my way, in the coach, I fear I had rather brooded.

The only thing indeed that in this early outlook might have made me shrink again was the clear circumstance of her being so glad to see me. I perceived within half an hour that she was so glad—stout, simple, plain, clean, wholesome woman—as to be positively on her guard against showing it too much. I wondered even then a little why she should wish not to show it, and that, with reflection, with suspicion, might of course have made me uneasy.

But it was a comfort that there could be no uneasiness in a connection with anything so beatific as the radiant image of my little girl, the vision of whose angelic beauty had probably more than anything else to do with the restlessness that, before morning, made me several times rise and wander about my room to take in the whole picture and prospect; to watch, from my open window, the faint summer dawn, to look at such portions of the rest of the house as I could catch, and to listen, while, in the fading dusk, the first birds began to twitter, for the possible recurrence of a sound or two, less natural and not without, but within, that I had fancied I heard.

There had been a moment when I believed I recognized, faint and far, the cry of a child; there had been another when I found myself just consciously starting as at the passage, before my door, of a light footstep. But these fancies were not marked enough not to be thrown off, and it is only in the light, or the gloom, I should rather say, of other and subsequent matters that they now come back to me. To watch, teach, "form" little Flora would too evidently be the making of a happy and useful life. It had been agreed between us downstairs that after this first occasion I should have her as a matter of course at night, her small white bed being already arranged, to that end, in my room.

What I had undertaken was the whole care of her, and she had remained, just this last time, with Mrs. Grose only as an effect of our consideration for my inevitable strangeness and her natural timidity. In spite of this timidity—which the child herself, in the oddest way in the world, had been perfectly frank and brave about, allowing it, without a sign of uncomfortable consciousness, with the deep, sweet serenity indeed of one of Raphael's holy infants, to be discussed, to be imputed to her, and to determine us—I feel quite sure she would presently like me. It was part of what I already liked Mrs. Grose herself for, the pleasure I could see her feel in my admiration and wonder as I sat at supper with four tall candles and with my pupil, in a high chair and a bib, brightly facing me, between them, over bread and milk. There were naturally things that in Flora's presence could pass between us only as prodigious and gratified looks, obscure and roundabout allusions.

"And the little boy—does he look like her? Is he too so very remarkable?"

One wouldn't flatter a child. "Oh, miss, MOST remarkable. If you think well of this one!"—and she stood there with a plate in her hand, beaming at our companion, who looked from one of us to the other with placid heavenly eyes that contained nothing to check us.

"Yes; if I do—?"

"You WILL be carried away by the little gentleman!"

"Well, that, I think, is what I came for—to be carried away. I'm afraid, however," I remember feeling the impulse to add, "I'm rather easily carried away. I was carried away in London!"

I can still see Mrs. Grose's broad face as she took this in. "In Harley Street?"

"In Harley Street."

"Well, miss, you're not the first—and you won't be the last."

"Oh, I've no pretension," I could laugh, "to being the only one. My other pupil, at any rate, as I understand, comes back tomorrow?"

"Not tomorrow—Friday, miss. He arrives, as you did, by the coach, under care of the guard, and is to be met by the same carriage."

I forthwith expressed that the proper as well as the pleasant and friendly thing would be therefore that on the arrival of the public conveyance I should be in waiting for him with his little sister; an idea in which Mrs. Grose concurred so heartily that I somehow took her manner as a kind of comforting pledge-never falsified, thank heaven!—that we should on every question be quite at one. Oh, she was glad I was there!

What I felt the next day was, I suppose, nothing that could be fairly called a reaction from the cheer of my arrival; it was probably at the most only a slight oppression produced by a fuller measure of the scale, as I walked round them, gazed up at them, took them in, of my new circumstances. They had, as it were, an extent and mass for which I had not been prepared and in the presence of which I found myself, freshly, a little scared as well as a little proud. Lessons, in this agitation, certainly suffered some delay; I reflected that my first duty was, by the gentlest arts I could contrive, to win the child into the sense of knowing me.

I spent the day with her out-of-doors; I arranged with her, to her great satisfaction, that it should be she, she only, who might show me the place. She showed it step by step and room by room and secret by secret, with droll, delightful, childish talk about it and with the result, in half an hour, of our becoming immense friends. Young as she was, I was struck, throughout our little tour, with her confidence and courage with the way, in empty chambers and dull corridors, on crooked staircases that made me pause and even on the summit of an old machicolated square tower that made me dizzy, her morning music, her disposition to tell me so many more things than she asked, rang out and led me on.

I have not seen Bly since the day I left it, and I daresay that to my older and more informed eyes it would now appear sufficiently contracted. But as my little conductress, with her hair of gold and her frock of blue, danced before me round corners and pattered down passages, I had the view of a castle of romance inhabited by a rosy sprite, such a place as would somehow, for diversion of the young idea, take all colour out of storybooks and fairytales. Wasn't it just a storybook over which I had fallen adoze and adream? No; it was a big, ugly, antique, but convenient house, embodying a few features of a building still older, half-replaced and half-utilized, in which I had the fancy of our being almost as lost as a handful of passengers in a great drifting ship. Well, I was, strangely, at the helm!

2

This came home to me when, two days later, I drove over with Flora to meet, as Mrs. Grose said, the little gentleman; and all the more for an incident that, presenting itself the second evening, had deeply disconcerted me. The first day had been, on the whole, as I have expressed, reassuring; but I was to see it wind up in keen apprehension. The postbag, that evening—it came late—contained a letter for me, which, however, in the hand of my employer, I found to be composed but of a few words enclosing another, addressed to himself, with a seal still unbroken. "This, I recognize, is from the headmaster, and the headmaster's an awful bore. Read him, please; deal with him; but mind you don't report. Not a word. I'm off!"

I broke the seal with a great effort—so great a one that I was a long time coming to it; took the unopened missive at last up to my room and only attacked it just before going to bed. I had better have let it wait till morning, for it gave me a second sleepless night. With no counsel to take, the next day, I was full of distress; and it finally got so the better of me that I determined to open myself at least to Mrs. Grose.

"What does it mean? The child's dismissed his school."

She gave me a look that I remarked at the moment; then, visibly, with a quick blankness, seemed to try to take it back. "But aren't they all—?"

"Sent home—yes. But only for the holidays. Miles may never go back at all."

Consciously, under my attention, she reddened. "They won't take him?"

"They absolutely decline."

At this she raised her eyes, which she had turned from me; I saw them fill with good tears. "What has he done?"

I hesitated; then I judged best simply to hand her my letter-which, however, had the effect of making her, without taking it, simply put her hands behind her. She shook her head sadly. "Such things are not for me, miss."

My counsellor couldn't read! I winced at my mistake, which I attenuated as I could, and opened my letter again to repeat it to her; then, faltering in the act and folding it up once more, I put it back in my pocket. "Is he really BAD?"

The tears were still in her eyes. "Do the gentlemen say so?"

"They go into no particulars. They simply express their regret that it should be impossible to keep him. That can have only one meaning." Mrs. Grose listened with dumb emotion; she forbore to ask me what this meaning might be; so that, presently, to put the thing with some coherence and with the mere aid of her presence to my own mind, I went on: "That he's an injury to the others."

At this, with one of the quick turns of simple folk, she suddenly flamed up. "Master Miles! HIM an injury?"

There was such a flood of good faith in it that, though I had not yet seen the child, my very fears made me jump to the absurdity of the idea. I found myself, to meet my friend the better, offering it, on the spot, sarcastically. "To his poor little innocent mates!"

"It's too dreadful," cried Mrs. Grose, "to say such cruel things! Why, he's scarce ten years old."

"Yes, yes; it would be incredible."

She was evidently grateful for such a profession. "See him, miss, first. THEN believe it!" I felt forthwith a new impatience to see him; it was the beginning of a curiosity that, for all the next hours, was to deepen almost to pain. Mrs. Grose was aware, I could judge, of what she had produced in me, and she followed it up with assurance. "You might as well believe it of the little lady. Bless her," she added the next moment—"LOOK at her!"

I turned and saw that Flora, whom, ten minutes before, I had established in the schoolroom with a sheet of white paper, a pencil, and a copy of nice "round o's," now presented herself to view at the open door. She expressed in her little way an extraordinary detachment from disagreeable duties, looking to me, however, with a great childish light that seemed to offer it as a mere result of the affection she had conceived for my person, which had rendered necessary that she should follow me. I needed nothing more than this to feel the full force of Mrs. Grose's comparison, and, catching my pupil in my arms, covered her with kisses in which there was a sob of atonement.

Nonetheless, the rest of the day I watched for further occasion to approach my colleague, especially as, toward evening, I began to fancy she rather sought to avoid me. I overtook her, I remember, on the staircase; we went down together, and at the bottom I detained her, holding her there with a hand on her arm. "I take what you said to me at noon as a declaration that YOU'VE never known him to be bad."

She threw back her head; she had clearly, by this time, and very honestly, adopted an attitude. "Oh, never known him—I don't pretend THAT!"

I was upset again. "Then you HAVE known him—?"

"Yes indeed, miss, thank God!"

On reflection I accepted this. "You mean that a boy who never is—?"

"Is no boy for ME!"

I held her tighter. "You like them with the spirit to be naughty?" Then, keeping pace with her answer, "So do I!" I eagerly brought out. "But not to the degree to contaminate—"

"To contaminate?"—my big word left her at a loss. I explained it. "To corrupt."

She stared, taking my meaning in; but it produced in her an odd laugh. "Are you afraid he'll corrupt YOU?" She put the question with such a fine bold humour that, with a laugh, a little silly doubtless, to match her own, I gave way for the time to the apprehension of ridicule.

But the next day, as the hour for my drive approached, I cropped up in another place. "What was the lady who was here before?"

"The last governess? She was also young and pretty—almost as young and almost as pretty, miss, even as you."

"Ah, then, I hope her youth and her beauty helped her!" I recollect throwing off. "He seems to like us young and pretty!"

"Oh, he DID," Mrs. Grose assented: "it was the way he liked everyone!" She had no sooner spoken indeed than she caught herself up. "I mean that's HIS way—the master's."

I was struck. "But of whom did you speak first?"

She looked blank, but she coloured. "Why, of HIM."

"Of the master?"

"Of who else?"

There was so obviously no one else that the next moment I had lost my impression of her having accidentally said more than she meant; and I merely asked what I wanted to know. "Did SHE see anything in the boy—?"

"That wasn't right? She never told me."

I had a scruple, but I overcame it. "Was she careful—particular?"

Mrs. Grose appeared to try to be conscientious. "About some things—yes."

"But not about all?"

Again she considered. "Well, miss—she's gone. I won't tell tales."

"I quite understand your feeling," I hastened to reply; but I thought it, after an instant, not opposed to this concession to pursue: "Did she die here?"

"No—she went off."

I don't know what there was in this brevity of Mrs. Grose's that struck me as ambiguous. "Went off to die?" Mrs. Grose looked straight out of the window, but I felt that, hypothetically, I had a right to know what young persons engaged for Bly were expected to do. "She was taken ill, you mean, and went home?"

"She was not taken ill, so far as appeared, in this house. She left it, at the end of the year, to go home, as she said, for a short holiday, to which the time she had put in had certainly given her a right. We had then a young woman—a nursemaid who had stayed on and who was a good girl and clever; and SHE took the children altogether for the interval. But our young lady never came back, and at the very moment I was expecting her I heard from the master that she was dead."

I turned this over. "But of what?"

"He never told me! But please, miss," said Mrs. Grose, "I must get to my work."

3

Her thus turning her back on me was fortunately not, for my just preoccupations, a snub that could check the growth of our mutual esteem. We met, after I had brought home little Miles, more intimately than ever on the ground of my stupefaction, my general emotion: so monstrous was I then ready to pronounce it that such a child as had now been revealed to me should be under an interdict. I was a little late on the scene, and I felt, as he stood wistfully looking out for me before the door of the inn at which the coach had put him down, that I had seen him, on the instant, without and within, in the great glow of freshness, the same positive fragrance of purity, in which I had, from the first moment, seen his little sister.

He was incredibly beautiful, and Mrs. Grose had put her finger on it: everything but a sort of passion of tenderness for him was swept away by his presence. What I then and there took him to my heart for was something divine that I have never found to the same degree in any child—his indescribable little air of knowing nothing in the world but love. It would have been impossible to carry a bad name with a greater sweetness of innocence, and by the time I had got back to Bly with him I remained merely bewildered—so far, that is, as I was not outraged—by the sense of the horrible letter locked up in my room, in a drawer. As soon as I could compass a private word with Mrs. Grose I declared to her that it was grotesque.

She promptly understood me. "You mean the cruel charge—?"

"It doesn't live an instant. My dear woman, LOOK at him!"

She smiled at my pretention to have discovered his charm. "I assure you, miss, I do nothing else! What will you say, then?" she immediately added.

"In answer to the letter?" I had made up my mind. "Nothing."

"And to his uncle?"

I was incisive. "Nothing."

"And to the boy himself?"

I was wonderful. "Nothing."

She gave with her apron a great wipe to her mouth. "Then I'll stand by you. We'll see it out."

"We'll see it out!" I ardently echoed, giving her my hand to make it a vow.

She held me there a moment, then whisked up her apron again with her detached hand. "Would you mind, miss, if I used the freedom—"

"To kiss me? No!" I took the good creature in my arms and, after we had embraced like sisters, felt still more fortified and indignant.

This, at all events, was for the time: a time so full that, as I recall the way it went, it reminds me of all the art I now need to make it a little distinct. What I look back at with amazement is the situation I accepted. I had undertaken, with my companion, to see it out, and I was under a charm, apparently, that could smooth away the extent and the far and difficult connections of such an effort. I was lifted aloft on a great wave of infatuation and pity. I found it simple, in my ignorance, my confusion, and perhaps my conceit, to assume that I could deal with a boy whose education for the world was all on the point of beginning.

I am unable even to remember at this day what proposal I framed for the end of his holidays and the resumption of his studies. Lessons with me, indeed, that charming summer, we all had a theory that he was to have; but I now feel that, for weeks, the lessons must have been rather my own. I learned something—at first, certainly—that had not been one of the teachings of my small, smothered life; learned to be amused, and even amusing, and not to think for the morrow. It was the first time, in a manner, that I had known space and air and freedom, all the music of summer and all the mystery of nature. And then there was consideration—and consideration was sweet.

Oh, it was a trap—not designed, but deep—to my imagination, to my delicacy, perhaps to my vanity; to whatever, in me, was most excitable. The best way to picture it all is to say that I was off my guard. They gave me so little trouble—they were of a gentleness so extraordinary. I used to speculate—but even this with a dim disconnectedness—as to how the rough future (for all futures are rough!) would handle them and might bruise them. They had the bloom of health and happiness; and yet, as if I had been in charge of a pair of little grandees, of princes of the blood, for whom everything, to be right, would have to be enclosed and protected, the only form that, in my fancy, the afteryears could take for them was that of a romantic, a really royal extension of the garden and the park. It may be, of course, above all, that what suddenly broke into this gives the previous time a charm of stillness—that hush in which something gathers or crouches. The change was actually like the spring of a beast.

In the first weeks the days were long; they often, at their finest, gave me what I used to call my own hour, the hour when, for my pupils, teatime and bedtime having come and gone, I had, before my final retirement, a small interval alone. Much as I liked my companions, this hour was the thing in the day I liked most; and I liked it best of all when, as the light faded—or rather, I should say, the day lingered and the last calls of the last birds sounded, in a flushed sky, from the old trees—I could take a turn into the grounds and enjoy, almost with a sense of property that amused and flattered me, the beauty and dignity of the place.

It was a pleasure at these moments to feel myself tranquil and justified; doubtless, perhaps, also to reflect that by my discretion, my quiet good sense and general high propriety, I was giving pleasure—if he ever thought of it!—to the person to whose pressure I had responded. What I was doing was what he had earnestly hoped and directly asked of me, and that I COULD, after all, do it proved even a greater joy than I had expected. I daresay I fancied myself, in short, a remarkable young woman and took comfort in the faith that this would more publicly appear. Well, I needed to be remarkable to offer a front to the remarkable things that presently gave their first sign.

It was plump, one afternoon, in the middle of my very hour: the children were tucked away, and I had come out for my stroll. One of the thoughts that, as I don't in the least shrink now from noting, used to be with me in these wanderings was that it would be as charming as a charming story suddenly to meet someone. Someone would appear there at the turn of a path and would stand before me and smile and approve. I didn't ask more than that—I only asked that he should KNOW; and the only way to be sure he knew would be to see it, and the kind light of it, in his handsome face.

That was exactly present to me—by which I mean the face was—when, on the first of these occasions, at the end of a long June day, I stopped short on emerging from one of the plantations and coming into view of the house. What arrested me on the spot—and with a shock much greater than any vision had allowed for—was the sense that my imagination had, in a flash, turned real. He did stand there!—but high up, beyond the lawn and at the very top of the tower to which, on that first morning, little Flora had conducted me. This tower was one of a pair—square, incongruous, crenelated structures—that were distinguished, for some reason, though I could see little difference, as the new and the old.

They flanked opposite ends of the house and were probably architectural absurdities, redeemed in a measure indeed by not being wholly disengaged nor of a height too pretentious, dating, in their gingerbread antiquity, from a romantic revival that was already a respectable past. I admired them, had fancies about them, for we could all profit in a degree, especially when they loomed through the dusk, by the grandeur of their actual battlements; yet it was not at such an elevation that the figure I had so often invoked seemed most in place.

It produced in me, this figure, in the clear twilight, I remember, two distinct gasps of emotion, which were, sharply, the shock of my first and that of my second surprise. My second was a violent perception of the mistake of my first: the man who met my eyes was not the person I had precipitately supposed. There came to me thus a bewilderment of vision of which, after these years, there is no living view that I can hope to give. An unknown man in a lonely place is a permitted object of fear to a young woman privately bred; and the figure that faced me was—a few more seconds assured me—as little anyone else I knew as it was the image that had been in my mind. I had not seen it in Harley Street—I had not seen it anywhere.

The place, moreover, in the strangest way in the world, had, on the instant, and by the very fact of its appearance, become a solitude. To me at least, making my statement here with a deliberation with which I have never made it, the whole feeling of the moment returns. It was as if, while I took in—what I did take in—all the rest of the scene had been stricken with death. I can hear again, as I write, the intense hush in which the sounds of evening dropped. The rooks stopped cawing in the golden sky, and the friendly hour lost, for the minute, all its voice. But there was no other change in nature, unless indeed it were a change that I saw with a stranger sharpness.

The gold was still in the sky, the clearness in the air, and the man who looked at me over the battlements was as definite as a picture in a frame. That's how I thought, with extraordinary quickness, of each person that he might have been and that he was not. We were confronted across our distance quite long enough for me to ask myself with intensity who then he was and to feel, as an effect of my inability to say, a wonder that in a few instants more became intense.

The great question, or one of these, is, afterward, I know, with regard to certain matters, the question of how long they have lasted. Well, this matter of mine, think what you will of it, lasted while I caught at a dozen possibilities, none of which made a difference for the better, that I could see, in there having been in the house—and for how long, above all?—a person of whom I was in ignorance. It lasted while I just bridled a little with the sense that my office demanded that there should be no such ignorance and no such person. It lasted while this visitant, at all events—and there was a touch of the strange freedom, as I remember, in the sign of familiarity of his wearing no hat—seemed to fix me, from his position, with just the question, just the scrutiny through the fading light, that his own presence provoked.

We were too far apart to call to each other, but there was a moment at which, at shorter range, some challenge between us, breaking the hush, would have been the right result of our straight mutual stare. He was in one of the angles, the one away from the house, very erect, as it struck me, and with both hands on the ledge. So I saw him as I see the letters I form on this page; then, exactly, after a minute, as if to add to the spectacle, he slowly changed his place—passed, looking at me hard all the while, to the opposite corner of the platform. Yes, I had the sharpest sense that during this transit he never took his eyes from me, and I can see at this moment the way his hand, as he went, passed from one of the crenelations to the next. He stopped at the other corner, but less long, and even as he turned away still markedly fixed me. He turned away; that was all I knew.

4

It was not that I didn't wait, on this occasion, for more, for I was rooted as deeply as I was shaken. Was there a "secret" at Bly—a mystery of Udolpho or an insane, an unmentionable relative kept in unsuspected confinement? I can't say how long I turned it over, or how long, in a confusion of curiosity and dread, I remained where I had had my collision; I only recall that when I re-entered the house darkness had quite closed in. Agitation, in the interval, certainly had held me and driven me, for I must, in circling about the place, have walked three miles; but I was to be, later on, so much more overwhelmed that this mere dawn of alarm was a comparatively human chill.

The most singular part of it, in fact—singular as the rest had been—was the part I became, in the hall, aware of in meeting Mrs. Grose. This picture comes back to me in the general train—the impression, as I received it on my return, of the wide white panelled space, bright in the lamplight and with its portraits and red carpet, and of the good surprised look of my friend, which immediately told me she had missed me. It came to me straightway, under her contact, that, with plain heartiness, mere relieved anxiety at my appearance, she knew nothing whatever that could bear upon the incident I had there ready for her. I had not suspected in advance that her comfortable face would pull me up, and I somehow measured the importance of what I had seen by my thus finding myself hesitate to mention it.

Scarce anything in the whole history seems to me so odd as this fact that my real beginning of fear was one, as I may say, with the instinct of sparing my companion. On the spot, accordingly, in the pleasant hall and with her eyes on me, I, for a reason that I couldn't then have phrased, achieved an inward resolution-offered a vague pretext for my lateness and, with the plea of the beauty of the night and of the heavy dew and wet feet, went as soon as possible to my room.

Here it was another affair; here, for many days after, it was a queer affair enough. There were hours, from day to day—or at least there were moments, snatched even from clear duties-when I had to shut myself up to think. It was not so much yet that I was more nervous than I could bear to be as that I was remarkably afraid of becoming so; for the truth I had now to turn over was, simply and clearly, the truth that I could arrive at no account whatever of the visitor with whom I had been so inexplicably and yet, as it seemed to me, so intimately concerned. It took little time to see that I could sound without forms of inquiry and without exciting remark any domestic complications.

The shock I had suffered must have sharpened all my senses; I felt sure, at the end of three days and as the result of mere closer attention, that I had not been practiced upon by the servants nor made the object of any "game." Of whatever it was that I knew, nothing was known around me. There was but one sane inference: someone had taken a liberty rather gross. That was what, repeatedly, I dipped into my room and locked the door to say to myself. We had been, collectively, subject to an intrusion; some unscrupulous traveller, curious in old houses, had made his way in unobserved, enjoyed the prospect from the best point of view, and then stolen out as he came. If he had given me such a bold hard stare, that was but a part of his indiscretion. The good thing, after all, was that we should surely see no more of him.

This was not so good a thing, I admit, as not to leave me to judge that what, essentially, made nothing else much signify was simply my charming work. My charming work was just my life with Miles and Flora, and through nothing could I so like it as through feeling that I could throw myself into it in trouble. The attraction of my small charges was a constant joy, leading me to wonder afresh at the vanity of my original fears, the distaste I had begun by entertaining for the probable gray prose of my office.

There was to be no gray prose, it appeared, and no long grind; so how could work not be charming that presented itself as daily beauty? It was all the romance of the nursery and the poetry of the schoolroom. I don't mean by this, of course, that we studied only fiction and verse; I mean I can express no otherwise the sort of interest my companions inspired. How can I describe that except by saying that instead of growing used to them—and it's a marvel for a governess: I call the sisterhood to witness!—I made constant fresh discoveries. There was one direction, assuredly, in which these discoveries stopped: deep obscurity continued to cover the region of the boy's conduct at school. It had been promptly given me, I have noted, to face that mystery without a pang.

Perhaps even it would be nearer the truth to say that—without a word—he himself had cleared it up. He had made the whole charge absurd. My conclusion bloomed there with the real rose flush of his innocence: he was only too fine and fair for the little horrid, unclean school world, and he had paid a price for it. I reflected acutely that the sense of such differences, such superiorities of quality, always, on the part of the majority-which could include even stupid, sordid headmasters—turn infallibly to the vindictive.

Both the children had a gentleness (it was their only fault, and it never made Miles a muff) that kept them—how shall I express it?—almost impersonal and certainly quite unpunishable. They were like the cherubs of the anecdote, who had—morally, at any rate—nothing to whack! I remember feeling with Miles in especial as if he had had, as it were, no history. We expect of a small child a scant one, but there was in this beautiful little boy something extraordinarily sensitive, yet extraordinarily happy, that, more than in any creature of his age I have seen, struck me as beginning anew each day. He had never for a second suffered. I took this as a direct disproof of his having really been chastised. If he had been wicked he would have "caught" it, and I should have caught it by the rebound—I should have found the trace.

I found nothing at all, and he was therefore an angel. He never spoke of his school, never mentioned a comrade or a master; and I, for my part, was quite too much disgusted to allude to them. Of course I was under the spell, and the wonderful part is that, even at the time, I perfectly knew I was. But I gave myself up to it; it was an antidote to any pain, and I had more pains than one. I was in receipt in these days of disturbing letters from home, where things were not going well. But with my children, what things in the world mattered? That was the question I used to put to my scrappy retirements. I was dazzled by their loveliness.

There was a Sunday—to get on—when it rained with such force and for so many hours that there could be no procession to church; in consequence of which, as the day declined, I had arranged with Mrs. Grose that, should the evening show improvement, we would attend together the late service. The rain happily stopped, and I prepared for our walk, which, through the park and by the good road to the village, would be a matter of twenty minutes. Coming downstairs to meet my colleague in the hall, I remembered a pair of gloves that had required three stitches and that had received them—with a publicity perhaps not edifying—while I sat with the children at their tea, served on Sundays, by exception, in that cold, clean temple of mahogany and brass, the "grown-up" dining room.

The gloves had been dropped there, and I turned in to recover them. The day was gray enough, but the afternoon light still lingered, and it enabled me, on crossing the threshold, not only to recognize, on a chair near the wide window, then closed, the articles I wanted, but to become aware of a person on the other side of the window and looking straight in. One step into the room had sufficed; my vision was instantaneous; it was all there. The person looking straight in was the person who had already appeared to me. He appeared thus again with I won't say greater distinctness, for that was impossible, but with a nearness that represented a forward stride in our intercourse and made me, as I met him, catch my breath and turn cold.

He was the same—he was the same, and seen, this time, as he had been seen before, from the waist up, the window, though the dining room was on the ground floor, not going down to the terrace on which he stood. His face was close to the glass, yet the effect of this better view was, strangely, only to show me how intense the former had been. He remained but a few seconds-long enough to convince me he also saw and recognized; but it was as if I had been looking at him for years and had known him always.

Something, however, happened this time that had not happened before; his stare into my face, through the glass and across the room, was as deep and hard as then, but it quitted me for a moment during which I could still watch it, see it fix successively several other things. On the spot there came to me the added shock of a certitude that it was not for me he had come there. He had come for someone else. The flash of this knowledge—for it was knowledge in the midst of dread—produced in me the most extraordinary effect, started as I stood there, a sudden vibration of duty and courage. I say courage because I was beyond all doubt already far gone. I bounded straight out of the door again, reached that of the house, got, in an instant, upon the drive, and, passing along the terrace as fast as I could rush, turned a corner and came full in sight. But it was in sight of nothing now—my visitor had vanished. I stopped, I almost dropped, with the real relief of this; but I took in the whole scene—I gave him time to reappear. I call it time, but how long was it? I can't speak to the purpose today of the duration of these things.

That kind of measure must have left me: they couldn't have lasted as they actually appeared to me to last. The terrace and the whole place, the lawn and the garden beyond it, all I could see of the park, were empty with a great emptiness. There were shrubberies and big trees, but I remember the clear assurance I felt that none of them concealed him. He was there or was not there: not there if I didn't see him. I got hold of this; then, instinctively, instead of returning as I had come, went to the window. It was confusedly present to me that I ought to place myself where he had stood. I did so; I applied my face to the pane and looked, as he had looked, into the room.

As if, at this moment, to show me exactly what his range had been, Mrs. Grose, as I had done for himself just before, came in from the hall. With this I had the full image of a repetition of what had already occurred. She saw me as I had seen my own visitant; she pulled up short as I had done; I gave her something of the shock that I had received. She turned white, and this made me ask myself if I had blanched as much. She stared, in short, and retreated on just MY lines, and I knew she had then passed out and come round to me and that I should presently meet her. I remained where I was, and while I waited I thought of more things than one. But there's only one I take space to mention. I wondered why SHE should be scared.

5

Oh, she let me know as soon as, round the corner of the

house, she loomed again into view. "What in the name of goodness is the matter—?" She was now flushed and out of breath.

I said nothing till she came quite near. "With me?" I must have made a wonderful face. "Do I show it?"

"You're as white as a sheet. You look awful."

I considered; I could meet on this, without scruple, any innocence. My need to respect the bloom of Mrs. Grose's had dropped, without a rustle, from my shoulders, and if I wavered for the instant it was not with what I kept back. I put out my hand to her and she took it; I held her hard a little, liking to feel her close to me. There was a kind of support in the shy heave of her surprise. "You came for me for church, of course, but I can't go."

"Has anything happened?"

"Yes. You must know now. Did I look very queer?"

"Through this window? Dreadful!"

"Well," I said, "I've been frightened." Mrs. Grose's eyes expressed plainly that SHE had no wish to be, yet also that she knew too well her place not to be ready to share with me any marked inconvenience. Oh, it was quite settled that she MUST share! "Just what you saw from the dining room a minute ago was the effect of that. What *I* saw—just before—was much worse."

Her hand tightened. "What was it?"

"An extraordinary man. Looking in."

"What extraordinary man?"

"I haven't the least idea."

Mrs. Grose gazed round us in vain. "Then where is he gone?"

"I know still less."

"Have you seen him before?"

"Yes—once. On the old tower."

She could only look at me harder. "Do you mean he's a stranger?"

"Oh, very much!"

"Yet you didn't tell me?"

"No—for reasons. But now that you've guessed—"

Mrs. Grose's round eyes encountered this charge. "Ah, I haven't guessed!" she said very simply. "How can I if YOU don't imagine?"

"I don't in the very least."

"You've seen him nowhere but on the tower?"

"And on this spot just now."

Mrs. Grose looked round again. "What was he doing on the tower?"

"Only standing there and looking down at me."

She thought a minute. "Was he a gentleman?"

I found I had no need to think. "No." She gazed in deeper wonder. "No."

"Then nobody about the place? Nobody from the village?"

"Nobody—nobody. I didn't tell you, but I made sure."

She breathed a vague relief: this was, oddly, so much to the good. It only went indeed a little way. "But if he isn't a gentleman—"

"What IS he? He's a horror."

"A horror?"

"He's—God help me if I know WHAT he is!"

Mrs. Grose looked round once more; she fixed her eyes on the duskier distance, then, pulling herself together, turned to me with abrupt inconsequence. "It's time we should be at church."

"Oh, I'm not fit for church!"

"Won't it do you good?"

"It won't do THEM—! I nodded at the house.

"The children?"

"I can't leave them now."

"You're afraid—?"

I spoke boldly. "I'm afraid of HIM."

Mrs. Grose's large face showed me, at this, for the first time, the faraway faint glimmer of a consciousness more acute: I somehow made out in it the delayed dawn of an idea I myself had not given her and that was as yet quite obscure to me. It comes back to me that I thought instantly of this as something I could get from her; and I felt it to be connected with the desire she presently showed to know more. "When was it—on the tower?"

"About the middle of the month. At this same hour."

"Almost at dark," said Mrs. Grose.

"Oh, no, not nearly. I saw him as I see you."

"Then how did he get in?"

"And how did he get out?" I laughed. "I had no opportunity to ask him! This evening, you see," I pursued, "he has not been able to get in."

"He only peeps?"

"I hope it will be confined to that!" She had now let go my hand; she turned away a little. I waited an instant; then I brought out: "Go to church. Goodbye. I must watch."

Slowly she faced me again. "Do you fear for them?"

We met in another long look. "Don't YOU?" Instead of answering she came nearer to the window and, for a minute, applied her face to the glass. "You see how he could see," I meanwhile went on.

She didn't move. "How long was he here?"

"Till I came out. I came to meet him."

Mrs. Grose at last turned round, and there was still more in her face. "*I* couldn't have come out."

"Neither could I!" I laughed again. "But I did come. I have my duty."

"So have I mine," she replied; after which she added: "What is he like?"

"I've been dying to tell you. But he's like nobody."

"Nobody?" she echoed.

"He has no hat." Then seeing in her face that she already, in this, with a deeper dismay, found a touch of picture, I quickly added stroke to stroke. "He has red hair, very red, close-curling, and a pale face, long in shape, with straight, good features and little, rather queer whiskers that are as red as his hair. His eyebrows are, somehow, darker; they look particularly arched and as if they might move a good deal. His eyes are sharp, strange—awfully; but I only know clearly that they're rather small and very fixed. His mouth's wide, and his lips are thin, and except for his little whiskers he's quite clean-shaven. He gives me a sort of sense of looking like an actor."

"An actor!" It was impossible to resemble one less, at least, than Mrs. Grose at that moment.

"I've never seen one, but so I suppose them. He's tall, active, erect," I continued, "but never—no, never!—a gentleman."

My companion's face had blanched as I went on; her round eyes started and her mild mouth gaped. "A gentleman?" she gasped, confounded, stupefied: "a gentleman HE?"

"You know him then?"

She visibly tried to hold herself. "But he IS handsome?"

I saw the way to help her. "Remarkably!"

"And dressed—?"

"In somebody's clothes." "They're smart, but they're not his own."

She broke into a breathless affirmative groan: "They're the master's!"

I caught it up. "You DO know him?"

She faltered but a second. "Quint!" she cried.

"Quint?"

"Peter Quint—his own man, his valet, when he was here!"

"When the master was?"

Gaping still, but meeting me, she pieced it all together. "He never wore his hat, but he did wear—well, there were waistcoats missed. They were both here—last year. Then the master went, and Quint was alone."

I followed, but halting a little. "Alone?"

"Alone with US." Then, as from a deeper depth, "In charge," she added.

"And what became of him?"

She hung fire so long that I was still more mystified. "He went, too," she brought out at last.

"Went where?"

Her expression, at this, became extraordinary. "God knows where! He died."

"Died?" I almost shrieked.

She seemed fairly to square herself, plant herself more firmly to utter the wonder of it. "Yes. Mr. Quint is dead."

6

It took of course more than that particular passage to place us together in presence of what we had now to live with as we could—my dreadful liability to impressions of the order so vividly exemplified, and my companion's knowledge, henceforth—a knowledge half consternation and half compassion-of that liability. There had been, this evening, after the revelation left me, for an hour, so prostrate—there had been, for either of us, no attendance on any service but a little service of tears and vows, of prayers and promises, a climax to the series of mutual challenges and pledges that had straightway ensued on our retreating together to the schoolroom and shutting ourselves up there to have everything out.

The result of our having everything out was simply to reduce our situation to the last rigor of its elements. She herself had seen nothing, not the shadow of a shadow, and nobody in the house but the governess was in the governess's plight; yet she accepted without directly impugning my sanity the truth as I gave it to her, and ended by showing me, on this ground, an awe-stricken tenderness, an expression of the sense of my more than questionable privilege, of which the very breath has remained with me as that of the sweetest of human charities.

What was settled between us, accordingly, that night, was that we thought we might bear things together; and I was not even sure that, in spite of her exemption, it was she who had the best of the burden. I knew at this hour, I think, as well as I knew later, what I was capable of meeting to shelter my pupils; but it took me some time to be wholly sure of what my honest ally was prepared for to keep terms with so compromising a contract. I was queer company enough—quite as queer as the company I received; but as I trace over what we went through I see how much common ground we must have found in the one idea that, by good fortune, COULD steady us.

It was the idea, the second movement, that led me straight out, as I may say, of the inner chamber of my dread. I could take the air in the court, at least, and there Mrs. Grose could join me. Perfectly can I recall now the particular way strength came to me before we separated for the night. We had gone over and over every feature of what I had seen.

"He was looking for someone else, you say—someone who was not you?"

"He was looking for little Miles." A portentous clearness now possessed me. "THAT'S whom he was looking for."

"But how do you know?"

"I know, I know, I know!" My exaltation grew. "And YOU know, my dear!"

She didn't deny this, but I required, I felt, not even so much telling as that. She resumed in a moment, at any rate: "What if HE should see him?"

"Little Miles? That's what he wants!"

She looked immensely scared again. "The child?"

"Heaven forbid! The man. He wants to appear to THEM." That he might was an awful conception, and yet, somehow, I could keep it at bay; which, moreover, as we lingered there, was what I succeeded in practically proving. I had an absolute certainty that I should see again what I had already seen, but something within me said that by offering myself bravely as the sole subject of such experience, by accepting, by inviting, by surmounting it all, I should serve as an expiatory victim and guard the tranquility of my companions. The children, in especial, I should thus fence about and absolutely save. I recall one of the last things I said that night to Mrs. Grose.

"It does strike me that my pupils have never mentioned—"

She looked at me hard as I musingly pulled up. "His having been here and the time they were with him?"

"The time they were with him, and his name, his presence, his history, in any way."

"Oh, the little lady doesn't remember. She never heard or

knew."

"The circumstances of his death?" I thought with some intensity. "Perhaps not. But Miles would remember—Miles would know."

"Ah, don't try him!" broke from Mrs. Grose.

I returned her the look she had given me. "Don't be afraid." I continued to think. "It IS rather odd."

"That he has never spoken of him?"

"Never by the least allusion. And you tell me they were 'great friends'?"

"Oh, it wasn't HIM!" Mrs. Grose with emphasis declared. "It was Quint's own fancy. To play with him, I mean—to spoil him." She paused a moment; then she added: "Quint was much too free."

This gave me, straight from my vision of his face—SUCH a face!—a sudden sickness of disgust. "Too free with MY boy?"

"Too free with everyone!"

I forbore, for the moment, to analyze this description further than by the reflection that a part of it applied to several of the members of the household, of the half-dozen maids and men who were still of our small colony. But there was everything, for our apprehension, in the lucky fact that no discomfortable legend, no perturbation of scullions, had ever, within anyone's memory attached to the kind old place. It had neither bad name nor ill fame, and Mrs. Grose, most apparently, only desired to cling to me and to quake in silence. I even put her, the very last thing of all, to the test. It was when, at midnight, she had her hand on the schoolroom door to take leave. "I have it from you then—for it's of great importance—that he was definitely and admittedly bad?"

"Oh, not admittedly. *I* knew it—but the master didn't."

"And you never told him?"

"Well, he didn't like tale-bearing—he hated complaints. He was terribly short with anything of that kind, and if people were all right to HIM—"

"He wouldn't be bothered with more?" This squared well

enough with my impressions of him: he was not a trouble-loving gentleman, nor so very particular perhaps about some of the company HE kept. All the same, I pressed my interlocutress. "I promise you I would have told!"

She felt my discrimination. "I daresay I was wrong. But, really, I was afraid."

"Afraid of what?"

"Of things that man could do. Quint was so clever—he was so deep."

I took this in still more than, probably, I showed. "You weren't afraid of anything else? Not of his effect—?"

"His effect?" she repeated with a face of anguish and waiting while I faltered.

"On innocent little precious lives. They were in your charge."

"No, they were not in mine!" she roundly and distressfully returned. "The master believed in him and placed him here because he was supposed not to be well and the country air so good for him. So he had everything to say. Yes"—she let me have it—"even about THEM."

"Them—that creature?" I had to smother a kind of howl. "And you could bear it!"

"No. I couldn't—and I can't now!" And the poor woman burst into tears.

A rigid control, from the next day, was, as I have said, to follow them; yet how often and how passionately, for a week, we came back together to the subject! Much as we had discussed it that Sunday night, I was, in the immediate later hours in especial—for it may be imagined whether I slept—still haunted with the shadow of something she had not told me. I myself had kept back nothing, but there was a word Mrs. Grose had kept back. I was sure, moreover, by morning, that this was not from a failure of frankness, but because on every side there were fears.

It seems to me indeed, in retrospect, that by the time the morrow's sun was high I had restlessly read into the fact before us almost all the meaning they were to receive from subsequent and more cruel occurrences. What they gave me above all was just the sinister figure of the living man—the dead one would keep awhile!—and of the months he had continuously passed at Bly, which, added up, made a formidable stretch. The limit of this evil time had arrived only when, on the dawn of a winter's morning, Peter Quint was found, by a laborer going to early work, stone dead on the road from the village: a catastrophe explained—superficially at least—by a visible wound to his head; such a wound as might have been produced—and as, on the final evidence, HAD been—by a fatal slip, in the dark and after leaving the public house, on the steepish icy slope, a wrong path altogether, at the bottom of which he lay.

The icy slope, the turn mistaken at night and in liquor, accounted for much—practically, in the end and after the inquest and boundless chatter, for everything; but there had been matters in his life—strange passages and perils, secret disorders, vices more than suspected—that would have accounted for a good deal more.

I scarce know how to put my story into words that shall be a credible picture of my state of mind; but I was in these days literally able to find a joy in the extraordinary flight of heroism the occasion demanded of me. I now saw that I had been asked for a service admirable and difficult; and there would be a greatness in letting it be seen—oh, in the right quarter!—that I could succeed where many another girl might have failed. It was an immense help to me—I confess I rather applaud myself as I look back!—that I saw my service so strongly and so simply. I was there to protect and defend the little creatures in the world the most bereaved and the most lovable, the appeal of whose helplessness had suddenly become only too explicit, a deep, constant ache of one's own committed heart.

We were cut off, really, together; we were united in our danger. They had nothing but me, and I—well, I had THEM. It was in short a magnificent chance. This chance presented itself to me in an image richly material. I was a screen—I was to stand before them. The more I saw, the less they would. I began to watch them in a stifled suspense, a disguised excitement that might well, had it continued too long, have turned to something like madness. What saved me, as I now see, was that it turned to something else altogether. It didn't last as suspense—it was superseded by horrible proofs. Proofs, I say, yes—from the moment I really took hold.

This moment dated from an afternoon hour that I happened to spend in the grounds with the younger of my pupils alone. We had left Miles indoors, on the red cushion of a deep window seat; he had wished to finish a book, and I had been glad to encourage a purpose so laudable in a young man whose only defect was an occasional excess of the restless. His sister, on the contrary, had been alert to come out, and I strolled with her half an hour, seeking the shade, for the sun was still high and the day exceptionally warm. I was aware afresh, with her, as we went, of how, like her brother, she contrived—it was the charming thing in both children—to let me alone without appearing to drop me and to accompany me without appearing to surround.

They were never importunate and yet never listless. My attention to them all really went to seeing them amuse themselves immensely without me: this was a spectacle they seemed actively to prepare and that engaged me as an active admirer. I walked in a world of their invention—they had no occasion whatever to draw upon mine; so that my time was taken only with being, for them, some remarkable person or thing that the game of the moment required and that was merely, thanks to my superior, my exalted stamp, a happy and highly distinguished sinecure. I forget what I was on the present occasion; I only remember that I was something very important and very quiet and that Flora was playing very hard. We were on the edge of the lake, and, as we had lately begun geography, the lake was the Sea of Azof.

Suddenly, in these circumstances, I became aware that, on the other side of the Sea of Azof, we had an interested spectator. The way this knowledge gathered in me was the strangest thing in the world—the strangest, that is, except the very much stranger in which it quickly merged itself. I had sat down with a piece of work—for I was something or other that could sit—on the old stone bench which overlooked the pond; and in this position I began to take in with certitude, and yet without direct vision, the presence, at a distance, of a third person. The old trees, the thick shrubbery, made a great and pleasant shade, but it was all suffused with the brightness of the hot, still hour.

There was no ambiguity in anything; none whatever, at least, in the conviction I from one moment to another found myself forming as to what I should see straight before me and across the lake as a consequence of raising my eyes. They were attached at this juncture to the stitching in which I was engaged, and I can feel once more the spasm of my effort not to move them till I should so have steadied myself as to be able to make up my mind what to do.

There was an alien object in view—a figure whose right of presence I instantly, passionately questioned. I recollect counting over perfectly the possibilities, reminding myself that nothing was more natural, for instance, then the appearance of one of the men about the place, or even of a messenger, a postman, or a tradesman's boy, from the village. That reminder had as little effect on my practical certitude as I was conscious—still even without looking—of its having upon the character and attitude of our visitor. Nothing was more natural than that these things should be the other things that they absolutely were not.

Of the positive identity of the apparition I would assure myself as soon as the small clock of my courage should have ticked out the right second; meanwhile, with an effort that was already sharp enough, I transferred my eyes straight to little Flora, who, at the moment, was about ten yards away. My heart had stood still for an instant with the wonder and terror of the question whether she too would see; and I held my breath while I waited for what a cry from her, what some sudden innocent sign either of interest or of alarm, would tell me. I waited, but nothing came; then, in the first place—and there is something more dire in this, I feel, than in anything I have to relate—I was determined by a sense that, within a minute, all sounds from her had previously dropped; and, in the second, by the circumstance that, also within the minute, she had, in her play, turned her back to the water.

This was her attitude when I at last looked at her—looked with the confirmed conviction that we were still, together, under direct personal notice. She had picked up a small flat piece of wood, which happened to have in it a little hole that had evidently suggested to her the idea of sticking in another fragment that might figure as a mast and make the thing a boat. This second morsel, as I watched her, she was very markedly and intently attempting to tighten in its place. My apprehension of what she was doing sustained me so that after some seconds I felt I was ready for more. Then I again shifted my eyes—I faced what I had to face.

7

I got hold of Mrs. Grose as soon after this as I could; and I can give no intelligible account of how I fought out the interval. Yet I still hear myself cry as I fairly threw myself into her arms: "They KNOW—it's too monstrous: they know, they know!"

"And what on earth—?" I felt her incredulity as she held me.

"Why, all that WE know—and heaven knows what else besides!" Then, as she released me, I made it out to her, made it out perhaps only now with full coherency even to myself. "Two hours ago, in the garden"—I could scarce articulate—"Flora SAW!"

Mrs. Grose took it as she might have taken a blow in the stomach. "She has told you?" she panted.

"Not a word—that's the horror. She kept it to herself! The child of eight, THAT child!" Unutterable still, for me, was the stupefaction of it.

Mrs. Grose, of course, could only gape the wider. "Then how do you know?"

"I was there—I saw with my eyes: saw that she was perfectly aware."

"Do you mean aware of HIM?"

"No—of HER." I was conscious as I spoke that I looked prodigious things, for I got the slow reflection of them in my companion's face. "Another person—this time; but a figure of quite as unmistakable horror and evil: a woman in black, pale and dreadful—with such an air also, and such a face!—on the other side of the lake. I was there with the child—quiet for the hour; and in the midst of it she came."

"Came how—from where?"

"From where they come from! She just appeared and stood there—but not so near."

"And without coming nearer?"

"Oh, for the effect and the feeling, she might have been as close as you!"

My friend, with an odd impulse, fell back a step. "Was she someone you've never seen?"

"Yes. But someone the child has. Someone YOU have." Then, to show how I had thought it all out: "My predecessor—the one who died."

"Miss Jessel?"

"Miss Jessel. You don't believe me?" I pressed.

She turned right and left in her distress. "How can you be sure?"

This drew from me, in the state of my nerves, a flash of impatience. "Then ask Flora—SHE'S sure!" But I had no sooner spoken than I caught myself up. "No, for God's sake, DON'T! She'll say she isn't—she'll lie!"

Mrs. Grose was not too bewildered instinctively to protest. "Ah, how CAN you?"

"Because I'm clear. Flora doesn't want me to know."

"It's only then to spare you."

"No, no—there are depths, depths! The more I go over it, the more I see in it, and the more I see in it, the more I fear. I don't know what I DON'T see—what I DON'T fear!"

Mrs. Grose tried to keep up with me. "You mean you're afraid of seeing her again?"

"Oh, no; that's nothing—now!" Then I explained. "It's of NOT seeing her."

But my companion only looked wan. "I don't understand you."

"Why, it's that the child may keep it up—and that the child assuredly WILL—without my knowing it."

At the image of this possibility Mrs. Grose for a moment collapsed, yet presently to pull herself together again, as if from the positive force of the sense of what, should we yield an inch, there would really be to give way to. "Dear, dear—we must keep our heads! And after all, if she doesn't mind it—!" She even tried a grim joke. "Perhaps she likes it!"

"Likes SUCH things—a scrap of an infant!"

"Isn't it just a proof of her blessed innocence?" my friend bravely inquired.

She brought me, for the instant, almost round. "Oh, we must clutch at THAT—we must cling to it! If it isn't a proof of what you say, it's a proof of—God knows what! For the woman's a horror of horrors."

Mrs. Grose, at this, fixed her eyes a minute on the ground; then at last raising them, "Tell me how you know," she said.

"Then you admit it's what she was?" I cried.

"Tell me how you know," my friend simply repeated.

"Know? By seeing her! By the way she looked."

"At you, do you mean—so wickedly?"

"Dear me, no—I could have borne that. She gave me never a glance. She only fixed the child."

Mrs. Grose tried to see it. "Fixed her?"

"Ah, with such awful eyes!"

She stared at mine as if they might really have resembled them. "Do you mean of dislike?"

"God help us, no. Of something much worse."

"Worse than dislike?—this left her indeed at a loss.

"With a determination—indescribable. With a kind of fury of intention."

I made her turn pale. "Intention?"

"To get hold of her." Mrs. Grose—her eyes just lingering on mine—gave a shudder and walked to the window; and while she stood there looking out I completed my statement. "THAT'S what Flora knows."

After a little she turned round. "The person was in black, you say?"

"In mourning—rather poor, almost shabby. But—yes—with extraordinary beauty." I now recognized to what I had at last, stroke by stroke, brought the victim of my confidence, for she quite visibly weighed this. "Oh, handsome—very, very," I insisted; "wonderfully handsome. But infamous."

She slowly came back to me. "Miss Jessel—WAS infamous." She once more took my hand in both her own, holding it as tight as if to fortify me against the increase of alarm I might draw from this disclosure. "They were both infamous," she finally said.

So, for a little, we faced it once more together; and I found absolutely a degree of help in seeing it now so straight. "I appreciate," I said, "the great decency of your not having hitherto spoken; but the time has certainly come to give me the whole thing." She appeared to assent to this, but still only in silence; seeing which I went on: "I must have it now. Of what did she die? Come, there was something between them."

"There was everything."

"In spite of the difference—?"

"Oh, of their rank, their condition"—she brought it woefully out. "SHE was a lady."

I turned it over; I again saw. "Yes—she was a lady."

"And he so dreadfully below," said Mrs. Grose.

I felt that I doubtless needn't press too hard, in such company, on the place of a servant in the scale; but there was nothing to prevent an acceptance of my companion's own measure of my predecessor's abasement. There was a way to deal with that, and I dealt; the more readily for my full vision—on the evidence—of our employer's late clever, good-looking "own" man; impudent, assured, spoiled, depraved. "The fellow was a hound."

Mrs. Grose considered as if it were perhaps a little a case for a sense of shades. "I've never seen one like him. He did what he wished."

"With HER?"

"With them all."

It was as if now in my friend's own eyes Miss Jessel had again appeared. I seemed at any rate, for an instant, to see their evocation of her as distinctly as I had seen her by the pond; and I brought out with decision: "It must have been also what SHE wished!"

Mrs. Grose's face signified that it had been indeed, but she said at the same time: "Poor woman—she paid for it!"

"Then you do know what she died of?" I asked.

"No—I know nothing. I wanted not to know; I was glad enough I didn't; and I thanked heaven she was well out of this!"

"Yet you had, then, your idea—"

"Of her real reason for leaving? Oh, yes—as to that. She couldn't have stayed. Fancy it here—for a governess! And afterward I imagined—and I still imagine. And what I imagine is dreadful."

"Not so dreadful as what *I* do," I replied; on which I must have shown her—as I was indeed but too conscious—a front of miserable defeat. It brought out again all her compassion for me, and at the renewed touch of her kindness my power to resist broke down. I burst, as I had, the other time, made her burst, into tears; she took me to her motherly breast, and my lamentation overflowed. "I don't do it!" I sobbed in despair; "I don't save or shield them! It's far worse than I dreamed—they're lost!"

8

What I had said to Mrs. Grose was true enough: there were in the matter I had put before her depths and possibilities that I lacked resolution to sound; so that when we met once more in the wonder of it we were of a common mind about the duty of resistance to extravagant fancies. We were to keep our heads if we should keep nothing else—difficult indeed as that might be in the face of what, in our prodigious experience, was least to be questioned. Late that night, while the house slept, we had another talk in my room, when she went all the way with me as to its being beyond doubt that I had seen exactly what I had seen.

To hold her perfectly in the pinch of that, I found I had only to ask her how, if I had "made it up," I came to be able to give, of each of the persons appearing to me, a picture disclosing, to the last detail, their special marks—a portrait on the exhibition of which she had instantly recognized and named them. She wished of course—small blame to her!—to sink the whole subject; and I was quick to assure her that my own interest in it had now violently taken the form of a search for the way to escape from it. I encountered her on the ground of a probability that with recurrence—for recurrence we took for granted—I should get used to my danger, distinctly professing that my personal exposure had suddenly become the least of my discomforts. It was my new suspicion that was intolerable; and yet even to this complication the later hours of the day had brought a little ease.

On leaving her, after my first outbreak, I had of course returned to my pupils, associating the right remedy for my dismay with that sense of their charm which I had already found to be a thing I could positively cultivate and which had never failed me yet. I had simply, in other words, plunged afresh into Flora's special society and there become aware—it was almost a luxury!-that she could put her little conscious hand straight upon the spot that ached. She had looked at me in sweet speculation and then had accused me to my face of having "cried." I had supposed I had brushed away the ugly signs: but I could literally-for the time, at all events—rejoice, under this fathomless charity, that they had not entirely disappeared.

To gaze into the depths of blue of the child's eyes and pronounce their loveliness a trick of premature cunning was to be guilty of a cynicism in preference to which I naturally preferred to abjure my judgment and, so far as might be, my agitation. I couldn't abjure for merely wanting to, but I could repeat to Mrs.

Grose—as I did there, over and over, in the small hours—that with their voices in the air, their pressure on one's heart, and their fragrant faces against one's cheek, everything fell to the ground but their incapacity and their beauty. It was a pity that, somehow, to settle this once for all, I had equally to re-enumerate the signs of subtlety that, in the afternoon, by the lake had made a miracle of my show of self-possession.

It was a pity to be obliged to reinvestigate the certitude of the moment itself and repeat how it had come to me as a revelation that the inconceivable communion I then surprised was a matter, for either party, of habit. It was a pity that I should have had to quaver out again the reasons for my not having, in my delusion, so much as questioned that the little girl saw our visitant even as I actually saw Mrs. Grose herself, and that she wanted, by just so much as she did thus see, to make me suppose she didn't, and at the same time, without showing anything, arrive at a guess as to whether I myself did! It was a pity that I needed once more to describe the portentous little activity by which she sought to divert my attention—the perceptible increase of movement, the greater intensity of play, the singing, the gabbling of nonsense, and the invitation to romp.

Yet if I had not indulged, to prove there was nothing in it, in this review, I should have missed the two or three dim elements of comfort that still remained to me. I should not for instance have been able to asseverate to my friend that I was certain-which was so much to the good—that *I* at least had not betrayed myself. I should not have been prompted, by stress of need, by desperation of mind—I scarce know what to call it—to invoke such further aid to intelligence as might spring from pushing my colleague fairly to the wall.

She had told me, bit by bit, under pressure, a great deal; but a small shifty spot on the wrong side of it all still sometimes brushed my brow like the wing of a bat; and I remember how on this occasion—for the sleeping house and the concentration alike of our danger and our watch seemed to help—I felt the importance of giving the last jerk to the curtain. "I don't believe anything so horrible," I recollect saying; "no, let us put it definitely, my dear, that I don't. But if I did, you know, there's a thing I should require now, just without sparing you the least bit more—oh, not a scrap, come!—to get out of you. What was it you had in mind when, in our distress, before Miles came back, over the letter from his school, you said, under my insistence, that you didn't pretend for him that he had not literally EVER been 'bad'? He has NOT literally 'ever,' in these weeks that I myself have lived with him and so closely watched him; he has been an imperturbable little prodigy of delightful, lovable goodness. Therefore you might perfectly have made the claim for him if you had not, as it happened, seen an exception to take. What was your exception, and to what passage in your personal observation of him did you refer?"

It was a dreadfully austere inquiry, but levity was not our note, and, at any rate, before the gray dawn admonished us to separate I had got my answer. What my friend had had in mind proved to be immensely to the purpose. It was neither more nor less than the circumstance that for a period of several months Quint and the boy had been perpetually together. It was in fact the very appropriate truth that she had ventured to criticize the propriety, to hint at the incongruity, of so close an alliance, and even to go so far on the subject as a frank overture to Miss Jessel. Miss Jessel had, with a most strange manner, requested her to mind her business, and the good woman had, on this, directly approached little Miles. What she had said to him, since I pressed, was that SHE liked to see young gentlemen not forget their station.

I pressed again, of course, at this. "You reminded him that Quint was only a base menial?"

"As you might say! And it was his answer, for one thing, that was bad."

"And for another thing?" I waited. "He repeated your words to Quint?"

"No, not that. It's just what he WOULDN'T!" she could still impress upon me. "I was sure, at any rate," she added, "that he didn't. But he denied certain occasions."

"What occasions?"

"When they had been about together quite as if Quint were his tutor—and a very grand one—and Miss Jessel only for the little lady. When he had gone off with the fellow, I mean, and spent hours with him."

"He then prevaricated about it—he said he hadn't?" Her assent was clear enough to cause me to add in a moment: "I see. He lied."

"Oh!" Mrs. Grose mumbled. This was a suggestion that it didn't matter; which indeed she backed up by a further remark. "You see, after all, Miss Jessel didn't mind. She didn't forbid him."

I considered. "Did he put that to you as a justification?"

At this she dropped again. "No, he never spoke of it."

"Never mentioned her in connection with Quint?"

She saw, visibly flushing, where I was coming out. "Well, he didn't show anything. He denied," she repeated; "he denied."

Lord, how I pressed her now! "So that you could see he knew what was between the two wretches?"

"I don't know—I don't know!" the poor woman groaned.

"You do know, you dear thing," I replied; "only you haven't my dreadful boldness of mind, and you keep back, out of timidity and modesty and delicacy, even the impression that, in the past, when you had, without my aid, to flounder about in silence, most of all made you miserable. But I shall get it out of you yet! There was something in the boy that suggested to you," I continued, "that he covered and concealed their relation."

"Oh, he couldn't prevent—"

"Your learning the truth? I daresay! But, heavens," I fell, with vehemence, athinking, "what it shows that they must, to that extent, have succeeded in making of him!"

"Ah, nothing that's not nice NOW!" Mrs. Grose lugubriously pleaded.

"I don't wonder you looked queer," I persisted, "when I mentioned to you the letter from his school!"

"I doubt if I looked as queer as you!" she retorted with homely force. "And if he was so bad then as that comes to, how is he such an angel now?"

"Yes, indeed—and if he was a fiend at school! How, how, how? Well," I said in my torment, "you must put it to me again, but I shall not be able to tell you for some days. Only, put it to me again!" I cried in a way that made my friend stare. "There are directions in which I must not for the present let myself go." Meanwhile I returned to her first example—the one to which she had just previously referred—of the boy's happy capacity for an occasional slip. "If Quint—on your remonstrance at the time you speak of—was a base menial, one of the things Miles said to you, I find myself guessing, was that you were another." Again her admission was so adequate that I continued: "And you forgave him that?"

"Wouldn't YOU?"

"Oh, yes!" And we exchanged there, in the stillness, a sound of the oddest amusement. Then I went on: "At all events, while he was with the man—"

"Miss Flora was with the woman. It suited them all!"

It suited me, too, I felt, only too well; by which I mean that it suited exactly the particularly deadly view I was in the very act of forbidding myself to entertain. But I so far succeeded in checking the expression of this view that I will throw, just here, no further light on it than may be offered by the mention of my final observation to Mrs. Grose. "His having lied and been impudent are, I confess, less engaging specimens than I had hoped to have from you of the outbreak in him of the little natural man. Still," I mused, "They must do, for they make me feel more than ever that I must watch."

It made me blush, the next minute, to see in my friend's face how much more unreservedly she had forgiven him than her anecdote struck me as presenting to my own tenderness an occasion for doing. This came out when, at the schoolroom door, she quitted me. "Surely you don't accuse HIM—"

"Of carrying on an intercourse that he conceals from me?

Ah, remember that, until further evidence, I now accuse nobody." Then, before shutting her out to go, by another passage, to her own place, "I must just wait," I wound up.

9

I waited and waited, and the days, as they elapsed, took something from my consternation. A very few of them, in fact, passing, in constant sight of my pupils, without a fresh incident, sufficed to give to grievous fancies and even to odious memories a kind of brush of the sponge. I have spoken of the surrender to their extraordinary childish grace as a thing I could actively cultivate, and it may be imagined if I neglected now to address myself to this source for whatever it would yield. Stranger than I can express, certainly, was the effort to struggle against my new lights; it would doubtless have been, however, a greater tension still had it not been so frequently successful.

I used to wonder how my little charges could help guessing that I thought strange things about them; and the circumstances that these things only made them more interesting was not by itself a direct aid to keeping them in the dark. I trembled lest they should see that they WERE so immensely more interesting. Putting things at the worst, at all events, as in meditation I so often did, any clouding of their innocence could only be—blameless and foredoomed as they were—a reason the more for taking risks. There were moments when, by an irresistible impulse, I found myself catching them up and pressing them to my heart.

As soon as I had done so I used to say to myself: "What will they think of that? Doesn't it betray too much?" It would have been easy to get into a sad, wild tangle about how much I might betray; but the real account, I feel, of the hours of peace that I could still enjoy was that the immediate charm of my companions was a beguilement still effective even under the shadow of the possibility that it was studied. For if it occurred to me that I might occasionally excite suspicion by the little outbreaks of my sharper passion for them, so too I remember wondering if I mightn't see a queerness in the traceable increase of their own demonstrations.

They were at this period extravagantly and preternaturally fond of me; which, after all, I could reflect, was no more than a graceful response in children perpetually bowed over and hugged. The homage of which they were so lavish succeeded, in truth, for my nerves, quite as well as if I never appeared to myself, as I may say, literally to catch them at a purpose in it. They had never, I think, wanted to do so many things for their poor protectress; I mean—though they got their lessons better and better, which was naturally what would please her most—in the way of diverting, entertaining, surprising her; reading her passages, telling her stories, acting her charades, pouncing out at her, in disguises, as animals and historical characters, and above all astonishing her by the "pieces" they had secretly got by heart and could interminably recite. I should never get to the bottom—were I to let myself go even now—of the prodigious private commentary, all under still more private correction, with which, in these days, I overscored their full hours.

They had shown me from the first a facility for everything, a general faculty which, taking a fresh start, achieved remarkable flights. They got their little tasks as if they loved them, and indulged, from the mere exuberance of the gift, in the most unimposed little miracles of memory. They not only popped out at me as tigers and as Romans, but as Shakespeareans, astronomers, and navigators. This was so singularly the case that it had presumably much to do with the fact as to which, at the present day, I am at a loss for a different explanation: I allude to my unnatural composure on the subject of another school for Miles.

What I remember is that I was content not, for the time, to open the question, and that contentment must have sprung from the sense of his perpetually striking show of cleverness. He was too clever for a bad governess, for a parson's daughter, to spoil; and the strangest if not the brightest thread in the pensive embroidery I just spoke of was the impression I might have got, if I had dared to work it out, that he was under some influence operating in his small intellectual life as a tremendous incitement.

If it was easy to reflect, however, that such a boy could postpone school, it was at least as marked that for such a boy to have been "kicked out" by a schoolmaster was a mystification without end. Let me add that in their company now—and I was careful almost never to be out of it—I could follow no scent very far. We lived in a cloud of music and love and success and private theatricals. The musical sense in each of the children was of the quickest, but the elder in especial had a marvellous knack of catching and repeating. The schoolroom piano broke into all gruesome fancies; and when that failed there were confabulations in corners, with a sequel of one of them going out in the highest spirits in order to "come in" as something new. I had had brothers myself, and it was no revelation to me that little girls could be slavish idolaters of little boys.

What surpassed everything was that there was a little boy in the world who could have for the inferior age, sex, and intelligence so fine a consideration. They were extraordinarily at one, and to say that they never either quarrelled or complained is to make the note of praise coarse for their quality of sweetness. Sometimes, indeed, when I dropped into coarseness, I perhaps came across traces of little understandings between them by which one of them should keep me occupied while the other slipped away. There is a naive side, I suppose, in all diplomacy; but if my pupils practiced upon me, it was surely with the minimum of grossness. It was all in the other quarter that, after a lull, the grossness broke out.

I find that I really hang back; but I must take my plunge. In going on with the record of what was hideous at Bly, I not only challenge the most liberal faith—for which I little care; but—and this is another matter—I renew what I myself suffered, I again push my way through it to the end. There came suddenly an hour after which, as I look back, the affair seems to me to have been all pure suffering; but I have at least reached the heart of it, and the straightest road out is doubtless to advance.

One evening—with nothing to lead up or to prepare it—I

felt the cold touch of the impression that had breathed on me the night of my arrival and which, much lighter then, as I have mentioned, I should probably have made little of in memory had my subsequent sojourn been less agitated. I had not gone to bed; I sat reading by a couple of candles. There was a roomful of old books at Bly—last-century fiction, some of it, which, to the extent of a distinctly deprecated renown, but never to so much as that of a stray specimen, had reached the sequestered home and appealed to the unavowed curiosity of my youth.

I remember that the book I had in my hand was Fielding's *Amelia*; also that I was wholly awake. I recall further both a general conviction that it was horribly late and a particular objection to looking at my watch. I figure, finally, that the white curtain draping, in the fashion of those days, the head of Flora's little bed, shrouded, as I had assured myself long before, the perfection of childish rest. I recollect in short that, though I was deeply interested in my author, I found myself, at the turn of a page and with his spell all scattered, looking straight up from him and hard at the door of my room.

There was a moment during which I listened, reminded of the faint sense I had had, the first night, of there being something undefinably astir in the house, and noted the soft breath of the open casement just move the half-drawn blind. Then, with all the marks of a deliberation that must have seemed magnificent had there been anyone to admire it, I laid down my book, rose to my feet, and, taking a candle, went straight out of the room and, from the passage, on which my light made little impression, noiselessly closed and locked the door.

I can say now neither what determined nor what guided me, but I went straight along the lobby, holding my candle high, till I came within sight of the tall window that presided over the great turn of the staircase. At this point I precipitately found myself aware of three things. They were practically simultaneous, yet they had flashes of succession. My candle, under a bold flourish, went out, and I perceived, by the uncovered window, that the yielding dusk of earliest morning rendered it unnecessary. Without it, the next instant, I saw that there was someone on the stair. I speak of sequences, but I required no lapse of seconds to stiffen myself for a third encounter with Quint.

The apparition had reached the landing halfway up and was therefore on the spot nearest the window, where at sight of me, it stopped short and fixed me exactly as it had fixed me from the tower and from the garden. He knew me as well as I knew him; and so, in the cold, faint twilight, with a glimmer in the high glass and another on the polish of the oak stair below, we faced each other in our common intensity. He was absolutely, on this occasion, a living, detestable, dangerous presence. But that was not the wonder of wonders; I reserve this distinction for quite another circumstance: the circumstance that dread had unmistakably quitted me and that there was nothing in me there that didn't meet and measure him.

I had plenty of anguish after that extraordinary moment, but I had, thank God, no terror. And he knew I had not—I found myself at the end of an instant magnificently aware of this. I felt, in a fierce rigor of confidence, that if I stood my ground a minute I should cease—for the time, at least—to have him to reckon with; and during the minute, accordingly, the thing was as human and hideous as a real interview: hideous just because it WAS human, as human as to have met alone, in the small hours, in a sleeping house, some enemy, some adventurer, some criminal. It was the dead silence of our long gaze at such close quarters that gave the whole horror, huge as it was, its only note of the unnatural.

If I had met a murderer in such a place and at such an hour, we still at least would have spoken. Something would have passed, in life, between us; if nothing had passed, one of us would have moved. The moment was so prolonged that it would have taken but little more to make me doubt if even *I* were in life. I can't express what followed it save by saying that the silence itself—which was indeed in a manner an attestation of my strength—became the element into which I saw the figure disappear; in which I definitely saw it turn as I might have seen the low wretch to which it had once belonged turn on receipt of an order, and pass, with my eyes on the villainous back that no hunch could have more disfigured, straight down the staircase and into the darkness in which the next bend was lost.

10

I remained awhile at the top of the stair, but with the effect presently of understanding that when my visitor had gone, he had gone: then I returned to my room. The foremost thing I saw there by the light of the candle I had left burning was that Flora's little bed was empty; and on this I caught my breath with all the terror that, five minutes before, I had been able to resist. I dashed at the place in which I had left her lying and over which (for the small silk counterpane and the sheets were disarranged) the white curtains had been deceivingly pulled forward; then my step, to my unutterable relief, produced an answering sound: I perceived an agitation of the window blind, and the child, ducking down, emerged rosily from the other side of it.

She stood there in so much of her candour and so little of her nightgown, with her pink bare feet and the golden glow of her curls. She looked intensely grave, and I had never had such a sense of losing an advantage acquired (the thrill of which had just been so prodigious) as on my consciousness that she addressed me with a reproach. "You naughty: where HAVE you been?"—instead of challenging her own irregularity I found myself arraigned and explaining. She herself explained, for that matter, with the loveliest, eagerest simplicity. She had known suddenly, as she lay there, that I was out of the room, and had jumped up to see what had become of me.

I had dropped, with the joy of her reappearance, back into my chair—feeling then, and then only, a little faint; and she had pattered straight over to me, thrown herself upon my knee, given herself to be held with the flame of the candle full in the wonderful little face that was still flushed with sleep. I remember closing my eyes an instant, yieldingly, consciously, as before the excess of something beautiful that shone out of the blue of her own. "You were looking for me out of the window?" I said. "You thought I might be walking in the grounds?"

"Well, you know, I thought someone was"—she never blanched as she smiled out that at me.

Oh, how I looked at her now! "And did you see anyone?"

"Ah, NO!" she returned, almost with the full privilege of childish inconsequence, resentfully, though with a long sweetness in her little drawl of the negative.

At that moment, in the state of my nerves, I absolutely believed she lied; and if I once more closed my eyes it was before the dazzle of the three or four possible ways in which I might take this up. One of these, for a moment, tempted me with such singular intensity that, to withstand it, I must have gripped my little girl with a spasm that, wonderfully, she submitted to without a cry or a sign of fright. Why not break out at her on the spot and have it all over?—give it to her straight in her lovely little lighted face? "You see, you see, you KNOW that you do and that you already quite suspect I believe it; therefore, why not frankly confess it to me, so that we may at least live with it together and learn perhaps, in the strangeness of our fate, where we are and what it means?"

This solicitation dropped, alas, as it came: if I could immediately have succumbed to it I might have spared myself—well, you'll see what. Instead of succumbing I sprang again to my feet, looked at her bed, and took a helpless middle way. "Why did you pull the curtain over the place to make me think you were still there?"

Flora luminously considered; after which, with her little divine smile: "Because I don't like to frighten you!"

"But if I had, by your idea, gone out—?"

She absolutely declined to be puzzled; she turned her eyes to the flame of the candle as if the question were as irrelevant, or at any rate as impersonal, as Mrs. Marcet or nine-times-nine. "Oh, but you know," she quite adequately answered, "that you might come back, you dear, and that you HAVE!" And after a little, when she had got into bed, I had, for a long time, by almost sitting on her to hold her hand, to prove that I recognized the pertinence of my return.

You may imagine the general complexion, from that moment, of my nights. I repeatedly sat up till I didn't know when; I selected moments when my roommate unmistakably slept, and, stealing out, took noiseless turns in the passage and even pushed as far as to where I had last met Quint. But I never met him there again; and I may as well say at once that I on no other occasion saw him in the house. I just missed, on the staircase, on the other hand, a different adventure. Looking down it from the top I once recognized the presence of a woman seated on one of the lower steps with her back presented to me, her body half-bowed and her head, in an attitude of woe, in her hands. I had been there but an instant, however, when she vanished without looking round at me.

I knew, nonetheless, exactly what dreadful face she had to show; and I wondered whether, if instead of being above I had been below, I should have had, for going up, the same nerve I had lately shown Quint. Well, there continued to be plenty of chance for nerve. On the eleventh night after my latest encounter with that gentleman—they were all numbered now—I had an alarm that perilously skirted it and that indeed, from the particular quality of its unexpectedness, proved quite my sharpest shock. It was precisely the first night during this series that, weary with watching, I had felt that I might again without laxity lay myself down at my old hour. I slept immediately and, as I afterward knew, till about one o'clock; but when I woke it was to sit straight up, as completely roused as if a hand had shook me. I had left a light burning, but it was now out, and I felt an instant certainty that Flora had extinguished it. This brought me to my feet and straight, in the darkness, to her bed, which I found she had left. A glance at the window enlightened me further, and the striking of a match completed the picture.

The child had again got up—this time blowing out the taper, and had again, for some purpose of observation or response, squeezed in behind the blind and was peering out into the night. That she now saw—as she had not, I had satisfied myself, the previous time—was proved to me by the fact that she was disturbed neither by my reillumination nor by the haste I made to get into slippers and into a wrap. Hidden, protected, absorbed, she evidently rested on the sill—the casement opened forward—and gave herself up. There was a great still moon to help her, and this fact had counted in my quick decision. She was face to face with the apparition we had met at the lake, and could now communicate with it as she had not then been able to do.

What I, on my side, had to care for was, without disturbing her, to reach, from the corridor, some other window in the same quarter. I got to the door without her hearing me; I got out of it, closed it, and listened, from the other side, for some sound from her. While I stood in the passage I had my eyes on her brother's door, which was but ten steps off and which, indescribably, produced in me a renewal of the strange impulse that I lately spoke of as my temptation. What if I should go straight in and march to HIS window?—what if, by risking to his boyish bewilderment a revelation of my motive, I should throw across the rest of the mystery the long halter of my boldness?

This thought held me sufficiently to make me cross to his threshold and pause again. I preternaturally listened; I figured to myself what might portentously be; I wondered if his bed were also empty and he too were secretly at watch. It was a deep, soundless minute, at the end of which my impulse failed. He was quiet; he might be innocent; the risk was hideous; I turned away. There was a figure in the grounds—a figure prowling for a sight, the visitor with whom Flora was engaged; but it was not the visitor most concerned with my boy. I hesitated afresh, but on other grounds and only for a few seconds; then I had made my choice.

There were empty rooms at Bly, and it was only a question of choosing the right one. The right one suddenly presented itself to me as the lower one—though high above the gardens—in the solid corner of the house that I have spoken of as the old tower. This was a large, square chamber, arranged with some state as a bedroom, the extravagant size of which made it so inconvenient that it had not for years, though kept by Mrs. Grose in exemplary order, been occupied. I had often admired it and I knew my way about in it; I had only, after just faltering at the first chill gloom of its disuse, to pass across it and unbolt as quietly as I could one of the shutters.

Achieving this transit, I uncovered the glass without a sound and, applying my face to the pane, was able, the darkness without being much less than within, to see that I commanded the right direction. Then I saw something more. The moon made the night extraordinarily penetrable and showed me on the lawn a person, diminished by distance, who stood there motionless and as if fascinated, looking up to where I had appeared—looking, that is, not so much straight at me as at something that was apparently above me. There was clearly another person above me—there was a person on the tower; but the presence on the lawn was not in the least what I had conceived and had confidently hurried to meet. The presence on the lawn—I felt sick as I made it out—was poor little Miles himself.

11

It was not till late next day that I spoke to Mrs. Grose; the rigor with which I kept my pupils in sight making it often difficult to meet her privately, and the more as we each felt the importance of not provoking—on the part of the servants quite as much as on that of the children—any suspicion of a secret flurry or that of a discussion of mysteries. I drew a great security in this particular from her mere smooth aspect. There was nothing in her fresh face to pass on to others my horrible confidences. She believed me, I was sure, absolutely: if she hadn't I don't know what would have become of me, for I couldn't have borne the business alone. But she was a magnificent monument to the blessing of a want of imagination, and if she could see in our little charges nothing but their beauty and amiability, their happiness and cleverness, she had no direct communication with the sources of my trouble.

If they had been at all visibly blighted or battered, she would doubtless have grown, on tracing it back, haggard enough to match them; as matters stood, however, I could feel her, when she surveyed them, with her large white arms folded and the habit of serenity in all her look, thank the Lord's mercy that if they were ruined the pieces would still serve. Flights of fancy gave place, in her mind, to a steady fireside glow, and I had already begun to perceive how, with the development of the conviction that—as time went on without a public accident-our young things could, after all, look out for themselves, she addressed her greatest solicitude to the sad case presented by their instructress. That, for myself, was a sound simplification: I could engage that, to the world, my face should tell no tales, but it would have been, in the conditions, an immense added strain to find myself anxious about hers.

At the hour I now speak of she had joined me, under pressure, on the terrace, where, with the lapse of the season, the afternoon sun was now agreeable; and we sat there together while, before us, at a distance, but within call if we wished, the children strolled to and fro in one of their most manageable moods. They moved slowly, in unison, below us, over the lawn, the boy, as they went, reading aloud from a storybook and passing his arm round his sister to keep her quite in touch. Mrs. Grose watched them with positive placidity; then I caught the suppressed intellectual creak with which she conscientiously turned to take from me a view of the back of the tapestry.

I had made her a receptacle of lurid things, but there was an odd recognition of my superiority—my accomplishments and my function—in her patience under my pain. She offered her mind to my disclosures as, had I wished to mix a witch's broth and proposed it with assurance, she would have held out a large clean saucepan. This had become thoroughly her attitude by the time that, in my recital of the events of the night, I reached the point of what Miles had said to me when, after seeing him, at such a monstrous hour, almost on the very spot where he happened now to be, I had gone down to bring him in; choosing then, at the window, with a concentrated need of not alarming the house, rather that method than a signal more resonant.

I had left her meanwhile in little doubt of my small hope of representing with success even to her actual sympathy my sense of the real splendour of the little inspiration with which, after I had got him into the house, the boy met my final articulate challenge. As soon as I appeared in the moonlight on the terrace, he had come to me as straight as possible; on which I had taken his hand without a word and led him, through the dark spaces, up the staircase where Quint had so hungrily hovered for him, along the lobby where I had listened and trembled, and so to his forsaken room.

Not a sound, on the way, had passed between us, and I had wondered—oh, HOW I had wondered!—if he were groping about in his little mind for something plausible and not too grotesque. It would tax his invention, certainly, and I felt, this time, over his real embarrassment, a curious thrill of triumph. It was a sharp trap for the inscrutable! He couldn't play any longer at innocence; so how the deuce would he get out of it? There beat in me indeed, with the passionate throb of this question an equal dumb appeal as to how the deuce *I* should. I was confronted at last, as never yet, with all the risk attached even now to sounding my own horrid note.

I remember in fact that as we pushed into his little chamber, where the bed had not been slept in at all and the window, uncovered to the moonlight, made the place so clear that there was no need of striking a match—I remember how I suddenly dropped, sank upon the edge of the bed from the force of the idea that he must know how he really, as they say, "had" me. He could do what he liked, with all his cleverness to help him, so long as I should continue to defer to the old tradition of the criminality of those caretakers of the young who minister to superstitions and fears. He "had" me indeed, and in a cleft stick; for who would ever absolve me, who would consent that I should go unhung, if, by the faintest tremor of an overture, I were the first to introduce into our perfect intercourse an element so dire?

No, no: it was useless to attempt to convey to Mrs. Grose, just as it is scarcely less so to attempt to suggest here, how, in our short, stiff brush in the dark, he fairly shook me with admiration. I was of course thoroughly kind and merciful; never, never yet had I placed on his little shoulders hands of such tenderness as those with which, while I rested against the bed, I held him there well under fire. I had no alternative but, in form at least, to put it to him.

"You must tell me now—and all the truth. What did you go out for? What were you doing there?"

I can still see his wonderful smile, the whites of his beautiful eyes, and the uncovering of his little teeth shine to me in the dusk. "If I tell you why, will you understand?" My heart, at this, leaped into my mouth. WOULD he tell me why? I found no sound on my lips to press it, and I was aware of replying only with a vague, repeated, grimacing nod. He was gentleness itself, and while I wagged my head at him he stood there more than ever a little fairy prince. It was his brightness indeed that gave me a respite. Would it be so great if he were really going to tell me? "Well," he said at last, "just exactly in order that you should do this."

"Do what?"

"Think me—for a change—BAD!" I shall never forget the sweetness and gaiety with which he brought out the word, nor how, on top of it, he bent forward and kissed me. It was practically the end of everything. I met his kiss and I had to make, while I folded him for a minute in my arms, the most stupendous effort not to cry. He had given exactly the account of himself that permitted least of my going behind it, and it was only with the effect of confirming my acceptance of it that, as I presently glanced about the room, I could say—

"Then you didn't undress at all?"

He fairly glittered in the gloom. "Not at all. I sat up and read."

"And when did you go down?"

"At midnight. When I'm bad I AM bad!"

"I see, I see—it's charming. But how could you be sure I would know it?"

"Oh, I arranged that with Flora." His answers rang out with a readiness! "She was to get up and look out."

"Which is what she did do." It was I who fell into the trap!

"So she disturbed you, and, to see what she was looking at, you also looked—you saw."

"While you," I concurred, "caught your death in the night air!"

He literally bloomed so from this exploit that he could afford radiantly to assent. "How otherwise should I have been bad enough?" he asked. Then, after another embrace, the incident and our interview closed on my recognition of all the reserves of goodness that, for his joke, he had been able to draw upon.

12

The particular impression I had received proved in the morning light, I repeat, not quite successfully presentable to Mrs. Grose, though I reinforced it with the mention of still another remark that he had made before we separated. "It all lies in half a dozen words," I said to her, "words that really settle the matter. 'Think, you know, what I MIGHT do!' He threw that off to show me how good he is. He knows down to the ground what he 'might' do. That's what he gave them a taste of at school."

"Lord, you do change!" cried my friend.

"I don't change—I simply make it out. The four, depend upon it, perpetually meet. If on either of these last nights you had been with either child, you would clearly have understood. The more I've watched and waited the more I've felt that if there were nothing else to make it sure it would be made so by the systematic silence of each. NEVER, by a slip of the tongue, have they so much as alluded to either of their old friends, any more than Miles has alluded to his expulsion.

"Oh, yes, we may sit here and look at them, and they may show off to us there to their fill; but even while they pretend to be lost in their fairytale they're steeped in their vision of the dead restored. He's not reading to her," I declared; "they're talking of THEM—they're talking horrors! I go on, I know, as if I were crazy; and it's a wonder I'm not. What I've seen would have made YOU so; but it has only made me more lucid, made me get hold of still other things."

My lucidity must have seemed awful, but the charming creatures who were victims of it, passing and repassing in their interlocked sweetness, gave my colleague something to hold on by; and I felt how tight she held as, without stirring in the breath of my passion, she covered them still with her eyes. "Of what other things have you got hold?"

"Why, of the very things that have delighted, fascinated, and yet, at bottom, as I now so strangely see, mystified and troubled me. Their more than earthly beauty, their absolutely unnatural goodness. It's a game," I went on; "it's a policy and a fraud!"

"On the part of little darlings—?"

"As yet mere lovely babies? Yes, mad as that seems!" The very act of bringing it out really helped me to trace it—follow it all up and piece it all together. "They haven't been good—they've only been absent. It has been easy to live with them, because they're simply leading a life of their own. They're not mine-they're not ours. They're his and they're hers!"

"Quint's and that woman's?"

"Quint's and that woman's. They want to get to them."

Oh, how, at this, poor Mrs. Grose appeared to study them! "But for what?"

"For the love of all the evil that, in those dreadful days, the pair put into them. And to ply them with that evil still, to keep up the work of demons, is what brings the others back."

"Laws!" said my friend under her breath. The exclamation was homely, but it revealed a real acceptance of my further proof of what, in the bad time—for there had been a worse even than this!—must have occurred. There could have been no such justification for me as the plain assent of her experience to whatever depth of depravity I found credible in our brace of scoundrels. It was in obvious submission of memory that she brought out after a moment: "They WERE rascals! But what can they now do?" she pursued.

"Do?" I echoed so loud that Miles and Flora, as they passed at their distance, paused an instant in their walk and looked at us. "Don't they do enough?" I demanded in a lower tone, while the children, having smiled and nodded and kissed hands to us, resumed their exhibition. We were held by it a minute; then I answered: "They can destroy them!" At this my companion did turn, but the inquiry she launched was a silent one, the effect of which was to make me more explicit. "They don't know, as yet, quite how—but they're trying hard. They're seen only across, as it were, and beyond—in strange places and on high places, the top of towers, the roof of houses, the outside of windows, the further edge of pools; but there's a deep design, on either side, to shorten the distance and overcome the obstacle; and the success of the tempters is only a question of time. They've only to keep to their suggestions of danger."

"For the children to come?"

"And perish in the attempt!" Mrs. Grose slowly got up, and I scrupulously added: "Unless, of course, we can prevent!"

Standing there before me while I kept my seat, she visibly turned things over. "Their uncle must do the preventing. He must take them away."

"And who's to make him?"

She had been scanning the distance, but she now dropped on me a foolish face. "You, miss."

"By writing to him that his house is poisoned and his little nephew and niece mad?"

"But if they ARE, miss?"

"And if I am myself, you mean? That's charming news to be sent him by a governess whose prime undertaking was to give him no worry."

Mrs. Grose considered, following the children again. "Yes, he do hate worry. That was the great reason—"

"Why those fiends took him in so long? No doubt, though his indifference must have been awful. As I'm not a fiend, at any rate, I shouldn't take him in."

My companion, after an instant and for all answer, sat down again and grasped my arm. "Make him at any rate come to you."

I stared. "To ME?" I had a sudden fear of what she might do. "'Him'?"

"He ought to BE here—he ought to help."

I quickly rose, and I think I must have shown her a queerer face than ever yet. "You see me asking him for a visit?" No, with her eyes on my face she evidently couldn't. Instead of it even—as a woman reads another—she could see what I myself saw: his derision, his amusement, his contempt for the breakdown of my resignation at being left alone and for the fine machinery I had set in motion to attract his attention to my slighted charms. She didn't know—no one knew—how proud I had been to serve him and to stick to our terms; yet she nonetheless took the measure, I think, of the warning I now gave her. "If you should so lose your head as to appeal to him for me—"

She was really frightened. "Yes, miss?"

"I would leave, on the spot, both him and you."

13

It was all very well to join them, but speaking to them proved quite as much as ever an effort beyond my strength—offered, in close quarters, difficulties as insurmountable as before. This situation continued a month, and with new aggravations and particular notes, the note above all, sharper and sharper, of the small ironic consciousness on the part of my pupils. It was not, I am as sure today as I was sure then, my mere infernal imagination: it was absolutely traceable that they were aware of my predicament and that this strange relation made, in a manner, for a long time, the air in which we moved.

I don't mean that they had their tongues in their cheeks or did anything vulgar, for that was not one of their dangers: I do mean, on the other hand, that the element of the unnamed and untouched became, between us, greater than any other, and that so much avoidance could not have been so successfully effected without a great deal of tacit arrangement. It was as if, at moments, we were perpetually coming into sight of subjects before which we must stop short, turning suddenly out of alleys that we perceived to be blind, closing with a little bang that made us look at each other—for, like all bangs, it was something louder than we had intended—the doors we had indiscreetly opened.

All roads lead to Rome, and there were times when it might have struck us that almost every branch of study or subject of conversation skirted forbidden ground. Forbidden ground was the question of the return of the dead in general and of whatever, in especial, might survive, in memory, of the friends little children had lost. There were days when I could have sworn that one of them had, with a small invisible nudge, said to the other: "She thinks she'll do it this time—but she WON'T!"

To "do it" would have been to indulge for instance—and for once in a way—in some direct reference to the lady who had prepared them for my discipline. They had a delightful endless appetite for passages in my own history, to which I had again and again treated them; they were in possession of everything that had ever happened to me, had had, with every circumstance the story of my smallest adventures and of those of my brothers and sisters and of the cat and the dog at home, as well as many particulars of the eccentric nature of my father, of the furniture and arrangement of our house, and of the conversation of the old women of our village.

There were things enough, taking one with another, to chatter about, if one went very fast and knew by instinct when to go round. They pulled with an art of their own the strings of my invention and my memory; and nothing else perhaps, when I thought of such occasions afterward, gave me so the suspicion of being watched from under cover. It was in any case over MY life, MY past, and MY friends alone that we could take anything like our ease—a state of affairs that led them sometimes without the least pertinence to break out into sociable reminders. I was invited—with no visible connection—to repeat afresh Goody

Gosling's celebrated *mot* or to confirm the details already supplied as to the cleverness of the vicarage pony.

It was partly at such junctures as these and partly at quite different ones that, with the turn my matters had now taken, my predicament, as I have called it, grew most sensible. The fact that the days passed for me without another encounter ought, it would have appeared, to have done something toward soothing my nerves. Since the light brush, that second night on the upper landing, of the presence of a woman at the foot of the stair, I had seen nothing, whether in or out of the house, that one had better not have seen. There was many a corner round which I expected to come upon Quint, and many a situation that, in a merely sinister way, would have favoured the appearance of Miss Jessel. The summer had turned, the summer had gone; the autumn had dropped upon Bly and had blown out half our lights.

The place, with its gray sky and withered garlands, its bared spaces and scattered dead leaves, was like a theatre after the performance—all strewn with crumpled playbills. There were exactly states of the air, conditions of sound and of stillness, unspeakable impressions of the KIND of ministering moment, that brought back to me, long enough to catch it, the feeling of the medium in which, that June evening out of doors, I had had my first sight of Quint, and in which, too, at those other instants, I had, after seeing him through the window, looked for him in vain in the circle of shrubbery.

I recognized the signs, the portents—I recognized the moment, the spot. But they remained unaccompanied and empty, and I continued unmolested; if unmolested one could call a young woman whose sensibility had, in the most extraordinary fashion, not declined but deepened. I had said in my talk with Mrs. Grose on that horrid scene of Flora's by the lake—and had perplexed her by so saying—that it would from that moment distress me much more to lose my power than to keep it. I had then expressed what was vividly in my mind: the truth that, whether the children really saw or not—since, that is, it was not yet definitely proved—I greatly preferred, as a safeguard, the fullness of my own exposure.

I was ready to know the very worst that was to be known. What I had then had an ugly glimpse of was that my eyes might be sealed just while theirs were most opened. Well, my eyes WERE sealed, it appeared, at present—a consummation for which it seemed blasphemous not to thank God. There was, alas, a difficulty about that: I would have thanked him with all my soul had I not had in a proportionate measure this conviction of the secret of my pupils.

How can I retrace today the strange steps of my obsession? There were times of our being together when I would have been ready to swear that, literally, in my presence, but with my direct sense of it closed, they had visitors who were known and were welcome. Then it was that, had I not been deterred by the very chance that such an injury might prove greater than the injury to be averted, my exultation would have broken out. "They're here, they're here, you little wretches," I would have cried, "and you can't deny it now!" The little wretches denied it with all the added volume of their sociability and their tenderness, in just the crystal depths of which—like the flash of a fish in a stream—the mockery of their advantage peeped up.

The shock, in truth, had sunk into me still deeper than I knew on the night when, looking out to see either Quint or Miss Jessel under the stars, I had beheld the boy over whose rest I watched and who had immediately brought in with him-had straightway, there, turned it on me—the lovely upward look with which, from the battlements above me, the hideous apparition of Quint had played. If it was a question of a scare, my discovery on this occasion had scared me more than any other, and it was in the condition of nerves produced by it that I made my actual inductions.

They harassed me so that sometimes, at odd moments, I shut myself up audibly to rehearse—it was at once a fantastic relief and a renewed despair—the manner in which I might come to the point. I approached it from one side and the other while, in my room, I flung myself about, but I always broke down in the monstrous utterance of names. As they died away on my lips, I said to myself that I should indeed help them to represent something infamous, if, by pronouncing them, I should violate as rare a little case of instinctive delicacy as any schoolroom, probably, had ever known.

When I said to myself: "THEY have the manners to be silent, and you, trusted as you are, the baseness to speak!" I felt myself crimson and I covered my face with my hands. After these secret scenes I chattered more than ever, going on volubly enough till one of our prodigious, palpable hushes occurred—I can call them nothing else—the strange, dizzy lift or swim (I try for terms!) into a stillness, a pause of all life, that had nothing to do with the more or less noise that at the moment we might be engaged in making and that I could hear through any deepened exhilaration or quickened recitation or louder strum of the piano. Then it was that the others, the outsiders, were there. Though they were not angels, they "passed," as the French say, causing me, while they stayed, to tremble with the fear of their addressing to their younger victims some yet more infernal message or more vivid image than they had thought good enough for myself.

What it was most impossible to get rid of was the cruel idea that, whatever I had seen, Miles and Flora saw MORE—things terrible and unguessable and that sprang from dreadful passages of intercourse in the past. Such things naturally left on the surface, for the time, a chill which we vociferously denied that we felt; and we had, all three, with repetition, got into such splendid training that we went, each time, almost automatically, to mark the close of the incident, through the very same movements. It was striking of the children, at all events, to kiss me inveterately with a kind of wild irrelevance and never to fail—one or the other—of the precious question that had helped us through many a peril. "When do you think he WILL come? Don't you think we OUGHT to write?"—there was nothing like that inquiry, we found by experience, for carrying off an awkwardness.

"He" of course was their uncle in Harley Street; and we lived in much profusion of theory that he might at any moment arrive to mingle in our circle. It was impossible to have given less encouragement than he had done to such a doctrine, but if we had not had the doctrine to fall back upon we should have deprived each other of some of our finest exhibitions. He never wrote to them—that may have been selfish, but it was a part of the flattery of his trust of me; for the way in which a man pays his highest tribute to a woman is apt to be but by the more festal celebration of one of the sacred laws of his comfort; and I held that I carried out the spirit of the pledge given not to appeal to him when I let my charges understand that their own letters were but charming literary exercises.

They were too beautiful to be posted; I kept them myself; I have them all to this hour. This was a rule indeed which only added to the satiric effect of my being plied with the supposition that he might at any moment be among us. It was exactly as if my charges knew how almost more awkward than anything else that might be for me. There appears to me, moreover, as I look back, no note in all this more extraordinary than the mere fact that, in spite of my tension and of their triumph, I never lost patience with them. Adorable they must in truth have been, I now reflect, that I didn't in these days hate them! Would exasperation, however, if relief had longer been postponed, finally have betrayed me? It little matters, for relief arrived. I call it relief, though it was only the relief that a snap brings to a strain or the burst of a thunderstorm to a day of suffocation. It was at least change, and it came with a rush.

14

Walking to church a certain Sunday morning, I had little Miles at my side and his sister, in advance of us and at Mrs. Grose's, well in sight. It was a crisp, clear day, the first of its order for some time; the night had brought a touch of frost, and the autumn air, bright and sharp, made the church bells almost gay. It was an odd accident of thought that I should have happened at such a moment to be particularly and very gratefully struck with the obedience of my little charges. Why did they never resent my inexorable, my perpetual society? Something or other had brought nearer home to me that I had all but pinned the boy to my shawl and that, in the way our companions were marshalled before me, I might have appeared to provide against some danger of rebellion.

I was like a gaoler with an eye to possible surprises and escapes. But all this belonged—I mean their magnificent little surrender—just to the special array of the facts that were most abysmal. Turned out for Sunday by his uncle's tailor, who had had a free hand and a notion of pretty waistcoats and of his grand little air, Miles's whole title to independence, the rights of his sex and situation, were so stamped upon him that if he had suddenly struck for freedom I should have had nothing to say. I was by the strangest of chances wondering how I should meet him when the revolution unmistakably occurred. I call it a revolution because I now see how, with the word he spoke, the curtain rose on the last act of my dreadful drama, and the catastrophe was precipitated. "Look here, my dear, you know," he charmingly said, "when in the world, please, am I going back to school?"

Transcribed here the speech sounds harmless enough, particularly as uttered in the sweet, high, casual pipe with which, at all interlocutors, but above all at his eternal governess, he threw off intonations as if he were tossing roses. There was something in them that always made one "catch," and I caught, at any rate, now so effectually that I stopped as short as if one of the trees of the park had fallen across the road. There was something new, on the spot, between us, and he was perfectly aware that I recognized it, though, to enable me to do so, he had no need to look a whit less candid and charming than usual. I could feel in him how he already, from my at first finding nothing to reply, perceived the advantage he had gained.

I was so slow to find anything that he had plenty of time, after a minute, to continue with his suggestive but inconclusive smile: "You know, my dear, that for a fellow to be with a lady ALWAYS—!" His "my dear" was constantly on his lips for me, and nothing could have expressed more the exact shade of the sentiment with which I desired to inspire my pupils than its fond familiarity. It was so respectfully easy.

But, oh, how I felt that at present I must pick my own phrases! I remember that, to gain time, I tried to laugh, and I seemed to see in the beautiful face with which he watched me how ugly and queer I looked. "And always with the same lady?" I returned.

He neither blanched nor winked. The whole thing was virtually out between us. "Ah, of course, she's a jolly, 'perfect' lady; but, after all, I'm a fellow, don't you see? that's—well, getting on."

I lingered there with him an instant ever so kindly. "Yes, you're getting on." Oh, but I felt helpless!

I have kept to this day the heartbreaking little idea of how he seemed to know that and to play with it. "And you can't say I've not been awfully good, can you?"

I laid my hand on his shoulder, for, though I felt how much better it would have been to walk on, I was not yet quite able. "No, I can't say that, Miles."

"Except just that one night, you know—!"

"That one night?" I couldn't look as straight as he.

"Why, when I went down—went out of the house."

"Oh, yes. But I forget what you did it for."

"You forget?"—he spoke with the sweet extravagance of childish reproach. "Why, it was to show you I could!"

"Oh, yes, you could."

"And I can again."

I felt that I might, perhaps, after all, succeed in keeping my wits about me. "Certainly. But you won't."

"No, not THAT again. It was nothing."

"It was nothing," I said. "But we must go on."

He resumed our walk with me, passing his hand into my arm. "Then when AM I going back?"

I wore, in turning it over, my most responsible air. "Were you very happy at school?"

He just considered. "Oh, I'm happy enough anywhere!"

"Well, then," I quavered, "if you're just as happy here—!"

"Ah, but that isn't everything! Of course YOU know a lot—"

"But you hint that you know almost as much?" I risked as he paused.

"Not half I want to!" Miles honestly professed. "But it isn't so much that."

"What is it, then?"

"Well—I want to see more life."

"I see; I see." We had arrived within sight of the church and of various persons, including several of the household of Bly, on their way to it and clustered about the door to see us go in. I quickened our step; I wanted to get there before the question between us opened up much further; I reflected hungrily that, for more than an hour, he would have to be silent; and I thought with envy of the comparative dusk of the pew and of the almost spiritual help of the hassock on which I might bend my knees. I seemed literally to be running a race with some confusion to which he was about to reduce me, but I felt that he had got in first when, before we had even entered the churchyard, he threw out—

"I want my own sort!"

It literally made me bound forward. "There are not many of your own sort, Miles!" I laughed. "Unless perhaps dear little Flora!"

"You really compare me to a baby girl?"

This found me singularly weak. "Don't you, then, LOVE our sweet Flora?"

"If I didn't—and you, too; if I didn't—!" he repeated as if retreating for a jump, yet leaving his thought so unfinished that, after we had come into the gate, another stop, which he imposed on me by the pressure of his arm, had become inevitable. Mrs. Grose and Flora had passed into the church, the other worshippers had followed, and we were, for the minute, alone among the old, thick graves. We had paused, on the path from the gate, by a low, oblong, tablelike tomb.

"Yes, if you didn't—?"

He looked, while I waited, at the graves. "Well, you know what!" But he didn't move, and he presently produced something that made me drop straight down on the stone slab, as if suddenly to rest. "Does my uncle think what YOU think?"

I markedly rested. "How do you know what I think?"

"Ah, well, of course I don't; for it strikes me you never tell me. But I mean does HE know?"

"Know what, Miles?"

"Why, the way I'm going on."

I perceived quickly enough that I could make, to this inquiry, no answer that would not involve something of a sacrifice of my employer. Yet it appeared to me that we were all, at Bly, sufficiently sacrificed to make that venial. "I don't think your uncle much cares."

Miles, on this, stood looking at me. "Then don't you think he can be made to?"

"In what way?"

"Why, by his coming down."

"But who'll get him to come down?"

"*I* will!" the boy said with extraordinary brightness and emphasis. He gave me another look charged with that expression and then marched off alone into church.

15

The business was practically settled from the moment I never followed him. It was a pitiful surrender to agitation, but my being aware of this had somehow no power to restore me. I only sat there on my tomb and read into what my little friend had said to me the fullness of its meaning; by the time I had grasped the whole of which I had also embraced, for absence, the pretext that I was ashamed to offer my pupils and the rest of the congregation such an example of delay. What I said to myself above all was that Miles had got something out of me and that the proof of it, for him, would be just this awkward collapse. He had got out of me that there was something I was much afraid of and that he should probably be able to make use of my fear to gain, for his own purpose, more freedom.

My fear was of having to deal with the intolerable question of the grounds of his dismissal from school, for that was really but the question of the horrors gathered behind. That his uncle should arrive to treat with me of these things was a solution that, strictly speaking, I ought now to have desired to bring on; but I could so little face the ugliness and the pain of it that I simply procrastinated and lived from hand to mouth.

The boy, to my deep discomposure, was immensely in the right, was in a position to say to me: "Either you clear up with my guardian the mystery of this interruption of my studies, or you cease to expect me to lead with you a life that's so unnatural for a boy." What was so unnatural for the particular boy I was concerned with was this sudden revelation of a consciousness and a plan.

That was what really overcame me, what prevented my going in. I walked round the church, hesitating, hovering; I reflected that I had already, with him, hurt myself beyond repair. Therefore I could patch up nothing, and it was too extreme an effort to squeeze beside him into the pew: he would be so much more sure than ever to pass his arm into mine and make me sit there for an hour in close, silent contact with his commentary on our talk. For the first minute since his arrival I wanted to get away from him. As I paused beneath the high east window and listened to the sounds of worship, I was taken with an impulse that might master me, I felt, completely should I give it the least encouragement.

I might easily put an end to my predicament by getting away altogether. Here was my chance; there was no one to stop me; I could give the whole thing up—turn my back and retreat. It was only a question of hurrying again, for a few preparations, to the house which the attendance at church of so many of the servants would practically have left unoccupied. No one, in short, could blame me if I should just drive desperately off. What was it to get away if I got away only till dinner? That would be in a couple of hours, at the end of which—I had the acute prevision—my little pupils would play at innocent wonder about my nonappearance in their train.

"What DID you do, you naughty, bad thing? Why in the world, to worry us so—and take our thoughts off, too, don't you know?—did you desert us at the very door?" I couldn't meet such questions nor, as they asked them, their false little lovely eyes; yet it was all so exactly what I should have to meet that, as the prospect grew sharp to me, I at last let myself go.

I got, so far as the immediate moment was concerned, away; I came straight out of the churchyard and, thinking hard, retraced my steps through the park. It seemed to me that by the time I reached the house I had made up my mind I would fly. The Sunday stillness both of the approaches and of the interior, in which I met no one, fairly excited me with a sense of opportunity. Were I to get off quickly, this way, I should get off without a scene, without a word. My quickness would have to be remarkable, however, and the question of a conveyance was the great one to settle.

Tormented, in the hall, with difficulties and obstacles, I remember sinking down at the foot of the staircase—suddenly collapsing there on the lowest step and then, with a revulsion, recalling that it was exactly where more than a month before, in the darkness of night and just so bowed with evil things, I had seen the specter of the most horrible of women. At this I was able to straighten myself; I went the rest of the way up; I made, in my bewilderment, for the schoolroom, where there were objects belonging to me that I should have to take. But I opened the door to find again, in a flash, my eyes unsealed. In the presence of what I saw I reeled straight back upon my resistance.

Seated at my own table in clear noonday light I saw a person whom, without my previous experience, I should have taken at the first blush for some housemaid who might have stayed at home to look after the place and who, availing herself of rare relief from observation and of the schoolroom table and my pens, ink, and paper, had applied herself to the considerable effort of a letter to her sweetheart. There was an effort in the way that, while her arms rested on the table, her hands with evident weariness supported her head; but at the moment I took this in I had already become aware that, in spite of my entrance, her attitude strangely persisted.

Then it was—with the very act of its announcing itself—that her identity flared up in a change of posture. She rose, not as if she had heard me, but with an indescribable grand melancholy of indifference and detachment, and, within a dozen feet of me, stood there as my vile predecessor. Dishonoured and tragic, she was all before me; but even as I fixed and, for memory, secured it, the awful image passed away. Dark as midnight in her black dress, her haggard beauty and her unutterable woe, she had looked at me long enough to appear to say that her right to sit at my table was as good as mine to sit at hers.

While these instants lasted, indeed, I had the extraordinary chill of feeling that it was I who was the intruder. It was as a wild protest against it that, actually addressing her—"You terrible, miserable woman!"—I heard myself break into a sound that, by the open door, rang through the long passage and the empty house. She looked at me as if she heard me, but I had recovered myself and cleared the air. There was nothing in the room the next minute but the sunshine and a sense that I must stay.

16

I had so perfectly expected that the return of my pupils would be marked by a demonstration that I was freshly upset at having to take into account that they were dumb about my absence. Instead of gaily denouncing and caressing me, they made no allusion to my having failed them, and I was left, for the time, on perceiving that she too said nothing, to study Mrs. Grose's odd face. I did this to such purpose that I made sure they had in some way bribed her to silence; a silence that, however, I would engage to break down on the first private opportunity.

This opportunity came before tea: I secured five minutes with her in the housekeeper's room, where, in the twilight, amid a smell of lately baked bread, but with the place all swept and garnished, I found her sitting in pained placidity before the fire. So I see her still, so I see her best: facing the flame from her straight chair in the dusky, shining room, a large clean image of the "put away"—of drawers closed and locked and rest without a remedy.

"Oh, yes, they asked me to say nothing; and to please them-so long as they were there—of course I promised. But what had happened to you?"

"I only went with you for the walk," I said. "I had then to come back to meet a friend."

She showed her surprise. "A friend—YOU?"

"Oh, yes, I have a couple!" I laughed. "But did the children give you a reason?"

"For not alluding to your leaving us? Yes; they said you would like it better. Do you like it better?"

My face had made her rueful. "No, I like it worse!" But after an instant I added: "Did they say why I should like it better?"

"No; Master Miles only said, 'We must do nothing but what she likes!'"

"I wish indeed he would. And what did Flora say?"

"Miss Flora was too sweet. She said, 'Oh, of course, of course!'—and I said the same."

I thought a moment. "You were too sweet, too—I can hear you all. But nonetheless, between Miles and me, it's now all out."

"All out?" My companion stared. "But what, miss?"

"Everything. It doesn't matter. I've made up my mind. I came home, my dear," I went on, "for a talk with Miss Jessel."

I had by this time formed the habit of having Mrs. Grose literally well in hand in advance of my sounding that note; so that even now, as she bravely blinked under the signal of my word, I could keep her comparatively firm. "A talk! Do you mean she spoke?"

"It came to that. I found her, on my return, in the schoolroom."

"And what did she say?" I can hear the good woman still, and the candour of her stupefaction.

"That she suffers the torments—!"

It was this, of a truth, that made her, as she filled out my picture, gape. "Do you mean," she faltered, "—of the lost?"

"Of the lost. Of the damned. And that's why, to share them-" I faltered myself with the horror of it.

But my companion, with less imagination, kept me up. "To share them—?"

"She wants Flora." Mrs. Grose might, as I gave it to her, fairly have fallen away from me had I not been prepared. I still held her there, to show I was. "As I've told you, however, it doesn't matter."

"Because you've made up your mind? But to what?"

"To everything."

"And what do you call 'everything'?"

"Why, sending for their uncle."

"Oh, miss, in pity do," my friend broke out. "ah, but I will, I WILL! I see it's the only way. What's 'out,' as I told you, with Miles is that if he thinks I'm afraid to—and has ideas of what he gains by that—he shall see he's mistaken. Yes, yes; his uncle shall have it here from me on the spot (and before the boy himself, if necessary) that if I'm to be reproached with having done nothing again about more school—"

"Yes, miss—" my companion pressed me.

"Well, there's that awful reason."

There were now clearly so many of these for my poor colleague that she was excusable for being vague. "But—a—which?"

"Why, the letter from his old place."

"You'll show it to the master?"

"I ought to have done so on the instant."

"Oh, no!" said Mrs. Grose with decision.

"I'll put it before him," I went on inexorably, "that I can't undertake to work the question on behalf of a child who has been expelled—"

"For we've never in the least known what!" Mrs. Grose declared.

"For wickedness. For what else—when he's so clever and beautiful and perfect? Is he stupid? Is he untidy? Is he infirm? Is he ill-natured? He's exquisite—so it can be only THAT; and that would open up the whole thing. After all," I said, "it's their uncle's fault. If he left here such people—!"

"He didn't really in the least know them. The fault's mine." She had turned quite pale.

"Well, you shan't suffer," I answered.

"The children shan't!" she emphatically returned.

I was silent awhile; we looked at each other. "Then what am I to tell him?"

"You needn't tell him anything. *I'll* tell him."

I measured this. "Do you mean you'll write—?" Remembering she couldn't, I caught myself up. "How do you communicate?"

"I tell the bailiff. HE writes."

"And should you like him to write our story?"

My question had a sarcastic force that I had not fully intended, and it made her, after a moment, inconsequently break down. The tears were again in her eyes. "Ah, miss, YOU write!"

"Well—tonight," I at last answered; and on this we separated.

17

I went so far, in the evening, as to make a beginning. The weather had changed back, a great wind was abroad, and beneath the lamp, in my room, with Flora at peace beside me, I sat for a long time before a blank sheet of paper and listened to the lash of the rain and the batter of the gusts. Finally I went out, taking a candle; I crossed the passage and listened a minute at Miles's door. What, under my endless obsession, I had been impelled to listen for was some betrayal of his not being at rest, and I presently caught one, but not in the form I had expected. His voice tinkled out. "I say, you there—come in." It was a gaiety in the gloom!

I went in with my light and found him, in bed, very wide awake, but very much at his ease. "Well, what are YOU up to?" he asked with a grace of sociability in which it occurred to me that Mrs. Grose, had she been present, might have looked in vain for proof that anything was "out."

I stood over him with my candle. "How did you know I was there?"

"Why, of course I heard you. Did you fancy you made no noise? You're like a troop of cavalry!" he beautifully laughed.

"Then you weren't asleep?"

"Not much! I lie awake and think."

I had put my candle, designedly, a short way off, and then, as he held out his friendly old hand to me, had sat down on the edge of his bed. "What is it," I asked, "that you think of?"

"What in the world, my dear, but YOU?"

"Ah, the pride I take in your appreciation doesn't insist on that! I had so far rather you slept."

"Well, I think also, you know, of this queer business of ours."

I marked the coolness of his firm little hand. "Of what queer business, Miles?"

"Why, the way you bring me up. And all the rest!"

I fairly held my breath a minute, and even from my glimmering taper there was light enough to show how he smiled up at me from his pillow. "What do you mean by all the rest?"

"Oh, you know, you know!"

I could say nothing for a minute, though I felt, as I held his hand and our eyes continued to meet, that my silence had all the air of admitting his charge and that nothing in the whole world of reality was perhaps at that moment so fabulous as our actual relation. "Certainly you shall go back to school," I said, "if it be that that troubles you. But not to the old place—we must find another, a better. How could I know it did trouble you, this question, when you never told me so, never spoke of it at all?" His clear, listening face, framed in its smooth whiteness, made him for the minute as appealing as some wistful patient in a children's hospital; and I would have given, as the resemblance came to me, all I possessed on earth really to be the nurse or the sister of charity who might have helped to cure him. Well, even as it was, I perhaps might help! "Do you know you've never said a word to me about your school—I mean the old one; never mentioned it in any way?"

He seemed to wonder; he smiled with the same loveliness. But he clearly gained time; he waited, he called for guidance. "Haven't I?" It wasn't for ME to help him—it was for the thing I had met!

Something in his tone and the expression of his face, as I got this from him, set my heart aching with such a pang as it had never yet known; so unutterably touching was it to see his little brain puzzled and his little resources taxed to play, under the spell laid on him, a part of innocence and consistency. "No, never—from the hour you came back. You've never mentioned to me one of your masters, one of your comrades, nor the least little thing that ever happened to you at school. Never, little Miles—no, never—have you given me an inkling of anything that MAY have happened there.

"Therefore you can fancy how much I'm in the dark. Until you came out, that way, this morning, you had, since the first hour I saw you, scarce even made a reference to anything in your previous life. You seemed so perfectly to accept the present." It was extraordinary how my absolute conviction of his secret precocity (or whatever I might call the poison of an influence that I dared but half to phrase) made him, in spite of the faint breath of his inward trouble, appear as accessible as an older person—imposed him almost as an intellectual equal. "I thought you wanted to go on as you are."

It struck me that at this he just faintly coloured. He gave, at any rate, like a convalescent slightly fatigued, a languid shake of his head. "I don't—I don't. I want to get away."

"You're tired of Bly?"

"Oh, no, I like Bly."

"Well, then—?"

"Oh, YOU know what a boy wants!"

I felt that I didn't know so well as Miles, and I took temporary refuge. "You want to go to your uncle?"

Again, at this, with his sweet ironic face, he made a movement on the pillow. "Ah, you can't get off with that!"

I was silent a little, and it was I, now, I think, who changed colour. "My dear, I don't want to get off!"

"You can't, even if you do. You can't, you can't!"—he lay beautifully staring. "My uncle must come down, and you must completely settle things."

"If we do," I returned with some spirit, "you may be sure it will be to take you quite away."

"Well, don't you understand that that's exactly what I'm working for? You'll have to tell him—about the way you've let it all drop: you'll have to tell him a tremendous lot!"

The exultation with which he uttered this helped me somehow, for the instant, to meet him rather more. "And how much will YOU, Miles, have to tell him? There are things he'll ask you!"

He turned it over. "Very likely. But what things?"

"The things you've never told me. To make up his mind what to do with you. He can't send you back—"

"Oh, I don't want to go back!" he broke in. "I want a new field."

He said it with admirable serenity, with positive unimpeachable gaiety; and doubtless it was that very note that most evoked for me the poignancy, the unnatural childish tragedy, of his probable reappearance at the end of three months with all this bravado and still more dishonour. It overwhelmed me now that I should never be able to bear that, and it made me let myself go. I threw myself upon him and in the tenderness of my pity I embraced him. "Dear little Miles, dear little Miles—!"

My face was close to his, and he let me kiss him, simply taking it with indulgent good humour. "Well, old lady?"

"Is there nothing—nothing at all that you want to tell me?"

He turned off a little, facing round toward the wall and holding up his hand to look at as one had seen sick children look. "I've told you—I told you this morning."

Oh, I was sorry for him! "That you just want me not to worry you?"

He looked round at me now, as if in recognition of my understanding him; then ever so gently, "To let me alone," he replied.

There was even a singular little dignity in it, something that made me release him, yet, when I had slowly risen, linger beside him. God knows I never wished to harass him, but I felt that merely, at this, to turn my back on him was to abandon or, to put it more truly, to lose him. "I've just begun a letter to your uncle," I said.

"Well, then, finish it!"

I waited a minute. "What happened before?"

He gazed up at me again. "Before what?"

"Before you came back. And before you went away."

For some time he was silent, but he continued to meet my eyes. "What happened?"

It made me, the sound of the words, in which it seemed to me that I caught for the very first time a small faint quaver of consenting consciousness—it made me drop on my knees beside the bed and seize once more the chance of possessing him. "Dear little Miles, dear little Miles, if you KNEW how I want to help you! It's only that, it's nothing but that, and I'd rather die than give you a pain or do you a wrong—I'd rather die than hurt a hair of you. Dear little Miles"—oh, I brought it out now even if I SHOULD go too far—"I just want you to help me to save you!"

But I knew in a moment after this that I had gone too far. The answer to my appeal was instantaneous, but it came in the form of an extraordinary blast and chill, a gust of frozen air, and a shake of the room as great as if, in the wild wind, the casement had crashed in. The boy gave a loud, high shriek, which, lost in the rest of the shock of sound, might have seemed, indistinctly, though I was so close to him, a note either of jubilation or of terror. I jumped to my feet again and was conscious of darkness. So for a moment we remained, while I stared about me and saw that the drawn curtains were unstirred and the window tight. "Why, the candle's out!" I then cried.

"It was I who blew it, dear!" said Miles.

18

The next day, after lessons, Mrs. Grose found a moment to say to me quietly: "Have you written, miss?"

"Yes—I've written." But I didn't add—for the hour—that my letter, sealed and directed, was still in my pocket. There would be time enough to send it before the messenger should go to the village. Meanwhile there had been, on the part of my pupils, no more brilliant, more exemplary morning. It was exactly as if they had both had at heart to gloss over any recent little friction. They performed the dizziest feats of arithmetic, soaring quite out of MY feeble range, and perpetrated, in higher spirits than ever, geographical and historical jokes. It was conspicuous of course in Miles in particular that he appeared to wish to show how easily he could let me down.

This child, to my memory, really lives in a setting of beauty and misery that no words can translate; there was a distinction all his own in every impulse he revealed; never was a small natural creature, to the uninitiated eye all frankness and freedom, a more ingenious, a more extraordinary little gentleman. I had perpetually to guard against the wonder of contemplation into which my initiated view betrayed me; to check the irrelevant gaze and discouraged sigh in which I constantly both attacked and renounced the enigma of what such a little gentleman could have done that deserved a penalty. Say that, by the dark prodigy I knew, the imagination of all evil HAD been opened up to him: all the justice within me ached for the proof that it could ever have flowered into an act.

He had never, at any rate, been such a little gentleman as when, after our early dinner on this dreadful day, he came round to me and asked if I shouldn't like him, for half an hour, to play to me. David playing to Saul could never have shown a finer sense of the occasion. It was literally a charming exhibition of tact, of magnanimity, and quite tantamount to his saying outright: "The true knights we love to read about never push an advantage too far. I know what you mean now: you mean that—to be let alone yourself and not followed up—you'll cease to worry and spy upon me, won't keep me so close to you, will let me go and come. Well, I 'come,' you see—but I don't go! There'll be plenty of time for that. I do really delight in your society, and I only want to show you that I contended for a principle."

It may be imagined whether I resisted this appeal or failed to accompany him again, hand in hand, to the schoolroom. He sat down at the old piano and played as he had never played; and if there are those who think he had better have been kicking a football I can only say that I wholly agree with them. For at the end of a time that under his influence I had quite ceased to measure, I started up with a strange sense of having literally slept at my post. It was after luncheon, and by the schoolroom fire, and yet I hadn't really, in the least, slept: I had only done something much worse—I had forgotten. Where, all this time, was Flora? When I put the question to Miles, he played on a minute before answering and then could only say: "Why, my dear, how do *I* know?"—breaking moreover into a happy laugh which, immediately after, as if it were a vocal accompaniment, he prolonged into incoherent, extravagant song.

I went straight to my room, but his sister was not there; then, before going downstairs, I looked into several others. As she was nowhere about she would surely be with Mrs. Grose, whom, in the comfort of that theory, I accordingly proceeded in quest of. I found her where I had found her the evening before, but she met my quick challenge with blank, scared ignorance. She had only supposed that, after the repast, I had carried off both the children; as to which she was quite in her right, for it was the very first time I had allowed the little girl out of my sight without some special provision.

Of course now indeed she might be with the maids, so that the immediate thing was to look for her without an air of alarm. This we promptly arranged between us; but when, ten minutes later and in pursuance of our arrangement, we met in the hall, it was only to report on either side that after guarded inquiries we had altogether failed to trace her. For a minute there, apart from observation, we exchanged mute alarms, and I could feel with what high interest my friend returned me all those I had from the first given her.

"She'll be above," she presently said—"in one of the rooms you haven't searched."

"No; she's at a distance." I had made up my mind. "She has gone out."

Mrs. Grose stared. "Without a hat?"

I naturally also looked volumes. "Isn't that woman always without one?"

"She's with HER?"

"She's with HER!" I declared. "We must find them."

My hand was on my friend's arm, but she failed for the moment, confronted with such an account of the matter, to respond to my pressure. She communed, on the contrary, on the spot, with her uneasiness. "And where's Master Miles?"

"Oh, HE'S with Quint. They're in the schoolroom."

"Lord, miss!" My view, I was myself aware—and therefore I suppose my tone—had never yet reached so calm an assurance.

"The trick's played," I went on; "they've successfully worked their plan. He found the most divine little way to keep me quiet while she went off."

"'Divine'?" Mrs. Grose bewilderedly echoed.

"Infernal, then!" I almost cheerfully rejoined. "He has provided for himself as well. But come!"

She had helplessly gloomed at the upper regions. "You leave him—?"

"So long with Quint? Yes—I don't mind that now."

She always ended, at these moments, by getting possession of my hand, and in this manner she could at present still stay me. But after gasping an instant at my sudden resignation, "Because of your letter?" she eagerly brought out.

I quickly, by way of answer, felt for my letter, drew it forth, held it up, and then, freeing myself, went and laid it on the great hall table. "Luke will take it," I said as I came back. I reached the house door and opened it; I was already on the steps.

My companion still demurred: the storm of the night and the early morning had dropped, but the afternoon was damp and gray. I came down to the drive while she stood in the doorway. "You go with nothing on?"

"What do I care when the child has nothing? I can't wait to dress," I cried, "and if you must do so, I leave you. Try meanwhile, yourself, upstairs."

"With THEM?" Oh, on this, the poor woman promptly joined me!

19

We went straight to the lake, as it was called at Bly, and I daresay rightly called, though I reflect that it may in fact have been a sheet of water less remarkable than it appeared to my untraveled eyes. My acquaintance with sheets of water was small, and the pool of Bly, at all events on the few occasions of my consenting, under the protection of my pupils, to affront its surface in the old flat-bottomed boat moored there for our use, had impressed me both with its extent and its agitation.

The usual place of embarkation was half a mile from the house, but I had an intimate conviction that, wherever Flora might be, she was not near home. She had not given me the slip for any small adventure, and, since the day of the very great one that I had shared with her by the pond, I had been aware, in our walks, of the quarter to which she most inclined. This was why I had now given to Mrs. Grose's steps so marked a direction—a direction that made her, when she perceived it, oppose a resistance that showed me she was freshly mystified. "You're going to the water, Miss?—you think she's IN—?"

"She may be, though the depth is, I believe, nowhere very great. But what I judge most likely is that she's on the spot from which, the other day, we saw together what I told you."

"When she pretended not to see—?"

"With that astounding self-possession? I've always been sure she wanted to go back alone. And now her brother has managed it for her."

Mrs. Grose still stood where she had stopped. "You suppose they really TALK of them?"

"I could meet this with a confidence! They say things that, if we heard them, would simply appal us."

"And if she IS there—"

"Yes?"

"Then Miss Jessel is?"

"Beyond a doubt. You shall see."

"Oh, thank you!" my friend cried, planted so firm that, taking it in, I went straight on without her. By the time I reached the pool, however, she was close behind me, and I knew that, whatever, to her apprehension, might befall me, the exposure of my society struck her as her least danger. She exhaled a moan of relief as we at last came in sight of the greater part of the water without a sight of the child. There was no trace of Flora on that nearer side of the bank where my observation of her had been most startling, and none on the opposite edge, where, save for a margin of some twenty yards, a thick copse came down to the water.

The pond, oblong in shape, had a width so scant compared to its length that, with its ends out of view, it might have been taken for a scant river. We looked at the empty expanse, and then I felt the suggestion of my friend's eyes. I knew what she meant and I replied with a negative headshake.

"No, no; wait! She has taken the boat."

My companion stared at the vacant mooring place and then again across the lake. "Then where is it?"

"Our not seeing it is the strongest of proofs. She has used it to go over, and then has managed to hide it."

"All alone—that child?"

"She's not alone, and at such times she's not a child: she's an old, old woman." I scanned all the visible shore while Mrs. Grose took again, into the queer element I offered her, one of her plunges of submission; then I pointed out that the boat might perfectly be in a small refuge formed by one of the recesses of the pool, an indentation masked, for the hither side, by a projection of the bank and by a clump of trees growing close to the water.

"But if the boat's there, where on earth's SHE?" my colleague anxiously asked.

"That's exactly what we must learn." And I started to walk further.

"By going all the way round?"

"Certainly, far as it is. It will take us but ten minutes, but it's far enough to have made the child prefer not to walk. She went straight over."

"Laws!" cried my friend again; the chain of my logic was ever too much for her. It dragged her at my heels even now, and when we had got halfway round—a devious, tiresome process, on ground much broken and by a path choked with overgrowth—I paused to give her breath. I sustained her with a grateful arm, assuring her that she might hugely help me; and this started us afresh, so that in the course of but few minutes more we reached a point from which we found the boat to be where I had supposed it.

It had been intentionally left as much as possible out of sight and was tied to one of the stakes of a fence that came, just there, down to the brink and that had been an assistance to disembarking. I recognized, as I looked at the pair of short, thick oars, quite safely drawn up, the prodigious character of the feat for a little girl; but I had lived, by this time, too long among wonders and had panted to too many livelier measures. There was a gate in the fence, through which we passed, and that brought us, after a trifling interval, more into the open. Then, "There she is!" we both exclaimed at once.

Flora, a short way off, stood before us on the grass and smiled as if her performance was now complete. The next thing she did, however, was to stoop straight down and pluck—quite as if it were all she was there for—a big, ugly spray of withered fern. I instantly became sure she had just come out of the copse. She waited for us, not herself taking a step, and I was conscious of the rare solemnity with which we presently approached her. She smiled and smiled, and we met; but it was all done in a silence by this time flagrantly ominous. Mrs. Grose was the first to break the spell: she threw herself on her knees and, drawing the child to her breast, clasped in a long embrace the little tender, yielding body.

While this dumb convulsion lasted I could only watch it—which I did the more intently when I saw Flora's face peep at me over our companion's shoulder. It was serious now—the flicker had left it; but it strengthened the pang with which I at that moment envied Mrs. Grose the simplicity of HER relation. Still, all this while, nothing more passed between us save that Flora had let her foolish fern again drop to the ground. What she and I had virtually said to each other was that pretexts were useless now. When Mrs. Grose finally got up she kept the child's hand, so that the two were still before me; and the singular reticence of our communion was even more marked in the frank look she launched me. "I'll be hanged," it said, "if *I'll* speak!"

It was Flora who, gazing all over me in candid wonder, was the first. She was struck with our bareheaded aspect. "Why, where are your things?"

"Where yours are, my dear!" I promptly returned.

She had already got back her gaiety, and appeared to take this as an answer quite sufficient. "And where's Miles?" she went on.

There was something in the small valour of it that quite finished me: these three words from her were, in a flash like the glitter of a drawn blade, the jostle of the cup that my hand, for weeks and weeks, had held high and full to the brim that now, even before speaking, I felt overflow in a deluge. "I'll tell you if you'll tell ME—" I heard myself say, then heard the tremor in which it broke.

"Well, what?"

Mrs. Grose's suspense blazed at me, but it was too late now, and I brought the thing out handsomely. "Where, my pet, is Miss Jessel?"

20

Just as in the churchyard with Miles, the whole thing was upon us. Much as I had made of the fact that this name had never once, between us, been sounded, the quick, smitten glare with which the child's face now received it fairly likened my breach of the silence to the smash of a pane of glass. It added to the interposing cry, as if to stay the blow, that Mrs. Grose, at the same instant, uttered over my violence—the shriek of a creature scared, or rather wounded, which, in turn, within a few seconds, was completed by a gasp of my own. I seized my colleague's arm. "She's there, she's there!"

Miss Jessel stood before us on the opposite bank exactly as she had stood the other time, and I remember, strangely, as the first feeling now produced in me, my thrill of joy at having brought on a proof. She was there, and I was justified; she was there, and I was neither cruel nor mad. She was there for poor scared Mrs. Grose, but she was there most for Flora; and no moment of my monstrous time was perhaps so extraordinary as that in which I consciously threw out to her—with the sense that, pale and ravenous demon as she was, she would catch and understand it—an inarticulate message of gratitude. She rose erect on the spot my friend and I had lately quitted, and there was not, in all the long reach of her desire, an inch of her evil that fell short.

This first vividness of vision and emotion were things of a few seconds, during which Mrs. Grose's dazed blink across to where I pointed struck me as a sovereign sign that she too at last saw, just as it carried my own eyes precipitately to the child. The revelation then of the manner in which Flora was affected startled me, in truth, far more than it would have done to find her also merely agitated, for direct dismay was of course not what I had expected. Prepared and on her guard as our pursuit had actually made her, she would repress every betrayal; and I was therefore shaken, on the spot, by my first glimpse of the particular one for which I had not allowed.

To see her, without a convulsion of her small pink face, not even feign to glance in the direction of the prodigy I announced, but only, instead of that, turn at ME an expression of hard, still gravity, an expression absolutely new and unprecedented and that appeared to read and accuse and judge me—this was a stroke that somehow converted the little girl herself into the very presence that could make me quail. I quailed even though my certitude that she thoroughly saw was never greater than at that instant, and in the immediate need to defend myself I called it passionately to witness.

"She's there, you little unhappy thing—there, there, THERE, and you see her as well as you see me!" I had said shortly before to Mrs. Grose that she was not at these times a child, but an old, old woman, and that description of her could not have been more strikingly confirmed than in the way in which, for all answer to this, she simply showed me, without a concession, an admission, of her eyes, a countenance of deeper and deeper, of indeed suddenly quite fixed, reprobation. I was by this time—if I can put the whole thing at all together—more appalled at what I may properly call her manner than at anything else, though it was simultaneously with this that I became aware of having Mrs. Grose also, and very formidably, to reckon with. My elder companion, the next moment, at any rate, blotted out everything but her own flushed face and her loud, shocked protest, a burst of high disapproval. "What a dreadful turn, to be sure, miss! Where on earth do you see anything?"

I could only grasp her more quickly yet, for even while she spoke the hideous plain presence stood undimmed and undaunted. It had already lasted a minute, and it lasted while I continued, seizing my colleague, quite thrusting her at it and presenting her to it, to insist with my pointing hand. "You don't see her exactly as WE see?—you mean to say you don't now—NOW? She's as big as a blazing fire! Only look, dearest woman, LOOK—!" She looked, even as I did, and gave me, with her deep groan of negation, repulsion, compassion—the mixture with her pity of her relief at her exemption—a sense, touching to me even then, that she would have backed me up if she could.

I might well have needed that, for with this hard blow of the proof that her eyes were hopelessly sealed I felt my own situation horribly crumble, I felt—I saw—my livid predecessor press, from her position, on my defeat, and I was conscious, more than all, of what I should have from this instant to deal with in the astounding little attitude of Flora. Into this attitude Mrs. Grose immediately and violently entered, breaking, even while there pierced through my sense of ruin a prodigious private triumph, into breathless reassurance.

"She isn't there, little lady, and nobody's there—and you never see nothing, my sweet! How can poor Miss Jessel—when poor Miss Jessel's dead and buried? WE know, don't we, love?"—and she appealed, blundering in, to the child. "It's all a mere mistake and a worry and a joke—and we'll go home as fast as we can!"

Our companion, on this, had responded with a strange, quick primness of propriety, and they were again, with Mrs. Grose on her feet, united, as it were, in pained opposition to me. Flora continued to fix me with her small mask of reprobation, and even at that minute I prayed God to forgive me for seeming to see that, as she stood there holding tight to our friend's dress, her incomparable childish beauty had suddenly failed, had quite vanished.

I've said it already—she was literally, she was hideously, hard; she had turned common and almost ugly. "I don't know what you mean. I see nobody. I see nothing. I never HAVE. I think you're cruel. I don't like you!" Then, after this deliverance, which might have been that of a vulgarly pert little girl in the street, she hugged Mrs. Grose more closely and buried in her skirts the dreadful little face.

In this position she produced an almost furious wail. "Take me away, take me away—oh, take me away from HER!"

"From ME?" I panted.

"From you—from you!" she cried.

Even Mrs. Grose looked across at me dismayed, while I had nothing to do but communicate again with the figure that, on the opposite bank, without a movement, as rigidly still as if catching, beyond the interval, our voices, was as vividly there for my disaster as it was not there for my service. The wretched child had spoken exactly as if she had got from some outside source each of her stabbing little words, and I could therefore, in the full despair of all I had to accept, but sadly shake my head at her.

"If I had ever doubted, all my doubt would at present have gone. I've been living with the miserable truth, and now it has only too much closed round me. Of course I've lost you: I've interfered, and you've seen—under HER dictation"—with which I faced, over the pool again, our infernal witness—"the easy and perfect way to meet it. I've done my best, but I've lost you. Goodbye." For Mrs. Grose I had an imperative, an almost frantic "Go, go!" before which, in infinite distress, but mutely possessed of the little girl and clearly convinced, in spite of her blindness, that something awful had occurred and some collapse engulfed us, she retreated, by the way we had come, as fast as she could move.

Of what first happened when I was left alone I had no subsequent memory. I only knew that at the end of, I suppose, a quarter of an hour, an odorous dampness and roughness, chilling and piercing my trouble, had made me understand that I must have thrown myself, on my face, on the ground and given way to a wildness of grief. I must have lain there long and cried and sobbed, for when I raised my head the day was almost done. I got up and looked a moment, through the twilight, at the gray pool and its blank, haunted edge, and then I took, back to the house, my dreary and difficult course.

When I reached the gate in the fence the boat, to my surprise, was gone, so that I had a fresh reflection to make on Flora's extraordinary command of the situation. She passed that night, by the most tacit, and I should add, were not the word so grotesque a false note, the happiest of arrangements, with Mrs. Grose. I saw neither of them on my return, but, on the other hand, as by an ambiguous compensation, I saw a great deal of Miles. I saw—I can use no other phrase—so much of him that it was as if it were more than it had ever been.

No evening I had passed at Bly had the portentous quality of this one; in spite of which—and in spite also of the deeper depths of consternation that had opened beneath my feet—there was literally, in the ebbing actual, an extraordinarily sweet sadness. On reaching the house I had never so much as looked for the boy; I had simply gone straight to my room to change what I was wearing and to take in, at a glance, much material testimony to Flora's rupture. Her little belongings had all been removed.

When later, by the schoolroom fire, I was served with tea by the usual maid, I indulged, on the article of my other pupil, in no inquiry whatever. He had his freedom now—he might have it to the end! Well, he did have it; and it consisted—in part at least—of his coming in at about eight o'clock and sitting down with me in silence. On the removal of the tea things I had blown out the candles and drawn my chair closer: I was conscious of a mortal coldness and felt as if I should never again be warm. So, when he appeared, I was sitting in the glow with my thoughts. He paused a moment by the door as if to look at me; then—as if to share them—came to the other side of the hearth and sank into a chair. We sat there in absolute stillness; yet he wanted, I felt, to be with me.

21

Before a new day, in my room, had fully broken, my eyes opened to Mrs. Grose, who had come to my bedside with worse news. Flora was so markedly feverish that an illness was perhaps at hand; she had passed a night of extreme unrest, a night agitated above all by fears that had for their subject not in the least her former, but wholly her present, governess. It was not against the possible re-entrance of Miss Jessel on the scene that she protested—it was conspicuously and passionately against mine. I was promptly on my feet of course, and with an immense deal to ask; the more that my friend had discernibly now girded her loins to meet me once more. This I felt as soon as I had put to her the question of her sense of the child's sincerity as against my own. "She persists in denying to you that she saw, or has ever seen, anything?"

My visitor's trouble, truly, was great. "Ah, miss, it isn't a matter on which I can push her! Yet it isn't either, I must say, as if I much needed to. It has made her, every inch of her, quite old."

"Oh, I see her perfectly from here. She resents, for all the world like some high little personage, the imputation on her truthfulness and, as it were, her respectability. 'Miss Jessel indeed—SHE!' Ah, she's 'respectable,' the chit! The impression she gave me there yesterday was, I assure you, the very strangest of all; it was quite beyond any of the others. I DID put my foot in it! She'll never speak to me again."

Hideous and obscure as it all was, it held Mrs. Grose briefly silent; then she granted my point with a frankness which, I made sure, had more behind it. "I think indeed, miss, she never will. She do have a grand manner about it!"

"And that manner"—I summed it up—"is practically what's the matter with her now!"

Oh, that manner, I could see in my visitor's face, and not a little else besides! "She asks me every three minutes if I think you're coming in."

"I see—I see." I, too, on my side, had so much more than worked it out. "Has she said to you since yesterday—except to repudiate her familiarity with anything so dreadful—a single other word about Miss Jessel?"

"Not one, miss. And of course you know," my friend added, "I took it from her, by the lake, that, just then and there at least, there WAS nobody."

"Rather! and, naturally, you take it from her still."

"I don't contradict her. What else can I do?"

"Nothing in the world! You've the cleverest little person to deal with. They've made them—their two friends, I mean—still cleverer even than nature did; for it was wondrous material to play on! Flora has now her grievance, and she'll work it to the end."

"Yes, miss; but to WHAT end?"

"Why, that of dealing with me to her uncle. She'll make me out to him the lowest creature—!"

I winced at the fair show of the scene in Mrs. Grose's face; she looked for a minute as if she sharply saw them together. "And him who thinks so well of you!"

"He has an odd way—it comes over me now," I laughed,"—of proving it! But that doesn't matter. What Flora wants, of course, is to get rid of me."

My companion bravely concurred. "Never again to so much as look at you."

"So that what you've come to me now for," I asked, "is to speed me on my way?" Before she had time to reply, however, I had her in check. "I've a better idea—the result of my reflections. My going WOULD seem the right thing, and on Sunday I was terribly near it. Yet that won't do. It's YOU who must go. You must take Flora."

My visitor, at this, did speculate. "But where in the world—?"

"Away from here. Away from THEM. Away, even most of all, now, from me. Straight to her uncle."

"Only to tell on you—?"

"No, not 'only'! To leave me, in addition, with my remedy."

She was still vague. "And what IS your remedy?"

"Your loyalty, to begin with. And then Miles's."

She looked at me hard. "Do you think he—?"

"Won't, if he has the chance, turn on me? Yes, I venture still to think it. At all events, I want to try. Get off with his sister as soon as possible and leave me with him alone." I was amazed, myself, at the spirit I had still in reserve, and therefore perhaps a trifle the more disconcerted at the way in which, in spite of this fine example of it, she hesitated. "There's one thing, of course," I went on: "they mustn't, before she goes, see each other for three seconds." Then it came over me that, in spite of Flora's presumable sequestration from the instant of her return from the pool, it might already be too late. "Do you mean," I anxiously asked, "that they HAVE met?"

At this she quite flushed. "Ah, miss, I'm not such a fool as that! If I've been obliged to leave her three or four times, it has been each time with one of the maids, and at present, though she's alone, she's locked in safe. And yet—and yet!" There were too many things.

"And yet what?"

"Well, are you so sure of the little gentleman?"

"I'm not sure of anything but YOU. But I have, since last evening, a new hope. I think he wants to give me an opening. I do believe that—poor little exquisite wretch!—he wants to speak. Last evening, in the firelight and the silence, he sat with me for two hours as if it were just coming."

Mrs. Grose looked hard, through the window, at the gray, gathering day. "And did it come?"

"No, though I waited and waited, I confess it didn't, and it was without a breach of the silence or so much as a faint allusion to his sister's condition and absence that we at last kissed for good night. All the same," I continued, "I can't, if her uncle sees her, consent to his seeing her brother without my having given the boy—and most of all because things have got so bad—a little more time."

My friend appeared on this ground more reluctant than I could quite understand. "What do you mean by more time?"

"Well, a day or two—really to bring it out. He'll then be on MY side—of which you see the importance. If nothing comes, I shall only fail, and you will, at the worst, have helped me by doing, on your arrival in town, whatever you may have found possible." So I put it before her, but she continued for a little so inscrutably embarrassed that I came again to her aid. "Unless, indeed," I wound up, "you really want NOT to go."

I could see it, in her face, at last clear itself; she put out her hand to me as a pledge. "I'll go—I'll go. I'll go this morning."

I wanted to be very just. "If you SHOULD wish still to wait, I would engage she shouldn't see me."

"No, no: it's the place itself. She must leave it." She held me a moment with heavy eyes, then brought out the rest. "Your idea's the right one. I myself, miss—"

"Well?"

"I can't stay."

The look she gave me with it made me jump at possibilities. "You mean that, since yesterday, you HAVE seen—?"

She shook her head with dignity. "I've HEARD—!"

"Heard?"

"From that child—horrors! There!" she sighed with tragic relief. "On my honour, miss, she says things—!" But at this evocation she broke down; she dropped, with a sudden sob, upon my sofa and, as I had seen her do before, gave way to all the grief of it.

It was quite in another manner that I, for my part, let myself go. "Oh, thank God!"

She sprang up again at this, drying her eyes with a groan. "'Thank God'?"

"It so justifies me!"

"It does that, miss!"

I couldn't have desired more emphasis, but I just hesitated. "She's so horrible?"

I saw my colleague scarce knew how to put it. "Really shocking."

"And about me?"

"About you, miss—since you must have it. It's beyond everything, for a young lady; and I can't think wherever she must have picked up—"

"The appalling language she applied to me? I can, then!" I broke in with a laugh that was doubtless significant enough.

It only, in truth, left my friend still more grave. "Well, perhaps I ought to also—since I've heard some of it before! Yet I can't bear it," the poor woman went on while, with the same movement, she glanced, on my dressing table, at the face of my watch. "But I must go back."

I kept her, however. "Ah, if you can't bear it—!"

"How can I stop with her, you mean? Why, just FOR that: to get her away. Far from this," she pursued, "far from THEM-"

"She may be different? She may be free?" I seized her almost with joy. "Then, in spite of yesterday, you BELIEVE—"

"In such doings?" Her simple description of them required, in the light of her expression, to be carried no further, and she gave me the whole thing as she had never done. "I believe."

Yes, it was a joy, and we were still shoulder to shoulder: if I might continue sure of that I should care but little what else happened. My support in the presence of disaster would be the same as it had been in my early need of confidence, and if my friend would answer for my honesty, I would answer for all the rest. On the point of taking leave of her, nonetheless, I was to some extent embarrassed. "There's one thing, of course—it occurs to me—to remember. My letter, giving the alarm, will have reached town before you."

I now perceived still more how she had been beating about the bush and how weary at last it had made her. "Your letter won't have got there. Your letter never went."

"What then became of it?"

"Goodness knows! Master Miles—"

"Do you mean HE took it?" I gasped.

She hung fire, but she overcame her reluctance. "I mean that I saw yesterday, when I came back with Miss Flora, that it wasn't where you had put it. Later in the evening I had the chance to question Luke, and he declared that he had neither noticed nor touched it." We could only exchange, on this, one of our deeper mutual soundings, and it was Mrs. Grose who first brought up the plumb with an almost elated "You see!"

"Yes, I see that if Miles took it instead he probably will have read it and destroyed it."

"And don't you see anything else?"

I faced her a moment with a sad smile. "It strikes me that by this time your eyes are open even wider than mine."

They proved to be so indeed, but she could still blush, almost, to show it. "I make out now what he must have done at school." And she gave, in her simple sharpness, an almost droll disillusioned nod. "He stole!"

I turned it over—I tried to be more judicial. "Well—perhaps."

She looked as if she found me unexpectedly calm. "He stole LETTERS!"

She couldn't know my reasons for a calmness after all pretty shallow; so I showed them off as I might. "I hope then it was to more purpose than in this case! The note, at any rate, that I put on the table yesterday," I pursued, "will have given him so scant an advantage—for it contained only the bare demand for an interview—that he is already much ashamed of having gone so far for so little, and that what he had on his mind last evening was precisely the need of confession." I seemed to myself, for the instant, to have mastered it, to see it all. "Leave us, leave us"—I was already, at the door, hurrying her off. "I'll get it out of him. He'll meet me—he'll confess. If he confesses, he's saved. And if he's saved—"

"Then YOU are?" The dear woman kissed me on this, and I took her farewell. "I'll save you without him!" she cried as she went.

22

Yet it was when she had got off—and I missed her on the spot—that the great pinch really came. If I had counted on what it would give me to find myself alone with Miles, I speedily perceived, at least, that it would give me a measure. No hour of my stay in fact was so assailed with apprehensions as that of my coming down to learn that the carriage containing Mrs. Grose and my younger pupil had already rolled out of the gates. Now

I WAS, I said to myself, face to face with the elements, and for much of the rest of the day, while I fought my weakness, I could consider that I had been supremely rash. It was a tighter place still than I had yet turned round in; all the more that, for the first time, I could see in the aspect of others a confused reflection of the crisis. What had happened naturally caused them all to stare; there was too little of the explained, throw out whatever we might, in the suddenness of my colleague's act.

The maids and the men looked blank; the effect of which on my nerves was an aggravation until I saw the necessity of making it a positive aid. It was precisely, in short, by just clutching the helm that I avoided total wreck; and I dare say that, to bear up at all, I became, that morning, very grand and very dry. I welcomed the consciousness that I was charged with much to do, and I caused it to be known as well that, left thus to myself, I was quite remarkably firm. I wandered with that manner, for the next hour or two, all over the place and looked, I have no doubt, as if I were ready for any onset. So, for the benefit of whom it might concern, I paraded with a sick heart.

The person it appeared least to concern proved to be, till dinner, little Miles himself. My perambulations had given me, meanwhile, no glimpse of him, but they had tended to make more public the change taking place in our relation as a consequence of his having at the piano, the day before, kept me, in Flora's interest, so beguiled and befooled. The stamp of publicity had of course been fully given by her confinement and departure, and the change itself was now ushered in by our non-observance of the regular custom of the schoolroom.

He had already disappeared when, on my way down, I pushed open his door, and I learned below that he had breakfasted—in the presence of a couple of the maids—with Mrs. Grose and his sister. He had then gone out, as he said, for a stroll; than which nothing, I reflected, could better have expressed his frank view of the abrupt transformation of my office. What he would not permit this office to consist of was yet to be settled: there was a queer relief, at all events—I mean for myself in especial—in the renouncement of one pretension.

If so much had sprung to the surface, I scarce put it too strongly in saying that what had perhaps sprung highest was the absurdity of our prolonging the fiction that I had anything more to teach him. It sufficiently stuck out that, by tacit little tricks in which even more than myself he carried out the care for my dignity, I had had to appeal to him to let me off straining to meet him on the ground of his true capacity.

He had at any rate his freedom now; I was never to touch it again; as I had amply shown, moreover, when, on his joining me in the schoolroom the previous night, I had uttered, on the subject of the interval just concluded, neither challenge nor hint. I had too much, from this moment, my other ideas. Yet when he at last arrived, the difficulty of applying them, the accumulations of my problem, were brought straight home to me by the beautiful little presence on which what had occurred had as yet, for the eye, dropped neither stain nor shadow.

To mark, for the house, the high state I cultivated I decreed that my meals with the boy should be served, as we called it, downstairs; so that I had been awaiting him in the ponderous pomp of the room outside of the window of which I had had from Mrs. Grose, that first scared Sunday, my flash of something it would scarce have done to call light. Here at present I felt afresh—for I had felt it again and again—how my equilibrium depended on the success of my rigid will, the will to shut my eyes as tight as possible to the truth that what I had to deal with was, revoltingly, against nature.

I could only get on at all by taking "nature" into my confidence and my account, by treating my monstrous ordeal as a push in a direction unusual, of course, and unpleasant, but demanding, after all, for a fair front, only another turn of the screw of ordinary human virtue. No attempt, nonetheless, could well require more tact than just this attempt to supply, one's self, ALL the nature. How could I put even a little of that article into a suppression of reference to what had occurred? How, on the other hand, could I make reference without a new plunge into the hideous obscure?

Well, a sort of answer, after a time, had come to me, and it was so far confirmed as that I was met, incontestably, by the quickened vision of what was rare in my little companion. It was indeed as if he had found even now—as he had so often found at lessons—still some other delicate way to ease me off. Wasn't there light in the fact which, as we shared our solitude, broke out with a specious glitter it had never yet quite worn?—the fact that (opportunity aiding, precious opportunity which had now come) it would be preposterous, with a child so endowed, to forego the help one might wrest from absolute intelligence?

What had his intelligence been given him for but to save him? Mightn't one, to reach his mind, risk the stretch of an angular arm over his character? It was as if, when we were face to face in the dining room, he had literally shown me the way. The roast mutton was on the table, and I had dispensed with attendance. Miles, before he sat down, stood a moment with his hands in his pockets and looked at the joint, on which he seemed on the point of passing some humorous judgment. But what he presently produced was: "I say, my dear, is she really very awfully ill?"

"Little Flora? Not so bad but that she'll presently be better. London will set her up. Bly had ceased to agree with her. Come here and take your mutton."

He alertly obeyed me, carried the plate carefully to his seat, and, when he was established, went on. "Did Bly disagree with her so terribly suddenly?"

"Not so suddenly as you might think. One had seen it coming on."

"Then why didn't you get her off before?"

"Before what?"

"Before she became too ill to travel."

I found myself prompt. "She's NOT too ill to travel: she only might have become so if she had stayed. This was just the moment to seize. The journey will dissipate the influence"—oh, I was grand!—"and carry it off."

"I see, I see"—Miles, for that matter, was grand, too. He settled to his repast with the charming little "table manner" that, from the day of his arrival, had relieved me of all grossness of admonition. Whatever he had been driven from school for, it was not for ugly feeding. He was irreproachable, as always, today; but he was unmistakably more conscious. He was discernibly trying to take for granted more things than he found, without assistance, quite easy; and he dropped into peaceful silence while he felt his situation.

Our meal was of the briefest—mine a vain pretence, and I had the things immediately removed. While this was done Miles stood again with his hands in his little pockets and his back to me—stood and looked out of the wide window through which, that other day, I had seen what pulled me up. We continued silent while the maid was with us—as silent, it whimsically occurred to me, as some young couple who, on their wedding journey, at the inn, feel shy in the presence of the waiter. He turned round only when the waiter had left us. "Well—so we're alone!"

23

"Oh, more or less." I fancy my smile was pale. "Not absolutely. We shouldn't like that!" I went on.

"No—I suppose we shouldn't. Of course we have the others."

"We have the others—we have indeed the others," I concurred.

"Yet even though we have them," he returned, still with his hands in his pockets and planted there in front of me, "they don't much count, do they?"

I made the best of it, but I felt wan. "It depends on what you call 'much'!"

"Yes"—with all accommodation—"everything depends!" On this, however, he faced to the window again and presently reached it with his vague, restless, cogitating step. He remained there awhile, with his forehead against the glass, in contemplation of the stupid shrubs I knew and the dull things of November. I had always my hypocrisy of "work," behind which, now, I gained the sofa. Steadying myself with it there as I had repeatedly done at those moments of torment that I have described as the moments of my knowing the children to be given to something from which I was barred, I sufficiently obeyed my habit of being prepared for the worst.

But an extraordinary impression dropped on me as I extracted a meaning from the boy's embarrassed back—none other than the impression that I was not barred now. This inference grew in a few minutes to sharp intensity and seemed bound up with the direct perception that it was positively HE who was. The frames and squares of the great window were a kind of image, for him, of a kind of failure. I felt that I saw him, at any rate, shut in or shut out. He was admirable, but not comfortable: I took it in with a throb of hope. Wasn't he looking, through the haunted pane, for something he couldn't see?—and wasn't it the first time in the whole business that he had known such a lapse?

The first, the very first: I found it a splendid portent. It made him anxious, though he watched himself; he had been anxious all day and, even while in his usual sweet little manner he sat at table, had needed all his small strange genius to give it a gloss. When he at last turned round to meet me, it was almost as if this genius had succumbed. "Well, I think I'm glad Bly agrees with ME!"

"You would certainly seem to have seen, these twenty-four hours, a good deal more of it than for some time before. I hope," I went on bravely, "that you've been enjoying yourself."

"Oh, yes, I've been ever so far; all round about—miles and miles away. I've never been so free."

He had really a manner of his own, and I could only try to keep up with him. "Well, do you like it?"

He stood there smiling; then at last he put into two words-"Do YOU?"—more discrimination than I had ever heard two words contain. Before I had time to deal with that, however, he continued as if with the sense that this was an impertinence to be softened. "Nothing could be more charming than the way you take it, for of course if we're alone together now it's you that are alone most. But I hope," he threw in, "you don't particularly mind!"

"Having to do with you?" I asked. "My dear child, how can I help minding? Though I've renounced all claim to your company—you're so beyond me—I at least greatly enjoy it. What else should I stay on for?"

He looked at me more directly, and the expression of his face, graver now, struck me as the most beautiful I had ever found in it. "You stay on just for THAT?"

"Certainly. I stay on as your friend and from the tremendous interest I take in you till something can be done for you that may be more worth your while. That needn't surprise you." My voice trembled so that I felt it impossible to suppress the shake. "Don't you remember how I told you, when I came and sat on your bed the night of the storm, that there was nothing in the world I wouldn't do for you?"

"Yes, yes!" He, on his side, more and more visibly nervous, had a tone to master; but he was so much more successful than I that, laughing out through his gravity, he could pretend we were pleasantly jesting. "Only that, I think, was to get me to do something for YOU!"

"It was partly to get you to do something," I conceded. "But, you know, you didn't do it."

"Oh, yes," he said with the brightest superficial eagerness, "you wanted me to tell you something."

"That's it. Out, straight out. What you have on your mind, you know."

"Ah, then, is THAT what you've stayed over for?"

He spoke with a gaiety through which I could still catch the finest little quiver of resentful passion; but I can't begin to express the effect upon me of an implication of surrender even so faint. It was as if what I had yearned for had come at last only to astonish me. "Well, yes—I may as well make a clean breast of it, it was precisely for that."

He waited so long that I supposed it for the purpose of repudiating the assumption on which my action had been founded; but what he finally said was: "Do you mean now—here?"

"There couldn't be a better place or time." He looked round him uneasily, and I had the rare—oh, the queer!—impression of the very first symptom I had seen in him of the approach of immediate fear. It was as if he were suddenly afraid of me—which struck me indeed as perhaps the best thing to make him. Yet in the very pang of the effort I felt it vain to try sternness, and I heard myself the next instant so gentle as to be almost grotesque. "You want so to go out again?"

"Awfully!" He smiled at me heroically, and the touching little bravery of it was enhanced by his actually flushing with pain. He had picked up his hat, which he had brought in, and stood twirling it in a way that gave me, even as I was just nearly reaching port, a perverse horror of what I was doing. To do it in ANY way was an act of violence, for what did it consist of but the obtrusion of the idea of grossness and guilt on a small helpless creature who had been for me a revelation of the possibilities of beautiful intercourse?

Wasn't it base to create for a being so exquisite a mere alien awkwardness? I suppose I now read into our situation a clearness it couldn't have had at the time, for I seem to see our poor eyes already lighted with some spark of a prevision of the anguish that was to come. So we circled about, with terrors and scruples, like fighters not daring to close. But it was for each other we feared! That kept us a little longer suspended and unbruised. "I'll tell you everything," Miles said—"I mean I'll tell you anything you like. You'll stay on with me, and we shall both be all right, and I WILL tell you—I WILL. But not now."

"Why not now?"

My insistence turned him from me and kept him once more at his window in a silence during which, between us, you might have heard a pin drop. Then he was before me again with the air of a person for whom, outside, someone who had frankly to be reckoned with was waiting. "I have to see Luke."

I had not yet reduced him to quite so vulgar a lie, and I felt proportionately ashamed. But, horrible as it was, his lies made up my truth. I achieved thoughtfully a few loops of my knitting. "Well, then, go to Luke, and I'll wait for what you promise. Only, in return for that, satisfy, before you leave me, one very much smaller request."

He looked as if he felt he had succeeded enough to be able still a little to bargain. "Very much smaller—?"

"Yes, a mere fraction of the whole. Tell me"—oh, my work preoccupied me, and I was offhand!—"if, yesterday afternoon, from the table in the hall, you took, you know, my letter."

24

My sense of how he received this suffered for a minute from something that I can describe only as a fierce split of my attention—a stroke that at first, as I sprang straight up, reduced me to the mere blind movement of getting hold of him, drawing him close, and, while I just fell for support against the nearest piece of furniture, instinctively keeping him with his back to the window. The appearance was full upon us that I had already had to deal with here: Peter Quint had come into view like a sentinel before a prison. The next thing I saw was that, from outside, he had reached the window, and then I knew that, close to the glass and glaring in through it, he offered once more to the room his white face of damnation.

It represents but grossly what took place within me at the sight to say that on the second my decision was made; yet I believe that no woman so overwhelmed ever in so short a time recovered her grasp of the ACT. It came to me in the very horror of the immediate presence that the act would be, seeing and facing what I saw and faced, to keep the boy himself unaware. The inspiration—I can call it by no other name—was that I felt how voluntarily, how transcendently, I MIGHT. It was like fighting with a demon for a human soul, and when I had fairly so appraised it I saw how the human soul—held out, in the tremor of my hands, at arm's length—had a perfect dew of sweat on a lovely childish forehead. The face that was close to mine was as white as the face against the glass, and out of it presently came a sound, not low nor weak, but as if from much further away, that I drank like a waft of fragrance.

"Yes—I took it."

At this, with a moan of joy, I enfolded, I drew him close; and while I held him to my breast, where I could feel in the sudden fever of his little body the tremendous pulse of his little heart, I kept my eyes on the thing at the window and saw it move and shift its posture. I have likened it to a sentinel, but its slow wheel, for a moment, was rather the prowl of a baffled beast. My present quickened courage, however, was such that, not too much to let it through, I had to shade, as it were, my flame. Meanwhile the glare of the face was again at the window, the scoundrel fixed as if to watch and wait. It was the very confidence that I might now defy him, as well as the positive certitude, by this time, of the child's unconsciousness, that made me go on. "What did you take it for?"

"To see what you said about me."

"You opened the letter?"

"I opened it."

My eyes were now, as I held him off a little again, on Miles's own face, in which the collapse of mockery showed me how complete was the ravage of uneasiness. What was prodigious was that at last, by my success, his sense was sealed and his communication stopped: he knew that he was in presence, but knew not of what, and knew still less that I also was and that I did know. And what did this strain of trouble matter when my eyes went back to the window only to see that the air was clear again and—by my personal triumph—the influence quenched? There was nothing there. I felt that the cause was mine and that I should surely get ALL. "And you found nothing!"—I let my elation out.

He gave the most mournful, thoughtful little headshake. "Nothing."

"Nothing, nothing!" I almost shouted in my joy.

"Nothing, nothing," he sadly repeated.

I kissed his forehead; it was drenched. "So what have you done with it?"

"I've burned it."

"Burned it?" It was now or never. "Is that what you did at school?"

Oh, what this brought up! "At school?"

"Did you take letters?—or other things?"

"Other things?" He appeared now to be thinking of something far off and that reached him only through the pressure of his anxiety. Yet it did reach him. "Did I STEAL?"

I felt myself redden to the roots of my hair as well as wonder if it were more strange to put to a gentleman such a question or to see him take it with allowances that gave the very distance of his fall in the world. "Was it for that you mightn't go back?"

The only thing he felt was rather a dreary little surprise. "Did you know I mightn't go back?"

"I know everything."

He gave me at this the longest and strangest look. "Everything?"

"Everything. Therefore DID you—?" But I couldn't say it again.

Miles could, very simply. "No. I didn't steal."

My face must have shown him I believed him utterly; yet my hands—but it was for pure tenderness—shook him as if to ask him why, if it was all for nothing, he had condemned me to months of torment. "What then did you do?"

He looked in vague pain all round the top of the room and drew his breath, two or three times over, as if with difficulty. He might have been standing at the bottom of the sea and raising his eyes to some faint green twilight. "Well—I said things."

"Only that?"

"They thought it was enough!"

"To turn you out for?"

Never, truly, had a person "turned out" shown so little to explain it as this little person! He appeared to weigh my question, but in a manner quite detached and almost helpless. "Well,

I suppose I oughtn't."

"But to whom did you say them?"

He evidently tried to remember, but it dropped—he had lost it. "I don't know!"

He almost smiled at me in the desolation of his surrender, which was indeed practically, by this time, so complete that I ought to have left it there. But I was infatuated—I was blind with victory, though even then the very effect that was to have brought him so much nearer was already that of added separation. "Was it to everyone?" I asked.

"No; it was only to—" But he gave a sick little headshake. "I don't remember their names."

"Were they then so many?"

"No—only a few. Those I liked."

Those he liked? I seemed to float not into clearness, but into a darker obscure, and within a minute there had come to me out of my very pity the appalling alarm of his being perhaps innocent. It was for the instant confounding and bottomless, for if he WERE innocent, what then on earth was *I*? Paralyzed, while it lasted, by the mere brush of the question, I let him go a little, so that, with a deep-drawn sigh, he turned away from me again; which, as he faced toward the clear window, I suffered, feeling that I had nothing now there to keep him from. "And did they repeat what you said?" I went on after a moment.

He was soon at some distance from me, still breathing hard and again with the air, though now without anger for it, of being confined against his will. Once more, as he had done before, he looked up at the dim day as if, of what had hitherto sustained him, nothing was left but an unspeakable anxiety. "Oh, yes," he nevertheless replied—"they must have repeated them. To those THEY liked," he added.

There was, somehow, less of it than I had expected; but I turned it over. "And these things came round—?"

"To the masters? Oh, yes!" he answered very simply. "But I didn't know they'd tell."

"The masters? They didn't—they've never told. That's why I

ask you."

He turned to me again his little beautiful fevered face. "Yes, it was too bad."

"Too bad?"

"What I suppose I sometimes said. To write home."

I can't name the exquisite pathos of the contradiction given to such a speech by such a speaker; I only know that the next instant I heard myself throw off with homely force: "Stuff and nonsense!" But the next after that I must have sounded stern enough. "What WERE these things?"

My sternness was all for his judge, his executioner; yet it made him avert himself again, and that movement made ME, with a single bound and an irrepressible cry, spring straight upon him. For there again, against the glass, as if to blight his confession and stay his answer, was the hideous author of our woe—the white face of damnation. I felt a sick swim at the drop of my victory and all the return of my battle, so that the wildness of my veritable leap only served as a great betrayal. I saw him, from the midst of my act, meet it with a divination, and on the perception that even now he only guessed, and that the window was still to his own eyes free, I let the impulse flame up to convert the climax of his dismay into the very proof of his liberation. "No more, no more, no more!" I shrieked, as I tried to press him against me, to my visitant.

"Is she HERE?" Miles panted as he caught with his sealed eyes the direction of my words. Then as his strange "she" staggered me and, with a gasp, I echoed it, "Miss Jessel, Miss Jessel!" he with a sudden fury gave me back.

I seized, stupefied, his supposition—some sequel to what we had done to Flora, but this made me only want to show him that it was better still than that. "It's not Miss Jessel! But it's at the window—straight before us. It's THERE—the coward horror, there for the last time!"

At this, after a second in which his head made the movement of a baffled dog's on a scent and then gave a frantic little shake for air and light, he was at me in a white rage, bewildered, glaring vainly over the place and missing wholly, though it now, to my sense, filled the room like the taste of poison, the wide, overwhelming presence. "It's HE?"

I was so determined to have all my proof that I flashed into ice to challenge him. "Whom do you mean by 'he'?"

"Peter Quint—you devil!" His face gave again, round the room, its convulsed supplication. "WHERE?"

They are in my ears still, his supreme surrender of the name and his tribute to my devotion. "What does he matter now, my own?—what will he EVER matter? *I* have you," I launched at the beast, "but he has lost you forever!" Then, for the demonstration of my work, "There, THERE!" I said to Miles.

But he had already jerked straight round, stared, glared again, and seen but the quiet day. With the stroke of the loss I was so proud of he uttered the cry of a creature hurled over an abyss, and the grasp with which I recovered him might have been that of catching him in his fall. I caught him, yes, I held him—it may be imagined with what a passion; but at the end of a minute I began to feel what it truly was that I held. We were alone with the quiet day, and his little heart, dispossessed, had stopped.

The Man-Wolf

A.K.A. HUGH THE WOLF

By Erckmann-Chatrian

CHAPTER 1

About Christmas time in the year 18—, as I was lying fast asleep at the Cygne at Fribourg, my old friend Gideon Sperver broke abruptly into my room, crying—

"Fritz, I have good news for you; I am going to take you to Nideck, two leagues from this place. You know Nideck, the finest baronial castle in the country, a grand monument of the glory of our forefathers?"

Now I had not seen Sperver, who was my foster-father, for sixteen years; he had grown a full beard in that time, a huge fox-skin cap covered his head, and he was holding his lantern close under my nose. It was, therefore, only natural that I should answer—

"In the first place let us do things in order. Tell me who you are."

"Who I am? What! don't you remember Gideon Sperver, the Schwartzwald huntsman? You would not be so ungrateful, would you? Was it not I who taught you to set a trap, to lay wait for the foxes along the skirts of the woods, to start the dogs after the wild birds? Do you remember me now? Look at my left ear, with a frost-bite."

"Now I know you; that left ear of yours has done it; Shake hands."

Sperver, passing the back of his hand across his eyes, went

on—

"You know Nideck?"

"Of course I do—by reputation; what have you to do there?"

"I am the count's chief huntsman."

"And who has sent you?"

"The young Countess Odile."

"Very good. How soon are we to start?"

"This moment. The matter is urgent; the old count is very ill, and his daughter has begged me not to lose a moment. The horses are quite ready."

"But, Gideon, my dear fellow, just look out at the weather; it has been snowing three days without cessation."

"Oh, nonsense; we are not going out boar-hunting; put on your thick coat, buckle on your spurs, and let us prepare to start. I will order something to eat first." And he went out, first adding, "Be sure to put on your cape."

I could never refuse old Gideon anything; from my childhood he could do anything with me with a nod or a sign; so I equipped myself and came into the coffee-room.

"I knew," he said, "that you would not let me go back without you. Eat every bit of this slice of ham, and let us drink a stirrup cup, for the horses are getting impatient. I have had your portmanteau put in."

"My portmanteau! what is that for?"

"Yes, it will be all right; you will have to stay a few days at Nideck, that is indispensable, and I will tell you why presently."

So we went down into the courtyard.

At that moment two horsemen arrived, evidently tired out with riding, their horses in a perfect lather of foam. Sperver, who had always been a great admirer of a fine horse, expressed his surprise and admiration at these splendid animals.

"What beauties! They are of the Wallachian breed, I can see, as finely formed as deer, and as swift. Nicholas, throw a cloth over them quickly, or they will take cold."

The travellers, muffled in Siberian furs, passed close by us just as we were going to mount. I could only discern the long brown moustache of one, and his singularly bright and sparkling eyes.

They entered the hotel.

The groom was holding our horses by the bridle. He wished us *bon voyage*, removed his hand, and we were off.

Sperver rode a pure Mecklemburg. I was mounted on a stout cob bred in the Ardennes, full of fire; we flew over the snowy ground. In ten minutes we had left Fribourg behind us.

The sky was beginning to clear up. As far as the eye could reach we could distinguish neither road, path, nor track. Our only company were the ravens of the Black Forest spreading their hollow wings wide over the banks of snow, trying one place after another unsuccessfully for food, and croaking, "Misery! misery!"

Gideon, with his weather-beaten countenance, his fur cloak and cap, galloped on ahead, whistling airs from the *Freyschuetz*; sometimes as he turned I could see the sparkling drops of moisture hanging from his long moustache.

"Well, Fritz, my boy, this is a fine winter's morning."

"So it is, but it is rather severe; don't you think so?"

"I am fond of a clear hard frost," he replied; "it promotes circulation. If our old minister Tobias had but the courage to start out in weather like this he would soon put an end to his rheumatic pains."

I smiled, I am afraid, involuntarily.

After an hour of this rapid pace Sperver slackened his speed and let me come abreast of him.

"Fritz, I shall have to tell you the object of this journey at some time, I suppose?"

"I was beginning to think I ought to know what I am going about."

"A good many doctors have already been consulted."

"Indeed!"

"Yes, some came from Berlin in great wigs who only asked to see the patient's tongue. Others from Switzerland examined him another way. The doctors from Paris stared at their patient through magnifying glasses to learn something from his physiognomy. But all their learning was wasted, and they got large fees in reward of their ignorance."

"Is that the way you speak of us medical gentlemen?"

"I am not alluding to you at all. I have too much respect for you, and if I should happen to break my leg I don't know that there is another that I should prefer to yourself to treat me as a patient, but you have not discovered an optical instrument yet to tell what is going on inside of us."

"How do you know that?"

At this reply the worthy fellow looked at me doubtfully as if he thought me a quack like the rest, yet he replied—

"Well, Fritz, if you have indeed such a glass it will be wanted now, for the count's complaint is internal; it is a terrible kind of illness, something like madness. You know that madness shows itself in either nine hours, nine days, or nine weeks?"

"So it is said; but not having noticed this myself, I cannot say that it is so."

"Still you know there are agues which return at periods of either three, six, or nine years. There are singular works in this machinery of ours. Whenever this human clockwork is wound up in some particular way, fever, or indigestion, or toothache returns at the very hour and day."

"Why, Gideon, I am quite aware of that; those periodical complaints are the greatest trouble we have."

"I am sorry to hear it, for the count's complaint is periodical; it comes back every year, on the same day, at the same hour; his mouth runs over with foam, his eyes stand out white and staring, like great billiard-balls; he shakes from head to foot, and he gnashes with his teeth."

"Perhaps this man has had serious troubles to go through?"

"No, he has not. If his daughter would but consent to be married he would be the happiest man alive. He is rich and powerful and full of honours. He possesses everything that the rest of the world is coveting. Unfortunately his daughter persists in refusing every offer of marriage. She consecrates her life to

God, and it harasses him to think that the ancient house of Nideck will become extinct."

"How did his illness come on?" I asked.

"Suddenly, ten years ago," was the reply.

All at once the honest fellow seemed to be recollecting himself. He took from his pocket a short pipe, filled it, and having lighted it—

"One evening," said he, "I was sitting alone with the count in the armoury of the castle. It was about Christmas time. We had been hunting wild boars the whole day in the valleys of the Rhethal, and had returned at night bringing home with us two of our boar-hounds ripped open from head to tail. It was just as cold as it is to-night, with snow and frost. The count was pacing up and down the room with his chin upon his breast and his hands crossed behind him, like a man in profound thought. From time to time he stopped to watch the gathering snow on the high windows, and I was warming myself in the chimney corner, bewailing my dead hounds, and bestowing maledictions on all the wild boars that infest the Schwartzwald. Everybody at Nideck had been asleep a couple of hours, and not a sound could be heard but the tread and the clank of the count's heavy spurred boots upon the flags. I remember well that a crow, no doubt driven by a gust of wind, came flapping its wings against the window-panes, uttering a discordant shriek, and how the sheets of snow fell from the windows, and the windows suddenly changed from white to black—"

"But what has all this to do with your master's illness?" I interrupted.

"Let me go on—you will soon see. At that cry the count suddenly gathered himself together with a shuddering movement, his eyes became fixed with a glassy stare, his cheeks were bloodless, and he bent his head forward just like a hunter catching the sound of his approaching game. I went on warming myself, and I thought, 'Won't he soon go to bed now?' for, to tell you the truth, I was overcome with fatigue. All these details, Fritz, are still present in my memory. Scarcely had the bird of ill omen croaked its unearthly cry when the old clock struck eleven. At that moment the count turns on his heel—he listens, his lips tremble, I can see him staggering like a drunken man. He stretches out his hands, his jaws are tightly clenched, his eyes staring and white.

"I cried, 'My lord, what is the matter?' but he began to laugh discordantly like a madman, stumbled, and fell upon the stone floor, face downwards. I called for help; servants came round. Sebalt took the count by the shoulders; we removed him to a bed near the window; but just as I was loosening the count's neckerchief—for I was afraid it was apoplexy—the countess came and flung herself upon the body of her father, uttering such heartrending cries that the very remembrance of them makes me shudder."

Here Gideon took his pipe from his lips, knocked the ashes out upon the pommel of his saddle, and pursued his tale in a saddened voice.

"From that day, Fritz, none but evil days have come upon Nideck, and better times seem to be far off. Every year at the same day and hour the count has shuddering fits. The malady lasts from a week to a fortnight, during which he howls and yells so frightfully that it makes a man's blood run cold to hear him. Then he slowly recovers his usual health. He is still pale and weak, and moves trembling from one chair to another, starting at the least noise or movement, and fearful of his own shadow. The young countess, the sweetest creature in the world, never leaves his side; but he cannot endure her while the fit is upon him. He roars at her, 'Go, leave me this moment! I have enough to endure without seeing you hanging about me!' It is a horrible sight. I am always close at his heels in the chase, I who sound the horn when he has killed the forest beasts; I am at the head of all his retainers, and I would give my life for his sake; yet when he is at his worst I can hardly keep off my hands from his throat, I am so horrified at the way in which he treats his beautiful daughter."

Sperver looked dangerously wroth for a moment, clapped both his spurs to his mount, and we rode on at a hard gallop.

I had fallen into a reverie. The cure of a complaint of this description appeared to me more than doubtful, even impossible. It was evidently a mental disorder. To fight against it with any hope of success it would be needful to trace it back to its origin, and this would, no doubt, be too remote for successful investigation.

All these reflections perplexed me greatly. The old huntsman's story, far from strengthening my hopes, only depressed me—not a very favourable condition to insure success. At about three we came in sight of the ancient castle of Nideck on the verge of the horizon. In spite of the great distance we could distinguish the projecting turrets, apparently suspended from the angles of the edifice. It was but a dim outline barely distinguishable from the blue sky, but soon the red points of the Vosges became visible.

At that moment Sperver drew in his bridle and said—

"Fritz, we shall have to get there before night—onward!"

But it was in vain that he spurred and lashed. The horse stood rooted to the ground, his ears thrown back, his nostrils dilated, his sides panting, his legs firmly planted in an attitude of resistance.

"What is the matter with the beast?" cried Gideon in astonishment. "Do you see anything, Fritz? Surely—"

He broke off abruptly, pointing with his whip at a dark form in the snow fifty yards off, on the slope of the hill.

"The Black Plague!" he exclaimed with a voice of distress which almost robbed me of my self-possession.

Following the indication of his outstretched whip I discerned with astonishment an aged woman crouching on the snowy ground, with her arms clasped about her knees, and so tattered that her red elbows came through her tattered sleeves. A few ragged locks of grey hung about her long, scraggy, red, and vulture-like neck.

Strange to say, a bundle of some kind lay upon her knees, and her haggard eyes were directed upon distant objects in the white landscape.

Spencer drew off to the left, giving the hideous object as

wide a berth as he could, and I had some difficulty in following him.

"Now," I cried, "what is all this for? Are you joking?"

"Joking?—assuredly not! I never joke about such serious matters. I am not given to superstition, but I confess that I am alarmed at this meeting!"

Then turning his head, and noticing that the old woman had not moved, and that her eyes were fixed upon the same one spot, he appeared to gather a little courage.

"Fritz," he said solemnly, "you are a man of learning—you know many things of which I know nothing at all. Well, I can tell you this, that a man is in the wrong who laughs at a thing because he can't understand it. I have good reasons for calling this woman the Black Plague. She is known by that name in the whole Black Forest, but here at Nideck she has earned that title by supreme right."

And the good man pursued his way without further observation.

"Now, Sperver, just explain what you mean," I asked, "for I don't understand you."

"That woman is the ruin of us all. She is a witch. She is the cause of it all. It is she who is killing the count by inches."

"How is that possible?" I exclaimed. "How could she exercise such a baneful influence?"

"I cannot tell how it is. All I know is, that on the very day that the attack comes on, at the very moment, if you will ascend the beacon tower, you will see the Black Plague squatting down like a dark speck on the snow just between the Tiefenbach and the castle of Nideck. She sits there alone, crouching close to the snow. Every day she comes a little nearer, and every day the attacks grow worse. You would think he hears her approach. Sometimes on the first day, when the fits of trembling have come over him, he has said to me, 'Gideon, I feel her coming.' I hold him by the arms and restrain the shuddering somewhat, but he still repeats, stammering and struggling with his agony, and his eyes staring and fixed, 'She is coming—nearer—oh—oh—she comes!'

"Then I go up Hugh Lupus's tower; I survey the country. You know I have a keen eye for distant objects. At last, amidst the grey mists afar off, between sky and earth, I can just make out a dark speck. The next morning that black spot has grown larger. The Count of Nideck goes to bed with chattering teeth. The next day again we can make out the figure of the old hag; the fierce attacks begin; the count cries out. The day after, the witch is at the foot of the mountain, and the consequence is that the count's jaws are set like a vice; his mouth foams; his eyes turn in his head. Vile creature! Twenty times I have had her within gunshot, and the count has bid me shed no blood. 'No, Sperver, no; let us have no bloodshed.' Poor man, he is sparing the life of the wretch who is draining his life from him, for she is killing him, Fritz; he is reduced to skin and bone."

My good friend Gideon was in too great a rage with the unhappy woman to make it possible to bring him back to calm reason. Besides, who can draw the limits around the region of possibility? Every day we see the range of reality extending more widely. Unseen and unknown influences, marvellous correspondences, invisible bonds, some kind of mysterious magnetism, are, on the one hand, proclaimed as undoubted facts, and denied on the other with irony and scepticism, and yet who can say that after a while there will not be some astonishing revelations breaking in in the midst of us all when we least expect it? In the midst of so much ignorance it seems easy to lay a claim to wisdom and shrewdness.

I therefore only begged Sperver to moderate his anger, and by no means to fire upon the Black Plague, warning him that such a proceeding would bring serious misfortune upon him.

"Pooh!" he cried; "at the very worst they could but hang me."

But that, I remarked, was a good deal for an honest man to suffer.

"Not at all," he cried; "it is but one kind of death out of many. You are suffocated, that is all. I would just as soon die of that as of a hammer falling on my head, as in apoplexy, or not to be able to sleep, or smoke, or swallow, or digest my food."

"You, Gideon, with your grey beard, you have learnt a peculiar mode of reasoning."

"Grey beard or not, that is my way of seeing things. I always keep a ball in my double-barrelled gun at the witch's service; from time to time I put in a fresh charge, and if I get the chance—"

He only added an expressive gesture.

"Quite wrong, Sperver, quite wrong. I agree with the Count of Nideck, and I say no bloodshed. Oceans cannot wipe away blood shed in anger. Think of that, and discharge that barrel against the first boar you meet."

These words seemed to make some impression upon the old huntsman; he hung down his head and looked thoughtful.

We were then climbing the wooded steeps which separate the poor village of Tiefenbach from the Castle of Nideck.

Night had closed in. As it always happens with us after a bright clear winter's day, snow was again beginning to fall, heavy flakes dropped and melted upon our horses' manes, who were beginning now to pluck up their spirits at the near prospect of the comfortable stable.

Now and then Sperver looked over his shoulder with evident uneasiness; and I myself was not altogether free from a feeling of apprehension in thinking of the strange account which the huntsman had given me of his master's complaint.

Besides all this, there is a certain harmony between external nature and the spirit of a man, and I know of nothing more depressing than a gloomy forest loaded in every branch with thick snow and hoar frost, and moaning in the north wind. The gaunt and weird-looking trunks of the tall pines and the gnarled and massive oaks look mournfully upon you, and fill you with melancholy thoughts.

As we ascended the rocky eminence the oaks became fewer, and scattered birches, straight and white as marble pillars, divided the dark green of the forest pines, when in a moment, as we issued from a thicket, the ancient stronghold stood before us in a heavy mass, its dark surface studded with brilliant points of light.

Sperver had pulled up before a deep gateway between two towers, barred in by an iron grating.

"Here we are," he cried, throwing the reins on the horses' necks.

He laid hold of the deer's-foot bell-handle, and the clear sound of a bell broke the stillness.

After waiting a few minutes the light of a lantern flickered in the deep archway, showing us in its semicircular frame of ruddy light the figure of a humpbacked dwarf, yellow-bearded, broad-shouldered, and wrapped in furs from head to foot.

You might have thought him, in the deep shadow, some gnome or evil spirit of earth realised out of the dreams of the Niebelungen Lieder.

He came towards us at a very leisurely pace, and laid his great flat features close against the massive grating, straining his eyes, and trying to make us out in the darkness in which we were standing.

"Is that you, Sperver?" he asked in a hoarse voice.

"Open at once, Knapwurst," was the quick reply. "Don't you know how cold it is?"

"Oh! I know you now," cried the little man; "there's no mistaking you. You always speak as if you were going to gobble people up."

The door opened, and the dwarf, examining me with his lantern, with an odd expression in his face, received me with "*Willkommen, herr* doctor," but which seemed to say besides, "Here is another who will have to go away again as others have done." Then he quietly closed the door, whilst we alighted, and came to take our horses by the bridle.

CHAPTER 2

Following Sperver, who ascended the staircase with rapid steps, I was still able to convince myself that the Castle of Nideck had not an undeserved reputation.

It was a true stronghold, partly cut out of the rock, such as used formerly to be called a *château d'ambuscade*. Its lofty vaulted arches re-echoed afar with our steps, and the outside air blowing with sharp gusts through the loopholes—narrow slits made for the archers of former days—caused our torches to flare and flicker from space to space over the faintly-illuminated protruding lines of the arches as they caught the uncertain light.

Sperver knew every nook and corner of this vast place. He turned now to the right and now to the left, and I followed him breathless. At last he stopped on a spacious landing, and said to me—

"Now, Fritz, I will leave you for a minute with the people of the castle to inform the young Countess Odile of your arrival."

"Do just what you think right."

"Then you will find the head butler, Tobias Offenloch, an old soldier of the regiment of Nideck. He campaigned in France under the count; and you will see his wife, a Frenchwoman, Marie Lagoutte, who pretends that she comes of a high family."

"And why should she not?"

"Of course she might; but, between ourselves, she was nothing but a *cantiniere* in the Grande Armee. She brought in Tobias Offenloch upon her cart, with one of his legs gone, and he has married her out of gratitude. You understand?"

"That will do, but open, for I am numb with cold."

And I was about to push on; but Sperver, as obstinate as any other good German, was not going to let me off without edifying me upon the history of the people with whom my lot was going to be cast for awhile, and holding me by the frogs of my fur coat he went on—

"There's, besides, Sebalt Kraft, the master of the hounds; he is rather a dismal fellow, but he has not his equal at sounding the horn; and there will be Karl Trumpf, the butler, and Christian Becker, and everybody, unless they have all gone to bed."

Thereupon Sperver pushed open the door, and I stood in some surprise on the threshold of a high, dark hall, the guard room of the old lords of Nideck.

My eyes fell at first upon the three windows at the farther end, looking out upon the sheer rocky precipice. On the right stood an old sideboard in dark oak, and upon it a cask, glasses, and bottles; on the left a Gothic chimney overhung with its heavy massive mantelpiece, empurpled by the brilliant roaring fire underneath, and ornamented on both front and sides with wood-carvings representing scenes from boar-hunts in the Middle Ages, and along the centre of the apartment a long table, upon which stood a huge lamp throwing its light upon a dozen pewter tankards.

At one glance I saw all this; but the human portion of the scene interested me most.

I recognised the *major-domo*, or head butler, by his wooden leg, of which I had already heard; he was of low stature, round, fat, and rosy, and his knees seldom coming within an easy range of his eyesight; a nose red and bulbous like a ripe raspberry; on his head he wore a huge hemp-coloured wig, bulging out over his fat poll; a coat of light green plush, with steel buttons as large as a five-*franc* piece; velvet breeches, silk stockings, and shoes garnished with silver buckles. He was just with his hand upon the top of the cask, with an air of inexpressible satisfaction beaming upon his ruddy features, and his eyes glowing in profile, from the reflection of the fire, like a couple of watch-glasses.

His wife, the worthy Marie Lagoutte, her spare figure draped in voluminous folds, her long and sallow face like a skin of chamois leather, was playing at cards with two servants who were gravely seated on straight-backed armchairs. Certain small split pegs were seated astride across the nose of the old woman and that of another player, whilst the third was significantly and cunningly winking his eye and seeming to enjoy seeing them victimised upon these new Caudine Forks.

"How many cards?" he was asking.

"Two," answered the old woman.

"And you, Christian?"

"Two."

"Aha! now I have got you, then. Cut the king—now the ace—here's one, here's another. Another peg, mother! This will teach you once more not to brag about French games."

"Monsieur Christian, you don't treat the fair sex with proper respect."

"At cards you respect nobody."

"But you see I have no room left!"

"Pooh, on a nose like yours there's always room for more!"

At that moment Sperver cried—

"Mates, here I am!"

"Ha! Gideon, back already?"

Marie Lagoutte shook off her numerous pegs with a jerk of her head. The big butler drank off his glass. Everybody turned our way.

"Is *monseigneur* better?"

The butler answered with a doubtful ejaculation.

"Is he just the same?"

"Much about," answered Marie Lagoutte, who never took her eyes off me.

Sperver noticed this.

"Let me introduce to you my foster-son, Doctor Fritz, from the Black Forest," he answered proudly. "Now we shall see a change, Master Tobie. Now that Fritz has come the abominable fits will be put an end to. If I had but been listened to earlier—but better late than never."

Marie Lagoutte was still watching us, and her scrutiny seemed satisfactory, for, addressing the *major-domo*, she said—

"Now, Monsieur Offenloch, hand the doctor a chair; move about a little, do! There you stand with your mouth wide open, just like a fish. Ah, sir, these Germans!"

And the good man, jumping up as if moved by a spring, came to take off my cloak.

"Permit me, sir."

"You are very kind, my dear lady."

"Give it to me. What terrible weather! Ah, *monsieur*, what a dreadful country this is!"

"So *monseigneur* is neither better nor worse," said Sperver, shaking the snow off his cap; "we are not too late, then. Ho, Kasper! Kasper!"

A little man, who had one shoulder higher than the other, and his face spotted with innumerable freckles, came out of the chimney corner.

"Here I am!"

"Very good; now get ready for this gentleman the bedroom at the end of the long gallery—Hugh's room; you know which I mean."

"Yes, Sperver, in a minute."

"And you will take with you, as you go, the doctor's knapsack. Knapwurst will give it you. As for supper—"

"Never you mind. That is my business."

"Very well, then. I will depend upon you."

The little man went out, and Gideon, after taking off his cape, left us to go and inform the young countess of my arrival.

I was rather overpowered with the attentions of Marie Lagoutte.

"Give up that place of yours, Sebalt," she cried to the kennel-keeper. "You are roasted enough by this time. Sit near the fire, *monsieur le docteur*; you must have very cold feet. Stretch out your legs; that's the way."

Then, holding out her snuff-box to me—

"Do you take snuff?"

"No, dear madam, with many thanks."

"That is a pity," she answered, filling both nostrils. "It is the most delightful habit."

She slipped her snuff-box back into her apron pocket, and went on—

"You are come not a bit too soon. *Monseigneur* had his second attack yesterday; it was an awful attack, was it not, Monsieur Offenloch?"

"Furious indeed," answered the head butler gravely.

"It is not surprising," she continued, "when a man takes no nourishment. Fancy, *monsieur*, that for two days he has never tasted broth!"

"Nor a glass of wine," added the *major-domo,* crossing his hands over his portly, well-lined person.

As it seemed expected of me, I expressed my surprise, on which Tobias Offenloch came to sit at my right hand, and said—

"Doctor, take my advice; order him a bottle a day of *Marcobrunner.*"

"And," chimed in Marie Lagoutte, "a wing of a chicken at every meal. The poor man is frightfully thin."

"We have got *Marcobrunner* sixty years in bottle," added the *major-domo*, "for it is a mistake of Madame Offenloch's to suppose that the French drank it all. And you had better order, while you are about it, now and then, a good bottle of Johannisberg. That is the best wine to set a man up again."

"Time was," remarked the master of the hounds in a dismal voice—"time was when *monseigneur* hunted twice a week; then he was well; when he left off hunting, then he fell ill."

"Of course it could not be otherwise," observed Marie Lagoutte. "The open air gives you an appetite. The doctor had better order him to hunt three times a week to make up for lost time."

"Two would be enough," replied the man of dogs with the same gravity; "quite enough. The hounds must have their rest. Dogs have just as much right to rest as we have."

There was a few moments' silence, during which I could hear the wind beating against the window-panes, and rush, sighing and wailing, through the loopholes into the towers.

Sebalt sat with legs across, and his elbow resting on his knee, gazing into the fire with unspeakable dolefulness. Marie Lagoutte, after having refreshed herself with a fresh pinch, was settling her snuff into shape in its box, while I sat thinking on the strange habit people indulge in of pressing their advice upon those who don't want it.

At this moment the *major-domo* rose.

"Will you have a glass of wine, doctor?" said he, leaning over the back of my armchair.

"Thank you, but I never drink before seeing a patient."

"What! not even one little glass?"

"Not the smallest glass you could offer me."

He opened his eyes wide and looked with astonishment at his wife.

"The doctor is right," she said. "I am quite of his opinion. I prefer to drink with my meat, and to take a glass of cognac afterwards. That is what the ladies do in France. Cognac is more fashionable than *kirschwasser!*"

Marie Lagoutte had hardly finished with her dissertation when Sperver opened the door quietly and beckoned me to follow him.

I bowed to the "honourable company," and as I was entering the passage I could hear that lady saying to her husband—

"That is a nice young man. He would have made a good-looking soldier."

Sperver looked uneasy, but said nothing. I was full of my own thoughts.

A few steps under the darkling vaults of Nideck completely effaced from my memory the queer figures of Tobias and Marie Lagoutte, poor harmless creatures, existing like bats under the mighty wing of the vulture.

Soon Gideon brought me into a sumptuous apartment hung with violet-coloured velvet, relieved with gold. A bronze lamp stood in a corner, its brightness toned down by a globe of ground crystal; thick carpets, soft as the turf on the hills, made our steps noiseless. It seemed a fit abode for silence and meditation.

On entering Sperver lifted the heavy draperies which fell around an ogee window. I observed him straining his eyes to discover something in the darkened distance; he was trying to make out whether the witch still lay there crouching down upon the snow in the midst of the plain; but he could see nothing, for there was deep darkness over all.

But I had gone on a few steps, and came in sight, by the faint rays of the lamp, of a pale, delicate figure seated in a Gothic chair not far from the sick man. It was Odile of Nideck. Her long black silk dress, her gentle expression of calm self-devotion and complete resignation, the ideal angel-like cast of her sweet features, recalled to one's mind those mysterious creations of the pencil in the Middle Ages when painting was pursued as a true art, but which modern imitators have found themselves obliged to give up in despair, while at the same time they never can forget them.

I cannot say what thoughts passed rapidly through my mind at the sight of this fair creature, but certainly much of devotion mingled with my sentiments. A sense of music and harmony swept sadly through by soul, with faint impressions of the old ballads of my childhood—of those pious songs with which the kind nurses of the Black Forest rock to peaceful sleep our infant sorrows.

At my approach Odile rose.

"You are very welcome, *monsieur le docteur*," she said with touching kindness and simplicity; then, pointing with her finger to a recess where lay the count, she added, "There is my father."

I bowed respectfully and without answering, for I felt deeply affected, and drew near to my patient.

Sperver, standing at the head of the bed, held up the lamp with one hand, holding his far cap in the other. Odile stood at my left hand. The light, softened by the subdued light of the globe of ground crystal, fell softly on the face of the count.

At once I was struck with a strangeness in the physiognomy of the Count of Nideck, and in spite of all the admiration which his lovely daughter had at once obtained from me, my first conclusion was, "What an old wolf!"

And such he seemed to be indeed. A grey head, covered with short, close hair, strangely full behind the ears, and drawn out in the face to a portentous length, the narrowness of his forehead up to its summit widening over the eyebrows, which were shaggy and met, pointing downwards over the bridge of the nose, imperfectly shading with their sable outline the cold and inexpressive eyes; the short, rough beard, irregularly spread over the angular and bony outline of the mouth—every feature of this man's dreadful countenance made me shudder, and strange notions crossed my mind about the mysterious affinities between man and the lower creation.

But I resisted my first impressions and took the sick man's hand. It was dry and wiry, yet small and strong; I found the pulse quick, feverish, and denoting great irritability.

What was I to do?

I stood considering; on the one side stood the young lady, anxiously trying to read a little hope in my face; on the other Sperver, equally anxious and watching my every movement. A painful constraint lay, therefore, upon me, yet I saw that there was nothing definite that could be attempted yet.

I dropped the arm and listened to the breathing. From time to time a convulsive sob heaved the sick man's heart, after which followed a succession of quick, short respirations. A kind of nightmare was evidently weighing him down—epilepsy, perhaps, or tetanus. But what could be the cause or origin?

I turned round full of painful thoughts.

"Is there any hope, sir?" asked the young countess.

"Yesterday's crisis is drawing to its close," I answered; "we must see if we can prevent its recurrence."

"Is there any possibility of it, sir?"

I was about to answer in general medical terms, not daring to venture any positive assertions, when the distant sound of the bell at the gate fell upon our ears.

"Visitors," said Sperver.

There was a moment's silence.

"Go and see who it is," said Odile, whose brow was for a minute shaded with anxiety. "How can one be hospitable to strangers at such a time? It is hardly possible!"

But the door opened, and a rosy face, with golden hair, appeared in the shadow, and said in a whisper—

"It is the Baron of Zimmer-Bluderich, with a servant, and he asks for shelter in the Nideck. He has lost his way among the mountains."

"Very well, Gretchen," answered the young countess, kindly; "go and tell the steward to attend to the Baron de Zimmer. Inform him that the count is very ill, and that this alone prevents him from doing the honours as he would wish. Wake up some of our people to wait on him, and let everything be done properly."

Nothing could exceed the sweet and noble simplicity of the young *chatelaine* in giving her orders. If an air of distinction seems hereditary in some families it is surely because the exercise of the duties conferred by the possession of wealth has a natural tendency to ennoble the whole character and bearing.

These thoughts passed through my mind whilst admiring the grace and gentleness in every movement of Odile of Nideck, and that clearness and purity of outline which is only found marked in the features of the higher aristocracy, and I could recall nothing to my recollection equal to this ideal beauty.

"Go now, Gretchen," said the young countess, "and make haste."

The attendant went out, and I stood a few seconds under the influence of the charm of her manner.

Odile turned round, and addressing me, "You see, sir," said she with a sad smile, "one may not indulge in grief without a pause; we must divide ourselves between our affection within and the world without."

"True, madam," I replied; "souls of the highest order are for the common property and advantage of the unhappy—the lost wayfarer, the sick, the hungry poor—each has his claim for a share, for God has made them like the stars of heaven to give light and pleasure to all."

The deep-fringed eyelids veiled the blue eyes for a moment, while Sperver pressed my hand.

Presently she pursued—

"Ah, if you could but restore my father's health!"

"As I have had the pleasure to inform you, madam, the crisis is past; the return must be anticipated, if possible."

"Do you hope that it may?"

"With God's help, madam, it is not impossible; I will think carefully over it."

Odile, much moved, came with me to the door. Sperver and I crossed the ante-room, where a few servants were waiting for the orders of their mistress. We had just entered the corridor when Gideon, who was walking first, turned quickly round, and, placing both his hands on my shoulders, said—

"Come, Fritz; I am to be depended upon for keeping a secret; what is your opinion?"

"I think there is no cause of apprehension for tonight."

"I know that—so you told the countess—but how about tomorrow?"

"Tomorrow?"

"Yes; don't turn round. I suppose you cannot prevent the return of the complaint; do you think, Fritz, he will die of it?"

"It is possible, but hardly probable."

"Well done!" cried the good man, springing from the ground with joy; "if you don't think so, that means that you are sure."

And taking my arm, he drew me into the gallery. We had just reached it when the Baron of Zimmer-Bluderich and his groom appeared there also, marshalled by Sebalt with a lighted torch in his hand. They were on their way to their chambers, and those two figures, with their cloaks flung over their shoulders, their loose Hungarian boots up to the knees, the body closely girt with long dark-green laced and frogged tunics, and the bear-skin cap closely and warmly covering the head, were very picturesque objects by the flickering light of the pine-torch.

"There," whispered Sperver, "if I am not very much mistaken, those are our Fribourg friends; they have followed very close upon our heels."

"You are quite right: they are the men; I recognise the younger by his tall, slender figure, his aquiline nose, and his long, drooping moustache."

They disappeared through a side passage.

Gideon took a torch from the wall, and guided me through

quite a maze of corridors, aisles, narrow and wide passages, under high vaulted roofs and under low-built arches; who could remember? There seemed no end.

"Here is the hall of the margraves," said he; "here is the portrait-gallery, and this is the chapel, where no mass has been said since Louis the Bold became a Protestant."

All these particulars had very little interest for me.

After reaching the end we had again to go down steps; at last we happily came to the end of our journey before a low massive door. Sperver took a huge key out of his pocket, and handing me the torch, said—

"Mind the light—look out!"

At the same time he pushed open the door, and the cold outside air rushed into the narrow passage. The torch flared and sent out a volley of sparks in all directions. I thought I saw a dark abyss before me, and recoiled with fear.

"Ha, ha, ha!" cried the huntsman, opening his mouth from ear to ear, "you are surely not afraid, Fritz? Come on; don't be frightened! We are upon the parapet between the castle and the old tower."

And my friend advanced to set me the example.

The narrow granite-walled platform was deep in snow, swept in swirling banks by the angry winds. Anyone who had seen our flaring torch from below would have asked, "What are they doing up there in the clouds? what can they want at this time of the night?"

Perhaps, I thought within myself, the witch is looking up at us, and that idea gave me a fit of shuddering. I drew closer together the folds of my horseman's cloak, and with my hand upon my hat, I set off after Sperver at a run; he was raising the light above his head to show me the road, and was moving forward rapidly.

We rushed into the tower and then into Hugh Lupus's chamber. A bright fire saluted us here with its cheerful rays; how delightful to be once more sheltered by thick walls!

I had stopped while Sperver closed the door, and contemplating this ancient abode, I cried—

"Thank God! we shall rest now!"

"With a well-furnished table before us," added Gideon. "Don't stand there with your nose in the air, but rather consider what is before you—a leg of a kid, a couple of roast fowls, a pike fresh caught, with parsley sauce; cold meats and hot wines, that's what I like. Kasper has attended to my orders like a real good fellow."

Gideon spoke the truth. The meats were cold and the wines were warm, for in front of the fire stood a row of small bottles under the gentle influence of the heat.

At the sight of these good things my appetite rose in me wonderfully. But Sperver, who understood what is comfortable, stopped me.

"Fritz," said he, "don't let us be in too great a hurry; we have plenty of time; the fowls won't fly away. Your boots must hurt you. After eight hours on horseback it is pleasant to take off one's boots, that's my principle. Now sit down, put your boot between my knees; there goes one off, now the other, that's the way; now put your feet into these slippers, take off your cloak and throw this lighter coat over your shoulders. Now we are ready."

And with his cheery summons I sat down with him to work, one on each side of the table, remembering the German proverb—*Thirst comes from the evil one, but good wine from the Powers above*.

Chapter 3

We ate with the vigorous appetite which ten hours in the snows of the Black Forest would be sure to provoke.

Sperver making indiscriminate attacks upon the kid, the fowls, and the fish, murmured with his mouth full—

"The woods, the lakes and rivers, and the heathery hills are full of good things!"

Then he leaned over the back of his chair, and laying his hand on the first bottle that came to hand, he added—

"And we have hills green in spring, purple in autumn when

the grapes ripen. Your health, Fritz!"

"Yours, Gideon!"

We were a wonder to behold. We reciprocally admired each other.

The fire crackled, the forks rattled, teeth were in full activity, bottles gurgled, glasses jingled, while outside the wintry blast, the high moaning mountain winds, were mournfully chanting the dirge of the year, that strange wailing hymn with which they accompany the shock of the tempest and the swift rush of the grey clouds charged with snow and hail, while the pale moon lights up the grim and ghastly battle scene.

But we were snug under cover, and our appetite was fading away into history. Sperver had filled the "*wieder komm*," the "come again," with old wine of Brumberg; the sparkling froth fringed its ample borders; he presented it to me, saying—

"Drink the health of Yeri-Hans, lord of Nideck. Drink to the last drop, and show them that you mean it!"

Which was done.

Then he filled it again, and repeating with a voice that re-echoed among the old walls, "To the recovery of my noble master, the high and mighty lord of Nideck," he drained it also.

Then a feeling of satisfied repletion stole gently over us, and we felt pleased with everything.

I fell back in my chair, with my face directed to the ceiling, and my arms hanging lazily down. I began dreamily to consider what sort of a place I had got into.

It was a low vaulted ceiling cut out of the live rock, almost oven-shaped, and hardly twelve feet high at the highest point. At the farther end I saw a sort of deep recess where lay my bed on the ground, and consisting, as I thought I could see, of a huge bear-skin above, and I could not tell what below, and within this yet another smaller niche with a figure of the Virgin Mary carved out of the same granite, and crowned with a bunch of withered grass.

"You are looking over your room," said Spencer. "*Parbleu!* it is none of the biggest or grandest, not quite like the rooms in the castle. We are now in Hugh Lupus's tower, a place as old as the mountain itself, going as far back as the days of Charlemagne. In those days, as you see, people had not yet learned to build arches high, round, or pointed. They worked right into the rock."

"Well, for all that, you have put me in strange lodgings."

"Don't be mistaken, Fritz; it is the place of honour. It is here that the count put all his most distinguished friends. Mind that: Hugh Lupus's tower is the most honourable accommodation we have."

"And who was Hugh Lupus?"

"Why, Hugh the Wolf, to be sure. He was the head of the family of Nideck, a rough-and-ready warrior, I can tell you. He came to settle up here with a score of horsemen and halberdiers of his following. They climbed up this rock—the highest rock amongst these mountains. You will see this tomorrow. They constructed this tower, and proclaimed, 'Now we are the masters! Woe befall the miserable wretches who shall pass without paying toll to us! We will tear the wool off their backs, and their hide too, if need be. From this watch-tower we shall command a view of the far distance all round. The passes of the Rhethal, of Steinbach, Koche Plate, and of the whole line of the Black Forest are under our eye. Let the Jew pedlars and the dealers beware!' And the noble fellows did what they promised. Hugh the Wolf was at their head. Knapwurst told me all about it sitting up one night."

"Who is Knapwurst?"

"That little humpback who opened the gate for us. He is an odd fellow, Fritz, and almost lives in the library."

"So you have a man of learning at Nideck?"

"Yes, we have, the rascal! Instead of confining himself to the porter's lodge, his proper place, all the day over he is amongst the dusty books and parchments belonging to the family. He comes and goes along the shelves of the library just like a big cat. Knapwurst knows our story better than we know it ourselves. He would tell you the longest tales, Fritz, if you would only let him. He calls them chronicles—ha, ha!"

And Sperver, with the wine mounting a little into his head, began to laugh, he could hardly say why.

"So then, Gideon, you call this tower, Hugh's tower the Hugh Lupus tower?"

"Haven't I told you so already? What are you so astonished at?"

"Nothing particular."

"But you are. I can see it in your face. You are thinking of something strange. What is it?"

"Oh, never mind! It is not the name of the tower which surprises me. What I am wondering at is, how it is that you, an old poacher, who had never lived anywhere since you were a boy but amongst the fir forests, between the snowy summits of the Wald Horn and the passes of the Rhethal—you who, during all your prime of life, thought it the finest of fun to laugh at the count's gamekeepers, and to scour the mountain paths of the Schwartzwald, and boat the bushes there, and breathe the free air, and bask in the bright sunshine amongst the hills and valleys—here I find you, at the end of sixteen years of such a life, shut up in this red granite hole. That is what surprises me and what I cannot understand. Come, Sperver, light your pipe, and tell me all about it."

The old poacher took out of his leathern jacket a bit of a blackened pipe; he filled it at his leisure, gathered up in the hollow of his hand a live ember, which he placed upon the bowl of his pipe; then with his eyes dreamily cast up to the ceiling he answered meditatively—

"Old falcons, gerfalcons, and hawks, when they have long swept the plains, end their lives in a hole in a rock. Sure enough I am fond of the wide expanse of sky and land. I always was fond of it; but instead of perching by night upon a high branch of a tall tree, rocked by the wind, I now prefer to return to my cavern, to drink a glass, to pick a bone of venison, and dry my plumage before a warm fire. The Count of Nideck does not disdain Sperver, the old hawk, the true man of the woods. One evening, meeting me by moonlight, he frankly said to me, 'Old comrade, you hunt only by night. Come and hunt by day with me. You have a sharp beak and strong claws. Well, hunt away, if such is your nature; but hunt by my licence, for I am the eagle upon these mountains, and my name is Nideck!'"

Sperver was silent a few minutes; then he resumed—

"That was just what suited me, and now I hunt as I used to do, and I quietly drink along with a friend my bottle of *Affenthal* or—"

At that moment there was a shock that made the door vibrate; Sperver stopped and listened.

"It is a gust of wind," I said.

"No, it is something else. Don't you hear the scratching of claws? It is a dog that has escaped. Open, Lieverle, open, Blitzen!" cried the huntsman, rising; but he had not gone a couple of steps when a formidable-looking hound of the Danish breed broke into the tower, and ran to lay his heavy paws on his master's shoulders, licking his beard and his cheeks with his long rose-coloured tongue, uttering all the while short barks and yelps expressive of his joy.

Sperver had passed his arm round the dog's neck, and, turning to me, said—

"Fritz, what man could love me as this dog does? Do look at this head, these eyes, these teeth!"

He uncovered the animal's teeth, displaying a set of fangs that would have pulled down and rent a buffalo. Then repelling him with difficulty, for the dog was re-doubling his caresses—

"Down, Lieverle. I know you love me. If you did not, who would?"

Never had I seen so tremendous a dog as this Lieverle. His height attained two feet and a half. He would have been a most formidable creature in an attack. His forehead was broad, flat, and covered with fine soft hair; his eye was keen, his paws of great length, his sides and legs a woven mass of muscles and nerves, broad over the back and shoulders, slender and tapering towards the hind legs. But he had no scent. If such monstrous and powerful hounds were endowed with the scent of the terrier there would soon be an end of game.

Sperver had returned to his seat, and was passing his hand over Lieverle's massive head with pride, and enumerating to me his excellent qualities.

Lieverle seemed to understand him.

"See, Fritz, that dog will throttle a wolf with one snap of his jaws. For courage and strength, he is perfection. He is not five years old, but he is in his prime. I need not tell you that he is trained to hunt the boar. Every time we come across a herd of them I tremble for Lieverle; his attack is too straightforward, he flies on the game as straight as an arrow. That is why I am afraid of the brutes' tusks. Lie down, Lieverle, lie on your back!"

The dog obeyed, and presented to view his flesh-coloured sides.

"Look, Fritz, at that long white seam without any hair upon it from under the thigh right up to the chest. A boar did that. Poor creature! he was holding him fast by the ear and would not let go; we tracked the two by the blood. I was the first up with them. Seeing my Lieverle I gave a shout, I jumped off my horse, I caught him between my arms, flung him into my cloak, and brought him home. I was almost beside myself. Happily the vital parts had not been wounded. I sewed up his belly in spite of his howling and yelling, for he suffered fearfully; but in three days he was already licking his wound, and a dog who licks himself is already saved. You remember that, Lieverle, hey! and aren't we fonder of each other now than ever?"

I was quite moved with the affection of the man for that dog, and of the dog for his master; they seemed to look into the very depths of each other's souls. The dog wagged his tail, and the man had tears in his eyes.

Sperver went on—

"What amazing strength! Do you see, Fritz, he has burst his cord to get to me—a rope of six strands; he found out my track and here he is! Here, Lieverle, catch!"

And he threw to him the remains of the leg of kid. The jaws opened wide and closed again with a terrible crash, and Sperver, looking at me significantly, said—

"Fritz, if he were to grip you by your breeches you would not get away so easily!"

"Nor any one else, I suppose."

The dog went to stretch himself at his ease full length under the mantelshelf with the leg fast between his mighty paws. He began to tear it into pieces. Sperver looked at him out of the corner of his eye with great satisfaction. The bone was fast falling into small fragments in the powerful mill that was crashing it. Lieverle was partial to marrow!

"Aha! Fritz, if you were requested to fetch that bone away from him, what would you say?"

"I should think it a mission requiring extraordinary delicacy and tact."

Then we broke out into a hearty laugh, and Sperver, seated in his leathern easy chair, with his left arm thrown back over his head, one of his manly legs over a stool, and the other in front of a huge log, which was dripping at its end with the oozing sap, and darted volumes of light grey smoke to the roof.

I was still contemplating the dog, when, suddenly recollecting our broken conversation, I went on—

"Now, Sperver, you have not told me everything. When you left the mountain for the castle was it not on account of the death of Gertrude, your good, excellent wife?"

Gideon frowned, and a tear dimmed his eye; he drew himself up, and shaking out the ashes of his pipe upon his thumbnail, he said—

"True, my wife is dead. That drove me from the woods. I could not look upon the valley of Roche Creuse without pain. I turned my flight in this direction: I hunt less in the woods, and I can see it all from higher up, and if by chance the pack tails off in that direction I let them go. I turn back and try to think of something else."

Sperver had grown taciturn. With his head drooped upon his breast, his eyes fixed on the stone floor, he sat silent. I felt sorry to have awoke these melancholy recollections in him. Then, my thoughts once more returning to the Black Plague grovelling in the snow, I felt a shivering of horror.

How strange! just one word had sent us into a train of unhappy thoughts. A whole world of remembrances was called up by a chance.

I know not how long this silence lasted, when a growl, deep, long, and terrible, like distant thunder, made us start.

We looked at the dog. The half-gnawed bone was still between his forepaws, but with head raised high, ears cocked up, and flashing eye, he was listening intently—listening to the silence as it were, and an angry quivering ran down the length of his back.

Sperver and I fixed on each other anxious eyes; yet there was not a sound, not a breath outside, for the wind had gone down; nothing could be heard but the deep protracted growl which came from deep down the chest of the noble hound.

Suddenly he sprang up and bounded impetuously against the wall with a hoarse, rough bark of fearful loudness. The walls reechoed just as if a clap of thunder had rattled the casements.

Lieverle, with his head low down, seemed to want to see through the granite, and his lips drawn back from his teeth discovered them to the very gums, displaying two close rows of fangs white as ivory. Still he growled. For a moment he would stop abruptly with his nose snuffing close to the wall, next the floor, with strong respirations; then he would rise again in a fresh rage, and with his forepaws seemed as if he would break through the granite.

We watched in silence without being able to understand what caused his excitement.

Another yell of rage more terrible than the first made us spring from our seats.

"Lieverle! what possesses you? Are you going mad?"

He seized a log and began to sound the wall, which only returned the dead, hard sound of a wall of solid rock. There was no hollow in it; yet the dog stood in the posture of attack.

"Decidedly you must have been dreaming bad dreams," said

the huntsman. "Come, lie down, and don't worry us any more with your nonsense."

At that moment a noise outside reached our ears. The door opened, and the fat honest countenance of Tobias Offenloch with his lantern in one hand and his stick in the other, his three-cornered hat on his head, appeared, smiling and jovial, in the opening.

"*Salut! l'honorable compagnie!*" he cried as he entered; "what are you doing here?"

"It was that rascal Lieverle who made all that row. Just fancy—he set himself up against that wall as if he smelt a thief. What could he mean?"

"Why *parbleu!* he heard the dot, dot of my wooden leg, to be sure, stumping up the tower-stairs," answered the jolly fellow, laughing.

Then setting his lantern on the table—

"That will teach you, friend Gideon, to tie up your dogs. You are foolishly weak over your dogs—very foolishly. Those beasts of yours won't be satisfied till they have put us all out of doors. Just this minute I met Blitzen in the long gallery: he sprang at my leg—see there are the marks of his teeth in proof of what I say; and it is quite a new leg—a brute of a hound!"

"Tie up my dogs! That's rather a new idea," said the huntsman. "Dogs tied up are good for nothing at all; they grow too wild. Besides, was not Lieverle tied up, after all? See his broken cord."

"What I tell you is not on my own account. When they come near me I always hold up my stick and put my wooden leg foremost—that is my discipline. I say, dogs in their kennels, cats on the roof, and the people in the castle."

Tobias sat down after thus delivering himself of his sentiments, and with both elbows on the table, his eyes expanding with delight, he confided to us that just now he was a bachelor.

"You don't mean that!"

"Yes, Marie Anne is sitting up with Gertrude in *monseigneur's* ante-room."

"Then you are in no hurry to go away?"

"No, none at all. I should like to stay in your company."

"How unfortunate that you should have come in so late!" remarked Sperver; "all the bottles are empty."

The disappointment of the discomfited *major-domo* excited my compassion. The poor man would so gladly have enjoyed his widowhood. But in spite of my endeavours to repress it a long yawn extended wide my mouth.

"Well, another time," said he, rising. "What is only put off is not given up."

And he took his lantern.

"Good night, gentlemen."

"Stop—wait for me," cried Gideon. "I can see Fritz is sleepy; we will go down together."

"Very gladly, Sperver; on our way we will have a word with Trumpf, the butler. He is downstairs with the rest, and Knapwurst is telling them tales."

"All right. Goodnight, Fritz."

"Goodnight, Gideon. Don't forget to send for me if the count is taken worse."

"I will do as you wish. Lieverle, come."

They went out, and as they were crossing the platform I could hear the Nideck clock strike eleven. I was tired out and soon fell asleep.

Chapter 4

Daylight was beginning to tinge with bluish grey the only window in my dungeon tower when I was roused out of my niche in the granite by the prolonged distant notes of a hunting horn.

There is nothing more sad and melancholy than the wail of this instrument when the day begins to struggle with the night—when not a sigh nor a sound besides comes to molest the solitary reign of silence; it is especially the last long note which spreads in widening waves over the immensity of the plain beneath, awaking the distant, far-off echoes amongst the mountains, that has in it a poetic element that stirs up the depths of the soul.

Leaning upon my elbow in my bear-skin I lay listening to the plaintive sound, which suggested something of the feudal ages. The contemplation of my chamber, the ancient den of the Wolf of Nideck, with its low, dark arch, threatening almost to come down to crush the occupant; and further on that small leaden window, just touching the ceiling, more wide than high, and deeply recessed in the wall, added to the reality of the impression.

I arose quickly and ran to open the window wide.

Then presented itself to my astonished eyes such a wondrous spectacle as no mortal tongue, no pen of man, can describe—the wide prospect that the eagle, the denizen of the high Alps, sweeps with his far reaching ken every morning at the rising of the deep purple veil that overhung the horizon by night mountains farther off! mountains far away! and yet again in the blue distance—mountains still, blending with the grey mists of the morning in the shadowy horizon!—motionless billows that sink into peace and stillness in the blue distance of the plains of Lorraine. Such is a faint idea of the mighty scenery of the Vosges, boundless forests, silver lakes, dazzling crests, ridges, and peaks projecting their clear outlines upon the steel-blue of the valleys clothed in snow. Beyond this, infinite space!

Could any enthusiasm of poet or skill of painter attain the sublime elevation of such a scene as that?

I stood mute with admiration. At every moment the details stood out more clearly in the advancing light of morning; hamlets, farmhouses, villages, seemed to rise and peep out of every undulation of the land. A little more attention brought more and more numerous objects into view.

I had leaned out of my window rapt in contemplation for more than a quarter of an hour when a hand was laid lightly upon my shoulder; I turned round startled, when the calm figure and quiet smile of Gideon saluted me with—

"*Guten Tag*, Fritz! Good morning!"

Then he also rested his arms on the window, smoking his short pipe. He extended his hand and said—

"Look, Fritz, and admire! You are a son of the Black Forest, and you must admire all that. Look there below; there is Roche Creuse. Do you see it? Don't you remember Gertrude? How far off those times seem now!"

Sperver brushed away a tear. What could I say?

We sat long contemplating and meditating over this grand spectacle. From time to time the old poacher, noticing me with my eyes fixed upon some distant object, would explain—

"That is the Wald Horn; this is the Tiefenthal; there's the fall of the Steinbach; it has stopped running now; it is hanging down in great fringed sheets, like the curtains over the shoulder of the Harberg—a cold winter's cloak! Down there is a path that leads to Fribourg; in a fortnight's time it will be difficult to trace it."

Thus our time passed away.

I could not tear myself away from so beautiful a prospect. A few birds of prey, with wings hollowed into a graceful curve sharp-pointed at each end, the fan-shaped tail spread out, were silently sweeping round the rock-hewn tower; herons flew unscathed above them, owing their safety from the grasp of the sharp claws and the tearing beak to the elevation of their flight.

Not a cloud marred the beauty of the blue sky; all the snow had fallen to earth; once more the huntsman's horn awoke the echoes.

"That is my friend Sebalt lamenting down there," said Sperver. "He knows everything about horses and dogs, and he sounds the hunter's horn better than any man in Germany. Listen, Fritz, how soft and mellow the notes are! Poor Sebalt! he is pining away over *monseigneur's* illness; he cannot hunt as he used to do. His only comfort is to get up every morning at sunrise on to the Altenberg and play the count's favourite airs. He thinks he shall be able to cure him that way!"

Sperver, with the good taste of a man who appreciates beautiful scenery, had offered no interruption to my contemplations; but when, my eyes dazzled and swimming with so much light, I turned round to the darkness of the tower, he said to me—

"Fritz, it's all right; the count has had no fresh attack."

These words brought me back to a sense of the realities of life.

"Ah, I am very glad!"

"It is all owing to you, Fritz."

"What do you mean? I have not prescribed yet."

"What signifies? You were there; that was enough."

"You are only joking, Gideon! What is the use of my being present if I don't prescribe?"

"Why, you bring him good luck!"

I looked straight at him, but he was not even smiling!

"Yes, Fritz, you are just a messenger of good; the last two years the lord had another attack the next day after the first, then a third and a fourth. You have put an end to that. What can be clearer?"

"Well, to me it is not so very clear; on the contrary, it is very obscure."

"We are never too old to learn," the good man went on. "Fritz, there are messengers of evil and there are messengers of good. Now that rascal Knapwurst, he is a sure messenger of ill. If ever I meet him as I am going out hunting I am sure of some misadventure; my gun misses fire, or I sprain my ankle, or a dog gets ripped up!—all sorts of mischief come. So, being quite aware of this, I always try and set off at early daybreak, before that author of mischief, who sleeps like a dormouse, has opened his eyes; or else I slip out by a back way by the postern gate. Don't you see?"

"I understand you very well, but your ideas seem to me very strange, Gideon."

"You, Fritz," he went on, without noticing my interruption, "you are a most excellent lad; Heaven has covered your head with innumerable blessings; just one glance at your jolly countenance, your frank, clear eyes, your good-natured smile, is enough to make any one happy. You positively bring good luck with you. I have always said so, and now would you like to have a proof?"

"Yes, indeed I should. It would be worthwhile to know how much there is in me without my having any knowledge of it."

"Well," said he, grasping my wrist, "look down there!"

He pointed to a hillock at a couple of gunshots from the castle.

"Do you see there a rock half-buried in the snow, with a ragged bush by its side?"

"Quite well."

"Do you see anything near?"

"No."

"Well, there is a reason for that. You have driven away the Black Plague! Every year at the second attack there she was holding her feet between her hands. By night she lighted a fire; she warmed herself and boiled roots. She bore a curse with her. This morning the very first thing which I did was to get up here. I climbed up the beacon tower; I looked well all round; the old hag was nowhere to be seen. I shaded my eyes with my hand. I looked up and down, right and left, and everywhere; not a sign of the creature anywhere. She had scented you evidently."

And the good fellow, in a fit of enthusiasm, shook me warmly by the hand, crying with unchecked emotion—

"Ah, Fritz, how glad I am that I brought you here! The witch *will* be sold, eh?"

Well, I confess I felt a little ashamed that I had been all my life such a very well-deserving young man without knowing anything of the circumstance myself.

"So, Sperver," I said, "the count has spent a good night?"

"A very good one."

"Then I am very well pleased. Let us go down."

We again traversed the high parapet, and I was now better able to examine this way of access, the ramparts of which arose from a prodigious depth; and they were extended along the sharp narrow ridge of the rock down to the very bottom of the valley. It was a long flight of jagged precipitous steps descending from the wolf's den, or rather eagle's nest, down to the deep valley below.

Gazing down I felt giddy, and recoiling in alarm to the middle of the platform, I hastily descended down the path which led to the main building.

We had already traversed several great corridors when a great open door stood before us. I looked in, and descried, at the top of a double ladder, the little gnome Knapwurst, whose strange appearance had struck me the night before.

The hall itself attracted my attention by its imposing aspect. It was the receptacle of the archives of the house of Nideck, a high, dark, dusty apartment, with long Gothic windows, reaching from the angle of the ceiling to within a couple of yards from the floor.

There were collected along spacious shelves, by the care of the old abbots, not only all the documents, title-deeds, and family genealogies of the house of Nideck, establishing their rights and their alliances, and connections with all the great historic families of Germany, but besides these there were all the chronicles of the Black Forest, the collected works of the old Minnesinger, and great folio volumes from the presses of Gutenberg and Faust, entitled to equal veneration on account of their remarkable history and of the enduring solidity of their binding. The deep shadows of the groined vaults, their arches divided by massive ribs, and descending partly down the cold grey walls, reminded one of the gloomy cloisters of the Middle Ages. And amidst these characteristic surroundings sat an ugly dwarf on the top of his ladder, with a red-edged volume upon his bony knees, his head half-buried in a rough fur cap, small grey eyes, wide misshapen mouth, humps on back and shoulders, a most uninviting object, the familiar spirit—the rat, as Sperver would have it—of this last refuge of all the learning belonging to the princely race of Nideck.

But a truly historical importance belonged to this chamber in the long series of family portraits, filling almost entirely one side of the ancient library. All were there, men and women; from Hugh the Wolf to Yeri-Hans, the present owner; from the first rough daub of barbarous times to the perfect work of the best modern painters.

My attention was naturally drawn in that direction.

Hugh I., a bald-headed figure, seemed to glare upon you like a wolf stealing upon you round the corner of a wood. His grey bloodshot eyes, his red beard, and his large hairy ears gave him a fearful and ferocious aspect.

Next to him, like the lamb next to the wolf, was the portrait of a lady of youthful years, with gentle blue eyes, hands crossed on the breast over a book of devotions, and tresses of fair long silky hair encircling her sweet countenance with a glorious golden aureola. This picture struck me by its wonderful resemblance to Odile of Nideck.

I have never seen anything more lovely and more charming than this old painting on wood, which was stiff enough indeed in its outline, but delightfully refreshing and ingenuous.

I had examined this picture attentively for some minutes when another female portrait, hanging at its side, drew my attention reluctantly away. Here was a woman of the true Visigoth type, with a wide low forehead, yellowish eyes, prominent cheek-bones, red hair, and a nose hooked like an eagle's beak.

That woman must have been an excellent match for Hugh, thought I, and I began to consider the costume, which answered perfectly to the energy displayed in the head, for the right hand rested upon a sword, and an iron breastplate inclosed the figure.

I should have some difficulty in expressing the thoughts which passed through my mind in the examination of these three portraits. My eye passed from the one to the other with singular curiosity.

Sperver, standing at the library door, had aroused the attention of Knapwurst with a sharp whistle, which made that worthy send a glance in his direction, though it did not succeed in fetching him down from his elevation.

"Is it me that you are whistling to like a dog?" said the dwarf.

"I am, you vermin! It is an honour you don't deserve."

"Just listen to me, Sperver," replied the little man with sublime scorn; "you cannot spit so high as my shoe!" which he contemptuously held out.

"Suppose I were to come up?"

"If you come up a single step I'll squash you flat with this volume!"

Gideon laughed, and replied—

"Don't get angry, friend; I don't mean to do you any harm; on the contrary, I greatly respect you for your learning; but what I want to know is what you are doing here so early in the morning, by lamplight? You look as if you had spent the night here."

"So I have; I have been reading all night."

"Are not the days long enough for you to read in?"

"No; I am following out an important inquiry, and I don't mean to sleep until I am satisfied."

"Indeed; and what may this very important question be?"

"I have to ascertain under what circumstances Ludwig of Nideck discovered my ancestor, Otto the Dwarf, in the forests of Thuringia. You know, Sperver, that my ancestor Otto was only a cubit high—that is, a foot and a-half. He delighted the world with his wisdom, and made an honourable figure at the coronation of Duke Rudolphe. Count Ludwig had him inclosed in a cold roast peacock, served up in all his plumage. It was at that time one of the greatest delicacies, served up garnished all round with sucking pigs, gilded and silvered. During the banquet Otto kept spreading the peacock's tail, and all the lords, courtiers, and ladies of high birth were astonished and delighted at this wonderful piece of mechanism. At last he came out, sword in hand, and shouted with a loud voice—"Long live Duke Rudolphe!" and the cry was repeated with acclamations by the whole table. Bernard Herzog makes mention of this event, but he has neglected to inform us where this dwarf came from, whether he was of lofty lineage or of base extraction, which latter, however, is very improbable, for the lower sort of people have not so much sense as that."

I was astounded at so much pride in so diminutive a being,

yet my curiosity prevented me from showing too much of my feelings, for he alone could supply me with information upon the portraits that accompanied that of Hugh Lupus.

"Monsieur Knapwurst," I began very respectfully, "would you oblige me by enlightening me upon certain historic doubts?"

"Speak, sir, without any constraint; on the subject of family history and chronicles I am entirely at your service. Other matters don't interest me."

"I desire to learn some particulars respecting the two portraits on each side of the founder of this race."

"Aha!" cried Knapwurst with a glow of satisfaction lighting up his hideous features; "you mean Hedwige and Huldine, the two wives of Hugh Lupus."

And laying down his volume he descended from his ladder to speak more at his ease. His eyes glistened, and the delight of gratified vanity beamed from them as he displayed his vast erudition.

When he had arrived at my side he bowed to me with ceremonious gravity. Sperver stood behind us, very well satisfied that I was admiring the dwarf of Nideck. In spite of the ill luck which, in his opinion, accompanied the little monster's appearance, he respected and boasted of his superior knowledge.

"Sir," said Knapwurst, pointing with his yellow hand to the portraits, "Hugh of Nideck, the first of his illustrious race, married, in 832, Hedwige of Lutzelbourg, who brought to him in dowry the counties of Giromani and Haut Barr, the castles of Geroldseck, Teufelshorn, and others. Hugh Lupus had no issue by his first wife, who died young, in the year of our Lord 837. Then Hugh, having become lord and owner of the dowry, refused to give it up, and there were terrible battles between himself and his brothers-in-law. But his second wife, Huldine, whom you see there in a steel breastplate, aided him by her sage counsel. It is unknown whence or of what family she came, but for all that she saved Hugh's life, who had been made prisoner by Frantz of Lutzelbourg. He was to have been hanged that very day, and a gibbet had already been set up on the ramparts, when Huldine, at the head of her husband's vassals, whom she had armed and inspired with her own courage, bravely broke in, released Hugh, and hung Frantz in his place. Hugh had married his wife in 842, and had three children by her."

"So," I resumed pensively, "the first of these wives was called Hedwige, and the descendants of Nideck are not related to her?"

"Not at all."

"Are you quite sure?"

"I can show you our genealogical tree; Hedwige had no children; Huldine, the second wife, had three."

"That is surprising to me."

"Why so?"

"I thought I traced a resemblance."

"Oho! resemblance! Rubbish!" cried Knapwurst with a discordant laugh. "See—look at this wooden snuff-box; in it you see a portrait of my great-grandfather, Hanswurst. His nose is as long and as pointed as an extinguisher, and his jaws like nutcrackers. How does that affect his being the grandfather of me—of a man with finely-formed features and an agreeable mouth?"

"Oh no!—of course not."

"Well, so it is with the Nidecks. They may some of them be like Hedwige, but for all that Huldine is the head of their ancestry. See the genealogical tree. Now, sir, are you satisfied?"

Then we separated—Knapwurst and I—excellent friends.

Chapter 5

"Nevertheless," thought I, "there is the likeness. It is not chance. What is chance? There is no such thing; it is nonsense to talk of chance. It must be something higher!"

I was following my friend Sperver, deep in thought, who had now resumed his walk down the corridor. The portrait of Hedwige, in all its artless simplicity, mingled in my mind with the face of Odile.

Suddenly Gideon stopped, and, raising my eyes, I saw that we were standing before the count's door.

"Come in, Fritz," he said, "and I will give the dogs a feed. When the master's away the servants neglect their duty; I will come for you by-and-by."

I entered, more desirous of seeing the young lady than the count her father; I was blaming myself for my remissness, but there is no controlling one's interest and affections. I was much surprised to see in the half-light of the alcove the reclining figure of the count leaning upon his elbow and observing me with profound attention. I was so little prepared for this examination that I stood rather dispossessed of self-command.

"Come nearer, *monsieur le docteur*," he said in a weak but firm voice, holding out his hand. "My faithful Sperver has often mentioned your name to me; and I was anxious to make your acquaintance."

"Let us hope, my lord, that it will be continued under more favourable circumstances. A little patience, and we shall avert this attack."

"I think not," he replied. "I feel my time drawing near."

"You are mistaken, my lord."

"No; Nature grants us, as a last favour, to have a presentiment of our approaching end."

"How often I have seen such presentiments falsified!" I said with a smile.

He fixed his eyes searchingly upon me, as is usual with patients expressing anxiety about their prospects. It is a difficult moment for the doctor. The moral strength of his patient depends upon the expression of the firmness of his convictions; the eye of the sufferer penetrates into the innermost soul of his consciousness; if he believes that he can discover any hint or shade of doubt, his fate is sealed; depression sets in; the secret springs that maintain the elasticity of the spirit give way, and the disorder has it all its own way.

I stood my examination firmly and successfully, and the count seemed to regain confidence; he again pressed my hand, and resigned himself calmly and confidently to my treatment.

Not until then did I perceive Mademoiselle Odile and an old

lady, no doubt her governess, seated by her bedside at the other end of the alcove.

They silently saluted me, and suddenly the picture in the library reappeared before me.

"It is she," I said, "Hugh's first wife. There is the fair and noble brow, there are the long lashes, and that sad, unfathomable smile. Oh, how much past telling lies in a woman's smile! Seek not, then, for unmixed joy and pleasure! Her smile serves but to veil untold sorrows, anxiety for the future, even heartrending cares. The maid, the wife, the mother, smile and smile, even when the heart is breaking and the abyss is opening. O woman! this is thy part in the mortal struggle of human life!"

I was pursuing these reflections when the lord of Nideck began to speak—

"If my dear child Odile would but consult my wishes I believe my health would return."

I looked towards the young countess; she fixed her eyes on the floor, and seemed to be praying silently.

"Yes," the sick man went on, "I should then return to life; the prospect of seeing myself surrounded by a young family, and of pressing grandchildren to my heart, and beholding the succession to my house, would revive me."

At the mild and gentle tone of entreaty in which this was said I felt deeply moved with compassion; but the young lady made no reply.

In a minute or two the count, who kept his watchful eyes upon her, went on—

"Odile, you refuse to make your father a happy man? I only ask for a faint hope. I fix no time. I won't limit your choice. We will go to court. There you will have a hundred opportunities of marrying with distinction and with honour. Who would not be proud to win my daughter's hand? You shall be perfectly free to decide for yourself."

He paused.

There is nothing more painful to a stranger than these family quarrels. There are such contending interests, so many private motives, at work, that mere modesty should make it our duty to place ourselves out of hearing of such discussions. I felt pained, and would gladly have retired. But the circumstances of the case forbade this.

"My dear father," said Odile, as if to evade any further discussion, "you will get better. Heaven will not take you from those who love you. If you but knew the fervour with which I pray for you!"

"That is not an answer," said the count drily. "What objection can you make to my proposal? Is it not fair and natural? Am I to be deprived of the consolations vouchsafed to the neediest and most wretched? You know I have acted towards you openly and frankly."

"You have, my father."

"Then give me your reason for your refusal."

"My resolution is formed—I have consecrated myself to God."

So much firmness in so frail a being made me tremble. She stood like the sculptured Madonna in Hugh's tower, calm and immovable, however weak in appearance.

The eyes of the count kindled with an ominous fire. I tried to make the young countess understand by signs how gladly I would hear her give the least hope, and calm his rising passion; but she seemed not to see me.

"So," he cried in a smothered tone, as if he were strangling—"so you will look on and see your father perish? A word would restore him to life, and you refuse to speak that one word?"

"Life is not in the hand of man, for it is God's gift; my word can be of no avail."

"Those are nothing but pious maxims," answered the count scornfully, "to release you from your plain duty. But has not God said, '*Honour thy father and thy mother?*'"

"I do honour you," she replied gently. "But it is my duty not to marry."

I could hear the grinding and gnashing of the man's teeth. He lay apparently calm, but presently turned abruptly and cried—

"Leave me; the sight of you is offensive to me!"

And addressing me as I stood by agitated with conflicting feelings—

"Doctor," he cried with a savage grin, "have you any violent malignant poison about you to give me—something that will destroy me like a thunderbolt? It would be a mercy to poison me like a dog, rather than let me suffer as I am doing."

His features writhed convulsively, his colour became livid.

Odile rose and advanced to the door.

"Stay!" he howled furiously—"stay till I have cursed you!"

So far I had stood by without speaking, not venturing to interfere between Father and Daughter, but now I could refrain no longer.

"*Monseigneur*," I cried, "for the sake of your own health, for the sake of mere justice and fairness, do calm yourself; your life is at stake."

"What matters my life? what matters the future? Is there a knife here to put an end to me? Let me die!"

His excitement rose every minute. I seemed to dread lest in some frenzied moment he should spring from the bed and destroy his child's life. But she, calm though deadly pale, knelt at the door, which was standing open, and outside I could see Sperver, whose features betrayed the deepest anxiety. He drew near without noise, and bending towards Odile—

"Oh, *mademoiselle!*" he whispered—"*mademoiselle*, the count is such a worthy, good man. If you would but just say only, 'Perhaps—by-and-by—we will see.'"

She made no reply, and did not change her attitude.

At this moment I persuaded the Lord of Nideck to take a few drops of *laudanum*; he sank back with a sigh, and soon his panting and irregular breathing became more measured under the influence of a deep and heavy slumber.

Odile arose, and her aged friend, who had not opened her lips, went out with her. Sperver and I watched their slowly retreating figures. There was a calm grandeur in the step of the young countess which seemed to express a consciousness of duty fulfilled.

When she had disappeared down the long corridor Gideon turned towards me.

"Well, Fritz," he said gravely, "what is your opinion?"

I bent my head down without answering. This girl's incredible firmness astonished and bewildered me.

Chapter 6

Sperver's indignation was mounting.

"There's the happiness and felicity of the rich! What is the good of being master of Nideck, with castles, forests, lakes, and all the best parts of the Black Forest, when an innocent looking damsel comes and says to you in her sweet soft voice, 'Is that your will? Well, it is not mine. Do you say I must? Well, I say no, I won't.' Is it not awful? Would it not be better to be a woodcutter's son and live quietly upon the wages of your day's work? Come on, Fritz; let us be off. I am suffocating here; I want to get into the open air."

And the good fellow, seizing my arm, dragged me down the corridor.

It was now about nine. The sky had been fair when we got up, but now the clouds had again covered the dreary earth, the north wind was raising the snow in ghostly eddies against the window-panes, and I could scarcely distinguish the summits of the neighbouring mountains.

We were going down the stairs which led into the hall, when, at a turn in the corridor, we found ourselves face to face with Tobias Offenloch, the worthy *major-domo*, in a great state of palpitation.

"Halloo!" he cried, closing our way with his stick right across the passage; "where are you off to in such a hurry? What about our breakfast?"

"Breakfast! which breakfast do you mean?" asked Sperver.

"What do you mean by pretending to forget what breakfast? Are not you and I to breakfast this very morning with Doctor Fritz?"

"Aha! so we are! I had forgotten all about it."

And Offenloch burst into a great laugh which divided his jolly face from ear to ear.

"Ha, ha! this is rather beyond a joke. And I was afraid of being too late! Come, let us be moving. Kasper is upstairs waiting. I ordered him to lay the breakfast in your room; I thought we should be more comfortable there. Goodbye for the present, doctor."

"Are you not coming up with us?" asked Sperver.

"No, I am going to tell the countess that the Baron de Zimmer-Bluderich begs the honour to thank her in person before he leaves the castle."

"The Baron de Zimmer?"

"Yes, that stranger who came yesterday in the middle of the night."

"Well, you must make haste."

"Yes, I shall not be long. Before you have done uncorking the bottles I shall be with you again."

And he hobbled away as fast as he could.

The mention of breakfast had given a different turn to Sperver's thoughts.

"Exactly so," he observed, turning back; "the best way to drown all your cares is to drink a draught of good wine. I am very glad we are going to breakfast in my room. Under those great high vaults in the fencing-school, sitting round a small table, you feel just like mice nibbling a nut in a corner of a big church. Here we are, Fritz. Just listen to the wind whistling through the arrow-slits. In half-an-hour there will be a storm."

He pushed the door open; and Kasper, who was only drumming with his fingers upon the window-panes, seemed very glad to see us. That little man had flaxen hair and a snub nose. Sperver had made him his *factotum*; it was he who took to pieces and cleaned his guns, mended the riding-horses' harness, fed the dogs in his absence, and superintended in the kitchen the preparation of his favourite dishes. On grand occasions he was outrider. He now stood with a napkin over his arm, and was gravely uncorking the long-necked bottle of Rhenish.

"Kasper," said his master, as soon as he had surveyed this satisfactory state of things—"Kasper, I was very well pleased with you yesterday; everything was excellent; the roast kid, the chicken, and the fish. I like fair-play, and when a man has done his duty I like to tell him so. To-day I am quite as well satisfied. The boar's head looks excellent with its white-wine sauce; so does the crayfish soup. Isn't it your opinion too, Fritz?"

I assented.

"Well," said Sperver, "since it is so, you shall have the honour of filling our glasses. I mean to raise you step by step, for you are a very deserving fellow."

Kasper looked down bashfully and blushed; he seemed to enjoy his master's praises.

We took our places, and I was wondering at this quondam poacher, who in years gone by was content to cook his own potatoes in his cottage, now assuming all the airs of a great *seigneur*. Had he been born Lord of Nideck he could not have put on a more noble and dignified attitude at table. A single glance brought Kasper to his side, made him bring such and such a bottle, or bring the dish he required.

We were just going to attack the boar's head when Master Tobias appeared in person, followed by no less a personage than the Baron of Zimmer-Bluderich, attended by his groom.

We rose from our seats. The young baron advanced to meet us with head uncovered. It was a noble-looking head, pale and haughty, with a surrounding of fine dark hair. He stopped before Sperver.

"*Monsieur*," said he in that pure Saxon accent which no other dialect can approach, "I am come to ask you for information as to this locality. Madame la Comtesse de Nideck tells me that no one knows these mountains so well as yourself."

"That is quite true, *monseigneur*, and I am quite at your service."

"Circumstances of great urgency oblige me to start in the midst of the storm," replied the baron, pointing to the window-panes thickly covered with flakes of snow. "I must reach Wald Horn, six leagues from this place!"

"That will be a hard matter, my lord, for all the roads are blocked up with snow."

"I am aware of that, but necessity obliges."

"You must have a guide, then. I will go, if you will allow me, to Sebalt Kraft, the head huntsman at Nideck. He knows the mountains almost as well as I do."

"I am much obliged to you for your kind offers, and I am very grateful, but still I cannot accept them. Your instructions will be quite sufficient."

Sperver bowed, then advancing to a window, he opened it wide. A furious blast of wind rushed in, driving the whirling snow as far as the corridor, and slammed the door with a crash.

I remained by my chair, leaning on its back. Kasper slunk into a corner. Sperver and the baron, with his groom, stood at the open window.

"Gentlemen," said Sperver with a loud voice to make himself heard above the howling winds, and with arm extended, "you see the country mapped out before you. If the weather was fair I would take you up into the tower, and then we could see the whole of the Black Forest at our feet, but it is no use now. Here you can see the peak of the Altenberg. Farther on behind that white ridge you may see the Wald Horn, beaten by a furious storm. You must make straight for the Wald Horn. From the summit of the rock, which seems formed like a mitre, and is called Roche Fendue, you will see three peaks, the Behrenkopp, the Geierstein, and the Trielfels. It is by this last one at the right that you must proceed. There is a torrent across the valley of the Rhethal, but it must be frozen now.

"In any case, if you can get no farther, you will find on your left, on following the bank, a cavern half-way up the hill, called Roche Creuse. You can spend the night there, and to-morrow very likely, if the wind falls, you will see the Wald Horn before you. If you are lucky enough to meet with a charcoal-burner, he might, perhaps, show you where there is a ford over the stream;

but I doubt whether one will be found anywhere on such a day as this. There are none from our neighbourhood. Only be careful to go right round the base of the Behrenkopp, for you could not get down the other side. It is a precipice."

During these observations I was watching Sperver, whose clear, energetic tones indicated the different points in the road with the greatest precision, and I watched, too, the young baron, who was listening with the closest attention. No obstacle seemed to alarm him. The old groom seemed not less bent upon the enterprise.

Just as they were leaving the window a momentary light broke through the grey snow-clouds—just one of those moments when the eddying wind lays hold of the falling clouds of snow and flings them back again like floating garments of white. Then for a moment there was a glimpse of the distance. The three peaks stood out behind the Altenberg. The description which Sperver had given of invisible objects became visible for a few moments; then the air again was veiled in ghostly clouds of flying snow.

"Thank you," said the baron. "Now I have seen the point I am to make for; and, thanks to your explanations, I hope to reach it."

Sperver bowed without answering. The young man and his servant, having saluted us, retired slowly and gravely.

Gideon shut the window, and addressing Master Tobias and me, said—

"The deuce must be in the man to start off in such horrible weather as this. I could hardly turn out a wolf on such a day as this. However, it is their business, not mine. I seem to remember that young man's face, and his servant's too. Now let us drink! Maitre Tobie, your health!"

I had gone to the window, and as the Baron Zimmer and his groom mounted on horseback in the middle of the courtyard, in spite of the snow which was filling the air, I saw at the left in a turret, pierced with long Gothic windows, the pale countenance of Odile directed long and anxiously towards the young man.

"Halloo, Fritz! what are you doing?"

"I am only looking at those strangers' horses."

"Oh, the Wallachians! I saw them this morning in the stable. They are splendid animals."

The horsemen galloped away at full speed, and the curtain in the turret-window dropped.

Chapter 7

Several uneventful days followed. My life at Nideck was becoming dull and monotonous. Every morning there was the doleful bugle-call of the huntsman, whose occupation was gone; then came a visit to the count; after that breakfast, with Sperver's interminable speculations upon the Black Plague, the incessant gossiping and chattering of Marie Lagoutte, Maitre Tobias, and all that pack of idle servants, who had nothing to do but eat and drink, smoke, and go to sleep. The only man who had any kind of individual existence was Knapwurst, who sat buried up to the tip of his red nose in old chronicles all the day long, careless of the cold so long as there was anything left to find out in his curious researches.

My weariness of all this may easily be imagined. Ten times had Sperver taken me over the stables and the kennels; the dogs were beginning to know me. I knew by heart all the coarse pleasantries of the *major-domo* over his bottles and Marie Lagoutte's invariable replies. Sebalt's melancholy was infecting me; I would gladly have blown a little on his horn to tell the mountains of my *ennui*, and my eyes were incessantly directed towards Fribourg.

Still the disorder of Yeri-Hans, lord of Nideck, was taking its usual course, and this gave my only occupation any serious interest. All the particulars which Sperver had made me acquainted with appeared clearly before me; sometimes the count, waking up with a start, would half rise, and supported on his elbow, with neck outstretched and haggard eyes, would mutter, "She is coming, she is coming!"

Then Gideon would shake his head and ascend the signal-tower, but neither right nor left could the Black Plague be discovered.

After long reflection upon this strange malady I had come to the conclusion that the sufferer was insane. The strange influence that the old hag exercised over him, his alternate phases of madness and lucidity, all confirmed me in this view.

Medical men who have given especial attention to the subject of mental aberrations are well aware that periodical madness is of not unfrequent occurrence. In some cases the illness appears several times in the year, in others at only particular seasons of the year. I know at Fribourg an old lady who for thirty years past has regularly presented herself at the door of the asylum. At her own request they place her in confinement; then the unhappy woman every night passes through the terrible scenes of the French Revolution, of which she was a witness in her youth. She trembles in the hands of the executioner; she fancies herself drenched with the blood of the victims; she weeps and cries aloud incessantly. In the course of a few weeks the mind returns to its wonted seat, and she is restored to liberty with the full expectation that she will return again in a year.

"The Count of Nideck is suffering from a similar attack," I said; "unknown chains unite his fate with that of the Black Plague. Who can tell?" thought I; "that woman once was young, perhaps beautiful!"

And my imagination, once launched, carried me into the interesting regions of romance; but I was careful to tell no one what I thought. If I had opened out those conjectures to Sperver he would never have forgiven me for imagining that there could have been any intimacy between his master and the Black Plague; and as for Mademoiselle Odile, I dared not suggest insanity to her.

The poor young lady was evidently most unhappy. Her refusal to marry had so embittered the count against her that he could scarcely endure to have her in his presence. He bitterly reproached her with her ingratitude and disobedience, and expatiated upon the cruelty of ungrateful children. Sometimes even violent curses followed his daughter's visits. Things at last were so bad that I thought myself obliged to interfere. I therefore waited one evening on the countess in the antechamber and entreated her to relinquish her personal attendance upon her father. But here arose, contrary to all expectations, quite an unforeseen obstacle. In spite of all my entreaties she steadily insisted on watching by her father and nursing him as she had done hitherto.

"It is my duty," she repeated, "and no arguments will shake my purpose," she said firmly.

"Madam," I replied as a last effort, "the medical profession, too, has its duties, and an honourable man must fulfil them even to harshness and cruelty; your presence is killing your father."

I shall remember all my life the sudden change in the expression of the face of Odile.

My solemn words of warning seemed to cause the blood to flow back to the heart; her face became white as marble, and her large blue eyes, fixed steadily upon mine, seemed to read into the most secret recesses of my soul.

"Is that possible, sir?" she stammered; "upon your honour, do you declare this? Tell me truly!"

"Yes, madam, upon my honour."

There was a long and painful silence, only broken at last by these words in a low voice:—

"Let God's will be done!"

And with downcast eyes she withdrew.

The day after this scene, about eight in the morning, I was pacing up and down in Hugh Lupus's tower, thinking of the count's illness, of which I could not foretell the issue—and I was thinking too of my patients at Fribourg, whom I might lose by too prolonged an absence—when three discreet taps upon my door turned my thoughts into another channel.

"Come in!"

The door opened, and Marie Lagoutte stood within, dropping me a low curtsey.

This old dame's visit put me out, and I was going to beg her to postpone her visit, when something mysterious in her countenance caught my attention. She had thrown over her shoulders a red-and-green shawl; she was biting her lips, with her head down, and as soon as she had closed the door she opened it again, and peeped out, to make sure that no one had followed her.

"What does she want with me?" I thought; "what is the meaning of all these precautions?"

And I was quite puzzled.

"*Monsieur le Docteur,*" said the worthy lady, advancing towards me, "I beg your pardon for disturbing you so early in the morning, but I have a very serious thing to tell you."

"Pray tell me all about it, then."

"It is the count."

"Indeed!"

"Yes, sir; you know that I sat up with him last night."

"I know. Pray sit down."

She sat before me in a great armchair, and I could not help noticing the energetic character of her head, which on the evening of my arrival at the castle had only seemed to me grotesque.

"Doctor," she resumed after a short pause and with her dark eyes upon me, "you know I am not timid or easily frightened. I have seen so many dreadful things in the course of my life that I am astonished at nothing now. When you have seen Marengo, Austerlitz, and Moscow, there is nothing left that can put you out."

"I am sure of that, ma'am."

"I don't want to boast; that is not my reason for telling you this; but it is to show you that I am not an escaped lunatic, and that you may believe me when I tell you what I say I have seen."

This was becoming interesting.

"Well," the good woman resumed, "last night, between nine and ten, just as I was going to bed, Offenloch came in and said to me, 'Marie, you will have to sit up with the count tonight.' At first I felt surprised. 'What! is not *mademoiselle* going to sit up?' 'No, *mademoiselle* is poorly, and you will have to take her place.' Poor girl, she is ill; I knew that would be the end of it, I told her so a hundred times; but it is always so. Young people won't believe those who are older; and then, it is her Father. So I took my knitting, said good night to Tobias, and went into *monseigneur's* room. Sperver was there waiting for me, and went to bed; so there I was, all alone."

Here the good woman stopped a moment, indulged in a pinch of snuff, and tried to arrange her thoughts. I listened with eager attention for what was coming.

"About half-past ten," she went on, "I was sitting near the bed, and from time to time drew the curtain to see what the count was doing; he made no movement; he was sleeping as quietly as a child. It was all right until eleven o'clock, then I began to feel tired. An old woman, sir, cannot help herself—she must drop off to sleep in spite of everything. I did not think anything was going to happen, and I said to myself, 'He is sure to sleep till daylight.' About twelve the wind went down; the big windows had been rattling, but now they were quiet. I got up to see if anything was stirring outside.

"It was all as black as ink; so I came back to my armchair. I took another look at the patient; I saw that he had not stirred an inch, and I took up my knitting; but in a few minutes more I began nodding, nodding, and I dropped right off to sleep. I could not help it, the armchair was so soft and the room was so warm, who could have helped it? I had been asleep an hour, I suppose, when a sharp current of wind woke me up. I opened my eyes, and what do you think I saw? The tall middle window was wide open, the curtains were drawn, and there in the opening stood the count in his white nightdress, right on the windowsill."

"The count?"

"Yes."

"Nay, it is impossible; he cannot move!"

"So I thought too; but that is just how I saw him. He was standing with a torch in his hand; the night was so dark and the air so still that the flame stood up quite straight."

I gazed upon Marie Anne with astonishment.

"First of all," she said, after a moment's silence, "to see that long, thin man standing there with his bare legs, I can assure you it had such an effect upon me! I wanted to scream; but then I thought, 'Perhaps he is walking in his sleep; if I shout he will wake up, he will jump down, and then—' So I did not say a word, but I stared and stared till I saw him lift up his torch in the air over his head, then he lowered it, then up again and down again, and he did this three times, just like a man making signals; then he threw it down upon the ramparts, shut the window, drew the curtains, passed before me without speaking, and got into bed muttering some words I could not make out."

"Are you sure you saw all that, ma'am?"

"Quite sure."

"Well, it is strange."

"I know it is; but it is true. Ah! it did astonish me at first, and then when I saw him get into bed again and cross his hands over his breast just as if nothing had happened, I said to myself, 'Marie Anne, you have had a bad dream; it cannot be true;' and so I went to the window, and there I saw the torch still burning; it had fallen into a bush near the third gate, and there it was shining just like a spark of fire. There was no denying it."

Marie Lagoutte looked at me a few moments without speaking.

"You may be sure, doctor, that after that I had no more sleep; I sat watching and ready for anything. Every moment I fancied I could hear something behind the arm-chair. I was not afraid—it was not that—but I was uneasy and restless. When morning came, very early I ran and woke Offenloch and sent him to the count. Passing down the corridor I noticed that there was no torch in the first ring, and I came down and found it near the narrow path to the Schwartzwald; there it is!"

And the good woman took from under her apron the end of a torch, which she threw upon the table.

I was confounded.

How had that man, whom I had seen the night before feeble and exhausted, been able to rise, walk, lift up and close down that heavy window? What was the meaning of that signal by night? I seemed to myself to witness this strange, mysterious scene, and my thoughts went off at once to the Black Plague. When I aroused myself from this contemplation of my own thoughts, I saw Marie Lagoutte rising and preparing to go.

"You have done quite right," I said as I took her to the door, "to tell me of these things, and I am much obliged to you. Have you told anyone else of this adventure?"

"No one, sir; such things are only to be told to the priest and the doctor."

"Come, I see you are a very wise, sensible woman."

These words were exchanged at the door of my tower. At this moment Sperver appeared at the end of the gallery, followed by his friend Sebalt.

"Fritz!" he shouted, "I have got news to tell you."

"Oh, come!" thought I, "more news! This is a strange condition of things."

Marie Lagoutte had disappeared, and the huntsman and his friend entered the tower.

Chapter 8

On the countenance of Sperver was an expression of suppressed wrath, on that of his companion bitter irony. This worthy sportsman, whose woeful physiognomy had struck me on my first arrival at Nideck, was as thin and dry as a lath. His hunting-jacket was girded tightly about him by his belt, from which hung a hunting-knife with a horn handle; long leathern gaiters came above his knees; the horn went over his shoulder from right to left, the wide-expanded opening under his arm; on his head a wide-brimmed hat, with a heron's plume in the buckle. His profile, coming to a point in a reddish tuft, looked not unlike a goat's.

"Yes," cried Sperver, "I have got strange things to tell you."

He threw himself in a chair, seizing his head between his

clenched hands, while dismal Sebalt calmly drew his horn over his head and laid it on the table.

"Now, Sebalt," cried Gideon, "speak out."

"The witch is hanging about the castle."

This piece of intelligence would have failed to interest me before seeing Marie Lagoutte, but now it struck more forcibly. There certainly was some mysterious connection between the lord of Nideck and that old woman. I knew nothing of the nature of this connection, and I felt that, at whatever cost, I must know it.

"Just wait a moment, friends," said I to Sperver and his comrade. "I want to know, first of all, where does this Black Pest come from?"

Sperver stared at me with astonishment.

"Come from? Who can tell that?"

"Very well, you can't. But when does she come within sight of Nideck?"

"As I told you, ten days before Christmas, at the same time every year."

"And how long does she stay?"

"A fortnight or three weeks."

"Is she ever seen before? Not even on her way? Nor after?"

"No."

"Then we shall have to catch her, seize upon her," I cried. "This is contrary to nature. We must find out where she comes from, what she wants here, what she is."

"Lay hold of her!" exclaimed Sperver; "seize her! Do you mean it?" and he shook his head. "Fritz, your advice is good enough in its way, but it is easier said than done. I could very easily send a bullet after her, almost at any time; but the count won't consent to that measure; and as for catching in any other way than by powder and shot, why, you had better go first and catch a squirrel by the tail! Listen to Sebalt's story, and you shall judge for yourself."

The master of the hounds, sitting on the table with his long legs crossed, fixed his eyes mournfully upon me, and began his tale.

"This morning, as I was coming down from the Altenberg, I followed the hollow road to Nideck. The snow filled it up entirely. I was going on my way, thinking of nothing particular, when I noticed a foot-track; it was deep down, and went across the road. The person had come down the bank and gone up on the other side. It was not a soft hare's foot, which hardly leaves an impression, it was not forked like a wild boar's track, it was not like a cloven hoof, such as the wolf's—it was a deep hole. I stopped and stooped down, and cleared away the loose snow that fell round, and came upon the very track of the Black Pest!"

"Are you sure it was that?"

"Of course I am. I know the old woman by her foot better than by her figure, for I always go, sir, with my eyes on the ground. I know everybody by their tracks; and as for this one, a child might know it."

"What, then, distinguishes this foot so particularly?"

"It is so small that you could cover it with your hand; it is finely shaped, the heel is rather long, the outline clean, the great toe lies close to the other toes, and they are all as fine as if they were in a lady's slipper. It is a lovely foot. Twenty years ago I should have fallen in love with a foot like that. Whenever I come across it, it has such an effect upon me! No one would believe that such a foot could belong to the Black Plague."

And the poor fellow, joining his hands together, contemplated the stone floor with doleful eyes.

"Well, Sebalt, what next?" asked Sperver impatiently.

"Ah, yes, to be sure! Well, I recognised that track and started off in pursuit. I was hoping to catch the creature in her lair, but I will tell you the way she took me. I climbed up the bank by the roadside, only two gunshots from Nideck. I go along the hill, keeping the track on my right; it led along the side of the wood in the Rhethal. All at once it jumps over the ditch into the wood. I stuck to it, but, happening to look a little to my left, I saw another track which had, been following the Black Plague. I stopped short: was it Sperver's? or Kasper Trumpfs? or whose?

I came to it, and you may fancy how astounded I was when I saw that it was nobody from our place! I know every foot in the Schwartzwald from Fribourg to Nideck.

"That foot was like none of ours. It must have come from a distance. The boot—for it was a kind of well-made, soft gentleman's boot, with spurs, which leave a little print behind them—the boot was not round at the toes, but square. The sole was thin, and bent with every step, and it had no nails in it. The walk was rapid, and the short steps were like those of a young man of twenty to five-and-twenty. I noticed the stitches in the side leather at once, and I think I never saw finer."

"Who can this be?" Sperver exclaimed.

Sebalt raised his shoulders and extended his hands, but said nothing.

"Who can have any object in following the old woman?" I asked Sperver.

"No one on earth can tell," was the reply.

And so we sat a few minutes meditating over what we had heard.

At last he went on again with his narrative:—

"I kept following the track; it went up the next ridge through the pine-forest. When it doubled round the Koche Fendue I said to myself, 'Ah, you accursed plague! If there was much game of your sort there would not be much sport; it would be preferable to work like a nigger!' So we all three arrive—the two tracks and I—at the top of the Schneeberg. There the wind had been blowing hard; the snow was knee-deep—but no matter! I must get on! I got to the edge of the torrent of the Steinbach, and there I lost the track. I halted, and I saw that, after trying up and down in several directions, the gentleman's boots had gone down the Tiefenbach. That was a bad sign. I looked along the other side of the torrent, but there was no appearance of a track there—none at all! The old hag had paddled up and down the stream to throw any one off the scent who should try to follow her. Where was I to go to?—right, or left, or straight on? Not knowing, I came back to Nideck."

"You haven't told us about her breakfast," said Sperver.

"No, I was forgetting. At the foot of Roche Fendue I saw there had been a fire; there was a black place; I laid my hand upon it, thinking it might be warm, which would have proved that the Black Plague had not gone far; but it was as cold as ice. Close by I saw a wire trap in the bushes. It seems the creature knows how to snare game. A hare had been caught in it; the print of its body was still plain, lying flat in the snow. The witch had lighted the fire to cook it; she had had a good breakfast, I'll be bound."

At this Sperver cried indignantly—

"Just fancy that old witch living on meat while so many honest folks in our villages have nothing better than potatoes to eat! That's what upsets me, Fritz! Ah! if I had but—"

But his thoughts remained untold; he turned deadly pale, and all three of us, in a moment, stood rigid and motionless, staring with horror at each other's ghastly countenances.

A yell—the howling cry of the wolf in the long, cold days of winter—the cry which none can imagine who has not heard the most fearful and harrowing of all bestial sounds—that fearful cry was echoing through the castle not far from us! It rose up the spiral staircase, it filled the massive building as if the hungry, savage beast was at our door!

Travellers speak of the deep roar of the lion troubling the silence of the night amidst the rocky deserts of Africa; but while the tropical regions, sultry and baked, resound with the vibrations of the mighty voice of the savage monarch of the desert, making the air tremble with the distant thunder of his awful cry, the vast snowy deserts of the North too have their characteristic cry—a strange, lamentable yell that seems to suit the character of the dreary winter scene. That voice of the Northern desert is the howl of the wolf!

The instant after this awful sound had broken upon the silence followed another formidable body of discordant sounds—the baying and yelling of sixty hounds—answering from the ramparts of Nideck. The whole pack gave voice at the same moment—the deep bay of the bloodhound, the sharp cry of the pointer, the plaintive yelpings of the spaniels, and the melancholy howl of the mastiffs, all mingling in confusion with the rattling of dog-chains, the shaking of the kennels under the struggles of the hounds to get loose; and, dominating over all, the long, dismal, prolonged note of the wolf's monotonous howl; his was the leading part in this horrible canine concert!

Sperver sprang from his seat and ran out upon the platform to see if a wolf had dropped into the moat. But no—the howling came from neither. Then turning to us he cried—

"Fritz! Sebalt!—come, come quickly!"

We flew down the steps four at a time and rushed into the fencing-school. Here we heard the cry of the wolf alone, prolonged beneath the echoing arches the distant barking and yelling of the pack became almost inaudible in the distance; the dogs were hoarse with rage and excitement, their chains were getting entangled together. Perhaps they were strangling each other.

Sperver drew the keen blade of his hunting-knife. Sebalt did the same; they preceded me down the gallery.

Then the fearful sounds became our guide to the sick man's room. Sperver spoke no more; he hurried forward. Sebalt stretched his long legs. I felt a shuddering horror creep through my whole frame—a horrible presentiment of something shocking and abominable came over us.

As we approached the apartments of the count we met the whole household afoot—the gamekeepers, the huntsmen, the kennel-keepers, the scullions were all mingled and jostling each other, asking—

"What is the matter? Where are those cries coming from?"

Without stopping we ran into the passage which led into the count's bedroom, where we met poor Marie Lagoutte, who alone had had the courage to penetrate thither before us. She was holding in her arms the young countess, who had fainted, her head falling back, her hair flowing down behind her; she was carrying her away as fast as she could.

We passed her so rapidly that we scarcely had time to witness this sad sight. But it has since returned to my memory, and the pale face of Odile lying on the ample shoulders of the good servant still makes a vivid impression upon my memory, resembling the poor lamb presenting its throat to the knife without a complaint, dying with fear before the stroke falls.

At last we had reached the count's chamber.

The howling came from behind his door.

We stole fearful glances at one another without attempting to account for the hideous noise, or explaining the presence of such a wild guest in the house. Indeed, we had no time; our ideas were in dire and utter confusion.

Sperver hastily pushed the door open, and, knife in hand, was darting into the room; but he stood arrested on the threshold motionless as a stone.

Never have I seen such a picture of horror as he displayed standing rooted there, with his eyes starting from his head, and his mouth wide open and gasping for breath.

I gazed over his shoulder, and the sight that met my eyes made the blood run chill as snow in my veins.

The lord of Nideck, crouching on all fours upon his bed, with his arms bending forward, his head carried low, his eyes glaring with fierce fires, was uttering loud, protracted howlings!

He was the wolf!

That low receding forehead, that sharp-pointed face, that foxy-looking beard, bristling off both cheeks; the long meagre figure, the sinewy limbs, the face, the cry. The attitude, declared the presence of the wild beast half-hidden, half-revealed under a human mask!

At times he would stop for a second and listen attentively with head awry, and then the crimson hangings would tremble with the quivering of his limbs, like foliage shaken by the wind; then the melancholy wail would open afresh.

Sperver, Sebalt, and I stood nailed to the floor; we held our breath, petrified with fear.

Suddenly the count stopped. As a wild beast scents the wind, he lifted his head and listened again.

There, there, far away, down among the thick fir forests, whitened with dense patches of snow, a cry was heard in reply—weak at first; then the sound rose and swelled in a long protracted howl, drowning the feebler efforts of the hounds: it was the she-wolf answering the wolf!

Sperver, turning round awe-stricken, his countenance pale as ashes, pointed to the mountain, and murmured low—

"Listen—there's the witch!"

And the count still crouching motionless, but with his head now raised in the attitude of attention, his neck outstretched, his eyes burning, seemed to understand the meaning of that distant voice, lost amidst the passes and peaks of the Schwartzwald, and a kind of fearful joy gleamed in his savage features.

At this moment, Sperver, unable or unwilling to restrain himself any longer, cried in a voice broken with emotion—

"Count of Nideck—what are you doing?"

The count fell back thunderstruck. We rushed into the room to his help. It was time. The third attack had commenced, and it was terrible to witness!

Chapter 9

The lord of Nideck was in a dying state.

What can science do in presence of the great mortal strife between Death and Life? At the supreme hour, when the invisible wrestlers are writhed together body to body and limb to limb, panting, each in turn overthrowing and overthrown, what avails the healing art? One can but watch, and tremble, and listen!

At times the struggle seems suspended—a truce has sounded; Life has retired into her hold. She is resting; she is collecting the courage of despair. But the relentless enemy beats at the gates; he bursts in; then Life springs to the rescue, and again grapples with her adversary. The strife is renewed with fresh fuel added to the fire of mortal energy as the fatal issue draws closer and nearer.

And the exhausted patient, himself the field of battle, weltering in the cold sweat of death, the eye set and the arm powerless, can do nothing for himself. His breathing, sometimes short, broken, and distressing, sometimes long, deep, laboured, and heavy, indicates the varying phases of this dreadful struggle.

The bystanders watch each other's faces, and they think, "The day will come when we in our turns shall be the field of the same strife, and victorious Death will bear us away into the grave, his den, as the spider carries away the fly." But the true life, the only life, the soul, spreading her immortal wings, will speed her flight to another world, with the exulting cry, "I have fought the good fight. I have finished my course. I have kept the faith!" And Death, disappointed of its prey, will look up at the emancipated being, unable to follow, and holding in its clutches only a cold and decaying corpse, soon to be a handful of dust. "*O death, where is thy sting? O grave, where is thy victory?*" O best and only consolation, the hope and belief in the final triumph of justice, the certainty of immortal life through Jesus Christ the Saviour! Cruel indeed is he who would rob man of the chief brightness and glory of life!

Towards midnight the Count of Nideck seemed almost gone; the agony of death was at hand; the broken, weakened pulse indicated the sinking of the vital powers; then, it might return to a more active state; but there seemed no hope.

My only duty left was to stay and see this unhappy man die.

I was exhausted with fatigue and anxiety; whatever art could do I had tried.

I told Sperver to sit up, and close his master's eyes in death. The poor faithful fellow was in the utmost distress; he reproached himself with his involuntary cry—"Count of Nideck—what are you doing?" and tore his hair in bitter repentance.

I went away alone to Hugh Lupus's tower, having had scarcely any time to take food, but I did not feel the want of it.

There was a bright fire on the hearth; I threw myself dressed upon the bed, and sleep soon came to relieve my weight of apprehension—that heavy sleep broken by the consciousness that you may any minute be awoke by tears and lamentations.

I was sleeping thus, with my face turned towards the fire, and as it often happens, the flame fitfully rising, and falling threw a fluttering, flickering light like those of ruddy flapping wings against the walls, and wearied still more my dropping eyelids.

Lost in a dreamy slumber, I was half opening my eyes to see the cause of these alternate lights and shadows, but the strangest sight surprised me.

Close by the hearth, hardly revealed by the feeble light of a few dying embers, I recognised with dismay the dark profile of the Black Plague!

She sat upon a low stool, and was evidently warming herself.

At first I thought myself deceived by my senses, which would have been natural enough after the exciting scenes of the last few days; I raised myself upon my elbow, gazing with my eyes starting with fear and horror.

It was she indeed! I lay horrified, for there she sat calm and immovable, with her hands clasped over her skinny knees, just as I had seen her in the snow, with her long scraggy neck outstretched, her hooked nose, her compressed lips.

How had the Black Pest got here? How had she found her way into this high tower crowning the dangerous precipices? Everything that Sperver had told me of this mysterious being seemed to be coming true! And now the unaccountable behaviour of Lieverle, growling so fiercely against the wall, seemed clear as the daylight. I huddled myself close up into the alcove, hardly daring to breathe, and staring upon this motionless profile just as a mouse out of its hole fixes its paralysed stare upon the cat that is watching for it.

The old woman stirred no more than the rock-hewn pillars on each side of the hearthstone, and her lips were mumbling inarticulate sounds.

My heart was palpitating, my fears increased momentarily during the long silence, made more startling by the motionless supernatural figure that sat there before me.

This had lasted a quarter of an hour when, the fire catching a splinter of fir-wood, a flash of light broke out, the shaving twisted and flamed, and a few rays of light flared to the end of the room.

That luminous jet was sufficient to show me that the creature was clothed in an old dress of rich purple silk as stiff as cardboard, with a violet pattern; there was a massive bracelet upon her left wrist, and a gold arrow stuck through her thick grey hair twisted over the back of her head. It was like an apparition out of the ages past.

Still the Plague could have had no hostile intentions towards me, or she might easily have taken advantage of my sleep to have put them in execution.

That thought was beginning to give me some confidence, when suddenly she rose from her seat and with slow steps approached my bed, holding in her hand a torch which she had just lighted. I then observed that her eyes were fixed and haggard.

I made an effort to rise and cry aloud, but not a muscle of my body would obey my wishes, not a breath came to my lips; and the old woman, bending over me between the curtains, fixed her stony stare upon me with a strange unearthly smile. I wanted to call for help, I wanted to drive her from me, but her petrifying stare seemed to fascinate and paralyse me, just as that of the serpent fixes the little bird motionless before it.

During this speechless contemplation minutes seemed like hours. What was she about to do? I was ready for any event.

Suddenly she turned her head, went round upon her heel, listened, strode across the room, and opened the door.

At last I recovered a little courage; an effort of the will brought me to my feet as if I were acted on by a spring; I darted after her footsteps; she with one hand was holding her torch on high, and with the other kept the door open.

I was about to seize her by the hair, when at the end of the long gallery, under the Gothic archway of the castle leading to the ramparts, I saw—a tall figure.

It was the Count of Nideck!

The Count of Nideck, whom I had thought a dying man,

clad in a huge wolf-skin thrown with its upper jaw projecting grimly over his eyes like a visor, the formidable claws hanging over each shoulder, and the tail dragging behind him along the flags.

He wore stout heavy shoes, a silver clasp gathered the wolf-skin round his neck, and his whole aspect, but for the ice-cold deathly expression of his face, proclaimed the man born for command—the master!

In the presence of such an imposing personage my ideas became vague and confused. Flight was no longer possible, yet I had the presence of mind to throw myself into the embrasure of the window.

The count entered my room with his eyes fixed on the old woman and his features unrelaxed. They spoke to one another in hoarse whispers, so low that I could not distinguish a word. But there was no mistaking their gestures. The woman was pointing to the bed.

They approached the fireplace on tiptoe. There in the dark shadow of the recess at its side the Black Plague, with a horrible smile, unrolled a large bag.

As soon as the count saw the bag he made a bound towards the bed and kneeled upon it with one knee; there was a shaking of the curtains, his body disappeared beneath their folds, and I could only see one leg still resting on the floor, and the wolf's tail undulating irregularly from side to side.

They seemed to be acting a murder in ghastly pantomime. No real scene, however frightful, could have agitated me more than this mute representation of some horrible deed.

Then the old woman ran to his assistance, carrying the bag with her. Again the curtains shook and the shadows crossed the walls; but the most horrible of all was that I fancied I saw a pool of blood creeping across the floor and slowly reaching the hearth. But it was only the snow that had clung to the count's boots, and was melting in the heat.

I was still gazing upon this dark stream, feeling my dry tongue cleave to the roof of my mouth, when there was a great movement; the old woman and the count were stuffing the sheets of the bed into the sack, they were thrusting and stamping them in with just the same haste as a dog scratching at a hole, then the lord of Nideck flung this unshapely bundle over his shoulder and made for the door; a sheet was dragging behind him, and the old woman followed him torch in hand. They went across the court.

My knees were almost giving way under me; they knocked together for fear. I prayed for strength.

In a couple of minutes I was on their footsteps, dragged forward by a sudden irresistible impulse.

I crossed the court at a run, and was just going to enter the door of the tower when I perceived a deep but narrow pit at my feet, down which went a winding staircase, and there far below I could see the torch describing a spiral course around the stone rail like a little star; at last it was lost in the distance.

Now I also descended the first steps of this newly-discovered staircase, directing my course after this distant light; suddenly it vanished. The old woman and the count had reached the bottom of the precipice. Supported by the stone rail I continued my descent, safe to be able to mount again if I found my further progress stopped.

Soon I came to the last step; I looked around me, and discovered on my left hand a narrow streak of moonlight shining under a low door, through the nettles and brambles; I kicked a way through these obstacles, clearing the snow away with my feet, and then found that I was at the very foot of the keep—Hugh's donjon tower.

Who would have supposed that such a hole would have led up into the castle? Who had shown it to the old woman? I did not stay to satisfy myself on these points.

The vast plain lay spread before me bathed in a light almost equal to that of day. On the right lay extended wide the dark line of the Black Forest with its craggy rocks, its gullies, its passes stretching away as far as the sight could reach.

The night air was keen and sharp, but perfectly calm, and I

felt myself awakened to the highest degree, almost as if my senses were volatilised by the still and ice-cold air.

My first examination of the horizon was for the figures of the count and his strange companion. I soon distinguished their tall dark forms standing out sharply against the star-spangled purple heavens. I nearly overtook them at the bottom of the ravine.

The count was moving with deliberate steps, the imaginary winding-sheet dragging slowly after him. There was an automatic precision in the movements of both.

I kept six or eight yards behind them down the hollow road to the Altenberg, now in the shade, now in the full light, for the moon was shining with astonishing brilliancy. A few clouds floated idly across the zenith, seeming to want to clasp her in their long arms, but she ever eluded their grasp, and her rays, keen as a blade of steel, cut me to the marrow of my bones.

I could have wished to turn back, but some invisible power impelled me onwards to follow this funeral procession in pantomime. Even to this day I fancy still I can see the rough mountain path through the Black Forest, I can hear the crisp snow crackling under foot, and the dead leaves rustling in the light north wind; I can see myself following those two silent beings, but I cannot understand what mysterious power drew me in their footsteps.

At last we reach the forest, and advance amongst the tall bare-branched, beeches; the dark shadows of their higher boughs intersect the lower branches, and fall broken upon the snow-encumbered road. Sometimes I fancy I can hear steps behind me; I turn sharply round, but can see no one.

We had just reached the long rocky ridge that forms the crest of the Altenberg; behind it flows the torrent of the Schneeberg, but in winter no current is visible; scarcely does a mere thread of its blue waters trickle under the thick crust of ice. Here the deep solitude is broken by no murmuring brooks, no warblings of birds, no thunder of the waterfall. In the vast unbroken solitudes the awful silence is terrible.

The Count of Nideck and the old woman found a gap in the

face of the rock, up which they mounted straight with marvellous celerity, whilst I had to pull myself up by the help of the bushes.

Hardly had they reached the ridge of the crags, which came almost to a point, when I was within three yards of them, and I beheld beyond a dreadful precipice of which I could not see the bottom. At the left hung in the air like a vast sheet the fall of the Schneeberg, a mass of ice. That resemblance to an immense wave taking the precipice at one bound, bearing trees on its breast, fringed with the bushes, and winding out the long ivy sprays, which exhibit in their delicate tracery the form of the rigid glassy billow; that mere semblance of movement amidst the stillness and immovableness of death, and the presence of those two speechless creatures pursuing their ghastly work with automatic precision, added to the terror with which I already trembled.

Nature herself seemed to shrink with horror.

The count had laid down his burden; the old woman and he took it up together, swung it for a moment over the edge of the precipice, then the long shroud floated over the abyss, and the imaginary murderers in silence bent forward to see it fall.

That long white sheet floating in the air is still present before my eyes. It descends, it falls like a wild swan shot in the clouds, spreading its wide wings, the long neck thrown back, whirling down to earth to die.

The white burden disappeared in the dark depths of the precipice.

At last the cloud which I had long seen threatening to cover the moon's bright disc veiled her in its steel-blue folds, and her rays ceased to shine.

The old woman, holding the count by the hand and dragging him forward with hurried steps, came for a moment into view.

The cloud had overshadowed the moon, and I could not move out of their way without danger of falling over the precipice.

After a few minutes, during which I lay as close as I could, there was a rift in the cloud. I looked out again. I stood alone on the point of the peak with the snow up to my knees.

Full of horror and apprehension, I descended from my perilous position, and ran to the castle in as much consternation as if I had been guilty of some great crime.

As for the lord of Nideck and his companion, I lost sight of them.

Chapter 10

I wandered around the castle of Nideck unable to find the exit from which I had commenced my melancholy journey.

So much anxiety and uneasiness were beginning to tell upon my mind; I staggered on, wondering if I was not mad, unable to believe in what I had seen, and yet alarmed at the clearness of my own perceptions.

My mind in confusion passed in review that strange man waving his torch overhead in the darkness, howling like a wolf, coldly and accurately going through all the details of an imaginary murder without the omission of one ghastly detail or circumstance, then escaping and committing to the furious torrent the secret of his crime; these things all harassed my mind, hurried confusedly past my eyes, and made me feel as if I were labouring under a nightmare.

Lost in the snow, I ran to and fro panting and alarmed, and unable to judge which way to direct my steps.

As day drew near the cold became sharper; I shivered, I execrated Sperver for having brought me from Fribourg to bear a part in this hideous adventure.

At last, exhausted, my beard a mass of ice, my ears nearly frostbitten, I discovered the gate and rang the bell with all my might.

It was then about four in the morning. Knapwurst made me wait a terribly long time. His little lodge, cut in the rock, remained silent; I thought the little humpbacked wretch would never have done dressing; for of course I supposed he would be in bed and asleep.

I rang again.

This time his grotesque figure appeared abruptly, and he cried to me from the door in a fury—

"Who are you?"

"I?—Doctor Fritz."

"Oh, that alters the case," and he went back into his lodge for a lantern, crossed the outer court where the snow came up to his middle, and staring at me through the grating, he exclaimed—

"I beg your pardon, Doctor Fritz; I thought you would be asleep up there in Hugh Lupus's tower. Were *you* ringing? Now that explains why Sperver came to me about midnight to ask if anybody had gone out. I said no, which was quite true, for I never saw you going out."

"But pray, Monsieur Knapwurst, do for pity's sake let me in, and I will tell you all about that by-and-by."

"Come, come, sir, a little patience."

And the hunchback, with the slowest deliberation, undid the padlock and slipped the bars, whilst my teeth were chattering, and I stood shivering from head to foot.

"You are very cold, doctor," said the diminutive man, "and you cannot get into the castle. Sperver has fastened the inside door, I don't know why; he does not usually do so; the outer gate is enough. Come in here and get warm. You won't find my little hole very inviting, though. It is nothing but a sty, but when a man is as cold as you are he is not apt to be particular."

Without replying to his chatter I followed him in as quickly as I could.

We went into the hut, and in spite of my complete state of numbness, I could not help admiring the state of picturesque disorder in which I found the place. The slate roof leaning against the rock, and resting by its other side on a wall not more than six feet high, showed the smoky, blackened rafters from end to end.

The whole edifice consisted of but one apartment, furnished with a very uninviting bed, which the dwarf did not often take the trouble to make, and two small windows with hexagonal panes, weather-stained with the rainbow tints of mother-of-pearl. A large square table filled up the middle, and it would be difficult to account for that massive oak slab being got in unless by supposing it to have been there before the hut was built.

On shelves against the wall were rolls of parchment, and old books great and small. Wide open on the table lay a fine black-letter volume, with illuminations, bound in vellum, clasped and cornered with silver, apparently a collection of old chronicles. Besides there was nothing but two leathern arm-chairs, bearing on them the unmistakable impression of the misshapen figure of this learned gentleman.

I need not stay to do more than mention the pens, the jar of tobacco, five or six pipes lying here and there, and in a corner a small cast-iron stove, with its low, open door wide open, and throwing out now and then a volley of bright sparks; and to complete the picture, the cat arching her back, and spitting threateningly at me with her armed paw uplifted.

All this scene was tinted with that deep rich amber light in which the old Flemish painters delighted, and of which they alone possessed the secret, and never left it to the generations after them.

"So you went out last night, doctor?" inquired my host, after we had both installed ourselves, and while I had my hands in a warm place upon the stove.

"Yes, pretty early," I answered. "I had to look after a patient."

This brief explanation seemed to satisfy the little hunchback, and he lighted his blackened boxwood pipe, which was hanging over his chin.

"You don't smoke, doctor?"

"I beg your pardon, I do."

"Well, fill any one of these pipes. I was here," he said, spreading his yellow hand over the open volume. "I was reading the chronicles of Hertzog when you came."

"Ah, that accounts for the time I had to wait! Of course you stayed to finish the chapter?" I said, smiling.

He owned it, grinning, and we both laughed together.

"But if I had known it was you," he said, "I should have finished the chapter another time."

There was a short silence, during which I was observing the very peculiar physiognomy of this misshapen being—those long deep wrinkles that moated in his wide mouth, his small eyes with the crow's feet at the outer corners, that contorted nose, bulbous at its end, and especially that huge double-storied forehead of his. The whole figure reminded me not a little of the received pictures of Socrates, and while warming myself and listening to the crackling of the fire, I went off into contemplations on the very diversified fortunes of mankind.

"Here is this dwarf," I thought, "an ill-shaped, stunted caricature, banished into a corner of Nideck, and living just like the cricket that chirps beneath the hearthstone. Here is this little Knapwurst, who in the midst of excitement, grand hunts, gallant trains of horsemen coming and going, the barking of the hounds, the trampling of the horses, and the shouts of the hunters, is living quietly all alone, buried in his books, and thinking of nothing but the times long gone by, whilst joy or sorrow, songs or tears, fill the world around him, while spring and summer, autumn and winter, come and look in through his dim windows, by turns brightening, warming, and benumbing the face of nature outside.

"Whilst men in the outer world are subject to the gentle influences of love, or the sterner impulses of ambition or avarice, hoping, coveting, longing, and desiring, he neither hopes, nor desires, nor covets anything. As long as he is smoking his pipe, with his eyes feasting on a musty parchment, he lives in the enjoyment of dreams, and he goes into raptures over things long, long ago gone by, or which have never existed at all; it is all one to him. 'Hertzog says so and so, somebody else tells the tale a different way,' and he is perfectly happy! His leathery face gets more and more deeply wrinkled, his broken angular back bends into sharper angles and corners, his pointed elbows dig beds for themselves in the oak table, his skinny fingers bury themselves in his cheeks, his piggish grey eyes get redder over manuscripts,

Latin, Greek, or mediaeval. He falls into raptures, he smacks his lips, he licks his chops like a cat over a dainty dish, and then he throws himself upon that dirty litter, with his knees up to his chin, and he thinks he has had a delightful day! Oh, Providence of God, is a man's duty best done, are his responsibilities best discharged, at the top or at the bottom of the scale of human life?"

But the snow was melting away from my legs, the balmy warmth of the stove was shedding a pleasant influence over my feelings, and I felt myself reviving in this mixed atmosphere of tobacco-smoke and burning pine-wood.

Knapwurst gravely laid his pipe on the table, and reverently spreading his hand upon the folio, said in a voice that seemed to issue from the bottom of his consciousness; or, if you like it better, from the bottom of a twenty-gallon cask—

"Doctor Fritz, here is the law and the prophets!"

"How so? what do you mean?"

"Parchment—old parchment—that is what I love! These old yellow, rusty, worm-eaten leaves are all that is left to us of the past, from the days of Charlemagne until this day. The oldest families disappear, the old parchments remain. Where would be the glory of the Hohenstauffens, the Leiningens, the Nidecks, and of so many other families of renown? Where would be the fame of their titles, their deeds of arms, their magnificent armour, their expeditions to the Holy Land, their alliances, their claims to remote antiquity, their conquests once complete, now long ago annulled? Where would be all those grand claims to historic fame without these parchments? Nowhere at all. Those high and mighty barons, those great dukes and princes, would be as if they had never been—they and everything that related to them far and near. Their strong castles, their palaces, their fortresses fall and moulder away into masses of ruin, vague remembrancers! Of all that greatness one monument alone remains—the chronicles, the songs of bards and minnesingers. Parchment alone remains!"

He sat silent for a moment, and then pursued his reflections.

"And in those distant times, while knights and squires rode out to war, and fought and conquered or fought and fell over the possession of a nook in a forest, or a title, or a smaller matter still, with what scorn and contempt did they not look down upon the wretched little scribbler, the man of mere letters and jargon, half-clothed in untanned hides, his only weapon an inkhorn at his belt, his pennon the feather of a goosequill! How they laughed at him, calling him an atom or a flea, good for nothing!

'He does nothing, he cannot even collect our taxes, or look after our estates, whilst we bold riders, armed to the teeth, sword in hand and lance on thigh, we fight, and we are the finest fellows in the land!' So they said when they saw the poor devil dragging himself on foot after their horses' heels, shivering in winter and sweating in summer, rusting and decaying in old age. Well, what has happened? That flea, that vermin, has kept them in the memory of men longer than their castles stood, long after their arms and their armour had rusted in the ground. I love those old parchments. I respect and revere them. Like ivy, they clothe the ruins and keep the ancient walls from crumbling into dust and perishing in oblivion!"

Having thus delivered himself, a solemn expression stole over his features, and his own eloquence made the tears of moved affection to steal down his furrowed cheeks.

The poor hunchback evidently loved those who had borne with and protected his unwarlike but clever ancestors. And after all he spoke truly, and there was profound good sense in his words.

I was surprised, and said, "Monsieur Knapwurst, do you know Latin?"

"Yes, sir," he answered, but without conceit, "both Latin and Greek. I taught myself. Old grammars were quite enough; there were some old books of the count's, thrown by as rubbish; they fell into my hands, and I devoured them. A little while after the count, hearing me drop a Latin quotation, was quite astonished, and said, 'When did you learn Latin, Knapwurst?' 'I taught myself, *monseigneur*.' He asked me a few questions, to which I gave pretty good answers. '*Parbleu!*' he cried, 'Knapwurst knows more than I do; he shall keep my records.' So he gave me the keys of the archives; that was thirty years ago. Since that time I have read every word. Sometimes, when the count sees me mounted upon my ladder, he says, 'What are you doing now, Knapwurst?' 'I am reading the family archives, *monseigneur*.' 'Aha! is that what you enjoy?' 'Yes, very much.' 'Come, come, I am glad to hear it, Knapwurst; but for you, who would know anything about the glory of the house of Nideck?' And off he goes laughing. I do just as I please."

"So he is a very good master, is he?"

"Oh, Doctor Fritz, he is the kindest-hearted master! he is so frank and so pleasant!" cried the dwarf, with hands clasped. "He has but one fault."

"And what may that be?"

"He has no ambition."

"How do you prove that?"

"Why, he might have been anything he pleased. Think of a Nideck, one of the very noblest families in Germany! He had but to ask to be made a minister or a field-marshal. Well! he desired nothing of the sort. When he was no longer a young man he retired from political life. Except that he was in the campaign in France at the head of a regiment he raised at his own expense, he has always lived far away from noise and battle; plain and simple, and almost unknown, he seemed to think of nothing but his hunting."

These details were deeply interesting to me. The conversation was of its own accord taking just the turn I wished it to take, and I resolved to get my advantage out of it.

"So the count has never had any exciting deeds in hand?"

"None, Doctor Fritz, none whatever; and that is the pity. A noble excitement is the glory of great families. It is a misfortune for a noble race when a member of it is devoid of ambition; he allows his family to sink below its level. I could give you many examples. That which would be very fortunate in a trader's family is the greatest misfortune in a nobleman's."

I was astonished; for all my theories upon the count's past life were falling to the earth.

"Still, Monsieur Knapwurst, the lord of Nideck has had great sorrows, had he not?"

"Such as what?"

"The loss of his wife."

"Yes, you are right there; his wife was an angel; he married her for love. She was a Zaan, one of the oldest and best nobility of Alsace, but a family ruined by the Revolution. The Countess Odile was the delight of her husband. She died of a decline which carried her off after five years' illness. Every plan was tried to save her life. They travelled in Italy together but she returned worse than she went, and died a few weeks after their return. The count was almost broken-hearted, and for two years he shut himself up and would see no one. He neglected his hounds and his horses. Time at last calmed his grief, but there is always a remainder of grief," said the hunchback, pointing with his finger to his heart; "you understand very well, there is still a bleeding wound. Old wounds you know, make themselves felt in change of weather—and old sorrows too—in spring when the flowers bloom again, and in autumn when the dead leaves cover the soil. But the count would not marry again; all his love is given to his daughter."

"So the marriage was a happy one throughout?"

"Happy! why it was a blessing for everybody."

I said no more. It was plain that the count had not committed, and could not have committed, a crime. I was obliged to yield to evidence. But, then, what was the meaning of that scene at night, that strange connection with the Black Pest, that fearful acting, that remorse in a dream, which impelled the guilty to betray their past atrocities?

I lost myself in vain conjectures.

Knapwurst relighted his pipe, and handed me one, which I accepted.

By that time the icy numbness which had laid hold of me

had nearly passed away, and I was enjoying that pleasant sense of relief which follows great fatigue when by the chimney-corner in a comfortable easy-chair, veiled in wreaths of tobacco-smoke, you yield to the luxury of repose, and listen idly to the duet between the chirping of a cricket on the hearth and the hissing of the burning log.

So we sat for a quarter of an hour.

At last I ventured to remark—

"But sometimes the count gets angry with his daughter?"

Knapwurst started, and fixing a sinister, almost a fierce and hostile eye upon me, answered—

"I know, I know!"

I watched him narrowly, thinking I might learn something now in support of my theory, but he simply added ironically—

"The towers of Nideck are high, and slander flies too low to reach their elevation!"

"No doubt; but still it is a fact, is it not?"

"Oh yes, so it is; but after all it is only a craze, an effect of his complaint. As soon as the crisis is past all his love for *mademoiselle* comes back. I assure you, sir, that a lover of twenty could not be more devoted, more affectionate, than he is. That young girl is his pride and his joy. A dozen times have I seen him riding away to get a dress, or flowers, or what not, for her. He went off alone, and brought back the articles in triumph, blowing his horn. He would have entrusted so delicate a commission to no one, not even to Sperver, whom he is so fond of. *Mademoiselle* never dares express a wish in his hearing lest he should start off and fulfil it at once. The lord of Nideck is the worthiest master, the tenderest father, and the kindest and most upright of men. Those poachers who are forever infesting our woods, the old Count Ludwig would have strung them up without mercy; our count winks at them; he even turns them into gamekeepers. Look at Sperver! why, if Count Ludwig was alive, Sperver's bones would long ago have been rattling in chains; instead of which he is head huntsman at the castle."

All my theories were now in a state of disorganisation. I laid my head between my hands and thought a long while.

Knapwurst, supposing that I was asleep, had turned to his folio again.

The grey dawn was now peeping in, and the lamp turning pale. Indistinct voices were audible in the castle.

Suddenly there was a noise of hurried steps outside. I saw some one pass before the window, the door opened abruptly, and Gideon appeared at the threshold.

Chapter 11

Sperver's pale face and glowing eyes announced that events were on their way. Yet he was calm, and did not seem surprised at my presence in Knapwurst's room.

"Fritz," he said briefly, "I am come to fetch you." I rose without answering and followed him. Scarcely were we out of the hut when he took me by the arm and drew me on to the castle.

"Mademoiselle Odile wants to see you," he whispered.

"What! is she ill?"

"No, she is much better, but something or other that is strange is going on. This morning about one o'clock, thinking that the count was nearly breathing his last, I went to wake the countess; with my hand on the bell my heart failed me. 'Why should I break her heart?' I said to myself, 'She will learn her misfortune only too soon; and then to wake her up in the middle of the night, weak and frail as she is, after such shocks, might kill her at a stroke.' I took a few minutes to consider, and then I resolved I would take it all on myself. I returned to the count's room. I looked in—not a soul was there! Impossible! the man was in the last agonies of death. I ran into the corridor like a madman. No one was there! Into the long gallery—no one!

"Then I lost my presence of mind, and rushing again into the young countess's room, I rang again. This time she appeared, crying out—'Is my father dead?' 'No.' 'Has he disappeared?' 'Yes, madam. I had gone out for a minute—when I came in again—' 'And Doctor Fritz, where is he?' 'In Hugh Lupus's tower.' 'In *that* tower?' She started. She threw a dressing-gown around her, took her lamp, and went out. I stayed behind. A quarter of an hour after she came back, her feet covered with snow, and so pale and so cold! She set her lamp upon the chimney-piece, and looking at me fixedly, said—'Was it you who put the doctor into that tower?' 'Yes, madam.' 'Unhappy man! you will never know the extent of the harm you have done.' I was about to answer, but she interrupted me—'No more; go and fasten every door and lie down. I will sit up. Tomorrow morning you will find Doctor Fritz at Knapwurst's, and bring him to me. Make no noise, and mind, you have seen nothing and know nothing!'"

"Is that all, Sperver?" I asked.

He nodded gravely.

"And about the count?"

"He is in again. He is better."

We had got to the antechamber. Gideon knocked at the door gently, then he opened it, announcing—"Doctor Fritz."

I took a pace forward, and stood in the presence of Odile. Sperver had retired, closing the door.

A strange impression crossed my mind at the sight of the young countess standing pale and still, leaning upon the back of an arm-chair, her eyes of feverish brightness, and robed in a long dress of rich black velvet. But she stood calm and firm.

"Doctor," she said, motioning me to a chair, "pray sit down; I have a very serious matter to speak to you about."

I obeyed in silence.

In her turn she sat down and seemed to be collecting her thoughts.

"Providence or an evil destiny, I know not which, has made you witness of a mystery in which lies involved the honour of my family."

So she knew it all!

I sat confounded and astonished.

"Madam, believe me, it was but by chance—"

"It is useless," she interrupted; "I know it all, and it is frightful!"

Then, in a heartrending appealing voice, she cried—

"My father is not a guilty man!"

I shuddered, and with hands outstretched cried—

"Madam, I know it; I know that the life of your father has been one of the noblest and loveliest."

Odile had half-risen from her seat, as if to protest, by anticipation, against any supposition that might be injurious to her father. Hearing me myself taking up his defence, she sank back again, and covering her face with her hands, the tears began to flow.

"God bless you, sir!" she exclaimed. "I should have died with the very thought that a breath of suspicion was harboured against him."

"Ah! madam, who could possibly attach any reality to the action of a somnambulist?"

"That is quite true, sir; I had had that thought myself, but appearances—pardon me—yet I feared—still I knew Doctor Fritz was a man of honour."

"Pray, madam, be calm."

"No," she cried, "let me weep on. It is such a relief; for ten years I have suffered in secret. Oh, how I suffered! That secret, so long shut up in my breast, was killing me. I should soon have died, like my dear mother. God has had pity upon me, and has sent you, and made you share it with me. Let me tell you all, sir, do let me!"

She could speak no more. Sobs and tears broke her voice. So it always is with proud and lofty natures. After having conquered grief, and imprisoned it, buried, and, as it were, crushed down in the secret depths of the mind, they seem happy, or, at any rate, indifferent to the eyes of the uninformed around, and the eye of the most watchful observer might be mistaken; but let a sudden shock break the seal, an unexpected rending of a portion of the veil, then, as with the crash of a thunderstorm, the tower in which the sufferer hid his sorrow falls in ruins to the ground. The conquered foe rises more fierce than before his defeat and captivity; he shakes with fury the prison doors, the frame trembles with long shudderings, sobs and sighs heave the breast, the tears, too long contained within bounds, overflow their swollen banks, bounding and rushing as if after the heavy rain of a thunderstorm.

Such was Odile.

At length she lifted her beautiful head; she wiped her tear-stained cheeks, and with her arm on the elbow of her chair, her cheek resting on her hand, and her eyes tenderly fixed on a picture on the wall, she resumed in slow and melancholy tones:—

"When I go back into the past, sir, when I return to my first impressions, my mother's is the picture before me. She was a tall, pale, and silent woman. She was still young at the period to which I am referring. She was scarcely thirty, and yet you would have thought her fifty. Her brow was silvered round with hair white as snow; her thin, hollow cheeks, her sharp, clear profile—her lips ever closed together with an expression of pain—gave to her features a strange character in which pride and pain seemed to contend for the mastery. There was nothing left of the elasticity of youth in that aged woman of thirty—nothing but her tall, upright figure, her brilliant eyes, and her voice, which was always as gentle and as sweet as a dream of childhood.

"She often walked up and down for hours in this very room, with her head hanging down, and I, an unthinking child, ran happily along by her side, never aware that my mother was sad, never understanding the meaning of the deep melancholy revealed by those furrows that traversed her fair brow. I knew nothing of the past, to me the present was joy and happiness, and oh! the future!—the dark, miserable future!—there was none! My only future was tomorrow's play!"

Odile smiled bitterly and went on:—

"Sometimes I would happen, in my noisy play, to disturb my mother in her silent walk; then she would stop, look down, and, seeing me at her feet, would slowly bend, kiss me with an absent smile, and then again resume her interrupted walk and her sad gait. Since then, sir, whenever I have desired to search back in my memory for remembrances of my early days that tall, pale woman has risen before me, the image of melancholy. There she is," pointing to a picture on the wall—"there she is!—not such as illness made her as my father supposes, but that fatal and terrible secret. See!"

I turned round, and as my eye dwelt upon the portrait the lady pointed to, I shuddered.

It was a long, pale, thin face, cold and rigid as death, and only luridly lighted up by two dark, deep-set eyes, fixed, burning, and of a terrible intensity.

There was a moment's silence.

"How much that woman must have suffered!" I said to myself with a pain striking at my heart.

"I know not how my mother made that terrible discovery," added Odile, "but she became aware of the mysterious attraction of the Black Pest and their meetings in Hugh Lupus's tower; she knew it all—all! She never suspected my father—ah no!—but she perished away by slow degrees under this consuming influence! and I myself am dying."

I bowed my head into my hands and wept in silence.

"One night," she went on, "one night—I was only ten—and my mother, with the remains of her superhuman energy, for she was near her end that night, came to me when I lay asleep. It was in winter; a stony cold hand caught me by the wrist. I looked up. Before me stood a tall woman; in one hand she held a flaming torch, with the other she held me by the arm. Her robe was sprinkled with snow. There was a convulsive movement in all her limbs and her eyes were fired with a gloomy light through the long locks of white hair which hung in disorder round her face. It was my mother; and she said, 'Odile, my child, get up and dress! You must know it all!' Then taking me to Hugh Lupus's tower she showed me the open subterranean passage. 'Your father will come out that way,' she said, pointing to the tower; 'he will come out with the she-wolf; don't be frightened, he won't see you.'

"And presently my father, bearing his funereal burden, came out with the old woman. My mother took me in her arms and followed; she showed me the dismal scene on the Altenberg of which you know. 'Look, my child,' she said; 'you must for I—am going to die soon. You will have to keep that secret. You alone are to sit up with your father,' she said impressively—'you alone. The honour of your family depends upon you!' And so we returned. A fortnight after my mother died, leaving me her will to accomplish and her example to follow. I have scrupulously obeyed her injunctions as a sacred command, but oh, at what a sacrifice! You have seen it all. I have been obliged to disobey my father and to rend his heart. If I had married I should have brought a stranger into the house and betrayed the secret of our race. I resisted.

"No one in this castle knows of the somnambulism of my father, and but for yesterday's crisis, which broke down my strength completely and prevented me from sitting up with my father, I should still have been its sole depositary. God has decreed otherwise, and has placed the honour and reputation of my family in your keeping. I might demand of you, sir, a solemn promise never to reveal what you have seen to-night. I should have a right to do so."

"Madam," I said, rising, "I am ready."

"No, sir," she replied with much dignity, "I will not put such an affront upon you. Oaths fail to bind base men, and honour alone is a sufficient guarantee for the upright. You will keep that secret, sir, I know you will keep it, because it is your duty to do so. But I expect more than this of you, much more, and this is why I consider myself obliged to tell you all!"

She rose slowly from her seat.

"Doctor Fritz," she resumed in a voice which made every nerve within me quiver with deep emotion, "my strength is unequal to my burden; I bend beneath it. I need a helper, a friend. Will you be that friend?"

"Madam," I replied, rising from my seat, "I gratefully accept your offer of friendship. I cannot tell you how proud I am of your confidence; but still, allow me to unite with it one condition."

"Pray speak, sir."

"I mean that I will accept that title of friend with all the duties and obligations which it shall impose upon me."

"What duties do you mean?"

"There is a mystery overhanging your family; that mystery must be discovered and solved at any cost. That Black Pest must be apprehended. We must find out where she comes from, what she is, and what she wants!"

"Oh, but that is impossible!" she said with a movement of despair.

"Who can tell that, madam? Perhaps Divine Providence may have had a design connected with me in sending Sperver to fetch me here."

"You are right, sir. God never acts without consummate wisdom. Do whatever you think right. I give my approval in advance."

I raised to my lips the hand which she tremblingly placed in mine, and went out full of admiration for this frail and feeble woman, who was, nevertheless, so strong in the time of trial. Is anything grander than duty nobly accomplished?

Chapter 12

An hour after the conversation with Odile, Sperver and I were riding hard, and leaving Nideck rapidly behind us.

The huntsman, bending forward over his horse's neck, encouraged him with voice and action.

He rode so fast that his tall Mecklemburger, her mane flying, tail outstretched, and legs extended wide, seemed almost motionless, so swiftly did she cleave the air. As for my little Ardenne pony, I think he was running right away with his rider. Lieverle accompanied us, flying alongside of us like an arrow from the bow. A whirlwind seemed to sweep us in our headlong way.

The towers of Nideck were far away, and Sperver was keeping ahead as usual when I shouted—

"Halloo, comrade, pull up! Halt! Before we go any farther let us know what we are about."

He faced round.

"Only just tell me, Fritz, is it right or is it left?"

"No; that won't do. It is of the first importance that you should know the object of our journey. In short, we are going to catch the hag."

A flush of pleasure brightened up the long sallow face of the old poacher, and his eyes sparkled.

"Ha, ha!" he cried, "I knew we should come to that at last!"

And he slipped his rifle round from his shoulder into his hand.

This significant action roused me.

"Wait, Sperver; we are not going to kill the Black Pest, but to take her alive!"

"Alive?"

"No doubt, and it will spare you a good deal of remorse perhaps if I declare to you that the life of this old woman is bound up with that of your master. The ball that hits her hits your lord."

Sperver gazed at me in astonishment.

"Is this really true, Fritz?"

"Positively true."

There was a long silence; our mounts, Fox and Rappel, tossed their heads at each other as if in the act of saluting one another, scraping up the snow with their hoofs in congratulation upon so pleasant an expedition. Lieverle opened wide his red mouth, gaping with impatience, extending and bending his long meagre body like a snake, and Sperver sat motionless, his hand still upon his gun.

"Well, let us try and catch her alive. We will put on gloves if we have to touch her, but it is not so easy as you think, Fritz."

And pointing out with extended hand the panorama of mountains which lay unrolled about us like a vast amphitheatre, he added—

"Look! there's the Altenberg, the Schneeberg, the Oxenhorn, the Rhethal, the Behrenkopf, and if we only got up a little higher we should see fifty more mountain-tops far away, right into the Palatinate. There are rocks and ravines, passes and valleys, torrents and waterfalls, forests, and more mountains; here beeches, there firs, then oaks, and the old woman has got all that for her camping-ground. She tramps everywhere, and lives in a hole wherever she pleases. She has a sure foot, a keen eye, and can scent you a couple of miles off. How are you going to catch her, then?"

"If it was an easy matter where would be the merit? I should not then have chosen you to take a part in it."

"That is all very fine, Fritz. If we only had one end of her trail, who knows but with courage and perseverance—"

"As for her trail, don't trouble about that; that's my business."

"Yours?"

"Yes, mine."

"What do you know about following up a trail?"

"Why should not I?"

"Oh, if you are so sure of it, and you know more about it than I do, of course march on, and I'll follow!"

It was easy to see that the old hunter was vexed that I should presume to trespass upon his special province; therefore, only laughing inwardly, I required no repetition of the request to lead on, and I turned sharply to the left, sure of coming across the old woman's trail, who, after having left the count at the postern gate, must have crossed the plain to reach the mountain. Sperver rode behind me now, whistling rather contemptuously, and I could hear him now and then grumbling—

"What is the use of looking for the track of the she-wolf in the plain? Of course she went along the forest side just as usual. But it seems she has altered her habits, and now walks about with her hands in her pockets, like a respectable Fribourg tradesman out for a walk."

I turned a deaf ear to his hints, but in a moment I heard him utter an exclamation of surprise; then, fixing a keen eye upon me, he said—

"Fritz, you know more than you choose to tell."

"How so, Gideon?"

"The track that I should have been a week finding, you have got it at once. Come, that's not all right!"

"Where do you see it, then?"

"Oh, don't pretend to be looking at your feet."

And pointing out to me at some distance a scarcely perceptible white streak in the snow—

"There she is!"

Immediately he galloped up to it; I followed in a couple of minutes; we had dismounted, and were examining the track of the Black Pest.

"I should like to know," cried Sperver, "how that track came here?"

"Don't let that trouble you," I replied.

"You are right, Fritz; don't mind what I say; sometimes I do speak rather at random. What we want now is to know where that track will lead us to."

And now the huntsman knelt on the ground.

I was all ears; he was closely examining.

"It is a fresh track," he pronounced, "last night's. It is a strange thing, Fritz, during the count's last attack that old witch was hanging about the castle."

Then examining with greater care—

"She passed here between three and four o'clock this morning."

"How can you tell that?"

"It is quite a fresh track; there is sleet all round it. Last night, about twelve, I came out to shut the doors; there was sleet falling then, there is none upon the footsteps, therefore she has passed since."

"That is true enough, Sperver, but it may have been made much later; for instance, at eight or nine."

"No, look, there is frost upon it! The fog that freezes on the snow only comes at daybreak. The creature passed here after the sleet and before the fog—that is, about three or four this morning."

I was astonished at Sperver's exactitude.

He rose from his knee, clapping his hands together to get rid of the snow, and looking at me thoughtfully, as if speaking to himself, said—

"It is twelve, is it not, Fritz?"

"A quarter to twelve."

"Very well; then the old woman has got seven hours' start of us. We must follow upon her trail step by step; on horseback we can do it in half the time, and, if she is still going, about seven or eight to-night we have got her, Fritz. Now then, we're off."

And we started afresh upon the track. It led us straight to the mountains.

Galloping away, Sperver said—

"If good luck only would have it that she had rested an hour or two in a hole in a rock, we might be up with her before the daylight is gone."

"Let us hope so, Gideon."

"Oh, don't think of it. The old she-wolf is always moving; she never tires; she tramps along all the hollows in the Black Forest. We must not flatter ourselves with vain hopes. If, perhaps, she has stopped on her journey, so much the better for us; and if she still keeps going, we won't let that discourage us. Come on at a gallop."

It is a very strange feeling to be hunting down a fellow-creature; for, after all, that unhappy woman was of our own kind and nature; endowed like ourselves with an immortal soul to be saved, she felt, and thought, and reflected like ourselves. It is true that a strange perversion of human nature had brought her near to the nature of the wolf, and that some great mystery overshadowed her being. No doubt a wandering life had obliterated the moral sense in her, and even almost effaced the human character; but still nothing in the world can give one man a right to exercise over another the dominion of the man over the brute.

And yet a burning ardour hurried us on in pursuit; my blood was at fever heat; I was determined to stand at no obstacle in laying hold of this extraordinary being. A wolf-hunt or a boar-hunt would not have excited me near so much.

The snow was flying in our rear; sometimes splinters of ice, bitten off by the horse-shoes, like shavings of iron from machinery, whizzed past our ears.

Sperver, sometimes with his nose in the air and his red moustache floating in the wind, sometimes with his grey eyes intently following the track, reminded me of those famous Cossacks that I had seen pass through Germany when I was a boy; and his tall, lanky horse, muscular and full-maned, its body as slender as a greyhound's, completed the illusion.

Lieverle, in a high state of enthusiasm and excitement, took bounds sometimes as high as our horses' backs, and I could not but tremble at the thought that when we came up at last with the Pest he might tear her in pieces before we could prevent him.

But the old woman gave us all the trouble she could; on every hill she doubled, at every hillock there was a false track.

"After all, it is easy here," cried Sperver, "to what it will be in the wood. We shall have to keep our eyes open there! Do you see the accursed beast? Here she has confused the track! There she has been amusing herself sweeping the trail, and then from that height which is exposed to the wind she has slipped down to the stream, and has crept along through the cresses to get to the underwood. But for those two footsteps she would have sold us completely."

We had just reached the edge of a pine-forest. In woods of this description the snow never reaches the ground except in the open spaces between the trees, the dense foliage intercepting it in its fall. This was a difficult part of our enterprise. Sperver dismounted to see our way better, and placed me on his left so as not to be hindered by my shadow.

Here were large spaces covered with dead leaves and the needles and cones of the fir-trees, which retain no footprint. It was, therefore, only in the open patches where the snow had fallen on the ground that Sperver found the track again.

It took us an hour to get through this thicket. The old poacher bit his moustache with excitement and vexation, and his long nose visibly bent into a hook. When I was only opening my mouth to speak, he would impatiently say—

"Don't speak—it bothers me!"

At last we descended a valley to the left and Gideon pointing to the track of the she-wolf outside the edge of the brushwood, triumphantly remarked—

"There is no feint in this sortie, for once. We may follow this track confidently."

"Why so?"

"Because the Pest has a habit every time she doubles of going three paces to the right; then she retraces her steps four, five, or six in the other direction, and jumps away into a clear place. But when she thinks she has sufficiently disguised her trail she breaks out without troubling herself to make any feints. There now! What did I say? Now she is burrowing beneath the brushwood like a wild boar, and it won't be so difficult to follow her up."

"Well, let us put the track between us and smoke a pipe."

We halted, and the honest fellow, whose countenance was beginning to brighten up, looking up at me with enthusiasm, cried—

"Fritz, if we have luck this will be one of the finest days in my life. If we catch the old hag I will strap her across my horse behind me like a bundle of old rags. There is only one thing troubles me."

"And what is that?"

"That I forgot my bugle. I should have liked to have sounded the return on getting near the castle! Ha, ha, ha!"

He lighted his stump of a pipe and we galloped off again.

The track of the she-wolf now passed on to the heights of the forest by so steep an ascent that several times we had to dismount and lead our horses by the bridle.

"There she is, turning to the right," said Sperver. "In this direction the mountains are craggy; perhaps one of us will have to lead both horses while the other climbs to look after the trail. But don't you think the light is going?"

The landscape now was assuming an aspect of grandeur and magnificence. Vast grey rocks, sparkling with long icicles, raised here and there their sharp peaks like breakers amidst a snowy sea.

There is nothing more sadly impressive than the aspect of winter in a mountainous region. The jagged crests of the precipices, the deep, dark ravines, the woods sparkling with boar-frost like diamonds, all form a picture of desertion, desolation, and unspeakable melancholy. The silence is so profound that you hear a dead leaf rustling on the snow, or the needle of the fir dropping to the ground. Such a silence is oppressive as the tomb; it urges on the mind the idea of man's nothingness in the vastness of creation.

How frail a being is man! Two winters together, without a summer between, would sweep him off the earth!

At times we felt it a necessity to be saying something if only to show that we were keeping up our spirits.

"Ah, we are getting on! How fearfully cold! Lieverle, what is the matter? what have you found now?"

Unfortunately Fox and Rappel were beginning to tire; they sank deeper in the snow and no longer neighed joyfully.

And added to this the endless mazes of the Black Forest wearied us too. The old woman affected this solitary region greatly; here she had trotted round a deserted charcoal-burner's hut; farther on she had torn out the roots that projected from a moss-grown rock; there she had sat at the foot of a tree, and that very recently—not more than two hours since, for the track was quite fresh—and our hope and our ardour rose together. But the daylight was slowly fading away!

Very strangely, ever since our departure from Nideck we had met neither wood-cutters, nor charcoal-burners, nor timber-carriers. At this season the silence and solitude of the Black Forest is as deep as that of the North-American steppes.

At five o'clock it was almost dark. Sperver halted and said—

"Fritz, my lad, we have started a couple of hours too late. The she-wolf has had too long a start. In ten minutes it will be as dark as a dungeon. The best way would be to reach Roche Creuse, which is twenty minutes' ride from here, light a good fire, and eat our provisions and empty our flasks. When the moon is up we will follow the trail again, and unless the old hag is the foul fiend himself, ten to one we shall find her dead and stiff with cold against the foot of a tree, for nothing can live after such a tremendous tramp in weather like this. Sebalt is the best walker in the Black Forest, and he would not have stood it. Come, Fritz, what is your opinion?"

"I am not so mad as to think differently. Besides, I am perishing with hunger!"

"Well, let us start again."

He took the lead and passed into a close and narrow glen between two precipitous faces of rock. The fir-trees met over our heads; under our feet ran a mere thread of the stream, and from time to time some ray from above was dimly reflected in the depths below and glinted with a dull leaden light.

The darkness was now such that I thought it prudent to drop my bridle on Rappel's neck. The steps of our horses on the slippery gravel awoke strange discordant sounds like the screaming of monkeys at play. The echoes from rock to rock caught up and repeated every sound, and in the distance a tiny space of deep blue widened as we advanced; it was the issue from the glen.

"Fritz," said Sperver, "we are in the bed of the Tunkelbach. This is the wildest spot in the Black Forest. The end is a pit called La Marmite du Grand Gueulard, the muckle-mouthed giant's kettle. In the spring, when the snow is melting, the Tunkelbach hurls all its waters into it, a depth of two hundred feet. There is an awful uproar; the waters dash down and then splash up again and fall in spray on all the hills around. Sometimes it even fills the Roche Creuse, but just now it must be as dry as a powder-flask."

Whilst I was listening to Gideon's explanations I was at the same time meditating upon this dark and fearful glen, and I reflected that the instinct which attracts the brutes into such retreats as these, far from the light of heaven, away from everything bright and cheerful, must partake of the nature of remorse. Those animals which love the open sunshine—the goat aloft upon a high conspicuous peak, the horse flying across the wide plain, the dog capering round his master, the bird bathed in sunlight—all breathe joy and happiness; they bask, and sing, and rejoice in dancing and delight. The kid nibbling the tender grass under the shade of the great trees is as poetic an object as the shelter that it loves; the fierce boar is as rough as the tangled brakes through which he loves to run his huge bristly back; the eagle is as proud and lofty as the sky-piercing crags on which he perches as his home; the lion is as majestic as the arching vaults of the caves where he makes his den; but the wolf, the fox, and the ferret seek the darkness that conforms to their ugly deeds; fear and remorse dog their steps.

I was still dreamily pursuing these thoughts, and I was beginning to feel the keen air moving upon my face, for we were approaching the outlet of the gorge, when all at once a red light struck the rock a hundred feet above us, purpling the dark green of the fir-trees and lighting up the wreaths of snow.

"Ha!" cried Sperver, "we have got her at last!"

My heart leaped; we stood, closely pressed, the one against the other.

The dog growled low and deep.

"Cannot she escape?" I asked in a whisper.

"No; she is caught like a rat in a trap. There is no way out of La Marmite du Grand Gueulard but this, and everywhere all round the rocks are two hundred feet high. Now, vile hag, I hold you!"

He alighted in the ice-cold stream, handing me his bridle. I caught in the silence the click of the lock of his gun, and that slight noise threw me into a tremor of apprehension.

"Sperver, what are you about?"

"Don't be alarmed; it is only to frighten her."

"Very well, then, but no blood. Remember what I told you—the ball which strikes the Pest slays the count!"

"Don't trouble yourself," was the answer.

He went away without further parley. I could hear the splash of his feet in the water; then I saw his tall figure emerge at the opening of the dark glen, black against a purple background. He stood five minutes motionless. Attentive, bending forward, I looked and listened, still moving onward. As he returned I was but a few yards from him.

"Hark!" he whispered mysteriously. "Look there!"

At the end of the hollow, scooped out perpendicularly like a quarry in the mountain side, I saw a bright fire unrolling its golden spires beneath the vault of a cave, and before the fire sat a man with his hands clasped about his knees, whom I recognised by his dress as the Baron de Zimmer-Bluderich.

He sat motionless, his forehead resting between his hands. Behind him lay a dark gaunt form extended on the ground. Farther on, his horse, half lost in the shade, reared his neck, gazed on us with eyes fixed, ears erect, and nostrils distended.

I stood rooted to the ground.

How did the Baron de Zimmer happen to be in that lonely wilderness at such a time? What did he want here? Had he lost his way?

The most contradictory conjectures were passing in confusion through my excited brain, and I could not tell what conclusion to arrive at, when the baron's horse began to neigh, and the master raised his head.

"Well, Donner, what is the matter now?" said he.

Then he, too, directed his gaze our way, straining his eyes through the darkness.

That pale face, with its strongly-marked features, thin lips, and thick black eyebrows meeting together, and forming a deep hollow on the brow in the form of a long vertical wrinkle, would have struck me with admiration at any other time; while now an inexplicable anxiety laid hold of me, and I was filled with vague apprehensions.

Suddenly the young man exclaimed—

"Who goes there?"

"I, *monseigneur*," answered Sperver, coming forward—

"Sperver, chief huntsman to the lord of Nideck."

A flash shot from the baron's quick eye; not a muscle of his countenance quailed. He rose to his feet, gathering his *pelisse* over his shoulders. I drew towards me the horses and the dog, and this animal suddenly began howling fearfully.

Is not every one, more or less, subject to superstitious fears? At these dismal sounds I trembled, and a cold shudder crept through my whole body.

Sperver and the baron stood at a distance of fifty yards from each other; the first immovable in the midst of the deep glen, his gun unslung from his shoulder, the other erect upon the level platform outside of the cave, carrying his head high, fixing on us a haughty eye and a proud look of superiority.

"What do you want here?" he asked aggressively.

"We are looking for a woman," replied the old poacher—"a woman who comes every year prowling about Nideck, and our orders are to take her."

"Has she stolen anything?"

"No."

"Has she committed murder?"

"No, *monseigneur*."

"Then what do you want with her? What right have you to pursue her?"

"And you—what right have you over her?" answered Sperver with an ironical smile. "See, there she is. I can see her at the bottom of the cave. What right have you to meddle with our affairs? Don't you know that we are here in the domains of Nideck, and that we administer justice and execute our own decrees?"

The young man changed colour, and said coldly—

"I have no account to render to you."

"Beware," replied Sperver. "I am come with proposals of peace and conciliation. I am here on behalf of the lord Yeri-Hans. I am in the execution of my duty, and you are putting yourself in the wrong."

"Your duty!" cried the young man bitterly. "If you talk about your duty you will oblige me to do mine!"

"Well, do it!" cried the huntsman, whose features were becoming disturbed with anger.

"No," replied the baron, "I am not responsible to you, and you shall not come here!"

"That's what we shall soon see!" said Sperver, drawing nearer to the cave.

The young man drew his hunting-knife. Perceiving this menacing action, I was about to dart between them, but happily the hound which I was holding by his collar slipped from me with a violent shock and threw me on the ground. I thought the baron would be lost, but at that instant a wild shriek rose from the dark bottom of the cavern, and as I rose to my feet I saw the old woman standing erect before the fire, her tattered garments hanging loosely about her, her grey and tangled locks floating wildly in the wind; she flung her bony arms in the air and uttered prolonged piercing howls like the cry of agony of the hungry wolf in the long cold nights of winter when famine is gnawing his entrails.

Never in my life have I seen a more fearful apparition. Sperver, motionless, his eyes riveted on the fearful object before him, and his mouth open with astonishment, stood as if rooted to the earth. But the powerful dog, surprised himself at this unexpected sight, stood still for a moment; then with a bend of his bristling back in preparation for a mighty leap, he made a rush with a deep, impatient growl which made me tremble. The platform before the cave was about eight or nine feet from the level where we stood, or he would have reached it at a single bound. I can yet hear him clearing a way through the snowy brambles, the baron flinging himself before the woman with a piercing cry, "My mother!" then the dog taking another spring, and Sperver, quick as lightning, raising his gun, and bringing down the poor animal dead at the young man's feet.

This was but the work of a second. The gulf had been illuminated with a momentary flash, and the wild echoes were vibrating with the explosion from rock to rock, till it died in the far distance. Then silence again settled on the gloomy scene, as darkness after the lightning.

When the smoke of the explosion had cleared away I saw Lieverle lying outstretched at the foot of the rock, and the woman fainting in the arms of the young man. Sperver, pale with concentrated rage and excitement, and eyeing the young baron darkly, dropped the butt of his gun to the ground, his features discomposed, and his eyes half-hid in his gloomy frown.

"Seigneur de Bluderich," he cried, with his hand extended, "I have killed my best friend to save the life of that unhappy woman, your mother! Thank God that her life is bound up with that of the Count of Nideck! Take her away! take her hence, and never let her return here again; if you do I cannot answer for what old Sperver may be driven to do!"

Then, with a glance at the poor dog—

"Oh! Lieverle, Lieverle!" he cried, "was it to end thus? Come, Fritz, let us go. I cannot stay here. I might do something that I should have to repent of!"

And, laying hold of Fox by the mane, he was going to throw himself into the saddle, but suddenly his feelings of distress overcame all restraint, and bowing his head upon his horse's neck, he burst into sobs and tears, and wept like a child.

Chapter 13

Sperver had gone, bearing the body of poor Lieverle in his cloak. I had declined to follow; my sense of duty kept me by this unhappy woman, and I could not leave her without violence to my own feelings.

Besides, I must confess I was curious to see a little more closely this strange mysterious being, and therefore as soon as Sperver had disappeared in the darkness of the glen I began to climb up to reach the cavern.

There I beheld a strange sight.

Extended upon a large cloak of white fur lay the aged woman in a long and ragged robe of purple, her fingers clutching her breast, a golden arrow through her grey hair.

Never shall I forget the figure of this strange woman; her

vulture-like features distorted with the last agonies of death, her eyes set, her gasping mouth, were fearful to look upon. Such might have been the terrible Queen Fredegonde.

The baron, on his knees at her side, was trying to restore her to animation; but I saw at a glance that the wretched creature was dying, and it was not without a profound sense of pity that I took her by the arm.

"Leave *madame* alone—don't touch her," cried the young man with irritation.

"I am a surgeon, *monseigneur*."

He looked in silence at me for a moment, then rising, said—

"Pardon me, sir; pray forgive my hasty language."

He trembled with excitement, scarcely yet subdued, and presently he went on—

"What is your opinion, sir?"

"It is over—she is dead!"

Then, without speaking another word, he sat upon a large stone, with his forehead resting upon his hand and his elbow on his knee, his eyes motionless, as still as a statue.

I sat near the fire, watching the flames rising to the vaulted roof of the cave, and casting lurid reflections upon the rigid features of the corpse.

We had sat there an hour as motionless as statues, each deep in thought, when, suddenly lifting his head, the baron said—

"Sir, all this utterly confounds me. Here is my mother—for twenty-six years I thought I knew her—and now an abyss of horrible mysteries opens before me. You are a doctor; tell me, did you ever know anything so dreadful?"

"*Monseigneur*," I replied, "the Count of Nideck is afflicted with a complaint strikingly similar to that from which your mother appears to have suffered. If you feel enough confidence in me to communicate to me the facts which you have yourself observed, I will gladly tell you what I know myself; for perhaps this exchange of our experiences might supply me with the means to save my patient."

"Willingly, sir," he replied, and without any further prelude he informed me that the Baroness de Bluderich, a member of one of the noblest families in Saxony, took, every year towards autumn, a journey into Italy, with no attendant besides an old man-servant, who possessed her entire confidence; that that man, being at the point of death, had desired a private interview with the son of his old master, and that at that last hour, prompted, no doubt, by the pangs of remorse, he had told the young man that his mother's visit to Italy was only a pretence to enable her to make, you observed, a certain excursion into the Black Forest, the object of which was unknown to himself, but which must have had something fearful in its character, since the baroness returned always in a state of physical prostration, ragged, half dead, and that weeks of rest alone could restore her after the hideous labours of those few days.

This was the purport of the old servant's disclosures to the young baron, who believed that in so doing he was only fulfilling his duty.

The son, anxious at any sacrifice to know the truth of this account, had, that very year, ascertained it, first by following his mother to Baden, and then by penetrating on her track into the gorges of the Black Forest. The footsteps which Sebalt had tracked in the woods were his.

When the baron had thus imparted his knowledge to me, I thought I ought not to conceal from him the mysterious influence which the appearance of the old woman in the neighbourhood of the castle exercised over the count, nor the other circumstances of this unaccountable series of events.

We were both amazed at the extraordinary coincidence between the facts narrated, the mysterious attraction which these beings unconsciously exercised the one over the other, the tragic drama which they performed in union, the familiarity which the old woman had shown with the castle, and its most secret passages, without any previous examination of them; the costume which she had discovered in which to carry out this secret act, and which could only have been rummaged out of some mysterious retreat revealed to her by the strange instinct of insanity. Finally, we were agreed that there are unknown, unfathomed depths in our being, and that the mystery of death is not the only secret which God has veiled from our eyes, although it may seem to us the most important.

But the darkness of night was beginning to yield to the pale tints of early dawn. A bat was sounding the departure of the hours of darkness with a singular note resembling the gurgling of liquid from a narrow bottle-neck. A neighing of horses was heard far up the defile; then, with the first rays of dawn, we distinguished a sledge driven by the baron's servant; its bottom was littered with straw; on this the body was laid.

I mounted my horse, who seemed not sorry to use his limbs again, which had been numbed by standing upon ice and snow the whole night through. I rode after the sledge to the exit from the defile, when, after a grave salutation—the usual token of courtesy between the nobility and the people—they drove off in the direction of Hirschland and I rode towards the towers of Nideck.

At nine I was in the presence of Mademoiselle Odile, to whom I gave a faithful narrative of all that had taken place.

Then repairing to the count's apartments, I found him in a very satisfactory state of improvement. He felt very weak, as was to be expected after the terrible shocks of such crises as he had gone through, but had returned to the full possession of his clear faculties, and the fever had left him the evening before. There was, therefore, every prospect of a speedy cure.

A few days later, seeing the old lord in a state of convalescence, I expressed a desire to return to Fribourg, but he entreated me so earnestly to stay altogether at Nideck, and offered me terms so honourable and advantageous, that I felt myself unable to refuse compliance with his wishes.

I shall long remember the first boar-hunt in which I had the honour to join with the count, and especially the magnificent return home in a torchlight procession after having sat in the saddle for twelve hours together.

I had just had supper, and was going up into Hugh Lupus's tower completely knocked up, when, passing Sperver's room, whose door was half open, shouts and cries of joy reached my ears. I stopped, when the most jovial spectacle burst upon me. Around the massive oaken table beamed twenty square rosy faces, bright and ruddy with health and fun.

The hob and nobbing of the glasses gave out an incessant tinkling and clattering. There was sitting Sperver with his bossy forehead, his moustaches bedewed with Rhenish wine, his eyes sparkling, and his grey hair rather disordered; at his right was Marie Lagoutte, on his left Knapwurst. He was raising aloft the ancient silver-gilt and chased goblet dimmed with age, and on his manly chest glittered the silver plate of his shoulder-belt, for, according to his custom on a hunting day, he was still wearing the uniform of his office.

The colour of Marie Lagoutte's cheeks, rather redder even than usual, told of an evening of jollity, and her broad cap-frills seemed as if they were wanting to fly all abroad; she sat laughing, now with one, then with another.

Knapwurst, squatting in his armchair, with his head on a level with Sperver's elbow, looked like a big pumpkin. Then came Tobias Offenloch, so red that you would have thought he had bathed his face in the red wine, leaning back with his wig upon the chair-back and his wooden leg extended under the table. Farther on loomed the melancholy long face of Sebalt, who was peeping with a sickly smile into the bottom of his wine-glass.

Besides these worthies there were present the waiting-people, men and women servants, comprising all that little community which springs up around the board of the great people of the land and belongs to them as the ivy, and the moss, and the wild convolvulus belong to the monarch of the forests.

Upon the groaning board lay a vast ham, displaying its concentric circles of pink and white. Then among the gaily-patterned plates and dishes came the long-necked bottles containing the produce of the vineyards that border the broad and flowing Rhine—long German pipes with little silver chains, and long shining blades of steel.

The light of the lamp shed over the whole scene its amber-coloured hue and left in the shade the old grey and time-stained walls, where hung in ample numbers the brazen convolutions of the hunting-horns and bugles.

What an original picture! The vaulted roof was ringing with the joyous shouts of laughter.

Sperver, as I have already told, was lifting high the full bumper and singing the song of Black Hatto, the Burgrave,

"*I am king on these mountains of mine,*"

while the rosy dew of Affenthal hung trembling from his long moustaches. As soon as he caught sight of me he stopped, and holding out his hand—

"Fritz," said he, "we only wanted you. It is a long time since I felt so comfortable as I do tonight. You are welcome, old boy!"

As I gazed upon him with surprise—for since the death of Lieverle I had never seen him smile—he added more seriously—

"We are celebrating the return of *monseigneur* to his health, and Knapwurst is telling us stories."

All the guests turned my way, and I was saluted with kindly welcomes on all sides.

I was dragged in by Sebalt, seated near Marie Lagoutte, and found a large glass of Bohemian wine in my hand before I could quite understand the meaning of it all.

The old hall was echoing with merry peals of laughter, and Sperver, throwing his arm round my neck, holding his cup high, and with an attempt at gravity which showed plainly that the wine was up in his head, he shouted—

"Here is my son! He and I—I and he—until death! Here's the health of Doctor Fritz!"

Knapwurst, standing as high as he was able upon the seat of his armchair, not unlike a turnip half divided in two, leaned towards me and held me out his glass. Marie Lagoutte shook out the long streamers of her cap, and Sebalt, upright before his chair, as gaunt and lean as the shade of the wild *jaeger* amongst the heather, repeated, "Your health, Doctor Fritz!" whilst the flakes of silvery foam ran down his cup and floated gently down upon the stone-flagged floor.

Then there was a moment's silence. Every guest drank. Then, with a single clash, every glass was set vigorously down upon the table.

"Bravo!" cried Sperver.

Then turning to me—

"Fritz, we have already drunk to the health of the count and of Mademoiselle Odile; you will do the same."

Twice had I to drain the cup before the vigilant eyes of the whole table. Then I too began to look grave. Could it have been drunken gravity? A luminous radiance seemed shed on every object; faces stood out brightly from the darkness, and looked more nearly upon me; in truth, there were youthful faces and aged, pretty and ugly, but all alike beamed upon me kindly, and lovingly, and tenderly; but it was the youngest, at the other end of the table, whose bright eyes attracted me, and we exchanged long and wistful glances, full of affection and sympathy!

Sperver kept on humming and laughing. Suddenly putting his hand upon the dwarf's misshapen back, he cried—

"Silence! Here is Knapwurst, our historian and chronicler! He is preparing to speak. This hump holds all the history of the house of Nideck from the beginning of time!"

The little hunchback, not at all indignant at so ambiguous a compliment, directed his benevolent eyes upon the face of the huntsman, and replied—

"You, Sperver, you are one of the *reiters* whose story I have been telling you. You have the arm, and the courage, and the whiskers of a *reiter* of old! If that window opened wide, and a *reiter* was to hold out his hand at the end of his long arm to you, what would you say to him?"

"I would say, 'You are welcome, comrade; sit down and drink. You will find the wine just as good and the girls just as pretty as they were in the days of old Hugh Lupus.' Look!"

And he pointed with his glass at the jolly young faces that

brightened the farther end of the table.

Certainly the damsels of Nideck were lovely. Some were blushing with pleasure to hear their own praises; others half-veiled their rosy cheeks with their long drooping eyelashes, while one or two seemed rather to prefer to display their, sweet blue eyes by raising them to the smoky ceiling. I wondered at my own insensibility that I had never before noticed these fair roses blooming in the towers of the ancient manor.

"Silence!" cried Sperver for the second time. "Our friend Knapwurst is going to tell us again the legend he related to us just now."

"Won't you have another instead?" asked the hunchback.

"No. I like this best."

"I know better ones than that."

"Knapwurst," insisted the huntsman, raising his finger impressively, "I have reasons for wishing to hear the same again and no other. Cut it shorter if you like. There is a great deal in it. Now, Fritz, listen!"

The dwarf, rather under the influence of the sparkling wine he had taken, rested his elbows on the table, and with his cheeks clutched in his bony fingers, and his eyes starting from his head with his concentrated efforts to speak with becoming seriousness, he cried as if he were publishing a proclamation—

"Bernard Hertzog relates that the burgrave Hugh, surnamed Lupus, or the Wolf, when he was old, used to wear a cowl, which was a kind of knitted cap that covered in the crest of the knight's helmet when engaged in fighting. When the helmet tired him he would take it off and put on the knitted cowl, and its long cape fell around his shoulders.

"Up to his eighty-second year Hugh still wore his armour, though he could hardly breathe in it.

"Then he sent for Otto of Burlach, his chaplain, his eldest son Hugh, his second son Berthold, and his daughter the red-haired Bertha, wife of a Saxon chief named Bluderich, and said to them—

"'Your mother the she-wolf has bequeathed you her claws;

her blood flows, mingled with mine, in your veins. In you the wolf's blood will flow from generation to generation; it shall weep and howl among the snows of the Black Forest. Some will say, "Hark! The wind howls!" others, "No, it is the owl hooting!" But not so; it is your blood, mine and the blood of the she-wolf who drove me to murder Hedwige, my wife before God and the Church. She died under my bloody hands! Cursed be the she-wolf! for it is written, "I will visit the sins of the fathers upon the children." The crime of the father shall be visited upon the children until justice shall have been satisfied!'

"Then old Hugh the Wolf died.

"From that dreary day the north wind has howled across the wilds, and the owl has hooted in the dark, and travellers by night know not that it is the blood of the she-wolf weeping for the day of vengeance that will come, whose blood will be renewed from generation to generation—so says Hertzog—until the day when the first wife of Hugh, Hedwige the Fair, shall reappear at Nideck under the form of an angel to comfort and to forgive!"

Then Sperver, rising from his seat, took a lamp and demanded of Knapwurst the keys of the library, and beckoned to me to follow him.

We rapidly traversed the long dark gallery, then the armoury, and soon the archive-chamber appeared at the end of the great corridor.

All noises had died away in the distance. The place seemed quite deserted.

Once or twice I turned round, and could then see with a creeping feeling of dread our two long fantastic shadows in ghostly fashion writhing in strange distortions upon the high tapestry.

Sperver quickly opened the old oak door, and with torch uplifted, his hair all bristling in disorder, and excited features, walked in the first. Standing before the portrait of Hedwige, whose likeness to the young countess had struck me at our first visit to the library, he addressed me in these solemn words:—

"Here is she who was to return to comfort and pity me! She

has returned! At this moment she is downstairs with the old count. Look well, Fritz; do you recognise her? Is it not Odile?"

Then turning to the picture of Hugh's second wife—

"There," he said, "is Huldine, the she-wolf. For a thousand years she has wept in the deep gorges amongst the pine forests of the Schwartzwald; she was the cause of the death of poor Lieverle; but henceforward the lords of Nideck may rest securely, for justice is done, and the good angel of this lordly house has returned!"

Squire Toby's Will

by J. Sheridan le Fanu

Many persons accustomed to travel the old York and London road, in the days of stage-coaches, will remember passing, in the afternoon, say, of an autumn day, in their journey to the capital, about three miles south of the town of Applebury and a mile and a half before you reach the old Angel Inn, a large black-and-white house, as those old-fashioned cage-work habitations are termed, dilapidated and weather-stained, with broad lattice windows glimmering all over in the evening sun with little diamond panes, and thrown into relief by a dense background of ancient elms. A wide avenue, now overgrown like a churchyard with grass and weeds, and flanked by double rows of the same dark trees, old and gigantic, with here and there a gap in their solemn files, and sometimes a fallen tree lying across on the avenue, leads up to the hall door.

Looking up its sombre and lifeless avenue from the top of the London coach, as I have often done, you are struck with so many signs of desertion and decay,—the tufted grass sprouting in the chinks of the steps and window-stones, the smokeless chimneys over which the jackdaws are wheeling, the absence of human life and all its evidence, that you conclude at once that the place is uninhabited and abandoned to decay. The name of this ancient house is Gylingden Hall. Tall hedges and old timber quickly shroud the old place from view, and about a quarter of a mile further on you pass, embowered in melancholy trees, a small and ruinous Saxon chapel, which, time out of mind, has been the burying-place of the family of Marston, and partakes of the neglect and desolation which brood over their ancient dwelling-place.

The grand melancholy of the secluded valley of Gylingden, lonely as an enchanted forest, in which the crows returning to their roosts among the trees, and the straggling deer who peep from beneath their branches, seem to hold a wild and undisturbed dominion, heightens the forlorn aspect of Gylingden Hall.

Of late years repairs have been neglected, and here and there the roof is stripped, and 'the stitch in time' has been wanting. At the side of the house exposed to the gales that sweep through the valley like a torrent through its channel, there is not a perfect window left, and the shutters but imperfectly exclude the rain. The ceilings and walls are mildewed and green with damp stains. Here and there, where the drip falls from the ceiling, the floors are rotting. On stormy nights, as the guard described, you can hear the doors clapping in the old house, as far away as old Gryston bridge, and the howl and sobbing of the wind through its empty galleries.

About seventy years ago died the old Squire, Toby Marston, famous in that part of the world for his hounds, his hospitality and his vices. He had done kind things, and he had fought duels: he had given away money and he had horse-whipped people. He carried with him some blessings and a good many curses, and left behind him an amount of debts and charges upon the estates which appalled his two sons, who had no taste for business or accounts, and had never suspected, till that wicked, openhanded and swearing old gentleman died, how very nearly he had run the estates into insolvency.

They met in Gylingden Hall. They had the will before them, and lawyers to interpret, and information without stint, as to the encumbrances with which the deceased had saddled them, The will was so framed as to set the two brothers instantly at deadly feud.

These brothers differed in some points; but in one material

characteristic they resembled one another, and also their departed father. They never went into a quarrel by halves, and once in, they did not stick at trifles.

The elder, Scroope Marston, the more dangerous man of the two, had never been a favourite of the old Squire. He had no taste for the sports of the field and the pleasures of a rustic life. He was no athlete, and he certainly was not handsome. All this the Squire resented. The young man, who had no respect for him, and outgrew his fear of his violence as he came to manhood, retorted. This aversion, therefore, in the ill-conditioned old man grew into positive hatred. He used to wish that d——d pippin-squeezing, humpbacked rascal Scroope, out of the way of better men—meaning his younger son Charles; and in his cups would talk in a way which even the old and young fellows who followed his hounds, and drank his port, and could stand a reasonable amount of brutality, did not like.

Scroope Marston was slightly deformed, and he had the lean sallow face, piercing black eyes, and black lank hair, which sometimes accompany deformity.

'I'm no feyther o' that hog-backed creature. I'm no sire of his'n, d——n him! I'd as soon call that tongs son o' mine,' the old man used to bawl, in allusion to his son's long, lank limbs: 'Charlie's a man, but that's a jack-an-ape. He has no good nature; there's nothing handy, nor manly, nor no one turn of a Marston in him.'

And when he was pretty drunk, the old Squire used to swear he should never 'sit at the head o' that board; nor frighten away folk from Gylingden Hall wi' his d——d hatchet face ' the black loon!'

Handsome Charlie was the man for his money. He knew what a horse was, and could sit to his bottle; and the lasses were all clean *mad* about him. He was a Marston every inch of his six foot two.

Handsome Charlie and he, however, had also had a row or two. The old Squire was free with horsewhip as with his tongue, and on occasion when neither weapon was quite practicable, had been known to give a fellow 'a tap o' his knuckles.' Handsome Charlie, however, thought there was a period at which personal chastisement should cease; and one night, when the port was flowing, there was some allusion to Marion Hayward, the miller's daughter, which for some reason the old gentleman did not like. Being 'in liquor,' and having clearer ideas about pugilism than self-government, he struck out, to the surprise of all present, at Handsome Charlie. The youth threw back his head scientifically, and nothing followed but the crash of a decanter on the floor. But the old Squire's blood was up, and he bounced from his chair. Up jumped Handsome Charlie, resolved to stand no nonsense. Drunken Squire Lilbourne, intending to mediate, fell flat on the floor, and cut his ear among the glasses. Handsome Charlie caught the thump which the old Squire discharged at him upon his open hand, and catching him by the cravat, swung him with his back to the wall. They said the old man never looked so purple, nor his eyes so goggle before; and then Handsome Charlie pinioned him tight to the wall by both arms.

'Well, I say—come, don't you talk no more nonsense o' that sort, and I won't lick you,' croaked the old Squire. 'You stopped that un clever, you did. Didn't he? Come, Charlie, man, gie us your hand, I say, and sit down again, lad.' And so the battle ended; and I believe it was the last time the Squire raised his hand to Handsome Charlie.

But those days were over. Old Toby Marston lay cold and quiet enough now, under the drip of the mighty ash-tree within the Saxon ruin where so many of the old Marston race returned to dust, and were forgotten. The weather-stained top boots and leather breeches, the three-cornered cocked hat to which old gentlemen of that day still clung, and the well-known red waistcoat that reached below his hips, and the fierce pug face of the old Squire, were now but a picture of memory. And the brothers between whom he had planted an irreconcilable quarrel were now in their new mourning suits, with the gloss still on, debating furiously across the table in the great oak parlour, which had so often resounded to the banter and coarse songs, the oaths and laughter of the congenial neighbours whom the old Squire of Gylingden Hall loved to assemble there.

These young gentlemen, who had grown up in Gylingden Hall, were not accustomed to bridle their tongues, nor, if need be, to hesitate about a blow. Neither had been at the old man's funeral. His death had been sudden. Having been helped to his bed in that hilarious and quarrelsome state which was induced by port and punch, he was found dead in the morning—his head hanging over the side of the bed, and his face very black and swollen.

Now the Squire's will despoiled his eldest son of Gylingden, which had descended to the heir time out of mind. Scroope Marston was furious. His deep stern voice was heard inveighing against his dead father and living brother, and the heavy thumps on the table with which he enforced his stormy recriminations resounded through the large chamber. Then broke in Charles's rougher voice, and then came a quick alternation of short sentences, and then both voices together in growing loudness and anger, and at last, swelling the tumult, the expostulations of pacific and frightened lawyers, and at last a sudden breakup of the conference. Scroope broke out of the room, his pale furious face showing whiter against his long black hair, his dark fierce eyes blazing, his hands clenched, and looking more ungainly and deformed than ever in the convulsions of his fury.

Very violent words must have passed between them; for Charlie, though he was the winning man, was almost as angry as Scroope. The elder brother was for holding possession of the house, and putting his rival to legal process to oust him. But his legal advisers were clearly against it. So, with a heart boiling over with gall, up he went to London, and found the firm who had managed his father's business fair and communicative enough. They looked into the settlements, and found that Gylingden was expected. It was very odd, but so it was, specially excepted; so that the right of the old Squire to deal with it by his will could not be questioned.

Notwithstanding all this, Scroope, breathing vengeance and

aggression, and quite willing to wreck himself provided he could run his brother down, assailed Handsome Charlie, and battered old Squire Toby's will in the Prerogative Court and also at common law, and the feud between the brothers was knit, and every month their exasperation was heightened.

Scroope was beaten, and defeat did not soften him. Charles might have forgiven hard words; but he had been himself worsted during the long campaign in some of those skirmishes, special motions and so forth, that constitute the episodes of a legal epic like that in which the Marston brothers figured as opposing combatants; and the blight of law costs had touched him, too, with the usual effect upon the temper of a man of embarrassed means.

Years flew, and brought no healing on their wings. On the contrary, the deep corrosion of this hatred bit deeper by time. Neither brother married. But an accident of a different kind befell the younger, Charles Marston, which abridged his enjoyments very materially.

This was a bad fall from his hunter. There were severe fractures, and there was concussion of the brain. For some time it was thought that he could not recover. He disappointed these evil auguries, however. He did recover, but changed in two essential particulars. He had received an injury in his hip, which doomed him never more to sit in the saddle. And the rollicking animal spirits which hitherto had never failed him, had now taken flight forever.

He had been for five days in a state of coma—absolute insensibility—and when he recovered consciousness he was haunted by an indescribable anxiety.

Tom Cooper, who had been butler in the palmy days of Gylingden Hall, under old Squire Toby, still maintained his post with old-fashioned fidelity, in these days of faded splendour and frugal house-keeping. Twenty years had passed since the death of his old master. He had grown lean, and stooped, and his face, dark with the peculiar brown of age, furrowed and gnarled, and his temper, except with his master, had waxed surly.

His master had visited Bath and Buxton, and came back, as he went, lame, and halting gloomily about with the aid of a stick. When the hunter was sold, the last tradition of the old life at Gylingden disappeared. The young Squire, as he was still called, excluded by his mischance from the hunting Field, dropped into a solitary way of life, and halted slowly and solitarily about the old place, seldom raising his eyes, and with an appearance of indescribable gloom.

Old Cooper could talk freely on occasion with his master; and one day he said, as he handed him his hat and stick in the hall:

'You should rouse yourself up a bit, Master Charles!'

'It's past rousing with me, old Cooper.'

'It's just this, I'm thinking: there's something on your mind, and you won't tell no one. There's no good keeping it on your stomach. You'll be a deal lighter if you tell it. Come, now, what is it, Master Charlie?'

The Squire looked with his round gray eyes straight into Cooper's eyes. He felt that there was a sort of spell broken. It was like the old rule of the ghost who can't speak till it is spoken to. He looked earnestly into old Cooper's face for some seconds, and sighed deeply.

'It ain't the first good guess you've made in your day, old Cooper, and I'm glad you've spoke. It's bin on my mind, sure enough, ever since I had that fall. Come in here after me, and shut the door.'

The Squire pushed open the door of the oak parlour, and looked round on the pictures abstractedly. He had not been there for some time, and, seating himself on the table, he looked again for a while in Cooper's face before he spoke.

'It's not a great deal, Cooper, but it troubles me, and I would not tell it to the parson nor the doctor; for God knows what they'd say, though there's nothing to signify in it. But you were always true to the family, and I don't mind if I tell you.'

''Tis as safe with Cooper. Master Charles. is if 'twas locked in a chest, and sunk in a well.'

'It's only this,' said Charles Marston, looking down on the end of his stick, with which he was tracing lines and circles, 'all the time I was lying like dead, as you thought, after the fall, I was with the old master.' He raised his eyes to Coopers's again as he spoke, and with an awful oath he repeated—'I was with him, Cooper!'

'He was a good man, sir, in his way,' repeated old Cooper, returning his gaze with awe. 'He was a good master to me, and a good father to you, and I hope he's happy. May God rest him!'

'Well,' said Squire Charles, 'it's only this: the whole of that time I was with him, or he was with me—I don't know which. The upshot is, we were together, and I thought I'd never get out of his hands again, and all the time he was bullying me about some one thing; and if it was to save my life, Tom Cooper, by—from the time I waked I never could call to mind what it was; and I think I'd give that hand to know; and if you can think of anything it might be—for God's sake! Don't be afraid, Tom Cooper, but speak it out, for he threatened me hard, and it was surely him.'

Here ensued a silence.

'And what did you think it might be yourself, Master Charles?' said Cooper.

'I hadn't thought of aught that's likely. I'll never hit on't—*never*. I thought it might happen he knew something about that d—— humpbacked villain, Scroope, that swore before Lawyer Gingham I made away with a paper of settlements—me and father; and, as I hope to be saved, Tom Cooper, there never was a bigger lie! I'd a had the law of him for them identical words, and cast him for more than he's worth; only Lawyer Gingham never goes into nothing for me since money grew scarce in Gylingden; and I can't change my lawyer, I owe him such a hatful of money. But he did, he swore he'd hang me yet for it. He said it in them identical words—he'd never rest till he *hanged* me for it, and I think it was, like enough, something about *that*, the old master was troubled; but it's enough to drive a man mad. I *can't* bring it to mind—I can't remember a word he said, only he threatened awful, and looked—Lord a mercy on us!—frightful bad.'

'There's no need he should. May the Lord a-mercy on him!' said the old butler.

'No, of course; and you're not to tell a soul, Cooper—not a living soul, mind, that I said he looked bad, nor nothing about it.'

'God forbid!' said old Cooper, shaking his head. 'But I was thinking, sir, it might ha' been about the slight that's bin so long put on him by having no stone over him, and never a scratch o' a chisel to say who he is.'

'Ay! well, I didn't think o' that. Put on your hat, old Cooper, and come clown wi' me; for I'll look after that, at any rate.'

There is a bye-path leading by a turnstile to the park, and thence to the picturesque old burying-place, which lies in a nook by the roadside, embowered in ancient trees. It was a fine autumnal sunset, and melancholy lights and long shadows spread their peculiar effects over the landscape as 'Handsome Charlie' and the old butler made their way slowly toward the place where Handsome Charlie was himself to lie at last.

'Which of the dogs made that howling all last night?' asked the Squire, when they had got on a little way.

''Twas a strange dog, Master Charlie, in front of the house; ours was all in the yard—a white dog wi' a black head, he looked to be, and he was smelling round then' mounting-steps the old master, God be wi' him! set up, the time his knee was bad. When the tyke got up a' top of them, howlin' up at the windows, I'd like to shy something at him.'

'Hullo! Is that like him?' said the Squire, stopping short, and pointing with his stick at a dirty-white dog, with a large black head, which was scampering round them in a wide circle, half crouching with that air of uncertainty and deprecation which dogs so well know how to assume.

He whistled the dog up. He was a large, half-starved bull dog.

'That fellow has made a long journey—thin as a whipping post, and stained all over, and his claws worn to the stumps,' said the Squire, musingly. 'He isn't a bad dog, Cooper. My father liked a good bull dog, and knew a cur from a good' un.'

The dog was looking up into the Squire's face with the peculiar grim visage of his kind, and the Squire was thinking irreverently how strong a likeness it presented to the character of his father's fierce pug features when he was clutching his horsewhip and swearing at a keeper.

'If I did right I'd shoot him. He'll worry the cattle, and kill our dogs,' said the Squire. 'Hey, Cooper' I'll tell the keeper to look after him, That fellow could pull down a sheep, and he shan't live on my mutton.'

But the dog was not to be shaken off. He looked wistfully after the Squire, and after they had got a little way on, he followed timidly.

It was vain trying to drive him off. The dog ran round them in wide circles, like the infernal dog in *Faust*; only he left no track of thin flame behind him, These manoeuvres were executed with a sort of beseeching air, which flattered and touched the object of this odd preference. So he called him up again, patted him and then and there in a manner adopted him.

The dog now followed their steps dutifully, as if he had belonged to Handsome Charlie all his days. Cooper unlocked the little iron door, and the dog walked in close behind their heels, and followed them as they visited the roofless chapel.

The Marstons were lying under the floor of this little building in rows. There is not a vault. Each has his distinct grave closed in a lining of masonry. Each is surmounted by a stone kist, on the upper flag of which is enclosed his epitaph, except that of poor old Squire Toby. Over him was nothing but the grass and the line of masonry which indicate the site of the kist, whenever his family should afford him one like the rest.

'Well, it does look shabby. It's the elder brother's business; but if he won't, I'll see to it myself, and I'll take care, old boy, to cut sharp and deep in it, that the elder son having refused to lend a hand the stone was put there by the younger.'

They strolled round this little burial ground. The sun was now below the horizon, and the red metallic glow from the clouds, still illuminated by the departed sun, mingled luridly with the twilight. When Charlie peeped again into the little chapel, he saw the ugly dog stretched upon Squire Toby's grave, looking at least twice his natural length, and performing such antics as made the young Squire stare. If you have ever seen a cat stretched on the floor, with a bunch of Valerian, straining, writhing, rubbing its jaws in long-drawn caresses, and in the absorption of a sensual ecstasy, you have seen a phenomenon resembling that which Handsome Charlie witnessed on looking in.

The head of the brute looked so large, its body so long and thin, and its joints so ungainly and dislocated, that the Squire, with old Cooper beside him, looked on with a feeling of disgust and astonishment, which, in a moment or two more, brought the Squire's stick down upon him with a couple of heavy thumps. The beast awakened from his ecstasy, sprang to the head of the grave, and there on a sudden, thick and bandy as before, confronted the Squire, who stood at its foot, with a terrible grin, and eyes that glared with the peculiar green of canine fury.

The next moment the dog was crouching abjectly at the Squire's feet.

'Well, he's a rum 'un!' said old Cooper, looking hard at him.

'I like him,' said the Squire.

'I don't,' said Cooper.

'But he shan't come in here again,' said the Squire.

'I shouldn't wonder if he was a witch,' said old Cooper, who remembered more tales of witchcraft than are now current in that part of the world.

'He's a good dog,' said the Squire, dreamily. 'I remember the time I'd a given a handful for him—but I'll never be good for nothing again. Come along.'

And he stooped down and patted him. So up jumped the dog and looked up in his face, as if watching for some sign, ever so slight, which he might obey.

Cooper did not like a bone under that dog's skin. He could not imagine what his master saw to admire in him. He kept him all night in the gun-room, and the dog accompanied him in his halting rambles about the place. The fonder his master grew of him, the less did Cooper and the other servants like him.

'He hasn't a point of a good dog about him,' Cooper would growl. 'I think Master Charlie be blind. And old Captain (an old red parrot, who sat chained to a perch in the oak parlour, and conversed with himself, and nibbled at his claws and bit his perch all day),—old Captain, the only living thing, except one or two of us, and the Squire himself, that remembers the old master, the minute he saw the dog, screeched as if he was struck, shakin' his feathers out quite wild, and drops down, poor old soul, a-hangin' by his foot, in a fit.'

But there is no accounting for fancies, and the Squire was one of those dogged persons who persist more obstinately in their whims the more they are opposed, But Charles Marston's health suffered by his lameness. The transition frown habitual and violent exercise to such a life as his privation now consigned him to, was never made without a risk to health; and a host of dyspeptic annoyances, the existence of which he had never dreamed of before, now beset him in sad earnest. Among these was the now not unfrequent troubling of his sleep with dreams and nightmares.

In these his canine favourite invariably had a part and was generally a central, and sometimes a solitary figure. In these visions the dog seemed to stretch himself up the side of the Squire's bed, and in dilated proportions to sit at his feet, with a horrible likeness to the pug features of old Squire Toby, with his tricks of wagging his head and throwing up his chin; and then he would talk to him about Scroope, and tell him 'all wasn't straight,' and that he 'must make it up wi' Scroope,' that he, the old Squire, had 'served him an ill turn,' that 'time was nigh up,' and that 'fair was fair,' and he was 'troubled where he was, about Scroope.'

Then in his dream this semi-human brute would approach his face to his, crawling and crouching up his body, heavy as lead, till the facc of the beast was laid on his, with the same odious caresses and stretchings and writhings which he had seen over the old Squire's grave. Then Charlie would wake up with a gasp and a howl, and start upright in the bed, bathed in a cold moisture, and fancy he saw something white sliding off the foot of the bed. Sometimes he thought it might be the curtain with white lining that slipped down, or the coverlet disturbed by his uneasy turnings; but he always fancied, at such moments, that he saw something white sliding hastily off the bed; and always when he had been visited by such dreams the dog next morning was more than usually caressing and servile, as if to obliterate, by a more than ordinary welcome, the sentiment of disgust which the horror of the night had left behind it.

The doctor half-satisfied the Squire that there was nothing in these dreams, which, in one shape or another, invariably attended forms of indigestion such as he was suffering from.

For a while, as if to corroborate this theory, the dog ceased altogether to figure in them. But at last there came a vision in which, more unpleasantly than before, he did resume his old place.

In his nightmare the room seemed all but dark; he heard what he knew to be the dog walking from the door round his bed slowly, to the side from which he always had come upon it. A portion of the room was uncarpeted, and he said he distinctly heard the peculiar tread of a dog, in which the faint clatter of the claws is audible. It was a light stealthy step, but at every tread the whole room shook heavily; he felt something place itself at the foot of his bed, and saw a pair of green eyes staring at him in the dark, from which he could not remove his own. Then he heard, as he thought, the old Squire Toby say—'The eleventh hour be passed, Charlie, and ye've done nothing—you and I 'a done Scroope a wrong!' and then came a good deal more, and then—'The time's nigh up, it's going to strike.' And with a long low growl, the thing began to creep up upon his feet; the growl continued, and he saw the reflection of the upturned green eyes upon the bedclothes, as it began slowly to stretch itself up his body towards his face.

With a loud scream, he waked. The light, which of late the

Squire was accustomed to have in his bed-room, had accidentally gone out. He was afraid to get up, or even to look about the room for some time; so sure did he feel of seeing the green eyes in the dark fixed on him from some corner. He had hardly recovered from the first agony which nightmare leaves behind it, and was beginning to collect his thoughts, when he heard the clock strike twelve. And he bethought him of the words 'the eleventh hour be passed—time's nigh up—it's going to strike!' and he almost feared that he would hear the voice reopening the subject.

Next morning the Squire came down looking ill.

'Do you know a room, old Cooper,' said he, 'they used to call King Herod's chamber?'

'Ay, sir; the story of King Herod was on the walls o't when I was a boy.'

'There's a closet off it—is there?'

'I can't be sure o' that; but 'tisn't worth your looking at, now; the hangings was rotten, and took off the walls, before you was born; and there's nou't there but some old broken things and lumber. I seed them put there myself by poor Twinks; he was blind of an eye, and footman afterwards. You'll remember Twinks? He died here, about the time o' the great snow. There was a deal o' work to bury him, poor fellow!'

'Get the key, old Cooper; I'll look at the room,' said the Squire.

'And what the devil can you want to look at it for?' said Cooper, with the old-world privilege of a rustic butler.

'And what the devil's that to you? But I don't mind if I tell you. I don't want that dog in the gun-room, and I'll put him somewhere else; and I don't care if I put him there.'

'A bulldog in a bedroom! Oons, sir! the folks 'ill say you're clean mad!'

'Well, let them; get you the key and let us look at the room.'

'You'd shoot him if you did right, Master Charlie. You never heard what a noise he kept up all last night in the gun-room, walking to and fro growling like a tiger in a show; and, say what you like, the dog's not worth his feed; he hasn't a point of a dog; he's a bad dog.'

'I know a dog better than you—and he's a good dog!' said the Squire, testily.

'If you was a judge of a dog you'd hang that 'un,' said Cooper.

'I'm not going to hang him, so there's an end. Go you, and get the key; and don't be talking, mind, when you go down. I may change my mind.'

Now this freak of visiting King Herod's room had, in truth, a totally different object from that pretended by the Squire. The voice in his nightmare had uttered a particular direction, which haunted him, and would give him no peace until he had tested it. So far from liking that dog to-day, he was beginning to regard it with a horrible suspicion; and if old Cooper had not stirred his obstinate temper by seeming to dictate, I dare say he would have got rid of the inmate effectually before evening.

Up to the third story, long disused, he and old Cooper mounted. At the end of a dusty gallery, the room lay. The old tapestry, from which the spacious chamber had taken its name, had long given place to modern paper, and this was mildewed, and in some places hanging from the walls. A thick mantle of dust lay over the floor. Some broken chairs and boards, thick with dust, lay, along with other lumber, piled together at one end of the room.

They entered the closet, which was quite empty. The Squire looked round, and you could hardly have said whether he was relieved or disappointed.

'No furniture here,' said the Squire, and looked through the dusty window. 'Did you say anything to me lately—I don't mean this morning—about this room, or the closet—or anything—I forget?'

'Lor' bless you! Not I. I han't been thinkin' o' this room this forty year.'

'Is there any sort of old furniture called a *buffet*—do you remember?' asked the Squire.

'A buffet? Why, yes—to be sure—there was a buffet, sure enough, in this closet, now you bring it to my mind,' said Cooper. 'But it's papered over.'

'And what is it?'

'A little cupboard in the wall,' answered the old man.

'Ho—I see—and there's such a thing here, is there, under the paper? Show me whereabouts it was.'

'Well—I think it was somewhere about here,' answered he, rapping his knuckles along the wall opposite the window. 'Ay, there it is,' he added, as the hollow sound of a wooden door was returned to his knock.

The Squire pulled the loose paper from the wall, and disclosed the doors of a small press, about two feet square, fixed in the wall.

'The very thing for my buckles and pistols, and the rest of my gimcracks,' said the Squire. 'Come away, we'll leave the dog where he is. Have you the key of that little press?'

No, he had not. The old master had emptied and locked it up, and desired that it should be papered over, and that was the history of it.

Down came the Squire, and took a strong turn-screw from his gun-case; and quietly he reascended to King Herod's room, and, with little trouble, forced the door of the small press in the closet wall. There were in it some letters and cancelled leases, and also a parchment deed which he took to the window and read with much agitation. It was a supplemental deed executed about a fortnight after the others, and previously to his father's marriage, placing Gylingden under strict settlement to the elder son, in what is called 'tail male.' Handsome Charlie, in his fraternal litigation, had acquired a smattering of technical knowledge, and he perfectly well knew that the effect of this would be not only to transfer the house and lands to his brother Scroope, but to leave him at the mercy of that exasperated brother, who might recover from him personally every guinea he had ever received by way of rent, from the date of his father's death.

It was a dismal, clouded day, with something threatening in

its aspect, and the darkness, where he stood, was made deeper by the top of one of the huge old trees overhanging the window.

In a state of awful confusion he attempted to think over his position. He placed the deed in his pocket, and nearly made up his mind to destroy it. A short time ago he would not have hesitated for a moment under such circumstances; but now his health and his nerves were shattered, and he was under a supernatural alarm which the strange discovery of this deed had powerfully confirmed.

In this state of profound agitation he heard a sniffing at the closet-door, and then an impatient scratch and a long low growl. He screwed his courage up, and, not knowing what to expect, threw the door open and saw the dog, not in his dream-shape, but wriggling with joy, and crouching and fawning with eager submission; and then wandering about the closet, the brute growled awfully into the corners of it, and Seemed in an unappeasable agitation.

Then the dog returned and fawned and crouched again at his feet.

After the first moment was over, the sensations of abhorrence and fear began to subside, and he almost reproached himself for requiting the affection of this poor friendless brute with the antipathy which he had really done nothing to earn.

The dog pattered after him down the stairs. Oddly enough, the sight of this animal, after the first revulsion, reassured him; *it was*, in his eyes, so attached, so good-natured and palpably so mere a dog.

By the hour of evening the Squire had resolved on a middle course; he would not inform his brother of his discovery, nor yet would he destroy the deed. He would never marry. He was past that time. He would leave a letter, explaining the discovery of the deed, addressed to the only surviving trustee—who had probably forgotten everything about it—and having seen out his own tenure, he would provide that all should be set right after his death. Was not that fair? At all events it quite satisfied what he called his conscience, and he thought it a devilish good compromise for his brother; and he went out, towards sunset, to take his usual walk.

Returning in the darkening twilight, the dog, as usual attending him, began to grow frisky and wild, at first scampering round him in great circles, as before, nearly at the top of his speed, his great head between his paws as he raced. Gradually more excited grew the pace and narrow his circuit, louder and fiercer his continuous growl, and the Squire stopped and grasped his stick hard, for the lurid eyes and grin of the brute threatened an attack. Turning round and round as the excited brute encircled him, and striking vainly at him with his stick, he grew at last so tired that he almost despaired of keeping him longer at bay; when on a sudden the dog stopped short and crawled up to his feet wriggling and crouching submissively.

Nothing could be more apologetic and abject; and when the Squire dealt him two heavy thumps with his stick, the dog whimpered only, and writhed and licked his feet. The Squire sat down on a prostrate tree; and his dumb companion, recovering his wonted spirits immediately, began to sniff and nuzzle among the roots. The Squire felt in his breast-pocket for the deed—it was safe; and again he pondered, in this loneliest of spots, on the question whether he should preserve it for restoration after his death to his brother, or destroy it forthwith. He began rather to lean toward the latter solution, when the long low growl of the dog not far off startled him.

He was sitting in a melancholy grove of old trees, that slants gently westward. Exactly the same odd effect of light I have before described—a faint red glow reflected downward from the upper sky, after the sun had set, now gave to the growing darkness a lurid uncertainty. This grove, which lies in a gentle hollow, owing to its circumscribed horizon on all but one side, has a peculiar character of loneliness.

He got up and peeped over a sort of barrier, accidentally formed of the trunks of felled trees laid one over the other, and saw the dog straining up the other side of it, and hideously stretched out, his ugly head looking in consequence twice the natural size. His dream was coming over him again. And now between the trunks the brute's ungainly head was thrust, and the long neck came straining through, and the body, twining after it like a huge white lizard; and as it came striving and twisting through, it growled and glared as if it would devour him.

As swiftly as his lameness would allow, the Squire hurried from this solitary spot towards the house. What thoughts exactly passed through his mind as he did so, I am sure he could not have told. But when the dog came up with him it seemed appeased, and even in high good *humour*, and no longer resembled the brute that haunted his dreams.

That night, near ten o'clock, the Squire, a good deal agitated, sent for the keeper, and told him that he believed the dog was mad, and that he must shoot him. He might shoot the dog in the gun-room, where he was—a grain of shot or two in the wainscot did not matter, and the dog must not have a chance of getting out.

The Squire gave the gamekeeper his double-barrelled gun, loaded with heavy shot. He did not go with him beyond the hall. He placed his hand on the keeper's arm; the keeper said his hand trembled, and that he looked 'as white as curds.'

'Listen a bit!' said the Squire under his breath.

They heard the dog in a state of high excitement in the room—growling ominously, jumping on the window-stool and down again, and running round the room.

'You'll need to be sharp, mind—don't give him a chance—slip in edgeways, d'ye see? and give him both barrels!'

'Not the first mad dog I've knocked over, sir,' said the man, looking very serious as he cocked the gun.

As the keeper opened the door, the dog had sprung into the empty grate. He said he 'never see sich a stark, staring devil.' The beast made a twist round, as if, he thought, to jump up the chimney—'but that wasn't to be done at no price'—and he made a yell—not like a dog—like a man caught in a mill-crank, and before he could spring *at the keeper, he fired* one barrel into him. The dog leaped towards him, and rolled over, receiving the second barrel in his head, as he lay snorting at the keeper's feet!

'I never seed the like; I never heard a screech like that!' said the keeper, recoiling. 'It makes a fellow feel queer.'

'Quite dead?' asked the Squire.

'Not a stir in him, sir,' said the man, pulling him along the floor by the neck.

'Throw him outside the hall-door now,' said the Squire; 'and mind you pitch him outside the gate tonight—old Cooper says he's a witch,' and the pale Squire smiled, 'so he shan't lie in Gylingden.'

Never was man more relieved than the Squire, and he slept better for a week after this than he had done for many weeks before.

It behooves us all to act promptly on our good resolutions. There is a determined gravitation towards evil, which, if left to itself, will bear down first intentions. If at one moment of superstitious fear the Squire had made up his mind to a great sacrifice, and resolved in the matter of that deed so strangely recovered to act honestly by his brother, that resolution very soon gave place to the compromise with fraud which so conveniently postponed the restitution to the period when further enjoyment on his part was impossible. Then came more tidings of Scroope's violent and minatory language, with always the same burthen—that he would leave no stone unturned to show that there had existed a deed which Charles had either secreted or destroyed, and that he would never rest till he had hanged him.

This of course was wild talk. At first it had only enraged him; but, with his recent guilty knowledge and suppression, had come fear. His danger was the existence of the deed, and little by little he brought himself to a resolution to destroy it. There were many falterings and recoils before he could bring himself to commit this crime. At length, however, he did it, and got rid of the custody of that which at any time might become the instrument of disgrace and ruin. There was relief in this, but also the new and terrible sense of actual guilt.

He had got pretty well rid of his supernatural qualms. It was a different kind of trouble that agitated him now.

But this night, he imagined, he was awakened by a violent shaking of his bed. He could see, in the very imperfect light, two figures at the foot of it, holding each a bed-post. One of these he half-fancied was his brother Scroope, but the other was the old Squire—of that he was sure—and he fancied that they had shaken him up from his sleep. Squire Toby was talking as Charlie wakened, and he heard him say:

'Put out of our own house by you! It won't hold for long. We'll come in together, friendly, and stay. Forewarned, wi' yer eyes open, ye did it; and now Scroope'll hang you! We'll hang you together! Look at me, you devil's limb.'

And the old Squire tremblingly stretched his face, torn with shot and bloody, and growing every moment more and more into the likeness of the dog, and began to stretch himself out and climb the bed over the foot-board; and he saw the figure at the other side, little more than a black shadow, begin also to scale the bed; and there was instantly a dreadful confusion and uproar in the room, and such a gabbling and laughing; he could not catch the words; but, with a scream, he woke, and found himself standing on the floor. The phantoms and the clamour were gone, but a crash and ringing of fragments was in his ears. The great china bowl, from which for generations the Marstons of Gylingden had been baptized, had failed from the mantelpiece, and was smashed on the hearth-stone.

'I've bin dreamin' all night about Mr. Scroope, and I wouldn't wonder, old Cooper, if he was dead,' said the Squire, when he came down in the morning.

'God forbid! I was adreamed about him, too, sir: I dreamed he was dammin' and sinkin' about a hole was burnt in his coat, and the old master, God be wi' him! said—quite plain—I'd 'a swore 'twas himself' 'Cooper, get up, ye d——land-loupin' thief, and lend a hand to hang him—for he's a daft cur, and no dog o' mine.' 'Twas the dog shot over night, I do suppose, as was runnin' in my old head. I thought old master gied me a punch wi' his knuckles, and says I, wakenin' up, 'At yer service, sir'; and for a while I couldn't get it out o' my head, master was in the room still.'

Letters from town soon convinced the Squire that his brother Scroope, so far from being dead, was particularly active; and Charlie's attorney wrote to say, in serious alarm, that he had heard, accidentally, that he intended setting up a case, of a supplementary deed of settlement, of which he had secondary evidence, which would give him Gylingden. And at this menace Handsome Charlie snapped his fingers, and wrote courageously to his attorney; abiding what might follow with, however, a secret foreboding.

Scroope threatened loudly now, and swore after his bitter fashion, and reiterated his old promise of hanging that cheat at last. In the midst of these menaces and preparations, however, a sudden peace proclaimed itself: Scroope died, without time even to make provisions for a posthumous attack upon his brother. It was one of those cases of disease of the heart in which death is as sudden as by a bullet.

Charlie's exultation was undisguised. It was shocking. Not, of course, altogether malignant. For there was the expansion consequent on the removal of a secret fear. There was also the comic piece of luck, that only the day before Scroope had destroyed his old will, which left to a stranger every farthing he possessed, intending in a day or two to execute another to the same person, charged with the express condition of prosecuting the suit against Charlie.

The result was that all his possessions went unconditionally to his brother Charles as his heir. Here were grounds for abundance of savage elation. But there was also the deep-seated hatred of half a life of mutual and persistent aggression and revilings; and Handsome Charlie was capable of nursing a grudge, and enjoying a revenge with his whole heart.

He would gladly have prevented his brother's being buried in the old Gylingden chapel, where he wished to lie; but his lawyers doubted his power, and he was not quite proof against the scandal which would attend his turning back the funeral, which would, he knew, be attended by some of the country gentry and others, with an hereditary regard for the Marstons.

But he warned his servants that not one of them were to attend it; promising, with oaths and curses not to be disregarded, that any one of them who did so, should find the door shut in his face on his return.

I don't think, with the exception of old Cooper, that the servants cared for this prohibition, except as it baulked a curiosity always strong in the solitude of the country. Cooper was very much vexed that the eldest son of the old Squire should be buried in the old family chapel, and no sign of decent respect from Gylingden Hall. He asked his master whether he would not, at least, have some wine and refreshments in the oak parlour, in case any of the country gentlemen who paid this respect to the old family should come up to the house? But the Squire only swore at him, told him to mind his own business, and ordered him to say, if such a thing happened, that he was out, and no preparations made, and, in fact, to send them away as they came. Cooper expostulated stoutly, and the Squire grew angrier; and after a tempestuous scene, took his hat and stick and walked out, just as the funeral descending the valley from the direction of the 'Old Angel Inn' came in sight.

Old Cooper prowled about disconsolately, and counted the carriages as well as he could from the gate. When the funeral was over, and they began to drive away, he returned to the hall, the door of which lay open, and as usual deserted. Before he reached it quite, a mourning coach drove up, and two gentlemen in black cloaks, and with crapes to their hats, got out, and without looking to the right or the left, went up the steps into the house. Cooper followed them slowly. The carriage had, he supposed, gone round to the yard, for, when he reached the door, it was no longer there.

So he followed the two mourners into the house. In the hall he found a fellow servant, who said he had seen two gentlemen, in black cloaks, pass through the hall, and go up the stairs without removing their hats, or asking leave of anyone. This was very odd, old Cooper thought, and a great liberty; so upstairs he went to make them out.

But he could not find them then, nor ever. And from that hour the house was troubled.

In a little time there was not one of the servants who had not something to tell. Steps and voices followed them sometimes in the passages, and tittering whispers, always minatory, scared them at the corners of the galleries, or from dark recesses; so that they would return panic-stricken to be rebuked by thin Mrs. Beckett, who looked on such stories as worse than idle. But Mrs. Beckett herself, a short time after, took a very different view of the matter.

She had herself begun to hear these voices, and with this formidable aggravation, that they came always when she was at her prayers, which she had been punctual in saying all her life, and utterly interrupted them. She was scared at such moments by dropping words and sentences, which grew, as she persisted, into threats and blasphemies.

These voices were not always in the room. They called, as she fancied, through the walls, very thick in that old house, from the neighbouring apartments, sometimes on one side, sometimes on the other; sometimes they seemed to holloa from distant lobbies, and came muffled, but threateningly, through the long panelled passages. As they approached they grew furious, as if several voices were speaking together. Whenever, as I said, this worthy woman applied herself to her devotions, these horrible sentences came hurrying towards the door, and, in panic, she would start from her knees, and all then would subside except the thumping of her heart against her stays, and the dreadful tremors of her nerves.

What these voices said, Mrs. Beckett never could quite remember one minute after they had ceased speaking; one sentence chased another away; gibe and menace and impious denunciation, each hideously articulate, were lost as soon as heard. And this added to the effect of these terrifying mockeries and invectives, that she could not, by any effort, retain their exact import, although their horrible character remained vividly present to her mind.

For a long time the Squire seemed to be the only person in the house absolutely unconscious of these annoyances. Mrs. Beckett had twice made up her mind within the week to leave. A prudent woman, however, who has been comfortable for more than twenty years in a place, thinks oftener than twice before she leaves it. She and old Cooper were the only servants in the house who remembered the good old housekeeping in Squire Toby's day. The others were few, and such as could hardly be accounted regular servants. Meg Dobbs, who acted as housemaid, would not sleep in the house, but walked home, in trepidation, to her father's, at the gatehouse, under the escort of her little brother, every night. Old Mrs. Beckett, who was high and mighty with the make-shift servants of fallen Gylingden, let herself down all at once, and made Mrs. Kymes and the kitchen-maid move their beds into her large and faded room, and there, very frankly, shared her nightly terrors with them.

Old Cooper was testy and captious about these stories. He was already uncomfortable enough by reason of the entrance of the two muffled figures into the house, about which there could be no mistake. His own eyes had seen them. He refused to credit the stories of the women, and affected to think that the two mourners might have left the house and driven away, on finding no one to receive them.

Old Cooper was summoned at night to the oak parlour, where the Squire was smoking.

'I say, Cooper,' said the Squire, looking pale and angry, 'what for ha' you been frightenin' they crazy women wi' your plaguy stories? D——me, if you see ghosts here it's no place for you, and it's time you should pack. I won't be left without servants. Here has been old Beckett, wi' the cook and the kitchenmaid, as white as pipeclay, all in a row, to tell me I must have a parson to sleep among them, and preach down the devil! Upon my soul, you're a wise old body, filling their heads wi' maggots! And Meg goes down to the lodge every night, afeared to lie in the house—all your doing, wi' your old wives' stories—ye withered old Tom o' Bedlam!'

'I'm not to blame, Master Charles. 'Tisn't along o' no stories o' mine, for I'm never done tellin' 'era it's all vanity and vapours. Mrs. Beckett 'ill tell you that, and there's been many a wry word betwixt us on the head o't. Whate'er I may *think*,' said old Cooper, significantly, and looked askance, with the sternness of fear in the Squire's face.

The Squire averted his eyes, and muttered angrily to himself, and turned away to knock the ashes out of his pipe on the hob, and then turning suddenly round upon Cooper again, he spoke, with a pale face, but not quite so angrily as before.

'I know you're no fool, old Cooper, when you like. Suppose there was such a thing as a ghost here, don't you see, it ain't to them snipe-headed women it' id go to tell its story. What ails you, man, that you should think aught about it, but just what *I* think? You had a good headpiece o' yer own once, Cooper, don't be you clappin' a goosecap over it, as my poor father used to say; d—— it old boy, you mustn't let 'em be fools, settin' one another wild wi' their blether, and makin' the folk talk what they shouldn't, about Gylingden and the family. I don't think ye'd like that, old Cooper, I'm sure ye wouldn't. The women has gone out o' the kitchen, make up a bit o' fire, and get your pipe. I'll go to you, when I finish this one, and we'll smoke a bit together, and a glass o' brandy and water.'

Down went the old butler, not altogether unused to such condescensions in that disorderly and lonely household; and let not those who can choose their company, be too hard on the Squire who couldn't.

When he had got things tidy, as he said, he sat down in that big old kitchen, with his feet on the fender, the kitchen candle burning in a great brass candlestick, which stood on the deal table at his elbow, with the brandy bottle and tumblers beside it, and Cooper's pipe also in readiness. And these preparations completed, the old butler, who had remembered other generations and better times, fell into rumination, and so, gradually, into a deep sleep.

Old Cooper was half awakened by someone laughing low, near his head. He was dreaming of old times in the hall, and fancied one of 'the young gentlemen' going to play him a trick, and he mumbled something in his sleep, from which he was awakened by a stern deep voice, saying, 'You wern't at the funeral; I might take your life, I'll take your ear.' At the same moment, the side of his head received a violent push, and he started to his feet. The fire had gone down, and he was chilled. The candle was expiring in the socket, and threw on the white wall long shadows, that danced up and down from the ceiling to the ground, and their black outlines he fancied resembled the two men in cloaks, whom he remembered with a profound horror.

He took the candle, with all the haste he could, getting along the passage, on whose wails the same dance of black shadows was continued, very anxious to reach his room before the light should go out. He was startled half out of his wits by the sudden clang of his master's bell, close over his head, ringing furiously.

'Ha, ha! There it goes—yes, sure enough,' said Cooper, reassuring himself with the sound of his own voice, as he hastened on, hearing more and more distinct every moment the same furious ringing. 'He's fell asleep, like me; that's it, and his lights is out, I lay you fifty—'

When he turned the handle of the door of the oak parlour, the Squire wildly called, 'Who's there?' in the tone of a man who expects a robber.

'It's me, old Cooper, all right, Master Charlie, you didn't come to the kitchen after all, sir.'

'I'm very bad, Cooper; I don't know how I've been. Did you meet anything?' asked the Squire.

'No,' said Cooper.

They stared at one another.

'Come here—stay here! Don't you leave me! Look round the room, and say is all right; and gie us your hand, old Cooper, for I must hold it.' The Squire's was damp and cold, and trembled very much. It was not very far from daybreak now.

After a time he spoke again:'I 'a done many a thing I shouldn't; I'm not fit to go, and wi' God's blessin' I'll look to it—why shouldn't I' I'm as lame as old Billy—I'll never be able to do any good no more, and I'll give over drinking, and marry, as I ought to 'a done long ago—none o' yet fine ladies, but a good homely wench; there's Farmer Crump's youngest daughter, a good lass, and discreet. What for shouldn't I take her? She'd take care o' me, and wouldn't bring a head full o' romances here, and *mantua*-makers' trumpery, and I'll talk with the parson, and I'll do what's fair wi' everyone and mind, I said I'm sorry for many a thing I 'a done.'

A wild cold dawn had by this time broken. The Squire, Cooper said, looked 'awful bad,' as he got his hat and stick, and sallied out for a walk, instead of going to his bed, as Cooper besought him, looking so wild and distracted, that it was plain his object was simply to escape from the house. It was twelve o'clock when the Squire walked into the kitchen, where he was sure of finding some of the servants, looking as if ten years had passed over him since yesterday. He pulled a stool by tile fire, without speaking a word, and sat down. Cooper had sent to Applebury for the doctor, who had just arrived, but the Squire would not go to him. 'If he wants to see me, he may come here,' he muttered as often as Cooper urged him. So the doctor did come, charily enough, and found the Squire very much worse than he had expected.

The Squire resisted the order to get to his bed. But the doctor insisted under a threat of death, at which his patient quailed.

'Well, I'll do what you say—only this—you must let old Cooper and Dick Keeper stay wi' me. I mustn't be left alone, and they must keep awake o' nights; and stay a while, do *you*. When I get round a bit, I'll go and live in a town. It's dull livin' here, now that I can't do nou't, as I used, and I'll live a better life, mind ye; ye heard me say that, and I don't care who laughs, and I'll talk wi' the parson. I like 'em to laugh, hang 'em, it's a sign I'm doin' right, at last.'

The doctor sent a couple of nurses from the County Hospital, not choosing to trust his patient to the management he had selected, and he went down himself to Gylingden to meet them in the evening. Old Cooper was ordered to occupy the dressing room, and sit up at night, which satisfied the Squire, who was in a strangely excited state, very low, and threatened, the doctor said, with fever.

The clergyman came, an old, gentle, 'book-learned' man, and talked and prayed with him late that evening. After he had gone the Squire called the nurses to his bedside, and said: 'There's a fellow sometimes comes; you'll never mind him. He looks in at the door and beckons—a thin, hump-backed chap in mourning, wi' black gloves on; ye'll know him by his lean face, as brown as the wainscot: don't ye mind his smilin'. You don't go out to him, nor ask him in; he won't say nou't; and if he grows anger'd and looks awry at ye, don't be afeared, for he can't hurt ye, and he'll grow tired waitin', and go away; and for God's sake mind ye don't ask him in, nor go out after him!'

The nurses put their heads together when this was over, and held afterwards a whispering conference with old Cooper. 'Law bless ye!—no, there's no madman in the house,' he protested; 'not a soul but what ye saw—it's just a trifle o' the fever in his head—no more.'

The Squire grew worse as the night wore on. He was heavy and delirious, talking of all sorts of things—of wine, and dogs, and lawyers; and then he began to talk, as it were, to his brother Scroope. As he did so, Mrs. Oliver, the nurse, who was sitting up alone with him, heard, as she thought, a hand softly laid on the door handle outside, and a stealthy attempt to turn it. 'Lord bless us! Who's there?' she cried, and her heart jumped into her mouth as she thought of the hump-backed man ill black, who was to put in his head smiling and beckoning—'Mr. Cooper! Sir! Are you there?' she cried. 'Come here, Mr. Cooper, please—do, sir, quick!'

Old Cooper, called up from his doze by the fire, stumbled in from the dressing room, and Mrs. Oliver seized him tightly as he emerged.

'The man with the hump has been atryin' the door, Mr. Cooper, as sure as I am here.' The Squire was moaning and mumbling in his fever, understanding nothing, as she spoke. 'No, no! Mrs. Oliver, ma'am, it's impossible, for there's no sich man in the house: what is Master Charlie sayin'?'

'He's saying *Scroope* every minute, whatever he means by that, and—and—hisht!—listen—there's the handle again,' and, with a loud scream, she added—'Look at his head and neck in at the door!' and in her tremor she strained old Cooper in an agonizing embrace.

The candle was flaring, and there was a wavering shadow at the door that looked like the head of a man with a long neck, and a longish sharp nose, peeping in and drawing back.

'Don't be a d—— fool, ma'am!' cried Cooper, very white, and shaking her with all his might. 'It's only the candle, I tell you—nothing in life but that. Don't you see?' and he raised the light. 'And I'm sure there was no one at the door, and I'll try, if you let me go.'

The other nurse was asleep on a sofa, and Mrs. Oliver called her up in a panic, for company, as old Cooper opened the door. There was no one near it, but at the angle of the gallery was a shadow resembling that which he had seen in the room. He raised the candle a little, and it seemed to beckon with a long hand as the head drew back. 'Shadow from the candle!' exclaimed Cooper aloud, resolved not to yield to Mrs. Oliver's panic; and, candle in hand, he walked to the corner.

There was nothing. He could not forbear peeping down the long gallery from this point, and as he moved the light, he saw precisely the same sort of shadow, a little further down, and as he advanced the same withdrawal, and beckon. 'Gammon!' said he; 'it is nou't but the candle.' And on he went, growing half angry and half frightened at the persistency with which this ugly shadow—a literal shadow he was sure it was—presented itself. As he drew near the point where it now appeared, it seemed to collect itself, and nearly dissolve in the central panel of an old carved cabinet which he was now approaching.

In the centre panel of this is a sort of boss carved into a wolf's head.

The light fell oddly upon this, and the fugitive shadow seemed to be breaking up, and rearranging itself oddly. The eyeball gleamed with a point of reflected light, which glittered also upon the grinning mouth, and he saw the long, sharp nose of Scroope Marston, and his fierce eve looking at him, he thought, with a steadfast meaning.

Old Cooper stood gazing upon this sight, unable to move, till he saw the face, and the figure that belonged to it, begin gradually to emerge from the wood. At the same time he heard voices approaching rapidly up a side gallery, and Cooper, with a loud 'Lord a-mercy on us!' turned and ran back again, pursued by a sound that seemed to shake the old house like a mighty gust of wind.

Into his master's room burst old Cooper, half wild with fear, and clapped the door and turned the key in a twinkling, looking as if he had been pursued by murderers.

'Did you hear it?' whispered Cooper, now standing near the dressing room door. They all listened, but not a sound from without disturbed the utter stillness of night. 'God bless us! I doubt it's my old head that's gone crazy!' exclaimed Cooper.

He would tell them nothing but that he was himself 'an old fool,' to be frightened by their talk, and that 'the rattle of a window, or the dropping o' a pin' was enough to scare him now; and so he helped himself through that night with brandy, and sat up talking by his master's fire.

The Squire recovered slowly from his brain fever, but not perfectly.

A very little thing, the doctor said, would suffice to upset him. He was not yet sufficiently strong to remove for change of scene and air, which were necessary for his complete restoration.

Cooper slept in the dressing room, and was now his only nightly attendant. The ways of the invalid were odd: he liked, half sitting up in his bed, to smoke his churchwarden o' nights, and made old Cooper smoke, for company, at the fireside. As the

Squire and his humble friend indulged in it, smoking is a taciturn pleasure, and it was not until the master of Gylingden had finished his third pipe that he essayed conversation, and when he did, the subject was not such as Cooper would have chosen.

'I say, old Cooper, look in my face, and don't be afeared to speak out,' said the Squire, looking at him with a steady, cunning smile; 'you know all this time, as well as I do, who's in the house. You needn't deny—hey?—Scroope and my father?'

'Don't you be talking like that, Charlie,' said old Cooper, rather sternly and frightened, after a long silence, still looking in his face, which did not change.

'What's the good o' shammin', Cooper? Scroope's took the hearin' o' yer right ear—you know he did. He's looking angry. He's nigh took my life wi' this fever. But he's not done wi' me yet, and he looks awful wicked. Ye saw him—ye know ye did.'

Cooper was awfully frightened, and the odd smile on the Squire's lips frightened him still more. He dropped his pipe, and stood gazing in silence at his master, and feeling as if he were in a dream.

'If ye think so, ye should not be smiling like that.' said Cooper, grimly.

'I'm tired, Cooper, and it's as well to smile as t' other thing; so I'll even smile while I can. You know what they mean to do wi' me. That's all I wanted to say. Now, lad, go on wi' yer pipe—I'm goin' asleep.'

So the Squire turned over in his bed, and lay down serenely, with his head on the pillow. Old Cooper looked at him, and glanced at the door, and then half-filled his tumbler with brandy, and drank it off, and felt better, and got to his bed in the dressing room.

In the dead of night he was suddenly awakened by the Squire, who was standing, in his dressing gown and slippers, by his bed.

'I've brought you a bit o' present. I got the rents o' Hazelden yesterday, and ye'll keep that for yourself—it's a fifty—and give t' other to Nelly Carwell, tomorrow; I'll sleep the sounder; and I saw Scroope since; he's not such a bad 'un after all, old fellow!

He's got a crape over his face—for I told him I couldn't bear it; and I'd do many a thing for him now. I never could stand shilly-shally. Good night, old Cooper!'

And the Squire laid his trembling hand kindly on the old man's shoulder, and returned to his own room. 'I don't half like how he is. Doctor don't come half often enough. I don't like that queer smile o' his, and his hand was as cold as death. I hope in God his brain's not a-turnin'!' With these reflections, he turned to the pleasanter subject of his present, and at last fell asleep.

In the morning, when he went into the Squire's room, the Squire had left his bed. 'Never mind; he'll come back, like a bad shillin',' thought old Cooper, preparing the room as usual. But he did not return. Then began an uneasiness, succeeded by a panic, when it began to be plain that the Squire was not in the house. What had become of him? None of his clothes, but his dressing gown and slippers, were missing. Had he left the house, in his present sickly state, in that garb? and, if so, could he be in his right senses; and was there a chance of his surviving a cold, a damp night, so passed, in the open air?

Tom Edwards was up to the house, and told them that, walking a mile or so that morning, at four o'clock—there being no moon—along with Farmer Nokes, who was driving his cart to market, in the dark, three men walked, in front of the horse, not twenty yards before them, all the way from Gylingden Lodge to the burial ground, the gate of which was opened for them from within, and the three men entered, and the gate was shut. Tom Edwards thought they were gone in to make preparation for a funeral of some member of tile Marston family. But the occurrence seemed to Cooper, who knew there was no such thing, horribly ominous.

He now commenced a careful search, and at last bethought him of the lonely upper story and King Herod's chamber. He saw nothing changed there, but the closet door was shut, and, dark as was the morning, something, like a large white knot sticking out over the door, caught his eye.

The door resisted his efforts to open it for a time; some great weight forced it down against the floor; at length, however, it did yield a little, and a heavy crash, shaking the whole floor, and sending an echo flying through all the silent corridors, with a sound like receding laughter, half stunned him.

When he pushed open the door, his master was lying dead upon the floor. His cravat was drawn halter-wise tight round his throat, and had done its work well. The body was cold, and had been long dead.

In due course the coroner held his inquest, and the jury pronounced that 'the deceased, Charles Marston, had died by his own hand, in a state of temporary insanity.' But old Cooper had his own opinion about the Squire's death, though his lips were sealed, and he never spoke about it. He went and lived for the residue of days in York, where there are still people who remember him, a taciturn and surly old man, who attended church regularly, and also drank a little, and was known to have saved some money.

Spinach

By E. F. Benson

Ludovic Byron and his sister Sylvia had adopted these pretty, though quite incredible names because those for which their injudicious parents and god-parents were responsible were not so suitable, though quite as incredible. They rightly felt that there was a lack of spiritual suggestiveness in Thomas and Caroline Carrot which would be a decided handicap in their psychical careers, and would cool rather than kindle the faith of those inquirers who were so eager to have séances with the Byrons.

The change, however, had not been made without earnest thought on their parts, for they were two very scrupulous young people, and wondered whether it would be "acting a lie" thus to profess to be what they were not, and whether, in consequence, the clearness of their psychical sight would be dimmed. But they found to their great joy that their spiritual guides or controls, Asteria and Violetta, communicated quite as freely with the Byrons as with the Carrots, and by now they called each other by their assumed names quite naturally, and had almost themselves forgotten that they had ever been other than what they were styled on their neat professional engagement cards.

While it would be tedious to trace Ludovic's progress from the time when it was first revealed to him that he had rare mediumistic gifts down to the present day, when he was quite at the head of his interesting profession, it is necessary to explain the manner in which his powers were manifested. When the circle was assembled (fees payable in advance), he composed himself in his chair, and seemed to sink into a sort of trance, in which Asteria took possession of him and communicated through his mouth with the devotees. Asteria, when living on the material plane, had been a Greek maiden of ancient Athens, who had become a Christian and suffered martyrdom in Rome about the same time as St. Peter. She had wonderful things to tell them all about her experiences on this earth, a little vague, perhaps, as was only natural after so long a lapse of time, but she spoke dreamily yet convincingly about the Parthenon and the Forum and the Aegean sea (so blue) and the catacombs (so black), and the beautiful Italian and Greek sunsets, and this was all the more remarkable because Ludovic had never been outside the country of his birth.

But far more interesting to the circle, any of whom could take a ticket for Rome or Athens and see the sunsets and the catacombs for themselves, were the encouraging things she said about her present existence. Everyone was wonderfully happy and busy helping those who had lately passed over to the other side, and they all lived in an industrious ecstasy of spiritual progress. There were refreshments and relaxations as well, quantities of the most beautiful flowers and exquisite fruits and crystal rivers and azure mountains, and flowing robes and delightful habitations. None of these things was precisely material; you "thought" a flower or a robe, and there it was!

Asteria knew many of the friends and relatives, who had passed over, of Ludovic's circle, and they sent through her loving messages and sweet thoughts. There was George, for instance did any of the sitters know George? Very often somebody did know George. George was the late husband of one of the sitters, or the father of another, or the little son, who had passed over, of a third, and so George would say how happy he was, and how much love he sent. Then Asteria would tell them that Jane wanted to talk to her dear one, and if nobody knew Jane, it was Mary. And Asteria explained quite satisfactorily how it was that, among all the thousands who were continually passing over, just those who had friends and relations among the ladies and gentlemen who sat with Ludovic Byron were clever enough to "spot" Asteria as being his spiritual guide, who would put them into communication with their loved ones. This was due to currents of sympathy which immediately drew them to her.

Then, when the *séance* had gone on for some time, Asteria would say that the power was getting weak, and she would bid them goodbye and fade into silence. Presently Ludovic came out of his trance, and they would all tell him how wonderful it had been. At other *séances* he would not go into trance at all, but Asteria used his hand and his pencil, and wrote pages of automatic script in quaint, slightly foreign English, with here and there a word in strange and undecipherable characters, which was probably Greek. George and Jane and Mary were then dictating to Asteria, who caused Ludovic to write down what she said, and sometimes they were very playful, and did not like their wife's hat or their husband's tie, just by way of showing that they were really there. And then any member of the circle could ask Asteria questions, and she gave them beautiful answers.

Sylvia and her guide, Violetta, were not in so advanced a stage of development as Ludovic and Asteria; indeed, it was only lately that Sylvia had discovered that she had psychical gifts and had got into touch with her guide. Violetta had been a Florentine lady of noble birth, and was born (on the material plane) in the year 1452, which was a very interesting date, as it made her an exact contemporary of Savonarola and Leonardo da Vinci. She had often heard Savonarola preach, and had seen Leonardo at his easel, and it was splendid to know that Savonarola often preached now to enraptured audiences, and that Leonardo was producing pictures vastly superior to anything he had done on earth. They were not material pictures exactly, but thought-pictures. He thought them, and there the pictures were. This corresponded precisely with what Asteria had said about the flowers, and was, therefore, corroborative evidence.

This winter and spring had been a very busy time for Ludovic, and Mrs. Sapson, one of the most regular attendants at his seances, had been trying to persuade him to go for a short holiday. He was very unwilling to do so, for he was giving five full *séances* every day (which naturally "mounted up,") and he was loth to abandon, even for a short time, the work that so many people found so enlightening. But then Mrs. Sapson had been very clever, and had asked Asteria at one of the *séances* whether he ought not to take a rest, and Asteria distinctly said: "Wisdom counsels prudence; be it so." After the *séance* was over, therefore, Mrs. Sapson, strong in spiritual support, renewed her arguments with redoubled force. She was a large, emphatic widow, who received no end of messages from her husband, William. He had been a choleric stockbroker on this plane, but his character had marvellously mellowed and improved, and now he knew what a waste of time it had been to make so much money and lose so much temper ,

"Dear Mr. Ludovic," she said, "you must have a rest. You can't fly in the face of sweet Asteria. Besides. I have just got a lovely plan for you. I own a charming little cottage near Rye, which is vacant. My tenant has—has suddenly quitted it. It is a dear little place, everything quite ready for you. No expense at all, except what you eat and drink, and sea-bathing and golf at your door. Such a place for quiet and meditation, and—who knows—some wonderful visitor (not earthly, of course, for there are no bothering neighbours) might come to you there."

Of course, this charming offer made a great difference. Ludovic felt that he could give up his spiritual work for a fortnight with less of a wrench than was possible when he thought that he would have to pay for lodgings. He expressed his gratitude in suitable terms, and promised to consult Sylvia, who at the moment was engaged with Violetta . She leaped at the idea when it was referred to her, and the matter was instantly settled.

The two were chatting together on the eve of their departure.

"Wonderfully kind of Mrs. Sapson," said Ludovic. "But it's odd that she didn't offer us the cottage before. She was wanting me to take a holiday a month ago."

"Perhaps the tenant has only just left," said Sylvia.

"That may be so. Dear me, the country and sea-breezes! How nice. But I don't mean to be idle."

"Golf?" suggested Sylvia. "Isn't it very difficult?"

He walked across to the table and took up a square parcel, which had just been delivered.

"No, not golf," he said. "But I am going to take up spirit photography. It pays very I mean it's very helpful. So I've bought a camera and some rolls of films, and the developing and fixing solutions. I shall do it all myself. I used to photograph when I was a boy."

"That must have cost a good deal of money," said Sylvia, who had a great gift for economy.

"Ten pounds, but don't look pained; I think it's worth it. Besides, we get our lodging free. And if I have the power of spirit-photography, it will repay us over and over again."

"Explain the process to me," said Sylvia.

"Well, it's very mysterious, but there's no doubt that if a medium who has got the gift takes a photograph, there sometimes appears on the negative what is called an 'extra.' In other words, if I took a photograph of you, there might appear on the film not only your photograph, but that of some spirit, connected with you or the place, standing by you, or perhaps its face floating in the air near you. It would make another branch of our work, it would bring in fresh clients. The old ones too; I think they want something new. Mrs. Sapson would love a photograph of herself with her William leaning over her shoulder. Anyhow, it's worth trying. I shall practise down at the cottage."

He put the parcel containing the photographic apparatus with other property for packing, and made himself comfortable in his chair.

"I want you to work, too," he said. "I want you to develop your *rapport* with Violetta. There's nothing like practice. Mediumistic power is just as much a gift as music. But you must practice on the piano to be able to play."

The two were alone, and the utmost confidence existed between them. They talked to each other with a frankness which would have appalled their sitters.

"Sometimes I wonder whether I have any mediumistic power at all," she said. "I get in a dreamy sort of state when I am writing automatic script, but is Violetta really communicating, or am I only putting down the thoughts of my sub-conscious self? Or when Asteria speaks through you is she really an independent intelligence, or is she part of your own?"

Ludovic was in a very candid mood.

"I don't know, and I don't care," he said. "But my conscious self certainly can't invent all the things Asteria says, so they come from outside my normal perceptions. And then, after all, Asteria tells things about George and Jane, and so on, concerning their life on earth, which I never knew at all."

"But their relations who are sitting with you know them," said Sylvia. "Isn't it possible that you may get at those facts through telepathy?"

"Yes, but then that's extremely clever of me if I do," said Ludovic. "And it's just as reasonable to say that it's Asteria. Besides, if it's all me, how do you account for it that Asteria sometimes says something which goes against all my intentions and inclinations? For instance, when she said '*Wisdom counsels prudence: be it so*,' in answer to Mrs. Sapson's asking if I was not overworked and wanted a holiday, that quite contradicted my own wishes. I didn't want to go for a holiday at all. Therefore it looks as if Asteria was an external intelligence controlling me."

"Sub-consciously you might have known you wanted a holiday," said the ingenious Sylvia.

"That's far-fetched. Better stick to Asteria. Besides, I sincerely believe that sometimes things come to me from outside my consciousness. And I don't know—not always, that's to say—what Asteria has been telling them while I'm in trance. Sometimes it really astonishes me."

He poured out a moderate whisky-and-soda.

"I'm looking forward to a holiday from *séances*," he said, "now that it's settled, for, frankly, Asteria has been a little thin and feeble lately. And I'm not sure that Mrs. Sapson doesn't think so, too. I think she feels that she's heard about all that Asteria has got to say, and it would never do to lose her as a sitter. That's why I should very much like to find that I can produce spirit photographs. It—it would vary the menu."

They took with them a grim and capable general servant called Gramsby, and arrived next afternoon at Mrs. Sapson's cottage. It was romantically situated near a range of great sand-dunes which ran along the coast, and was only a few minutes' walk from the sea. The place was very remote; a minute village with a shop or two and a cluster of fishermen's huts stood half a mile away, and inland there stretched the empty levels of the Romney marsh away to Rye, which smouldered distantly in the afternoon sunlight. The cottage itself was an enchanting abode, built of timber and rough-cast, with a broad verandah facing south, and a gay little garden in front.

Inside, on the ground floor, there were kitchen and dining-room, and a large living-room with access to the verandah. This was well and plainly furnished and had an open fireplace with a wide hearth for a wood fire and an immense chimney. Logs were ready laid there and, indeed, the whole house had the aspect of having been lately tenanted. Upstairs there were sunny bedrooms facing south, which, overlooking the sand-dunes, gave a restful view of the sea beyond; it was impossible to conceive a more tranquil haven for an overworked medium.

They had a hasty cup of tea, and hurried out to enjoy the last hours of daylight in exploration among the sand-dunes and along the beach, and came back soon after sunset. Though the day had been warm, the evening air had a nip in it, and Sylvia gave a little shiver as they stepped in from the verandah to the sitting-room.

"It's rather cold," she said. "I think I'll light the fire."

Ludovic shared her sensations.

"An excellent idea," he said. "And we'll draw the curtains and be cosy. What a charming room! I shall take some interiors to-morrow Time exposure, I think they told me, for an interior."

Their supper was soon ready, and presently they came back

to the sitting-room and laid out a hectic Patience. But they were both strangely absent-minded, neglecting the most glaring opportunities for getting spaces and putting up kings.

"I can't concentrate on it tonight," said Ludovic. "I feel as if someone was trying to attract my attention. . . . I wonder if Asteria wants to communicate."

Sylvia looked up at him.

"Now it's very odd that you should say that," she observed. "I feel exactly as if Violetta was wanting to come through, and yet it doesn't seem quite like Violetta."

He gave an uneasy glance round the room. "A curious sensation," he said. "I have the consciousness of some presence here, which isn't quite Asteria. But it may be she. Tiresome of her, if it is, for she ought to know I came down here for a holiday, considering that she recommended it herself. I think I'll get a pencil and paper, and see if she wants to say anything."

He composed himself in a chair, with the stationery for Asteria on his knee.

"Ask her a question or two, Sylvia," he said, "when I go off."

Sylvia waited till her brother's eyelids fluttered and fell.

"Is that you, Asteria?" she asked.

His hand twitched and quivered. Then the pencil scribbled "Certainly not" in large, firm letters, quite unlike Asteria's pretty writing.

Sylvia asked if it was Violetta, but got an emphatic denial.

"Who is it, then?" she said.

And then a very absurd thing happened. The pencil spelt out "Thomas Spinach."

Sylvia was puzzled for a moment. Then the explanation occurred to her, and she laughed.

"Wake up, dear," she said to Ludovic. "It says it is Thomas Spinach. Of course, that's your sub-conscious self trying to remember Carrot."

But Ludovic did not stir, and to her surprise the pencil began writing again.

"I don't know who you are," wrote the unknown control.

"But I'm Spinach, young Spinach. And"—there was a long pause—"I want you to help me. I can't remember . . . I'm very unhappy."

As she followed the words, there suddenly came a very loud rap on the wall just above her, which considerably startled her, for why, if "Spinach" was an attempt on the part of Ludovic's sub-consciousness to write "Carrot," should he announce his presence? She sprang up, and shook Ludovic by the shoulder.

"Wake up," she said. "There's a strange spirit here, and I don't like it. Wake up, Ludovic."

He came drowsily to himself.

"Hullo!" he said. "Anything been happening? was it Asteria?"

His eye fell on the paper,

"What's all this?" he said. "Thomas Spinach? That's only me. My sub-consciousness said it was Asparagus once."

"But look what it has been writing," said Sylvia.

He read it.

"That's queer," he said. "That can't be me. I'm not very unhappy. I don't want my own help. I know who I am."

He jumped up.

"Most interesting," he said. "It looks like a new control. Young Spinach must be powerful, too; he came through the first time he tried. We'll investigate this, Sylvia. It would be fine to get a new control for our *séances*."

"But not tonight, Ludovic," said she. "I really shouldn't sleep if you went on now. And he's violent. He made the loudest rap I ever heard."

"Did he, indeed?" said Ludovic. "I must have been in deep trance then, for I never heard it. We'll certainly try to snap him with the camera tomorrow."

The morning was bright and sunny, and directly after breakfast Ludovic set to work with his photography. The first three or four films showed nothing but impenetrable blackness, and a consultation of his handbook convinced him that they must have been over-exposed. He corrected this, and after a few errors on the other side, produced a negative which quite clearly showed Sylvia sitting by the long window into the verandah. This, though it revealed no "extra," was an encouraging achievement, and he took half a dozen more exposures with which he hurried away into the small dark cupboard under the stairs, where he had installed his developing and fixing baths. Shortly afterwards Sylvia heard her name called in crowing, exultant tones, and ran to see what had happened.

"Don't open the door," he called, "or you'll spoil it. But I've got a picture of you with a magnificent extra—a face hanging in the air by your shoulder."

"How lovely!" shouted Sylvia. "Do be quick and fix it."

There was no sort of doubt about it. There she sat by the window, and close by her was a strange, inexplicable face. So much could be seen from the negative, and when a print was taken of it, the details were wonderfully clear. It was the face of a young man; his handsome features wore an expression of agonized entreaty.

"Poor boy!" said Sylvia, sympathetically. "So good looking, too, but somehow I don't like him."

Then a brilliant idea struck her.

"Oh, Ludovic!" she said. "Is it young Spinach?"

He snatched the print from her.

"I must fix it," he said, "or it will be ruined. Of course it's young Spinach. Who else could it be, I should like to know? We'll find out more about him this evening. Fancy obtaining that the very first morning!"

They spent the afternoon on the beach, in order to get in an elevated frame of mind by contemplating the beauties of nature, and after a light supper, prepared for a double *séance*. Two hooks, so to speak, were baited for Spinach, for in one chair sat Sylvia, with pencil and paper, ready to take down his slightest word, and in another Ludovic, similarly equipped. They both let themselves sink into that drowsy and vacant condition which they knew to be favourable to communications from the unseen, but for a long time they neither of them got a bite. Then Ludovic heard the dash and clatter of his sister's pencil, suddenly beginning to write very rapidly, and this aroused in him disturbing feelings of envy and jealousy, for something was coming through to Sylvia and not to him.

This inharmonious emotion quite dissipated the tranquillity which was a *sine qua non* of the receptive state, and he got up to see what was coming through to her. Probably some mawkish rubbish from Violetta about Savonarola's sermons. But the moment he saw her paper he was thrilled to the marrow.

"Yes, I'm Thomas Spinach," he read, "and I'm very unhappy. I came and stood by you this morning when the man was photographing. I want you to help me. Oh, do help me! It's something I've forgotten, though it is so important. I want you to look everywhere and see if you can't find something very unusual, and tell them. It is somewhere here. It must be, because I put it there, and I hardly like to tell you what it is, because it's terrible. . . ."

The pencil stopped. Ludovic was wildly excited, and his jealousy of Sylvia was almost forgotten. After all, it was he who had taken Spinach's photograph. . . .

Sylvia's hand continued idle so long that Ludovic, in order to stir it into activity again, began to ask questions.

"Have you passed over. Spinach?" he said.

Her hand began to write in a swift and irritated manner. "Of course I have," it scribbled. "Otherwise I should know where it was."

"Used you to live here?" asked Ludovic. "And when did you pass over?"

"Yes, I lived here," came the answer. "I passed over a week ago. Very suddenly. There was a thunderstorm that night, and I had just finished it all, and was in the garden cooling down, when lightning struck me, and when I came to on this side, you understand—I couldn't remember where it was."

"Where what was?" asked Ludovic. "Do you mean the thing you had finished? What was it you had finished?"

The pencil seemed to give a loud squeak, as if it was a slate pencil.

"Oh, here it is again," it wrote in trembling characters. "I can't go on now. It's terrible. Tm so frightened. Please, please find it."

Just as on the previous evening, there came an appalling rap somewhere on the wall close to him, and, seriously startled, Ludovic sprang up, and shook Sylvia into consciousness. Whoever this spirit was, it was not a good, kind, mild one like Asteria, who, whenever she rapped, did so very softly and pleasantly.

Sylvia yawned and stretched herself.

"Spinach?" she said, drowsily. "Any Spinach?"

"Yes, dear, quantities," said Ludovic

"And what did he say? Oh, I went off deep then, Ludovic. I don't know what's been happening. Violetta isn't nearly so powerful. Such an odd feeling! Did I write all that?"

"Yes, in answer to some pretty good questions of mine," he said. "It's really wonderful. We're on the track of young Spinach, or, rather, he's on ours."

Sylvia was reading her manuscript.

"'I passed over a week ago,'" she said. "'Very suddenly—there was a thunderstorm that night' Why, Ludovic, there was! That's quite true. You slept through it, but I didn't, and I remember reading in the paper that it had been very violent in the Rye district. How strange!"

Ludovic clicked his fingers.

"I know what I'll do," he said. "I shall send a telegram to Mrs. Sapson Give me a piece of paper. She said that wonderful visitors might perhaps come to me here."

Sylvia grasped his thoughts.

"I see!" she cried. "You mean to tell her that her late tenant, young Thomas Spinach, who was killed by lightning last week, has communicated with us. That will impress her tremendously, if you think she's had enough of Asteria. Indeed, I shouldn't wonder if she lent us this cottage just in order to test us, and see if we really received messages from the other side. What a score!"

She hastily scribbled on a leaf of her writing-block, counting up the words on her fingers. Her economical mind exerted itself to contrive the message in exactly twelve words.

"There!" she read out triumphantly. "Listen! 'Sapson, 29, Brompton Avenue, London. Tenant Spinach killed last week, thunderstorm, communicated.' Just twelve. You needn't sign it, as it will have the Rye postmark."

"My dear," said he, "it's no time for such petty economies. Better spend a few pence more and make it impressive and rather more intelligible. Give me some paper; I asked you before. And we must make it clear that it's not a chance word of local gossip that has inspired it I shall tell her about the photograph, too."

Before they went to bed, Ludovic composed a more explicit telegram, and in the course of the next morning he received an enthusiastic reply from Mrs. Sapson,

"All quite correct and most wonderful," she wrote. "Delighted you have got into communication. Find out more, and ask him about his uncle. Wire again if fresh revelations occur."

In order to secure themselves from the possibility of interruption, Sylvia gave Gramsby an afternoon out, which she proposed to spend in the excitements of Rye, and as soon as she was gone the mediums prepared for a *séance*. As Spinach seemed to fancy Sylvia, she composed herself for the trance-condition, with pencil and paper handy, and Ludovic sat by to ask questions. Very soon Sylvia's eyes closed, her head fell forward, and the pencil she held began to tremble violently, like a motorcar ready to start.

"Are you Spinach?" asked Ludovic, observing these signs of possession. Instantly the pencil began to write.

"Yes; have you found it?"

"We don't know what it is," said Ludovic. Then he remembered Mrs. Sapson's telegram. "Has it anything to do with your uncle?" he asked.

There was a long pause. Then the pencil began to move again.

"Please find him," it wrote.

"But how are we to find your uncle?" asked Ludovic. "We don't know where to look or what he's like. Tell us where to look."

The pencil moved in a most agitated fashion.

"I don't know," it wrote. "If I knew I would tell you. But it's somewhere about. I had just put it somewhere, when the lightning came and killed me, and I can't remember. My memory's gone like—like after concussion of the brain."

An uneasy thought struck Ludovic. Why did young Spinach allude to his uncle as "it"?

"Is your uncle dead?" he asked. "Is it his body that you mean by 'it'?"

Sylvia's fingers writhed as if in mortal agony. Then the pencil jerked out, "Yes."

Ludovic, accustomed as he was to spirits, felt an icy shudder run through him. But he waited in silence, for the pencil looked as if it had something more to write. Then, great heavens! it came.

"I will tell you all," it wrote. "I killed him, and I can't remember where I put him."

A spasm of moral indignation seized Ludovic.

"That was very wrong of you," he justly observed. "But we'll try to help you if you will tell us all about it. Come; you're dead. Nobody can hang you."

Shocked as Ludovic was, and extremely uneasy also at the thought of the proximity not only of the spirit of a murderer, but the corpse of young Spinach's uncle, it was only natural that he should feel an overwhelming professional interest in the revelations that appeared to be imminent. It would be a glorious thing for his career to receive from a departed spirit the first-hand account of this undetected crime, and to be able to corroborate it by the discovery of the corpse. Though he had come down here for a holiday, the chance of such a unique piece of work made him feel quite rested already, for it was impossible to conceive a more magnificent advertisement.

What a wonderful confirmation it would be also to Mrs.

Sapson's wavering faith in his psychical powers. She would publish the news of it far and wide, and the *séances* would be more popular than ever. Moreover, there was the chance of learning all sorts of fresh information about the conditions that prevailed on the other side, of a far more sensational and exciting quality than the method of the production of thought-flowers and flowing robes and general love and helpfulness. . . . He waited with the intensest expectation for anything that Spinach might vouchsafe.

At last it began, and now there was no need for further questions, for the pencil streamed across the page. Sheet after sheet of the writing-block was filled, and twice Ludovic had to sharpen Sylvia's pencil, for the point was quite worn down with these remarkable disclosures, and only made illegible scratches on the paper. For half an hour it careered over the sheets; then finally it made a great scrawl, and Sylvia's hand dropped inert She stretched and yawned, and came to herself.

The next hour was the most absorbing that Ludovic had ever spent in his professional work. Together they read the account of the crime Alexander Spinach, the uncle, was the most wicked of elderly gentlemen, who made his nephew's life an intolerable burden to him. He had found out that the orphan boy had committed a petty forgery with regard to a cheque which he had signed with his uncle's name, and, holding exposure and arrest over his head, had made him work for him day and night, fishing and farming and doing the work of the house without a penny-piece of wages, while he himself boozed his days away in the chimney-corner.

Long brooding over his wrongs and the misery of his life made young Spinach (very properly, as he still thought) determine to kill the odious old wretch, and he adroitly poisoned his whisky with weed-killer. He went out to his work next morning as usual, leaving the corpse in the locked-up house, and casually mentioned to the folk he came across that his uncle had gone up to London and would probably not be back for some time. When he returned in the evening he hid the body somewhere, meaning to dig a handsome excavation in the garden, and having buried it, plant some useful vegetables above it But hardly had he made this temporary disposition of the corpse, than he was struck by lightning in the terrific storm that visited the district a week ago, and killed. When he came to himself on the spiritual plane, he could not remember what he had done with the body.

So far the story was ordinary enough, apart from the interest in the manner of its communication, but now came that part of the confession which these ardent young psychicists saw would be a veritable gold mine to them. For on emerging on the other side, young Spinach found himself terrifyingly haunted not by the spirit, but by the body of his uncle. Just as on the material plane, so he explained, murderers are sometimes haunted by the spirit of their victim, so on the spiritual plane, quite logically, they may be haunted by the body of their victim. His uncle's bodily and palpable presence grimly pursued him wherever he went; even as he gathered sweet thought-flowers or thought-fruits, the terrible body appeared.

If he woke at night he found it watching by his bed, if he bathed in the crystal rivers it swam beside him, and he had learned that he could never find peace till it was given proper burial No doubt, he said, Ludovic had heard of the skeletons of murdered folk being walled up in secret chambers, and how their spirits haunted the place till their bones were discovered and interred The converse was true on the other side, and while murdered corpses lay about unburied in the material world, their bodies haunted the perpetrator of the crime.

It was here that poor young Spinach's difficulty came in. The sudden lightning-stroke had bereft him of all memory of what he was doing just before, and, puzzle as he might, he could not recollect where he had put the corpse. . . . Then he broke out into passionate entreaties: "Help me, help me, kind mediums," he wrote. "I know it is somewhere about, so search for it and get it buried. He was an awful old man and I can't describe the agony of being haunted by his beastly body. Find it and have it buried, and then I shall be free from its dreadful presence."

They read this unique document together by the fading light, strung up to the highest pitch of professional interest, and yet peering awfully round from time to time in vague apprehension of what might happen next. During the *séance* the wind had got up, and now it was moaning round the corners of the house, and dusk was falling rapidly, with prospects of a wild night to follow. The curtains bulged and bellied in the draught, hollow voices sounded in the chimney, and Sylvia clung to her brother.

"I don't like it," she wailed. "I don't like this spirit of Spinach; Violetta and Asteria are far preferable. And then there's ' It.' It is somewhere about, and it may be anyrwhere."

Ludovic made an attempt at gaiety.

"It may be anywhere, as you say," he remarked, "but it actually is somewhere. And we've got to find it, dear. Better find it before it gets dark. And think of the sensation there will be when we publish the account of how, in answer to the entreaty of a remorseful spirit."

"But he isn't remorseful," said Sylvia. "There's not a word of remorse, but only terror at being haunted. There's not only a corpse about, but the spirit of an unrepentant murderer. It isn't pleasant. I would sooner be in expensive lodgings than here."

"Oh, nonsense," said Ludovic. "Besides, young Spinach is friendly enough to us. We're his one hope. And if we find it, he will certainly be very grateful. I shouldn't wonder if he sent us many more revelations. Even as it is, how deeply interesting. Nobody ever guessed that there were material ghosts in the spiritual world. But now we must get busy and search for Alexander. Fix your mind on what a tremendously paying experience this will be. Now, where shall we begin? There's the house and the garden."

"Oh, I hope it will be in the garden," said Sylvia. "But there's no chance of that, for he meant to bury it in the garden afterwards."

"True. We'll begin with the house, then. Now most murderers bury the body under the floor of the kitchen, cover it with quicklime, and fill in with cement."

"But he wouldn't have had time for that," said Sylvia. "Besides, this was to be only a temporary resting-place."

"Perhaps he cut it up," said Ludovic, "and we shall find a piece here and a piece there."

The search began. In the growing dusk, with the wild wind increasing to a gale, they annealed themselves for the gruesome business. They investigated the coal cellar, they peered into housemaids' cupboards, and with quaking hearts examined the woodshed. Here there were signs that its contents had been disturbed, and the sight of an old boot peeping out from behind some logs nearly caused Sylvia to collapse. Then Ludovic got a ladder, and, climbing up to the roof, interrogated the water-tank, from the contents of which they had already drunk. But all their explorations were in vain; there was no sign of the corpse. For a nerve-racking hour they persevered, and a dismal idea occurred to Ludovic.

"It can't be a practical joke on the part of Spinach, can it?" he said "That would be in the worst possible taste. Good gracious, what's that?"

There came a loud tapping at the front door, and Sylvia hid her face on his shoulder.

"That's Spinach," she whispered. "That terrible Spinach!"

They tottered to the door and opened it. On the threshold was a man, who told them he was the carrier from Rye, and brought a note for Miss Byron.

"I'm going back in half an hour, miss," he said, "if there's any answer. A box, I understood."

The note was from Gramsby, who, though unwilling to "upset" them, declined to come back to the cottage. She had heard things, and she didn't like it, and she would be obliged if they would pack her box and send it in.

"The coward!" said Sylvia, trembling violently. "She shan't have her box unless she comes to fetch it"

They went back into the sitting-room, lit the fire, and made it as cheerful as they could with many candles. Their flames wagged ominously in the eddying draughts, and the two drew their chairs close to the hearth. By now the full fury of the gale was unloosed, the whole house shuddered at the blasts, doors creaked, curtains whispered, flurries of rain were flung against the windows, and strange noises and stirrings muttered in the chimney.

"I shall just get warm," said Ludovic, "and then go on with the search. I shan't know a moment's peace till I find it."

"I shan't know a moment's peace when you do!" wailed Sylvia.

They were sitting in the fire almost, and suddenly something up the chimney caught Ludovic's eye.

"What's that?" he said.

He got a candle and held it up the chimney.

"It's a rope," he said, "tied round a staple in the wall."

His look met hers, and read the answering horror there.

"I'm going to undo it," he said. "Step back, Sylvia."

There was no need to say that, for she had already retreated to the farthest corner of the room. He pulled the rope off the staple and let it go.

There was a scrambling, shuffling noise from high up in the chimney, and in a cloud of soot It fell, with a heavy thud, sprawling across the hearth.

They fled into the night; the carrier had only just got to the garden gate.

"Take us into Rye," cried Ludovic. "Take us to the police-station. Murder has been done."

******

The account of these amazing events duly appeared in all the psychical papers and many others. Long queues of would-be sitters formed up for the Byron *séances*, in the hopes of getting fresh revelations from young Spinach. But from association with Asteria and Violetta he gradually became quite commonplace, and only told them about thought-flowers and white robes.

The Signal-Man

A.K.A. No. 1 Branch Line, The Signalman

By Charles Dickens

"Halloa! Below there!"

When he heard a voice thus calling to him, he was standing at the door of his box, with a flag in his hand, furled round its short pole. One would have thought, considering the nature of the ground, that he could not have doubted from what quarter the voice came; but instead of looking up to where I stood on the top of the steep cutting nearly over his head, he turned himself about, and looked down the Line. There was something remarkable in his manner of doing so, though I could not have said for my life what. But I know it was remarkable enough to attract my notice, even though his figure was foreshortened and shadowed, down in the deep trench, and mine was high above him, so steeped in the glow of an angry sunset, that I had shaded my eyes with my hand before I saw him at all.

"Halloa! Below!"

From looking down the Line, he turned himself about again, and, raising his eyes, saw my figure high above him.

"Is there any path by which I can come down and speak to you?"

He looked up at me without replying, and I looked down at him without pressing him too soon with a repetition of my idle question. Just then there came a vague vibration in the earth and air, quickly changing into a violent pulsation, and an oncoming rush that caused me to start back, as though it had force to draw me down. When such vapour as rose to my height from this rapid train had passed me, and was skimming away over the landscape, I looked down again, and saw him refurling the flag he had shown while the train went by.

I repeated my inquiry. After a pause, during which he seemed to regard me with fixed attention, he motioned with his rolled-up flag towards a point on my level, some two or three hundred yards distant. I called down to him, "All right!" and made for that point. There, by dint of looking closely about me, I found a rough zigzag descending path notched out, which I followed.

The cutting was extremely deep, and unusually precipitate. It was made through a clammy stone, that became oozier and wetter as I went down. For these reasons, I found the way long enough to give me time to recall a singular air of reluctance or compulsion with which he had pointed out the path.

When I came down low enough upon the zigzag descent to see him again, I saw that he was standing between the rails on the way by which the train had lately passed, in an attitude as if he were waiting for me to appear. He had his left hand at his chin, and that left elbow rested on his right hand, crossed over his breast. His attitude was one of such expectation and watchfulness that I stopped a moment, wondering at it.

I resumed my downward way, and stepping out upon the level of the railroad, and drawing nearer to him, saw that he was a dark sallow man, with a dark beard and rather heavy eyebrows. His post was in as solitary and dismal a place as ever I saw. On either side, a dripping-wet wall of jagged stone, excluding all view but a strip of sky; the perspective one way only a crooked prolongation of this great dungeon; the shorter perspective in the other direction terminating in a gloomy red light, and the gloomier entrance to a black tunnel, in whose massive architecture there was a barbarous, depressing, and forbidding air. So little sunlight ever found its way to this spot, that it had an earthy, deadly smell; and so much cold wind rushed through it, that it struck chill to me, as if I had left the natural world.

Before he stirred, I was near enough to him to have touched

him. Not even then removing his eyes from mine, he stepped back one step, and lifted his hand.

This was a lonesome post to occupy (I said), and it had riveted my attention when I looked down from up yonder. A visitor was a rarity, I should suppose; not an unwelcome rarity, I hoped? In me, he merely saw a man who had been shut up within narrow limits all his life, and who, being at last set free, had a newly-awakened interest in these great works. To such purpose I spoke to him; but I am far from sure of the terms I used; for, besides that I am not happy in opening any conversation, there was something in the man that daunted me.

He directed a most curious look towards the red light near the tunnel's mouth, and looked all about it, as if something were missing from it, and then looked at me.

That light was part of his charge? Was it not?

He answered in a low voice,—"Don't you know it is?"

The monstrous thought came into my mind, as I perused the fixed eyes and the saturnine face, that this was a spirit, not a man. I have speculated since, whether there may have been infection in his mind.

In my turn, I stepped back. But in making the action, I detected in his eyes some latent fear of me. This put the monstrous thought to flight.

"You look at me," I said, forcing a smile, "as if you had a dread of me."

"I was doubtful," he returned, "whether I had seen you before."

"Where?"

He pointed to the red light he had looked at.

"There?" I said.

Intently watchful of me, he replied (but without sound), "Yes."

"My good fellow, what should I do there? However, be that as it may, I never was there, you may swear."

"I think I may," he rejoined. "Yes; I am sure I may."

His manner cleared, like my own. He replied to my remarks

with readiness, and in well-chosen words. Had he much to do there? Yes; that was to say, he had enough responsibility to bear; but exactness and watchfulness were what was required of him, and of actual work—manual labour—he had next to none. To change that signal, to trim those lights, and to turn this iron handle now and then, was all he had to do under that head. Regarding those many long and lonely hours of which I seemed to make so much, he could only say that the routine of his life had shaped itself into that form, and he had grown used to it. He had taught himself a language down here,—if only to know it by sight, and to have formed his own crude ideas of its pronunciation, could be called learning it.

He had also worked at fractions and decimals, and tried a little algebra; but he was, and had been as a boy, a poor hand at figures. Was it necessary for him when on duty always to remain in that channel of damp air, and could he never rise into the sunshine from between those high stone walls? Why, that depended upon times and circumstances. Under some conditions there would be less upon the Line than under others, and the same held good as to certain hours of the day and night. In bright weather, he did choose occasions for getting a little above these lower shadows; but, being at all times liable to be called by his electric bell, and at such times listening for it with redoubled anxiety, the relief was less than I would suppose.

He took me into his box, where there was a fire, a desk for an official book in which he had to make certain entries, a telegraphic instrument with its dial, face, and needles, and the little bell of which he had spoken. On my trusting that he would excuse the remark that he had been well educated, and (I hoped I might say without offence) perhaps educated above that station, he observed that instances of slight incongruity in such wise would rarely be found wanting among large bodies of men; that he had heard it was so in workhouses, in the police force, even in that last desperate resource, the army; and that he knew it was so, more or less, in any great railway staff. He had been, when young (if I could believe it, sitting in that hut,—he scarcely could), a student of natural philosophy, and had attended lectures; but he had run wild, misused his opportunities, gone down, and never risen again. He had no complaint to offer about that. He had made his bed, and he lay upon it. It was far too late to make another.

All that I have here condensed he said in a quiet manner, with his grave dark regards divided between me and the fire. He threw in the word, "Sir," from time to time, and especially when he referred to his youth,—as though to request me to understand that he claimed to be nothing but what I found him. He was several times interrupted by the little bell, and had to read off messages, and send replies. Once he had to stand without the door, and display a flag as a train passed, and make some verbal communication to the driver. In the discharge of his duties, I observed him to be remarkably exact and vigilant, breaking off his discourse at a syllable, and remaining silent until what he had to do was done.

In a word, I should have set this man down as one of the safest of men to be employed in that capacity, but for the circumstance that while he was speaking to me he twice broke off with a fallen colour, turned his face towards the little bell when it did *not* ring, opened the door of the hut (which was kept shut to exclude the unhealthy damp), and looked out towards the red light near the mouth of the tunnel. On both of those occasions, he came back to the fire with the inexplicable air upon him which I had remarked, without being able to define, when we were so far asunder.

Said I, when I rose to leave him, "You almost make me think that I have met with a contented man."

(I am afraid I must acknowledge that I said it to lead him on.)

"I believe I used to be so," he rejoined, in the low voice in which he had first spoken; "but I am troubled, sir, I am troubled."

He would have recalled the words if he could. He had said them, however, and I took them up quickly.

"With what? What is your trouble?"

"It is very difficult to impart, sir. It is very, very difficult to speak of. If ever you make me another visit, I will try to tell you."

"But I expressly intend to make you another visit. Say, when shall it be?"

"I go off early in the morning, and I shall be on again at ten tomorrow night, sir."

"I will come at eleven."

He thanked me, and went out at the door with me. "I'll show my white light, sir," he said, in his peculiar low voice, "till you have found the way up. When you have found it, don't call out! And when you are at the top, don't call out!"

His manner seemed to make the place strike colder to me, but I said no more than, "Very well."

"And when you come down to-morrow night, don't call out! Let me ask you a parting question. What made you cry, 'Halloa! Below there!' tonight?"

"Heaven knows," said I. "I cried something to that effect—"

"Not to that effect, sir. Those were the very words. I know them well."

"Admit those were the very words. I said them, no doubt, because I saw you below."

"For no other reason?"

"What other reason could I possibly have?"

"You had no feeling that they were conveyed to you in any supernatural way?"

"No."

He wished me goodnight, and held up his light. I walked by the side of the down Line of rails (with a very disagreeable sensation of a train coming behind me) until I found the path. It was easier to mount than to descend, and I got back to my inn without any adventure.

Punctual to my appointment, I placed my foot on the first notch of the zigzag next night, as the distant clocks were striking eleven. He was waiting for me at the bottom, with his white light on. "I have not called out," I said, when we came close together; "may I speak now?"

"By all means, sir."

"Goodnight, then, and here's my hand."

"Goodnight, sir, and here's mine." With that we walked side by side to his box, entered it, closed the door, and sat down by the fire.

"I have made up my mind, sir," he began, bending forward as soon as we were seated, and speaking in a tone but a little above a whisper, "that you shall not have to ask me twice what troubles me. I took you for someone else yesterday evening. That troubles me."

"That mistake?"

"No. That someone else."

"Who is it?"

"I don't know."

"Like me?"

"I don't know. I never saw the face. The left arm is across the face, and the right arm is waved,—violently waved. This way."

I followed his action with my eyes, and it was the action of an arm gesticulating, with the utmost passion and vehemence, "For God's sake, clear the way!"

"One moonlight night," said the man, "I was sitting here, when I heard a voice cry, 'Halloa! Below there!' I started up, looked from that door, and saw this Someone else standing by the red light near the tunnel, waving as I just now showed you. The voice seemed hoarse with shouting, and it cried, 'Look out! Look out!' And then again, 'Halloa! Below there! Look out!' I caught up my lamp, turned it on red, and ran towards the figure, calling, 'What's wrong? What has happened? Where?' It stood just outside the blackness of the tunnel. I advanced so close upon it that I wondered at its keeping the sleeve across its eyes. I ran right up at it, and had my hand stretched out to pull the sleeve away, when it was gone."

"Into the tunnel?" said I.

"No. I ran on into the tunnel, five hundred yards. I stopped, and held my lamp above my head, and saw the figures of the measured distance, and saw the wet stains stealing down the walls and trickling through the arch. I ran out again faster than I had run in (for I had a mortal abhorrence of the place upon me), and I looked all round the red light with my own red light, and I went up the iron ladder to the gallery atop of it, and I came down again, and ran back here. I telegraphed both ways, 'An alarm has been given. Is anything wrong?' The answer came back, both ways, 'All well.'"

Resisting the slow touch of a frozen finger tracing out my spine, I showed him how that this figure must be a deception of his sense of sight; and how that figures, originating in disease of the delicate nerves that minister to the functions of the eye, were known to have often troubled patients, some of whom had become conscious of the nature of their affliction, and had even proved it by experiments upon themselves. "As to an imaginary cry," said I, "do but listen for a moment to the wind in this unnatural valley while we speak so low, and to the wild harp it makes of the telegraph wires."

That was all very well, he returned, after we had sat listening for a while, and he ought to know something of the wind and the wires,—he who so often passed long winter nights there, alone and watching. But he would beg to remark that he had not finished.

I asked his pardon, and he slowly added these words, touching my arm,—

"Within six hours after the Appearance, the memorable accident on this Line happened, and within ten hours the dead and wounded were brought along through the tunnel over the spot where the figure had stood."

A disagreeable shudder crept over me, but I did my best against it. It was not to be denied, I rejoined, that this was a remarkable coincidence, calculated deeply to impress his mind. But it was unquestionable that remarkable coincidences did continually occur, and they must be taken into account in dealing with such a subject. Though to be sure I must admit, I added (for I thought

I saw that he was going to bring the objection to bear upon me), men of common sense did not allow much for coincidences in making the ordinary calculations of life.

He again begged to remark that he had not finished.

I again begged his pardon for being betrayed into interruptions.

"This," he said, again laying his hand upon my arm, and glancing over his shoulder with hollow eyes, "was just a year ago. Six or seven months passed, and I had recovered from the surprise and shock, when one morning, as the day was breaking, I, standing at the door, looked towards the red light, and saw the spectre again." He stopped, with a fixed look at me.

"Did it cry out?"

"No. It was silent."

"Did it wave its arm?"

"No. It leaned against the shaft of the light, with both hands before the face. Like this."

Once more I followed his action with my eyes. It was an action of mourning. I have seen such an attitude in stone figures on tombs.

"Did you go up to it?"

"I came in and sat down, partly to collect my thoughts, partly because it had turned me faint. When I went to the door again, daylight was above me, and the ghost was gone."

"But nothing followed? Nothing came of this?"

He touched me on the arm with his forefinger twice or thrice giving a ghastly nod each time:—

"That very day, as a train came out of the tunnel, I noticed, at a carriage window on my side, what looked like a confusion of hands and heads, and something waved. I saw it just in time to signal the driver, Stop! He shut off, and put his brake on, but the train drifted past here a hundred and fifty yards or more. I ran after it, and, as I went along, heard terrible screams and cries. A beautiful young lady had died instantaneously in one of the compartments, and was brought in here, and laid down on this floor between us."

Involuntarily I pushed my chair back, as I looked from the boards at which he pointed to himself.

"True, sir. True. Precisely as it happened, so I tell it you."

I could think of nothing to say, to any purpose, and my mouth was very dry. The wind and the wires took up the story with a long lamenting wail.

He resumed. "Now, sir, mark this, and judge how my mind is troubled. The spectre came back a week ago. Ever since, it has been there, now and again, by fits and starts."

"At the light?"

"At the Danger-light."

"What does it seem to do?"

He repeated, if possible with increased passion and vehemence, that former gesticulation of, "For God's sake, clear the way!"

Then he went on. "I have no peace or rest for it. It calls to me, for many minutes together, in an agonised manner, 'Below there! Look out! Look out!' It stands waving to me. It rings my little bell—"

I caught at that. "Did it ring your bell yesterday evening when I was here, and you went to the door?"

"Twice."

"Why, see," said I, "how your imagination misleads you. My eyes were on the bell, and my ears were open to the bell, and if I am a living man, it did *not* ring at those times. No, nor at any other time, except when it was rung in the natural course of physical things by the station communicating with you."

He shook his head. "I have never made a mistake as to that yet, sir. I have never confused the spectre's ring with the man's. The ghost's ring is a strange vibration in the bell that it derives from nothing else, and I have not asserted that the bell stirs to the eye. I don't wonder that you failed to hear it. But I heard it."

"And did the spectre seem to be there, when you looked out?"

"It *was* there."'

"Both times?"

He repeated firmly: "Both times."

"Will you come to the door with me, and look for it now?"

He bit his under lip as though he were somewhat unwilling, but arose. I opened the door, and stood on the step, while he stood in the doorway. There was the Danger-light. There was the dismal mouth of the tunnel. There were the high, wet stone walls of the cutting. There were the stars above them.

"Do you see it?" I asked him, taking particular note of his face. His eyes were prominent and strained, but not very much more so, perhaps, than my own had been when I had directed them earnestly towards the same spot.

"No," he answered. "It is not there."

"Agreed," said I.

We went in again, shut the door, and resumed our seats. I was thinking how best to improve this advantage, if it might be called one, when he took up the conversation in such a matter-of-course way, so assuming that there could be no serious question of fact between us, that I felt myself placed in the weakest of positions.

"By this time you will fully understand, sir," he said, "that what troubles me so dreadfully is the question, What does the spectre mean?"

I was not sure, I told him, that I did fully understand.

"What is its warning against?" he said, ruminating, with his eyes on the fire, and only by times turning them on me. "What is the danger? Where is the danger? There is danger overhanging somewhere on the Line. Some dreadful calamity will happen. It is not to be doubted this third time, after what has gone before. But surely this is a cruel haunting of me. What can I do?"

He pulled out his handkerchief, and wiped the drops from his heated forehead.

"If I telegraph Danger, on either side of me, or on both, I can give no reason for it," he went on, wiping the palms of his hands. "I should get into trouble, and do no good. They would think I was mad. This is the way it would work,—Message: 'Danger!

Take care!' Answer: 'What Danger? Where?' Message: 'Don't know. But, for God's sake, take care!' They would displace me. What else could they do?"

His pain of mind was most pitiable to see. It was the mental torture of a conscientious man, oppressed beyond endurance by an unintelligible responsibility involving life.

"When it first stood under the Danger-light," he went on, putting his dark hair back from his head, and drawing his hands outward across and across his temples in an extremity of feverish distress, "why not tell me where that accident was to happen,-if it must happen? Why not tell me how it could be averted,—if it could have been averted? When on its second coming it hid its face, why not tell me, instead, 'She is going to die. Let them keep her at home'? If it came, on those two occasions, only to show me that its warnings were true, and so to prepare me for the third, why not warn me plainly now? And I, Lord help me! A mere poor signal-man on this solitary station! Why not go to somebody with credit to be believed, and power to act?"

When I saw him in this state, I saw that for the poor man's sake, as well as for the public safety, what I had to do for the time was to compose his mind. Therefore, setting aside all question of reality or unreality between us, I represented to him that whoever thoroughly discharged his duty must do well, and that at least it was his comfort that he understood his duty, though he did not understand these confounding Appearances. In this effort I succeeded far better than in the attempt to reason him out of his conviction. He became calm; the occupations incidental to his post as the night advanced began to make larger demands on his attention: and I left him at two in the morning. I had offered to stay through the night, but he would not hear of it.

That I more than once looked back at the red light as I ascended the pathway, that I did not like the red light, and that I should have slept but poorly if my bed had been under it, I see no reason to conceal. Nor did I like the two sequences of the accident and the dead girl. I see no reason to conceal that either.

But what ran most in my thoughts was the consideration how

ought I to act, having become the recipient of this disclosure? I had proved the man to be intelligent, vigilant, painstaking, and exact; but how long might he remain so, in his state of mind? Though in a subordinate position, still he held a most important trust, and would I (for instance) like to stake my own life on the chances of his continuing to execute it with precision?

Unable to overcome a feeling that there would be something treacherous in my communicating what he had told me to his superiors in the Company, without first being plain with himself and proposing a middle course to him, I ultimately resolved to offer to accompany him (otherwise keeping his secret for the present) to the wisest medical practitioner we could hear of in those parts, and to take his opinion. A change in his time of duty would come round next night, he had apprised me, and he would be off an hour or two after sunrise, and on again soon after sunset. I had appointed to return accordingly.

Next evening was a lovely evening, and I walked out early to enjoy it. The sun was not yet quite down when I traversed the field-path near the top of the deep cutting. I would extend my walk for an hour, I said to myself, half an hour on and half an hour back, and it would then be time to go to my signal-man's box.

Before pursuing my stroll, I stepped to the brink, and mechanically looked down, from the point from which I had first seen him. I cannot describe the thrill that seized upon me, when, close at the mouth of the tunnel, I saw the appearance of a man, with his left sleeve across his eyes, passionately waving his right arm.

The nameless horror that oppressed me passed in a moment, for in a moment I saw that this appearance of a man was a man indeed, and that there was a little group of other men, standing at a short distance, to whom he seemed to be rehearsing the gesture he made. The Danger-light was not yet lighted. Against its shaft, a little low hut, entirely new to me, had been made of some wooden supports and tarpaulin. It looked no bigger than a bed.

With an irresistible sense that something was wrong,—with a flashing self-reproachful fear that fatal mischief had come of my leaving the man there, and causing no one to be sent to overlook or correct what he did,—I descended the notched path with all the speed I could make.

"What is the matter?" I asked the men.

"Signal-man killed this morning, sir."

"Not the man belonging to that box?"

"Yes, sir."

"Not the man I know?"

"You will recognise him, sir, if you knew him," said the man who spoke for the others, solemnly uncovering his own head, and raising an end of the tarpaulin, "for his face is quite composed."

"O, how did this happen, how did this happen?" I asked, turning from one to another as the hut closed in again.

"He was cut down by an engine, sir. No man in England knew his work better. But somehow he was not clear of the outer rail. It was just at broad day. He had struck the light, and had the lamp in his hand. As the engine came out of the tunnel, his back was towards her, and she cut him down. That man drove her, and was showing how it happened. Show the gentleman, Tom."

The man, who wore a rough dark dress, stepped back to his former place at the mouth of the tunnel.

"Coming round the curve in the tunnel, sir," he said, "I saw him at the end, like as if I saw him down a perspective-glass. There was no time to check speed, and I knew him to be very careful. As he didn't seem to take heed of the whistle, I shut it off when we were running down upon him, and called to him as loud as I could call."

"What did you say?"

"I said, 'Below there! Look out! Look out! For God's sake, clear the way!'"

I started.

"Ah! it was a dreadful time, sir. I never left off calling to him.

I put this arm before my eyes not to see, and I waved this arm to the last; but it was no use."

Without prolonging the narrative to dwell on any one of its curious circumstances more than on any other, I may, in closing it, point out the coincidence that the warning of the Engine-Driver included, not only the words which the unfortunate Signal-man had repeated to me as haunting him, but also the words which I myself—not he—had attached, and that only in my own mind, to the gesticulation he had imitated.

Schalken the Painter

By J. Sheridan le Fanu

For he is not a man as I am that
we should come together; neither is
there any that might lay his hand
upon us both. Let him, therefore,
take his rod away from me, and let
not his fear terrify me.

There exists, at this moment, in good preservation a remarkable work of Schalken's. The curious management of its lights constitutes, as usual in his pieces, the chief apparent merit of the picture. I say *apparent*, for in its subject, and not in its handling, however exquisite, consists its real value. The picture represents the interior of what might be a chamber in some antique religious building; and its foreground is occupied by a female figure, in a species of white robe, part of which is arranged so as to form a veil.

The dress, however, is not that of any religious order. In her hand the figure bears a lamp, by which alone her figure and face are illuminated; and her features wear such an arch smile, as well becomes a pretty woman when practising some prankish roguery; in the background, and, excepting where the dim red light of an expiring fire serves to define the form, in total shadow, stands the figure of a man dressed in the old Flemish fashion, in an attitude of alarm, his hand being placed upon the hilt of his sword, which he appears to be in the act of drawing.

There are some pictures, which impress one, I know not how,

with a conviction that they represent not the mere ideal shapes and combinations which have floated through the imagination of the artist, but scenes, faces, and situations which have actually existed. There is in that strange picture, something that stamps it as the representation of a reality.

And such in truth it is, for it faithfully records a remarkable and mysterious occurrence, and perpetuates, in the face of the female figure, which occupies the most prominent place in the design, an accurate portrait of Rose Velderkaust, the niece of Gerard Douw, the first, and, I believe, the only love of Godfrey Schalken. My great grandfather knew the painter well; and from Schalken himself he learned the fearful story of the painting, and from him too he ultimately received the picture itself as a bequest. The story and the picture have become heirlooms in my family, and having described the latter, I shall, if you please, attempt to relate the tradition which has descended with the canvas.

There are few forms on which the mantle of romance hangs more ungracefully than upon that of the uncouth Schalken—the boorish but most cunning worker in oils, whose pieces delight the critics of our day almost as much as his manners disgusted the refined of his own; and yet this man, so rude, so dogged, so slovenly, in the midst of his celebrity, had in his obscure, but happier days, played the hero in a wild romance of mystery and passion.

When Schalken studied under the immortal Gerard Douw, he was a very young man; and in spite of his phlegmatic temperament, he at once fell over head and ears in love with the beautiful niece of his wealthy master. Rose Velderkaust was still younger than he, having not yet attained her seventeenth year, and, if tradition speaks truth, possessed all the soft and dimpling charms of the fair, light-haired Flemish maidens. The young painter loved honestly and fervently. His frank adoration was rewarded. He declared his love, and extracted a faltering confession in return. He was the happiest and proudest painter in all Christendom. But there was somewhat to dash his elation; he was poor and undistinguished. He dared not ask old Gerard for the hand of his sweet ward. He must first win a reputation and a competence.

There were, therefore, many dread uncertainties and cold days before him; he had to fight his way against sore odds. But he had won the heart of dear Rose Velderkaust, and that was half the battle. It is needless to say his exertions were redoubled, and his lasting celebrity proves that his industry was not unrewarded by success.

These ardent labours, and worse still, the hopes that elevated and beguiled them, were however, destined to experience a sudden interruption—of a character so strange and mysterious as to baffle all inquiry and to throw over the events themselves a shadow of preternatural horror.

Schalken had one evening outstayed all his fellow-pupils, and still pursued his work in the deserted room. As the daylight was fast falling, he laid aside his colours, and applied himself to the completion of a sketch on which he had expressed extraordinary pains. It was a religious composition, and represented the temptations of a pot-bellied Saint Anthony. The young artist, however destitute of elevation, had, nevertheless, discernment enough to be dissatisfied with his own work, and many were the patient erasures and improvements which saint and devil underwent, yet all in vain. The large, old-fashioned room was silent, and, with the exception of himself, quite emptied of its usual inmates.

An hour had thus passed away, nearly two, without any improved result. Daylight had already declined, and twilight was deepening into the darkness of night. The patience of the young painter was exhausted, and he stood before his unfinished production, angry and mortified, one hand buried in the folds of his long hair, and the other holding the piece of charcoal which had so ill-performed its office, and which he now rubbed, without much regard to the sable streaks it produced, with irritable pressure upon his ample Flemish inexpressibles. "Curse the subject!" said the young man aloud; "curse the picture, the devils, the saint—"

At this moment a short, sudden sniff uttered close beside him made the artist turn sharply round, and he now, for the first time, became aware that his labours had been overlooked by a stranger. Within about a yard and half, and rather behind him, there stood the figure of an elderly man in a cloak and broad-brimmed, conical hat; in his hand, which was protected with a heavy gauntlet-shaped glove, he carried a long ebony walking-stick, surmounted with what appeared, as it glittered dimly in the twilight, to be a massive head of gold, and upon his breast, through the folds of the cloak, there shone the links of a rich chain of the same metal. The room was so obscure that nothing further of the appearance of the figure could be ascertained, and his hat threw his features into profound shadow.

It would not have been easy to conjecture the age of the intruder; but a quantity of dark hair escaping from beneath this sombre hat, as well as his firm and upright carriage served to indicate that his years could not yet exceed threescore, or thereabouts. There was an air of gravity and importance about the garb of the person, and something indescribably odd, I might say awful, in the perfect, stone-like stillness of the figure, that effectually checked the testy comment which had at once risen to the lips of the irritated artist. He, therefore, as soon as he had sufficiently recovered his surprise, asked the stranger, civilly, to be seated, and desired to know if he had any message to leave for his master.

"Tell Gerard Douw," said the unknown, without altering his attitude in the smallest degree, "that Minheer Vanderhausen, of Rotterdam, desires to speak with him on tomorrow evening at this hour, and if he please, in this room, upon matters of weight; that is all."

The stranger, having finished this message, turned abruptly, and, with a quick, but silent step quitted the room, before Schalken had time to say a word in reply. The young man felt a curiosity to see in what direction the burgher of Rotterdam would turn, on quitting the studio, and for that purpose he went directly to the window which commanded the door. A lobby of considerable extent intervened between the inner door of the painter's room and the street entrance, so that Schalken occupied the post of observation before the old man could possibly have reached the street. He watched in vain, however. There was no other mode of exit. Had the queer old man vanished, or was he lurking about the recesses of the lobby for some sinister purpose?

This last suggestion filled the mind of Schalken with a vague uneasiness, which was so unaccountably intense as to make him alike afraid to remain in the room alone, and reluctant to pass through the lobby. However, with an effort which appeared very disproportioned to the occasion, he summoned resolution to leave the room, and, having locked the door and thrust the key in his pocket, without looking to the right or left, he traversed the passage which had so recently, perhaps still, contained the person of his mysterious visitant, scarcely venturing to breathe till he had arrived in the open street.

"Minheer Vanderhausen!" said Gerard Douw within himself, as the appointed hour approached, "Minheer Vanderhausen, of Rotterdam! I never heard of the man till yesterday. What can he want of me? A portrait, perhaps, to be painted; or a poor relation to be apprenticed; or a collection to be valued; or—pshaw! there's no one in Rotterdam to leave me a legacy. Well, whatever the business may be, we shall soon know it all."

It was now the close of day, and again every easel, except that of Schalken, was deserted. Gerard Douw was pacing the apartment with the restless step of impatient expectation, sometimes pausing to glance over the work of one of his absent pupils, but more frequently placing himself at the window, from whence he might observe the passengers who threaded the obscure by-street in which his studio was placed.

"Said you not, Godfrey," exclaimed Douw, after a long and fruitful gaze from his post of observation, and turning to Schalken, "that the hour he appointed was about seven by the clock of the *Stadhouse*?"

"It had just told seven when I first saw him, sir," answered the student.

"The hour is close at hand, then," said the master, consulting a horologe as large and as round as an orange. "Minheer Vanderhausen from Rotterdam—is it not so?"

"Such was the name."

"And an elderly man, richly clad?" pursued Douw, musingly.

"As well as I might see," replied his pupil; "he could not be young, nor yet very old, neither; and his dress was rich and grave, as might become a citizen of wealth and consideration."

At this moment the sonorous boom of the *Stadhouse* clock told, stroke after stroke, the hour of seven; the eyes of both master and student were directed to the door; and it was not until the last peal of the bell had ceased to vibrate, that Douw exclaimed——

"So, so; we shall have his worship presently, that is, if he means to keep his hour; if not, you may wait for him, Godfrey, if you court his acquaintance. But what, after all, if it should prove but a mummery got up by Vankarp, or some such wag? I wish you had run all risks, and cudgelled the old *burgomaster* soundly. I'd wager a dozen of Rhenish, his worship would have unmasked, and pleaded old acquaintance in a trice."

"Here he comes, sir," said Schalken, in a low monitory tone; and instantly, upon turning towards the door, Gerard Douw observed the same figure which had, on the day before, so unexpectedly greeted his pupil Schalken.

There was something in the air of the figure which at once satisfied the painter that there was no masquerading in the case, and that he really stood in the presence of a man of worship; and so, without hesitation, he doffed his cap, and courteously saluting the stranger, requested him to be seated. The visitor waved his hand slightly, as if in acknowledgment of the courtesy, but remained standing.

"I have the honour to see Minheer Vanderhausen of Rotterdam?" said Gerard Douw.

"The same," was the laconic reply of his visitor.

"I understand your worship desires to speak with me," continued Douw, "and I am here by appointment to wait your commands."

"Is that a man of trust?" said Vanderhausen, turning towards Schalken, who stood at a little distance behind his master.

"Certainly," replied Gerard.

"Then let him take this box, and get the nearest jeweller or goldsmith to value its contents, and let him return hither with a certificate of the valuation."

At the same time, he placed a small case about nine inches square in the hands of Gerard Douw, who was as much amazed at its weight as at the strange abruptness with which it was handed to him. In accordance with the wishes of the stranger, he delivered it into the hands of Schalken, and repeating his direction, despatched him upon the mission.

Schalken disposed his precious charge securely beneath the folds of his cloak, and rapidly traversing two or three narrow streets, he stopped at a corner house, the lower part of which was then occupied by the shop of a Jewish goldsmith. He entered the shop, and calling the little Hebrew into the obscurity of its back recesses, he proceeded to lay before him Vanderhausen's casket.

On being examined by the light of a lamp, it appeared entirely cased with lead, the outer surface of which was much scraped and soiled, and nearly white with age. This having been partially removed, there appeared beneath a box of some hard wood; which also they forced open and after the removal of two or three folds of linen, they discovered its contents to be a mass of golden ingots, closely packed, and, as the Jew declared, of the most perfect quality.

Every ingot underwent the scrutiny of the little Jew, who seemed to feel an epicurean delight in touching and testing these morsels of the glorious metal; and each one of them was replaced in its berth with the exclamation: "*Mein Gott*, how very perfect! not one grain of alloy—beautiful, beautiful!" The task was at length finished, and the Jew certified under his hand the value of the ingots submitted to his examination, to amount to many thousand *rix*-dollars. With the desired document in his pocket, and the rich box of gold carefully pressed under his arm, and concealed by his cloak, he retraced his way, and entering the studio, found his master and the stranger in close conference. Schalken had no sooner left the room, in order to execute the commission he had taken in charge, than Vanderhausen addressed Gerard Douw in the following terms:——

"I cannot tarry with you tonight more than a few minutes, and so I shall shortly tell you the matter upon which I come. You visited the town of Rotterdam some four months ago, and then I saw in the church of St. Lawrence your niece, Rose Velderkaust. I desire to marry her; and if I satisfy you that I am wealthier than any husband you can dream of for her, I expect that you will forward my suit with your authority. If you approve my proposal, you must close with it here and now, for I cannot wait for calculations and delays."

Gerard Douw was hugely astonished by the nature of Minheer Vanderhausen's communication, but he did not venture to express surprise; for besides the motives supplied by prudence and politeness, the painter experienced a kind of chill and oppression like that which is said to intervene when one is placed in unconscious proximity with the object of a natural antipathy—an undefined but overpowering sensation, while standing in the presence of the eccentric stranger, which made him very unwilling to say anything which might reasonably offend him.

"I have no doubt," said Gerard, after two or three prefatory hems, "that the alliance which you propose would prove alike advantageous and honourable to my niece; but you must be aware that she has a will of her own, and may not acquiesce in what *we* may design for her advantage."

"Do not seek to deceive me, sir painter," said Vanderhausen; "you are her guardian—she is your ward—she is mine if *you* like to make her so."

The man of Rotterdam moved forward a little as he spoke, and Gerard Douw, he scarce knew why, inwardly prayed for the speedy return of Schalken.

"I desire," said the mysterious gentleman, "to place in your hands at once an evidence of my wealth, and a security for my liberal dealing with your niece. The lad will return in a minute or two with a sum in value five times the fortune which she has a right to expect from her husband. This shall lie in your hands, together with her dowry, and you may apply the united sum as suits her interest best; it shall be all exclusively hers while she lives: is that liberal?"

Douw assented, and inwardly acknowledged that fortune had been extraordinarily kind to his niece; the stranger, he thought, must be both wealthy and generous, and such an offer was not to be despised, though made by a humorist, and one of no very prepossessing presence. Rose had no very high pretensions for she had but a modest dowry, which she owed entirely to the generosity of her uncle; neither had she any right to raise exceptions on the score of birth, for her own origin was far from splendid, and as the other objections, Gerald resolved, and indeed, by the usages of the time, was warranted in resolving, not to listen to them for a moment.

"Sir" said he, addressing the stranger, "your offer is liberal, and whatever hesitation I may feel in closing with it immediately, arises solely from my not having the honour of knowing anything of your family or station. Upon these points you can, of course, satisfy me without difficulty?'

"As to my respectability," said the stranger, drily, "you must take that for granted at present; pester me with no inquiries; you can discover nothing more about me than I choose to make known. You shall have sufficient security for my respectability-my word, if you are honourable: if you are sordid, my gold."

"A testy old gentleman," thought Douw, "he must have his own way; but, all things considered, I am not justified to declining his offer. I will not pledge myself unnecessarily, however."

"You will not pledge yourself unnecessarily," said Vanderhausen, strangely uttering the very words which had just floated through the mind of his companion; "but you will do so if it is necessary, I presume; and I will show you that I consider it indispensable. If the gold I mean to leave in your hands satisfy you, and if you don't wish my proposal to be at once withdrawn, you must, before I leave this room, write your name to this engagement."

Having thus spoken, he placed a paper in the hands of the master, the contents of which expressed an engagement entered into by Gerard Douw, to give to Wilken Vanderhausen of Rotterdam, in marriage, Rose Velderkaust, and so forth, within one week of the date thereof. While the painter was employed in reading this covenant, by the light of a twinkling oil lamp in the far wall of the room, Schalken, as we have stated, entered the studio, and having delivered the box and the valuation of the Jew, into the hands of the stranger, he was about to retire, when Vanderhausen called to him to wait; and, presenting the case and the certificate to Gerard Douw, he paused in silence until he had satisfied himself, by an inspection of both, respecting the value of the pledge left in his hands. At length he said—

"Are you content?"

The painter said he would fain have another day to consider.

"Not an hour," said the suitor, apathetically.

"Well then," said Douw, with a sore effort, "I am content, it is a bargain."

"Then sign at once," said Vanderhausen, "for I am weary."

At the same time he produced a small case of writing materials, and Gerard signed the important document.

"Let this youth witness the covenant," said the old man; and Godfrey Schalken unconsciously attested the instrument which forever bereft him of his dear Rose Velderkaust.

The compact being thus completed, the strange visitor folded up the paper, and stowed it safely in an inner pocket.

"I will visit you tomorrow night at nine o'clock, at your own house, Gerard Douw, and will see the object of our contract;" and so saying Wilken Vanderhausen moved stiffly, but rapidly, out of the room.

Schalken, eager to resolve his doubts, had placed himself by the window, in order to watch the street entrance; but the experiment served only to support his suspicions, for the old man did not issue from the door. This was *very* strange, odd, nay fearful. He and his master returned together, and talked but little on the way, for each had his own subjects of reflection, of anxiety, and of hope. Schalken, however, did not know the ruin which menaced his dearest projects.

Gerard Douw knew nothing of the attachment which had sprung up between his pupil and his niece; and even if he had, it is doubtful whether he would have regarded its existence as any serious obstruction to the wishes of Minheer Vanderhausen. Marriages were then and there matters of traffic and calculation; and it would have appeared as absurd in the eyes of the guardian to make a mutual attachment an essential element in a contract of the sort, as it would have been to draw up his bonds and receipts in the language of romance.

The painter, however, did not communicate to his niece the important step which he had taken in her behalf, a forbearance caused not by any anticipated opposition on her part, but solely by a ludicrous consciousness that if she were to ask him for a description of her destined bridegroom, he would be forced to confess that he had not once seen his face, and if called upon, would find it absolutely impossible to identify him. Upon the next day, Gerard Douw, after dinner, called his niece to him and having scanned her person with an air of satisfaction, he took her hand, and looking upon her pretty innocent face with a smile of kindness, he said:——

"Rose, my girl, that face of yours will make your fortune." Rose blushed and smiled. "Such faces and such tempers seldom go together, and when they do, the compound is a love charm, few heads or hearts can resist; trust me, you will soon be a bride, girl. But this is trifling, and I am pressed for time, so make ready the large room by eight o'clock tonight, and give directions for supper at nine. I expect a friend; and observe me, child, do you trick yourself out handsomely. I will not have him think us poor or sluttish."

With these words he left her, and took his way to the room in which his pupils worked.

When the evening closed in, Gerard called Schalken, who was about to take his departure to his own obscure and comfortless lodgings, and asked him to come home and sup with Rose and Vanderhausen. The invitation was, of course, accepted and Gerard Douw and his pupil soon found themselves in the handsome and, even then, antique chamber, which had been prepared for the reception of the stranger. A cheerful wood fire blazed in the hearth, a little at one side of which an old-fashioned table, which shone in the firelight like burnished gold, was awaiting the supper, for which preparations were going forward; and ranged with exact regularity, stood the tall-backed chairs, whose ungracefulness was more than compensated by their comfort.

The little party, consisting of Rose, her uncle, and the artist, awaited the arrival of the expected visitor with considerable impatience. Nine o'clock at length came, and with it a summons at the street door, which being speedily answered, was followed by a slow and emphatic tread upon the staircase; the steps moved heavily across the lobby, the door of the room in which the party we have described were assembled slowly opened, and there entered a figure which startled, almost appalled, the phlegmatic Dutchmen, and nearly made Rose scream with terror. It was the form, and arrayed in the garb of Minheer Vanderhausen; the air, the gait, the height were the same, but the features had never been seen by any of the party before.

The stranger stopped at the door of the room, and displayed his form and face completely. He wore a dark-coloured cloth cloak, which was short and full, not falling quite to his knees; his legs were cased in dark purple silk stockings, and his shoes were adorned with roses of the same colour. The opening of the cloak in front showed the under-suit to consist of some very dark, perhaps sable material, and his hands were enclosed in a pair of heavy leather gloves, which ran up considerably above the wrist, in the manner of a gauntlet. In one hand he carried his walking-stick and his hat, which he had removed, and the other hung heavily by his side. A quantity of grizzled hair descended in long tresses from his head, and rested upon the plaits of a stiff ruff, which effectually concealed his neck.

So far all was well; but the face!—all the flesh of the face was coloured with the bluish leaden hue, which is sometimes produced by metallic medicines, administered in excessive quantities; the eyes showed an undue proportion of muddy white, and had a certain indefinable character of insanity; the hue of the lips bearing the usual relation to that of the face, was, consequently, nearly black; and the entire character of the face was sensual, malignant, and even satanic. It was remarkable that the worshipful stranger suffered as little as possible of his flesh to appear, and that during his visit he did not once remove his gloves. Having stood for some moments at the door, Gerard Douw at length found breath and collectedness to bid him welcome, and with a mute inclination of the head, the stranger stepped forward into the room.

There was something indescribably odd, even horrible, about all his motions, something undefinable, that was unnatural, unhuman; it was as if the limbs were guided and directed by a spirit unused to the management of bodily machinery. The stranger spoke hardly at all during his visit, which did not exceed half an hour; and the host himself could scarcely muster courage enough to utter the few necessary salutations and courtesies; and, indeed, such was the nervous terror which the presence of Vanderhausen inspired, that very little would have made all his entertainers fly in downright panic from the room. They had not so far lost all self-possession, however, as to fail to observe two strange peculiarities of their visitor.

During his stay his eyelids did not once close, or, indeed, move in the slightest degree; and farther, there was a deathlike stillness in his whole person, owing to the absence of the heaving motion of the chest, caused by the process of respiration. These two peculiarities, though when told they may appear trifling, produced a very striking and unpleasant effect when seen and observed. Vanderhausen at length relieved the painter of Leyden of his inauspicious presence; and with no trifling sense of relief the little party heard the street door close after him.

"Dear uncle," said Rose, "what a frightful man! I would not see him again for the wealth of the States."

"Tush, foolish girl," said Douw, whose sensations were anything but comfortable. "A man may be as ugly as the devil, and yet, if his heart and actions are good, he is worth all the pretty-faced perfumed puppies that walk the Mall. Rose, my girl, it is very true he has not thy pretty face, but I know him to be wealthy and liberal; and were he ten times more ugly, these two virtues would be enough to counter balance all his deformity, and if not sufficient actually to alter the shape and hue of his features, at least enough to prevent one thinking them so much amiss."

"Do you know, uncle," said Rose, "when I saw him standing at the door, I could not get it out of my head that I saw the old painted wooden figure that used to frighten me so much in the Church of St. Laurence at Rotterdam."

Gerard laughed, though he could not help inwardly acknowledging the justness of the comparison. He was resolved, however, as far as he could, to check his niece's disposition to dilate upon the ugliness of her intended bridegroom, although he was not a little pleased, as well as puzzled, to observe that she appeared totally exempt from that mysterious dread of the stranger which, he could not disguise it from himself, considerably affected him, as also his pupil Godfrey Schalken.

Early on the next day there arrived, from various quarters of the town, rich presents of silks, velvets, jewellery, and so forth, for Rose; and also a packet directed to Gerard Douw, which on being opened, was found to contain a contract of marriage, formally drawn up, between Wilken Vanderhausen of the *Boom-quay*, in Rotterdam, and Rose Velderkaust of Leyden, niece to Gerard Douw, master in the art of painting, also of the same city; and containing engagements on the part of Vanderhausen to make settlements upon his bride, far more splendid than he had before led her guardian to believe likely, and which were to be secured to her use in the most unexceptionable manner possible—the money being placed in the hand of Gerard Douw himself.

I have no sentimental scenes to describe, no cruelty of guardians, no magnanimity of wards, no agonies, or transport of lovers. The record I have to make is one of sordidness, levity, and heartlessness. In less than a week after the first interview which we have just described, the contract of marriage was fulfilled, and Schalken saw the prize which he would have risked existence to secure, carried off in solemn pomp by his repulsive rival. For two or three days he absented himself from the school; he then returned and worked, if with less cheerfulness, with far more dogged resolution than before; the stimulus of love had given place to that of ambition. Months passed away, and, contrary to his expectation, and, indeed, to the direct promise of the parties, Gerard Douw heard nothing of his niece or her worshipful spouse. The interest of the money, which was to have been demanded in quarterly sums, lay unclaimed in his hands.

He began to grow extremely uneasy. Minheer Vanderhausen's direction in Rotterdam he was fully possessed of; after some irresolution he finally determined to journey thither—a trifling undertaking, and easily accomplished—and thus to satisfy himself of the safety and comfort of his ward, for whom he entertained an honest and strong affection. His search was in vain, however; no one in Rotterdam had ever heard of Minheer Vanderhausen. Gerard Douw left not a house in the *Boom-quay* untried, but all in vain. No one could give him any information whatever touching the object of his inquiry, and he was obliged to return to Leyden nothing wiser and far more anxious, than when he had left it.

On his arrival he hastened to the establishment from which Vanderhausen had hired the lumbering, though, considering the times, most luxurious vehicle, which the bridal party had employed to convey them to Rotterdam. From the driver of this machine he learned, that having proceeded by slow stages, they had late in the evening approached Rotterdam; but that before they entered the city, and while yet nearly a mile from it, a small party of men, soberly clad, and after the old fashion, with peaked beards and moustaches, standing in the centre of the road, obstructed the further progress of the carriage. The driver reined in his horses, much fearing, from the obscurity of the hour, and the loneliness, of the road, that some mischief was intended.

His fears were, however, somewhat allayed by his observing that these strange men carried a large litter, of an antique shape, and which they immediately set down upon the pavement, whereupon the bridegroom, having opened the coach-door from within, descended, and having assisted his bride to do likewise, led her, weeping bitterly, and wringing her hands, to the litter, which they both entered. It was then raised by the men who surrounded it, and speedily carried towards the city, and before it had proceeded very far, the darkness concealed it from the view of the Dutch coachman. In the inside of the vehicle he found a purse, whose contents more than thrice paid the hire of the carriage and man. He saw and could tell nothing more of Minheer Vanderhausen and his beautiful lady.

This mystery was a source of profound anxiety and even grief to Gerard Douw. There was evidently fraud in the dealing of Vanderhausen with him, though for what purpose committed he could not imagine. He greatly doubted how far it was possible for a man possessing such a countenance to be anything but a villain, and every day that passed without his hearing from or of his niece, instead of inducing him to forget his fears, on the contrary tended more and more to aggravate them. The loss of her cheerful society tended also to depress his spirits; and in order to dispel the gloom, which often crept upon his mind after his daily occupations were over, he was wont frequently to ask Schalken to accompany him home, and share his otherwise solitary supper.

One evening, the painter and his pupil were sitting by the fire, having accomplished a comfortable meal, and had yielded to the silent and delicious melancholy of digestion, when their ruminations were disturbed by a loud sound at the street door, as if occasioned by some person rushing and scrambling vehemently against it. A domestic had run without delay to ascertain the cause of the disturbance, and they heard him twice or thrice interrogate the applicant for admission, but without eliciting any other answer but a sustained reiteration of the sounds. They heard him then open the hall-door, and immediately there followed a light and rapid tread on the staircase.

Schalken advanced towards the door. It opened before he reached it, and Rose rushed into the room. She looked wild, fierce and haggard with terror and exhaustion, but her dress surprised them as much as even her unexpected appearance. It consisted of a kind of white woollen wrapper, made close about the neck, and descending to the very ground. It was much deranged and travel-soiled. The poor creature had hardly entered the chamber when she fell senseless on the floor. With some difficulty they succeeded in reviving her, and on recovering her senses, she instantly exclaimed, in a tone of terror rather than mere impatience:—

"Wine! wine! quickly, or I'm lost!"

Astonished and almost scared at the strange agitation in which the call was made, they at once administered to her wishes, and she drank some wine with a haste and eagerness which surprised them. She had hardly swallowed it, when she exclaimed, with the same urgency:

"Food, for God's sake, food, at once, or I perish."

A considerable fragment of a roast joint was upon the table, and Schalken immediately began to cut some, but he was anticipated, for no sooner did she see it than she caught it, a more than mortal image of famine, and with her hands, and even with her teeth, she tore off the flesh, and swallowed it. When the paroxysm of hunger had been a little appeased, she appeared on a sudden overcome with shame, or it may have been that other more agitating thoughts overpowered and scared her, for she began to weep bitterly and to wring her hands.

"Oh, send for a minister of God," said she; "I am not safe till he comes; send for him speedily."

Gerard Douw despatched a messenger instantly, and prevailed on his niece to allow him to surrender his bed chamber to her use. He also persuaded her to retire to it at once to rest; her consent was extorted upon the condition that they would not leave her for a moment.

"Oh that the holy man were here," she said; "he can deliver me: the dead and the living can never be one: God has forbidden it."

With these mysterious words she surrendered herself to their guidance, and they proceeded to the chamber which Gerard Douw had assigned to her use.

"Do not, do not leave me for a moment," said she; "I am lost forever if you do."

Gerard Douw's chamber was approached through a spacious apartment, which they were now about to enter. He and Schalken each carried a candle, so that a sufficiency of light was cast upon all surrounding objects. They were now entering the large chamber, which as I have said, communicated with Douw's apartment, when Rose suddenly stopped, and, in a whisper which thrilled them both with horror, she said:——

"Oh, God! he is here! he is here! See, see! there he goes!"

She pointed towards the door of the inner room, and Schalken thought he saw a shadowy and ill-defined form gliding into that apartment. He drew his sword, and, raising the candle so as to throw its light with increased distinctness upon the objects in the room, he entered the chamber into which the shadow had glided. No figure was there—nothing but the furniture which belonged to the room, and yet he could not be deceived as to the fact that something had moved before them into the chamber. A sickening dread came upon him, and the cold perspiration broke out in heavy drops upon his forehead; nor was he more composed, when he heard the increased urgency and agony of entreaty, with which Rose implored them not to leave her for a moment.

"I saw him," said she; "he's here. I cannot be deceived; I know him; he's by me; he is with me; he's in the room. Then, for God's sake, as you would save me, do not stir from beside me."

They at length prevailed upon her to lie down upon the bed, where she continued to urge them to stay by her. She frequently uttered incoherent sentences, repeating, again and again, "the dead and the living cannot be one: God has forbidden it." And then again, "Rest to the wakeful—sleep to the sleep-walkers." These and such mysterious and broken sentences, she continued to utter until the clergyman arrived. Gerard Douw began to fear, naturally enough, that terror or ill-treatment, had unsettled the poor girl's intellect, and he half suspected, by the suddenness of her appearance, the unseasonableness of the hour, and above all, from the wildness and terror of her manner, that she had made her escape from some place of confinement for lunatics, and was in imminent fear of pursuit.

He resolved to summon medical advice as soon as the mind of his niece had been in some measure set at rest by the offices of the clergyman whose attendance she had so earnestly desired; and until this object had been attained, he did not venture to put any questions to her, which might possibly, by reviving painful or horrible recollections, increase her agitation. The clergyman soon arrived—a man of ascetic countenance and venerable age—one whom Gerard Douw respected very much, forasmuch as he was a veteran polemic, though one perhaps more dreaded as a combatant than beloved as a Christian—of pure morality, subtle brain, and frozen heart. He entered the chamber which communicated with that in which Rose reclined and immediately on his arrival, she requested him to pray for her, as for one who lay in the hands of Satan, and who could hope for deliverance only from heaven.

That you may distinctly understand all the circumstances of the event which I am going to describe, it is necessary to state the relative position of the parties who were engaged in it. The old clergyman and Schalken were in the anteroom of which I have already spoken; Rose lay in the inner chamber, the door of which was open; and by the side of the bed, at her urgent desire, stood her guardian; a candle burned in the bedchamber, and three were lighted in the outer apartment. The old man now cleared his voice as if about to commence, but before he had time to begin, a sudden gust of air blew out the candle which served to illuminate the room in which the poor girl lay, and she, with hurried alarm, exclaimed:——

"Godfrey, bring in another candle; the darkness is unsafe."

Gerard Douw forgetting for the moment her repeated injunctions, in the immediate impulse, stepped from the bedchamber into the other, in order to supply what she desired.

"Oh God! do not go, dear uncle," shrieked the unhappy girl—and at the same time she sprung from the bed, and darted after him, in order, by her grasp, to detain him. But the warning came too late, for scarcely had he passed the threshold, and hardly had his niece had time to utter the startling exclamation, when the door which divided the two rooms closed violently after him, as if swung by a strong blast of wind. Schalken and he both rushed to the door, but their united and desperate efforts could not avail so much as to shake it. Shriek after shriek burst from the inner chamber, with all the piercing loudness of despairing terror. Schalken and Douw applied every nerve to force open the door; but all in vain.

There was no sound of struggling from within, but the screams seemed to increase in loudness, and at the same time they heard the bolts of the latticed window withdrawn, and the window itself grated upon the sill as if thrown open. One *last* shriek, so long and piercing and agonized as to be scarcely human, swelled from the room, and suddenly there followed a death-like silence. A light step was heard crossing the floor, as if from the bed to the window; and almost at the same instant the door gave way, and, yielding to the pressure of the external applicants, nearly precipitated them into the room. It was empty. The window was open, and Schalken sprung to a chair and gazed out upon the street and canal below. He saw no form, but he saw, or thought he saw, the waters of the broad canal beneath settling ring after ring in heavy circles, as if a moment before disturbed by the submission of some ponderous body.

No trace of Rose was ever after found, nor was anything certain respecting her mysterious wooer discovered or even suspected—no clue whereby to trace the intricacies of the labyrinth and to arrive at its solution, presented itself. But an incident occurred, which, though it will not be received by our rational readers in lieu of evidence, produced nevertheless a strong and a lasting impression upon the mind of Schalken.

Many years after the events which we have detailed, Schalken, then residing far away received an intimation of his father's death, and of his intended burial upon a fixed day in the church of Rotterdam. It was necessary that a very considerable journey should be performed by the funeral procession, which as it will be readily believed, was not very numerously attended. Schalken with difficulty arrived in Rotterdam late in the day upon which the funeral was appointed to take place. It had not then arrived. Evening closed in, and still it did not appear.

Schalken strolled down to the church; he found it open; notice of the arrival of the funeral had been given, and the vault in which the body was to be laid had been opened. The sexton, on seeing a well-dressed gentleman, whose object was to attend the expected obsequies, pacing the aisle of the church, hospitably invited him to share with him the comforts of a blazing fire, which, as was his custom in winter time upon such occasions, he had kindled in the hearth of a chamber in which he was accustomed to await the arrival of such grisly guests and which communicated, by a flight of steps, with the vault below. In this chamber, Schalken and his entertainer seated themselves; and the sexton, after some fruitless attempts to engage his guest in conversation, was obliged to apply himself to his tobacco-pipe and can, to solace his solitude.

In spite of his grief and cares, the fatigues of a rapid journey of nearly forty hours gradually overcame the mind and body of Godfrey Schalken, and he sank into a deep sleep, from which he awakened by someone's shaking him gently by the shoulder. He first thought that the old sexton had called him, but *he* was no longer in the room. He roused himself, and as soon as he could clearly see what was around him, he perceived a female form, clothed in a kind of light robe of white, part of which was so disposed as to form a veil, and in her hand she carried a lamp. She was moving rather away from him, in the direction of the flight of steps which conducted towards the vaults.

Schalken felt a vague alarm at the sight of this figure and at the same time an irresistible impulse to follow its guidance. He followed it towards the vaults, but when it reached the head of the stairs, he paused; the figure paused also, and, turning gently round, displayed, by the light of the lamp it carried, the face and features of his first love, Rose Velderkaust.

There was nothing horrible, or even sad, in the countenance. On the contrary, it wore the same arch smile which used to enchant the artist long before in his happy days. A feeling of awe and interest, too intense to be resisted, prompted him to follow the spectre, if spectre it were. She descended the stairs-he followed—and turning to the left, through a narrow passage, she led him, to his infinite surprise, into what appeared to be an old-fashioned Dutch apartment, such as the pictures of Gerard Douw have served to immortalize. Abundance of costly antique furniture was disposed about the room, and in one corner stood a four-post bed, with heavy black cloth curtains around it; the figure frequently turned towards him with the same arch smile; and when she came to the side of the bed, she drew the curtains, and, by the light of the lamp, which she held towards its contents, she disclosed to the horror-stricken painter, sitting bolt upright in the bed, the livid and demoniac form of Vanderhausen.

Schalken had hardly seen him, when he fell senseless upon the floor, where he lay until discovered, on the next morning, by persons employed in closing the passages into the vaults. He was lying in a cell of considerable size, which had not been disturbed for a long time, and he had fallen beside a large coffin, which was supported upon small pillars, a security against the attacks of vermin.

To his dying day Schalken was satisfied of the reality of the vision which he had witnessed, and he has left behind him a curious evidence of the impression which it wrought upon his fancy, in a painting executed shortly after the event I have narrated, and which is valuable as exhibiting not only the peculiarities which have made Schalken's pictures sought after, but even more so as presenting a portrait of his early love, Rose Velderkaust, whose mysterious fate must always remain matter of speculation.

The Screaming Skull

FROM *WANDERING GHOSTS*

by F. Marion Crawford

I have often heard it scream. No, I am not nervous, I am not imaginative, and I never believed in ghosts, unless that thing is one. Whatever it is, it hates me almost as much as it hated Luke Pratt, and it screams at me.

If I were you, I would never tell ugly stories about ingenious ways of killing people, for you never can tell but that someone at the table may be tired of his or her nearest and dearest. I have always blamed myself for Mrs. Pratt's death, and I suppose I was responsible for it in a way, though heaven knows I never wished her anything but long life and happiness. If I had not told that story she might be alive yet. That is why the thing screams at me, I fancy.

She was a good little woman, with a sweet temper, all things considered, and a nice gentle voice; but I remember hearing her shriek once when she thought her little boy was killed by a pistol that went off though everyone was sure that it was not loaded. It was the same scream; exactly the same, with a sort of rising quaver at the end; do you know what I mean? Unmistakable.

The truth is, I had not realized that the doctor and his wife were not on good terms. They used to bicker a bit now and then when I was here, and I often noticed that little Mrs. Pratt got very red and bit her lip hard to keep her temper, while Luke grew pale and said the most offensive things. He was that sort when he was in the nursery, I remember, and afterwards at school. He was my cousin, you know; that is how I came by this house; after he died, and his boy Charley was killed in South Africa, there were no relations left. Yes, it's a pretty little property, just the sort of thing for an old sailor like me who has taken to gardening.

One always remembers one's mistakes much more vividly than one's cleverest things, doesn't one? I've often noticed it. I was dining with the Pratts one night, when I told them the story that afterwards made so much difference. It was a wet night in November, and the sea was moaning. Hush!—if you don't speak you will hear it now. . .

Do you hear the tide? Gloomy sound, isn't it? Sometimes, about this time of year—hallo!—there it is! Don't be frightened, man—it won't eat you—it's only a noise, after all! But I'm glad you've heard it, because there are always people who think it's the wind, or my imagination, or something. You won't hear it again tonight, I fancy, for it doesn't often come more than once. Yes—that's right. Put another stick on the fire, and a little more stuff into that weak mixture you're so fond of. Do you remember old Blauklot the carpenter, on that German ship that picked us up when the *Clontarf* went to the bottom? We were hove to in a howling gale one night, as snug as you please, with no land within five hundred miles, and the ship coming up and falling off as regularly as clockwork—"*Biddy te boor beebles ashore tis night, poys!*" old Blauklot sang out, as he went off to his quarters with the sail-maker. I often think of that, now that I'm ashore for good and all.

Yes, it was on a night like this, when I was at home for a spell, waiting to take the *Olympia* out on her first trip—it was on the next voyage that she broke the record, you remember—but that dates it. Ninety-two was the year, early in November.

The weather was dirty, Pratt was out of temper, and the dinner was bad, very bad indeed, which didn't improve matters, and cold, which made it worse. The poor little lady was very unhappy about it, and insisted on making a Welsh rarebit on the table to counteract the raw turnips and the half-boiled mutton. Pratt must have had a hard day. Perhaps he had lost a patient. At all events, he was in a nasty temper.

"My wife is trying to poison me, you see!" he said. "She'll succeed some day." I saw that she was hurt, and I made believe to laugh, and said that Mrs. Pratt was much too clever to get rid of her husband in such a simple way; and then I began to tell them about Japanese tricks with spun glass and chopped horsehair and the like.

Pratt was a doctor, and knew a lot more than I did about such things, but that only put me on my mettle, and I told a story about a woman in Ireland who did for three husbands before anyone suspected foul play.

Did you never hear that tale? The fourth husband managed to keep awake and caught her, and she was hanged. How did she do it? She drugged them, and poured melted lead into their ears through a little horn funnel when they were asleep. No—that's the wind whistling. It's backing up to the southward again. I can tell by the sound. Besides, the other thing doesn't often come more than once in an evening even at this time of year—when it happened. Yes, it was in November. Poor Mrs. Pratt died suddenly in her bed not long after I dined here.

I can fix the date, because I got the news in New York by the steamer that followed the *Olympia* when I took her out on her first trip. You had the *Leofric* the same year? Yes, I remember. What a pair of old buffers we are coming to be, you and I. Nearly fifty years since we were apprentices together on the *Clontarf*. Shall you ever forget old Blauklot? "*Biddy te boor beebles ashore, poys!*" Ha, ha! Take a little more, with all that water. It's the old Hulstkamp I found in the cellar when this house came to me, the same I brought Luke from Amsterdam five-and-twenty years ago. He had never touched a drop of it. Perhaps he's sorry now, poor fellow.

Where did I leave off? I told you that Mrs. Pratt died suddenly—yes. Luke must have been lonely here after she was dead, I should think; I came to see him now and then, and he looked worn and nervous, and told me that his practice was growing too heavy for him, though he wouldn't take an assistant on any account. Years went on, and his son was killed in South Africa, and after that he began to be queer. There was something about him not like other people. I believe he kept his senses in his profession to the end; there was no complaint of his having made mad mistakes in cases, or anything of that sort, but he had a look about him——

Luke was a red-headed man with a pale face when he was young, and he was never stout; in middle age he turned a sandy grey, and after his son died he grew thinner and thinner, till his head looked like a skull with parchment stretched over it very tight, and his eyes had a sort of glare in them that was very disagreeable to look at.

He had an old dog that poor Mrs. Pratt had been fond of, and that used to follow her everywhere. He was a bulldog, and the sweetest tempered beast you ever saw, though he had a way of hitching his upper lip behind one of his fangs that frightened strangers a good deal. Sometimes, of an evening, Pratt and Bumble—that was the dog's name—used to sit and look at each other a long time, thinking about old times, I suppose, when Luke's wife used to sit in that chair you've got. That was always her place, and this was the doctor's, where I'm sitting. Bumble used to climb up by the footstool—he was old and fat by that time, and could not jump much, and his teeth were getting shaky. He would look steadily at Luke, and Luke looked steadily at the dog, his face growing more and more like a skull with two little coals for eyes; and after about five minutes or so, though it may have been less, old Bumble would suddenly begin to shake all over, and all on a sudden he would set up an awful howl, as if he had been shot, and tumble out of the easy-chair and trot away, and hide himself under the sideboard, and lie there making odd noises.

Considering Pratt's looks in those last months, the thing is not surprising, you know. I'm not nervous or imaginative, but I can quite believe he might have sent a sensitive woman into hysterics—his head looked so much like a skull in parchment.

At last I came down one day before Christmas, when my ship was in dock and I had three weeks off. Bumble was not about, and I said casually that I supposed the old dog was dead.

"Yes," Pratt answered, and I thought there was something odd in his tone even before he went on after a little pause. "I killed him," he said presently. "I could stand it no longer."

I asked what it was that Luke could not stand, though I guessed well enough.

"He had a way of sitting in her chair and glaring at me, and then howling," Luke shivered a little. "He didn't suffer at all, poor old Bumble," he went on in a hurry, as if he thought I might imagine he had been cruel. "I put *dionine* into his drink to make him sleep soundly, and then I chloroformed him gradually, so that he could not have felt suffocated even if he was dreaming. It's been quieter since then."

I wondered what he meant, for the words slipped out as if he could not help saying them. I've understood since. He meant that he did not hear that noise so often after the dog was out of the way. Perhaps he thought at first that it was old Bumble in the yard howling at the moon, though it's not that kind of noise, is it? Besides, I know what it is, if Luke didn't. It's only a noise after all, and a noise never hurt anybody yet. But he was much more imaginative than I am. No doubt there really is something about this place that I don't understand; but when I don't understand a thing, I call it a phenomenon, and I don't take it for granted that it's going to kill me, as he did. I don't understand everything, by long odds, nor do you, nor does any man who has been to sea.

We used to talk of tidal waves, for instance, and we could not account for them; now we account for them by calling them submarine earthquakes, and we branch off into fifty theories, any one of which might make earthquakes quite comprehensible if we only knew what they were. I fell in with one of them once, and the inkstand flew straight up from the table against the ceiling of my cabin. The same thing happened to Captain Lecky—I dare say you've read about it in his "Wrinkles". Very good. If that sort of thing took place ashore, in this room for instance, a nervous person would talk about spirits and levitation and fifty things that mean nothing, instead of just quietly setting it down as a "phenomenon" that has not been explained yet. My view of that voice, you see.

Besides, what is there to prove that Luke killed his wife? I would not even suggest such a thing to anyone but you. After all, there was nothing but the coincidence that poor little Mrs. Pratt died suddenly in her bed a few days after I told that story at dinner. She was not the only woman who ever died like that. Luke got the doctor over from the next parish, and they agreed that she had died of something the matter with her heart Why not? It's common enough.

Of course, there was the ladle. I never told anybody about that, and, it made me start when I found it in the cupboard in the bedroom. It was new, too—a little tinned iron ladle that had not been in the fire more than once or twice, and there was some lead in it that had been melted, and stuck to the bottom of the bowl, all grey, with hardened dross on it. But that proves nothing. A country doctor is generally a handy man, who does everything for himself, and Luke may have had a dozen reasons for melting a little lead in a ladle. He was fond of sea-fishing, for instance, and he may have cast a sinker for a night-line; perhaps it was a weight for the hall clock, or something like that. All the same, when I found it I had a rather queer sensation, because it looked so much like the thing I had described when I told them the story. Do you understand? It affected me unpleasantly, and I threw it away; it's at the bottom of the sea a mile from the Spit, and it will be jolly well rusted beyond recognizing if it's ever washed up by the tide.

You see, Luke must have bought it in the village, years ago, for the man sells just such ladles still. I suppose they are used in cooking. In any case, there was no reason why an inquisitive housemaid should find such a thing lying about, with lead in it, and wonder what it was, and perhaps talk to the maid who heard me tell the story at dinner—for that girl married the plumber's son in the village, and may remember the whole thing.

You understand me, don't you? Now that Luke Pratt is dead and gone, and lies buried beside his wife, with an honest man's tombstone at his head, I should not care to stir up anything that could hurt his memory. They are both dead, and their son, too. There was trouble enough about Luke's death, as it was.

How? He was found dead on the beach one morning, and there was a coroner's inquest. There were marks on his throat, but he had not been robbed. The verdict was that he had come to his end "By the hands or teeth of some person or animal unknown," for half the jury thought it might have been a big dog that had thrown him down and gripped his windpipe, though the skin of his throat was not broken. No one knew at what time he had gone out, nor where he had been. He was found lying on his back above high-water mark, and an old cardboard bandbox that had belonged to his wife lay under his hand, open. The lid had fallen off. He seemed to have been carrying home a skull in the box—doctors are fond of collecting such things. It had rolled out and lay near his head, and it was a remarkably fine skull, rather small, beautifully shaped and very white, with perfect teeth. That is to say, the upper jaw was perfect, but there was no lower one at all, when I first saw it.

Yes, I found it here when I came. You see, it was very white and polished, like a thing meant to be kept under a glass case, and the people did not know where it came from, nor what to do with it; so they put it back into the bandbox and set it on the shelf of the cupboard in the best bedroom, and of course they showed it to me when I took possession. I was taken down to the beach, too, to be shown the place where Luke was found, and the old fisherman explained just how he was lying, and the skull beside him. The only point he could not explain was why the skull had rolled up the sloping sand towards Luke's head instead of rolling downhill to his feet. It did not seem odd to me at the time, but I have often thought of it since, for the place is rather steep. I'll take you there tomorrow if you like—I made a sort of cairn of stones there afterwards.

When he fell down, or was thrown down—whichever happened—the bandbox struck the sand, and the lid came off, and the thing came out and ought to have rolled down. But it didn't. It was close to his head almost touching it, and turned with the face towards it. I say it didn't strike me as odd when the man told me; but I could not help thinking about It afterwards, again and again, till I saw a picture of it all when I closed my eyes; and then I began to ask myself why the plaguey thing had rolled up instead of down, and why it had stopped near Luke's head instead of anywhere else, a yard away, for instance.

You naturally want to know what conclusion I reached, don't you? None that at all explained the rolling, at all events. But I got something else into my head, after a time, that made me feel downright uncomfortable.

Oh, I don't mean as to anything supernatural! There may be ghosts, or there may not be. If there are, I'm not inclined to believe that they can hurt living people except by frightening them, and, for my part, I would rather face any shape of ghost than a fog in the Channel when it's crowded. No. What bothered me was just a foolish idea, that's all, and I cannot tell how it began, nor what made it grow till it turned into a certainty.

I was thinking about Luke and his poor wife one evening over my pipe and a dull book, when it occurred to me that the skull might possibly be hers, and I have never got rid of the thought since. You'll tell me there's no sense in it, no doubt, that Mrs. Pratt was buried like a Christian and is lying in the churchyard where they put her, and that it's perfectly monstrous to suppose her husband kept her skull in her old bandbox in his bedroom. All the same, in the face of reason, and common sense, and probability, I'm convinced that he did. Doctors do all sorts of queer things that would make men like you and me feel creepy, and those are Just the things that don't seem probable, nor logical, nor sensible to us.

Then, don't you see?—if it really was her skull, poor woman, the only way of accounting for his having it is that he really killed her, and did it in that way, as the woman killed her husbands in the story, and that he was afraid there might be an examination some day which would betray him. You see, I told that too, and I believe it had really happened some fifty or sixty years ago. They dug up the three skulls, you know, and there was a small lump of lead rattling about in each one. That was what hanged the woman. Luke remembered that, I'm sure. I don't want to know what he did when he thought of it; my taste never ran in the direction of horrors, and I don't fancy you care for them either, do you? No. If you did, you might supply what is wanting to the story.

It must have been rather grim, eh? I wish I did not see the whole thing so distinctly, just as everything must have happened. He took it the night before she was buried, I'm sure, after the coffin had been shut, and when the servant girl was asleep. I would bet anything, that when he'd got it, he put something under the sheet in its place, to fill up and look like it. What do you suppose he put there, under the sheet?

I don't wonder you take me up on what I'm saying! First I tell you that I don't want to know what happened, and that I hate to think about horrors, and then I describe the whole thing to you as if I had seen it. I'm quite sure that it was her work-bag that he put there. I remember the bag very well, for she always used it of an evening; it was made of brown plush, and when it was stuffed full it was about the size of—you understand. Yes, there I am, at it again! You may laugh at me, but you don't live here alone, where it was done, and you didn't tell Luke the story about the melted lead. I'm not nervous, I tell you, but sometimes I begin to feel that I understand why some people are. I dwell on all this when I'm alone, and I dream of it, and when that thing screams—well, frankly, I don't like the noise any more than you do, though I should be used to it by this time.

I ought not to be nervous. I've sailed in a haunted ship. There was a Man in the Top, and two-thirds of the crew died of the West Coast fever inside of ten days after we anchored; but I was all right, then and afterwards. I have seen some ugly sights, too, just as you have, and all the rest of us. But nothing ever stuck in my head in the way this does.

You see, I've tried to get rid of the thing, but it doesn't like that. It wants to be there in its place, in Mrs. Pratt's bandbox in the cupboard in the best bedroom. It's not happy anywhere else. How do I know that? Because I've tried it. You don't suppose that I've not tried, do you? As long as it's there it only screams now and then, generally at this time of year, but if I put it out of the house it goes on all night, and no servant will stay here twenty-four hours. As it is, I've often been left alone and have been obliged to shift for myself for a fortnight at a time. No one from the village would ever pass a night under the roof now, and as for selling the place, or even letting it, that's out of the question. The old women say that if I stay here I shall come to a bad end myself before long.

I'm not afraid of that. You smile at the mere idea that anyone could take such nonsense seriously. Quite right. It's utterly blatant nonsense, I agree with you. Didn't I tell you that it's only a noise after all when you started and looked round as if you expected to see a ghost standing behind your chair?

I may be all wrong about the skull, and I like to think that I am when I can. It may be just a fine specimen which Luke got somewhere long ago, and what rattles about inside when you shake it may be nothing but a pebble, or a bit of hard clay, or anything. Skulls that have lain long in the ground generally have something inside them that rattles don't they? No, I've never tried to get it out, whatever it is; I'm afraid it might be lead, don't you see? And if it is, I don't want to know the fact, for I'd much rather not be sure. If it really is lead, I killed her quite as much as if I had done the deed myself. Anybody must see that, I should think. As long as I don't know for certain, I have the consolation of saying that it's all utterly ridiculous nonsense, that Mrs. Pratt died a natural death and that the beautiful skull belonged to Luke when he was a student in London. But if I were quite sure, I believe I should have to leave the house; indeed I do, most certainly. As it is, I had to give up trying to sleep in the best bedroom where the cupboard is.

You ask me why I don't throw it into the pond—yes, but please don't call it a "confounded bugbear"—it doesn't like being called names.

There! Lord, what a shriek! I told you so! You're quite pale, man. Fill up your pipe and draw your chair nearer to the fire, and take some more drink. Old Hollands never hurt anybody yet. I've seen a Dutchman in Java drink half a jug of *Hulstkamp* in a morning without turning a hair. I don't take much rum myself, because it doesn't agree with my rheumatism, but you are not rheumatic and it won't damage you Besides, it's a very damp night outside. The wind is howling again, and it will soon be in the south-west; do you hear how the windows rattle? The tide must have turned too, by the moaning.

We should not have heard the thing again if you had not said that. I'm pretty sure we should not. Oh yes, if you choose to describe it as a coincidence, you are quite welcome, but I would rather that you should not call the thing names again, if you don't mind. It may be that the poor little woman hears, and perhaps it hurts her, don't you know? Ghosts? No! You don't call anything a ghost that you can take in your hands and look at in broad daylight, and that rattles when you shake it Do you, now? But it's something that hears and understands; there's no doubt about that.

I tried sleeping in the best bedroom when I first came to the house just because it was the best and most comfortable, but I had to give it up It was their room, and there's the big bed she died in, and the cupboard is in the thickness of the wall, near the head, on the left. That's where it likes to be kept, in its bandbox. I only used the room for a fortnight after I came, and then I turned out and took the little room downstairs, next to the surgery, where Luke used to sleep when he expected to be called to a patient during the night.

I was always a good sleeper ashore; eight hours is my dose, eleven to seven when I'm alone, twelve to eight when I have a friend with me. But I could not sleep after three o'clock in the morning in that room—a quarter past, to be accurate—as a matter of fact, I timed it with my old pocket chronometer, which still keeps good time, and it was always at exactly seventeen minutes past three. I wonder whether that was the hour when she died?

It was not what you have heard. If it had been that, I could not have stood it two nights. It was just a start and a moan and hard breathing for a few seconds in the cupboard, and it could never have waked me under ordinary circumstances, I'm sure. I suppose you are like me in that, and we are just like other people who have been to sea. No natural sounds disturb us at all, not all the racket of a square-rigger hove to in a heavy gale, or rolling on her beam ends before the wind. But if a lead pencil gets adrift and rattles in the drawer of your cabin table you are awake in a moment. Just so—you always understand. Very well, the noise in the cupboard was no louder than that, but it waked me instantly.

I said it was like a "start". I know what I mean, but it's hard to explain without seeming to talk nonsense. Of course you cannot exactly "hear" a person "start"; at the most, you might hear the quick drawing of the breath between the parted lips and closed teeth, and the almost imperceptible sound of clothing that moved suddenly though very slightly. It was like that.

You know how one feels what a sailing vessel is going to do, two or three seconds before she does it, when one has the wheel. Riders say the same of a horse, but that's less strange, because the horse is a live animal with feelings of its own, and only poets and landsmen talk about a ship being alive, and all that. But I have always felt somehow that besides being a steaming machine or a sailing machine for carrying weights, a vessel at sea is a sensitive instrument, and a means of communication between nature and man, and most particularly the man at the wheel, if she is steered by hand. She takes her impressions directly from wind and sea, tide and stream, and transmits them to the man's hand, just as the wireless telegraphy picks up the interrupted currents aloft and turns them out below in the form of a message.

You see what I am driving at; I felt that something started in the cupboard, and I felt it so vividly that I heard it, though there may have' been nothing to hear, and the sound inside my head waked me suddenly. But I really heard the other noise. It was as if it were muffled inside a box, as far away as if it came through a long-distance telephone; and yet I knew that it was inside the cupboard near the head of my bed. My hair did not bristle and my blood did not run cold that time. I simply resented being waked up by something that had no business to make a noise, any more than a pencil should rattle in the drawer of my cabin table on board ship.

For I did not understand; I just supposed that the cupboard had some communication with the outside air, and that the wind had got in and was moaning through it with a sort of very faint screech. I struck a light and looked at my watch, and it was seventeen minutes past three. Then I turned over and went to sleep on my right ear. That's my good one; I'm pretty deaf with the other, for I struck the water with it when I was a lad in diving from the fore-topsail yard. Silly thing to do, it was, but the result is very convenient when I want to go to sleep when there's a noise.

That was the first night, and the same thing happened again and several times afterwards, but not regularly, though it was always at the same time, to a second; perhaps I was sometimes sleeping on my good ear, and sometimes not. I overhauled the cupboard and there was no way by which the wind could get in, or anything else, for the door makes a good fit, having been meant to keep out moths, I suppose; Mrs. Pratt must have kept her winter things in it, for it still smells of camphor and turpentine.

After about a fortnight I had had enough of the noises. So far I had said to myself that it would be silly to yield to it and take the skull out of the room. Things always look differently by daylight, don't they? But the voice grew louder—I suppose one may call it a voice—and it got inside my deaf ear, too, one night. I realized that when I was wide awake, for my good ear was jammed down on the pillow, and I ought not to have heard a foghorn in that position. But I heard that, and it made me lose my temper, unless it scared me, for sometimes the two are not far apart. I struck a light and got up, and I opened the cupboard, grabbed the bandbox and threw it out of the window, as far as I could.

Then my hair stood on end. The thing screamed in the air, like a shell from a twelve-inch gun. It fell on the other side of the road. The night was very dark, and I could not see it fall, but I know it fell beyond the road The window is just over the front door, it's fifteen yards to the fence, more or less, and the road is ten yards wide. There's a thick-set hedge beyond, along the glebe that belongs to the vicarage.

I did not sleep much more than night. It was not more than half an hour after I had thrown the bandbox out when I heard a shriek outside—like what we've had tonight, but worse, more despairing, I should call it; and it may have been my imagination, but I could have sworn that the screams came nearer and nearer each time. I lit a pipe, and walked up and down for a bit, and then took a book and sat up reading, but I'll be hanged if I can remember what I read nor even what the book was, for every now and then a shriek came up that would have made a dead man turn in his coffin.

A little before dawn someone knocked at the front door. There was no mistaking that for anything else, and I opened my window and looked down, for I guessed that someone wanted the doctor, supposing that the new man had taken Luke's house. It was rather a relief to hear a human knock after that awful noise.

You cannot see the door from above, owing to the little porch. The knocking came again, and I called out, asking who was there, but nobody answered, though the knock was repeated. I sang out again, and said that the doctor did not live here any longer. There was no answer, but it occurred to me that it might be some old countryman who was stone deaf. So I took my candle and went down to open the door. Upon my word, I was not thinking of the thing yet, and I had almost forgotten the other noises. I went down convinced that I should find somebody outside, on the doorstep, with a message. I set the candle on the hall table, so that the wind should not blow it out when I opened. While I was drawing the old-fashioned bolt I heard the knocking again. It was not loud, and it had a queer, hollow sound, now that I was close to it, I remember, but I certainly thought it was made by some person who wanted to get in.

It wasn't. There was nobody there, but as I opened the door inward, standing a little on one side, so as to see out at once, something rolled across the threshold and stopped against my foot.

I drew back as I felt it, for I knew what it was before I looked down. I cannot tell you how I knew, and it seemed unreasonable, for I am still quite sure that I had thrown it across the road. It's a French window, that opens wide, and I got a good swing when I flung it out. Besides, when I went out early in the morning, I found the bandbox beyond the thick hedge.

You may think it opened when I threw it, and that the skull dropped out; but that's impossible, for nobody could throw an empty cardboard box so far. It's out of the question; you might as well try to fling a ball of paper twenty-five yards, or a blown bird's egg.

To go back, I shut and bolted the hall door, picked the thing up carefully, and put it on the table beside the candle. I did that mechanically, as one instinctively does the right thing in danger without thinking at all—unless one does the opposite. It may seem odd, but I believe my first thought had been that somebody might come and find me there on the threshold while it was resting against my foot, lying a little on its side, and turning one hollow eye up at my face, as if it meant to accuse me. And the light and shadow from the candle played in the hollows of the eyes as it stood on the table, so that they seemed to open and shut at me. Then the candle went out quite unexpectedly, though the door was fastened and there was not the least draught; and I used up at least half a dozen matches before it would burn again.

I sat down rather suddenly, without quite knowing why. Probably I had been badly frightened, and perhaps you will admit there was no great shame in being scared. The thing had come home, and it wanted to go upstairs, back to its cupboard. I sat still and stared at it for a bit till I began to feel very cold; then I took it and carried it up and set it in its place, and I remember that I spoke to it, and promised that it should have its bandbox again in the morning.

You want to know whether I stayed in the room till daybreak? Yes but I kept a light burning, and sat up smoking and reading, most likely out of fright; plain, undeniable fear, and you need not call it cowardice either, for that's not the same thing. I could not have stayed alone with that thing in the cupboard; I should have been scared to death, though I'm not more timid than other people. Confound it all, man, it had crossed the road alone, and had got up the doorstep and had knocked to be let in.

When the dawn came, I put on my boots and went out to find the bandbox. I had to go a good way round, by the gate near the high road, and I found the box open and hanging on the other side of the hedge. It had caught on the twigs by the string, and the lid had fallen off and was lying on the ground below it. That shows that it did not open till it was well over; and if it had not opened as soon as it left my hand, what was inside it must have gone beyond the road too.

That's all. I took the box upstairs to the cupboard, and put the skull back and locked it up. When the girl brought me my breakfast she said she was sorry, but that she must go, and she did not care if she lost her month's wages. I looked at her, and her face was a sort of greenish yellowish white. I pretended to be surprised, and asked what was the matter; but that was of no use, for she just turned on me and wanted to know whether I meant to stay in a haunted house, and how long I expected to live if I did, for though she noticed I was sometimes a little hard of hearing, she did not believe that even I could sleep through those screams again—and if I could, why had I been moving about the house and opening and shutting the front door, between three and four in the morning? There was no answering that, since she had heard me, so off she went, and I was left to myself. I went down to the village during the morning and found a woman who was willing to come and do the little work there is and cook my dinner, on condition that she might go home every night.

As for me, I moved downstairs that day, and I have never tried to sleep in the best bedroom since. After a little while I got a brace of middle-aged Scotch servants from London, and things were quiet enough for a long time. I began by telling them that the house was in a very exposed position, and that the wind whistled round it a good deal in the autumn and winter, which had given it a bad name in the village, the Cornish people being inclined to superstition and telling ghost stories. The two hard-faced, sandy-haired sisters almost smiled, and they answered with great contempt that they had no great opinion of any Southern bogey whatever, having been in service in two English haunted houses, where they had never seen so much as the Boy in Grey, whom they reckoned no very particular rarity in Forfarshire.

They stayed with me several months, and while they were in the house we had peace and quiet. One of them is here again now, but she went away with her sister within the year. This one—she was the cook—married the sexton, who works in my garden. That's the way of it. It's a small village and he has not much to do, and he knows enough about flowers to help me nicely, besides doing most of the hard work; for though I'm fond of exercise, I'm getting a little stiff in the hinges. He's a sober, silent sort of fellow, who minds his own business, and he was a widower when I came here—Trehearn is his name, James Trehearn.

The Scottish sisters would not admit that there was anything wrong about the house, but when November came they gave me warning that they were going, on the ground that the chapel was such a long walk from here, being in the next parish, and that they could not possibly go to our church. But the younger one came back in the spring, and as soon as the banns could be published she was married to James Trehearn by the vicar, and she seems to have had no scruples about hearing him preach since then. I'm quite satisfied, if she is! The couple live in a small cottage that looks over the churchyard.

I suppose you are wondering what all this has to do with what I was talking about. I'm alone so much that when an old friend comes to see me, I sometimes go on talking just for the sake of hearing my own voice. But in this case there is really a connection of ideas. It was James Trehearn who buried poor Mrs. Pratt, and her husband after her in the same grave, and it's not far from the back of his cottage. That's the connection in my mind, you see. It's plain enough. He knows something; I'm quite sure that he does, though he's such a reticent beggar.

Yes, I'm alone in the house at night now, for Mrs. Trehearn does everything herself, and when I have a friend the sexton's niece comes in to wait on the table. He takes his wife home every evening in winter, but in summer, when there's light, she goes by herself. She's not a nervous woman, but she's less sure than she used to be that there are no bogies in England worth a Scotch-woman's notice. Isn't it amusing, the idea that Scotland has a monopoly of the supernatural? Odd sort of national pride, I call that, don't you?

That's a good fire, isn't it? When driftwood gets started at last there's nothing like it, I think. Yes, we get lots of it, for I'm sorry to say there are still a great many wrecks about here. It's a lonely coast, and you may have all the wood you want for the trouble of bringing it in. Trehearn and I borrow a cart now and then, and load it between here and the Spit. I hate a coal fire when I can get wood of any sort A log is company, even if it's only a piece of a deck beam or timber sawn off, and the salt in it makes pretty sparks. See how they fly, like Japanese hand-fireworks! Upon my word, with an old friend and a good fire and a pipe, one forgets all about that thing upstairs, especially now that the wind has moderated. It's only a lull, though, and it will blow a gale before morning.

You think you would like to see the skull? I've no objection. There's no reason why you shouldn't have a look at it, and you never saw a more perfect one in your life, except that there are two front teeth missing in the lower jaw.

Oh yes—I had not told you about the jaw yet. Trehearn found it in the garden last spring when he was digging a pit for a new asparagus bed. You know we make asparagus beds six or eight feet deep here. Yes, yes—I had forgotten to tell you that. He was digging straight down, just as he digs a grave; if you want a good asparagus bed made, I advise you to get a sexton to make it for you. Those fellows have a wonderful knack at that sort of digging.

Trehearn had got down about three feet when he cut into a mass of white lime in the side of the trench. He had noticed that the earth was a little looser there, though he says it had not been disturbed for a number of years. I suppose he thought that even old lime might not be good for asparagus, so he broke it out and threw it up. It was pretty hard, he says, in biggish lumps, and out of sheer force of habit he cracked the lumps with his spade as they lay outside the pit beside him; the jaw bone of the skull dropped out of one of the pieces. He thinks he must have knocked out the two front teeth in breaking up the lime, but he did not see them anywhere.

He's a very experienced man in such things, as you may imagine, and he said at once that the jaw had probably belonged to a young woman, and that the teeth had been complete when she died. He brought it to me, and asked me if I wanted to keep it; if I did not, he said he would drop it into the next grave he made in the churchyard, as he supposed it was a Christian jaw, and ought to have decent burial, wherever the rest of the body might be. I told him that doctors often put bones into quicklime to whiten them nicely, and that I supposed Dr Pratt had once had a little lime pit in the garden for that purpose, and had forgotten the jaw. Trehearn looked at me quietly.

"Maybe it fitted that skull that used to be in the cupboard upstairs, sir," he said. "Maybe Dr Pratt had put the skull into the lime to clean it, or something, and when he took it out he left the lower jaw behind. There's some human hair sticking in the lime, sir."

I saw there was, and that was what Trehearn said. If he did not suspect something, why in the world should he have suggested that the jaw might fit the skull? Besides, it did. That's proof that he knows more than he cares to tell. Do you suppose he looked before she was buried? Or perhaps—when he buried Luke in the same grave——

Well, well, it's of no use to go over that, is it? I said I would keep the jaw with the skull, and I took it upstairs and fitted it into its place. There's not the slightest doubt about the two belonging together, and together they are.

Trehearn knows several things. We were talking about plastering the kitchen a while ago, and he happened to remember that it had not been done since the very week when Mrs. Pratt died. He did not say that the mason must have left some lime on the place, but he thought it, and that it was the very same lime he had found in the asparagus pit. He knows a lot. Trehearn is one of your silent beggars who can put two and two together. That grave is very near the back of his cottage, too, and he's one of the quickest men with a spade I ever saw. If he wanted to know the truth, he could, and no one else would ever be the wiser unless he chose to tell. In a quiet village like ours, people don't go and spend the night in the churchyard to see whether the sexton potters about by himself between ten o'clock and daylight.

What is awful to think of, is Luke's deliberation, if he did it; his cool certainty that no one would find him out; above all, his nerve, for that must have been extraordinary. I sometimes think it's bad enough to live in the place where it was done, if it really was done. I always put in the condition, you see, for the sake of his memory, and a little bit for my own sake, too.

I'll go upstairs and fetch the box in a minute. Let me light my pipe; there's no hurry! We had supper early, and it's only half-past nine o'clock. I never let a friend go to bed before twelve, or with less than three glasses—you may have as many more as you like, but you shan't have less, for the sake of old times.

It's breezing up again, do you hear? That was only a lull just now, and we are going to have a bad night.

A thing happened that made me start a little when I found that the jaw fitted exactly. I'm not very easily startled in that way myself, but I have seen people make a quick movement, drawing their breath sharply, when they had thought they were alone and suddenly turned and saw someone very near them. Nobody can call that fear. You wouldn't, would you? No. Well, just when I had set the jaw in its place under the skull, the teeth closed sharply on my finger. It felt exactly as if it were biting me hard, and I confess that I jumped before I realized that I had been pressing the jaw and the skull together with my other hand. I assure you I was not at all nervous.

It was broad daylight, too, and a fine day, and the sun was streaming into the best bedroom. It would have been absurd to be nervous, and it was only a quick mistaken impression, but it really made me feel queer. Somehow it made me think of the funny verdict of the coroner's jury on Luke's death, "by the hand or teeth of some person or animal unknown". Ever since that I've wished I had seen those marks on his throat, though the lower jaw was missing then.

I have often seen a man do insane things with his hands that he does not realize at all. I once saw a man hanging on by an old awning stop with one hand, leaning backward, outboard, with all his weight on it, and he was just cutting the stop with the knife in his other hand when I got my arms round him. We were in mid-ocean, going twenty knots. He had not the smallest idea what he was doing; neither had I when I managed to pinch my finger between the teeth of that thing. I can feel it now. It was exactly as if it were alive and were trying to bite me. It would if it could, for I know it hates me, poor thing! Do you suppose that what rattles about inside is really a bit of lead?

Well, I'll get the box down presently, and if whatever it is happens to drop out into your hands, that's your affair. If it's only a clod of earth or a pebble, the whole matter would be off my mind, and I don't believe I should ever think of the skull again; but somehow I cannot bring myself to shake out the bit of hard stuff myself. The mere idea that it may be lead makes me confoundedly uncomfortable, yet I've got the conviction that I shall know before long. I shall certainly know. I'm sure Trehearn knows, but he's such a silent beggar

I'll go upstairs now and get it. What? You had better go with me? Ha, ha! do you think I'm afraid of a bandbox and a noise? Nonsense!

Bother the candle, it won't light! As if the ridiculous thing understood what it's wanted for! Look at that—the third match. They light fast enough for my pipe. There, do you see? It's a fresh box, just out of the tin safe where I keep the supply on account of the dampness. Oh, you think the wick of the candle may be damp, do you? All right, I'll light the beastly thing in the fire. That won't go out, at all events. Yes, it sputters a bit, but it will keep lighted now. It burns just like any other candle, doesn't it? The fact is, candles are not very good about here. I don't know where they come from, but they have a way of burning low occasionally, with a greenish flame that spits tiny sparks, and I'm often annoyed by their going out of themselves. It cannot be helped, for it will be long before we have electricity in our village. It really is rather a poor light, isn't it?

You think I had better leave you the candle and take the lamp, do you? I don't like to carry lamps about, that's the truth. I never dropped one in my life, but I have always thought I might, and it's so confoundedly dangerous if you do. Besides, I am pretty well used to these rotten candles by this time.

You may as well finish that glass while I'm getting it, for I don't mean to let you off with less than three before you go to bed. You won't have to go upstairs, either, for I've put you in the old study next to the surgery—that's where I live myself. The fact is, I never ask a friend to sleep upstairs now. The last man who did was Crackenthorpe, and he said he was kept awake all night. You remember old Crack, don't you? He stuck to the Service, and they've just made him an admiral. Yes, I'm off now—unless the candle goes out. I couldn't help asking if you remembered Crackenthorpe. If anyone had told us that the skinny little idiot he used to be was to turn out the most successful of the lot of us, we should have laughed at the idea, shouldn't we? You and I did not do badly, it's true—but I'm really going now. I don't mean to let you think that I've been putting it off by talking! As if there were anything to be afraid of! If I were scared, I should tell you so quite frankly, and get you to go upstairs with me.

★★★★★★

Here's the box. I brought it down very carefully, so as not to disturb it, poor thing. You see, if it were shaken, the jaw might get separated from it again, and I'm sure it wouldn't like that. Yes, the candle went out as I was coming downstairs, but that was the draught from the leaky window on the landing. Did you hear anything? Yes, there was another scream. Am I pale, do you say? That's nothing. My heart is a little queer sometimes, and I went upstairs too fast. In fact, that's one reason why I really prefer to live altogether on the ground floor.

Wherever the shriek came from, it was not from the skull, for I had the box in my hand when I heard the noise, and here it is now; so we have proved definitely that the screams are produced by something else. I've no doubt I shall find out some day what makes them. Some crevice in the wall, of course, or a crack in a chimney, or a chink in the frame of a window. That's the way all ghost stories end in real life. Do you know, I'm jolly glad I thought of going up and bringing it down for you to see, for that last shriek settles the question. To think that I should have been so weak as to fancy that the poor skull could really cry out like a living thing!

Now I'll open the box, and we'll take it out and look at it under the bright light. It's rather awful to think that the poor lady used to sit there, in your chair, evening after evening, in just the same light, isn't it? But then—I've made up my mind that it's all rubbish from beginning to end, and that it's just an old skull that Luke had when he was a student and perhaps he put it into the lime merely to whiten it, and could not find the jaw.

I made a seal on the string, you see, after I had put the jaw in its place, and I wrote on the cover. There's the old white label on it still, from the milliner's, addressed to Mrs. Pratt when the hat was sent to her, and as there was room I wrote on the edge: "A skull, once the property of the late Luke Pratt, MD." I don't quite know why I wrote that, unless it was with the idea of explaining how the thing happened to be in my possession. I cannot help wondering sometimes what sort of hat it was that came in the bandbox. What colour was it, do you think? Was it a gay spring hat with a bobbing feather and pretty ribands? Strange that the very same box should hold the head that wore the finery—perhaps. No—we made up our minds that it just came from the hospital in London where Luke did his time. It's far better to look at it in that light, isn't it? There's no more connection between that skull and poor Mrs. Pratt than there was between my story about the lead and——

Good Lord! Take the lamp—don't let it go out, if you can help it—I'll have the window fastened again in a second—I say, what a gale! There, it's out! I told you so! Never mind, there's the firelight—I've got the window shut—the bolt was only half down. Was the box blown off the table? Where the deuce is it? There! That won't open again, for I've put up the bar. Good dodge, an old-fashioned bar—there's nothing like it. Now, you find the bandbox while I light the lamp. Confound those wretched matches! Yes, a pipe spill is better—it must light in the fire—hadn't thought of it—thank you—there we are again. Now, where's the box? Yes, put it back on the table, and we'll open it.

That's the first time I have ever known the wind to burst that window open; but it was partly carelessness on my part when I last shut it. Yes, of course I heard the scream. It seemed to go all round the house before it broke in at the window. That proves that it's always been the wind and nothing else, doesn't it? When it was not the wind, it was my imagination I've always been a very imaginative man: I must have been, though I did not know it. As we grow older we understand ourselves better, don't you know?

I'll have a drop of the *Hulstkamp* neat, by way of an exception, since you are filling up your glass. That damp gust chilled me, and with my rheumatic tendency I'm very much afraid of a chill, for the cold sometimes seems to stick in my joints all winter when it once gets in.

By George, that's good stuff! I'll just light a fresh pipe, now that everything is snug again, and then we'll open the box. I'm so glad we heard that last scream together, with the skull here on the table between us, for a thing cannot possibly be in two places at the same time, and the noise most certainly came from outside, as any noise the wind makes must. You thought you heard it scream through the room after the window was burst open? Oh yes, so did I, but that was natural enough when everything was open. Of course we heard the wind. What could one expect?

Look here, please. I want you to see that the seal is intact before we open the box together. Will you take my glasses? No, you have your own. All right. The seal is sound, you see, and you can read the words of the motto easily. "*Sweet and low*"—that's it—because the poem goes on "*Wind of the Western Sea*", and says, "*blow him again to me*", and all that. Here is the seal on my watch chain, where it's hung for more than forty years. My poor little wife gave it to me when I was courting, and I never had any other. It was just like her to think of those words—she was always fond of Tennyson.

It's no use to cut the string, for it's fastened to the box, so I'll just break the wax and untie the knot, and afterwards we'll seal it up again. You see, I like to feel that the thing is safe in its place, and that nobody can take it out. Not that I should suspect Trehearn of meddling with it, but I always feel that he knows a lot more than he tells.

You see, I've managed it without breaking the string, though when I fastened it I never expected to open the bandbox again. The lid comes off easily enough. There! Now look!

What! Nothing in it! Empty! It's gone, man, the skull is

gone!

No, there's nothing the matter with me. I'm only trying to collect my thoughts. It's so strange. I'm positively certain that it was inside when I put on the seal last spring. I can't have imagined that: it's utterly impossible. If I ever took a stiff glass with a friend now and then, I would admit that I might have made some idiotic mistake when I had taken too much. But I don't, and I never did. A pint of ale at supper and half a go of rum at bedtime was the most I ever took in my good days. I believe it's always we sober fellows who get rheumatism and gout! Yet there was my seal, and there is the empty bandbox. That's plain enough.

I say, I don't half like this. It's not right. There's something wrong about it, in my opinion. You needn't talk to me about supernatural manifestations, for I don't believe in them, not a little bit! Somebody must have tampered with the seal and stolen the skull. Sometimes, when I go out to work in the garden in summer, I leave my watch and chain on the table. Trehearn must have taken the seal then, and used it, for he would be quite sure that I should not come in for at least an hour.

If it was not Trehearn—oh, don't talk to me about the possibility that the thing has got out by itself! If it has, it must be somewhere about the house, in some out-of-the-way corner, waiting. We may come upon it anywhere, waiting for us, don't you know?—just waiting in the dark. Then it will scream at me; it will shriek at me in the dark, for it hates me, I tell you!

The bandbox is quite empty. We are not dreaming, either of us. There, I turn it upside down.

What's that? Something fell out as I turned it over. It's on the floor, it's near your feet. I know it is, and we must find it. Help me to find it, man. Have you got it? For God's sake, give it to me, quickly!

Lead! I knew it when I heard it fall. I knew it couldn't be anything else by the little thud it made on the hearthrug. So it was lead after all and Luke did it.

I feel a little bit shaken up—not exactly nervous, you know, but badly shaken up, that's the fact. Anybody would, I should think. After all, you cannot say that it's fear of the thing, for I went up and brought it down—at least, I believed I was bringing it down, and that's the same thing, and by George, rather than give in to such silly nonsense, I'll take the box upstairs again and put it back in its place. It's not that. It's the certainty that the poor little woman came to her end in that way, by my fault, because I told the story. That's what is so dreadful. Somehow, I had always hoped that I should never be quite sure of it, but there is no doubting it now. Look at that!

Look at it! That little lump of lead with no particular shape. Think of what it did, man! Doesn't it make you shiver? He gave her something to make her sleep, of course, but there must have been one moment of awful agony. Think of having boiling lead poured into your brain. Think of it. She was dead before she could scream, but only think of—oh! there it is again—it's just outside—I know it's just outside—I can't keep it out of my head!—oh!—oh!

★★★★★★

You thought I had fainted? No, I wish I had, for it would have stopped sooner. It's all very well to say that it's only a noise, and that a noise never hurt anybody—you're as white as a shroud yourself. There's only one thing to be done, if we hope to close an eye tonight. We must find it and put it back into its bandbox and shut it up in the cupboard, where it likes to be I don't know how it got out, but it wants to get in again. That's why it screams so awfully tonight—it was never so bad as this—never since I first——

Bury it? Yes, if we can find it, we'll bury it, if it takes us all night. We'll bury it six feet deep and ram down the earth over it, so that it shall never get out again, and if it screams, we shall hardly hear it so deep down. Quick, we'll get the lantern and look for it. It cannot be far away; I'm sure it's just outside—it was coming in when I shut the window, I know it.

Yes, you're quite right. I'm losing my senses, and I must get hold of myself. Don't speak to me for a minute or two; I'll sit quite still and keep my eyes shut and repeat something I know. That's the best way.

"Add together the altitude, the latitude, and the polar distance, divide by two and subtract the altitude from the half-sum; then add the logarithm of the secant of the latitude, the cosecant of the polar distance, the cosine of the half-sum and the sine of the half-sum minus the altitude"—there! Don't say that I'm out of my senses, for my memory is all right, isn't it?

Of course, you may say that it's mechanical, and that we never forget the things we learned when we were boys and have used almost every day for a lifetime. But that's the very point. When a man is going crazy, it's the mechanical part of his mind that gets out of order and won't work right; he remembers things that never happened, or he sees things that aren't real, or he hears noises when there is perfect silence. That's not what is the matter with either of us, is it?

Come, we'll get the lantern and go round the house. It's not raining—only blowing like old boots, as we used to say. The lantern is in the cupboard under the stairs in the hall, and I always keep it trimmed in case of a wreck.

No use to look for the thing? I don't see how you can say that. It was nonsense to talk of burying it, of course, for it doesn't want to be buried; it wants to go back into its bandbox and be taken upstairs, poor thing! Trehearn took it out, I know, and made the seal over again. Perhaps he took it to the churchyard, and he may have meant well. I dare say he thought that it would not scream any more if it were quietly laid in consecrated ground, near where it belongs. But it has come home. Yes, that's it. He's not half a bad fellow, Trehearn, and rather religiously inclined, I think. Does not that sound natural, and reasonable, and well meant? He supposed it screamed because it was not decently buried—with the rest. But he was wrong. How should he know that it screams at me because it hates me, and because it's my fault that there was that little lump of lead in it?

No use to look for it, anyhow? Nonsense! I tell you it wants to be found—Hark! what's that knocking? Do you hear it?

Knock—knock—knock—three times, then a pause, and then again. It has a hollow sound, hasn't it?

It has come home. I've heard that knock before. It wants to come in and be taken upstairs in its box. It's at the front door.

Will you come with me? We'll take it in. Yes, I own that I don't like to go alone and open the door. The thing will roll in and stop against my foot, just as it did before, and the light will go out. I'm a good deal shaken by finding that bit of lead, and, besides, my heart isn't quite right—too much strong tobacco, perhaps. Besides, I'm quite willing to own that I'm a bit nervous tonight, if I never was before in my life.

That's right, come along! I'll take the box with me, so as not to come back. Do you hear the knocking? It's not like any other knocking I ever heard. If you will hold this door open, I can find the lantern under the stairs by the light from this room without bringing the lamp into the hall—it would only go out.

The thing knows we are coming—hark! It's impatient to get in. Don't shut the door till the lantern is ready, whatever you do. There will be the usual trouble with the matches, I suppose—no, the first one, by Jove! I tell you it wants to get in, so there's no trouble. All right with that door now; shut it, please. Now come and hold the lantern, for it's blowing so hard outside that I shall have to use both hands. That's it, hold the light low. Do you hear the knocking still? Here goes—I'll open just enough with my foot against the bottom of the door—now!

Catch it! it's only the wind that blows it across the floor, that's all—there s half a hurricane outside, I tell you! Have you got it? The bandbox is on the table. One minute, and I'll have the bar up. There!

Why did you throw it into the box so roughly? It doesn't like that, you know.

What do you say? Bitten your hand? Nonsense, man! You did just what I did. You pressed the jaws together with your other hand and pinched yourself. Let me see. You don't mean to say you have drawn blood? You must have squeezed hard by Jove, for the skin is certainly torn. I'll give you some carbolic solution for it before we go to bed, for they say a scratch from a skull's tooth may go bad and give trouble.

Come inside again and let me see it by the lamp. I'll bring the bandbox—never mind the lantern, it may just as well burn in the hall for I shall need it presently when I go up the stairs. Yes, shut the door if you will; it makes it more cheerful and bright. Is your finger still bleeding? I'll get you the carbolic in an instant; just let me see the thing.

Ugh! There's a drop of blood on the upper jaw. It's on the eyetooth. Ghastly, isn't it? When I saw it running along the floor of the hall, the strength almost went out of my hands, and I felt my knees bending, then I understood that it was the gale, driving it over the smooth boards. You don't blame me? No, I should think not! We were boys together, and we've seen a thing or two, and we may just as well own to each other that we were both in a beastly funk when it slid across the floor at you. No wonder you pinched your finger picking it up, after that, if I did the same thing out of sheer nervousness, in broad daylight, with the sun streaming in on me.

Strange that the jaw should stick to it so closely, isn't it? I suppose it's the dampness, for it shuts like a vice—I have wiped off the drop of blood, for it was not nice to look at. I'm not going to try to open the jaws, don't be afraid! I shall not play any tricks with the poor thing, but I'll just seal the box again, and we'll take it upstairs and put it away where it wants to be. The wax is on the writing-table by the window. Thank you. It will be long before I leave my seal lying about again, for Trehearn to use, I can tell you. Explain? I don't explain natural phenomena, but if you choose to think that Trehearn had hidden it somewhere in the bushes, and that the gale blew it to the house against the door, and made it knock, as if it wanted to be let in, you're not thinking the impossible, and I'm quite ready to agree with you.

Do you see that? You can swear that you've actually seen me seal it this time, in case anything of the kind should occur again. The wax fastens the strings to the lid, which cannot possibly be lifted, even enough to get in one finger. You're quite satisfied, aren't you? Yes. Besides, I shall lock the cupboard and keep the key in my pocket hereafter.

Now we can take the lantern and go upstairs. Do you know? I'm very much inclined to agree with your theory that the wind blew it against the house. I'll go ahead, for I know the stairs; just hold the lantern near my feet as we go up. How the wind howls and whistles! Did you feel the sand on the floor under your shoes as we crossed the hall?

Yes—this is the door of the best bedroom. Hold up the lantern, please. This side, by the head of the bed. I left the cupboard open when I got the box. Isn't it queer how the faint odour of women's dresses will hang about an old closet for years? This is the shelf. You've seen me set the box there, and now you see me turn the key and put it into my pocket. So that's done!

Goodnight. Are you sure you're quite comfortable? It's not much of a room, but I dare say you would as soon sleep here as upstairs tonight. If you want anything, sing out; there's only a lath and plaster partition between us. There's not so much wind on this side by half. There's the Hollands on the table, if you'll have one more nightcap. No? Well, do as you please. Goodnight again, and don't dream about that thing, if you can.

★★★★★★

The following paragraph appeared in the *Penraddon News*, 23rd November 1906:

> MYSTERIOUS DEATH OF
> A RETIRED SEA CAPTAIN
>
> The village of Tredcombe is much disturbed by the strange death of Captain Charles Braddock, and all sorts of impossible stories are circulating with regard to the circumstances, which certainly seem difficult of explanation. The retired captain, who had successfully commanded in his time the largest and fastest liners belonging to one of the principal transatlantic steamship companies, was found dead in his bed on Tuesday morning in his own cottage, a quarter of a mile from the village. An examination was

made at once by the local practitioner, which revealed the horrible fact that the deceased had been bitten in the throat by a human assailant, with such amazing force as to crush the windpipe and cause death. The marks of the teeth of both jaws were so plainly visible on the skin that they could be counted, but the perpetrator of the deed had evidently lost the two lower middle incisors.

It is hoped that this peculiarity may help to identify the murderer, who can only be a dangerous escaped maniac. The deceased, though over sixty-five years of age, is said to have been a hale man of considerable physical strength, and it is remarkable that no signs of any struggle were visible in the room, nor could it be ascertained how the murderer had entered the house. Warning has been sent to all the insane asylums in the United Kingdom, but as yet no information has been received regarding the escape of any dangerous patient.

The coroner's Jury returned the somewhat singular verdict that Captain Braddock came to his death "by the hands or teeth of some person unknown." The local surgeon is said to have expressed privately the opinion that the maniac is a woman, a view he deduces from the small size of the jaws, as shown by the marks of the teeth. The whole affair is shrouded in mystery. Captain Braddock was a widower, and lived alone. He leaves no children.

(Author's Note.—Students of ghost lore and haunted houses will find the foundation of the foregoing story in the legends about a skull which is still preserved in the farmhouse called Bettiscombe Manor, situated, I believe, on the Dorsetshire coast.)

Hertford O'Donnell's Warning

By Mrs. J. H. Riddell

Many a year ago, before chloroform was thought of, there lived in an old, rambling house, in Gerard Street, Soho, a young Irishman called Hertford O'Donnell.

After Hertford O'Donnell he was entitled to write M.R.C.S., for he had studied hard to gain this distinction, and the older surgeons at Guy's (his hospital) considered him, in their secret hearts, one of the most rising operators of the day.

Having said chloroform was unknown at the time this story opens, it will strike my readers that, if Hertford O'Donnell were a rising and successful operator in those days, of necessity he combined within himself a larger number of striking qualities than are by any means necessary to form a successful operator in these.

There was more than mere hand skill, more than even thorough knowledge of his profession, needful for the man who, dealing with conscious subjects, essayed to rid them of some of the diseases to which flesh is heir. There was greater courage required in the manipulator of old than is at present altogether essential. Then, as now, a thorough mastery of his instruments—a steady hand—a keen eye—a quick dexterity were indispensable to a good operator; but, added to all these things, there formerly required a pulse which knew no quickening—a mental strength which never faltered—a ready power of adaptation in unexpected circumstances—fertility of resource in difficult cases, and a rave front under all emergencies.

If I refrain from adding that a hard as well as a courageous heart was an important item in the programme, it is only out of deference to general opinion, which amongst other delusions, clings to the belief that courage and hardness are antagonistic qualities.

Hertford O'Donnell, however, was hard as steel. He understood his work, and he did it thoroughly; but he cared no more for quivering nerves and contracting muscles, for screams of agony, for faces white with pain, and teeth clenched in the extremity of anguish, than he did for the stony countenances of the dead which sometimes in the dissecting-room appalled younger and less experienced men.

He had no sentiment, and he had no sympathy. The human body was to him an ingenious piece of mechanism, which it was at once a pleasure and a profit to understand. Precisely as Brunei loved the Thames Tunnel, or any other singular engineering feat, so O'Donnell loved a patient on whom he operated successfully, more especially if the ailment possessed by the patient were of a rare and difficult character.

And for this reason he was much liked by all who came under his hands, for patients are apt to mistake a surgeon's interest in their cases for interest in themselves; and it was gratifying to John Dicks, plasterer, and Timothy Regan, labourer, to be the happy possessors of remarkable diseases, which produced a cordial understanding between themselves and the handsome Irishman.

If he were hard and cool at the moment of hewing them to pieces, that was all forgotten, or remembered only as a virtue, when, after being discharged from hospital like soldiers who have served in a severe campaign, they met Mr. O'Donnell in the street, and were accosted by that rising individual, just as though he considered himself nobody.

He had a royal memory, this stranger in a strange land, both for faces and cases; and like the rest of his countrymen he never felt it beneath his dignity to talk cordially to corduroy and fustian.

In London, as at Calgillan, he never held back his tongue from speaking a cheery or a kindly word. His manners were pliable enough if his heart were not; and the porters, and the patients, and the nurses, and the students at Guy's all were pleased to see Hertford O'Donnell.

Rain, hail, sunshine, it was all the same; there was a life and a brightness about the man which communicated itself to those with whom he came in contact. Let the mud in the streets be a foot deep, or the London fog thick as pea-soup, Mr. O'Donnell never lost his temper, never muttered a surly reply to the gate-keeper's salutation, but spoke out blithely and cheerfully to his pupils and his patients, to the sick and to the well, to those below and to those above him.

And yet, spite of all these good qualities—spite of his handsome face, his fine figure, his easy address, and his unquestionable skill as an operator, the dons, who acknowledged his talent, shook their heads gravely when two or three of them in private and solemn conclave talked confidentially of their younger brother.

If there were many things in his favour, there were more in his disfavour. He was Irish—not merely by the accident of birth, which might have been forgiven, since a man cannot be held accountable for such caprices of Nature, but by every other accident and design which is objectionable to the orthodox and respectable and representative English mind.

In speech, appearance, manner, habits, modes of expression, habits of life, Hertford O'Donnell was Irish. To the core of his heart he loved his native land which he, nevertheless, declared he never meant to revisit; and amongst the English he moved to all intents and purposes a foreigner, who was resolved, so said the great prophets at Guy's, to go to destruction as fast as he could, and let no man hinder him.

"He means to go the whole length of his tether," observed one of the ancient wise-acres to another; which speech implied a conviction that Hertford O'Donnell, having sold himself to the Evil One, had determined to dive the full length of his rope into wickedness before being pulled to the shore where even wickedness is negative—where there are no mad carouses, no wild, sinful excitement, nothing but impotent wailing and useless gnashing of teeth.

A reckless, graceless, clever, wicked devil—going to his natural home as fast as in London a man can possibly progress thither: this was the opinion his superiors held of the man who lived all alone with a housekeeper and her husband (who acted as butler) in his big house near Soho.

Gerard Street was not then an utterly shady and forgotten locality: carriage patients found their way to the rising surgeon—some great personages thought it not beneath them to fee an individual whose consulting rooms were situated on what was even then the wrong side of Regent Street. He was making money, and he was spending it: he was over head and ears in debt—useless, vulgar debt—senselessly contracted, never bravely faced. He had lived at an awful pace ever since he came to London, at a pace which only a man who hopes and expects to die young can ever travel.

Life, what good was it? death, was he a child, or a woman, or a coward, to be afraid of death's "afterwards?" God knew all about the trifle which had upset his coach better than the dons at Guy's; and he did not dread facing his Maker, and giving an account to Him even of the disreputable existence he had led since he came to London.

Hertford O'Donnell knew the world pretty well, and the ways thereof were to him as roads often traversed; therefore, when he said that at the day of judgment he felt certain he should come off better than many of those who censured him, it may be assumed that, although his views of *post-mortem* punishment were vague, unsatisfactory, and infidel, still his information as to the peccadilloes of his neighbours was such as consoled himself.

And yet, living all alone in the old house near Soho Square, grave thoughts would intrude frequently into the surgeon's mind—thoughts which were, so to say, italicized by peremptory letters, and still more peremptory visits from people who wanted money.

Although he had many acquaintances he had no single friend, and accordingly these thoughts were received and brooded over in solitude, in those hours when, after returning from dinner or supper, or congenial carouse, he sat in his dreary rooms smoking his pipe and considering means and ways, chances and certainties.

In good truth he had started in London with some vague idea that as his life in it would not be of long continuance, the pace at which he elected to travel could be of little consequence; but the years since his first entry into the metropolis were now piled one on the top of another, his youth was behind him, his chances of longevity, spite of the way he had striven to injure his constitution, quite as good as ever. He had come to that time in existence, to that narrow strip of tableland whence the ascent of youth and the descent of age are equally discernible—when, simply because he has lived for so many years, it strikes a man as possible he may have to live for just as many more, with the ability for hard work gone, with the boon companions scattered abroad, with the capacity for enjoying convivial meetings a mere memory, with small means perhaps, with no bright hopes, with the pomp and the equipage, and the fairy carriages, and the glamour which youth flings over earthly objects faded away like the pageant of yesterday, while the dreary ceremony of living has to be gone through today and tomorrow and the morrow after, as though the gay cavalcade and the martial music, and the glittering helmets and the prancing steeds were still accompanying the wayfarer to his journey's end.

Ah! my friends, there comes a moment when we must all leave the coach, with its four bright bays, its pleasant outside freight, its cheery company, its guard who blows the horn so merrily through villages and along lonely country roads.

Long before we reach that final stage, where the black business claims us for its own especial property, we have to bid goodbye to all easy, thoughtless journeying, and betake ourselves with what zest we will, to traversing the common of Reality. There is no royal road across it that ever I heard of. From the king on his throne to the labourer who vaguely imagines what manner of being a king is, we have all to tramp across that desert at one period of our lives, at all events; and that period usually is when, as I have said, a man starts to find the hopes, and the strength, and the buoyancy of youth left behind, while years and years of coming life lie stretching out before him.

The coach he has travelled by drops him here. There is no appeal, there is no help; therefore let him take off his hat and wish the new passengers good speed, without either envy or repining.

Behold, he has had his turn, and let whosoever will, mount on the box-seat of life again, and tip the coachman and handle the ribbons, he shall take that pleasant journey no more—no more forever.

Even supposing a man's spring time to have been a cold and ungenial one, with bitter easterly winds and nipping frosts, biting the buds and retarding the blossoms, still it was spring for all that—spring with the young green leaves sprouting eagerly, with the flowers unfolding tenderly, with the songs of birds and the rush of waters, with the summer before and the autumn afar off, and winter remote as death and eternity; but when once the trees have donned their summer foliage, when the pure white blossoms have disappeared, and a gorgeous red and orange and purple blaze of many-coloured flowers fills the gardens, then if there come a wet, dreary day, the idea of autumn and winter is not so difficult to realise. When once twelve o'clock is reached, the evening and night become facts, not possibilities; and it was of the afternoon, and the evening and the night, Hertford O'Donnell sat thinking on the Christmas Eve when I crave permission to introduce him to my readers.

A good-looking man ladies considered him. A tall, dark-complexioned, black-haired, straight-limbed, deeply, divinely blue-eyed fellow, with a soft voice, with a pleasant brogue, who had ridden like a Centaur over the loose stone walls in Connemara, who had danced all night at the Dublin balls, who had walked over the Bennebeola mountains, gun in hand, day after day without weariness, who had fished in every one of the hundred lakes you can behold from the top of that mountain near the Recess Hotel, who had led a mad, wild life in Trinity College, and a wilder, perhaps, while '*studying for a doctor*'—as the Irish phrase goes—in Dublin, and who, after the death of his eldest brother left him free to return to Calgillan and pursue the usual utterly useless, utterly purposeless, utterly pleasant life of an Irish gentleman possessed of health, birth, and expectations, suddenly kicked over the paternal traces, bade *adieu* to Calgillan Castle and the blandishments of a certain beautiful Miss Clifden, beloved of his mother, and laid out to be his wife, walked down the avenue without even so much company as a gossoon to carry his carpet bag, shook the dust from his feet at the lodge-gates, and took his seat on the coach, never once looking back at Calgillan, where his favourite mare was standing in the stable, his greyhounds chasing one another round the home paddock, his gun at half- cock in his dressing-room, and his fishing- tackle all in order and ready for use.

He had not kissed his mother or asked for his father's blessing; he left Miss Clifden arrayed in her bran-new riding-habit without a word of affection or regret; he had spoken no syllable of farewell to any servant about the place; only when the old woman at the lodge bade him good morning and God-blessed his handsome face, he recommended her bitterly to "look well at it, for she would never see it more."

Twelve years and a half had passed since then without either Nancy Blake or any other one of the Calgillan people having set eyes on Master Hertford's handsome face.

He had kept his vow made to himself; he had not written home; he had not been indebted to mother or father for even a tenpenny-piece during the whole of that time; he had lived without friends, and he had lived without God—so far as God ever lets a man live without him—and his own private conviction was that he could get on very well without either. One thing only he felt to be needful—money, money to keep him when the evil days of sickness, or age, or loss of practice came upon him. Though a spendthrift, he was not a simpleton. Around him he saw men who, having started with fairer prospects than his own, were nevertheless reduced to indigence; and he knew that what had happened to others might happen to himself.

An unlucky cut, slipping on a bit of orange-peel in the street, the merest accident imaginable, is sufficient to change opulence to beggary in the life's programme of an individual whose income depends on eye, on nerve, on hand; and besides the consciousness of this fact, Hertford O'Donnell knew that beyond a certain point in his profession progress was not easy.

It did not depend quite on the strength of his own bow or shield whether he counted his earnings by hundreds or thousands. Work may achieve competence; but mere work cannot, in a profession at all events, compass wealth.

He looked around him, and he perceived that the majority of great men—great and wealthy—had been indebted for their elevation more to the accidents of birth, patronage, connection, or marriage, than to personal ability.

Personal ability, no doubt, they possessed; but then, little Jones, who lived in Frith Street, and who could barely keep himself and his wife and family, had ability, too, only he lacked the concomitants of success.

He wanted something or someone to puff him into notoriety—a brother at court—a lord's leg to mend—a rich wife to give him prestige into society; and, lacking this something or someone, he had grown grey-haired and faint-hearted in the service of that world which utterly despises its most obsequious servants.

"Clatter along the streets with a pair of hired horses, snub the middle classes, and drive over the commonalty—that is the way to compass wealth and popularity in England," said Hertford O'Donnell, bitterly; and, as the man desired wealth and popularity, he sat before his fire, with a foot on each hob, and a short pipe in his mouth, considering how he might best obtain the means to clatter along the streets in his carriage, and splash plebeians with mud from his wheels like the best.

In Dublin he could, by reason of his name and connection, have done well; but then he was not in Dublin, neither did he want to be. The bitterest memories of his life were inseparable from the name of the Green Island, and he had no desire to return to it.

Besides, in Dublin, heiresses are not quite so plentiful as in London; and an heiress Hertford O'Donnell had decided would do more for him than years of steady work.

A rich wife could clear him of debt, introduce him to fashionable practice, afford him that measure of social respectability which a medical bachelor invariably lacks, deliver him from the loneliness of Gerard Street, and the domination of Mr. and Mrs. Coles.

To most men, deliberately bartering away their independence for money seems so prosaic a business that they strive to gloss it over even to themselves, and to assign every reason for their choice, save that which is really the influencing one.

Not so, however, with Hertford O'Donnell. He sat beside the fire scoffing over his proposed bargain—thinking of the lady's age—her money-bags—her desirable house in town—her seat in the country—her snobbishness—her folly.

"It would be a fitting ending," he sneered; "and why I did not settle the matter tonight passes my comprehension. I am not a coward, to be frightened with old women's tales; and yet I must have turned white. I felt I did, and she asked me whether I was ill. And then to think of my being such an idiot as to ask her if she had heard anything like a cry, as though she would be likely to hear *that*—she, with her poor *parvenu* blood, which, I often imagine, must have been mixed with some of her father's pickling vinegar. What the deuce could I have been dreaming about? I wonder what it really was;" and Hertford O'Donnell pushed his hair back from his forehead, and took another draught from the too familiar tumbler, which was placed conveniently on the chimneypiece.

"After expressly making up my mind to propose, too!" he mentally continued.

"Could it have been conscience—that myth, which somebody, who knew nothing of the matter, said, '*makes cowards of us all?*' I don't believe in conscience; and even if there be such a thing capable of being developed by sentiment and cultivation, why should it trouble me? I have no intention of wronging Miss Janet Price Ingot—not the least. Honestly and fairly I shall marry her; honestly and fairly I shall act by her. An old wife is not exactly an ornamental article of furniture in a man's house; and I do not know that the fact of her being well gilded makes her look any more ornamental. But she shall have no cause for complaint; and I will go and dine with her tomorrow, and settle the matter."

Having arrived at which resolution, Mr. O'Donnell arose, kicked down the fire—burning hollow—with the heel of his boot, knocked the ashes out of his pipe, emptied his tumbler, and bethought him it was time to go to bed. He was not in the habit of taking his rest so early as quarter to twelve o'clock; but he felt unusually weary—tired mentally and bodily—and lonely beyond all power of expression.

"The fair Janet would be better than this," he said, half aloud; and then with a start and a shiver, and a blanched face, he turned sharply round, whilst a low, sobbing, wailing cry echoed mournfully though the room. No form of words could give an idea of the sound. The plaintivenes of the Eolian harp—that plaintiveness which so soon affects and lowers the highest spirits—would have seemed wildly gay in comparison to the sadness of the cry which seemed floating in the air. As the summer wind comes and goes amongst the trees, so that mournful wail came and went—came and went. It came in a rush of sound, like a gradual *crescendo* managed by a skilful musician, and it died away like a lingering note, so that the listener could scarcely tell the exact moment when it faded away into silence.

I say faded away, for it disappeared as the coast line disappears in the twilight, and there was utter stillness in the apartment.

Then, for the first time, Hertford O'Donnell looked at his dog, and beholding the creature crouched into a corner beside the fireplace, called upon him to come out.

His voice sounded strange even to himself, and apparently the dog thought so too, for he made no effort to obey the summons.

"Come out, sir," his master repeated, and then the animal came crawling reluctantly forward, with his hair on end, his eyes almost starting from his head, trembling violently, as the surgeon, who caressed him, felt.

"So you heard it, Brian?" he said to the dog. "And so your ears are sharper than hers, old fellow? It's a mighty queer thing to think of, being favoured with a visit from a banshee in Gerard Street; and as the lady has travelled so far, I only wish. I knew whether there is any sort of refreshment she would like to take after her long journey."

He spoke loudly, and with a certain mocking defiance, seeming to think the phantom he addressed would reply; but when he stopped at the end of his sentence, no sound came through the stillness. There was utter silence in the room—silence broken only by the falling of the cinders on the hearth and the breathing of his dog.

"If my visitor would tell me," he proceeded, "for whom this lamentation is being made, whether for myself, or for some other member of my illustrious family, I should feel immensely obliged. It seems too much honour for a poor surgeon to have such attention paid him. Good heavens! What is that?" he exclaimed, as a ring, loud and peremptory, woke all the echoes in the house, and brought his housekeeper in a state of distressing *dishabille*, "out of her warm bed," so she subsequently stated, to the head of the staircase.

Across the hall Hertford O'Donnell strode, relieved at the prospect of speaking to any living being. He took no precaution of putting up the chain, but flung the door wide. A dozen burglars would have proved welcome in comparison to that ghostly intruder; and, as I have said, he threw the door open, admitting a rush of wet, cold air, which made poor Mrs. Coles' few remaining teeth chatter in her head.

"Who is there ?—what do you want?" asked the surgeon, seeing no person, and hearing no voice. "Who is there?—why the devil can't you speak?"

But when even this polite exhortation failed to elicit an answer, he passed out into the night and looked up the street, and down the street, to see nothing but the driving rain and the blinking lights.

"If this goes on much longer I shall soon think I must be either mad or drunk," he muttered, as he re-entered the house, and locked and bolted the door once more.

"Lord's sake! what is the matter, sir?" asked Mrs. Coles, from the upper flight, careful only to reveal the borders of her night-cap to Mr. O'Donnell's admiring gaze. "Is anybody killed?—have you to go out, sir?"

"It was only a runaway ring," he answered, trying to reassure himself with an explanation he did not in his heart believe.

"Runaway!—I'd runaway them," murmured Mrs. Coles, as she retired to the conjugal couch, where Coles was, to quote her own expression, "*snoring like a pig through it all.*" Almost immediately afterwards she heard her master ascend the stairs and close his bedroom-door.

"Madam will surely be too much of a gentlewoman to intrude here," thought the surgeon, scoffing even at his own fears; but when he lay down he did not put out his light, and he made Brian leap up and crouch on the coverlet beside him.

The man was fairly frightened, and would have thought it no discredit to his manhood to acknowledge as much. He was not afraid of death, he was not afraid of trouble, he was not afraid of danger; but he was afraid of the banshee; and as he lay with his hand on the dog's head, he thought over all the stories he had ever heard about this family retainer in the days of his youth. He had not thought about her for years and years. Never before had he heard her voice himself. When his brother died, she had not thought it necessary to travel up to Dublin and give him notice of the impending catastrophe.

"If she had, I would have gone down to Calgillan, and perhaps saved his life," considered the surgeon. "I wonder who this is for! If for me, that will settle my debts and my marriage. If I could be quite certain it was either of the old people, I would start for Ireland tomorrow."

And then vaguely his mind wandered on to think of every banshee story he had ever heard in his life—about the beautiful lady with the wreath of flowers, who sat on the rocks below Red Castle, in the County Antrim, lamenting till one of the sons died for love of her; about the Round Chamber at Dunluce, which was swept clean by the banshee every night; about the bed in a certain great house in Ireland, which was slept in constantly, although no human being ever passed in or out after dark; about that general officer who the night before Waterloo, said to a friend, "I have heard the banshee, and shall not come off the field alive tomorrow; break the news gently to poor Carry;" and who, nevertheless, coming safe off the field, had subsequently news about poor Carry broken tenderly and pitifully to him; about the lad who, aloft in the rigging, hearing through the night a sobbing and wailing coming over the waters, went down to the captain and told him he was afraid they were somehow out of their reckoning, just in time to save the ship, which, when morning broke, they found but for his warning would have been on the rocks. It was blowing great guns, and the sea was all in a fret and turmoil, and they could sometimes see in the trough of the waves, as down a valley, the cruel black reefs they had escaped.

On deck the captain stood speaking to the boy who had saved them, and asking how he knew of their danger; and when the lad told him, the captain laughed, and said her ladyship had been outwitted that time.

But the boy answered, with a grave shake of his head, that the warning was either for him or his, and that if he got safe to port there would be bad tidings waiting for him from home; whereupon the captain bade him go below, and get some brandy and lie down.

He got the brandy, and he lay down, but he never rose again; and when the storm abated—when a great calm succeeded to the previous tempest—there was a very solemn funeral at sea; and on their arrival at Liverpool the captain took a journey to Ireland to tell a widowed mother how her only son died, and to bear his few effects to the poor desolate soul.

And Hertford O'Donnell thought again about his own father riding full-chase across country, and hearing, as he galloped by a clump of plantation, something like a sobbing and wailing. The hounds were in full cry; but he still felt, as he afterwards expressed it, that there was something among those trees he could not pass; and so he jumped off his horse, and hung the reins over the branch of a fir, and beat the cover well, but not a thing could be find in it.

Then, for the first time in his life, Miles O'Donnell turned his horse's head *from* the hunt, and, within a mile of Calgillan, met a man running to tell him Mr. Martin's gun had burst, and hurt him badly.

And he remembered the story also, of how Mary O'Donnell, his great aunt, being married to a young Englishman, heard the banshee as she sat one evening waiting for his return; and of how she, thinking the bridge by which he often came home unsafe for horse and man, went out, in a great panic, to meet and entreat him to go round by the main road for her sake. Sir Everard was riding along in the moonlight, making straight for the bridge, when he beheld a figure dressed all in white upon it. Then there was a crash, and the figure disappeared.

The lady was rescued and brought back to the hall; but next morning there were two dead bodies within its walls—those of Lady Eyreton and her stillborn son.

Quicker than I write them, these memories chased one another through Hertford O'Donnell's brain; and there was one more terrible memory than any which would recur to him, concerning an Irish nobleman who, seated alone in his great town-house in London, heard the banshee, and rushed out to get rid of the phantom, which wailed in his ear, nevertheless, as he strode down Piccadilly. And then the surgeon remembered how he went with a friend to the Opera, feeling sure that there no banshee, unless she had a box, could find admittance, until suddenly he heard her singing up amongst the highest part of the scenery, with a terrible mournfulness, with a *pathos* which made the *prima donna's* tenderest notes seem harsh by comparison.

As he came out, some quarrel arose between him and a famous fire-eater, against whom he stumbled; and the result was that the next afternoon there was a new Lord ——, *vice* Lord ——, killed in a duel with Captain Bravo.

Memories like these are not the most enlivening possible; they are apt to make a man fanciful, and nervous, and wakeful; but as time ran on, Hertford O'Donnell fell asleep, with his candle still burning, and Brian's cold nose pressed against his hand.

He dreamt of his mother's family—the Hertfords, of Artingbury, Yorkshire, far-off relatives of Lord Hertford—so far off that even Mrs. O'Donnell held no clue to the genealogical maze.

He thought he was at Artingbury, fishing; that it was a misty summer's morning, and the fish rising beautifully. In his dream he hooked one after another, and the boy who was with him threw them into the basket.

At last there was one more difficult to land than the others; and the boy, in his eagerness to watch the sport, drew nearer and nearer to the brink, while the fisher, intent on his prey, failed to notice his companion's danger.

Suddenly there was a cry, a splash, and the boy disappeared from sight.

Next instant he rose again, however, and then, for the first time, Hertford O'Donnell saw his face.

It was one he knew well.

In a moment he plunged into the water, and struck out for the lad. He had him by the hair, he was turning to bring him back to land, when the stream suddenly changed into a wide, wild, shoreless sea, where the billows were chasing one another with a mad demoniac mirth.

For awhile O'Donnell kept the lad and himself afloat. They were swept under the waves, and came forth again, only to see larger wares rushing towards them; but through all the surgeon never loosened his hold until a tremendous billow engulfing them both, tore the boy from him.

With the horror of that he awoke, to hear a voice saying quite distinctly.

"Go to the hospital!—go at once!"

The surgeon started up in bed, rubbed his eyes, and looked about him. The candle was flickering faintly in its socket. Brian, with his ears pricked forward, had raised his head at his master's sudden jump.

Everything was quiet, but still those words were ringing in his ear—

"Go to the hospital!—go at once!"

The tremendous peal of the bell overnight, and this sentence, seemed to be simultaneous.

That he was wanted at Guy's—wanted imperatively—came to O'Donnell like an inspiration.

Neither sense nor reason had anything to do with the conviction that roused him out of bed, and made him dress as speedily as possible, and grope his way down the staircase, Brian following.

He opened the front door, and passed out into the darkness. The rain was over, and the stars were shining as he pursued his way down Newport Market, and thence, winding in and out in a south-east direction, through Lincoln's Inn Fields and Old Square to Chancery Lane, whence he proceeded to St. Paul's.

Along the deserted streets he resolutely continued his walk. He did not know what he was going to Guy's for. Some instinct was urging him on, and he neither strove to combat nor control it. Only once had the thought of turning back occurred, and that was at the archway leading into Old Square. There he had paused for a moment, asking himself whether he were not gone stark, staring mad; but Guy's seemed preferable to the haunted house in Gerard Street, and he walked resolutely on, determining to say, if any surprise were expressed at his appearance, that he had been sent for.

Sent for?—yea, truly; but by whom?

On through Cannon Street; on over London Bridge, where the lights flickered in the river, and the sullen plash of the water flowing beneath the arches, washing the stone piers, could be heard, now the human din was hushed and lulled to sleep. On, thinking of many things; of the days of his youth; of his dead brother; of his father's heavily encumbered estate; of the fortune his mother had vowed she would leave to some charity rather than to him, if he refused to marry according to her choice; of his wild life in London; of the terrible cry he had heard overnight—that terrible wail which he could not drive away from his memory even as he entered Guy's, and confronted the porter, who said—

"You have just been sent for, sir; did you meet the messenger?"

Like one in a dream, Hertford O'Donnell heard him; like one in a dream, also, he asked what was the matter.

"Bad accident, sir; fire: balcony gave way—unsafe—old building. Mother and child—a son; boy with compound fracture of thigh." This, the joint information of porter and house-surgeon, mingled together, and made a roar in Mr. O'Donnell's ears like the sound of the sea breaking on a shingly shore.

Only one sentence he understood perfectly—"Immediate amputation necessary." At this point he grew cool; he was the careful, cautious, successful surgeon in a moment.

"The boy, you say?" he answered; "Let me see him."

The Guy's Hospital of today may be different to the Guy's Hertford O'Donnell knew so well. Railways have, I believe, swept away the old operating room; railways may have changed the position of the old accident ward, to reach which, in the days of which I am writing, the two surgeons had to pass a staircase leading to the upper stories.

On the lower step of this staircase, partially in shadow, Hertford O'Donnell beheld, as he came forward, an old woman seated.

An old woman with streaming grey hair, with attenuated arms, with head bowed forward, with scanty clothing, with bare feet; who never looked up at their approach, but sat unnoticing, shaking her head and wringing her hands in an extremity of grief.

"Who is that?" asked Mr. O'Donnell, almost involuntarily.

"Who is what?" demanded his companion.

"That—that woman," was the reply.

"What woman?"

"There—are you blind?—seated on the bottom step of the staircase. What is she doing?" persisted Mr. O'Donnell.

"There is no woman near us," his companion answered, looking at the rising surgeon very much as though he suspected him of seeing double.

"No woman!" scoffed Hertford. "Do you expect me to disbelieve the evidence of my own eyes?" and he walked up to the figure, meaning to touch it.

But as he essayed to do so, the woman seemed to rise in the air and float away, with her arms stretched high up over her head, uttering such a wail of pain, and agony, and distress, as caused the Irishman's blood to curdle.

"My God! Did you hear that?" he said to his companion.

"What?" was the reply.

Then, although he knew the sound had fallen on deaf ears, he answered—

"The wail of the banshee! Some of my people are doomed!"

"I trust not," answered the house-surgeon, who had an idea, nevertheless, that Hertford O'Donnell's banshee lived in a whisky-bottle, and that she would someday make an end of that rising and clever operator.

With nerves utterly shaken, Mr. O'Donnell walked forward to the accident ward. There, with his face shaded from the light, lay his patient—a young boy, with a compound fracture of the thigh.

In that ward, in the face of actual pain or danger capable of relief, the surgeon had never known faltering nor fear; and now he carefully examined the injury, felt the pulse, inquired as to the treatment pursued, and ordered the sufferer to be carried to the operating room.

While he was looking out his instruments he heard the boy lying on the table murmur faintly—

"Tell her not to cry so—tell her not to cry."

"What is he talking about?" Hertford O'Donnell inquired.

"The nurse says he has been speaking about some woman crying ever since he came in—his mother, most likely," answered one of the attendants.

"He is delirious, then?" observed the surgeon.

"No, sir," pleaded the boy, excitedly. "No; it is that woman—that woman with the grey hair. I saw her looking from the upper window before the balcony gave way. She has never left me since, and she won't be quiet, wringing her hands and crying."

"Can you see her now?" Hertford O'Donnell inquired, stepping to the side of the table. "Point out where she stands."

Then the lad stretched forth a feeble finger in the direction of the door, where clearly, as he had seen her seated on the stairs, the surgeon saw a woman standing—a woman with grey hair and scanty clothing, and upstretched arms and bare feet.

"A word with you, sir," O'Donnell said to the house-surgeon, drawing him back from the table. "I cannot perform this operation; send for some other person. I am ill: I am incapable."

"But," pleaded the other, "there is no time to get anyone else. We sent for Mr. —— before we troubled you, but he was out of town, and all the rest of the surgeons live so far away. Mortification may set in at any moment, and—"

"Do you think you require to teach me my business?" was the reply. "I know the boy's life hangs on a thread, and that is the very reason I cannot operate. I am not fit for it. I tell you I have seen tonight that which unnerves me for anything. My hand is not steady. Send for someone else without delay. Say I am ill—dead!—what you please. Heavens! there she is again, right over the boy! Do you hear her?" and Hertford O'Donnell fell fainting on the floor.

He lay in that death-like swoon for hours; and when he returned to consciousness, the principal physician of Guy's was standing beside him in the cold grey light of the Christmas morning.

"The boy?" murmured O'Donnell, faintly.

"Now, my dear fellow, keep yourself quiet," was the reply.

"The boy?" he repeated, irritably. "Who operated?"

"No one," Dr. —— answered. "It would have been useless cruelty. Mortification had set in, and—"

Hertford O'Donnell turned his face to the wall, and his friend could not see it.

"Do not distress yourself," went on the physician, kindly. "Allington says he could not have survived the operation in any case. He was quite delirious from the first, raving about a woman with grey hair, and—"

"Yes, I know," Hertford O'Donnell interrupted; "and the boy had a mother, they told me, or I dreamt it."

"Yes, bruised and shaken, but not seriously injured."

"Has she blue eyes and fair hair—fair hair all rippling and wavy? Is she white as a lily, with just a faint flush of colour in her cheek? Is she young, and trusting, and innocent? No; I am wandering. She must be nearly thirty, now. Go, for God's sake, and tell me if you can find a woman that you could imagine having been as a girl such as I describe."

"Irish?" asked the doctor; and O'Donnell made a gesture of assent.

"It is she, then," was the reply; "a woman with the face of an angel."

"A woman who should have been my wife," the surgeon answered; "whose child was my son."

"Lord help you!" ejaculated the doctor. Then Hertford O'Donnell raised himself from the sofa where they had laid him, and told his companion the story of his life—how there had been bitter feud between his people and her people—how they were divided by old animosities and by difference of religion—how they had met by stealth, and exchanged rings and vows, all for nought—how his family had insulted hers, so that her father, wishful for her to marry a kinsman of his own, bore her off to a far-away land, and made her write him a letter of eternal farewell—how his own parents had kept all knowledge of the quarrel from him till she was utterly beyond his reach—how they had vowed to discard him unless he agreed to marry according to their wishes—how he left his home, and came to London, and pushed his fortune. All this Hertford O'Donnell repeated; and when he had finished, the bells were ringing for morning service—ringing loudly—ringing joyfully. "*Peace on earth, good will towards men.*" But there was little peace that morning for Hertford O'Donnell. He had to look on the face of his dead son, wherein he beheld, as though reflected, the face of the boy in his dream.

Stealthily he followed his friend, and beheld, with her eyes closed, her cheeks pale and pinched, her hair thinner, but still falling like a veil over her, the love of his youth, the only woman he had ever loved devotedly and unselfishly.

There is little space left here, to tell of how the two met at last—of how the stone of the years seemed suddenly rolled away from the tomb of their past, and their youth arose and returned to them even amid their tears.

She had been true to him, through persecution, through contumely, through kindness, which was more trying; through shame, and grief, and poverty, she had been loyal to the lover of her youth; and before the new year dawned there came a letter from Calgillan, saying that the banshee had been heard there, and praying Hertford, if he were still alive, to let bygones be bygones, in consideration of the long years of estrangement—the anguish and remorse of his afflicted parents.

More than that Hertford O'Donnell, if a reckless man, was an honourable; and so, on the Christmas Day when he was to have proposed for Miss Ingot, he went to that lady, and told her how he had wooed and won in the years of his youth one who after many days was miraculously restored to him; and from the hour in which he took her into his confidence he never thought her either vulgar or foolish, but rather he paid homage to the woman who, when she had heard the whole tale repeated, said, simply, "Ask her to come to me till you claim her—and God bless you both!"

Mr. Justice Harbottle

By J. Sheridan le Fanu

Prologue

On this case Doctor Hesselius has inscribed nothing more than the words, "Harman's Report," and a simple reference to his own extraordinary Essay on "The Interior Sense, and the Conditions of the Opening thereof."

The reference is to Vol. 1., Section 317, Note Za. The note to which reference is thus made, simply says:

> There are two accounts of the remarkable case of the Honourable Mr. Justice Harbottle, one furnished to me by Mrs. Trimmer, of Tunbridge Wells (June, 1805); the other at a much later date, by Anthony Harman, Esq. I much prefer the former; in the first place, because it is minute and detailed, and written, it seems to me, with more caution and knowledge; and in the next, because the letters from Dr. Hedstone, which are embodied in it, furnish matter of the highest value to a right apprehension of the nature of the case. It was one of the best declared cases of an opening of the interior sense, which I have met with.
>
> It was affected too, by the phenomenon, which occurs so frequently as to indicate a law of these eccentric conditions; that is to say, it exhibited what I may term, the contagious character of this sort of intrusion of the spirit-world upon the proper domain of matter. So soon as the spirit-action has established itself in the case of one patient, its developed energy begins to radiate, more or less effectually,

upon others. The interior vision of the child was opened; as was, also, that of its mother, Mrs. Pyneweck; and both the interior vision and hearing of the scullery-maid, were opened on the same occasion. After-appearances are the result of the law explained in Vol. 2, Section 17 to 49. The common centre of association, simultaneously recalled, unites, or *re*unites, as the case may be, for a period measured, as we see, in Section 37. The *maximum* will extend to days, the *minimum* is little more than a second. We see the operation of this principle perfectly displayed, in certain cases of lunacy, of epilepsy, of catalepsy, and of mania, of a peculiar and painful character, though unattended by incapacity of business.

The memorandum of the case of Judge Harbottle, which was written by Mrs. Trimmer, of Tunbridge Wells, which Doctor Hesselius thought the better of the two, I have been unable to discover among his papers. I found in his escritoire a note to the effect that he had lent the Report of Judge Harbottle's case, written by Mrs. Trimmer, to Dr. F. Heyne.

To that learned and able gentleman accordingly I wrote, and received from him, in his reply, which was full of alarms and regrets, on account of the uncertain safety of that "valuable MS.," a line written long since by Dr. Hesselius, which completely exonerated him, inasmuch as it acknowledged the safe return of the papers.

The narrative of Mr. Harman, is therefore, the only one available for this collection. The late Dr. Hesselius, in another passage of the note that I have cited, says, "As to the facts (non-medical) of the case, the narrative of Mr. Harman exactly tallies with that furnished by Mrs. Trimmer."

The strictly scientific view of the case would scarcely interest the popular reader; and, possibly, for the purposes of this selection, I should, even had I both papers to choose between, have preferred that of Mr. Harman, which is given, in full, in the following pages.

Chapter 1
The Judge's House

Thirty years ago, an elderly man, to whom I paid quarterly a small annuity charged on some property of mine, came on the quarter-day to receive it. He was a dry, sad, quiet man, who had known better days, and had always maintained an unexceptionable character. No better authority could be imagined for a ghost story.

He told me one, though with a manifest reluctance; he was drawn into the narration by his choosing to explain what I should not have remarked, that he had called two days earlier than that week after the strict day of payment, which he had usually allowed to elapse. His reason was a sudden determination to change his lodgings, and the consequent necessity of paying his rent a little before it was due.

He lodged in a dark street in Westminster, in a spacious old house, very warm, being wainscoted from top to bottom, and furnished with no undue abundance of windows, and those fitted with thick sashes and small panes.

This house was, as the bills upon the windows testified, offered to be sold or let. But no one seemed to care to look at it.

A thin matron, in rusty black silk, very taciturn, with large, steady, alarmed eyes, that seemed to look in your face, to read what you might have seen in the dark rooms and passages through which you had passed, was in charge of it, with a solitary "maid-of-all-work" under her command. My poor friend had taken lodgings in this house, on account of their extraordinary cheapness. He had occupied them for nearly a year without the slightest disturbance, and was the only tenant, under rent, in the house. He had two rooms; a sitting-room and a bedroom with a closet opening from it, in which he kept his books and papers locked up.

He had gone to his bed, having also locked the outer door. Unable to sleep, he had lighted a candle, and after having read for a time, had laid the book beside him. He heard the old clock at the stairhead strike one; and very shortly after, to his alarm, he saw the closet-door, which he thought he had locked, open stealthily, and a slight dark man, particularly sinister, and somewhere about fifty, dressed in mourning of a very antique fashion, such a suit as we see in Hogarth, entered the room on tip-toe. He was followed by an elder man, stout, and blotched with scurvy, and whose features, fixed as a corpse's, were stamped with dreadful force with a character of sensuality and villainy.

This old man wore a flowered silk dressing-gown and ruffles, and he remarked a gold ring on his finger, and on his head a cap of velvet, such as, in the days of *perukes*, gentlemen wore in undress.

This direful old man carried in his ringed and ruffled hand a coil of rope; and these two figures crossed the floor diagonally, passing the foot of his bed, from the closet door at the farther end of the room, at the left, near the window, to the door opening upon the lobby, close to the bed's head, at his right.

He did not attempt to describe his sensations as these figures passed so near him. He merely said, that so far from sleeping in that room again, no consideration the world could offer would induce him so much as to enter it again alone, even in the daylight. He found both doors, that of the closet, and that of the room opening upon the lobby, in the morning fast locked as he had left them before going to bed.

In answer to a question of mine, he said that neither appeared the least conscious of his presence. They did not seem to glide, but walked as living men do, but without any sound, and he felt a vibration on the floor as they crossed it. He so obviously suffered from speaking about the apparitions, that I asked him no more questions.

There were in his description, however, certain coincidences so very singular, as to induce me, by that very post, to write to a friend much my senior, then living in a remote part of England, for the information which I knew he could give me. He had himself more than once pointed out that old house to my attention, and told me, though very briefly, the strange story which I now asked him to give me in greater detail.

His answer satisfied me; and the following pages convey its substance.

Your letter (he wrote) tells me you desire some particulars about the closing years of the life of Mr. Justice Harbottle, one of the judges of the Court of Common Pleas. You refer, of course, to the extraordinary occurrences that made that period of his life long after a theme for "winter tales" and metaphysical speculation. I happen to know perhaps more than any other man living of those mysterious particulars.

The old family mansion, when I revisited London, more than thirty years ago, I examined for the last time. During the years that have passed since then, I hear that improvement, with its preliminary demolitions, has been doing wonders for the quarter of Westminster in which it stood. If I were quite certain that the house had been taken down, I should have no difficulty about naming the street in which it stood. As what I have to tell, however, is not likely to improve its letting value, and as I should not care to get into trouble, I prefer being silent on that particular point.

How old the house was, I can't tell. People said it was built by Roger Harbottle, a Turkey merchant, in the reign of King James I. I am not a good opinion upon such questions; but having been in it, though in its forlorn and deserted state, I can tell you in a general way what it was like. It was built of dark-red brick, and the door and windows were faced with stone that had turned yellow by time. It receded some feet from the line of the other houses in the street; and it had a florid and fanciful rail of iron about the broad steps that invited your ascent to the hall-door, in which were fixed, under a file of lamps among scrolls and twisted leaves, two immense "extinguishers," like the conical caps of fairies, into which, in old times, the footmen used to thrust their flambeaux when their chairs or coaches had set down their great people, in the hall or at the steps, as the case might be.

That hall is panelled up to the ceiling, and has a large fireplace. Two or three stately old rooms open from it at each side.

The windows of these are tall, with many small panes. Passing through the arch at the back of the hall, you come upon the wide and heavy well-staircase. There is a back staircase also. The mansion is large, and has not as much light, by any means, in proportion to its extent, as modern houses enjoy. When I saw it, it had long been untenanted, and had the gloomy reputation beside of a haunted house. Cobwebs floated from the ceilings or spanned the corners of the cornices, and dust lay thick over everything. The windows were stained with the dust and rain of fifty years, and darkness had thus grown darker.

When I made it my first visit, it was in company with my father, when I was still a boy, in the year 1808. I was about twelve years old, and my imagination impressible, as it always is at that age. I looked about me with great awe. I was here in the very centre and scene of those occurrences which I had heard recounted at the fireside at home, with so delightful a horror.

My father was an old bachelor of nearly sixty when he married. He had, when a child, seen Judge Harbottle on the bench in his robes and wig a dozen times at least before his death, which took place in 1748, and his appearance made a powerful and unpleasant impression, not only on his imagination, but upon his nerves.

The Judge was at that time a man of some sixty-seven years. He had a great mulberry-coloured face, a big, carbuncled nose, fierce eyes, and a grim and brutal mouth. My father, who was young at the time, thought it the most formidable face he had ever seen; for there were evidences of intellectual power in the formation and lines of the forehead. His voice was loud and harsh, and gave effect to the sarcasm which was his habitual weapon on the bench.

This old gentleman had the reputation of being about the wickedest man in England. Even on the bench he now and then showed his scorn of opinion. He had carried cases his own way, it was said, in spite of counsel, authorities, and even of juries, by a sort of cajolery, violence, and bamboozling, that somehow confused and overpowered resistance. He had never actually committed himself; he was too cunning to do that. He had the character of being, however, a dangerous and unscrupulous judge; but his character did not trouble him. The associates he chose for his hours of relaxation cared as little as he did about it.

Chapter 2
Mr. Peters

One night during the session of 1746 this old Judge went down in his chair to wait in one of the rooms of the House of Lords for the result of a division in which he and his order were interested.

This over, he was about to return to his house close by, in his chair; but the night had become so soft and fine that he changed his mind, sent it home empty, and with two footmen, each with a flambeau, set out on foot in preference. Gout had made him rather a slow pedestrian. It took him some time to get through the two or three streets he had to pass before reaching his house.

In one of those narrow streets of tall houses, perfectly silent at that hour, he overtook, slowly as he was walking, a very singular-looking old gentleman.

He had a bottle-green coat on, with a cape to it, and large stone buttons, a broad-leafed low-crowned hat, from under which a big powdered wig escaped; he stooped very much, and supported his bending knees with the aid of a crutch-handled cane, and so shuffled and tottered along painfully.

"I ask your pardon, sir," said this old man, in a very quavering voice, as the burly Judge came up with him, and he extended his hand feebly towards his arm.

Mr. Justice Harbottle saw that the man was by no means poorly dressed, and his manner that of a gentleman.

The Judge stopped short, and said, in his harsh peremptory tones, "Well, sir, how can I serve you?"

"Can you direct me to Judge Harbottle's house? I have some intelligence of the very last importance to communicate to him."

"Can you tell it before witnesses?" asked the Judge.

"By no means; it must reach *his* ear only," quavered the old man earnestly.

"If that be so, sir, you have only to accompany me a few steps farther to reach my house, and obtain a private audience; for I am Judge Harbottle."

With this invitation the infirm gentleman in the white wig complied very readily; and in another minute the stranger stood in what was then termed the front parlour of the Judge's house, *tete-a-tete* with that shrewd and dangerous functionary.

He had to sit down, being very much exhausted, and unable for a little time to speak; and then he had a fit of coughing, and after that a fit of gasping; and thus two or three minutes passed, during which the Judge dropped his *roquelaure* on an arm-chair, and threw his cocked-hat over that.

The venerable pedestrian in the white wig quickly recovered his voice. With closed doors they remained together for some time.

There were guests waiting in the drawing-rooms, and the sound of men's voices laughing, and then of a female voice singing to a harpsichord, were heard distinctly in the hall over the stairs; for old Judge Harbottle had arranged one of his dubious jollifications, such as might well make the hair of godly men's heads stand upright for that night.

This old gentleman in the powdered white wig, that rested on his stooped shoulders, must have had something to say that interested the Judge very much; for he would not have parted on easy terms with the ten minutes and upwards which that conference filched from the sort of revelry in which he most delighted, and in which he was the roaring king, and in some sort the tyrant also, of his company.

The footman who showed the aged gentleman out observed that the Judge's mulberry-coloured face, pimples and all, were bleached to a dingy yellow, and there was the abstraction of agitated thought in his manner, as he bid the stranger good-night. The servant saw that the conversation had been of serious import, and that the Judge was frightened.

Instead of stumping upstairs forthwith to his scandalous hilarities, his profane company, and his great china bowl of punch-the identical bowl from which a bygone Bishop of London, good easy man, had baptised this Judge's grandfather, now clinking round the rim with silver ladles, and hung with scrolls of lemon-peel—instead, I say, of stumping and clambering up the great staircase to the cavern of his Circean enchantment, he stood with his big nose flattened against the window-pane, watching the progress of the feeble old man, who clung stiffly to the iron rail as he got down, step by step, to the pavement.

The hall-door had hardly closed, when the old Judge was in the hall bawling hasty orders, with such stimulating expletives as old colonels under excitement sometimes indulge in now-a-days, with a stamp or two of his big foot, and a waving of his clenched fist in the air. He commanded the footman to overtake the old gentleman in the white wig, to offer him his protection on his way home, and in no case to show his face again without having ascertained where he lodged, and who he was, and all about him.

"By ——, sirrah! if you fail me in this, you doff my livery tonight!"

Forth bounced the stalwart footman, with his heavy cane under his arm, and skipped down the steps, and looked up and down the street after the singular figure, so easy to recognize.

What were his adventures I shall not tell you just now.

The old man, in the conference to which he had been admitted in that stately panelled room, had just told the Judge a very strange story. He might be himself a conspirator; he might possibly be crazed; or possibly his whole story was straight and true.

The aged gentleman in the bottle-green coat, in finding himself alone with Mr. Justice Harbottle, had become agitated. He said,

"There is, perhaps you are not aware, my lord, a prisoner in Shrewsbury jail, charged with having forged a bill of exchange for a hundred and twenty pounds, and his name is Lewis

Pyneweck, a grocer of that town."

"Is there?" says the Judge, who knew well that there was.

"Yes, my lord," says the old man.

"Then you had better say nothing to affect this case. If you do, by ——, I'll commit you! for I'm to try it," says the judge, with his terrible look and tone.

"I am not going to do anything of the kind, my lord; of him or his case I know nothing, and care nothing. But a fact has come to my knowledge which it behoves you to well consider."

"And what may that fact be?" inquired the Judge; "I'm in haste, sir, and beg you will use dispatch."

"It has come to my knowledge, my lord, that a secret tribunal is in process of formation, the object of which is to take cognisance of the conduct of the judges; and first, of *your* conduct, my lord; it is a wicked conspiracy."

"Who are of it?" demands the Judge.

"I know not a single name as yet. I know but the fact, my lord; it is most certainly true."

"I'll have you before the Privy Council, sir," says the Judge.

"That is what I most desire; but not for a day or two, my lord."

"And why so?"

"I have not as yet a single name, as I told your lordship; but I expect to have a list of the most forward men in it, and some other papers connected with the plot, in two or three days."

"You said one or two just now."

"About that time, my lord."

"Is this a Jacobite plot?"

"In the main I think it is, my lord."

"Why, then, it is political. I have tried no State prisoners, nor am like to try any such. How, then, doth it concern me?"

"From what I can gather, my lord, there are those in it who desire private revenges upon certain judges."

"What do they call their cabal?"

"The High Court of Appeal, my lord."

"Who are you, sir? What is your name?"

"Hugh Peters, my lord."

"That should be a Whig name?"

"It is, my lord." "Where do you lodge, Mr. Peters?"

"In Thames Street, my lord, over against the sign of the 'Three Kings.'"

"'Three Kings?' Take care one be not too many for you, Mr. Peters! How come you, an honest Whig, as you say, to be privy to a Jacobite plot? Answer me that."

"My lord, a person in whom I take an interest has been seduced to take a part in it; and being frightened at the unexpected wickedness of their plans, he is resolved to become an informer for the Crown."

"He resolves like a wise man, sir. What does he say of the persons? Who are in the plot? Doth he know them?"

"Only two, my lord; but he will be introduced to the club in a few days, and he will then have a list, and more exact information of their plans, and above all of their oaths, and their hours and places of meeting, with which he wishes to be acquainted before they can have any suspicions of his intentions. And being so informed, to whom, think you, my lord, had he best go then?"

"To the king's attorney-general straight. But you say this concerns me, sir, in particular? How about this prisoner, Lewis Pyneweck? Is he one of them?"

"I can't tell, my lord; but for some reason, it is thought your lordship will be well advised if you try him not. For if you do, it is feared 'twill shorten your days."

"So far as I can learn, Mr. Peters, this business smells pretty strong of blood and treason. The king's attorney-general will know how to deal with it. When shall I see you again, sir?"

"If you give me leave, my lord, either before your lordship's court sits, or after it rises, tomorrow. I should like to come and tell your lordship what has passed."

"Do so, Mr. Peters, at nine o'clock tomorrow morning. And see you play me no trick, sir, in this matter; if you do, by ——, sir, I'll lay you by the heels!"

"You need fear no trick from me, my lord; had I not wished to serve you, and acquit my own conscience, I never would have come all this way to talk with your lordship."

"I'm willing to believe you, Mr. Peters; I'm willing to believe you, sir."

And upon this they parted.

"He has either painted his face, or he is consumedly sick," thought the old Judge.

The light had shown more effectually upon his features as he turned to leave the room with a low bow, and they looked, he fancied, unnaturally chalky.

"D— him!" said the Judge ungraciously, as he began to scale the stairs: "he has half-spoiled my supper."

But if he had, no one but the Judge himself perceived it, and the evidence was all, as any one might perceive, the other way.

Chapter 3
Lewis Pyneweck

In the meantime the footman dispatched in pursuit of Mr. Peters speedily overtook that feeble gentleman. The old man stopped when he heard the sound of pursuing steps, but any alarms that may have crossed his mind seemed to disappear on his recognizing the livery. He very gratefully accepted the proffered assistance, and placed his tremulous arm within the servant's for support. They had not gone far, however, when the old man stopped suddenly, saying,

"Dear me! as I live, I have dropped it. You heard it fall. My eyes, I fear, won't serve me, and I'm unable to stoop low enough; but if *you* will look, you shall have half the find. It is a guinea; I carried it in my glove."

The street was silent and deserted. The footman had hardly descended to what he termed his "hunkers," and begun to search the pavement about the spot which the old man indicated, when Mr. Peters, who seemed very much exhausted, and breathed with difficulty, struck him a violent blow, from above, over the back of the head with a heavy instrument, and then another; and leaving him bleeding and senseless in the gutter, ran like a lamplighter down a lane to the right, and was gone.

When an hour later, the watchman brought the man in livery home, still stupid and covered with blood, Judge Harbottle cursed his servant roundly, swore he was drunk, threatened him with an indictment for taking bribes to betray his master, and cheered him with a perspective of the broad street leading from the Old Bailey to Tyburn, the cart's tail, and the hangman's lash.

Notwithstanding this demonstration, the Judge was pleased. It was a disguised "affidavit man," or footpad, no doubt, who had been employed to frighten him. The trick had fallen through.

A "court of appeal," such as the false Hugh Peters had indicated, with assassination for its sanction, would be an uncomfortable institution for a "hanging judge" like the Honourable Justice Harbottle. That sarcastic and ferocious administrator of the criminal code of England, at that time a rather pharisaical, bloody and heinous system of justice, had reasons of his own for choosing to try that very Lewis Pyneweck, on whose behalf this audacious trick was devised. Try him he would. No man living should take that morsel out of his mouth.

Of Lewis Pyneweck, of course, so far as the outer world could see, he knew nothing. He would try him after his fashion, without fear, favour, or affection.

But did he not remember a certain thin man, dressed in mourning, in whose house, in Shrewsbury, the Judge's lodgings used to be, until a scandal of ill-treating his wife came suddenly to light? A grocer with a demure look, a soft step, and a lean face as dark as mahogany, with a nose sharp and long, standing ever so little awry, and a pair of dark steady brown eyes under thinly-traced black brows—a man whose thin lips wore always a faint unpleasant smile.

Had not that scoundrel an account to settle with the Judge? had he not been troublesome lately? and was not his name Lewis Pyneweck, sometime grocer in Shrewsbury, and now prisoner in the jail of that town?

The reader may take it, if he pleases, as a sign that Judge Harbottle was a good Christian, that he suffered nothing ever from remorse. That was undoubtedly true. He had, nevertheless, done this grocer, forger, what you will, some five or six years before, a grievous wrong; but it was not that, but a possible scandal, and possible complications, that troubled the learned Judge now.

Did he not, as a lawyer, know, that to bring a man from his shop to the dock, the chances must be at least ninety-nine out of a hundred that he is guilty?

A weak man like his learned brother Withershins was not a judge to keep the high-roads safe, and make crime tremble. Old Judge Harbottle was the man to make the evil-disposed quiver, and to refresh the world with showers of wicked blood, and thus save the innocent, to the refrain of the ancient saw he loved to quote:

Foolish pity
Ruins a city.

In hanging that fellow he could not be wrong. The eye of a man accustomed to look upon the dock could not fail to read "villain" written sharp and clear in his plotting face. Of course he would try him, and no one else should.

A saucy-looking woman, still handsome, in a mob-cap gay with blue ribbons, in a *saque* of flowered silk, with lace and rings on, much too fine for the Judge's housekeeper, which nevertheless she was, peeped into his study next morning, and, seeing the Judge alone, stepped in.

"Here's another letter from him, come by the post this morning. Can't you do nothing for him?" she said wheedlingly, with her arm over his neck, and her delicate finger and thumb fiddling with the lobe of his purple ear.

"I'll try," said Judge Harbottle, not raising his eyes from the paper he was reading.

"I knew you'd do what I asked you," she said.

The Judge clapt his gouty claw over his heart, and made her an ironical bow.

"What," she asked, "will you do?"

"Hang him," said the Judge with a chuckle.

"You don't mean to; no, you don't, my little man," said she, surveying herself in a mirror on the wall.

"I'm d——d but I think you're falling in love with your husband at last!" said Judge Harbottle.

"I'm blest but I think you're growing jealous of him," replied the lady with a laugh. "But no; he was always a bad one to me; I've done with him long ago."

"And he with you, by George! When he took your fortune, and your spoons, and your ear-rings, he had all he wanted of you. He drove you from his house; and when he discovered you had made yourself comfortable, and found a good situation, he'd have taken your guineas, and your silver, and your ear-rings over again, and then allowed you half-a-dozen years more to make a new harvest for his mill. You don't wish him good; if you say you do, you lie."

She laughed a wicked, saucy laugh, and gave the terrible Rhadamanthus a playful tap on the chops.

"He wants me to send him money to fee a counsellor," she said, while her eyes wandered over the pictures on the wall, and back again to the looking-glass; and certainly she did not look as if his jeopardy troubled her very much.

"Confound his impudence, the *scoundrel*!" thundered the old Judge, throwing himself back in his chair, as he used to do *in furore* on the bench, and the lines of his mouth looked brutal, and his eyes ready to leap from their sockets. "If you answer his letter from my house to please yourself, you'll write your next from somebody else's to please me. You understand, my pretty witch, I'll not be pestered. Come, no pouting; whimpering won't do. You don't care a brass farthing for the villain, body or soul. You came here but to make a row. You are one of Mother Carey's chickens; and where you come, the storm is up. Get you gone, baggage! get you *gone*!" he repeated, with a stamp; for a knock at the hall-door made her instantaneous disappearance indispensable.

I need hardly say that the venerable Hugh Peters did not appear again. The Judge never mentioned him. But oddly enough, considering how he laughed to scorn the weak invention which he had blown into dust at the very first puff, his white-wigged visitor and the conference in the dark front parlour were often in his memory.

His shrewd eye told him that allowing for change of tints and such disguises as the playhouse affords every night, the features of this false old man, who had turned out too hard for his tall footman, were identical with those of Lewis Pyneweck.

Judge Harbottle made his registrar call upon the crown solicitor, and tell him that there was a man in town who bore a wonderful resemblance to a prisoner in Shrewsbury jail named Lewis Pyneweck, and to make inquiry through the post forthwith whether any one was personating Pyneweck in prison and whether he had thus or otherwise made his escape.

The prisoner was safe, however, and no question as to his identity.

Chapter 4

Interruption in Court

In due time Judge Harbottle went circuit; and in due time the judges were in Shrewsbury. News travelled slowly in those days, and newspapers, like the wagons and stage coaches, took matters easily. Mrs. Pyneweck, in the Judge's house, with a diminished household—the greater part of the Judge's servants having gone with him, for he had given up riding circuit, and travelled in his coach in state—kept house rather solitarily at home.

In spite of quarrels, in spite of mutual injuries—some of them, inflicted by herself, enormous—in spite of a married life of spited bickerings—a life in which there seemed no love or liking or forbearance, for years—now that Pyneweck stood in near danger of death, something like remorse came suddenly upon her. She knew that in Shrewsbury were transacting the scenes which were to determine his fate. She knew she did not love him; but she could not have supposed, even a fortnight before, that the hour of suspense could have affected her so powerfully.

She knew the day on which the trial was expected to take

place. She could not get it out of her head for a minute; she felt faint as it drew towards evening.

Two or three days passed; and then she knew that the trial must be over by this time. There were floods between London and Shrewsbury, and news was long delayed. She wished the floods would last forever. It was dreadful waiting to hear; dreadful to know that the event was over, and that she could not hear till self-willed rivers subsided; dreadful to know that they must subside and the news come at last.

She had some vague trust in the Judge's good nature, and much in the resources of chance and accident. She had contrived to send the money he wanted. He would not be without legal advice and energetic and skilled support.

At last the news did come—a long arrear all in a gush: a letter from a female friend in Shrewsbury; a return of the sentences, sent up for the Judge; and most important, because most easily got at, being told with great aplomb and brevity, the long-deferred intelligence of the Shrewsbury Assizes in the *Morning Advertiser*. Like an impatient reader of a novel, who reads the last page first, she read with dizzy eyes the list of the executions.

Two were respited, seven were hanged; and in that capital catalogue was this line:

"Lewis Pyneweck—forgery."

She had to read it a half-a-dozen times over before she was sure she understood it. Here was the paragraph:

> Sentence, Death—7.
>
> Executed accordingly, on Friday the 13th instant, to wit: Thomas Primer, *alias* Duck—highway robbery. Flora Guy—stealing to the value of 11s. 6d. Arthur Pounden—burglary. Matilda Mummery—riot. Lewis Pyneweck—forgery, bill of exchange.

And when she reached this, she read it over and over, feeling very cold and sick.

This buxom housekeeper was known in the house as Mrs. Carwell—Carwell being her maiden name, which she had resumed.

No one in the house except its master knew her history. Her introduction had been managed craftily. No one suspected that it had been concerted between her and the old reprobate in scarlet and ermine.

Flora Carwell ran up the stairs now, and snatched her little girl, hardly seven years of age, whom she met on the lobby, hurriedly up in her arms, and carried her into her bedroom, without well knowing what she was doing, and sat down, placing the child before her. She was not able to speak. She held the child before her, and looked in the little girl's wondering face, and burst into tears of horror.

She thought the Judge could have saved him. I daresay he could. For a time she was furious with him, and hugged and kissed her bewildered little girl, who returned her gaze with large round eyes.

That little girl had lost her father, and knew nothing of the matter. She had always been told that her father was dead long ago.

A woman, coarse, uneducated, vain, and violent, does not reason, or even feel, very distinctly; but in these tears of consternation were mingling a self-upbraiding. She felt afraid of that little child.

But Mrs. Carwell was a person who lived not upon sentiment, but upon beef and pudding; she consoled herself with punch; she did not trouble herself long even with resentments; she was a gross and material person, and could not mourn over the irrevocable for more than a limited number of hours, even if she would.

Judge Harbottle was soon in London again. Except the gout, this savage old epicurean never knew a day's sickness. He laughed, and coaxed, and bullied away the young woman's faint upbraidings, and in a little time Lewis Pyneweck troubled her no more; and the Judge secretly chuckled over the perfectly fair removal of a bore, who might have grown little by little into something very like a tyrant.

It was the lot of the Judge whose adventures I am now recounting to try criminal cases at the Old Bailey shortly after his return. He had commenced his charge to the jury in a case of forgery, and was, after his wont, thundering dead against the prisoner, with many a hard aggravation and cynical gibe, when suddenly all died away in silence, and, instead of looking at the jury, the eloquent Judge was gaping at some person in the body of the court.

Among the persons of small importance who stand and listen at the sides was one tall enough to show with a little prominence; a slight mean figure, dressed in seedy black, lean and dark of visage. He had just handed a letter to the crier, before he caught the Judge's eye.

That Judge descried, to his amazement, the features of Lewis Pyneweck. He had the usual faint thin-lipped smile; and with his blue chin raised in air, and as it seemed quite unconscious of the distinguished notice he has attracted, he was stretching his low cravat with his crooked fingers, while he slowly turned his head from side to side—a process which enabled the Judge to see distinctly a stripe of swollen blue round his neck, which indicated, he thought, the grip of the rope.

This man, with a few others, had got a footing on a step, from which he could better see the court. He now stepped down, and the Judge lost sight of him.

His lordship signed energetically with his hand in the direction in which this man had vanished. He turned to the tipstaff. His first effort to speak ended in a gasp. He cleared his throat, and told the astounded official to arrest that man who had interrupted the court.

"He's but this moment gone down *there*. Bring him in custody before me, within ten minutes' time, or I'll strip your gown from your shoulders and fine the sheriff!" he thundered, while his eyes flashed round the court in search of the functionary.

Attorneys, counsellors, idle spectators, gazed in the direction in which Mr. Justice Harbottle had shaken his gnarled old hand. They compared notes. Not one had seen any one making a disturbance. They asked one another if the Judge was losing his head.

Nothing came of the search. His lordship concluded his charge a great deal more tamely; and when the jury retired, he stared round the court with a wandering mind, and looked as if he would not have given sixpence to see the prisoner hanged.

Chapter 5
Caleb Searcher

The Judge had received the letter; had he known from whom it came, he would no doubt have read it instantaneously. As it was he simply read the direction:

To the Honourable
The Lord Justice
Elijah Harbottle,
One of his Majesty's Justices of
the Honourable Court of Common Pleas.

It remained forgotten in his pocket till he reached home.

When he pulled out that and others from the capacious pocket of his coat, it had its turn, as he sat in his library in his thick silk dressing-gown; and then he found its contents to be a closely-written letter, in a clerk's hand, and an enclosure in "secretary hand," as I believe the angular scrivinary of law-writings in those days was termed, engrossed on a bit of parchment about the size of this page. The letter said:

> MR. JUSTICE HARBOTTLE,—MY LORD,
> I am ordered by the High Court of Appeal to acquaint your lordship, in order to your better preparing yourself for your trial, that a true bill hath been sent down, and the indictment lieth against your lordship for the murder of one Lewis Pyneweck of Shrewsbury, citizen, wrongfully executed for the forgery of a bill of exchange, on the ——th day of—— last, by reason of the wilful perversion of the evidence, and the undue pressure put upon the jury, together with the illegal admission of evidence by your

lordship, well knowing the same to be illegal, by all which the promoter of the prosecution of the said indictment, before the High Court of Appeal, hath lost his life.

And the trial of the said indictment, I am farther ordered to acquaint your lordship, is fixed for the both day of—— next ensuing, by the right honourable the Lord Chief Justice Twofold, of the court aforesaid, to wit, the High Court of Appeal, on which day it will most certainly take place. And I am farther to acquaint your lordship, to prevent any surprise or miscarriage, that your case stands first for the said day, and that the said High Court of Appeal sits day and night, and never rises; and herewith, by order of the said court, I furnish your lordship with a copy (extract) of the record in this case, except of the indictment, whereof, notwithstanding, the substance and effect is supplied to your lordship in this Notice. And farther I am to inform you, that in case the jury then to try your lordship should find you guilty, the right honourable the Lord Chief Justice will, in passing sentence of death upon you, fix the day of execution for the 10th day of ——, being one calendar month from the day of your trial.

It was signed by:

CALEB SEARCHER,

Officer of the Crown Solicitor in the Kingdom of Life and Death.

The Judge glanced through the parchment.

"'Sblood! Do they think a man like me is to be bamboozled by their buffoonery?"

The Judge's coarse features were wrung into one of his sneers; but he was pale. Possibly, after all, there was a conspiracy on foot. It was queer. Did they mean to pistol him in his carriage? or did they only aim at frightening him?

Judge Harbottle had more than enough of animal courage. He was not afraid of highwaymen, and he had fought more than his share of duels, being a foul-mouthed advocate while he held briefs at the bar. No one questioned his fighting qualities. But with respect to this particular case of Pyneweck, he lived in a house of glass. Was there not his pretty, dark-eyed, over-dressed housekeeper, Mrs. Flora Carwell? Very easy for people who knew Shrewsbury to identify Mrs. Pyneweck, if once put upon the scent; and had he not stormed and worked hard in that case? Had he not made it hard sailing for the prisoner? Did he not know very well what the bar thought of it? It would be the worst scandal that ever blasted Judge.

So much there was intimidating in the matter but nothing more. The Judge was a little bit gloomy for a day or two after, and more testy with everyone than usual.

He locked up the papers; and about a week after he asked his housekeeper, one day, in the library:

"Had your husband never a brother?"

Mrs. Carwell squalled on this sudden introduction of the funereal topic, and cried exemplary "piggins full," as the Judge used pleasantly to say. But he was in no mood for trifling now, and he said sternly:

"Come, madam! this wearies me. Do it another time; and give me an answer to my question." So she did.

Pyneweck had no brother living. He once had one; but he died in Jamaica.

"How do you know he is dead?" asked the Judge.

"Because he told me so."

"Not the dead man."

"Pyneweck told me so."

"Is that all?" sneered the Judge.

He pondered this matter; and time went on. The Judge was growing a little morose, and less enjoying. The subject struck nearer to his thoughts than he fancied it could have done. But so it is with most undivulged vexations, and there was no one to whom he could tell this one.

It was now the ninth; and Mr Justice Harbottle was glad. He knew nothing would come of it. Still it bothered him; and to-morrow would see it well over.

[What of the paper I have cited? No one saw it during his life; no one, after his death. He spoke of it to Dr. Hedstone; and what purported to be "a copy," in the old Judge's handwriting, was found. The original was nowhere. Was it a copy of an illusion, incident to brain disease? Such is my belief.]

Chapter 6

Arrested

Judge Harbottle went this night to the play at Drury Lane. He was one of the old fellows who care nothing for late hours, and occasional knocking about in pursuit of pleasure. He had appointed with two cronies of Lincoln's Inn to come home in his coach with him to sup after the play.

They were not in his box, but were to meet him near the entrance, and get into his carriage there; and Mr. Justice Harbottle, who hated waiting, was looking a little impatiently from the window.

The Judge yawned.

He told the footman to watch for Counsellor Thavies and Counsellor Beller, who were coming; and, with another yawn, he laid his cocked hat on his knees, closed his eyes, leaned back in his corner, wrapped his mantle closer about him, and began to think of pretty Mrs. Abington.

And being a man who could sleep like a sailor, at a moment's notice, he was thinking of taking a nap. Those fellows had no business to keep a judge waiting.

He heard their voices now. Those rake-hell counsellors were laughing, and bantering, and sparring after their wont. The carriage swayed and jerked, as one got in, and then again as the other followed. The door clapped, and the coach was now jogging and rumbling over the pavement. The Judge was a little bit sulky. He did not care to sit up and open his eyes. Let them suppose he was asleep. He heard them laugh with more malice than good-humour, he thought, as they observed it. He would give them a d——d hard knock or two when they got to his door, and till then he would counterfeit his nap.

The clocks were chiming twelve. Beller and Thavies were silent as tombstones. They were generally loquacious and merry rascals.

The Judge suddenly felt himself roughly seized and thrust from his corner into the middle of the seat, and opening his eyes, instantly he found himself between his two companions.

Before he could blurt out the oath that was at his lips, he saw that they were two strangers—evil-looking fellows, each with a pistol in his hand, and dressed like Bow Street officers.

The Judge clutched at the check-string. The coach pulled up. He stared about him. They were not among houses; but through the windows, under a broad moonlight, he saw a black moor stretching lifelessly from right to left, with rotting trees, pointing fantastic branches in the air, standing here and there in groups, as if they held up their arms and twigs like fingers, in horrible glee at the Judge's coming.

A footman came to the window. He knew his long face and sunken eyes. He knew it was Dingly Chuff, fifteen years ago a footman in his service, whom he had turned off at a moment's notice, in a burst of jealousy, and indicted for a missing spoon. The man had died in prison of the jail-fever.

The Judge drew back in utter amazement. His armed companions signed mutely; and they were again gliding over this unknown moor.

The bloated and gouty old man, in his horror considered the question of resistance. But his athletic days were long over. This moor was a desert. There was no help to be had. He was in the hands of strange servants, even if his recognition turned out to be a delusion, and they were under the command of his captors. There was nothing for it but submission, for the present.

Suddenly the coach was brought nearly to a standstill, so that the prisoner saw an ominous sight from the window.

It was a gigantic gallows beside the road; it stood three-sided, and from each of its three broad beams at top depended in chains some eight or ten bodies, from several of which the cere-clothes had dropped away, leaving the skeletons swinging lightly by their chains. A tall ladder reached to the summit of the structure, and on the peat beneath lay bones.

On top of the dark transverse beam facing the road, from which, as from the other two completing the triangle of death, dangled a row of these unfortunates in chains, a hangman, with a pipe in his mouth, much as we see him in the famous print of the "Idle Apprentice," though here his perch was ever so much higher, was reclining at his ease and listlessly shying bones, from a little heap at his elbow, at the skeletons that hung round, bringing down now a rib or two, now a hand, now half a leg. A long-sighted man could have discerned that he was a dark fellow, lean; and from continually looking down on the earth from the elevation over which, in another sense, he always hung, his nose, his lips, his chin were pendulous and loose, and drawn down into a monstrous grotesque.

This fellow took his pipe from his mouth on seeing the coach, stood up, and cut some solemn capers high on his beam, and shook a new rope in the air, crying with a voice high and distant as the caw of a raven hovering over a gibbet, "A robe for Judge Harbottle!"

The coach was now driving on at its old swift pace.

So high a gallows as that, the Judge had never, even in his most hilarious moments, dreamed of. He thought, he must be raving. And the dead footman! He shook his ears and strained his eyelids; but if he was dreaming, he was unable to awake himself.

There was no good in threatening these scoundrels. A *brutum fulmen* might bring a real one on his head.

Any submission to get out of their hands; and then heaven and earth he would move to unearth and hunt them down.

Suddenly they drove round a corner of a vast white building, and under a *porte-cochere*.

Chapter 7
Chief-Justice Twofold

The Judge found himself in a corridor lighted with dingy oil lamps, the walls of bare stone; it looked like a passage in a prison. His guards placed him in the hands of other people. Here and there he saw bony and gigantic soldiers passing to and fro, with muskets over their shoulders. They looked straight before them, grinding their teeth, in bleak fury, with no noise but the clank of their shoes. He saw these by glimpses, round corners, and at the ends of passages, but he did not actually pass them by.

And now, passing under a narrow doorway, he found himself in the dock, confronting a judge in his scarlet robes, in a large court-house. There was nothing to elevate this Temple of Themis above its vulgar kind elsewhere. Dingy enough it looked, in spite of candles lighted in decent abundance. A case had just closed, and the last juror's back was seen escaping through the door in the wall of the jury-box. There were some dozen barristers, some fiddling with pen and ink, others buried in briefs, some beckoning, with the plumes of their pens, to their attorneys, of whom there were no lack; there were clerks to-ing and fro-ing, and the officers of the court, and the registrar, who was handing up a paper to the judge; and the tipstaff, who was presenting a note at the end of his wand to a king's counsel over the heads of the crowd between. If this was the High Court of Appeal, which never rose day or night, it might account for the pale and jaded aspect of everybody in it. An air of indescribable gloom hung upon the pallid features of all the people here; no one ever smiled; all looked more or less secretly suffering.

"The King against Elijah Harbottle!" shouted the officer.

"Is the appellant Lewis Pyneweck in court?" asked Chief-Justice Twofold, in a voice of thunder, that shook the woodwork of the court, and boomed down the corridors.

Up stood Pyneweck from his place at the table.

"Arraign the prisoner!" roared the Chief: and Judge Harbottle felt the panels of the dock round him, and the floor, and the rails quiver in the vibrations of that tremendous voice.

The prisoner, *in limine*, objected to this pretended court, as being a sham, and non-existent in point of law; and then, that, even if it were a court constituted by law (the Judge was growing dazed), it had not and could not have any jurisdiction to try him for his conduct on the bench.

Whereupon the chief-justice laughed suddenly, and every one in court, turning round upon the prisoner, laughed also, till the laugh grew and roared all round like a deafening acclamation; he saw nothing but glittering eyes and teeth, a universal stare and grin; but though all the voices laughed, not a single face of all those that concentrated their gaze upon him looked like a laughing face. The mirth subsided as suddenly as it began.

The indictment was read. Judge Harbottle actually pleaded! He pleaded "Not Guilty." A jury were sworn. The trial proceeded. Judge Harbottle was bewildered. This could not be real. He must be either mad, or *going* mad, he thought.

One thing could not fail to strike even him. This Chief-Justice Twofold, who was knocking him about at every turn with sneer and gibe, and roaring him down with his tremendous voice, was a dilated effigy of himself; an image of Mr. Justice Harbottle, at least double his size, and with all his fierce colouring, and his ferocity of eye and visage, enhanced awfully.

Nothing the prisoner could argue, cite, or state, was permitted to retard for a moment the march of the case towards its catastrophe.

The chief-justice seemed to feel his power over the jury, and to exult and riot in the display of it. He glared at them, he nodded to them; he seemed to have established an understanding with them. The lights were faint in that part of the court. The jurors were mere shadows, sitting in rows; the prisoner could see a dozen pair of white eyes shining, coldly, out of the darkness; and whenever the judge in his charge, which was contemptuously brief, nodded and grinned and gibed, the prisoner could see, in the obscurity, by the dip of all these rows of eyes together, that the jury nodded in acquiescence.

And now the charge was over, the huge chief-justice leaned back panting and gloating on the prisoner. Everyone in the court turned about, and gazed with steadfast hatred on the man in the dock. From the jury-box where the twelve sworn brethren were whispering together, a sound in the general stillness like a prolonged "hiss-s-s!" was heard; and then, in answer to the challenge of the officer, "How say you, gentlemen of the jury, guilty or not guilty?" came in a melancholy voice the finding, "Guilty."

The place seemed to the eyes of the prisoner to grow gradually darker and darker, till he could discern nothing distinctly but the lumen of the eyes that were turned upon him from every bench and side and corner and gallery of the building. The prisoner doubtless thought that he had quite enough to say, and conclusive, why sentence of death should not be pronounced upon him; but the lord chief-justice puffed it contemptuously away, like so much smoke, and proceeded to pass sentence of death upon the prisoner, having named the tenth of the ensuing month for his execution.

Before he had recovered the stun of this ominous farce, in obedience to the mandate, "Remove the prisoner," he was led from the dock. The lamps seemed all to have gone out, and there were stoves and charcoal-fires here and there, that threw a faint crimson light on the walls of the corridors through which he passed. The stones that composed them looked now enormous, cracked and unhewn.

He came into a vaulted smithy, where two men, naked to the waist, with heads like bulls, round shoulders, and the arms of giants, were welding red-hot chains together with hammers that pelted like thunderbolts.

They looked on the prisoner with fierce red eyes, and rested on their hammers for a minute; and said the elder to his companion, "Take out Elijah Harbottle's gyves;" and with a pincers he plucked the end which lay dazzling in the fire from the furnace.

"One end locks," said he, taking the cool end of the iron in one hand, while with the grip of a vice he seized the leg of the Judge, and locked the ring round his ankle. "The other," he said with a grin, "is welded."

The iron band that was to form the ring for the other leg lay still red hot upon the stone floor, with brilliant sparks sporting up and down its surface.

His companion, in his gigantic hands, seized the old Judge's other leg, and pressed his foot immovably to the stone floor; while his senior, in a twinkling, with a masterly application of pincers and hammer, sped the glowing bar around his ankle so tight that the skin and sinews smoked and bubbled again, and old Judge Harbottle uttered a yell that seemed to chill the very stones, and make the iron chains quiver on the wall.

Chains, vaults, smiths, and smithy all vanished in a moment; but the pain continued. Mr. Justice Harbottle was suffering torture all round the ankle on which the infernal smiths had just been operating.

His friends, Thavies and Beller, were startled by the Judge's roar in the midst of their elegant trifling about a marriage *a-la-mode* case which was going on. The Judge was in panic as well as pain. The street lamps and the light of his own hall door restored him.

"I'm very bad," growled he between his set teeth; "my foot's blazing. Who was he that hurt my foot? 'Tis the gout—'tis the gout!" he said, awaking completely. "How many hours have we been coming from the playhouse? 'Sblood, what has happened on the way? I've slept half the night!"

There had been no hitch or delay, and they had driven home at a good pace.

The Judge, however, was in gout; he was feverish too; and the attack, though very short, was sharp; and when, in about a fortnight, it subsided, his ferocious joviality did not return. He could not get this dream, as he chose to call it, out of his head.

Chapter 8

Somebody Has Got Into the House

People remarked that the Judge was in the vapours. His doctor said he should go for a fortnight to Buxton.

Whenever the Judge fell into a brown study, he was always conning over the terms of the sentence pronounced upon him in his vision—"in one calendar month from the date of this day;" and then the usual form, "and you shall be hanged by the neck till you are dead," etc. "That will be the 10th—I'm not much in the way of being hanged. I know what stuff dreams are, and I laugh at them; but this is continually in my thoughts, as if it forecast misfortune of some sort. I wish the day my dream gave me were passed and over. I wish I were well purged of my gout. I wish I were as I used to be. 'Tis nothing but vapours, nothing but a maggot." The copy of the parchment and letter which had announced his trial with many a snort and sneer he would read over and over again, and the scenery and people of his dream would rise about him in places the most unlikely, and steal him in a moment from all that surrounded him into a world of shadows.

The Judge had lost his iron energy and banter. He was growing taciturn and morose. The Bar remarked the change, as well they might. His friends thought him ill. The doctor said he was troubled with hypochondria, and that his gout was still lurking in his system, and ordered him to that ancient haunt of crutches and chalk-stones, Buxton.

The Judge's spirits were very low; he was frightened about himself; and he described to his housekeeper, having sent for her to his study to drink a dish of tea, his strange dream in his drive home from Drury Lane Playhouse. He was sinking into the state of nervous dejection in which men lose their faith in orthodox advice, and in despair consult quacks, astrologers, and nursery storytellers. Could such a dream mean that he was to have a fit, and so die on the both? She did not think so. On the contrary, it was certain some good luck must happen on that day.

The Judge kindled; and for the first time for many days, he looked for a minute or two like himself, and he tapped her on the cheek with the hand that was not in flannel.

"Odsbud! odsheart! you dear rogue! I had forgot. There is young Tom—yellow Tom, my nephew, you know, lies sick at Harrogate; why shouldn't he go that day as well as another, and if he does, I get an estate by it? Why, lookee, I asked Doctor

Hedstone yesterday if I was like to take a fit any time, and he laughed, and swore I was the last man in town to go off that way."

The Judge sent most of his servants down to Buxton to make his lodgings and all things comfortable for him. He was to follow in a day or two.

It was now the 9th; and the next day well over, he might laugh at his visions and auguries.

On the evening of the 9th, Dr. Hedstone's footman knocked at the Judge's door. The Doctor ran up the dusky stairs to the drawing-room. It was a March evening, near the hour of sunset, with an east wind whistling sharply through the chimney-stacks. A wood fire blazed cheerily on the hearth. And Judge Harbottle, in what was then called a brigadier-wig, with his red *roquelaure* on, helped the glowing effect of the darkened chamber, which looked red all over like a room on fire.

The Judge had his feet on a stool, and his huge grim purple face confronted the fire, and seemed to pant and swell, as the blaze alternately spread upward and collapsed. He had fallen again among his blue devils, and was thinking of retiring from the Bench, and of fifty other gloomy things.

But the Doctor, who was an energetic son of Aesculapius, would listen to no croaking, told the Judge he was full of gout, and in his present condition no judge even of his own case, but promised him leave to pronounce on all those melancholy questions, a fortnight later.

In the meantime the Judge must be very careful. He was overcharged with gout, and he must not provoke an attack, till the waters of Buxton should do that office for him, in their own salutary way.

The Doctor did not think him perhaps quite so well as he pretended, for he told him he wanted rest, and would be better if he went forthwith to his bed.

Mr. Gerningham, his valet, assisted him, and gave him his drops; and the Judge told him to wait in his bedroom till he should go to sleep.

Three persons that night had specially odd stories to tell.

The housekeeper had got rid of the trouble of amusing her little girl at this anxious time, by giving her leave to run about the sitting-rooms and look at the pictures and china, on the usual condition of touching nothing.

It was not until the last gleam of sunset had for some time faded, and the twilight had so deepened that she could no longer discern the colours on the china figures on the chimneypiece or in the cabinets, that the child returned to the housekeeper's room to find her mother.

To her she related, after some prattle about the china, and the pictures, and the Judge's two grand wigs in the dressing-room off the library, an adventure of an extraordinary kind.

In the hall was placed, as was customary in those times, the sedan-chair which the master of the house occasionally used, covered with stamped leather, and studded with gilt nails, and with its red silk blinds down. In this case, the doors of this old-fashioned conveyance were locked, the windows up, and, as I said, the blinds down, but not so closely that the curious child could not peep underneath one of them, and see into the interior.

A parting beam from the setting sun, admitted through the window of a back room, shot obliquely through the open door, and lighting on the chair, shone with a dull transparency through the crimson blind.

To her surprise, the child saw in the shadow a thin man, dressed in black, seated in it; he had sharp dark features; his nose, she fancied, a little awry, and his brown eyes were looking straight before him; his hand was on his thigh, and he stirred no more than the waxen figure she had seen at Southwark fair.

A child is so often lectured for asking questions, and on the propriety of silence, and the superior wisdom of its elders, that it accepts most things at last in good faith; and the little girl acquiesced respectfully in the occupation of the chair by this mahogany-faced person as being all right and proper.

It was not until she asked her mother who this man was, and

observed her scared face as she questioned her more minutely upon the appearance of the stranger, that she began to understand that she had seen something unaccountable.

Mrs. Carwell took the key of the chair from its nail over the footman's shelf, and led the child by the hand up to the hall, having a lighted candle in her other hand. She stopped at a distance from the chair, and placed the candlestick in the child's hand.

"Peep in, Margery, again, and try if there's anything there," she whispered; "hold the candle near the blind so as to throw its light through the curtain."

The child peeped, this time with a very solemn face, and intimated at once that he was gone.

"Look again, and be sure," urged her mother.

The little girl was quite certain; and Mrs. Carwell, with her mob-cap of lace and cherry-coloured ribbons, and her dark brown hair, not yet powdered, over a very pale face, unlocked the door, looked in, and beheld emptiness.

"All a mistake, child, you see."

"*There!* ma'am! see there! He's gone round the corner," said the child.

"Where?" said Mrs. Carwell, stepping backward a step.

"Into that room."

"Tut, child! 'twas the shadow," cried Mrs. Carwell, angrily, because she was frightened. "I moved the candle." But she clutched one of the poles of the chair, which leant against the wall in the corner, and pounded the floor furiously with one end of it, being afraid to pass the open door the child had pointed to.

The cook and two kitchen-maids came running upstairs, not knowing what to make of this unwonted alarm.

They all searched the room; but it was still and empty, and no sign of any one's having been there.

Some people may suppose that the direction given to her thoughts by this odd little incident will account for a very strange illusion which Mrs. Carwell herself experienced about two hours later.

Chapter 9

The judge Leaves His House

Mrs. Flora Carwell was going up the great staircase with a posset for the Judge in a china bowl, on a little silver tray.

Across the top of the well-staircase there runs a massive oak rail; and, raising her eyes accidentally, she saw an extremely odd-looking stranger, slim and long, leaning carelessly over with a pipe between his finger and thumb. Nose, lips, and chin seemed all to droop downward into extraordinary length, as he leant his odd peering face over the banister. In his other hand he held a coil of rope, one end of which escaped from under his elbow and hung over the rail.

Mrs. Carwell, who had no suspicion at the moment, that he was not a real person, and fancied that he was someone employed in cording the Judge's luggage, called to know what he was doing there.

Instead of answering, he turned about, and walked across the lobby, at about the same leisurely pace at which she was ascending, and entered a room, into which she followed him. It was an uncarpeted and unfurnished chamber. An open trunk lay upon the floor empty, and beside it the coil of rope; but except herself there her. Perhaps, when she was able to think it over, it was a relief to was no one in the room.

Mrs. Carwell was very much frightened, and now concluded that the child must have seen the same ghost that had just appeared to believe so; for the face, figure, and dress described by the child were awfully like Pyneweck; and this certainly was not he.

Very much scared and very hysterical, Mrs. Carwell ran down to her room, afraid to look over her shoulder, and got some companions about her, and wept, and talked, and drank more than one cordial, and talked and wept again, and so on, until, in those early days, it was ten o'clock, and time to go to bed.

A scullery maid remained up finishing some of her scouring and "scalding" for some time after the other servants—who, as I said, were few in number—that night had got to their beds.

This was a low-browed, broad-faced, intrepid wench with black hair, who did not "vally a ghost not a button," and treated the housekeeper's hysterics with measureless scorn.

The old house was quiet now. It was near twelve o'clock, no sounds were audible except the muffled wailing of the wintry winds, piping high among the roofs and chimneys, or rumbling at intervals, in under gusts, through the narrow channels of the street.

The spacious solitudes of the kitchen level were awfully dark, and this sceptical kitchen-wench was the only person now up and about the house. She hummed tunes to herself, for a time; and then stopped and listened; and then resumed her work again. At last, she was destined to be more terrified than even was the housekeeper.

There was a back kitchen in this house, and from this she heard, as if coming from below its foundations, a sound like heavy strokes, that seemed to shake the earth beneath her feet. Sometimes a dozen in sequence, at regular intervals; sometimes fewer. She walked out softly into the passage, and was surprised to see a dusky glow issuing from this room, as if from a charcoal fire.

The room seemed thick with smoke.

Looking in she very dimly beheld a monstrous figure, over a furnace, beating with a mighty hammer the rings and rivets of a chain.

The strokes, swift and heavy as they looked, sounded hollow and distant. The man stopped, and pointed to something on the floor, that, through the smoky haze, looked, the thought, like a dead body. She remarked no more; but the servants in the room close by, startled from their sleep by a hideous scream, found her in a swoon on the flags, close to the door, where she had just witnessed this ghastly vision.

Startled by the girl's incoherent asseverations that she had seen the Judge's corpse on the floor, two servants having first searched the lower part of the house, went rather frightened upstairs to inquire whether their master was well. They found him, not in his bed, but in his room. He had a table with candles burning at his bedside, and was getting on his clothes again; and he swore and cursed at them roundly in his old style, telling them that he had business, and that he would discharge on the spot any scoundrel who should dare to disturb him again.

So the invalid was left to his quietude.

In the morning it was rumoured here and there in the street that the Judge was dead. A servant was sent from the house three doors away, by Counsellor Traverse, to inquire at Judge Harbottle's hall door.

The servant who opened it was pale and reserved, and would only say that the Judge was ill. He had had a dangerous accident; Doctor Hedstone had been with him at seven o'clock in the morning.

There were averted looks, short answers, pale and frowning faces, and all the usual signs that there was a secret that sat heavily upon their minds and the time for disclosing which had not yet come. That time would arrive when the coroner had arrived, and the mortal scandal that had befallen the house could be no longer hidden. For that morning Mr. Justice Harbottle had been found hanging by the neck from the banister at the top of the great staircase, and quite dead.

There was not the smallest sign of any struggle or resistance. There had not been heard a cry or any other noise in the slightest degree indicative of violence. There was medical evidence to show that, in his atrabilious state, it was quite on the cards that he might have made away with himself. The jury found accordingly that it was a case of suicide. But to those who were acquainted with the strange story which Judge Harbottle had related to at least two persons, the fact that the catastrophe occurred on the morning of March 10th seemed a startling coincidence.

A few days after, the pomp of a great funeral attended him to the grave; and so, in the language of Scripture, *the rich man died, and was buried.*

Behold, it was a Dream!

By Rhoda Broughton

Chapter 1

Yesterday morning I received the following letter:

Weston House, Caulfield, ——shire.

My Dear Dinah,—You *must* come: I scorn all your excuses, and see through their flimsiness. I have no doubt that you are much better amused in Dublin, frolicking round ball-rooms with a succession of horse-soldiers, and watching Her Majesty's household troops play Polo in the Phoenix Park, but no matter—you *must* come. We have no particular inducements to hold out. We lead an exclusively bucolic, cow-milking, pig-fattening, roast-mutton-eating and to-bed-at-ten-o'clock-going life; but no matter—you *must* come. I want you to see how happy two dull elderly people may be, with no special brightness in their lot to make them so. My old man—he is surprisingly ugly at the first glance, but grows upon one afterwards—sends you his respects, and bids me say that he will meet you at *any* station on *any* day at *any* hour of the day or night. If you succeed in evading our persistence this time, you will be a cleverer woman than I take you for.

Ever yours affectionately, Jane Watson.

August 15th.

P.S.—We will invite our little scarlet-headed curate to dinner to meet you, so as to soften your fall from the society of the Plungers.

This is my answer:

My Dear Jane,—Kill the fat calf in all haste, and put the bake meats into the oven, for I will come. Do not, however, imagine that I am moved thereunto by the prospect of the bright-headed curate. Believe me, my dear, I am as yet at a distance of ten long good years from an addiction to the minor clergy. If I survive the crossing of that seething, heaving, tumbling abomination, St. George's Channel, you may expect me on Tuesday next. I have been groping for hours in 'Bradshaw's' darkness that may be felt, and I have arrived at length at this twilight result, that I may arrive at your station at 6.55 p.m. But the ways of 'Bradshaw' are not our ways, and I *may* either rush violently past or never attain it. If I do, and if on my arrival I see some rustic vehicle, guided by a startlingly ugly gentleman, awaiting me, I shall know from your wifely description that it is your 'old man.' Till Tuesday,
then,

Affectionately yours,

Dinah Bellairs.

August 17th.

I am as good as my word; on Tuesday I set off. For four mortal hours and a half I am disastrously, hideously, diabolically sick. For four hours and a half I curse the day on which I was born, the day on which Jane Watson was born, the day on which her old man was born, and lastly—but oh! not, *not* leastly—the day and the dock on which and in which the *Leinster's* plunging, courtseying, throbbing body was born. On arriving at Holyhead, feeling convinced from my sensations that, as the French say, I touch my last hour, I indistinctly request to be allowed to stay on board and *die*, then and there; but as the stewardess and my maid take a different view of my situation, and insist upon forcing my cloak and bonnet on my dying body and limp head, I at length succeed in staggering on deck and off the accursed boat.

I am then well shaken up for two or three hours in the Irish mail, and after crawling along a slow by-line for two or three hours more, am at length, at 6.55, landed, battered, tired, dust-blacked, and qualmish, at the little roadside station of Caulfield. My maid and I are the only passengers who descend. The train snorts its slow way onwards, and I am left gazing at the calm crimson death of the August sun, and smelling the sweet-peas in the station-master's garden border. I look round in search of Jane's promised tax-cart, and steel my nerves for the contemplation of her old man's unlovely features. But the only vehicle which I see is a tiny two-wheeled pony carriage, drawn by a small and tub-shaped bay pony and driven by a lady in a hat, whose face is turned expectantly towards me. I go up and recognise my friend, whom I have not seen for two years—not since before she fell in with her old man and espoused him.

"I thought it safest, after all, to come myself," she says with a bright laugh. "My old man looked so handsome this morning, that I thought you would never recognise him from my description. Get in, dear, and let us trot home as quickly as we can."

I comply, and for the next half hour sit (while the cool evening wind is blowing the dust off my hot and jaded face) stealing amazed glances at my companion's cheery features. *Cheery!* That is the very last word that, excepting in an ironical sense, any one would have applied to my friend Jane two years ago. Two years ago Jane was thirty-five, the elderly eldest daughter of a large family, hustled into obscurity, jostled, shelved, by half a dozen younger, fresher sisters; an elderly girl addicted to lachrymose verse about the gone and the dead and the for-ever-lost. Apparently the gone has come back, the dead resuscitated, the for-ever-lost been found again. The peaky sour virgin is transformed into a gracious matron, with a kindly, comely face, pleasure making and pleasure feeling. Oh, Happiness, what powder, or paste, or milk of roses, can make old cheeks young again in the cunning way that you do? If you would but bide steadily with us we might live forever, always young and always handsome.

My musings on Jane's metamorphosis, combined with a tired

headache, make me some- what silent, and indeed there is mostly a slackness of conversation between the two dearest allies on first meeting after absence—a sort of hesitating shiver before plunging into the sea of talk that both know lie in readiness for them.

"Have you got your harvest in yet?" I ask, more for the sake of not utterly holding my tongue than from any profound interest in the subject, as we jog briskly along between the yellow cornfields, where the dry bound sheaves are standing in golden rows in the red sunset light.

"Not yet," answers Jane; "we have only just begun to cut some of it. However, thank God, the weather looks as settled as possible; there is not a streak of watery lilac in the west."

My headache is almost gone and I am beginning to think kindly of dinner—a subject from which all day until now my mind has hastily turned with a sensation of hideous inward revolt—by the time that the fat pony pulls up before the old-world dark porch of a modest little house, which has bashfully hidden its original face under a veil of crowded clematis flowers and stalwart ivy. Set as in a picture-frame by the large drooped ivy-leaves, I see a tall and moderately hard-featured gentleman of middle age, perhaps, of the two, rather inclining towards elderly, smiling at us a little shyly.

"This is my old man," cries Jane, stepping gaily out, and giving him a friendly introductory pat on the shoulder. "Old man, this is Dinah"

Having thus been made known to each other we shake hands, but neither of us can arrive at anything pretty to say. Then I follow Jane into her little house, the little house for which she has so happily exchanged her tenth part of the large and noisy paternal mansion. It is an old house, and everything about it has the moderate shabbiness of old age and long and careful wear. Little thick-walled rooms, dark and cool, with flowers and flower scents lying in wait for you everywhere—a silent, fragrant, childless house. To me, who have had oily locomotives snorting and racing through my head all day, its dumb sweetness seems like heaven.

"And now that we have secured you, we do not mean to let you go in a hurry," says Jane hospitably that night at bedtime, lighting the candles on my dressing-table.

"You are determined to make my mouth water, I see," say I, interrupting a yawn to laugh. "Lone lorn me, who have neither old man nor dear little house, nor any prospect of ultimately attaining either."

"But if you honestly are not bored you will stay with us a good bit?" she says, laying her hand with kind entreaty on my sleeve. "St. George's Channel is not lightly to be faced again."

"Perhaps I shall stay until you are obliged to go away yourselves to get rid of me," return I, smiling. "Such things have happened. Yes, without joking, I will stay a month. Then, by the end of a month, if you have not found me out thoroughly, I think I may pass among men for a more amiable woman than I have ever yet had the reputation of."

A quarter of an hour later I am laying down my head among soft and snow-white pillows, and saying to myself that this delicious sensation of utter drowsy repose, of soft darkness and odorous quiet, is cheaply purchased even by the ridiculous anguish which my own sufferings, and—hardly less than my own sufferings—the demoniac sights and sounds afforded by my fellow passengers, caused me on board the accursed *Leinster*—

Built in the eclipse, and rigged with curses dark.

Chapter 2

"Well, I cannot say that you look much rested," says Jane next morning, coming in to greet me, smiling and fresh—(yes, sceptic of eighteen, even a woman of thirty-seven may look fresh in a print gown on an August morning, when she has a well of lasting quiet happiness inside her)—coming in with a bunch of creamy *gloire de Dijons* in her hand for the breakfast table. "You look infinitely more fagged than you did when I left you last night!"

"Do I?" say I, rather faintly.

"I am afraid you did not sleep much?" suggests Jane, a little crestfallen at the insult to her feather beds implied by my wakefulness. "Some people never can sleep the first night in a strange bed, and I stupidly forgot to ask whether you liked the feather bed or mattress at the top."

"Yes, I did sleep," I answer gloomily. "I wish to heaven I had not!"

"Wish—to—heaven—you—had—not?" repeats Jane slowly, with a slight astonished pause between each word. "My dear child, for what other purpose did you go to bed?"

"I—I—had bad dreams," say I, shuddering a little and then taking her hand, roses and all, in mine. "Dear Jane, do not think me quite run mad, but—but—have you got a 'Bradshaw' in the house?"

"A 'Bradshaw?' What on earth do you want with 'Bradshaw?'" says my hostess, her face lengthening considerably and a slight tincture of natural coldness coming into her tone.

"I know it seems rude—insultingly rude," say I, still holding her hand and speaking almost lachrymosely: "but do you know, my dear, I really am afraid that—that—I shall have to leave you—today?"

"To leave us?" repeats she, withdrawing her hand and growing angrily red. "What! when not twenty-four hours ago you settled to stay *a month* with us? What have we done between then and now to disgust you with us?"

"Nothing—nothing," cry I, eagerly; "how can you suggest such a thing? I never had a kinder welcome nor ever saw a place that charmed me more; but—but—"

"But what?" asks Jane, her colour subsiding and looking a little mollified.

"It is best to tell the truth, I suppose," say I, sighing, "even though I know that you will laugh at me—will call me vapourish—sottishly superstitious; but I had an awful and hideous dream last night."

"Is that all!" she says, looking relieved, and beginning to arrange her roses in an old china bowl. "And do you think that all dreams are confined to this house? I never heard before of their affecting any one special place more than another. Perhaps no sooner are you back in Dublin, in your own room and your own bed, than you will have a still worse and uglier one."

I shake my head. "But it was about this house—about *you*."

"About *me?*" she says, with an accent of a little aroused interest.

"About you and your husband," I answer earnestly. "Shall I tell it you? Whether you say 'Yes' or 'No' I must. Perhaps it came as a warning; such things have happened. Yes, say what you will, I cannot believe that any vision so consistent—so tangibly real and utterly free from the jumbled incongruities and unlikelinesses of ordinary dreams—could have meant nothing. Shall I begin?"

"By all means," answers Mrs. Watson, sitting down in an armchair and smiling easily. I am quite prepared to listen—and *disbelieve*."

"You know," say I, narratively, coming and standing close before her, "how utterly tired out I was when you left me last night. I could hardly answer your questions for yawning. I do not think that I was ten minutes in getting into bed, and it seemed like heaven when I laid my head down on the pillow. I felt as if I should sleep till the Day of Judgment. Well, you know, when one is asleep one has of course no measure of time, and I have no idea what hour it was *really*; but at some time, in the blackest and darkest of the night, I seemed to wake. It appeared as if a noise had woke me—a noise which at first neither frightened nor surprised me in the least, but which seemed quite natural, and which I accounted for in the muddled drowsy way in which one does account for things when half asleep.

"But as I gradually grew to fuller consciousness I found out, with a cold shudder, that the noise I heard was not one that belonged to the night; nothing that one could lay on wind in the chimney, or mice behind the wainscot, or ill-fitting boards. It was a sound of muffled struggling, and once I heard a sort of choked strangled cry. I sat up in bed, perfectly numbed with fright, and for a moment could hear nothing for the singing of the blood in my head, and the loud battering of my heart against my side. Then I thought that if it were anything bad—if I were going to be murdered—I had at least rather be in the light than the dark, and see in what sort of shape my fate was coming, so I slid out of bed and threw my dressing-gown over my shoulders. I had stupidly forgotten, in my weariness, over night, to put the matches by the bedside, and could not for the life of me recollect where they were. Also, my knowledge of the geography of the room was so small that in the utter blackness, without even the palest, grayest ray from the window to help me, I was by no means sure in which direction the door lay.

"I can feel *now* the pain of the blow I gave this right side against the sharp corner of the table in passing; I was quite surprised this morning not to find the mark of a bruise there. At last, in my groping, I came upon the handle and turned the key in the lock. It gave a little squeak, and again I stopped for a moment, overcome by ungovernable fear. Then I silently opened the door and looked out. You know that your door is exactly opposite mine. By the line of red light underneath it, I could see that at all events someone was awake and astir within, for the light was brighter than that given by a night-light. By the broader band of red light on the right side of it I could also perceive that the door was ajar. I stood stock still and listened.

"The two sounds of struggling and chokedly crying had both ceased. All the noise that remained was that as of some person quietly moving about on unbooted feet. 'Perhaps Jane's dog Smut is ill and she is sitting up with it; she was saying last night, I remember, that she was afraid it was beginning with the distemper. Perhaps either she or her old man have been taken with some trifling temporary sickness. Perhaps the noise of crying out that I certainly heard was one of them fighting with a nightmare.' Trying, by such like suggestions, to hearten myself up, I stole across the passage and peeped in—"

I pause in my narrative.

"Well?" says Jane, a little impatiently.

She has dropped her flowers. They lie in odorous dewy confusion in her lap. She is listening rather eagerly. I cover my face with my hands. "Oh! my dear," I cry, "I do not think I can go on. It was *too* dreadful! Now that I am telling it I seem to be doing and hearing it over again—"

"I do not call it very kind to keep me on the rack," she says, with a rather forced laugh. "Probably I am imagining something much worse than the reality. For heaven's sake speak up! What *did* you see?"

I take hold of her hand and continue. "You know that in your room the bed exactly faces the door. Well, when I looked in, looked in with eyes blinking at first, and dazzled by the long darkness they had been in, it seemed to me as if that bed were only one horrible sheet of crimson; but as my sight grew clearer I saw what it was that caused that frightful impression of universal red—" Again I pause with a gasp and feeling of oppressed breathing.

"Go on! go on!" cries my companion, leaning forward, and speaking with some petulance. "Are you never going to get to the point?"

"Jane," say I solemnly, "do not laugh at me, nor pooh pooh me, for it is God's truth—as clearly and vividly as I see you now, strong, flourishing, and alive, so clearly, so vividly, with no more of dream haziness nor of contradiction in details than there is in the view I now have of this room and of you—I saw you *both*—you and your husband, lying *dead*—*murdered*—drowned in your own blood!"

"What, both of us?" she says, trying to laugh, but her healthy cheek has rather paled.

"Both of you," I answer, with growing excitement. "You, Jane, had evidently been the one first attacked—taken off in your sleep—for you were lying just as you would have lain in slumber, only that across your throat from there to there" (touching first one ear and then the other), "there was a huge and yawning gash."

"Pleasant," replies she, with a slight shiver.

"I never saw any one dead," continue I earnestly, "never until last night. I had not the faintest idea how dead people looked, even people who died quietly, nor has any picture ever given me at all a clear conception of death's dread look. How then could I have *imagined* the hideous contraction and distortion of feature, the staring starting open eyes—glazed yet agonized—the tightly clenched teeth that go to make up the picture, that is *now, this very minute*, standing out in ugly vividness before my mind's eye?" I stop, but she does not avail herself of the pause to make any remark, neither does she look any longer at all laughingly inclined.

"And yet," continue I, with a voice shaken by emotion, "it was *you*, *very* you, not partly you and partly someone else, as is mostly the case in dreams, but as much *you*, as the *you* I am touching now" (laying my finger on her arm as I speak).

"And my old man, Robin," says poor Jane, rather tearfully, after a moment's silence, "what about him? Did you see him? Was he dead too?"

"It was evidently he whom I had heard struggling and crying," I answer with a strong shudder, which I cannot keep down, "for it was clear that he had fought for his life. He was lying half on the bed and half on the floor, and one clenched hand was grasping a great piece of the sheet; he was lying head downwards, as if, after his last struggle, he had fallen forwards. All his grey hair was reddened and stained, and I could see that the rift in his throat was as deep as that in yours."

"I wish you would stop," cries Jane, pale as ashes, and speaking with an accent of unwilling terror; "you are making me quite sick!"

"I *must* finish," I answer earnestly, "since it has come in time I am sure it has come for some purpose. Listen to me till the end; it is very near." She does not speak, and I take her silence for assent. "I was staring at you both in a stony way," I go on, "feeling—if I felt at all—that I was turning idiotic with horror—standing in exactly the same spot, with my neck craned to look round the door, and my eyes unable to stir from that hideous scarlet bed, when a slight noise, as of someone cautiously stepping on the carpet, turned my stony terror into a living quivering agony. I looked and saw a man with his back towards me walking across the room from the bed to the dressing-table. He was dressed in the dirty fustian of an ordinary workman, and in his hand he held a red wet sickle. When he reached the dressing-table he laid it down on the floor beside him, and began to collect all the rings, open the cases of the bracelets, and hurry the trinkets of all sorts into his pockets. While he was thus busy I caught a full view of the reflection of the face in the glass—" I stop for breath, my heart is panting almost as hardly as it seemed to pant during the awful moments I am describing.

"What was he like—what was he like?" cries Jane, greatly excited. "Did you see him distinctly enough to recollect his features again? Would you know him again if you saw him?"

"Should I know my own face if I saw it in the glass?" I ask scornfully. "I see every line of it *now* more clearly than I do yours, though that is before my eyes, and the other only before my memory—"

"Well, what was he like?—be quick, for heaven's sake."

"The first moment that I caught sight of him," continue I, speaking quickly, "I felt certain that he was Irish; to no other nationality could such a type of face have belonged. His wild rough hair fell down over his forehead, reaching his shagged and overhanging brows. He had the wide grinning slit of a mouth—the long nose, the cunningly twinkling eyes—that one so often sees, in combination with a shambling gait and ragged tail-coat, at the railway stations or in the harvest fields at this time of year." A pause. "I do not know how it came to me," I go on presently; "but I felt as convinced as if I had been told as if I had known it for a positive fact—that he was one of your own labourers—one of your own harvest men. Have you any Irishmen working for you?"

"Of course we have," answers Jane, rather sharply, "but that proves nothing. Do not they, as you observed just now, come over in droves at this time of the year for the harvest?"

"I am sorry," say I, sighing. "I wish you had not. Well, let me finish; I have just done—I had been holding the door-handle mechanically in my hand; I suppose I pulled it unconsciously towards me, for the door hinge creaked a little, but quite audibly. To my unspeakable horror the man turned round and saw me. Good God! he would cut my throat too with that red, *red* reaping hook! I tried to get into the passage and lock the door, but the key was on the inside. I tried to scream, I tried to run; but voice and legs disobeyed me. The bed and room and man began to dance before me; a black earthquake seemed to swallow me up, and I suppose I fell down in a swoon. When I awoke *really* the blessed morning had come, and a robin was singing outside my window on an apple bough. There—you have it all, and now let me look for a 'Bradshaw,' for I am so frightened and unhinged that go I must."

CHAPTER 3

"I must own that it has taken away appetite," I say, with rather a sickly smile, as we sit round the breakfast table. "I assure you that I mean no insult to your fresh eggs and bread-and-butter, but I simply *cannot* eat."

"It certainly was an exceptionally dreadful dream," says Jane, whose colour has returned, and who is a good deal fortified and reassured by the influences of breakfast and of her husband's scepticism; for a condensed and shortened version of my dream has been told to him, and he has easily laughed it to scorn. "Exceptionally dreadful, chiefly from its extreme consistency and precision of detail. But still, you know, dear, one has had hideous dreams oneself times out of mind and they never came to anything. I remember once I dreamt that all my teeth came out in my mouth at once—double ones and all; but that was ten years ago, and they still keep their situations, nor did I about that time lose any friend, which they say such a dream is a sign of."

"You say that some unaccountable instinct told you that the hero of your dream was one of my own men," says Robin, turning towards me with a covert smile of benevolent contempt for my superstitiousness; "did not I understand you to say so?"

"Yes," reply I, not in the least shaken by his hardly-veiled disbelief. "I do not know how it came to me, but I was as much persuaded of that, and am so still, as I am of my own identity."

"I will tell you of a plan then to prove the truth of your vision," returns he, smiling. "I will take you through the fields this morning and you shall see all my men at work, both the ordinary staff and the harvest casuals, Irish and all. If amongst them you find the counterpart of Jane's and my murderer" (a smile) "I will promise *then*—no, not even *then* can I promise to believe you, for there is such a family likeness between all Irishmen, at all events, between all the Irishmen that one sees *out* of Ireland."

"Take me," I say, eagerly, jumping up; "now, this *minute!* You cannot be more anxious nor half so anxious to prove me a false prophet as I am to be proved one."

"I am quite at your service," he answers, "as soon as you please. Jenny, get your hat and come too."

"And if we do *not* find him," says Jane, smiling playfully—I think I am growing pretty easy on that head—you will promise to eat a great deal of luncheon and never *mention* 'Bradshaw' again?"

"I promise," reply I, gravely. "And if, on the other hand, we *do* find him, you will promise to put no more obstacles in the way of my going, but will let me depart in peace without taking any offence thereat?"

"It is a bargain," she says gaily. "Witness, Robin."

So we set off in the bright dewiness of the morning on our walk over Robin's farm. It is a grand harvest day, and the whitened sheaves are everywhere drying, drying in the genial sun. We have been walking for an hour and both Jane and I are rather tired. The sun beats with all his late-summer strength on our heads and takes the force and spring out of our hot limbs.

"The hour of triumph is approaching," says Robin, with a quiet smile, as we draw near an open gate through which a loaded wain, shedding ripe wheat ears from its abundance as it crawls along, is passing. "And time for it too; it is a quarter past twelve and you have been on your legs for fully an hour. Miss Bellairs, you must make haste and find the murderer, for there is only one more field to do it in."

"Is not there?" I cry eagerly, "Oh, I *am* glad! Thank God, I begin to breathe again."

We pass through the open gate and begin to tread across the stubble, for almost the last load has gone.

"We must get nearer the hedge," says Robin, "or you will not see their faces; they are all at dinner."

We do as he suggests. In the shadow of the hedge we walk close in front of the row of heated labourers, who, sitting or lying on the hedge bank, are eating unattractive looking dinners. I scan one face after another—honest bovine English faces. I have seen a hundred thousand faces *like* each one of the faces now before me very like, but the exact counterpart of none. We are getting to the end of the row, I beginning to feel rather ashamed, though infinitely relieved, and to smile at my own expense. I look again, and my heart suddenly stands still and turns to stone within me. He is *there!*—not a hand-breadth from me! Great God! how well I have remembered his face, even to the unsightly smallpox seams, the shagged locks, the grinning slit mouth, the little sly base eyes. He is employed in no murderous occupation *now*; he is harmlessly cutting hunks of coarse bread and fat cold bacon with a clasp knife, but yet I have no more doubt that it is *he*—he whom I saw with the crimsoned sickle in his stained hand—than I have that it is I who am stonily, shiveringly, staring at him."

"Well, Miss Bellairs, who was right?" asks Robin's cheery voice at my elbow. "Perish 'Bradshaw' and all his labyrinths! Are you satisfied now? Good heavens!" (catching a sudden sight of my face) "How white you are! Do you mean to say that you have found him at last? Impossible!"

"Yes, I have found him," I answer in a low and unsteady tone. "I knew I should. Look, there he is!—close to us, the third from the end."

I turn away my head, unable to bear the hideous recollections and associations that the sight of the man calls up, and I suppose that they both look.

"Are you sure that you are not letting your imagination carry you away?" asks he presently, in a tone of gentle kindly remonstrance. "As I said before these fellows are all so much alike; they have all the same look of debased squalid cunning. Oblige me by looking once again, so as to be quite sure."

I obey. Reluctantly I look at him once again. Apparently, becoming aware that he is the object of our notice, he lifts his small dull eyes and looks back at me. It is the same face—they are the same eyes that turned from the plundered dressing-table to catch sight of me last night. "There is no mistake," I answer, shuddering from head to foot. "Take me away, please—as quick as you can—out of the field—home!"

They comply, and over the hot fields and through the hot noon air we step silently homewards. As we reach the cool and ivied porch of the house I speak for the first time. "You believe me *now?*"

He hesitates. "I was staggered for a moment, I will own," he answers, with candid gravity; "but I have been thinking it over, and on reflection I have come to the conclusion that the highly excited state of your imagination is answerable for the heightening of the resemblance which exists between all the Irish of that class into an identity with the particular Irishman you dreamed of, and whose face (by your own showing) you only saw dimly reflected in the glass."

"*Not* dimly," repeat I emphatically, "unless I now see that sun dimly" (pointing to him, as he gloriously, blindingly blazes from the sky). "You will not be warned by me then?" I continue passionately, after an interval. "You will run the risk of my dream coming true—you will stay on here in spite of it? Oh, if I could persuade you to go from home anywhere—anywhere—for a time, until the danger was past!"

"And leave the harvest to itself?" answers he, with a smile of quiet sarcasm; "be a loser of two hundred or three hundred pounds, probably, and a laughing-stock to my acquaintance into the bargain, and all for—what? A dream—a fancy—a nightmare!"

"But do you know anything of the man?—of his antecedents?—of his character?" I persist eagerly.

He shrugs his shoulders.

"Nothing whatever; nothing to his disadvantage, certainly. He came over with a lot of others a fortnight ago, and I engaged him for the harvesting. For anything I have heard to the contrary, he is a simple inoffensive fellow enough."

I am silenced, but not convinced. I turn to Jane. "You remember your promise: you will now put no more hindrances in the way of my going?"

"You do not mean to say that you are going, really?" says Jane, who is looking rather awed by what she calls the surprising coincidence, but is still a good deal heartened up by her husband's want of faith.

"I do," reply I, emphatically. "I should go stark staring mad if I were to sleep another night in that room. I shall go to Chester tonight, and cross tomorrow from Holyhead."

I do as I say. I make my maid, to her extreme surprise, repack my just unpacked wardrobe and take an afternoon train to Chester. As I drive away with bag and baggage down the leafy lane, I look back and see my two friends standing at their gate. Jane is leaning her head on her old man's shoulder, and looking rather wistfully after me: an expression of mingled regret for my departure and vexation at my folly clouding their kind and happy faces. At least my last living recollection of them is a pleasant one.

Chapter 4

The joy with which my family welcome my return is largely mingled with surprise, but still more largely with curiosity, as to the cause of my so sudden reappearance. But I keep my own counsel. I have a reluctance to give the real reason, and possess no inventive faculty in the way of lying, so I give none. I say, "I *am* back: is not that enough for you? Set your minds at rest, for that is as much as you will ever know about the matter."

For one thing, I am occasionally rather ashamed of my conduct. It is not that the impression produced by my dream is *effaced*, but that absence and distance from the scene and the persons of it have produced their natural weakening effect. Once or twice during the voyage, when writhing in laughable torments in the ladies' cabin of the steamboat, I said to myself, "Most likely you are a fool!" I therefore continually ward off the cross-questionings of my family with what defensive armour of silence and evasion I may.

"I feel convinced it was the husband," says one of my sisters, after a long catechism, which, as usual, has resulted in nothing. "You are too loyal to your friend to own it, but I always felt sure that any man who could take compassion on that poor peevish old Jane must be some wonderful freak of nature. Come, confess. Is not he a cross between an ourang-outang and a Methodist parson?"

"He is nothing of the kind," reply I, in some heat, recalling the libelled Robin's clean fresh-coloured *human* face. "You will be very lucky if you ever secure any one half so kind, pleasant, and gentleman-like."

Three days after my return, I receive a letter from Jane:

> Weston House, Caulfield.
>
> My Dear Dinah,—I hope you are safe home again, and that you have made up your mind that two crossings of St. George's Channel within forty-eight hours are almost as bad as having your throat cut, according to the programme you laid out for *us*. I have good news for you. Our murderer elect is *gone*. After hearing of the connection that there was to be between us, Robin naturally was rather interested in him, and found out his name, which is the melodious one of Watty Doolan. After asking his name he asked other things about him, and finding that he never did a stroke of work and was inclined to be tipsy and quarrelsome, he paid and packed him off at once. He is now, I hope, on his way back to his native shores, and if

he murder anybody it will be *you*, my dear. Goodbye, Dinah. Hardly yet have I forgiven you for the way in which you frightened me with your graphic description of poor Robin and me, with our heads loose and waggling.

Ever yours affectionately,

Jane Watson."

I fold up this note with a feeling of exceeding relief, and a thorough faith that I have been a superstitious hysterical fool. More resolved than ever am I to keep the reason for my return profoundly secret from my family. The next morning but one we are all in the breakfast-room after breakfast, hanging about, and looking at the papers. My sister has just thrown down the *Times*, with a pettish exclamation that there is nothing in it, and that it really is not worth while paying threepence a day to see nothing but advertisements and police reports. I pick it up as she throws it down, and look listlessly over its tall columns from top to bottom. Suddenly my listlessness vanishes. What is this that I am reading?—this in staring capitals?

SHOCKING TRAGEDY AT CAULFIELD. DOUBLE MURDER.

I am in the middle of the paragraph before I realise what it is.

From an early hour of the morning this village has been the scene of deep and painful excitement in consequence of the discovery of the atrocious murder of Mr. and Mrs. Watson, of Weston House, two of its most respected inhabitants. It appears that the deceased had retired to rest on Tuesday night at their usual hour, and in their usual health and spirits. The housemaid, on going to call them at the accustomed hour on Wednesday morning, received no answer, in spite of repeated knocking. She therefore at length opened the door and entered. The rest of the servants, attracted by her cries, rushed to the spot, and found the unfortunate gentleman and lady lying on the bed with their throats cut from ear to ear. Life must have been extinct for some hours, as they were both perfectly cold. The room presented a hideous spectacle, being literally swimming in blood. A reaping hook, evidently the instrument with which the crime was perpetrated, was picked up near the door. An Irish labourer of the name of Watty Doolan, discharged by the lamented gentleman a few days ago on account of misconduct, has already been arrested on strong suspicion, as at an early hour on Wednesday morning he was seen by a farm labourer, who was going to his work, washing his waistcoat at a retired spot in the stream which flows through the meadows below the scene of the murder. On being apprehended and searched, several small articles of jewellery, identified as having belonged to Mr. Watson, were discovered in his possession.

I drop the paper and sink into a chair, feeling deadly sick.

So you see that my dream came true, after all.

The facts narrated in the above story occurred in Ireland. The only liberty I have taken with them is in transplanting them to England.

Young Benjie

By Andrew Lang

Of all the maids of fair Scotland,
The fairest was Marjorie;
And young Benjie was her ae true love,
And a dear true love was he.

And wow but they were lovers dear,
And lov'd full constantlie;
But aye the mair when they fell out,
The sairer was their plea.

And they ha'e quarrell'd on a day,
Till Marjorie's heart grew wae;
And she said she'd chuse another luve,
And let young Benjie gae.

And he was stout and proud-hearted,
And thought o't bitterlie;
And he's gane by the wan moonlight,
To meet his Marjorie.

"Oh, open, open, my true love,
Oh, open and let me in!"—
"I dare na open, young Benjie,
My three brothers are within."—

"Ye lee, ye lee, ye bonnie burd,
Sae loud's I hear ye lie;
As I came by the Lowden banks,

They bade gude e'en to me.

"But fare ye weel, my ae fause love,
That I have lov'd sae lang!
It sets ye chuse another love,
And let young Benjie gang."

Then Marjorie turn'd her round about,
The tear blinding her e'e;
"I darena, darena let thee in,
But I'll come down to thee."

Then saft she smil'd, and said to him,
"Oh, what ill ha'e I done?"
He took her in his armis twa,
And threw her o'er the linn.

The stream was strong, the maid was stout,
And laith, laith to be dang;
But ere she wan the Lowden banks,
Her fair colour was wan.

Then up bespak her eldest brother
"Oh, see na ye what I see?"
And out then spak her second brother
"It is our sister Marjorie!"

Out then spak her eldest brother
"Oh, how shall we her ken?"
And out then spak her youngest brother
"There's a honey mark on her chin."

Then they've ta'en the comely corpse,
And laid it on the grund;
"O wha has kill'd our ae sister?
And how can he be found?

"The night it is her low lykewake,
The morn her burial day;
And we maun watch at mirk midnight,
And hear what she will say."

Wi' doors ajar, and candle-light,
And torches burning clear,
The streikit corpse, till still midnight,
They waked, but naething hear.

About the middle of the night
The cocks began to craw;
And at the dead hour of the night,
The corpse began to thraw.

"O, wha has done thee wrang, sister,
Or dared the deadly sin?
Wha was sae stout, and feared nae dout,
As thraw ye o'er the linn?"—

"Young Benjie was the first ae man
I laid my love upon;
He was sae stout and proud-hearted,
He threw me o'er the linn."—

"Sall we young Benjie head, sister,
Sall we young Benjie hang,
Or sall we pike out his twa gray e'en,
And punish him ere he gang?"—

"Ye maunna Benjie head, brothers,
Ye maunna Benjie hang;
But ye maun pike out his twa gray e'en.
And punish him ere he gang.

"Tie a green gravat round his neck,
And lead him out and in,
And the best ae servant about your house
To wait young Benjie on.

"And aye at every seven years' end,
Ye'll take him to the linn;
For that's the penance he maun drie,
To scug his deadly sin."

A List of The Stories Appearing in This Anthology Series

J. Sheridan le Fanu - Squire Toby's Will – Volume 2

J. Sheridan le Fanu - Schalken the Painter – Volume 2

J. Sheridan le Fanu - Mr. Justice Harbottle – Volume 2

J. Sheridan le Fanu - The Haunted Baronet – Volume 3

J. Sheridan le Fanu - The Watcher – Volume 3

J. Sheridan le Fanu - Madam Crowl's Ghost – Volume 4

J. Sheridan le Fanu - Carmilla – Volume 5

J. Sheridan le Fanu - The Room in the Dragon Volant – Volume 5

Lanoe Falconer - Cecilia de Noël – Volume 5

Mrs. H. D. Everett - The Death Mask – Volume 1

Mrs. H. D. Everett - Anne's Little Ghost – Volume 5

Mrs. Henry Wood - Featherston's Story – Volume 1

Mrs. Oliphant - A Beleaguered City – Volume 2

Mrs. Oliphant - The Open Door – Volume 3

Mrs. J. H. Riddell - The Last of Squire Ennismore – Volume 1

Mrs. J. H. Riddell - Hertford O'Donnell's Warning – Volume 2

Mrs. J. H. Riddell - The Uninhabited House – Volume 3

Rhoda Broughton - The Man With the Nose – Volume 1

Rhoda Broughton - Behold, it was a Dream! – Volume 2

Rhoda Broughton - Poor Pretty Bobby – Volume 3

Sir Walter Scott - The Tapestried Chamber – Volume 1

Sir Walter Scott - Wandering Willie's Tale – Volume 3

Sir Walter Scott - The Eve of Saint John – Volume 3

Sir Walter Scott - Glenfinlas – Volume 5

W. de Morgan - Alice-For-Short – Volume 4

W. M. Thackeray - The Notch on the Axe – Volume 3

Wilkie Collins - The Haunted Hotel – Volume 5

ALSO FROM LEONAUR

AVAILABLE IN SOFTCOVER OR HARDCOVER WITH DUST JACKET

THE LONG PATROL *by George Berrie*—A Novel of Light Horsemen from Gallipoli to the Palestine campaign of the First World War.

NAPOLEONIC WAR STORIES *by Arthur Quiller-Couch*—Tales of soldiers, spies, battles & sieges from the Peninsular & Waterloo campaingns.

THE FIRST DETECTIVE *by Edgar Allan Poe*—The Complete Auguste Dupin Stories—The Murders in the Rue Morgue, The Mystery of Marie Rogêt & The Purloined Letter.

THE COMPLETE DR NIKOLA—MAN OF MYSTERY: 1 *by Guy Boothby—A Bid for Fortune & Dr Nikola Returns*—Guy Boothby's Dr.Nikola adventures continue to fascinate readers and enthusiasts of crime and mystery fiction because—in the manner of Raffles, the gentleman cracksman—here is character far removed from the uncompromising goodness of Holmes and Watson or the uncompromising evil of Professor Moriarty.

THE COMPLETE DR NIKOLA—MAN OF MYSTERY: 2 *by Guy Boothby—The Lust of Hate, Dr Nikola's Experiment & Farewell, Nikola*—Guy Boothby's Dr.Nikola adventures continue to fascinate readers and enthusiasts of crime and mystery fiction because—in the manner of Raffles, the gentleman cracksman—here is character far removed from the uncompromising goodness of Holmes and Watson or the uncompromising evil of Professor Moriarty.

THE CASEBOOKS OF MR J. G. REEDER: BOOK 1 *by Edgar Wallace—Room 13, The Mind of Mr J. G. Reeder* and *Terror Keep*—Edgar Wallace's sleuth—whose territory is the London of the 1920s—is an unlikely figure, more bank clerk than detective in appearance, ever wearing his square topped bowler, frock coat, cravat and muffler, Mr Reeder is usually inseparable from his umbrella.

THE CASEBOOKS OF MR J. G. REEDER: BOOK 2 *by Edgar Wallace—Red Aces, Mr J. G. Reeder Returns, The Guv'nor* and *The Man Who Passed*—Edgar Wallace's sleuth—whose territory is the London of the 1920s—is an unlikely figure, more bank clerk than detective in appearance, ever wearing his square topped bowler, frock coat, cravat and muffler, Mr Reeder is usually inseparable from his umbrella.

THE COMPLETE FOUR JUST MEN: VOLUME 1 *by Edgar Wallace—The Four Just Men, The Council of Justice & The Just Men of Cordova*—disillusioned with a world where the wicked and the abusers of power perpetually go unpunished, the Just Men set about to rectify matters according to their own standards, and retribution is dispensed on swift and deadly wings.

LEONAUR

www.ingramcontent.com/pod-product-compliance
Lightning Source LLC
LaVergne TN
LVHW040824090826
845145LV00001BA/30